DATE DUE

Types of Prose Fiction

TYPES

OF

PROSE FICTION

Edited with an Introduction by

GEORGE P. ELLIOTT

Syracuse University

RANDOM HOUSE

NEW YORK

PREFATORY NOTE

THE PURPOSE OF THIS COLLECTION OF STORIES is to remind the reader of the dazzling variety of riches to be found in prose fiction and to provide some good examples of it for his pleasure.

The main purpose of the introductory essay is to suggest a way of talking about fiction which is ampler than the critical way dominant at present. This dominant way, which I call *Jamesianism*, has produced some first-rate fiction criticism—for example, Mark Schorer's essay, "Technique as Discovery." But it must not be allowed to become dogma, as it threatens to do in the United States, at least. Jamesianism derives from two chief sources: from the critical theories of Henry James, especially as they were codified by his prime disciple, Percy Lubbock, in *The Craft of Fiction;* and from The New Criticism, a school which applies structural, verbal, and symbolic exegesis most successfully to short poems, and which studies the creative power of words at the expense of their designative power. Here are some of the canons of Jamesianism: Flaubert and James are the Fathers of the art of fiction and their principal stories are its exemplars; perfection of form is a very great, if not the highest, good; the ideal short story ends in an epiphany (Joyce's term for a sudden revelation, or insight, or "opening"); the true novel is realistic and is coherent in all its parts; the writer's artistry matters more than his wisdom; the language of irony and indirection is preferable to fulfilled and fulfilling plain language. In the subtle, manicured shire of Jamesianism, one could spend a lifetime under strange illusions: that *War and Peace* and *Don Quixote*, though marvels, are somehow not to be taken seriously as works of art; that *The Betrothed* should be mentioned with politeness (if ever) only out of regard for the patriotic feelings of Italians; that Rabelais, *Pilgrim's Progress*, and *The Morte d'Arthur* exist as sources, precursors, Neanderthal novels; and that *Njal's Saga* and *The Tale of Genji*, those inconvenient masterworks, do not exist at all.

The Introduction sketches in four main types of stories, four loose categories no one of which is assumed to be superior to any other. There is nothing holy about categorizing. The writing and reading of fiction, the saying and hearing of stories, got along splendidly for eons with as muddy a set of categories as any in literary criticism. But, once started, the taxonomic process cannot easily be reversed. Take for example the names for works of fiction of a medium length, such as those in this collection: *novella, novelette, short novel, nouvelle, long short story*. Categorists are maddened by such loose, merely quantitative terms, and every so often they try to define the genre. But none of the would-be definitions stick, because, I suspect, there is no such genre. There seems to me no use in trying to domesticate the wilderness of fiction terminology (*picaresque novel, roman à clef, tale, confession, allegory*, etc.). What could be useful is to map the region roughly. The best compendious discussion of the types of prose fiction is Northrop Frye's essay in *The Anatomy of Criticism*. His fourfold division provides the frame to my essay.

A narrative may look like an account of actual happenings (realistic fiction) or even be one (autobiography); yet it must be as wholly imagined as the tallest tale, if it is to succeed. The fiction may propose ideas (anatomy and satire) or it may seem to be a tale as empty of ideas as a dream (romance). Ultimately, my thesis is that a good story is a narrative fantasy which generates an imaginative reality (and may or may not be an account or likeness of the actual world) and which incarnates an idea of moral reality (and may or may not present ideas openly).

These stories are all of "a certain length," because within this free scope can be collected every important variety of prose fiction, in pure or mixed form, except the full-length novel and the epiphanic short story, neither of which is currently in need of exemplification or defense. Within this medium range there exist a number of works of power, charm, and insight, many of which are not well enough known.

All these stories are in prose, not because prose is a better medium than verse for story telling, but in order to avoid three main complications. First, from Chaucer on, suitable verse narratives in English are well known and much anthologized, with a very few exceptions. Second, there is the question of what poetry can do with a narrative which prose cannot. It is true that "The Rime of the Ancient Mariner" could no more have been written in prose than "The Vicar of Tours" in verse, but except for being written in verse, how is *The Ring and the Book* more poetic than *Moby Dick?* Not only is such an issue juiceless, but also, happily, it is irrelevant to my thesis. Third, all important types of narrative which exist in verse (except for epic and ballad) exist in abundance in prose as well. Moreover, in verse one would be restricted to those composed in English or (they are few) well translated into English, whereas in prose one can range the world.

For convenience' sake I have arranged the stories in chronological order, even though the intention of the book has nothing to do with literary history. Indeed, the accident of chronological arrangement confounds any historical pattern of development by types. The first story is pure romance, the second is primarily, but not entirely, realistic, the next to last is satiric romance, and the last is anatomic realism with the effect, though not in the form, of spiritual biography. No progress there, no development, not even a pattern worth mentioning.

Few historical or biographical details about the composition or authors of these stories seem necessary; it is the stories that matter. Also, I hope to discourage that dubious classroom game of looking for pigeon-holes to put stories in. The categories that Frye proposed and I have followed have one legitimate use: by expanding a reader's appreciation of the manifold possibilities of fiction, to make it harder for him to demand that a story conform to a limited theory and easier for him to enjoy and talk about what a given story has done.

GEORGE P. ELLIOTT.

CONTENTS

Types of Prose Fiction

Introduction

A DEFENSE OF

FICTION

My lords, if you would hear a high tale of love and of death,
here is that of Tristan and Iseult.

Belloc's translation of Bedier's *The Romance of Tristan and Iseult*

I IMAGINE THAT THE IMPULSE to tell stories is as natural, and hence as little
in need of justification, as is the impulse to dance, and I take the listener as
female to the sayer's male, the desire of each needing the other for com-
pletion. I imagine further that the impulse to tell a story is like most impulses: not clear-cut and fixed, but blending with several other primitive
impulses, usually in combinations of every imaginable sort and degree. Of
these, the impulse to sing is pure and indisputable; a ballad is a story sung,
and almost every song has the germ, or the vestige, of a story in it (for the
reasons given in the Prefatory Note, I will not deal with narrative song).
I imagine there to be four other important impulses that mingle with the
story teller's: to dream, to tell what happened, to explain the nature of
things, and to make a likeness. I take them up in this order, which I imagine
to be the order of their sophistication.

Tale and Romance

. . . as I slept I dreamed a dream. I dreamed, and behold I saw. . . .

Bunyan: *Pilgrim's Progress*

So BEGINS the greatest of prose allegories. As many narratives do, it says it
is a dream but, more than most, *Pilgrim's Progress* affects the reader somewhat as a dream does. Kafka wrote stories more dream-like than Bunyan's,
for he was less impelled to instruct and advise the reader by interpreting
the dream as it went along. Some of *The Thousand and One Nights* are

even more purely dream-like than Kafka's tales; they do not compel interpretation at all, but exist in and of themselves. Yet they can be analyzed
by an external, imposed set of principles (such as psychoanalysis), pretty
much as dreams can be, and if they are good they may reveal something
of the truth. It is the fantasist's alchemy to obey the obscure laws of
dream and of story at once, in such a way that his words will stimulate the
same fantasy in the reader. If you recount to your friend what you dreamt
last night, he will not dream it, but merely look at it. If your tale-telling
and dreaming impulses become one, so that the dream is created while the
story is being told, then he may not only look at your fantasy but imagine
it as well. "*La poésie*," said Sainte-Beuve, "*ne consiste pas à tout dire, mais à
tout faire rêver.*"

My contention is that a good tale is like a dream, is unlike a dream, and
touches the truth.

Here are some of the ways in which a narrative fantasy is like a dream.
1) The people and images it evokes are vivid and particular. It is not despair
that Christian has to deal with, but Giant Despair of Doubting Castle, who
falls into fits even on sunshiny days. It is not by intellectual speculation that
K tries to discover what the Castle wants him to do, but by picking up
and talking into as actual a telephone as exists in literature. 2) Fantasy images
are particular, solid, immediate; yet around them there hovers a penumbra
of significance. Whether a cup is as symbolic as the Grail, a scientist as
representative as Frankenstein, the hero as loosely archetypal a lost-king's-
son as Tom Jones, the plight as phosphorescent with anxiety as that of "The
Pit and the Pendulum," this is certain: nothing is there just because in
ordinary life it would happen so to occur or so to appear. 3) The fantasy
puts disjunct parts of the world together in its own way, into a thing
radically different from the visible world. This is done partly in play, as
a relief from the tedium of life: for escape. In a good fantasy, it is also
done as a way of saying that the invisible world is not like the world we
see and commonly live in, but *thus*. Identity is impermanent: substitution,
metamorphosis, disguise are the stock in trade of romance. In "Qamar az-
Zaman," the hero's father, the King, fades out of the tale, but there fades
in a guardian old man, upon whose death Qamar az-Zaman has power to
become king in a new land and in his home.

In romances, in tales, in dream-like stories, all things are pure and highly
colored. The moon is not at the three quarters and dulled by dust in the
air, the third son wins, an infusion of herbs causes life-long love. Especially,
motives appear to be clear: malice, fidelity, courage, desire, revenge—all
the types of human impulses unpolluted. Desire is gratified or grandly
thwarted, but does not just peter out; evil abounds, but is recognized, and
justice triumphs; anguish is not interrupted by mosquito bites. Most of all,
there is the sense that matters have to be thus; there are laws—some strange,
some obscure, many usual—which cause and explain everything. Outrageous
coincidence is unexceptional in fantasy plots, because we feel secure that

what seems to be coincidence is really immanent destiny. (In a poor fantasy, the sense of destiny depreciates to a suspicion of author manipulation.) The dream-like sense of necessity, whether it is compulsive, as in Kafka, or easy and drifting, as in *The Thousand and One Nights,* comes from no natural determinism, for that philosophy holds that there is nothing moral about any decision; it comes from the sense that, no matter how hard the hero strives, the Jinn, the Gentlemen of the Castle, or the gods will make most of the important decisions at their whim, and will reward and punish according to a code that is humane (and therefore moral) only from time to time. It was not because of something he knew he had done or had meant to do that Joseph K was accused and shot; in the Grimms' tale, the dead girl's arm would quit growing from her grave only when her mother came to beat it with a stick.

It is not only because the laws of that world are strange that we feel released when we are in it. It is also because we are removed from the uncertainties of choice there: *If I were in his place it would be clear to me what I ought to do.* (How refreshingly strange!); *yet I know that whatever I choose to do the outcome of the event will probably be determined by powers I do not understand or of whose existence I may not even be aware* (How familiar, how true!).

Even the purest fantasy story is as unlike as it is like a dream. The dreamer has none of that distance from his dream which both teller and hearer have from a tale. Distance is one of the great goods of fiction—that distance midway between the abstractness of expository essay and the confrontation of drama, a wonderland distance permitting both a kind of extreme intimacy with characters and also a panorama of generations, both the full cold light of analysis and some of the heat of scene. The dream's images are so vivid and its emotions so pure, and, at the same time, the dreamer's consciousness is so dim, that the dream becomes reality for the dreamer: to dream is to be a solipsist. On the other hand, even a girl with *Dracula* in her hand at midnight, afraid to turn out the light and go to bed, knows as she stares at the billowing curtains that it is a book she holds and that this is her room she is in; if she loses herself further, if she mistakes a brother's snore in the next room for a vampire's chuckle, one says her state of mind is mildly pathological. For a reader not abnormally given to hallucinating, the images evoked by words simply are not so present to the mind, so immediate, as those of a dream, and if he is not hysterical his emotions are inhibited by his controlling consciousness. Psychologists conjecture that people can die of terror in their sleep. Who ever heard of someone's dying of terror while listening to a story? The girl fears going to bed because *Dracula* might stimulate such dreams as would terrify her too much.

A crucial difference between dream and story is language. A dream does not have to use language; most dreams do in fact use it, but not necessarily in the way a story-teller must. Each person is given language by his community, by those before and about him, and, among sane people, only the dreamer is released from the responsibility of giving language back to those about him in recognizable form. In this respect, dreaming is a kind of holiday from sanity, a region where *sinkboard* may inspire him with horror, *good morning* mean nothing, or *fiersh deply* fill him with erotic yearning. *Finnegans Wake*, a word-dream by the most solipsistic of writers, transforms language as freely as a dream does. In it, character, place, and story dissolve, and words metamorphose. Those who understand the book call it literature; yet so few will ever be able to understand it—and to do so they must so submit to Joyce's will—that the community who gave Joyce his language will never listen or even want to listen for long to what he has done to the language, marvelous though it may be. Insofar as a sayer's language is not understood by those to whom he is returning it, he has failed. If he is returning it only to a cabal, then one calls his writing esoteric, the justification for which is that there is no public language available for what he knows. Of *Finnegans Wake*, a sympathetic judgment is that it is a book of esoteric beauty and wisdom, the very form of·which demonstrates its basic assumption: the more real one's knowledge, the more private it is, and the less one can communicate it with common words in normal syntax. A harsh judgment is that the book is neither story, nor poem, nor dream, but a pseudo-dream based on a lie; a lie, because some of one's most real knowledge has come through stories which have communicated no less miraculously for being in the common tongue. Among these, none is greater than *Don Quixote*, which flowers from an assumption to which Joyce's is hostile. Cervantes assumes that, even as false or trivial dreams (like the romances that addled the Don's wits) reduce reality and as noble dreams (like Don Quixote's own) heighten it, so a literary analogue to a dream of the truth (like *Don Quixote* itself; unlike *Finnegans Wake*) magnifies reality by creating a communion of readers.

A good tale is seldom as purely fantastic as "Qamar az-Zaman," for usually the teller is moved also by the impulse to teach. The power of the teaching depends in good part on how intricately it has become the tale. No doubt Swift intended the story in *Gulliver's Travels* as a sort of vehicle separate from his message, and, of course, to some extent the two are separable. But Swift speaks better indirectly than directly, he is more tale-teller than philosopher: most of the power lies in the story. In the dreadful fourth voyage, that deepest of all excursions into misanthropy, the more potent meaning is to be found not in the message but in the story. Overtly, Swift meant that reason is vile man's one hope; but reason is exemplified in the Houyhnhnms, and the vapidity of their fictional effect quite undoes his conscious message. If the Houyhnhnms are the best we can hope for, why bother? For a natural story-teller, the truth he has to tell forms what he imagines to have happened, however much he may have intended, like Swift or Bunyan, to separate his message from the fantasy. A good story is the figure of a truth, but that truth is not always the author's consciously intended message.

Conversely, truth embodied in a story has a power it has in no other form. Jesus did not write theology, but told many stories; and we know him by the four versions of the story of his life. Moreover, unlike essay, fiction is not in danger of defining the truth too strictly. Who knows how many diverse sermons and exegeses have been stimulated by the story of Abraham and Isaac, each intended to expose *the* truth hidden in that story?

Fiction does not deal very much with those clear, definable sorts of truth which, like the circulation of blood, are merely tricky to expose or which, like the law of gravity, explain the behavior of things by a formula. Isolated, such formulas as stories yield may be wise and subtle, but more likely are limp and obvious: "We should love one another"; "You should change your life." Fiction deals with truths which, like love, are fully there only in the creation. If psychology, moral philosophy, and sociology could manage among them to encapsulate the truths of our behavior in accurate formulas, there would be no further use for story, except to amuse. But the contingencies of life, the possible combinations of factors, are too various. A man may know all the wise formulas about love, but until he has loved he has not possessed their wisdom. It is a wonder of fiction that it can both create and formulate truths for our possession. Story is endless.

In so pure a fantasy as "Qamar az-Zaman," the writer is quite unconcerned with telling the reader what actually happened, or with teaching him how things really are, or with showing him how things appear. Yet the story generates a vigor which would have been impossible if it did not have to do with the truth, a human truth of some substance. This is not to belittle the story's craftmanship. One's interest is engaged at the outset, and maintained without a lag, and one's expectations are fulfilled at the end. Moreover, the rules of that imaginary world are consistent, and those that govern the character's motives are purer versions of those that govern ours. In fiction, when the probable and the improbable conflict, the probable always wins; the author of "Qamar az-Zaman" succeeds perfectly at such a moment in keeping our attention on something else, so that we never ask that illusion-destroying question: "How can I be expected to believe this?" All the same, were this story not founded on some substratum of solid truth, it would be as flimsy as most science fiction, than which surely not even the romances Cervantes set out to satirize were flimsier.

A symptom of a story's excellence is that, as one reads along, one's mind enjoys a play of speculation about the story's meanings. In judging a book's value, one may consider the absence of such play far more damning than formal defects. Usually, this speculation leads to serious matters taken seriously, but a story may take them lightly, as "Qamar az-Zaman" does—not frivolously so much as rejoicingly: *How delightful the truth is.* As one reads the story along, one's mind dives beneath the surface of impossible events and is charmed to watch all manner of family sexual relationships form and dissolve. Since the writer has assumed that we too know that things are thus and so, he is freed from the burden of interpreting. Thinking about what this story deals with is an activity inseparable from enjoying it. It is not true that to enjoy it one needs to understand every part, but one does need to feel that it possesses a coherent significance there to be understood: that it was composed with authority. In the realm of pure fantasy, one wants to understand, not because one feels a compulsion or a moral obligation to do so, but because the writer has made it seem pleasing. Reading a good fantasy is like skin-diving just for the fun of seeing what is down there in the waterworld, and coming on a coffer full of gold.

Such fiction, though it is frequently looked at with condescension, is in no danger of disappearing. Tolkien's *Lord of the Rings* is three volumes of charming fantasy in the British manner. Amos Tutuola's *My Life in the Bush of Ghosts*, though it may sometimes sound allegorical, is always an extravagant fantasy. Faulkner's "Red Leaves" is a superb fantasy; perhaps it has been read and talked about less than most of his good, and even less than good, fiction just because it is so pure a fantasy as to seem out of the mainstream and not to be about anything much. But the outrageousness of human affairs is surely one of his grand themes and nowhere has it been more purely figured forth than in this tale.

Dreaming is one of the things we really do, and what actually happens sometimes takes fantastic forms (*The Conquest of Mexico*). Steadfastness to a dream of truth generates truth, and "real life" is commonly a blundering about in what merely seems to be. Does our belief in a god create him? Do we exist in the mind of God?

For lovely speculation of such a kind, read Unamuno's legend-like "St. Manuel Bueno, Martyr." After that, read his master, Cervantes, who is everyone's master at the grave play of so imagining what might be that it becomes what is.

Stories of What Happened: Autobiography

The storyteller's own experience of men and things, whether for good or ill—not only what he has passed through himself, but even events which he has only witnessed or been told of—has moved him to an emotion so passionate that he can no longer keep it shut up in his heart. Again and again something in his own life or in that around him will seem to the writer so important that he cannot bear to let it pass ino oblivion. There must never come a time, he feels, when men do not know about it.

Lady Murasaki: *The Tale of Genji*

About the impulse itself there is only this to add: it is not just writers who are so moved. To every writer many laymen come bearing a strange true story for him to bless for them by telling. The sadness is that they so seldom know how to make their impulse his; which is no doubt why they assure him he will make much money from their story or why they even, if they are rich, would pay him to tell it for them.

The three forms of telling what happened are biography, history, and autobiography.

Since biography became an important mode of writing at about the time humane scholarship became awed by scientific method, it has moved away from story-telling such as Plutarch's. However, biography (and history) lacks one of science's fundamental tools, the verification of hypothesis by experiment, and the variables and imponderables it deals with are beyond control—are, indeed, beyond identifying. Baffled, would-be scientific biography has put enormous emphasis on sheer fact. Since most of what most biographers know about what actually happened comes directly or indirectly through biased witnesses, i.e., is a form of hearsay, they have relied more and more on documents and letters. The result is that a great many "definitive" volumes of biography are as thorough and accurate as they claim, and are also boring beyond belief. Few men have been more fascinating than Byron; yet reading Marchand's three-volume fact-for-fact's-sake definitive life of Byron is like slogging through desert sand with nothing but oases of quotation for relief. An extreme of this is to be found in Jay Leyda's *The Melville Log,* a two-volume accumulation of documents pertaining to Melville's life: "Here, reader, are the materials with which you may compose your own biography of Melville." There is a kind of fascination to reading it, and also a kind of honesty to Leyda's abandonment of selectivity, of shaping, of art. Of course, accuracy and thoroughness are indispensable to excellent biography; the greatest of biographers, Boswell, was as scrupulous in his *Life of Johnson* as that contemporary scholar, Richard Ellmann, in his *James Joyce.* But the most important principle these two superb narratives demonstrate is that, quite as much as an interesting subject and a thoroughgoing accuracy, a biographer needs talent in his special art.

What is called a historical novel is nearly always a somewhat realistic romance set long enough ago to oblige the romancer to read up on events and customs so that he may embed his story in actual or actual-seeming details. The subject matter of history proper is large social forces, their creation, movement, corruption, interplay, ossification, destruction; individuals are portrayed (say, by Tacitus) as they cause, lead, or exemplify these forces. But the subject matter of fiction is the relationships among and within individuals as such, whatever their connection or lack of connection with society. These are mutually incompatible modes of representing character, history conceiving that personal qualities and relationships are important as they affect society at large, and fiction assuming that social forces are important as they affect the lives of its characters. How incompatible these two modes are may be demonstrated by the results of Tolstoy's trying to marry them in *War and Peace.* The greatness of the book surely has nothing to do with his portraits of actual persons, especially Napoleon and Kutuzov, or with his quarreling with the French historians and presenting his own theory of history. Indeed, while reading the novel one cares far less that the burning of Moscow actually took place than that Tolstoy vividly imagined it, far less that it was part of history than that the writer made it part of his imaginary characters' lives.

Nevertheless, a kind of stubborn value which an imaginary event lacks attaches to an actual event. In many ways, writers rely upon this to help them hold their readers. Kleist subtitles "Michael Kolhaas," "From an Old Chronicle;" Lady Murasaki pretends to appear from time to time in her own person as an eye-witness: "Indeed, the whole Court was in such a state of chatter and excitement that my head was in a whirl, and I forgot to make any note of the many and beautiful and interesting ceremonies that took place in the Palace at the time of this little Prince's birth." The reader naïvely likes the writer to say *I was there* or, at least, *This really happened*. Assured that it really did happen, a reader will put up with a score of defects he does not tolerate from story-tellers who make no such claim. Only knowledge that there was in fact the man Freud would support any reader through the three volumes of Jones's storyless, cottonwool biography of him.

The obvious value that attaches to narrating actual events is truth, reality. But, literarily, true-story is only one of many ways to achieve this value. The value is essential; the way is not. The truth of a story is its conformance to reality, and reality does not often manifest itself powerfully in actual events or lives. (Surely, sometimes it does: Buddha, the death of Socrates, Stalin's career.) It is the task of the biographer of a real person, as well as of a fictional one, to choose and arrange a sequence of apparent events so as to manifest to the reader their hidden reality. Essentially, the biographer, the autobiographer, and the writer of a fiction in the form of a biography or autobiography are engaged in the same literary task: *Behold the man*. There is an unbroken series of life-stories from the factual (Pepys' *Diary*, *Sinclair Lewis*), through mixtures of fact and fantasy (*Davy Crockett's Own Story*, *The Notebook of Malte Laurids Bridge*, *Portrait of the Artist as a Young Man*, *Heart of Darkness*), to the quite imaginary (*Clarissa*, *Dr. Jekyll and Mr. Hyde*).

There is another fairly important, though also non-essential, difference between the life-story of an actual person and that of an imaginary character: what actually happened sets a limit. It is one of the difficulties of the art of fiction—and hence of fiction theory and criticism—that its limits are indeterminable. It can include anything men do or imagine; it is especially attracted by strange and obscure motives; it blends with all the other forms of discourse: poetry, drama, essay, conversation, and self-communing. For this reason alone, there is a considerable security for both reader and writer in knowing that one important limit is set. This is the limit, not of the probable or even of the possible, but of the actual. A writer who is deficient in invention, and who is at the same time able to subordinate himself to another, is especially at ease in biography. Like a translator, who turns what a creator has given him from one language into another, the biographer turns into another arrangement of words what hearsay and documents (and sometimes direct experience) have given him. But the biographer is also much like a creative fiction writer, for most of the truth of the events will come, not from the irreducible brute facts, but from his conception of the man whom these facts reveal, and from his so ordering the facts as to reveal that man.

The Icelandic sagas began in the twelfth century as histories of the original settlers of Iceland, and the readers cared enough about this for the external forms to be preserved even in some of the later sagas that incorporated wild elements of European romances. But no one now reading for enjoyment and judging on literary grounds cares in any way whether Hrafnkel once existed or whether that profound consideration of law and anarchy, *Njal's Saga*, was based on an actual feud. Literarily, the one relevant statement to be made about the historicity of the good sagas is that the genealogies tying the characters, in epic fashion, to the clans of actual ninth and tenth century settlers are a nuisance to a reader now.

An excellent example of the irrelevance of factuality to a fiction's power is provided by a comparison of "Stephen Crane's Own Story" and "The Open Boat." The actual adventure, though plotless, is of the stuff of romantic episode, but Crane refused to exploit the possible romance just as he refused to exploit himself as participant autobiographically. Comparing the two versions of the event, we see that it is not fidelity to the facts of what happened that makes the story strong, but an ordering of those facts according to an idea, a vision. And neither of these versions strikes the reader as being truer to fact than Defoe's invented "True Relation of the Apparition of one Mrs. Veal." As a piece of writing, as a work of art, a well-executed imaginary document is precisely as authentic as an actual one, and this authenticity as such has little to do with the literary value of the work.

> Cast a cold eye
> On life, on death.
>   Yeats

Autobiography, whether real or imaginary, whether diary, letters, confession, or informal essay, has an advantage over biography in that the style itself helps create the character—reveals, betrays, masks, expresses him. The very magniloquence with which Augustine inveighs against literary artifice (like the paradox of his prayer, "O Lord, make me chaste, but not yet") creates one of the tensions which help make his confessions not only the first true autobiography but also a great one. One of the ways we appreciate the "opening" of the narrator's character in Bernanos's *Diary of a Country Priest* is by the "opening" of the style as the novel develops. Stendhal phrased another advantage early in his autobiographical *The Life of Henri Brulard*, in his discussion of the relative merits of writing it in the first or third person; he chose the first person, because in it he could better "record the inner movements of the soul." But against its advantages, autobiography has a serious disadvantage: it presents in acute form the general problem of a writer's keeping his distance from the character he is creating. Perhaps this problem is most severe when the character he is imagining is himself, past or present. Even a cursory reading in directly autobiographical writings shows how few such writers are able to conceive of themselves except in a literary stereotype: to read Sheila Graham's ghosted confessions is to learn less about her actual life or her connection with her lover, F. Scott Fitzgerald, than about *True Confessions* magazine clichés. It is harder than one would think to undress verbally even in private, harder yet to do it in public, hardest of all to do it in public without obscenity. Most good fiction is in the third person, and is not autobiographical in form, whatever it may be in fact.

The same problem, distance, presents itself to a writer of fictional autobiography whose central character is based not at all or only partly on himself: the frequent use of the first person singular tends to blur in a writer's mind the distinction between himself and his character. This is, of course, not always true. The epistolary story circumvents the problem by the letter writer's dramatic immediacy to the situation. The short story is less dangerous than the novel for a writer of fiction in autobiographical form, for in it the sustaining of the imagined personality does not last so long, and, frequently, the writer's intention is less to create character than to evoke the mood of an experience. Then, too, there are narratives in which the use of "I" is strategic; they are not properly autobiographies at all, not even in form: because *Moby Dick* is narrated by Ishmael, one knows while reading that at least one person will have survived the debacle, a security one badly needs; the "I" of *The Possessed* is little more than a way of heightening the illusion of actuality, like the "we" that appears from time to time in *Madame Bovary* or the "I" of *Robinson Crusoe*. Except in *Heart of Darkness*, Conrad's Marlow functions mainly as a voice—as a way of talking. However, of a good many first person novels, notoriously *David Copperfield* and *Great Expectations*, in which Dickens keeps David and Pip at a distance for a few chapters and then blurs in with them, one says that their excellence is in spite of the personal point of view.

For a reader, this problem of the writer's holding his distance from his character is the same whether the autobiography is fictional (*Lolita*), literal (*Boswell's Journals*), or somewhere in between (*Remembrance of Things Past*). The reader does not want to feel that the author at the time of writing the story is confusing his actual, immediate, pen-holding self with the self, real or fictional, that he is imagining—Nabokov with Humbert Humbert, Augustine the middle-aged Bishop of Hippo with Augustine the provincial young blade in Rome, Proust with Marcel. He wants the writer to look at the imagined self with the cold eye of detachment and honesty. Otherwise, the self-knowledge which could have included us ("nothing human is alien to me") will become the excluding mirror of self-consciousness or the obscuring murk of self-justification. The imagined character (like Boswell the doer) may be vain, self-indulgent, self-pitying, attitudinizing, self-justifying, self-lacerating; but the imagining author (like Boswell the writer) must see all this coldly for what it is and record what he sees with no special pleading. A striking example of a potentially strong confession ruined by lack of author-distance is Whittaker Chambers's *Witness*. Here are a public statement, a character, and a dark inner tangle worthy of a Dostoyevsky novel, all spoiled by a vain confusion of self-justification on the part not only of the imagined character but also of the imagining writer. An equally striking example of the reverse—a story in autobiographical form which succeeds in good part because of the author's control—is Unamuno's *Saint Manuel Bueno, Martyr*. In this story the relationship of narrator to the story narrated is of the essence, and Unamuno controls this relationship as surely as he creates it; indeed the control is part of the creating.

An author may put his consciousness of these considerations to good use. Gide, whose journals formidably intensify the coldness of distance with cold self-analysis, posthumously made it clear that *Strait Is the Gate* had been based immediately upon his own relationship with his wife. Yet, despite the novel's being cast in autobiographical form with a journal at its very core, the reader is not disturbed by knowing how intimately Gide was using his own experience; for at no point does the reader suffer either the embarrassment caused by an author's unintentional self-revelation or the fatal disillusionment that comes when he says to himself: "Aha, that is included not because the story demanded it, but because it occurred in actual life." Gide worked for years polishing the novel, removing from it every taint of special self-pleading. If this marvelously elegant story has an imperfection, it is the rather insubstantial quality of Jerome's character caused, no doubt, by Gide's fastidious concern to keep his immediate self clear of Jerome, as a consequence of which Jerome exists only in relationship to Alissa. This may be formally justified, but it does vitiate the character. It is not only Gide's eye that is cold.

At its best, the real author's consciousness of the necessity for him to keep his distance can become a delightful form-consciousness on the part of the supposed writer. The great bravura pieces of this sort are *Tristram Shandy* and *Confessions of Felix Krull*, in both of which novels a good share of the grace and quality come from the author's incomparable play with form-consciousness. Indeed, it is hard to imagine how such consciousness could be used more complexly than in *Felix Krull*. Felix is an artist whose material is his natural endowments and whose works of art are the selves which the world sees. He is the artist of himself. And at no point does he or the reader confuse who he pretended to be with who he is as writer, and at no point does Mann confuse himself with any of the Felixes. Surely it is not irrelevant that both Tristram and Felix take pleasure in the world, are fond of most of those about them, and are cordial with themselves.

A cold eye and a warm heart.

Of the three modes of telling what actually happened, autobiography has provided, for obvious reasons, much the largest tributary to the main stream of fiction. Not only has it contributed the most quantitatively; it has also exemplified in the most concentrated form how important honesty can be in story-telling.

The prime honesty, shared by all three, is fidelity to what happened—not a large matter, but one which only the naïve think easy. Every lawyer assumes that most people cannot report accurately the details of what they have observed, much less of what they have caused. Indeed, fidelity to fact is important enough so that, whenever the issue comes up (as it does in history especially), it becomes crucial. Herodotus the wonder-seeker was by far the better story-teller, but Thucydides, who was there or talked to those who were there, was the greater historian, and, finally, the greater writer.

There is an additional quality special to autobiography: the steadiness and sense of proportion it takes to know oneself. The difficulty of assigning and measuring responsibility for an act, the disentangling of character traits for clear presentation, the infinite complexity of motive—in no form of writing are these more important than in autobiography. Just as in no human endeavor is honesty more important than in self-scrutiny, so in no literary one is sincerity so essential as in autobiography.

Unfortunately, literary accomplishment is not dependent only upon a writer's sincerity. Finding the words by which to project his discoveries may be a gift denied him, so that he employs commonplaces, clichés, stereotypes that in a more sophisticated writer would betoken insincerity. Conversely, a good novelist can feign sincerity like a good actor. (The Greek word for actor was *hypocrite*). One feels when reading *Dangerous Acquaintances* that the letters Chaderlos de Laclos wrote for the imagined Mme. de Merteuil could not have been improved upon by the actual Mme. de Montmart upon whom Merteuil was modeled. To the reader and to the critic, the impression of honesty is more important than the writer's actual and literal sincerity. Perhaps the most one should say is that, granted a certain competence with language, one way for a writer to achieve the impression of fidelity to fact is to be faithful to fact, and that one way for a writer to impress the reader as sincere is for the man himself to be sincere, wearing the mask of himself. All the same, from the profoundest altitudes of self-honesty, each must call in his own voice. One cannot help believing that only St. Teresa could have written her Autobiography, or only Van Gogh his letters to his brother, and that no fiction in autobiographical form could have said what they said in a voice so absolutely true as theirs.

Story, and Speculation on the Nature of Things

> In the beginning was the Word, and the Word was with God, and the Word was God.
>
> John 1:1

So JOHN BEGAN the most important story he could tell. Matthew, Mark, and Luke, wishing to create primarily the image of a man, took the biographer's stance; genealogy, anecdote, scene, direct quotation are their chief instruments. But the Jesus of John's story is less visible than the penumbra Christ. It is not so much the man himself as his significance, with which John wants us to concern ourselves. In the fourth gospel, Christ's sayings, parables, and sermons sound as much like metaphysical John as like the Jesus of the synoptic three. In John, the impulse to teach, to explain the hidden nature of things, to speculate was at least as strong as the impulse to tell his story. Like Plato with the parable of the cave, like Augustine with events from his own life, like Bunyan with his imagined dream, like Kierkegaard, like any preacher, John used his story to illustrate his ideas, because he thought his ideas, the extractable meaning, were what made his story important.

As it merges with story, the speculative impulse takes several guises other than the apologue or illustrative story: the dialogue ("Rameau's Nephew"); creation of a character by presenting his ideas (Montaigne's *Essays*); anatomy (Burton's *Anatomy of Melancholy*); and narrative satire (*Gulliver's Travels*). (These are not logical categories, clearly defined and mutually exclusive.) The great age of this sort of writing was the sixteenth, seventeenth, and eighteenth centuries. Continental story-tellers overtly concerned with ideas still are regarded with esteem: Koestler, Camus, Hesse, Unamuno, Lagerkvist. But in English there are few; the most celebrated one in recent years is Durrell, who has spent very little of his life in an English-speaking country, and whose ideas, in any case, are vastly inferior to his romance. Satire in suitably "novelistic" mixture is still admissible, but the other kinds of idea-fiction are so apt to be looked at askance that very few are written. Partly this is due to the inscrutable shifts in taste from age to age; partly, however, it is due to the ascendancy of realistic fiction and of Jamesianism (for which James himself must not be held fully accountable). A shibboleth of contemporary fiction criticism holds that the characters and actions must speak for themselves without comment, that the writer ought to disappear into his fiction. For such reasons, this criticism rather looks down on a mode of writing which numbers among its purest practitioners, Rabelais and Montaigne, and among its less pure ones, Plato, Cervantes, Bunyan, Swift, Fielding, Sterne, Dostoyevsky, Joyce, and Mann—rather as Shakespeare used to be disparaged for having violated the three neo-Aristotelian unities. In criticism, one must think of Jamesianism as of the School of Boileau (which also was not without merit): *This too will pass*—though, God knows, it may take a while.

How can "Rameau's Nephew" be called fiction? True, it has no proper narrative, but it does have imagined characters projected by their dialogue; through their ideas and attitudes we come to know them. Then why is not Plato's *Symposium* a work of fiction? It is something of one. Both these dialogues, and the dialogue between Settembrini and Naphta in *The Magic Mountain*, exist in the ill-charted regions between philosophy and story. Whether they are called one thing or the other depends upon the stance they take—the direction they face. In *The Symposium*, Plato employs the scene and the characters as a way of heightening what he intended to be the main thing, his ideas; whereas in the Settembrini-Naphta scene, Mann, less than explaining the ideas for their own or the truth's sake, was showing how enlightened, civilized men employ and play with ideas, and how ideas can affect a young man not yet used to them. "Rameau's Nephew" lies somewhere between these two, though rather nearer Mann than Plato.

A philosopher proper is one who succeeds in disentangling ideas about the world from the world, and in making a fairly coherent system of his ideas. Such disentangling and ordering is greater in *The Symposium* than in "Rameau's Nephew"; in *The Republic*, it is greater still, and by the time of *The Laws*, the sense of dialogue has all but vanished—that sense of an intercourse of opinion among imagined characters. Such men as Voltaire, Dr. Johnson, Diderot, Jefferson, and Sade were thinkers of a sort; ideas animated them, and what they wrote was primarily concerned with ideas. Yet they were less concerned with disentangling or systematizing their ideas than with expressing them with persuasive elegance and turning them into social or private action. Such romances as *Zadig, Candide, Justine,* and *Rasselas* are vehicles for commenting on the world. These men are not interested in autobiography or self-expression; the Word is too important to them for that, as they believe. Indeed, it as an assumption of such a piece of "Rameau's Nephew" that the Word can become Man. This was Sade's assumption, too, though his novels are as dull as his ideas are vile. (It has turned out, alas, that he was as right as were the optimistic *philosophes* whose inversion he was. Man in a state of nature is good or is bad: how extraordinary it is that, for several generations, Europe accepted either of these notions, or the root notion that man is in a state of nature, or should be in it.)

Kleist's tales beautifully show how ideas which philosophy isolates and looks at separately are nevertheless bound up with the phenomenal world. In the first paragraph of *Michael Kohlhaas*, the theme of the story is announced: ". . . in short, the world would have had cause to bless his memory, had he not carried one virtue to excess. His sense of justice made him a robber and murderer." But the story does not in any divorceable way illustrate this theme. And this very tangle and difficulty is a good share of what the story is about: just as justice for Kohlhaas clings to and will not separate from the actual horses stolen from him and finally restored to him, so the idea of the story will not separate from the story itself but clearly lives in it.

Consider Ivan's fable, "The Grand Inquisitor." *The Brothers Karamazov* creates Ivan in the reader's mind primarily through a series of intellectual dialogues. For the most part, the ideas of these dialogues are present passionately and dramatically: the Word is fleshed. Ivan's conversations with the Devil illustrate his state of mind and illuminate his behavior on the witness stand, and the main event of the book, the murder, is Smerdyakov's incarnating Ivan's Word in action. So, his telling "The Grand Inquisitor" to Alyosha illustrates his agony of doubt and his intellectual's refusal to leave the mysteries alone. Just as the heart of the fable is the Inquisitor's defense of himself to the Christ, so Ivan defends (and exposes) himself to Alyosha by telling him the fable. Just as the Christ does not argue with the Inquisitor but gives him a kiss, so Alyosha, understanding that episode of Ivan's story as Ivan's plea for redeeming love, kisses him.

Now, all of this is sufficiently "novelistic," but it takes no account of the story of the Grand Inquisitor as such, nor of the ideas with which the story deals. Yet these, far more than its integration into the novel, give it its celebrity as the most brilliant autonomous passage in Dostoyevsky and the supreme fable about modern rationalist, progressivist, irreligious man— about the "socialist." Novelistically (structurally), the fable did not need to be as powerful or as intrinsically good as it is. The narrator's ideas in the first half of *Notes from Underground* are perhaps comparable to Ivan's in intrinsic interest, but their proliferation, their turbulence, their lack of an internal coherence such as the fable of the Grand Inquisitor affords, keeps them from flourishing apart from the Underground man himself. Raskolnikov's "Superman" theories are not so clear and forceful as Nietzsche's, and they are wholly integrated into his character and actions. But "The Grand Inquisitor" leads a life of its own. It does not positively contradict or damage anything else in the novel; its defect is its very excellence— according to that literary esthetic which holds that the structural coherence of ideas, not their power or truths, is all that matters as they occur in a story, poem, or play. No one, beginning with Dostoyevsky himself, would deny that Dostoyevsky's stories are marred by excesses and disproportions, nor should one deny that perfection of form is a noble ideal in art. But perfection is only one of several high goods, and when perfectionism is allowed to tyrannize, it can yield the judgment that, for the good of *The Brothers Karamazov*, "The Grand Inquisitor" should have been less beautiful, less powerful, less wise. To one for whom both the play and the truth of ideas are of high importance wherever they are found, even in a story, the judgment is monstrous. Not the least of the reasons for the greatness of this imperfect book is the extravagance of its intellectual energy, the exuberance of its wisdom.

An anatomy is an odd sort of writing, about as shapely as a gunnysack bulging with stores. Of all the kinds of literature it is the most bookish: it is full of allusions to other books; its lovers are bookish people (Dr. Johnson said that "Burton's *Anatomy of Melancholy* was the only book that ever took him out of bed two hours sooner than he wished to rise"); the anatomist is a scholar in the old sense, a man of learning most of whose experience comes from books. The impulse to anatomy still occurs, as evidenced by such books as those of Montagu Summers on the black arts; but, in effect, anatomy is extinct, for a mind strong enough to write a good anatomy has not for some time been allowed the necessary bagginess but is turned into what is now meant by a scholar. George Saintsbury, for example, might very well have been happier shuffling together an Anatomy of Books than machine-making all those histories and surveys he actually produced; despite the title, Frye's *Anatomy of Criticism* is intellectually rigid in its schema. The great intellectual good which science, would-be science, and awe of science have imposed upon scholars is not wisdom and certainly not play, but logical discipline. Literary scholars have been inspired with distrust of literature except as subject matter, as amusement, or as an impersonal, remote power to be revered; and scholars of all varieties (this has become especially virulent in America) have abandoned humane discourse, as being imprecise, in favor of a sort of sign language. Compare Havelock Ellis and Dr. Kinsey on sex. Though Ellis has scientific pretensions, the best thing about *The Psychology of Sex* is its ragbag accumulation of lore, and the language in which it is written, if not very high in the literary scale, is at least readable. In Kinsey there is not a trace of the anatomist left: he exactly defines his field; within it, he is statistically thorough; and he uses a sign language that has nothing to do with literary discourse—it is a version of the dumb hailing the deaf.

Though wildman bookishness may have become shy about displaying itself in full anatomy since the seventeenth century, still its *disjecta membra* are to be found strewn among stories, especially in such novels as *Tristram Shandy* and *Ulysses*, the main energy of which lies in their language rather than in the narrative or characters. *The Life and Opinions of Tristram Shandy* is the autobiography of an anatomist. Tristram is created in good part by his quirks of erudition and opinion, and the other characters are apprehended less as realistic personalities than as static, undeveloping "characters" dominated by one eccentricity, a hobbyhorse. Moreover, there is the rush of language, the parody, the fondness for odd or foreign words, the concern for (and superb control of) style, the love of digression, the display of erudition. Dickens has some of this, though not in so concentrated a form; so do the Melville of *Moby Dick* and the Twain of *Huckleberry Finn*. The Joyce of *Ulysses* has it all, in different proportions, and especially a gusto for wild, wonderful lists, for vulgar errors, and for puzzles. Contemporaneously, Saul Bellow is a rush-of-words writer of wildman fiction, for example in such a true "character" as quirky Tamkin in "Seize the Day"; the Nabokov of *Lolita* is more than half anatomist; the merits of Henry Miller's grotesque stories are those of anatomy; it is a pity that Aldous Huxley wrote any sort of fiction besides satiric anatomies. The indispensable tone for such fiction, the essential attitude towards its characters and events even when they are grimly painful, is comic. Sentiment, indignation, bewilderment, outrage—the comic tone overrides all, an awareness of absurdity. It is to be found, though nowhere else, in the sense of abundant delight with which the language talks about its subject or veers off towards anything else under the sun. It is in the voice of one who can not forget for long: *How impenetrably absurd the world is.*

Of the several ways in which speculating on the nature of things combines with story-telling, satire is by far the most frequent. Whether it is a Horatian impulse to laugh somewhat affectionately at or a Juvenalian drive mercilessly to scourge mankind for its foolishness, dishonesty, stupidity, filthy vice, corrupt institutions, vanity, and avarice, the satirist's clear intention is to say that things should be better arranged than thus. However disguisedly, he may also intend his satire to prod and sting his readers into arranging things better. But whether the reader goes into action and whether the writer wants him to, these are inessential, for satire is not propaganda. What is essential is a vision: for the writer to make the reader see men as being viler or sillier than they ought to be. This is Balzac's vision in *The Vicar of Tours*, and it is obvious that he had no propagandistic intentions in the story. For the effect of the story is not sharp or bitter; it is made ample and pleasant, as well as pathetic, by Balzac's appetite for human experience, the abundance of his interest, and his zest for understanding. The satire of the story (like Balzac's freely offered opinions on everything under the sun) serves as an ingredient in the whole concoction; it contributes to the whole without being the point of the story.

As a literary category, narrative satire is thoroughly unsatisfactory. Frye describes something called Menippean satire, a striking creature something like a gryphon: the ancient rhetoricians report having seen one, but unfortunately somewhere in the Dark Ages it lost its way, and has existed for centuries only in rumor. I suspect that the satiric impulse is not at all a narrative one, but takes as its pure form that sort of essay in either verse or prose which used to be called *a satire*. (*A satire* is nearly extinct now; neither Orwell nor his critics commonly refer to his essays as *satires*.) Usually, however, it merges with other literary impulses; formally, it becomes adjectival. *Tartuffe* is a satiric comedy; *Gargantua and Pantagruel* is a satiric anatomy (the two are very congenial); if *Animal Farm* survives, it will be as what it also was from the start, a tale for children, the visible half of a satiric allegory. The term *narrative satire* does not indicate a form but the blurred judgment that, whereas in *that* case, *Middlemarch*, for example, the satire is no more than a quality of tone, in *this* case, *A Tale of a Tub*, for example, the story exists for the convenience of the satire. There is another way of putting it: when a story-teller opens his revulsion full flood, as West did in *Miss Lonelyhearts* and as Swift did most savagely in Gulliver's fourth voyage, then the story itself becomes a figure of the satire. It should be judged only partly by the canon of realism in the one case, or of romance in the other. Everything in *Miss Lonelyhearts* could have happened; yet West did not select and arrange the events as a way of saying: "Life is like that." He did it to say: "This is dreadful; life ought not to be like this." It seems to be a realistic story, but as much as this it is a satire, a sermon given over to the illustration of an unstated text.

Making a Likeness: Realistic Fiction

Chekhov said: "You live badly, my friends. It is a shame to live like that." But his best stories, such as "The Duel," are not satires. They do not express horror, censure, or ridicule at the way people behave; they show the way people behave. Nor does Chekhov do this to illustrate a point, overtly to teach; he does it as one tells a tale or tells what happened, for its own sake.

I do not attribute to myself any guarantee of merit except that of painting a *real likeness* of nature.

Stendhal

Moderns are so used to having visual likenesses about them that they are apt not to realize how sophisticated it is to make one. To enjoy one is easy enough, but to make one is another matter. For a very long time, beasts and men in painting and sculpture obviously came from ideas—from dreams or ideals—rather than from observation of the appearance of actual individuals. In literary forms, realism signifies making a likeness with words, and it is worth while recalling just how recent a province realism is. According to standard European literary history of the main-currents sort, realistic fiction is a creation of the eighteenth century (sagas do not count, not being in The Great Tradition). The inhabitant of realism is not infrequently guilty of that provincial's arrogance which measures things by his own limited standards. F. Scott Fitzgerald said that if a writer began with an individual he would end with a type and if he began with a type, he would end with nothing. To repeat the mot without prefacing it with the phrase "in realistic writing," is to be guilty of a sleaziness. Fielding would have spat on the notion: "I describe not men, but manners; not an individual, but a species." It is not that realistic fiction as such is an inferior form of literature. Any province which can lay claim in whole or in part to most of European fiction for the past two centuries is one of the glories of literature—of its many glories, one.

The technique of striking off a visual likeness is not difficult to acquire. It needs no talent to take a snapshot or to make a death-mask. But making a likeness which is also art is another matter. In ancient Greece, portraiture was little practiced, not because it was beyond the artists, but because it was considered low; beauty was art's true business, and beauty was considered seldom or never to manifest itself in actuality—in appearances. During the centuries when portraiture was held to be high art, it was as much the painter's style as the subject's appearance that got onto the canvas: imagine the same person painted by Tintoretto, Holbein, Rembrandt, Gainsborough, and Goya. When somebody complained to Piscasso that his portrait of Gertrude Stein did not look like her, Picasso is reported to have said: "It will." Like any good painter, he was less interested in imitating Stein's appearance than in rearranging it so as to embody his idea of her; because he was a good painter, his idea seemed strange at first, but later it seemed more true than the mere appearance. It is only comparatively that a good portrait can be called real, true, or life-like.

In literature, as in painting, realism is the art of manifesting an idea by means of arranging the appearances of actual things into a recognizable likeness. When it is done well, one is likely not to penetrate to the idea, but to rest content with a clap of recognition, with saying: "Life is really like that." The danger is in the *really*.

Auden has written that one of the qualities he values highly in a young poet is the power to notice; indeed, in an age which puts such barriers of distraction and idea between seer and thing seen, to notice and to describe accurately is a moral virtue. He did not mean by this the irrelevant scrupulosity which drove Joyce to an excess of accuracy about the appearance of actual places in Dublin. He meant a fidelity to the actual for its own sake such as assisted Lawrence to describe so well a rearing horse; Hardy, a girl hoeing turnips; Twain, a raft on a river in fog. But, as such, regard for sensory experience is not very important in fiction. If so small a fidelity warrants being termed moral, how very important is fidelity to those gestures, inflections, glances, actions, and speeches which reveal fiction's main matter: the secret lives of individuals, the intricacies of their relationship to one another and to society, the movements of the soul. What realistic fiction imitates is not physical appearance as such. It is the developing relationships among characters, as revealed by their externally apprehensible behavior and their conscious thoughts—among characters, that is, whose physical, social, and psychological behavior conforms to what is there to be observed in life.

Realism assumes man under the aspect of nature. That the hardiest strain of realistic fiction should have arisen along with natural science is more than coincidence; they were both flora of the same new climate of opinion. In the latter part of the nineteenth century when scientific determinism was at its most presumptuous, naturalistic fiction shot off towards it away from the main stream of literature; nothing but a general acceptance of science's worst philosophical pretensions can explain the prestige of this dullest perversion of story-telling yet applauded, the extreme of which is that anti-story, the case history. Writers of good realistic fiction (Eliot, Crane), like supple and humane scientists, assume that men exist in a natural order, but that not everything about them can be known, or predicted. Unlike almost all other kinds of writing, naturalism and realism restrict their vision to what can be seen by natural light. Naturalism asserts that there is no other way of seeing than by that part of the spectrum visible to human eyes. Realism too will know only what can be seen, but it assumes that, both upward and downward in the range of "black," there are things, still in the natural order, which to imagine would stir the soggiest heart, especially things in our own souls of which we are not properly aware. "The Open Boat" is so fine a realistic story in good part because it brings these assumptions about nature up into action and image, confronts them, and rejoices in the mystery.

A realistic writer, like a scientist, may believe there is also a supernatural order, but he will admit it into his fiction only as it affects his character's naturally describable behavior. Prince André lying on the battlefield in *War and Peace* experiences something that profoundly affects and changes him.

What the reader knows is that he has a head wound, becomes indifferent to what had formerly been of greatest importance to him, and looks deeply into the sky. The experience as rendered is psychologically credible in the natural order, and it can be, but does not have to be, apprehended as somehow connected with the supernatural, the religious. That a character in a realistic story should believe an event to be providential, as Alyosha Karamazov does, is perfectly acceptable since there are such people in the natural world; but to hinge a realistic story on divine intervention, as Greene does in *The End of the Affair*, is to ruin it. There can be no miracles in *Middlemarch*, yet there must be mystery. Time, space, physical and biological laws, the mazes of psychology, social customs—these must all be as they are in life; yet there must be mystery. An ambiguous art, realistic fiction. One of its minor masterpieces is *The Turn of the Screw*, in which James goes right to the brink of "black," and peers as far into mystery as realism's ambiguities will penetrate: the apparitions are ghosts *according to the narrator*, the strangeness (but not unnaturalness) of whose mind the very story demonstrates. Whenever it is a question of the supernatural (as it is not for Narayan, who in *Grateful for Life and Death* assumes ghosts as part of the natural order), it must not be the ghosts or miracles which the likeness is of but the mind of the character who experiences what he believes to be ghosts or miracles. It is his state of mind which is "real."

If part of the over-valuation of realistic fiction comes from its verisimilitude, as much or more comes from the term *realistic* itself. Literarily, *realism* should refer only to the imitation of the actual, but in fact it is so closely associated with *reality* that it elevates whatever it touches (just as *nonrealistic fiction* has come to be not simply a neutral term, but slightly pejorative). But the largest part of the overrating comes from a philosophical agreement with the assumptions of realism. Good but quite small writers such as C. P. Snow and Katherine Anne Porter are often treated with the seriousness accorded those who belong to a Himalaya of literature; they may in themselves not be as grand as various individual mountains, yet they are treated as though they belonged to the range nearest reality. Many believe, or assume in a muddled sort of way, that reality is all—and only—that which can be apprehended by the senses and deduced by reason; for them, realism will be the most congenial kind of art, the truest. Many believe, more generally, that reality is an entity separate from the idea-making, fantasying mind; they are at least disposed in favor of realism. But for those who believe that reality is seldom manifested and is not only something to be imitated but is also something to be created, realism, like any other kind of art, is valuable as it transcends mere impact and becomes experience—that is, as it creates a reality of its own which is a figure of the hidden reality already there before the artist began. *War and Peace* made such a figure mainly in the realistic mode; *Don Quixote*, mainly in the mode of romance. But how could one presume to choose between these two magnificences?

All this about realistic fiction obviously has much in common with autobiography, and the overlap between the two is continuous and enormous. A writer may conceive of himself as a character, like the reporter in Crane's "The Open Boat," and the characters may present themselves auto-biographically, as in any epistolary story. Further, for place, characters, situations, costumes, and ways of speaking, every realistic fiction writer draws upon his experience in life far more than upon his imagination (Joyce worried whether he was deficient in invention). The difference may be seen when the examples are fairly pure. I know almost nothing of the man Augustine except what I have learned from his *Confessions;* from them, I intimately know a great deal about the motions of his soul, about a man moving towards the Infinite—indeed, about the soul itself; but from them I learn fictionally very little else—a little about the society of the time, something about his mother and less about four or five other people, almost nothing about the woman with whom he lived for several years and by whom he had a son (about whom I know only his name). I know nothing whatever about the person who wrote *Njal's Saga,* either externally or from reading the novel, and I suppose it was written by a man only because a learned friend instructs me that thirteenth-century Icelandic women did not, so far as is known, do such things as write sagas; but I learn from it a great deal about more than a score of persons (who may or may not have existed in fact), and about a particular society—indeed, about men's connection with Society; their hatred of the Law they need.

As for the craft of realistic fiction, James wrote about it at length, and Jamesianism has evolved most subtle elaborations upon his texts. When reading this body of criticism, one must remember that Cervantes, Tolstoy, and Dostoyevsky among them violate most of the principles it holds dear and that one should preface the words *fiction* and *novel* (as in Lubbock's *The Craft of Fiction* or James's *The Art of the Novel*) with the word *realistic.* Taking these precautions, one can learn much from Jamesianism.

The most important technical issue this criticism raises, one which has latterly become a special bugaboo for fiction writers, is point of view. Of course it is important for the writer to have a firm control of point of view, especially to maintain the proper distance from his subject. But one begins thinking of some wonderful stories that do not always pay attention to the rules: Dickens often failed to keep a proper distance in his novels, most egregiously when a child was dying; it was as though Hardy loved Tess so much that the pain of grinding her down and out was more than he could fully bear, so that he withdrew too far from her in the last, most tragic section of the novel; Fielding whenever he wished violated his story to speak to the reader. Also one remembers that James was not altogether pleased with Flaubert, whose formal perfection he, of course, hailed; that he thought the main business of fiction was to capture a felt sense of life, especially of moral life; that he could say that Tolstoy (whose novels at another time he lumped together with Dostoyevsky's as "fluid puddings") was "a reflector as vast as a natural lake; a monster harnessed to his great subject—all human life!" After such reflections, one decides that probably a writer need concern himself less and less about the technicalities of point of view as he gains in power and wisdom; the more powerful the story, the more point of view ceases to be a matter of craft and becomes an admonition to the story-teller to be wise.

In the hands of a master, a reader quite forgets about point of view, for it comes to seem that he is looking at reality truly. To do this, of course, he must stand somewhere, but the very doing, the high delight of true vision, makes him cease to notice any irregularities in what he is standing on. Lawrence in "The Virgin and the Gipsy" allows himself the greatest intimacy with any character he chooses—an irregular intimacy. But in the way that matters most he leaves them alone: at the moment of acting and speaking they are free to behave according to their own nature, and the author does not come between them and the reader but leaves them to connect as they will.

There are two accidental, but important, issues involved in Jamesianism's over-valuation of Flaubert, the first of which properly belongs to cultural history.

It has to do with the modern cult of The Artist. Flaubert dedicated himself to being an Artist of fiction as no predecessor had done—as James and Joyce supremely did, as Tolstoy and Chekhov utterly did not. *Madame Bovary* is, beyond cavil, a fine piece of craftsmanship; as a likeness, it has only one flaw of much consequence, the blind beggar's manipulated, almost purely symbolic appearance as Emma lies dying; the flaw is not grave. But I can think of no essential respect in which *Pride and Prejudice* is less well wrought, and if Jane Austen manipulated her plot considerably more than Flaubert did his, she did not thereby violate the essential relationships among the characters. In other words, part of the reason for *Madame Bovary's* prestige has been the irrelevant fact that Flaubert thought of himself as The Artist and spoke with great self-consciousness of his art as, say, Austen did not. In addition, that there was an attempt to suppress the novel on publication and that it triumphed over the enemy helped make Flaubert into an Artist-Hero; Austen has labored under the handicap of respectability even in her reputation.

The second matter that helps account for the excessive regard for *Madame Bovary's* importance has to do with Flaubert's criticism of provincial bourgeois society. Of all forms of literature, the realistic novel is the most directly concerned with social relationships, for in considerable part it defines its characters by the way they play their roles in society. For this reason, the writer cannot help criticizing the society he is writing about, which must also be quite similar to the society he knows by experience. (The frequent assertion that "the novel is a middle-class art" should read: "Most writers of realistic fiction write about the middle classes into which they were born.") Lady Murasaki thoroughly approves of the aristocratic customs, ideals, and arrangements which make Genji possible; Austen approves, with ironic reservations, of the rather functionless rural gentry she writes about;

Chekhov deplores late nineteenth-century Russia; Joyce devotes much of his force to attacking Ireland, the Catholic Church, the British Empire, the life of modern cities; Celine abandons himself to his loathing of all modern society. Whether the author's social views are expressed overtly like Dickens's in *Bleak House*, whether the characters present their opinions as some of Silone's do in *Bread and Wine* or the author analyzes them rather sociologically as Eliot does in *Middlemarch*, or whether neither author nor characters appear to have any such opinions as in Wharton's *Ethan Frome*, this much is certain: more than any other form of art, realistic fiction involves itself intimately in a system of social relationships, imitating a part of a society. The author's opinions about that society may be interesting, but they are usually inessential to the fiction. Such matters as these are always essential, for they affect action: the modes of courtship, the forms and extent of an employer's power over his employees, who owns the land a farmer works, what an unmarried girl is expected to do if she becomes pregnant and how she is looked at by her neighbors. Now, Flaubert's implicit thesis was one especially congenial to modern intellectuals: the life of the provincial bourgeoisie is deadly and deadening, most of all esthetically; by extension, modern society is deadening to the rare, sensitive soul, especially to The Artist. No doubt this is in good part true; it is one of the explicit themes in many first-rate fiction writers—Eliot, Chekhov. Yet it is not the whole truth; Austen, Balzac, Tanizaki (*The Makioka Sisters*), as well as the two named above, are not simply wrong to find living virtue in some of the members of bourgeois society. The danger is for this thesis to be accepted as dogma. When a reader so accepts it, he overrates a Flaubert or Joyce for confirming his prejudices, though the critic or reader may not acknowledge or even recognize this as the main reason for his over-valuation. No one satisfies these prejudices more thoroughly than James, who not only scorns bourgeois vulgarity but also makes the reader feel that anyone who has good taste is aristocratic, including any reader who has the good taste to like James.

The effect of this dogma can be most damaging to the novelist. *Madame Bovary* is an amazing work of likeness, from the parlor interiors to the course of Emma's love affairs. By reason of that very fact, it is not a satire, even though, like *Middlemarch*, it has a perceptible satiric tinge. Had it been clearly committed to satire as *Miss Lonelyhearts* is, then its partial truth would have been a distortion for the purpose of emphasis. But a realistic writer assumes the impersonal stance of one who is getting at as much of the whole truth as the likeness he is making can figure forth; his small image is meant to be in proportion to the larger reality of which it is a likeness. Flaubert maintains the stance of impersonality admirably. He treats every character with the same cold detachment. It is a coldness, however, not of the eye only but also of the heart. Except for the doctor called in to remedy Charles's bungling (the only character in the novel who comes off well) and except for Emma, Flaubert finds nothing human enough in his characters to respond to or to make us respond to with warmth, with admiration—perhaps with a certain pity for Charles, but a pity corrupted by disdain for his stupidity. (Tolstoy loathed adultery, but when he was preparing to write *Anna Karenina* he said that "his problem was to represent this woman as not guilty, but merely pitiful.") Flaubert's very coldness implies not only that the society is deadly but also that the persons in it are or will soon be entirely deadened—not most of them partially deadened, but all of them entirely.

Chekhov, who also knew and loathed the bourgeois society of the provinces, does not spare that society in his good fiction. In many of his lesser stories, he descends to something not much above analytic sociology. But in a story as successful as "The Duel," he does the better thing: he makes a likeness of that society and also penetrates to the inner nature of the individuals who live in it but do not just live in it. His comprehension of these people is that of the highest realistic fiction. Not everything about them demonstrates the power of social forces or comments upon these forces. They are coherent persons full of those sudden and continual contradictions without which a realistic character does not have a full life.

If there were a society as inescapably deadening as that which Flaubert asserted the society of his novel to be, then the most in realistic fiction which that society could be imagined to produce would be negligible, for in it every writer too would be deadened—as Flaubert himself was not, as Chekhov the humane, who did not hate the sin more than he felt for the sinner, knew many were not.

A cold eye but a warm heart.

Realistic fiction deals intimately with those actions and relations which are essentially moral. Just as a realistic writer must assume a certain stance toward the society he imagines, so he cannot help assuming a stance towards the moral life of his imagined people. It will be indistinguishable from a real-life stance towards moral issues. Bellow did not assume, so far as one can judge by reading "Seize the Day," a special story-telling stance towards Tommy Wilhelm's self-pity. Since in realistic fiction the author's moral stance towards his characters is also a stance towards actual people, a work of realistic fiction may be said to be in some way a work of life as well. And writers and critics of such fiction agree among themselves on moral matters no better than kings and philosophers.

There is a lesser consideration to be disposed of: which sorts of actions and thoughts is it immoral to present in fiction? The answer to this is clear: there is no moral reason to exclude any action or any thought from a story. That a Puritan who is willing to contemplate in a story the worst act his religion thinks possible, Judas' betrayal of Jesus, should be offended by an account of a man and woman fondling one another's genitals is perfectly reasonable, but it has less to do with morality than the Puritan thinks it does. It has to do with the feeling of broken taboos which is natural when one intrudes upon others in the performance of one of those bodily acts which each must do for himself. Moreover, if it is esthetically right and humanly true for a character to have the vilest of thoughts, then the moral problem becomes the literary one of tone, of distance, of keeping the idea the character's, and it is quite indefensible to suppress the thought as such. In sum: as man, novelist, and thinker, the Marquis de Sade is condemned, but there is no moral reason why he, his acts, and his thoughts could not be admitted into a good novel; the question, at once moral and esthetic, would be how he should be presented, with what sanction on the part of the novelist.

My contention is that a good work of fiction not only delights the reader but also is informed by a steady and adequate vision. The steadiness presents few difficulties, but *adequate vision* needs defending against both the moral relativist and the esthetician (who are not infrequently the same person).

The scientist assumes towards whatever he is studying the stance of pure inquiry: it is worth studying not because it is good or beautiful, but because it is. Zola in his fiction theoretically looked with the eyes of a naturalist, and his novels may be seen as the wreckage of a good romancer. The esthete assumes that a thing is interesting as it is beautiful or in some way esthetically pleasing. Gide obviously assumes this in that tiresome early book, *Fruits of the Earth*; but in *Strait Is the Gate*, his position as novelist is manifestly moral. It may or may not be true that as a man he took this position for esthetic reasons, to savor it and by doing so to savor Alissa's spiritual agony. But just as he purified the story of any sense of the extraneously autobiographical, so he purified it of his estheticism (if, in fact, that was his motive). The evidence for the accusation is not to be found in the story itself, and by the nature of the case all other evidence is inadmissible. In addition to taking the would-be scientist's or the esthete's stance, a story-teller may also proceed as though the issue did not exist and assume some local set of values, those of a game, for example. But the best such stories are very light of weight— nearly all science-fiction, Poe's "The Gold Bug," Thurber's "You Can Look It Up." When, as with *The Man Who Could Work Miracles* or *Alice in Wonderland*, such a story has some greater value, it is not because of the author's moral seriousness or whatever moral qualities the characters display, but because it is a fantasy. I know of no realistic story which takes a holiday from moral concern and also creates a considerable reality of its own.

A book's excellence should not be determined by its effect on the world or its writer's moralistic intentions; neither should it be judged according as it achieves or fails to achieve the judge's own set moral order. Such ways of judging led Plato in *The Republic* to condemn Homer (the story goes that *The Iliad* was under his pillow when he died). Tolstoy in *What is Art?* rated *Uncle Tom's Cabin* higher than his own novels, but when he had been writing *War and Peace* he defined his exalted ideal thus: "The aim of an artist is not to resolve a question irrefutably, but to compel one to love life in all its manifestations, and these are inexhaustible."

Moral order implies a set of laws, whether divinely ordained or natural, that exists apart from social conventions or from our knowledge and acceptance of it. A writer of realistic fiction is not to be judged as he believes in such an order or as he expounds it in his story, any more than he should be judged according as he holds to a psychological system and as this system conforms to the psychoanalytic one. To be sure, in a cloudy sort of way, writers agree on principles if they are stated generally and abstractly enough. It is good to help an unfortunate; brothers are rivals for their parents' affection; vengeance is natural but forgiveness is very good, etc. It is not these bleached bones of psychology or ethics that a story-teller cares about, but a person moving in the unpredictable flesh of decision and action. Dostoyevsky once said never to tell the reader what a character's deepest motive was. Exactly: let the bones be covered with meat. The realistic writer's concern is with the world of contingency, the world we daily live in, where it is hard to know what actually happened, harder yet to know and weigh the motives (moral and psychological) and consequences of an act, and quite impossible to judge an act, much less a man, with anything like absolute confidence. The impossibility of perfect sureness in the contingent world was what made Aquinas, the subtlest of minds, reluctant to deal with ethics. It was not the business of Tolstoy the novelist to preach against adultery or war. That he did not so preach in *Anna Karenina* is one of the reasons for its superiority to *War and Peace* as a work of art (though the latter is still superior as a work of life, the preaching in it being excisable and inessential); that his preaching was at the very heart of the story ruined *The Kreutzer Sonata*.

Mickey Spillane's vision is moral enough but not adequate. It is not even possible. The climax of *The Big Kill*, which is tough-guy realistic, consists of Mike Hammer's being saved by a crawling baby who shoots the villainess with a pistol in order to avenge his father's murder. Both Rousseauism and its inversion, Sadism, are as such inadequate. The veneer of conventionality is not adequate in *Moll Flanders*, and the commercial self-interest beneath the veneer is severely limiting. Murasaki's aristocratic stoicism is adequate, as are Manzoni's Catholicism, Chekhov's humane materialism, James's Manicheism, Richardson's use of bourgeois Protestantism (in *Clarissa*), Faulkner's pagan stoicism (in *The Hamlet*), and Dostoyevsky's Russian Orthodox Christianity. Murasaki's moral order was ample enough to permit her all the suppleness she was capable of; Richardson's was pinched and mean, but he did not stay within it (as he seemed to believe he was doing); Dostoyevsky's good fiction is the record of his struggle to create an order he could accept, rather than to reject all order or to accept one on mere authority. In every case, the writer was free to see actual behavior as amazing—undetermined and unexpected. Such freedom was not necessary to a Bunyan, who wrote an autobiography and an allegory, but it was necessary to Louisa May Alcott, James T. Farrell, and Jack London; their work is realistic enough so that the absence of this freedom gives the slick impression that in real life moral decision is clear and easy, or the fraudulent impression that it does not exist.

The vision of a realistic writer is not of a given or fixed moral order. It is of individuals' behavior as seen according to a social convention and a natural psychology, and in the light of their own and their author's beliefs. The trouble starts when he is a True Believer conceiving some social, psychological, or religious system as being rigidly right (Fast in *Spartacus*) or when he is confused in his grasp of them (Faulkner in *A Fable*). For his job is not proximately moral ("Poetry makes nothing happen," said Auden); it is not for him to improve us directly, teach us a given set of rules, or save us. His best job is to arouse and extend our wonder at the endless variety of human possibilities in the actual social, psychological, and moral world, and to enlarge our sense of communion with one another: *If life is like that, I am not alone.*

Don Quixote and *War and Peace*—these are the incomparable. The reality each imagines is of a supreme wisdom, delight, and scope. They do not give that singleness and purity of experience which a short story is capable of, nor do they admit of the special awe accorded to perfection. But if either of these novels were pared and proportioned à la Flaubert or James, it could not include so much or penetrate so far. Doubtless, God's reality is perfect, but my reality contains sillier fantasies than the flimsiest tale Cervantes included in his novel and stupider ideas than Tolstoy's tiresome theory of history. A perfect story is the work of a would-be god. A full story of a great man will be flawed; giving so much of himself to it, he cannot hide his own weaknesses. In his book I can see more of myself, as well as more of life, than in a godling's perfect book, and in more just proportions.

Don Quixote, the Knight of the White Moon's lance at his visor, preferring death to renouncing his devotion to Dulcinea; Natasha coming to the wounded André in the shed: these are for me the highest moments in story. They reach as far as translucent prose can go. That is, neither passage quoted out of context has anything like the power of Othello's last speech or of Priam's suing Achilles for Hector's body. It is not the words of the scenes which rise so high, only the scenes imagined as happening and the speeches as spoken in life, and they need the large body of their stories. Just as both are entirely realistic on the surface, so both are drenched in dream-like romance—not just *Don Quixote*, but *War and Peace* as well.

Tolstoy could write so realistically about the noble and rich because he was born to their class. Moreover, the fictional reality of the book is so powerful that one ceases to pay much attention to distinctions. If it seems so actual and is so real, why ask for more? But I imagine that it could be real only if it were also fabulous. ("Human kind," said Eliot, "cannot bear very much reality.") The army of one of the greatest conquerors in history is approaching a capital city which is in the throes of being evacuated and is about to be destroyed by fire. The family of as charming a young woman as exists in all literature has taken in a wounded officer whose people are trying to save him. This officer, by coincidence, is the young woman's former fiancé, a prince, capable of the highest spirituality, whom she had desperately offended by trying to elope with a scoundrel. When she discovers who the wounded man is, she goes in the dark to his bedside in her nightdress and purely begs the forgiveness which he purely grants. . . . Some of it did happen, all of it could have happened, it seems actual. True. But I imagine that its reality could not have been so great unless the likeness it created had found and held the form of moral dream.

The Tale of Qamar az-Zaman,

THE SON OF

KING SHAHRIMAN

FROM

The Arabian Nights

Translated by James A. Bellamy

Editor's Note

The earliest known evidence of the existence of the collection of tales that we call *The Arabian Nights* or, more precisely, *The Thousand and One Nights,* is from the ninth century. Whether the Tale of Qamar az-Zaman was already one of the collection then or whether it was added, as many of the tales were, during subsequent centuries, remains unknown. The best scholarly opinion is that the framework story of *The Thousand and One Nights* is Indian in origin and that "Qamar az-Zaman" is of Indian and Persian origin. The *Nights* were first introduced to the West in Galland's translation into French, 1704-1717. They have been translated many times into English, either through Galland or directly from Arabic, but the following is the only translation of the tale of Qamar into contemporary English.

In his translation, Professor Bellamy has omitted all framework material, the interpolated tale of Ni'am and Ni'mah, supposed to be related by the ex-Magian, Bahram, and most of the verses, which are probably later additions, interrupt the flow of the story, and have very little merit as poems. He has based his translation on the Egyptian recension in the edition published in Cairo.

The Tale of Qamar az-Zaman,

THE SON OF

KING SHAHRIMAN

HERE WAS IN ANCIENT TIMES A KING NAMED SHAHRIMAN, WHO WAS Lord of the Isles of Khalidan. He possessed armies, slaves, and retainers; however, he had grown old and feeble and had never been blessed with a son, which caused him much sadness and anxiety. He deliberated much about the matter, and finally complained to one of his viziers, saying: "I fear that the kingdom will be lost after I am dead, for I have no son to rule it after me."

"Perhaps God will produce a miracle," said the Vizier. "So rely on God, O King; go, perform the ritual ablutions and pray a prayer of two prostrations; then lie with your wife, and perhaps you will attain your desire."

So he lay with his wife, and she conceived at that time. When her months were completed, she gave birth to a boy who was like the unveiled full-moon on a dark night.

The King named his son Qamar az-Zaman (Moon of the Age), and rejoiced exceedingly. The people decorated the city for seven days; drums were beaten, and the glad tidings were published abroad.

The child was tended by both wet and dry nurses, and was reared in an atmosphere of affection and coddling until, by the age of fifteen years, he had become outstanding in grace and beauty, and was of a good stature and well-proportioned. His father loved him greatly and could not bear to be separated from him night or day.

One day King Shahriman complained to one of his viziers of his inordinate love for his son, and said: "O Vizier, I am afraid that the vicissitudes and calamities of fate will afflict my son, Qamar az-Zaman, so I should like to see him married during my lifetime."

[33]

"Know, O King," replied the Vizier, "that marriage is a virtue and there is nothing wrong with your marrying your son during your lifetime."

Thereupon the King said: "Bring my son, Qamar az-Zaman, to me."

Qamar az-Zaman appeared and lowered his head to the ground in modesty before his father, who spoke to him, saying: "O Qamar az-Zaman, I should like to see you married and rejoice in you during my lifetime."

"Father," his son replied, "I have no desire for marriage and my soul does not incline to women, for I have found that books are transmitted on their treachery and that volumes exist which deal with their guile. O father, marriage is something that I will never agree to, even were I given the cup of death to drink."

When King Shahriman heard his son speak in this way, the light of his face grew dark, and he was greatly distressed at Qamar az-Zaman's disobedience; but such was his love for him that he did not discuss the matter further, but rather he honored him and treated him kindly, in every way which would draw affection to the heart. All the while, Qamar az-Zaman increased daily in grace and beauty, and in charm and attractiveness.

The King waited patiently a whole year while his son grew to perfection in speech and in beauty, so that men were ravished by his beauty and every passing breeze told of his grace. He became a temptation to lovers and a garden to those who yearn. He was sweet in his manner of speaking; his face put the full-moon to shame; he possessed form and symmetry, wit and blandishments; and he seemed to be the branch of a ben-tree or a bamboo reed. His cheeks could substitute for red anemone, and his figure for the branch of a ben-tree.

When another full year had passed, King Shahriman summoned Qamar az-Zaman, and said: "My son, will you not listen to me?" Qamar az-Zaman, full of shame, fell upon the ground before his father in respect, and said: "O my father, how could I not listen to you, for God has commanded me to obey you and not to oppose you?"

"Know, O my son," said the King, "that I wish to marry you and rejoice in you during my lifetime, and bestow upon you the rule of my kingdom before I die."

When Qamar az-Zaman heard the words of his father, he hung his head for a while; then raising it, he spoke: "Father, this is something that I will never do, even though I were given the cup of death to drink. I know that God has imposed on me the duty of obeying you, but for the love of God, I beg of you, do not command me to marry, and do not think that I will ever marry in my whole life, for I have read in the books of the ancients and moderns, and I have learned of all the calamities and afflictions that have come upon them because of the temptations and the endless wiles of women and the catastrophes that they bring about."

When King Shahriman had heard his son speak these words, he made no reply because of his inordinate love for him, but favored and honored him even more. Then the assembly broke up, and thereafter the King summoned his Vizier and met with him alone.

"O Vizier," said the King, "tell me what I should do in the matter of my son, Qamar az-Zaman. I asked your advice about marrying him before investing him with power, and you counselled me to do so; you also advised me to speak to him on the matter of marriage. I have done so, but he has disobeyed me and behaved badly towards me, as you very well see."

"O King," replied the Vizier, "I advise you now to be patient another year. Then when you wish to speak to him again about marriage, do not do so in private, but speak to him on a day when you are holding court and all the emirs and viziers are present and all the soldiers are standing by. When they are all gathered together, send for your son, Qamar az-Zaman, and have him come before you. When he appears, speak to him of marriage in the presence of all the emirs, viziers, chamberlains, the palace guard, the councillors of state, the army, and the military leaders, and he will be ashamed before them, and unable to oppose you in their presence."

When the Vizier had spoken, King Shahriman rejoiced exceedingly. He considered that the idea of the Vizier was an excellent one, and he bestowed on him a splendid robe of honor.

So King Shahriman was patient with Qamar az-Zaman for another year. As each day passed, the son grew in grace and beauty, and in splendor and perfection, until he had almost attained his twentieth year. God clothed him in garments of beauty and crowned him with the crown of perfection. His eye was more bewitching than Harut and Marut, and the coquettishness of his glances was more seductive than Taghut. His cheeks shone with the redness of the dawn; his eyelids were contemptuous of the sharpest swords; the whiteness of his brow resembled the radiant moon; the black of his hair was like the dark night; his waist was more slender than a thread of gossamer, and his hips were heavier than a sand dune. Nightingales were aroused to sing at the sight of him; his waist complained at the heaviness of his hips; and his charms threw all men into confusion.

King Shahriman gave heed to the words of his Vizier and was patient for another year, until a holiday came round on which he held court with all the emirs, viziers, chamberlains, councillors of state, soldiers, and military leaders in attendance. Then the King sent for his son, Qamar az-Zaman, who, when he appeared, kissed the ground three times before his father, and stood with his arms folded behind his back.

"My son," his father said, "I have brought you here this time before this assembly with the whole army present, in order to command you to do something, so do not disobey me. This is that you marry, for I wish to marry you to a princess and rejoice in you before my death."

When Qamar az-Zaman heard his father speak these words, he lowered his head to the ground for a moment, then raised his eyes to his father, and in that moment, he was seized by the madness and boorishness of youth, and exclaimed: "I will never marry, though I were given the cup of death to drink. As for you, you are a silly old man: did I not refuse, when you asked me about marriage twice before?" Then, in his rage, Qamar az-Zaman unclasped his hands and shook his fist in the air in his father's presence.

His father was ashamed and embarrassed when this happened before the councillors of state while the army was present for the festival. He then recovered his kingly dignity and cried out against his son, and terrified him. Shouting to the slaves, he ordered them to seize and bind him. They did so, and brought him before the King, his head hanging in fear and dread, and his face and forehead crowned with sweat from the intensity of his shame and humiliation.

Then his father reviled and vilified him: "Woe to you, you whoreson and nursling of obscenity! How can this be your answer to me in the midst of my officers and soldiers? Up to now, no one has ever punished you, but you know that if one of my subjects had behaved thus, it would have been a serious offense indeed."

Then he ordered the slaves to remove his bonds and to imprison him in one of the towers of the palace. Servants went into the chamber that was in the tower and, after sweeping it out and washing down the tile floor, set up Qamar az-Zaman's bedstead, on which they spread a mattress and a leather coverlet. They gave him a pillow, a large lantern, and a candle, for the place was dark even in the daytime.

The slaves then brought Qamar az-Zaman into the chamber and stationed a eunuch at the door. Qamar az-Zaman lay down on the bed with a heavy heart and a broken spirit, blaming himself and regretting his conduct towards his father, now that regrets were of no avail.

"God frustrate marriage," he exclaimed, "and girls and deceitful women! Would that I had obeyed my father and married! If I had done so, it would have been better for me than this prison."

His father, in the meantime, remained upon the throne of his kingdom for the remainder of the day until sunset; then he retired with the Vizier and said: "O Vizier, when you advised me as you did, you became the cause of all that has happened between me and my son. What do you now advise?"

"O King," the Vizier replied, "leave your son in prison for fifteen days; then bring him before you and command him to marry, and he will surely not disobey."

The King accepted the Vizier's counsel, and retired for the night, his heart troubled on account of his son, because he loved him so dearly, having no other son than him. He had never been able to sleep unless he placed his arm under the neck of Qamar az-Zaman, so he spent this night with his mind in a turmoil, tossing and turning as if he were lying on a bed of burning coals. Anxieties assailed him and he shed many a tear, and he did not sleep the whole of that night.

When evening came, the eunuch brought Qamar az-Zaman the lantern, and, lighting a candle, he placed it in a candle-stick. He also brought him something to eat. Qamar az-Zaman ate a little, and continued to blame himself for behaving badly to his father, King Shahriman. "Did you not know," he said to himself, "that man is a hostage to his tongue, for it is a man's tongue that leads him to perdition?" He continued to blame and censure himself until he was overcome by tears. His broken heart was seared and he regretted intensely the words his tongue had uttered against the King. After he had finished eating, Qamar az-Zaman washed his hands, performed the ritual ablutions, prayed the sunset and evening prayers, and then sat down on the bed to read the Koran. He read the chapters of the Cow, the Family of Imran, Ya Sin, the Merciful, Blessed be the King, and the two Talismans, finishing with a prayer and supplication to God for protection. Before going to bed, he took off his clothes and changed into a nightshirt of fine silk, and bound around his head a piece of blue Marwazi cloth. He lay down to sleep on the bed on a mattress of satin of Ma'dan, which was the same on both sides, and was stuffed with ostrich feathers. Then, looking like the full moon on the fourteenth night of the month, Qamar az-Zaman covered himself with a silken sheet and fell asleep with the lantern lit at his feet and the candle burning at his head. He slept through the first watch of the night, not knowing what was stored up for him in the future or what He who knows the unseen had decreed.

It so happened that the chamber and tower were very old, and had been abandoned for many years. There was in the chamber an ancient Roman well in which dwelt a genie, one of the descendants of Iblis, the accursed one. Her name was Maymunah, and she was the daughter of Dimiryat, one of the famous kings of the Jinn.

When Qamar az-Zaman had slept through the first watch of the night, the Ifritah rose out of the Roman well, intending to lie in concealment near the heavens in order to eavesdrop. When she reached the rim of the well, she saw a light burning in the tower, contrary to custom. The Ifritah had been living in that place for many years, and she said to herself: "I have never seen anything like this." She was greatly amazed. It occurred to her that there must be a reason for this, so she went toward the light and found that it was coming from the tower room, which she then entered, finding the eunuch asleep at the door. When she entered the room, she saw that a bed had been set up, on which was the figure of a person sleeping, with a candle burning at his head and a lantern shining at his feet.

The Ifritah Maymunah was amazed at the light, so she went towards it little by little, folding her wings, and stopped beside the bed. She pulled down the sheet from Qamar az-Zaman's face and looked at him, standing there for a full hour, wondering at his beauty and grace. She saw that the radiance of his face was greater than that of the candle, for his face fairly sparkled with light. His eyes were dark and spoke the language of love. His cheeks were red; his eyelids drooped languidly; his eyebrows were arched like bows; and his body exhaled an aroma of musk.

When the Ifritah Maymunah, daughter of Dimiryat, saw him, she praised God, exclaiming: "Blessed be God, the best of creators!"—for she was one of the believing Jinn. And she continued to stare at him, repeating, "There is no god but God," and envying him his grace and beauty.

"By Allah," she said to herself, "I will not harm him and I will not let anyone else injure him! How could his people ever forget him here in this ruinous place? If one of our evil spirits should happen upon him at this time, he would ruin him!"

So saying, the Ifritah leaned over him and kissed him on the forehead;

then she drew the sheet up over his face and covered him with it. Opening her wings, she flew up towards the heavens, ascending from the tower chamber and rising in the air till she came near to the lowest heaven. Suddenly she heard the fluttering of wings flying in the air. She proceeded in the direction of the sound of the wings, and when she drew near, she discovered that they belonged to an Ifrit named Dahnash. She swooped down on him like a sparrow-hawk.

When Dahnash heard her and realized that it was Maymunah, daughter of the king of the Jinn, he was terribly afraid and his heart leaped into his throat. He begged for her protection, saying: "I conjure you by the most mighty name and the most noble talisman carven on the ring of Solomon that you treat me kindly and do me no harm!"

When Maymunah heard Dahnash speak these words, her heart felt compassion for him and she said: "You have conjured me with a mighty talisman, but I shall not free you unless you tell me where you are coming from at this hour."

"My lady," he replied, "I come from the farthest land of China and the inner isles, and I will tell you of a marvel that I have seen this night. If you find that I speak the truth, then let me go my way and write for me in your own hand a letter stating that I am your freedman, so that none of the high or low-flying Jinn nor those that plunge beneath the sea will oppress me."

"What is it that you have seen this night, O Dahnash?" asked Maymunah. "Tell me and do not hope to escape from my hands by lying. I swear by the carving on the seal-ring of Solomon, son of David—on them be peace—that if you lie, I will tear out your feathers with my hands, and I will rend your flesh and break your bones."

"If my words are not true," said Dahnash, son of the flying genie, Shamhurish, "do with me as you please, my lady.

"I have come this night from the inner isles of the land of China, which are the country of King Ghayur, Lord of the Isles and Seas and of the Seven Palaces. I have seen the daughter of this king, the most beautiful of God's creatures in this age. Indeed, I do not know how to describe her, for my tongue is incapable of doing her justice, but I shall mention to you some of her qualities by way of approximation.

"Her hair is black as a night of leave-taking and separation, and her face is as bright as the day of a lovers' meeting. Her nose is like the blade of a polished sword; her cheeks are like red wine or like red anemone. Her lips are like coral and carnelian. Her kisses are sweeter than wine whose taste quenches the torment of burning thirst. Her tongue is moved by a perfect intellect and a ready answer. Her bosom is a temptation to him who sees it —praised be He who created and fashioned it—joined to which are two braceleted arms. She has two breasts like two round boxes of ivory, from whose rising the sun and moon borrow light. Her belly has creases folded like the pleats in Egyptian Coptic cloth, going on to a slender waist which beggars the imagination. All this is above hips like a sand dune, which cause her to remain seated when she tries to rise, and keep her awake when she wishes to sleep. They are borne by two thighs like columns of pearl, which can carry the great load only because of what lies between them. As for her other qualities, no one can describe or depict them. This is all borne by two feet, the work of God the Guardian and Judge, so fine that I was amazed that they could carry what was above them. I will go no further than this, for the power of expression is inadequate to describe her and no indications can give her her full due.

"The father of this maid is a mighty king, a fighting knight, who traverses countries vast as the oceans both day and night; he fears not death, nor does dying cause him fright, for he is oppressive and tyrannical and conquering and repressive. He is the master of armies and hosts, climes and islands and seas, cities and abodes. He is named King Ghayur, Lord of the Isles and Seas, and the Seven Palaces.

"He loved this daughter whom I have described with a love so intense that he drew upon the wealth of all other kings and built for her seven palaces, each one unique in its own kind. The first palace was of crystal, the second of marble, the third of Chinese iron, the fourth of onyx and gemstones, the fifth of silver, the sixth of gold, and the seventh of precious jewels. These seven palaces he filled with all manner of splendid furnishings, gold and silver vessels, and all that gear which royalty requires, and commanded his daughter to dwell in each of the palaces for a part of the year and then move to another.

"The name of this queen was Budur. When her beauty became famous and her renown was spread abroad in the land, other kings sent to her father asking her hand in marriage.

"The King attempted to entice her into marrying, but she disapproved and said: 'O father, I have no purpose in ever marrying at all, for I am a lady and a queen who rules over men, and I do not want a man who would rule over me.'

"As often as she refused to wed, the desire of her suitors increased, and all the kings of the inner isles of China sent precious gifts and treasures to her father and corresponded with him about marrying her. Her father repeated his advice to her to marry numerous times, but she would not obey him. Finally she grew angry and said: 'Father, if you ever mention marriage to me one more time, I will take a sword and place its hilt on the ground and its point at my belly, and lean upon it till it comes out my back, and I will kill myself.'

"When her father heard these words, his face grew dark, and his heart was inflamed with anger against her. He was afraid that she might kill herself, and he was in a quandary as to what he should do about her and the kings who were writing to him asking her hand in marriage.

" 'If you must refuse to marry,' said he, 'then refrain from coming and going.' Then he shut her up in the house and confined her there, setting ten old women over her as stewardesses to guard her. He forbade her to go to the seven palaces, and let her know that he was angry. He also sent messages to the other kings, informing them that she had been afflicted with a mental derangement. A year has passed now, and she is still confined."

Then Dahnash the Ifrit said to the Ifritah: "O my lady, I go to her every night to gaze upon her and enjoy her face and kiss her on the forehead while she is sleeping. Because of my love for her I do her no harm and I do not mount her, for her beauty is so surpassing that anyone who sees her could never bring himself to do her an injury.

"I swear to you, my lady, that if you return with me and look upon her grace and beauty, her figure and symmetry, and then still wish to punish me or hold me captive, you may do so, for yours is the power to command and forbid."

Then Dahnash the Ifrit hung his head and lowered his wings to the ground.

Maymunah the Ifritah laughed at him and spat in his face, saying: "What is this girl you are talking about? She is nothing but a potsherd for wiping after making water! How could she be anything else, if you could only see my beloved. By Allah, I thought you had something marvelous or a remarkable story to relate, O accursed one. Tonight I saw a young man, at the sight of whom, even asleep, you would become paralyzed and stand drooling over him!"

"What about this young man?" asked Dahnash.

"The same thing happened to this boy as happened to your beloved whom you mentioned," replied Maymunah. "His father commanded him many times to marry, and he refused. When he disobeyed, his father grew angry and imprisoned him in the tower in which I live, and when I came out tonight I saw him."

"O my lady," said Dahnash, "show me this boy so I can see whether he is fairer than my beloved Queen Budur, for I do not believe that the like of my beloved is to be found anywhere in this age."

"You lie, O accursed one, most ill-fated of rebels and vilest of demons! I am sure that my beloved has no equal in these regions. Are you mad that you measure your beloved against my own?"

"God save you, my lady," replied Dahnash, "if you come with me to see my beloved and I go to see yours, then we shall know which is the fairer."

"That is what we must do, O accursed one, because you are a deceitful devil. However, I will not go with you, nor you with me, except on a wager. If your beloved girl whom you love and boast of turns out to be fairer than my young man, then you will win, but if my beloved is more beautiful, I shall win."

"My lady," said Dahnash, "I accept this condition and I am content. Come with me now to the Isles."

"My beloved's place is nearer," said Maymunah, "for it is just below us here; so descend with me to look at my beloved first, and then we shall go see yours."

"I hear and obey," Dahnash replied.

They descended and alighted at the chamber which was in the tower. Maymunah made Dahnash stand beside the bed, and she stretched out her hand and drew down the sheet from the face of Qamar az-Zaman, son of King Shahriman. His face was bright, resplendent, and luminous.

Maymunah gazed upon him, and then turning to Dahnash, she said: "Look, O accursed one, and do not be such a vile madman. I am a woman, and I am bewitched by him."

Dahnash bent over Qamar az-Zaman, and looked at him carefully for some time. Then he shook his head and said to Maymunah: "My lady, you are to be excused; one thing remains, however, and that is that men and women are not the same. By God's truth, your beloved is very like my own in grace and beauty, and in splendor and perfection. The two of them look as if they had been poured into the same mould of beauty."

When Maymunah heard these words, the light of her face grew dark, and she dealt him a heavy blow on the head with her wing that almost finished him.

"Swear by the light of the face of the Almighty, O accursed one," cried Maymunah, "that you will go this instant to your beloved whom you adore and bring her here to this place, so that we can put them together and look at them while they are sleeping side by side. Then we will see which is the fairer! If you do not do as I command you at once, I will burn you with my fire, I will strike you with the sparks of my malice, I will rend you to pieces in the desert, and I will make of you an example to all and sundry!"

"I grant you that, my lady," replied Dahnash, "for I know that my beloved is more beautiful and sweeter than yours."

Then the Ifrit Dahnash flew off at once, and Maymunah flew with him in order to watch him. They were gone for an hour and then returned, carrying between them the girl, who was dressed in a fine Venetian chemise, decorated with two fringes of gold and marvelous embroideries. They brought the maiden down and laid her beside the young man; then they uncovered their faces and saw that the two resembled each other so closely that they almost might have been twins, or brother and sister at least, each one a temptation to the pious.

Dahnash and Maymunah gazed upon the two for a while, and then the former said: "My beloved is more beautiful."

"No, mine is the fairer, woe to you, Dahnash," answered Maymunah. "Can you not see his grace and beauty, his form and symmetry?"

They continued the argument for a long time, each one reciting verses in praise of his beloved, but came to no agreement. Finally, Maymunah lost her temper and screamed at Dahnash, and was on the point of assaulting him. He humbled himself to her and softened his speech, saying: "The truth is not hard for you to find out. Forget what you say and what I say, for each of us only repeats that his beloved is more beautiful. Let us stop talking, and seek out someone on whom we can rely and let him decide the question between us."

"I agree," Maymunah said, and she stamped upon the ground with her foot. Immediately there arose out of the earth a one-eyed, mangy Ifrit, whose eye-sockets were split lengthwise in his face. On his head were seven horns and four braids of hair which hung down to the ground. His hands were those of a demon with the claws of a lion. His legs were like the legs of an elephant with hooves like those of an ass.

When the Ifrit rose out of the earth and saw Maymunah, he kissed the ground before her with great courtesy, and said: "What is your wish, my lady, daughter of the King?"

"O Qashqash," she replied, "I want you to judge between me and this cursed Dahnash."

Then she told him the tale from beginning to end. Thereupon the Ifrit looked at the faces of the boy and girl and saw that they were embracing, for they were sleeping with their arms around one another's neck. They resembled each other in grace and beauty, and were like one another in their elegance. Qashqash stared, and marveled at their grace and beauty; then, after a long while, he turned to Maymunah and Dahnash.

"By Allah," he said, "neither one is more or less fair than the other. They resemble one another exceedingly in beauty and grace, and in splendor and perfection. The only difference between them is the difference between male and female. My decision is that you should awaken each of them in turn without the knowledge of the other, and if one of them is seized with passion for the other, then that one is inferior in beauty and grace."

"That is a good judgment," said Maymunah; "I accept it."

"So do I," said Dahnash, and immediately he transformed himself into a flea and bit Qamar az-Zaman in a soft place on his neck. Qamar az-Zaman put his hand to his neck and scratched the place of the bite because of the sharpness of the pain. He moved to one side and discovered someone sleeping there whose breath was purer than musk and whose body was softer than cream. Qamar az-Zaman was greatly astonished and at once sat up to look at the person sleeping beside him. He found that it was a girl like a splendid pearl and a lofty dome, with a figure like the letter *alif*, five feet tall, with protruding breasts and rosy cheeks.

When Qamar az-Zaman saw the Lady Budur, daughter of King Ghayur, and observed her grace and beauty as she was sleeping beside him, he noticed that she was wearing a Venetian chemise without pajamas and a head kerchief of cloth-of-gold set with gems. Around her neck was a necklace of precious stones which no king could afford. He was utterly amazed. At the sight of her beauty, his passions were aroused, and God inspired him with desire to make love.

"God's will be done," he said, and turned her over with his hands and unfastened the collar of her chemise, which he pulled open. Her breasts and belly appeared, and as he gazed upon them, his love and desire for her increased. He attempted to rouse her, but she did not wake up for Dahnash had cast her into a profound sleep. Qamar az-Zaman moved her and shook her, saying: "Awake, my beloved, and see who I am. I am Qamar az-Zaman." But she did not awake or move her head. Qamar az-Zaman deliberated for a while, and then said to himself: "If my guess is right, this must be the girl whom my father wished me to marry, and for three years I refused. God willing, when morning comes I will tell my father to marry me to her, and I will not let half a day pass before I come to her and enjoy her grace and beauty."

Then Qamar az-Zaman bent over Budur to kiss her, and Maymunah trembled with shame, but Dahnash leapt for joy. But when he was about to kiss her on the mouth, he felt ashamed before God and turned his face aside.

"I shall be patient," he said to himself. "It may be that my father, when he became angry and imprisoned me here, brought me this bride and commanded her to sleep beside me in order to test me. He may have told her not to wake up if I should try to rouse her, and to inform him of whatever I do to her. It may even be that my father is hiding some place where I cannot see him to watch me and see everything I do to this girl. When morning comes, he will chide me and say: 'How can you say that you have no desire to marry, when you kissed and embraced this girl?' So I will stay away from her lest my feelings should be revealed to my father, and from this moment onward I will not touch her or even look at her. But I will take something from her which will be a sign for me and a reminder of her and a proof of our meeting."

Then Qamar az-Zaman raised the maiden's hand and from her little finger he removed her ring, which was worth a great amount of money, for its setting was of precious gems. He put it on his own little finger, turned his back to her and fell asleep.

Maymunah rejoiced when she saw this, and said to Dahnash and Qashqash: "Did you see my beloved Qamar az-Zaman and his continence in regard to this girl? This comes from the perfection of his good qualities. See how he looked upon the girl and her grace and beauty, and did not embrace her or even touch her with his hand, but turned his back and went to sleep."

"We saw the fine way in which he behaved," they answered.

Then Maymunah changed herself into a flea, and entered into the clothes of Budur, the beloved of Dahnash. She walked up her leg, climbed over her thigh, and advanced to a point four inches below her navel and bit her there.

Budur opened her eyes and sat up. She saw beside her a young man sleeping and snoring, whose cheeks were like red anemone and whose eyes would put to shame the lovely houris of Paradise. His mouth was like the seal of Solomon, and his saliva was sweet to the taste and more beneficial than a panacea.

When Queen Budur saw Qamar az-Zaman, she was seized with love, passion, and desire. "Alas, I am dishonored!" she exclaimed. "I do not know this strange young man; what does he mean, sleeping beside me in the same bed!"

She turned her eyes toward him and looked at him carefully, observing his beauty, charm, handsomeness, and grace.

"God's truth," she exclaimed, "he is a handsome young man, like the moon! My heart is almost torn with passion for him and infatuation with his grace and beauty. Alas, I am dishonored by him! By Allah, if I had known that this young man was the one who asked my father for my hand in marriage, I would never have refused him, but would have married him and enjoyed his beauty."

Then Queen Budur peered intently into Qamar az-Zaman's face, and said: "O my lord, love of my heart and light of my eyes, awake and enjoy my grace and beauty."

She moved him with her hand, but the Ifritah Maymunah had caused his head to be heavy and had cast him into a deep sleep, so Qamar az-Zaman did not awake. Then Queen Budur shook him hard with both hands and exclaimed: "By my life, you must obey me! Awake from your sleep and see the narcissus and the greenery; enjoy my belly and my navel, and caress me and play with me from now till morning. Get up, my lord; lean back on the pillow, and do not sleep!" But Qamar az-Zaman did not answer, and continued to snore in his sleep.

"Why are you so haughty with your grace and beauty, your elegance and charm?" asked Queen Budur. "I am just as beautiful as you. What is this that you are doing? Did they instruct you to turn away from me, or did my father, that old man of ill-omen, forbid you to speak to me tonight?" At this, Qamar az-Zaman, though still asleep, opened his eyes, and the love for him which God had placed in her heart increased even more. She gazed upon him, tortured as if with the pain of a thousand sorrows. Her heart throbbed, her vitals burned hot, and her limbs trembled.

"Speak to me, my beloved!" she cried. "Talk to me, my darling! Answer me! Tell me what your name is, for you have deprived me of my senses." All the while, Qamar az-Zaman remained submerged in sleep and did not answer a single word.

Queen Budur sighed. "Why are you so conceited?" she asked, and shook him again. She kissed his hand and seeing her ring upon his little finger, she moaned and said coquettishly: "Aha, by Allah, you are my lover, and you do love me, but now you seem to be flirting by turning away, although you came to me while I was asleep. I do not know how you behaved with me, but I shall not remove my ring from your finger."

Then she opened the pocket of his shirt, and bending over him she kissed his neck, and searched for something to take from him, but found that he had nothing there. She saw that he was wearing no pajamas, so she put her hand under the tail of his shirt, and felt his legs. Her hand slipped on the smoothness of his body, and fell upon his penis. Her bosom heaved and her breast fluttered—for the lust of women is stronger than that of men—and she was ashamed. Then she removed his ring and put it on her own finger as an exchange for hers. She kissed him on the mouth and on his hands, not leaving any spot unkissed. Finally, she took him in her arms and embraced him and, placing one arm beneath his neck and the other under his arm, she fell asleep at his side.

Maymunah was overjoyed at the sight of this and said to Dahnash: "Did you see, O accursed one, the passion for my darling which your beloved displayed, and the nobility and fondness which my beloved showed? There is no doubt that my beloved is better than yours. However, I forgive you."

Then she wrote out for him a certificate of release, and turning to

Qashqash, she said: "Go with him and help him carry his beloved back to her dwelling-place, for the night has passed, and I have not accomplished what I set out to do."

Dahnash and Qashqash picked up Budur and flew back with her to where she belonged and returned her to her bed. Maymunah remained alone with Qamar az-Zaman, gazing on him as he lay asleep, until the night was almost gone. Then she went about her business.

At the break of day Qamar az-Zaman awoke from his sleep and looked to the right and the left, but did not find the maiden with him.

"My father has done all this," he said to himself, "to make me want to marry the girl who was with me. He has taken her away secretly, so that my desire to marry will increase." Then he shouted to the eunuch who was sleeping at the door: "Woe to you, accursed one, get up!"

The eunuch arose, befuddled with sleep, and brought him the basin and ewer. Qamar az-Zaman went into the water closet and satisfied his needs. He came out again, performed the ritual ablutions, and after praying the morning prayer, sat down giving praise to God.

He then looked toward the eunuch who was standing before him, attentive to serve him, and said: "Woe to you, O Sawab! Who came here and took the girl away from my side while I was asleep?"

"What girl, my lord?" asked the eunuch.

"The girl who was sleeping with me last night."

The eunuch was alarmed at the words of Qamar az-Zaman, and said: "There was no girl with you, nor anyone else. Where could a girl have gotten in while I was sleeping in front of the door, which was locked? By Allah, my lord, no one came in to you, neither man nor woman!"

"You lie, O slave of misfortune! Do you think you have the power to deceive me by not telling where the girl who slept with me last night went, or who took her from me?"

"By Allah," said the eunuch, who was terrified, "I did not see any girl, or boy, my lord!"

Qamar az-Zaman was enraged at the words of the eunuch, and said: "They have instructed you to deceive me, accursed one. Come here!"

The eunuch came over to Qamar az-Zaman who seized him by the collar and flung him to the floor so hard that he farted. Then he beat him and kicked and choked him till he lost consciousness. After that, he tied him in the well-bucket and let him down till he reached the water, although it was winter and the day was bitter cold. He plunged the eunuch into the water and pulled him up again, and kept on doing this, plunging him down into the water and pulling him up again, while all the time the eunuch was shouting and screaming and crying for help.

"By God, O accursed one," said Qamar az-Zaman, "I shall not let you out of this well till you tell me all about this girl and who it was who took her from me while I was asleep."

"Save me from this well," cried the eunuch, "and I will tell you the truth!"

At once Qamar az-Zaman raised him and pulled him out of the well. He was almost dead from the cold and from the ducking, beating, and mistreatment he had suffered. He began to tremble like a reed in a high wind; his teeth chattered, for his clothes were all soaked from the water. When the eunuch saw that he was on the surface of the ground, he said to Qamar az-Zaman: "Let me go take off my clothes, my lord, and wring them out and and spread them in the sun, and put on some others. Then I will come to you immediately and tell you all about that young girl."

"By God, O slave of misfortune," cried Qamar az-Zaman, "if you had not seen death with your own eyes, you would never have confessed the truth! Go, do what you will, and come back quickly and tell me about this girl."

So the eunuch, still scarcely believing that he was saved, ran off quickly and did not stop until he came to King Shahriman. He found the Vizier with him, and they were talking together about Qamar az-Zaman. He heard the King say: "I did not sleep a wink last night because my heart was troubled about my son Qamar az-Zaman. I am afraid that something might happen to him because of that ancient tower, for there are no comforts in his prison."

"Do not be afraid for him, for, by Allah, nothing will hurt him. Leave him shut up for a month's time until his temper has cooled."

While they were talking, the eunuch suddenly burst in on them in his sad state, crying: "Oh my Lord and Master, your son has gone mad and has dealt with me thus, as you can see. He told me that a girl had spent the night with him and had left secretly, and he demanded that I tell him all about her, but I do not know anything about any girl."

When King Shahriman heard this report about his son, he cried out: "Alas, my poor son!" And he grew enraged at the Vizier who was the cause of it all, and said to him: "Go, find out what has happened to my son."

The Vizier hurried out, stumbling over the skirts of his cloak from fear of the King, and proceeded with the eunuch to the tower. The sun was high when the Vizier went in to Qamar az-Zaman. He found him sitting on the bed reading the Koran, and he greeted him and sat down at his side.

"My lord," said the Vizier, "this slave of ill-fortune has told us a tale that has disturbed and alarmed us, and the King has become very angry."

"What did he tell you, O Vizier," asked Qamar az-Zaman, "that disturbed my father? For, to tell the truth, it was me that he disturbed."

"He came to us in a shocking condition," replied the Vizier, "and said something ridiculous, and lied to us about you in a way that does not bear repeating, what with your youthful good health, your sound mind, and your eloquent tongue, and it is impossible that you should do anything wicked."

"What did this ill-omened slave say, O Vizier?" asked Qamar az-Zaman.

"He told us that you had gone mad and had told him that a girl was with you last night. Did you tell the eunuch that?"

"Now I see!" exclaimed Qamar az-Zaman. "It was you who instructed the eunuch to do what he did and forbade him to tell me of the girl who slept

with me last night, for you are smarter than the eunuch. Now tell me at
once, where is that pretty girl who slept in my arms last night? It was you
who sent her to me and ordered her to spend the night in my arms. I slept
with her till morning, and when I awoke I did not find her. So where is
she now?"

"O my Lord Qamar az-Zaman," replied the Vizier. "God preserve you!
By Allah, I swear, we did not send anyone to you last night. You slept alone,
for the door was locked and the eunuch slept in front of it. No girl came to
you, nor anyone else. Return to your senses, my lord, and do not occupy
your mind with such fancies."

Qamar az-Zaman grew angry at these words, and replied: "This girl is my
beloved. She is the beautiful one, the girl with black eyes and rosy cheeks,
whom I embraced last night!"

The Vizier was astonished to hear Qamar az-Zaman say such things. "Did
you see this girl last night with your own eyes while awake, or was it in a
dream?" he asked.

"You wicked old man," retorted Qamar az-Zaman. "Did you think I saw
her with my *ears?* I saw her with my own eyes while I was awake, and I
turned her over with my own hands, and spent half the night awake beside
her, gazing on her grace and beauty, and her charm and attractiveness. But
you had advised her not to talk to me, so she pretended to sleep. I slept beside her till morning, and when I awoke I did not find her."

"O my lord," said the Vizier, "perhaps you saw all this while asleep, and it
was only a tangle of dreams or fancies brought on by eating different food,
or perhaps a hallucination caused by evil spirits."

"You wicked old man!" cried Qamar az-Zaman. "How dare you make
fun of me by saying it was perhaps a tangle of dreams, when the eunuch
has confessed to me that there really was a girl, for he told me just now that
he would return and tell me all about her!"

Then Qamar az-Zaman got up and seized the Vizier by his beard. The
beard was quite long, and Qamar az-Zaman seized it and, twisting it
around his hand, he dragged him off the bed and threw him down on the
floor. The Vizier thought that life had almost departed from him because
of the pain of being plucked by the beard. Qamar az-Zaman proceeded to
kick him with his feet and pound him on the neck with his fists till the
Vizier was at the point of death.

The Vizier said to himself: "I deserve to escape more than that eunuch
slave who saved himself from this crazy boy with a lie, so I shall lie too and
save my life, for he is surely mad, there's no doubt of that."

"Forgive me, my lord!" cried the Vizier. "Your father ordered me not
to tell you anything about this girl, but I am weak and exhausted from being
beaten, for I am an old man and have no strength to endure a beating.
Calm down a little, and I will tell you about the girl."

Immediately Qamar az-Zaman left off beating him, and said: "Why did
you not tell me about her before I beat and insulted you? Get up, old man,
and tell me about her."

"Is it this girl with the beautiful face and the fine figure that you are asking me about?"

"Yes," replied Qamar az-Zaman. "Tell me, O Vizier. Who was it who brought her and had her sleep with me? Where is she now, that I may go to her myself? If my father, King Shahriman, did this to test me with the girl so that I might marry her, I agree to that, for he has done this and inflamed my heart for this girl, and then has kept her from me only because of my refusal to marry. So now I accept marriage and am content. Tell my father that, O Vizier, and advise him to marry me to this girl, for I will have no other, and my heart has never loved another. Arise and hurry to my father and advise him to hasten my marriage, and then return to me immediately."

The Vizier could scarcely believe he was saved from Qamar az-Zaman till he ran out of the tower and went to King Shahriman. When he entered, the King said: "How is it, O Vizier, that I see you in confusion? Who has done you such an injury that you run to me terrified?"

"I bring you news," said the Vizier.

"What news?"

"Your son, Qamar az-Zaman, has gone mad."

When the King heard these words, the light of his face grew dark, and he said: "Describe my son's madness to me, O Vizier."

"I hear and obey," replied the Vizier, and he informed the King of what his son had done.

"Rejoice, O Vizier," said the King, "for I give you glad tidings of the same sort as your tidings of my son's madness, the loss of favor and the cutting off of your head, O ill-omened Vizier and most miserable of emirs! For I know that you caused my son's madness by the wretched counsel and advice that you have given me from start to finish in this affair. By God, if any harm or madness has afflicted my son, I shall nail you to the palace dome and you will die a horrible death!"

Then the King rose to his feet and, taking the Vizier with him, went to the tower where Qamar az-Zaman was. When he entered, Qamar az-Zaman rose to greet his father; he came down quickly from the bed on which he had been sitting and kissed his hands. Then he stepped back and, with his hands folded behind his back, lowered his head to the floor before his father. He remained in this attitude for some time, then raised his head to his father and the tears flowed from his eyes and ran down his cheeks.

Thereupon his father arose and embraced his son, Qamar az-Zaman, kissed him on the forehead, and made him sit down beside him on the bed. Then he turned to the Vizier with an angry glance, saying: "O dog of a vizier, how can you say this and that about my son, Qamar az-Zaman, and cause my heart to be fearful for him?"

He then turned to his son, and said: "My son, what is today?"

"Today is Saturday, father," replied Qamar az-Zaman, "and tomorrow will be Sunday, the day after that will be Monday, and then come Tuesday, Wednesday, Thursday, and Friday."

"Qamar az-Zaman, my son!" exclaimed the King. "Praise be to God for your sanity! And what month is this?"

"This is Dhu l-Qa'dah," replied Qamar az-Zaman, "and next month will be Dhu l-Hijjah. Then come Muharram, Safar, Rabi' the First, Rabi' the Second, Jumada the First, Jumada the Last, Rajab, Sha'ban, Ramadan, and finally, Shawwal."

The King rejoiced greatly and spat in the face of the Vizier, saying: "You evil old man, how can you assert that my son, Qamar az-Zaman, is mad, when the truth is no one is mad but yourself?"

The Vizier shook his head and was about to say something, but then it occurred to him that he should bide his time for a little while to see what happened.

"O my son," the King said, "what is this story about your telling the eunuch and the Vizier that you slept with a beautiful maiden last night? What about this girl that you mentioned?"

When his father spoke these words, Qamar az-Zaman laughed and said: "Father, I have no strength left to bear this mockery, so do not say more, not a single word, for I am annoyed at what you are doing. I am content to marry, father, on condition that you marry me to the girl who slept with me last night, for I am sure that it was you who sent her to me to arouse my desire for her, and then took her from me before it was morning."

"God preserve your mind from madness, my son!" exclaimed King Shahriman. "What girl is this you insist I sent to you last night and then took her away before morning? By Allah, I know nothing about the matter! I urge you, in the name of Allah, to tell me, was this a tangle of dreams or fancies brought on by something you ate? You spent the night worried about marrying and obsessed with the thought of it. God curse marriage and the hour of marriage, and God curse him who advised it! You were doubtless disturbed in your mind on account of marriage, and saw in a dream that a pretty girl was embracing you, and you believed in your mind that you saw her while awake. All of this, my son, is only a tangle of dreams."

"Stop saying that!" cried Qamar az-Zaman. "And swear to me by Allah, the Creator, the Omniscient, the breaker of tyrants and the destroyer of kings, that you know nothing about this girl or where she is!"

"By God Almighty!" exclaimed the King. "By the God of Moses and Abraham, I swear I know nothing about her. It must be a tangle of dreams which you saw while asleep."

"I shall give you an analogy," said Qamar az-Zaman, "which will prove to you that this happened while I was awake. Could it happen," he asked, "that someone should see himself in a dream fighting in a furious battle, and then awake to find a bloody sword in his hand?"

"No, by Allah," said his father, "that could never happen."

"Well," continued Qamar az-Zaman, "I will tell you what happened. It seems to me that I awoke at midnight and found sleeping beside me a girl whose form and aspect were like my own. I embraced her and held her in my arms, and then I took off her ring and put it on my finger. Later on, she must have taken off my ring and put it on her own finger. I refrained from going any further, out of my feeling of modesty towards you, for I thought that you had sent her and were hiding somewhere to see what I would do, so I was ashamed to kiss her on the mouth. It occurred to me that you were testing me so as to make me want to marry. Then later, when I awoke early in the morning, I could not find any trace of the maiden nor any news of her, and this trouble with the eunuch and the Vizier took place. How can this be false, since the matter of the ring is true? If it were not for the ring, I would believe it was all a dream, but here is her ring on my little finger right now. Look at the ring, O King, and see how valuable it is."

Qamar az-Zaman handed the ring to his father, who took it and examined it, and then turned to his son, saying: "Indeed, there must be a great history and a mighty legend behind this ring, for what happened to you last night with this girl is a difficult matter. I do not know where this intruder came from, but the whole thing is the fault of the Vizier. I urge you, in God's name, my son, to be patient and perhaps He will show you a way out of this distress and give you release. My son, I am sure now that you are not mad, but only Allah can clear this matter up for you."

"Father," said Qamar az-Zaman, "will you search for this girl and bring her to me quickly? Otherwise I shall die of grief." Thus Qamar az-Zaman revealed his feelings, and, turning to his father humbly and with a broken heart, he burst into tears.

After a while the Vizier addressed the King, saying: "O Ruler of the Age, how long will you remain away from the army, shut up here with your son, Qamar az-Zaman? It may be that the order of the kingdom will be disturbed because you are away from the councillors of state. The intelligent man, when his body is afflicted by various ailments, must begin by treating the most grave. In my opinion, you should transport your son from this place to the pavilion in the palace overlooking the sea where you can stay with him. You should appoint Monday and Thursday in each week for the army and the Council of State. There the emirs, the viziers, chamberlains, and the palace guard, the councillors of state, your retainers, the military leaders, and the rest of the army and the subjects can come and present to you their affairs, and you can render decisions and pass judgments among them, and discuss and command and forbid. The remainder of the week you will remain with your son, Qamar az-Zaman. You can continue there until Allah shows you and him a way out of your straits. For you are not safe, O King, from the vicissitudes of fortune and the calamities of fate, and the intelligent man is always cautious."

When the King heard these words, he was struck by their wisdom and he considered them to be good advice and in his best interest, for he feared lest the order of the kingdom should be disturbed. So he arose at once and ordered that his son be moved from the tower to the pavilion which was in the palace overlooking the sea, to which one had access by a causeway twenty cubits wide running out into the sea. On all sides the pavilion had windows overlooking the sea; its floor was paved with colored marble and its ceiling was painted in many splendid colors picked out in gold and lapis lazuli. Silken carpets were spread there, the walls were covered with brocade, and curtains studded with gems were hung. Then Qamar az-Zaman was moved in.

Qamar az-Zaman lay awake nights because of the intensity of his love; his mind was continuously occupied, his face grew pale and his body became emaciated. His father, King Shahriman, sat at his head and grieved over him.

Every Monday and Thursday the King permitted those emirs, viziers, chamberlains, guards, councillors of state, and soldiers and subjects who wished to do so to enter the pavilion and perform their service to him till the end of the day; then they would go their own way, and the King would go in to his son, Qamar az-Zaman. He never left him by night or day, and continued in this fashion for many days.

Thus matters stood with Qamar az-Zaman. As for Queen Budur, however, when the genies brought her back and laid her upon her bed, only three hours of the night remained. When dawn came, she awoke from her sleep, sat up and looked to the right and the left, but did not see her beloved who had been in her arms. Her heart trembled and her senses left her, and she cried out in a loud voice which awakened all her slave-girls, attendants, and stewardesses. They all rushed in to her and the eldest of them approached her and said: "O my lady, what is the matter with you?"

"O evil old woman," she replied, "where is my beautiful young lover who slept in my arms last night? Tell me where he has gone."

When the stewardess heard this, her face became dark, for she was much afraid of being injured by her.

"My Lady Budur!" she exclaimed. "What kind of wicked talk is this?"

"Woe to you, wicked old crone!" cried the Lady Budur. "Where is my handsome young lover with the beautiful face, the black eyes, and the joined eyebrows who stayed with me from the evening almost till the break of day?"

"By Allah, I have not seen a young man or any one else," protested the old woman. "For heaven's sake, do not play this kind of unseemly joke, lest we should lose our lives, for this joke may reach your father, and then who will save us from his hand?"

"There was a young man who spent the night here with me," insisted Queen Budur, "and he had the handsomest face I have ever seen."

"God guard your sanity!" exclaimed the stewardess. "No one spent the night here with you."

Then Budur looked at her hand and found Qamar az-Zaman's ring on her finger, but not her own, and said to the stewardess: "Woe to you, O traitor, you are lying to me when you say that no one spent the night with me, and you swear by God falsely!"

"By Allah!" cried the stewardess. "I did not lie and I did not swear falsely!"

The Lady Budur became incensed at her and drawing a sword that she had nearby, struck her with it and killed her.

Immediately all the slave-girls and servants cried out against her, and went to her father and told him about her condition. The King came at once to his daughter, and said: "My daughter, what is the matter?"

"O my father!" she cried. "Where is the youth who slept beside me last night?"

Then she went out of her mind completely. She looked wildly right and left, and tore her clothes from top to bottom. When her father saw this, he ordered the eunuchs and the slave-girls to seize her. They seized and bound her, and put an iron chain around her neck and attached it to a window of the palace.

So matters stood with Queen Budur. Her father, King Ghayur, however, when he saw what had befallen the Lady Budur, was overwhelmed, for he loved her dearly and her well-being was of no small importance to him. He summoned his astrologers, physicians, and scribes, and said: "Whoever cures my daughter of her distemper, I will give him her hand in marriage and I will give him half my kingdom; but whoever tries to cure her and fails, his head will be cut off and hung up at the palace gate."

So he proceeded to cut off the heads of all those who went in to her but failed to cure her, and he hung them up on the palace gate. He continued thus till he had cut off forty heads and had crucified all the physicians. Ordinary people stayed away, seeing that the physicians had been unable to treat her, and her case was so difficult for men of science and the writers of talismans.

The Lady Budur's passion grew stronger, and the love and feeling that were in her did her great harm. She wept until her eyelids were inflamed and her cheeks had withered. In this manner she continued for a period of three years.

Queen Budur had a foster-brother named Marzuwan, who was away on a journey to remote countries and was absent this whole time. He loved her dearly with a love greater than brotherly affection. When he returned from his travels, he went in to see his mother and asked her about his sister, the Lady Budur.

"My son," his mother said, "your sister went mad three years ago. There is a chain of iron around her neck and the physicians are unable to treat her."

When Marzuwan heard these words, he said: "I must go to her; perhaps I will know what is wrong with her and will be able to treat her."

"You must indeed," said his mother, "but be patient till tomorrow so that I can devise some ruse to get you in."

Then his mother went to the palace of the Lady Budur and met with the eunuch charged with guarding the door. She gave him a present and said: "I have a married daughter who was raised with the Lady Budur. When this misfortune fell upon your mistress, my daughter's heart felt a great sympathy for her. I hope that you will out of kindness let my daughter come sometime to see her and then go away without anyone knowing about it."

"That will be possible only at night," replied the eunuch. "After the Sultan comes to see his daughter and leaves, you and your daughter can go in."

The old woman kissed the eunuch's hand and returned to her home. On the following night, when the time of the evening prayer came, she arose and took her son, Marzuwan, and dressed him in women's clothes. Then leading him by the hand, she brought him into the palace. After the King had left his daughter, she took him to the eunuch, who, when he saw her, arose and said: "Go in, but do not stay long."

When the old woman went in with her son, Marzuwan, he saw the Lady Budur in her sad state and greeted her. His mother took away his woman's clothing, after which Marzuwan brought out all the books he had with him and lit a candle. The Lady Budur looked at him and recognized him. "O my brother," she said, "you went away on a journey and we heard no news of you."

"True," he said, "but God brought me back safely, and I was about to start on another journey and was held back only by what I heard about you. My heart ached for your sake, so I have come, and perhaps I may recognize your ailment and be able to treat you."

"Do you think, my brother," said Budur, "that I am afflicted with madness?" then she recited these verses:

> "You are mad for the one you love," they said to me. "I know;
> Only the mad," said I, "have joy in life; 'tis sure.
> Yes, I am mad, so bring me the love who made me so,
> And blame me not, if madness finds in him a cure."

Marzuwan knew by this that she was in love, and said: "Tell me your story and what happened to you; perhaps God will show me some way to release you."

"Brother," said Budur, "hear my story. One night I awoke in the third watch of the night. I sat up and saw beside me a youth, the handsomest that ever could be, whom the tongue is too weak to describe, as if he were the branch of a ben-tree or a reed of bamboo. I thought it was my father who had ordered this so as to test me with him, for he had urged me to marry when the kings sought my hand and I refused. This thought kept me from waking him, for I feared if I embraced him, he would tell my father. When morning came, I saw his ring on my finger instead of my own. That is my story, brother. My heart was captivated by him from the moment I laid eyes on him, and because of my great love and passion, I cannot taste sleep and I have no occupation but to weep copious tears." So saying, she burst into a flood of tears. Then she continued: "O brother, what will you do for me in this affliction of mine?"

Marzuwan lowered his eyes to the ground a while in his astonishment, for he did not know what to do. Then he raised his head and said: "Everything that happened to you is true, but the story of this youth has me at my wit's end. However, I shall travel through all lands in search for your remedy; perhaps God will put it in my hand. So be patient and do not worry."

Then Marzuwan said farewell and, praying that she might remain steadfast, he left her. Returning to his mother's house, he slept there that night and on the morrow he made preparations for his journey and departed.

Marzuwan traveled from city to city and from isle to isle for a period of a whole month, and finally came to a city called Tayrab. As he journeyed, he would listen to people's conversations, thinking perhaps he might find some way to cure Queen Budur. Whenever he entered a city or passed through one, he heard that Queen Budur, the daughter of King Ghayur, had gone insane. He continued overhearing gossip to this effect until, when he came to the city of Tayrab, he heard that Qamar az-Zaman, the son of King Shahriman, was ill and afflicted by delusions and madness. He asked some of the people of that city about his country and his capital and was told that it was the Isles of Khalidan, which were a month's journey away by sea and a six months' journey by land.

Marzuwan then boarded a ship bound for the Isles of Khalidan. The ship was well-provisioned for the voyage and the wind was fair for a whole month. The city came in sight, and they approached and were on the point of landing, when suddenly a high wind rose, which blew down the yard-arm. The sails fell into the sea and the ship capsized with all that was in it. Each person tried to save himself, but Marzuwan was drawn by the force of the current till it brought him beneath the King's pavilion, in which dwelt Qamar az-Zaman. By a stroke of fate, the emirs and viziers had assembled in service to the King, who was sitting with Qamar az-Zaman's head lying in his lap while a eunuch fanned him. For two days Qamar az-Zaman had neither eaten nor drunk, and he had not uttered a word.

The Vizier, who was standing at his feet near the window which looked out over the sea, happened to raise his eyes and saw Marzuwan, who was near to perishing in the current and was almost at his last gasp. The heart of the Vizier was moved, so he approached the Sultan and, bowing his head, addressed him: "I ask leave to go down to the courtyard of the pavilion and open its gate in order to save someone who is on the point of drowning in the sea, and to deliver him from his straits. Perhaps God on account of this will release your son from his state."

"Everything that has befallen my son is your fault," replied the King, "and perhaps if you pull out this drowning man, he will discover our condition and look upon my son in his present state and take a malicious pleasure in my misfortune. I swear by God that if this person comes up and sees my son and goes out and talks to anyone about our secrets, I will cut off your head before his, for you are the cause of all that has happened to us, O Vizier, and no one else. So do as you please."

The Vizier arose and, opening the gate of the courtyard, went out about twenty paces onto the causeway. Then he waded into the sea and saw that Marzuwan was at the point of death. He stretched out his hand, and, seizing him by the hair, pulled him out of the water. Marzuwan was in a state of unconsciousness, for his belly was full of water, and his eyes were protruding. The Vizier worked over him till his breath returned; then he removed his clothes and gave him others and put on him a turban belonging to one of his slaves.

After he had done all this, the Vizier spoke to Marzuwan, saying: "You know that it was I who saved you from drowning, so do not be the cause of my death as well as your own."

"How could that be?" asked Marzuwan.

"Because you are now going to go up and pass among emirs and viziers, all of whom will be silent and speechless because of Qamar az-Zaman, the son of the Sultan."

When Marzuwan heared Qamar az-Zaman mentioned, he recognized the name, because he had heard him spoken of in the land. "Who is this Qamar az-Zaman?" he asked.

"He is the son of the Sultan, Shahriman," replied the Vizier, "and he is lying in bed, ill and distraught. He cannot tell night from day, and is near to departing this life and passing to the other world, because of the exhaustion of his body, for he is in burning pain by day and is tormented by night. We have despaired of his life and are certain that he will die. Take care not to look long at him, or even of looking at anything except where you put your feet; otherwise, you will lose your life and I mine."

"Please tell me about this young man you have described," said Marzuwan. "What is the cause of his sad condition?"

"I do not know any cause for it," replied the Vizier, "except that for three years his father had been trying to tempt him into marriage, but he refused. One morning he asserted that, while sleeping, he had seen at his side a girl whose beauty was indescribable and disturbing to the mind. He told us he had removed her ring and put it on his finger and that she had put his own ring on her finger, but we do not know the real truth of this story. So please go up with me, my son, to the pavilion, but do not look at the King's son. Then go your own way, for the Sultan's heart is full of wrath."

"By Allah," said Marzuwan to himself, "this is the one I have been looking for." Then he followed the Vizier up to the pavilion.

The Vizier sat down in his place at the feet of Qamar az-Zaman, but Marzuwan, without further ado, walked over to where Qamar az-Zaman lay and stood there staring at him. The Vizier almost died on the spot and made signs to him to go his way, but Marzuwan ignored him and continued to gaze at Qamar az-Zaman, for he knew he was the one he had been searching for.

"Praise be to God, who made their form, coloring, and cheeks alike!" he exclaimed.

Qamar az-Zaman opened his eyes and strained his ears to hear. When Marzuwan saw that Qamar az-Zaman was listening to the words he uttered, he recited the following verses:

> Why this ecstasy? Why so moved by song?
> What signifies this talk of beauty all day long?
> It must be love; your heart his arrow did not miss.
> All those wounded by his bow behave like this.
> 'Tis true; think not that by a sword thrust I will die;
> Nay, I am brought low by arrows from her eye.

I weep for one whose face by beauty is possessed;
Of all the nations by her peer not one is blessed.
When I am slain, revenge me not, I pray; but bid
Her tell you, friend, how it was lawful what she did.

When Qamar az-Zaman heard these verses, a feeling of ease and well-being descended upon his heart. His tongue moved in his mouth and he gestured with his hand to the Sultan, and said: "Let this young man come sit at my side."

When he heard his son, Qamar az-Zaman, speak, the King, who had been angry with the youth and had had the idea of cutting off his head, now rejoiced exceedingly. He arose and seated Marzuwan beside his son, and, turning to him, he asked him from what country he had come.

"From the inner isles of the land of King Ghayur, Lord of the Isles and Seas, and the Seven Palaces," replied Marzuwan.

"Perhaps my son Qamar az-Zaman's deliverance is to be at your hand."

Marzuwan turned to Qamar az-Zaman and spoke in his ear: "Take courage, be happy, and rejoice, and do not ask about the condition of her on whose account you have come to this pass, for you held your love in and became ill, whereas she let hers out and went mad. She is now imprisoned in the worst possible state with an iron chain around her neck. God willing, the cure for both of you is in my hands."

When Qamar az-Zaman heard these words, his spirit returned and he recovered. He directed his father to let him sit up and lean back against two cushions. The King rejoiced greatly, and, sending away all the emirs and viziers, he commanded that the pavilion be perfumed with saffron and that the city be decorated.

"By Allah, my son," he said to Marzuwan, "yours is a blessed face." Then he honored him greatly and ordered food brought to him. When it was brought in, he and Qamar az-Zaman ate together. Marzuwan spent the night with Qamar az-Zaman and the King stayed with them because of his great joy at the recovery of his son.

When morning came, Marzuwan told Qamar az-Zaman the whole story, and said: "I know the maid whom you met with. Her name is the Lady Budur, daughter of King Ghayur." Then he told him what had happened to the Lady Budur from beginning to end, and informed him of her great love for him.

"Everything that happened to her with her father happened to you with yours, and you and she are lovers without any doubt. So take courage and strengthen your resolve, for I shall bring you to her and unite you together."

As they ate and drank together, Marzuwan continued to encourage Qamar az-Zaman, until his spirit returned to him and he gradually recovered completely from his ailment. Marzuwan talked to him all the while, amusing and diverting him by recitations of poetry. Finally he arose and went to the baths, at which his father in his great joy ordered the city to be decorated. He distributed robes of honor, gave to charity, and released those who were in the prisons.

Then Marzuwan said to Qamar az-Zaman: "Know that I have come from

the Lady Budur only for one reason, and that is that I might deliver her
from her present plight. The only thing we have to do now is to devise
some stratagem to go to her, because your father cannot bear to be separated from you. Tomorrow ask your father for permission to go hunting
in the desert; take along a saddle bag full of money and ride a good horse
and take a spare horse with you. I will do likewise. Tell your father that
you want to divert yourself by seeing the desert and the countryside and
spending one night there. Tell him not to worry about you at all."

Qamar az-Zaman was overjoyed at what Marzuwan had said, and he went
at once to his father to ask permission to go hunting and spoke to him as
Marzuwan had bidden him. His father granted him permission, saying: "Do
not stay more than one night, and return on the morrow, for you know
that for me life is worth living only because of you, and I do not believe
that you are fully recovered from your sickness."

The King then equipped his son, Qamar az-Zaman, and Marzuwan for
their expedition and ordered that six horses be gotten ready for them, a
dromedary for the money, and a camel to carry the water and provisions,
but Qamar az-Zaman refused to let anyone come along to serve him.

His father bade him farewell and clasped him to his bosom, saying: "I
beg you, in God's name, do not stay away from me more than one night,
for tonight sleep will be denied me."

Qamar az-Zaman and Marzuwan went out and mounted their horses,
taking with them the dromedary with the money and the camel with the
water and provisions. They journeyed towards the desert and traveled all
the first day until evening, when they descended to eat and drink and feed
their riding animals and take their ease for a while. Then they remounted
and traveled onward. Thus they journeyed for the space of three days; then
on the fourth day they came in sight of a spacious forested area in which
they descended. Here Marzuwan took a camel and a horse and slaughtered
them, after which he cut their flesh into pieces and chopped up the bones.
Taking Qamar az-Zaman's shirt and trousers, he ripped them to pieces and
befouled them with the blood. He likewise tore up Qamar az-Zaman's coat,
stained it with the blood, and threw it down at a crossroads. Then they
ate and drank and resumed their journey.

Qamar az-Zaman asked Marzuwan about what he had done, and he replied: "Your father, King Shahriman, when you are gone for one night and
do not return to him, will mount up and ride after us until he comes to this
blood that I have left. He will see your clothing all torn and bloody and
will believe that you have met with some mishap from robbers or wild
beasts of the desert. He will give up hope for you and return to the city.
Thus by this ruse we will get to where we want to go."

"You have done well," said Qamar az-Zaman.

They traveled for many days and nights and Qamar az-Zaman wept all
the while till they drew near their destination. Then the Isles of King
Ghayur finally came in sight and Qamar az-Zaman rejoiced exceedingly and
thanked Marzuwan for what he had done.

They entered the city and stopped together at an inn where they rested from their journey for three days. After that, Marzuwan took Qamar az-Zaman into the baths and dressed him in the clothes of a merchant. He made for him a gold geomancer's table and a gold astrolabe. Then he said: "Arise, master, and go stand beneath the palace of the King, and cry out: I am the reckoner, the scribe, and the astrologer! Where is he who seeks? The King, when he hears you, will summon you and send you in to his daughter, your beloved. When she sees you, the madness will leave her; the King will be overjoyed at her recovery, and will marry you to her and share his kingdom with you, for this is the condition that he has laid upon himself."

Qamar az-Zaman followed the instructions of Marzuwan and left the inn, carrying with him the instruments we have mentioned. Proceeding to the palace of King Ghayur, he halted and cried out: "I am the scribe, the reckoner, the astrologer. I write talismans, I make strong amulets, I reckon up numbers, I draw talismans for buried treasure: where then is the seeker?"

It had been a long time since the people of the city had seen an astrologer or a reckoner, so when they heard this cry, they came and stood around him staring, amazed at the beauty of his face and the brightness of his youth.

"God save you, master," they said. "Do not do this thing to yourself out of a desire to marry the daughter of King Ghayur. Look and see those heads hanging up there. Their owners were all slain for that very reason, and their desires brought them to their evil end."

Qamar az-Zaman paid no heed to their words, but raised his voice, crying: "I am a scribe and a reckoner! I bring the seeker near to what he seeks."

The people became angry with him, and said: "You stupid, arrogant youth, take pity on your youth, your tender age, and your grace and beauty."

But Qamar az-Zaman shouted all the louder: "I am the astrologer, the reckoner! Is there anyone who seeks?"

While the people were trying to prevent Qamar az-Zaman from doing this, King Ghayur heard his shouting and the tumult of the people, and said to his vizier: "Go down and bring us this astrologer."

The vizier went down and fetched Qamar az-Zaman, and when he came into the King's presence, he kissed the ground before him. The King looked at him, then seated him beside himself, and turning to him, he said: "My son, for the sake of Allah, do not make yourself an astrologer, and do not submit to my conditions. For I have resolved that everyone who goes in to my daughter and does not cure her of her affliction shall have his head cut off, but I will marry her to whoever cures her. Do not be deceived by your grace and beauty and form and symmetry; by Allah, I swear, if your do not cure her, I will strike off your head!"

"I accept the conditions," insisted Qamar az-Zaman.

So the King called the judges to bear witness against him; then he turned him over to the eunuch, saying; "Take him to the Lady Budur." The eunuch took him by the hand to lead him into the antechamber, but Qamar az-Zaman went on ahead.

"Alas," said the eunuch, "do not hasten to your own perdition! By Allah, I have never seen an astrologer hasten to his perdition save yourself. But you do not know what catastrophes are before you!"

But Qamar az-Zaman paid him no heed. The eunuch stopped him before the curtain which hung over the door, and Qamar az-Zaman said: "Which do you prefer? Shall I treat your mistress and cure her from here, or shall I go in to her and cure her on the other side of the curtain?"

The eunuch was astonished at these words, and replied; "If you can cure her from here, you will show yourself to be all the more extraordinary."

Thereupon Qamar az-Zaman sat down behind the curtain, and taking out his inkwell and pen wrote on a sheet of paper the following words in rhymed prose:

Who suffers from his love rejection, his cure is in affection; he is sorely tried, despairing of life, he stands in dread, and is sure that soon he will be dead; no help comes to his grieving heart, to his sleepless eyes no aid against their burning smart; his days are spent in fire, his nights in torment of desire; his body is thin and wastes away, for no word comes from his beloved, his misery to allay.

Lovers' meeting is the heart's sole cure, only by God's grace can a rejected love endure; if ever I betray thee or thou me, may the traitor never true love see; for his is a finer soul who faithful e'er remains, to the love who his faithfulness disdains.

Then he wrote the signature:

From one who loves and yearns, a lover in confusion, distraught by passion and delusion, the slave of ecstasy and love, Qamar az-Zaman, son of King Shahriman, to the unique pearl of the age and the flower of the lovely houris, the Lady Budur, daughter of King Ghayur. Know that I am awake by night and by day in a wretched plight; from my wasting and illness I find no surcease, for my love and passion daily increase; sighing and weeping copious tears, the prisoner of love am I, the victim of passion, consumed in ecstasy; sickness is my only friend; wakeful, with sleepless eye, I am the slave whose tears will never end; ever burning is the fire of my heart, and the heat of my desire will ne'er depart.

At the end he wrote the following verse:

When we first met, thou gav'st thy ring for mine;
Return my ring, for here I send thee thine.

Qamar az-Zaman dropped the ring in the fold of the letter and handed it to the eunuch, who took it in to the Lady Budur. She received it from the hand of the eunuch, and opening it, found her ring inside. Then she read the paper, and when she learned that her lover was Qamar az-Zaman, and that he was standing behind the curtain, she almost went out of her mind with rapture, and her heart was eased and she rejoiced. She arose and bracing her feet against the wall, she leaned with all her strength against the chain of iron and broke it off her neck, and shattered the fetters. She ran out through the curtain and threw herself on Qamar az-Zaman and kissed him on the mouth like a pigeon feeding her young, embracing him in the intensity of her passion.

"My lord," she cried, "am I awake or dreaming? Has God really blessed us with reunion?" Then she praised God and thanked Him for re-uniting them after they had despaired.

When the eunuch saw her in this state, he ran to King Ghayur, and kissing the ground before him, said: "O my Lord, this astrologer is the wisest of them all. He treated your daughter while standing behind the curtain and did not go in to her."

"Is this true what you say?" demanded the King.

"O master," replied the eunuch, "go look at her and see how she broke the iron chains and went out to the astrologer, kissing and embracing him."

The King arose and went in to his daughter, who, when she saw him, arose and covered her head. Perceiving that she was recovered, her father rejoiced and kissed her on the forehead, since he loved her with a great love.

King Ghayur then turned to Qamar az-Zaman and asked him about himself and from what country he came. Qamar az-Zaman informed the King that he was the son of King Shahriman and related the story to him from beginning to end. He told the King everything that had happened between him and the Lady Budur and how they had exchanged rings, each taking the other's and putting it on his own finger.

The King was amazed, and said: "Your story must be recorded in books and read from generation to generation after you are gone."

Then the King summoned the judges and witnesses and wrote the marriage contract between Budur and Qamar az-Zaman. He ordered the city to be decorated for seven days and banquet tables to be set out with food. The city and the army decked themselves out in their best finery, and the glad tidings were published abroad. Finally, Qamar az-Zaman went in to his bride the Lady Budur.

The King rejoiced at her well-being and her marriage, and he praised God who had made her fall in love with a handsome young man who was a king's son. When she was unveiled to him, they were seen to resemble each other in grace and beauty, and in charm and attractiveness. Qamar az-Zaman slept that night with her and achieved his desires, and she enjoyed his grace and beauty. They stayed in each other's arms till morning.

On the following day, the King held another banquet and brought together all the people of the outer and the inner isles. The tables were laid and cloths were spread for a whole month.

After this, Qamar az-Zaman began to think again of his father. He saw him in a dream, saying to him: "O my son, is it thus that you treat me?" When he saw his father chiding him in a dream, he became sad and told his wife about it. Together she and Qamar az-Zaman went in to see her father, and told him what had happened. Qamar az-Zaman asked his permission to leave and was granted it.

"O my father," said the Lady Budur, "I cannot bear to be separated from him."

"Go with him," answered the King, and he gave her permission to remain with him for a whole year, but thereafter she should come to visit her father once each year. Budur and Qamar az-Zaman kissed the hand of her father in gratitude.

Then King Ghayur proceeded to equip his daughter and her husband for their trip. He made ready all things necessary for the journey, bringing forth horses and dromedaries for them and a litter for his daughter. He loaded mules and dromedaries with everything that they might require on the journey.

On the day of departure, King Ghayur said farewell to Qamar az-Zaman and bestowed on him a sumptuous robe of honor made of cloth-of-gold encrusted with gems. He presented him with a coffer of money, and commended his daughter, Budur, to his care. Then he went out with them, accompanying them as far as the boundary of the isles. Here he bade farewell to Qamar az-Zaman, and, going into his daughter's litter, he embraced her and wept. Coming out again, he went to her husband, Qamar az-Zaman, kissed him, and once again bade him farewell. Then commanding them to be on their way, he returned with his soldiers to the isles.

Qamar az-Zaman, his wife, the Lady Budur, and their attendants set out and traveled throughout the first, the second, and the third, and the fourth day. They continued on their way for the space of a whole month and finally descended in a wide meadow rich in green herbage. Here they set up their tents, ate and drank, and refreshed themselves.

The Lady Budur then fell asleep. Entering her tent, Qamar az-Zaman found her asleep, wearing a peach-colored chemise of silk through which everything could be seen. On her head was a kerchief of cloth-of-gold encrusted with gems. The breeze had raised her chemise till it lay above her navel at her breasts, and her belly was exposed, whiter than snow, each of whose folds could have contained an oke of ben-oil.

Qamar az-Zaman's love and passion for her increased, and he put his hand on the waistband of her pajamas and pulled on it, for his heart yearned for her. He suddenly caught sight of a red gemstone tied to her waistband, on which two lines of writing were incised in a language he could not read. Qamar az-Zaman was astonished, and said to himself: "If this stone were not of very great importance to her, she would not have tied it to the waistband of her pajamas this way, and she would not have hidden it in the dearest place of her so as not to be parted from it. What does she do with it and what is the secret of it?"

So he took it and brought it outside the tent to see it in the light. As he was examining it, suddenly a bird swooped down, snatched the gem from his hand, and, flying away a little distance, came to earth again still holding the stone. Qamar az-Zaman was fearful of losing it, so he ran after the bird, which at once proceeded to fly along ahead of Qamar az-Zaman at the same speed. Qamar az-Zaman followed the bird from hill to hill and from valley to valley until night fell and darkness closed in. The bird passed the night in the top of a lofty tree, while Qamar az-Zaman waited beneath it, pale and weak from hunger and fatigue, and thinking that he must surely perish. He wished to go back, but he no longer knew the way he had come, for the darkness had surprised him.

"There is no power or might save in God the Exalted, the Mighty!" he said, and then fell asleep at the foot of the tree. When morning came he awoke and saw that the bird had also awakened and was flying from the tree, so Qamar az-Zaman followed after. The bird flew on at the same speed at which Qamar az-Zaman walked.

"By Allah, how strange!" he exclaimed. "Yesterday this bird flew at the speed I ran, but today it knows that I am weary and cannot run, so it flies only as fast as I can walk. This is indeed amazing. I feel that I must follow this bird, whether it leads me to life or death, so I will follow it wherever it goes, for in any case, it will not stop except in some inhabited land."

So Qamar az-Zaman walked along beneath the bird, which spent each night in a tree. For ten days he followed it, living off the plants of the earth and drinking from rivers. On the tenth day, he approached a thriving city, through which the bird flitted in the twinkling of an eye and vanished from sight, leaving Qamar az-Zaman without any idea where it had gone.

Qamar az-Zaman was amazed and said: "Praise be to God, who has preserved me till I arrived at this city."

Then he sat down by the water and washed his hands, feet, and face. He rested for a while, recalling his former state of ease and considering his present state of loneliness, hunger, and fatigue.

After a while he arose and entered the gate of the city. He did not know where to go so he walked through the whole city. He had entered by the land-gate, and he walked until he came out by the sea-gate (for the city was located on the seacoast), without meeting a single one of its inhabitants. After coming out through the sea-gate, he kept on walking till he entered the gardens surrounding the city. He walked through the trees till he came to an olive grove and stopped at its gate. The caretaker came out and greeted him, saying: "Praise be to God who has brought you safely through the people of the city. Quick, come into this grove before anyone sees you!"

So Qamar az-Zaman went into the grove in perplexity. "What is there about this city?" he asked.

"The people of the city are all Magians," replied the caretaker. "I urge you in the name of Allah to tell me how you came to this place and what is the reason for your coming into our country."

Qamar az-Zaman told him everything that had happened to him, and the caretaker was greatly amazed.

"My son," he said, "the land of Islam is far from here, a four months' journey by sea and by land a full year. We have here a ship which sails each year, bearing trade goods to the nearest Moslem country. It goes from here to the Ebony Isles and thence to the Isles of Khalidan, whose king is called the Sultan Shahriman."

Qamar az-Zaman deliberated a long while, and decided that the best thing for him to do was to remain in the olive-grove and work with the caretaker for a share of the crop.

"Will you allow me to work in this grove," he asked the caretaker, "for a share of the crop?"

"I hear and obey," he replied. Then he taught Qamar az-Zaman how to direct the course of the water among the trees. He dressed him in a short blue tunic which reached his knees, and Qamar az-Zaman began to control the water and cut weeds with a hoe. He irrigated the trees, weeping copious tears and night and day reciting verses about his beloved Budur.

Thus matters lay with Qamar az-Zaman. As for his wife, the Lady Budur, daughter of King Ghayur, she awoke from her sleep and looked for her husband, Qamar az-Zaman, but did not find him. She noticed that her pajamas were loose, so she examined the knot and found that it was undone and that the gemstone was missing.

"By Allah, how strange!" she exclaimed. "Where is my beloved? It seems he has taken the gem and gone off, unaware of its secret. I wonder where he has gone. Some extraordinary thing must have compelled his departure, for he cannot bear to be away from me for a single hour. God curse that gem and the hour in which it was created!"

Then she deliberated for a while, and said to herself: "If I go out to the escort and tell them I have lost my husband, they will be seized with desire for me, so I must think of some ruse."

So she put on Qamar az-Zaman's clothes and a turban like his to which she bound a veil. She put a slave girl in her litter, and then, coming forth from her tent, she shouted at the slaves. They brought her the horse, and she mounted and commanded them to load up, which they did. Then they departed. She was able to conceal her identity because she resembled Qamar az-Zaman, and no one doubted that she was Qamar az-Zaman himself.

She continued journeying for some days and nights with her followers, till one day they approached a city overlooking the salt sea. She descended in its outskirts and had her tent set up there in order to take her repose. She asked about the city and was told that it was the City of Ebony, ruled by King Armanus, who had a daughter named Hayat an-Nufus.

Shortly thereafter King Armanus sent out a messenger to find out who the king was who had encamped in the outskirts of his city. When the messenger reached them he was told in reply to his questions that this was a king's son who was bound for the Isles of Khalidan and King Shahriman, but had lost his way.

The messenger returned and informed King Armanus, who at once set out with his ministers of state to meet the prince. When he approached the tent, the Lady Budur came out on foot, so the King descended and proceeded the rest of the way on foot. They greeted each other, and the King took her and brought her into the city to his palace. He ordered the dining cloths to be spread and the tables laid, and commanded that the Lady Budur be taken to the guesthouse, where she remained for three days.

Then King Armanus came to visit the Lady Budur. On that day she had gone to the baths, so she displayed a face like the full moon, a temptation to the world, at the sight of which moral virtue was rent in shreds. When King Armanus came in to her, she was wearing a robe of silk embroidered in gold and encrusted with gems.

"My son," the King addressed her, "know that I have grown to be an old man, and in my lifetime I have never been blessed with a son, but only a daughter who is like you in form and figure and in beauty and grace. I am now incapable of ruling. My son, would you like to remain in my country and dwell in my land? I will marry you to my daughter and give you my kingdom."

The Lady Budur hung her head and her brow was wet with shame.

"What shall I do?" she asked herself. "If I refuse him and depart, perhaps he will send an army after me to kill me, and if I obey him, I may be put to shame. But I have lost my beloved Qamar az-Zaman and I have no news of him. There is nothing for me to do but to consent to his desire and wait here till God decrees what shall be done."

Then the Lady Budur raised her head and submitted to the King, saying: "I hear and obey." The King rejoiced, and at once commanded the herald to proclaim festivities and illuminations throughout the Ebony Isles. He assembled the chamberlains, the palace guard, the emirs, viziers, and the councilors of state, and the judges of the city, and abdicated the throne, making the Lady Budur king in his stead. He invested her with the robes of state, and all the emirs came in to her, none of them doubting that she was a young man. Each one of them who looked at her wet his trousers at the sight of her extraordinary grace and beauty. Thus when Queen Budur became ruler, congratulations and best wishes for her resounded, and King Armanus began to prepare his daughter, Hayat an-Nufus, for the wedding.

After a few days they escorted the Lady Budur to Hayat an-Nufus, and the two of them seemed to be two moons joined together or two suns rising at the same time. Then, after lighting candles and making their bed, they closed the doors on them and let down curtains. The Lady Budur sat down with the Lady Hayat an-Nufus and thought about her beloved Qamar az-Zaman till her grief grew strong and she wept. Then she kissed the Lady Hayat an-Nufus on the mouth, but arose immediately, performed the ritual ablutions and prayed until the Lady Hayat an-Nufus fell asleep. Then the Lady Budur got into bed and, turning her back to Hayat an-Nufus, slept until morning.

When morning came, the King and his wife entered their daughter's room and asked her about her condition, and she told them what had happened.

In the meantime, Queen Budur came out and sat upon the royal throne, and all the emirs, the councilors of state, all the captains and the armies came to her and congratulated her on receiving the kingship and, kissing the ground before her, they showered blessings upon her. She inclined to them smiling, bestowing robes of honor on them, and granting fiefs to the emirs.

The army and the subjects loved her and wished her a long reign, thinking all the time that she was a man. She gave orders, made judgments, and administered justice. She released those who were in the prisons, remitted taxes, and, thus occupied, she sat in the council of state till nightfall.

Then she returned to the place prepared for her and found the Lady Hayat an-Nufus waiting. Sitting down beside her, she patted her on the shoulder and kissed her on the forehead and wept. Then rising, she brushed the tears from her eyes, and after performing the ritual ablutions, she prayed and did not cease till Hayat an-Nufus was overcome by sleep. Only then did Queen Budur come and sleep beside her till it was morning.

In the morning, after rising and praying the morning prayer, she sat upon the royal throne and gave orders, issued judgments, and administered justice. Meanwhile, King Armanus went into his daughter's chamber and asked her about her condition. She told him about everything that had happened, saying: "O father, I have never seen anyone more intelligent or more modest than my husband, only he weeps and sighs so much."

"Be patient my daughter," he said, "only the third night remains, and if he does not come in to you and take your virginity, I will come to a decision about him and take the necessary steps. I will remove him from the kingship and exile him from our country." He agreed with his daughter in this wise and resolved upon this decision.

When night came, Queen Budur arose and went from the council of state to the palace and entered the place prepared for her. She saw that the candles were lit and that Hayat an-Nufus was waiting, and recalled her husband and the things that had happened between them in so short a time, and she wept and sighed.

When finally she arose to go to pray, Hayat an-Nufus seized hold of the hem of her cloak and said: "O my lord, are you not ashamed before my father to neglect me for so long after the kindness he has done you?"

Upon hearing her speak thus, Queen Budur resumed her seat, and said: "My beloved, what is this you are saying?"

"What I am saying is that I have never seen anyone so pleased with himself as you. Is every handsome creature so much in love with his own beauty? However, I do not say this to make you desire me, but because I fear that King Armanus may harm you. For he has decided that if you do not come to me tonight and take my virginity he will remove you from the kingship tomorrow and banish you from his land. Perhaps if he becomes angry enough, he will even kill you. I pity you, my lord, and advise you well, but do as you think best."

When Queen Budur heard these words, she hung her head in confusion and said to herself: "If I oppose him, I am lost, and if I obey him, I will be disgraced. But I am now king over all the Ebony Isles and they are under my rule. I can never meet with Qamar az-Zaman except here, for there is no way to his country save through the Ebony Isles. So I will entrust my affair to God, for He is an excellent disposer."

Then Queen Budur said to Hayat an-Nufus: "O my beloved, my neglecting you and avoiding you is in spite of myself." Then she related to her the whole story from beginning to end and revealed herself, finally adding: "I beg you, in God's name, to conceal this matter and keep my secret until God joins me with my beloved Qamar az-Zaman, and after that, let come what may."

On hearing her story, Hayat an-Nufus was greatly amazed, and felt sympathy for her, and prayed that she might be united with her lover, Qamar az-Zaman.

"Do not fear, my sister," she said, "and do not be alarmed, but be patient till God decrees what is to be done. The heart of the nobly born is the grave of secrets, so I will not betray your secret." After this they played together, and embraced, and slept till near the time of the call to prayer.

Hayat an-Nufus arose and, taking a chicken, she slaughtered it and smeared herself with the blood. Then she stripped off her pajamas and cried out. Her servants came in to her and the slave girls began to trill with joy. Her mother came to her and remained until evening. Queen Budur, however, when morning came, arose, went to the baths and then prayed the morning prayer. Afterwards, she repaired to the council of state, sat on the throne, and attended to the affairs of state.

When King Armanus heard the hubbub of the women, he asked the reason for it, and was told that his daughter had been deflowered. The King rejoiced at the news and felt a great sense of relief and happiness, and gave many banquets in celebration of the event. Thus they continued for some time.

In the meantime, King Shahriman, after his son had gone out hunting with Marzuwan as was related before, waited till night, and when his son did not return, his mind became uneasy and he was unable to sleep because he was so greatly worried. Scarcely had dawn broken when he arose to wait for his son, who still had not arrived by midday. Then, realizing that Qamar az-Zaman had vanished, the King felt his heart was torn with anxiety for his son, and he wept until his clothing was soaked.

Then, drying his tears, he summoned his army to prepare to depart and undertake a long journey. The whole army mounted up and the Sultan rode out before them, his heart broken for his son and full of grief. He divided his army right and left and before and behind into six parts, and commanded them to meet at the crossroads on the following day.

The army and the soldiers split up as we said and the horsemen started off. They traveled through the remainder of the day until the darkness descended, and continued throughout the night till noon on the following day, at which time they reached a crossing of four ways, and they did not know which one he had followed. Here they found his rent garments and the torn flesh with the traces of blood remaining, each piece of which they examined carefully.

When the King saw these things, he uttered a loud cry from the depths of his heart, and cried out: "Alas, my son!" He beat his face, plucked out his beard, and rent his clothing, for he was sure that his son was dead. He wept and lamented exceedingly, and the whole army wept with him and poured dust on their heads, for they were sure that Qamar az-Zaman had perished.

Thus they spent the night, weeping and lamenting, until they were almost at the point of death. The King's heart was in anguish from his burning sighs, but finally he returned with his army to the city. The King was sure that his son was dead and believed that wild animals or robbers had torn him to pieces. He sent word throughout the Isles of Khalidan, and commanded that everyone should wear black in mourning for his son. He also had built for himself a house which he named "The House of Grief." Mondays and Thursdays the King spent in attending to the affairs of state among his soldiers and subjects, but, during the rest of the week, he retired to the House of Grief and lamented his son and composed elegies on him in verse.

In the meantime, Queen Budur, the daughter of King Ghayur, had become King in the Ebony Isles, and the people would point her out and say: "That is the son-in-law of Armanus." Every night, she slept with the Lady Hayat an-Nufus and complained of the absence of her husband, Qamar az-Zaman, and described to her his grace and beauty. Even when asleep she yearned to be reunited with him.

Meanwhile, Qamar az-Zaman was still living with the caretaker in the olive grove, weeping day and night, grieving, and reciting verses about the times of joy and happiness that he had once known. The caretaker told him that the ship would sail for the land of Islam at the end of the year. So Qamar az-Zaman continued thus, until one day he saw the people gathering together. He was surprised at this, but the caretaker came to him and said: "My son, work stops for today, so do not turn the water in among the trees. Today is a holiday on which people visit one another, so rest yourself and take a turn in the fields. Today I will see about a ship for you, since it won't be long now before I send you to the land of the Moslems."

The caretaker left the grove, and Qamar az-Zaman remained alone. He was depressed in spirits and his tears began to flow, and he continued weeping until he lost consciousness. When he awoke, he walked about in the grove, thinking of how fate had dealt with him and of his long separation and exile at which his mind became confused. Suddenly he stumbled and fell forward, his forehead striking against a tree root, so that his blood was mingled with his tears. Wiping off the blood and drying his tears, he bound up his forehead with a piece of cloth and continued to walk about in the grove in a distraught state of mind. Suddenly he saw two birds fighting in a tree. One of them overpowered the other and sank its beak into its opponent's neck, tearing it from the body. Then picking up the severed head, it flew away as the body of the slain bird fell to the ground at Qamar az-Zaman's feet. As Qamar az-Zaman was standing there, two great birds swooped down above him. One of them came to rest at the feet of the dead bird, the other at its head. They let down their wings over it and extended their necks towards it, weeping. Qamar az-Zaman wept over his distant wife as he watched the birds weeping over their dead companion. Then as he watched, the birds dug a grave and buried the slain bird, after which they flew off again into the air. Soon they returned, bringing with them the slayer and, after bringing him down to the grave of his victim, they attacked and killed him. Then they split open his belly and pulled out his entrails and poured his blood on the grave of the slain bird. Then they scattered his flesh and tore his skin to pieces; removing the rest of his vitals, they strewed them about. All this while Qamar az-Zaman was looking on amazed.

He happened to glance at the spot where they had killed the bird and noticed something glistening there. Drawing near, he found that it was the craw of the bird. Picking it up he opened it and found inside the gem which was the cause of his separation from his wife. When he saw it, he recognized it at once, and fell to the ground, fainting from joy. On awaking, he said to himself: "This is a sign of good and an omen that I shall meet my beloved." After examining it and passing it over his eyes, Qamar az-Zaman tied it to his arm, rejoicing at the good omen. He then arose and walked about waiting for the caretaker.

Qamar az-Zaman waited for the caretaker until nightfall, but he did not return, so he slept that night in his usual place. When morning came, he got up and went about his work. He bound his waist with a rope of palm fiber, and taking his ax and a basket, he pruned branches in the grove. Finally he came to a carob tree and struck the ax into its roots. The blow re-echoed with a hollow sound, so he removed the earth from the spot, and found there a trap door. This he opened, and going down, he came to another door, through which he passed, finding himself in a wide and ancient chamber dating from the time of Ad and Thamud, which was filled with red gold.

"The time of trouble is gone!'" he exclaimed. "And joy and happiness have come!"

He went up again to the grove and, closing the trap door as it had been, he went ahead with his work of irrigating the trees and continued till the close of day, at which time the caretaker returned.

"Rejoice, my son," the caretaker said, "for you are to return to your homeland. The merchants are ready to depart and, in three days' time, the ship will sail for the City of Ebony, which is the nearest Moslem city. When you arrive there, you will travel for six months by land before you come to the Isles of Khalidan and King Shahriman."

Qamar az-Zaman rejoiced and, kissing the caretaker's hand, he said: "Just as you have given me glad tidings, so will I give glad tidings to you." Then he told him about the underground chamber. The caretaker rejoiced, saying: "My son, I have been in this grove for eighty years, and have never found a thing. But you have been with me less than a year, and have discovered this marvelous thing. So it will be your provision and the means to make good your reverses, and a help toward reaching your people and rejoining the one you love."

"It must be divided between you and me," insisted Qamar az-Zaman.

Then taking the caretaker with him, he brought him down into the chamber and showed him the gold, which was stored in twenty great jars, making ten each for the caretaker and Qamar az-Zaman.

"My son," said the caretaker, "pack some casks for yourself with the sparrow-olives of this grove, for they do not exist in any other land, and the merchants here export them everywhere. Put the gold in the bottom of the casks and the olives on top of the gold. Then close them up and take them with you in the ship."

At once Qamar az-Zaman packed fifty casks with the gold and closed them up after placing olives on top. In one cask, along with the gold he concealed the gemstone that he had found.

Then he sat down and conversed with the caretaker. He was certain now that he would shortly rejoin his people, and he said to himself: "When I come to the Ebony Isles, I will journey thence to my father's country and ask about my beloved Budur. I wonder if she returned to her country, or whether she went on to my father's land, or whether some accident befell her on the way."

While he was waiting for the last days to pass, Qamar az-Zaman told the caretaker the story of the birds, at which he was greatly amazed.

One morning the caretaker awoke feeling ill and continued thus for two days. On the third day, his illness had increased so much that they despaired of his life, and Qamar az-Zaman was stricken with grief for the caretaker. That same day the ship-captain and the sailors came asking after the caretaker, and he informed them of his illness.

"Where then is the young man," they asked, "who wishes to sail with us to the Ebony Isles?"

"He is the poor slave who stands before you," replied Qamar az-Zaman. He ordered them to transport the casks to the ship, which they did at once. "Make haste," they said to him, "for the wind is fair."

"I hear and obey," replied Qamar az-Zaman, and he immediately brought his baggage to the ship. Then he returned to say farewell to the caretaker and found that he was at the point of death. Qamar az-Zaman remained with the caretaker until he died, after which he covered the body, prepared it for burial, and finally laid it away in the earth. Only then did he go down to the shore, where he found that the sails had been set and the ship was standing out to sea. It sailed on till it vanished from sight, to the dismay and perplexity of Qamar az-Zaman, who then returned, sad and distraught, to the grove, and poured dust upon his head.

When the ship departed, leaving Qamar az-Zaman behind, he rented the grove from its owner and hired a man to help him irrigate the trees. He went next to the trap door and, going down into the chamber, he packed the remaining gold into fifty casks, putting olives on the top. He asked about the ship and was told that it made the voyage only once a year.

His melancholy increased, for he was greatly distressed at what had befallen him, especially at the loss of the gem which belonged to the Lady Budur, so he wept by night and day and recited verses.

In the meantime, the ship sailing with a fair wind reached the Ebony Isles. Fate had decreed that Queen Budur should be sitting at a window where she saw the ship as it cast anchor on the shore. Her heart throbbed and immediately she rode down with the emirs and the chamberlains, and made her way to the shore. She stopped beside the ship where they were already engaged in transporting the merchandise to the warehouses and, summoning the captain, she asked him what his cargo was.

"O King," he replied, "I have with me in this ship drugs and medicines, kohls, slaves, and oils; fine, splendid fabrics and precious wares in such quantities that camels and mules could not carry them. Among them are all sorts of perfumes, incense, aloes wood, and tamarind, and sparrow-olives, the like of which is rarely seen in this country."

At once the Queen felt a craving for the olives and asked the captain the amount of olives he had with him.

"Fifty casks full," he answered. "However, the owner did not come with us, so let the King take of them as many as he pleases."

"Bring them out on the land so I may see them," she said. And the captain shouted to the sailors, and they brought out the fifty casks.

The Queen opened one of them and, after examining the olives, said to the captain: "I will take these fifty casks and pay you their price, whatever it may be."

"This has little value in our country," replied the captain, "but the owner who stayed behind is a poor man."

"What is the price?" she countered.

"A thousand dirhams."

"I will take them at a thousand dirhams," said the Queen. And she ordered them to be carried up to the palace.

When night came, she commanded that one of the casks be brought to her, and when it came she opened it while she and Hayat an-Nufus were alone together. She set before her a plate. When she poured some of the olives from the cask, a heap of red gold descended on to the plate.

"This is gold!" she exclaimed. And at once she examined the rest of the casks. She found them all full of gold, and the olives taken together would not have filled a single one of them. Searching through the gold, she came upon the gem, which she took and examined carefully. She discovered that it was the gem from the waistband of her pajamas, which Qamar az-Zaman had taken. When she realized this, she uttered a cry of joy and fell down in a faint.

When she recovered, she said to herself: "This gem was the cause of my separation from my beloved Qamar az-Zaman, but now it is a bearer of glad tidings." And she told the Lady Hayat an-Nufus that it was an omen of their reunion. When morning came, she sat upon the throne and had the ship-captain brought before her. When he came in to her presence, he kissed the ground before her.

"Where did you leave the owner of these olives?" she demanded.

"O King of the Age," he replied, "we left him in the land of the Magians, where he is the caretaker of an olive-grove."

"If you do not bring him to me," she said, "you cannot guess the harm that will befall you and your ship."

Then she ordered the warehouse of the merchants to be sealed up, and spoke to them, saying: "The owner of these olives is a debtor of mine who owes me money, and if he does not come, I will slay you all and confiscate your goods."

The merchants went to the captain and agreed with him to hire his ship to return a second time, begging him to save them from this tyrant. The captain descended into the ship and raised the sails. God granted him a safe voyage, and he arrived at the Isle of the Magians by night, and went up to the olive grove. Qamar az-Zaman had passed the night awake, thinking of his beloved and weeping over what had befallen him in this grove. When the captain knocked, Qamar az-Zaman opened the gate and went out to him, whereupon the sailors seized him and, carrying him off to the ship, at once set sail.

They sailed for many days and nights, and Qamar az-Zaman was at a loss to explain all this. When he asked them their reasons, they explained: "You are a debtor of the King of the Ebony Isles, the son-in-law of King Armanus, and have stolen his money, O unclean one!"

"By Allah!" he insisted, "in my whole life I have never been in that country and I do not know it!"

They continued sailing till they landed at the Ebony Isles where they brought him up to the Lady Budur. She recognized Qamar az-Zaman when she saw him, and ordered him to be left with the servants, who were commanded to take him into the bath. She then released the merchants and bestowed on the sea captain a robe of honor which was valued at ten thousand dinars. After this, she went in to Hayat an-Nufus and telling her what had happened, she said: "Keep this secret till I have accomplished my purpose, and I shall do a deed which will be recorded and read to kings and subjects alike after we are gone."

The servants took Qamar az-Zaman into the bath, as she had commanded, and dressed him in regal garments. When Qamar az-Zaman came out of the bath, he was fully restored and was like the branch of a ben-tree or a star whose aspect would put the sun and moon to shame.

Then he went to her and came into the palace. When she saw him, she compelled her heart to patience in order to accomplish her design. She generously bestowed on him slaves, servants, mules, and camels, and gave him treasures of money. She continued to advance Qamar az-Zaman from one post to the next, till finally she made him her Treasurer and turned over to him the finances of the kingdom, showing him great favor and bringing him near her own person. She informed the emirs of his new rank, and they all approved. Each day, Queen Budur increased his emoluments, but Qamar az-Zaman remained ignorant of her reasons for so honoring him. From his abundance of wealth he gave gifts and displayed great generosity, and he served King Armanus in such wise that the King came to love him. Likewise, the emirs, the upper classes, and the common people all loved him and began to swear by his life, an unusual mark of affection. All this time, Qamar az-Zaman continued in amazement at the honors shown him by Queen Budur.

"By Allah," he said to himself, "all this affection must be for some reason. Perhaps the King is doing me this great honor only for some corrupt purpose. I must ask his permission to leave the country."

He went to the Queen, and said: "O King, you have honored me excessively, but the most perfect honor would be to permit me to depart, while you take back all that you have bestowed on me."

The Queen smiled and asked: "What is it that makes you want to travel and face dangers, when you are at the pinnacle of honor here and are constantly increasing in my favor?"

"O King," replied Qamar az-Zaman, "if there is no reason for this honor, then indeed it is a most amazing thing, especially since you have conferred upon me ranks which by right ought to go to elderly sheiks, although I am only a young man."

"The reason is," said Queen Budur, "that I love you for your extraordinary grace and your marvelous splendid beauty, and if you let me have what I want from you, I will honor and favor you, and give you gifts, far more than I have done before. I will make you Vizier, in spite of your youth, just as the people made me ruler over them. I am of the same age as you are, and there is nothing strange today in young people ruling. What a fine poet was the one who said:

> It seems that men of Sodom do possess our age,
> For favoring the young today is all the rage.

When Qamar az-Zaman heard these words, he was ashamed and blushed till his cheeks were fiery red, and replied: "I have no need of this sort of honor which leads to the commission of forbidden acts. Nay, I would rather live poor in money, but rich in my manliness and perfection."

"I am not deceived by this virtue of yours," said Queen Budur, "since it stems from haughtiness and coquettishness. How well the poet said:

> "Leave off these painful words," he cried, when I
> For lovers' union would have set a date;
> But when I showed the color of my coin,
> "Oh well," said he, "I cannot flee from fate."

When Qamar az-Zaman heard these verses, he said: "O King, I do not have the habit of doing such things, and I have no strength to bear such burdens. They would be impossible even for one much older than I, so how could it be otherwise with me, seeing how young I am?"

At this, Queen Budur smiled and said: "It is strange indeed how error appears through the truth. If you are young, why do you fear forbidden things and the commission of sins, for you have not reached the age of responsibility. The sins of the young are not held against them, and they are not reprimanded for them. You have proved my point by your arguments, so it is your duty to go through with this union. After this, do not display such reluctance and aversion, for the command of God is fate foreordained. Indeed, I should fear more than you to fall into error."

When Qamar az-Zaman heard these words, his fear grew dark, and he said: "O King, there are many beautiful women and slave girls here with you, the like of which are not to be found elsewhere in this age. Why do you not manage with them and do without me? Go to any of them you please and leave me alone."

"You speak the truth," replied the Queen, "but the torment and agony brought on by loving you cannot be assuaged by one of them. When one's nature and disposition are corrupted, he will not hear and obey good counsel. So make an end to your arguments."

Qamar az-Zaman now realized that there was no way to avoid doing what she wanted.

"O King," he said, "if this thing must be, then promise me that you will do it no more than once even if one time is insufficient to put right your disordered nature, and that afterwards you will never ask me to do it again; thus perhaps God may make whole that which is corrupted in me."

"I promise you that," she replied, "in the hope that God will accept our repentance, and blot out this great sin of ours by His favor. The girdle of the firmament of forgiveness is not too narrow to go around us and grant us remission for our great offense and bring us out of the darkness of error into the light of rectitude."

Then she gave him a contract of agreement and swore by the Necessarily Existent One that this act would be performed by them only once, even should her passion for him bring her to death and destruction. On this condition, he arose and went with her to an isolated room so that she might extinguish the fire of her passion.

"There is no strength or power save in God the Exalted, the Mighty!" exclaimed Qamar az-Zaman. "This is decreed by the Almighty and the Omniscient." Then, with deepest shame, he loosened his trousers, his eyes flowing with tears from the intensity of his apprehension.

She smiled and drew him onto the bed with her, saying: "After tonight you will experience nothing that is repugnant to you." Then throwing her legs over his, she overwhelmed him with kisses and embraces.

"Run your hand between my thighs to the familiar thing," she said; "perhaps it will arise from its prostration and stand up."

"I am not good at this at all," cried Qamar az-Zaman in tears.

"By my life," she urged, "if you do as I bid you, you will like what is there."

So he put out his hand, sighing from the depths of his heart, and found her thighs softer than butter and smoother than silk. He enjoyed touching them, and he moved his hand about on every part of them till he reached the mound of many blessings and movements.

"Perhaps the King is a hermaphrodite and neither male nor female," said Qamar az-Zaman to himself, and then to her: "O King, I do not find a tool like that of men."

Queen Budur threw back her head and laughed, and said: "O my beloved, how quickly you have forgotten the nights we spent together!"

At once he recognized her and realized that she was his wife, Queen Budur, daughter of King Ghayur, Lord of the Isles and Seas, and they embraced and kissed each other and lay down together on the bed of reunion.

Afterwards, Queen Budur told him everything that had happened to her from beginning to end, and likewise he told her all that had happened to him. Then he reproached her, saying: "What possessed you to do what you did tonight?"

"Do not hold it against me," she replied. "I did it only as a joke, and also so that our delight and joy should be all the greater."

In the morning when it grew light, Queen Budur went to King Armanus, the father of Queen Hayat an-Nufus, and told him the truth about herself, that she was the wife of Qamar az-Zaman. She told him their story and the reason for their separation from each other, and informed him that his daughter Hayat an-Nufus was still a virgin.

When King Armanus, Lord of the Ebony Isles, heard Queen Budur's story, he was greatly amazed and ordered that it be written down in water of gold. Then he went to Qamar az-Zaman and said: "My son, would you like to become my son-in-law and marry my daughter Hayat an-Nufus?"

"First I must talk with Queen Budur about it," replied Qamar az-Zaman, "for she has an unlimited claim to my favor."

When he asked her about the matter, she replied: "This is an excellent idea; marry her, and I will be like a slave girl to her, for I am indebted to her for her favor and kindness, her goodness and forbearance, especially when we were living together, overwhelmed by her father's kindness."

When Qamar az-Zaman saw that Queen Budur was favorably inclined and that she entertained no feelings of jealousy for Hayat an-Nufus, he agreed with her on the marriage. He went to King Armanus and told him that Queen Budur favored the match and would be like a slave girl to Hayat an-Nufus. King Armanus rejoiced exceedingly on hearing this; immediately he went out and, seating himself on the royal throne, he summoned all the viziers, emirs, chamberlains, and councillors of state, and related to them the story of Qamar az-Zaman and Queen Budur from beginning to end. He informed them that he wished to marry his daughter to Qamar az-Zaman and make him ruler over them in the place of his wife, Queen Budur.

They replied that since Qamar az-Zaman was the husband of Queen Budur, who had ruled over them when they thought she was the King's son-in-law, they would now accept his rule and would be faithful servants to him and would not depart from submission to him.

The King rejoiced greatly at this and at once summoned the judges, the witnesses, and the councillors of state, and concluded the contract, marrying his daughter, Hayat an-Nufus, to Qamar az-Zaman. Then he celebrated, holding splendid banquets and bestowing precious robes of honor on all the emirs and generals of the army. Furthermore, he gave charity to the poor and miserable; he released all who were in the prisons, and announced to the world the good tidings of Qamar az-Zaman's elevation to the throne. Everyone prayed that he might be granted enduring power, good fortune, happiness, and honor.

Qamar az-Zaman, when he became ruler over them, remitted taxes, freed prisoners, and followed a praiseworthy course of action in general. He lived with his two wives in joy and happiness, and faithfully passed one night with each of them in turn. Thus he continued for a long period of time, his cares and sorrows dissipated, forgetting his father, Shahriman, and the position of honor and power that he had held with him.

Eventually God granted him two sons, one from each of his wives, like the two great luminaries, the sun and the moon. The elder, born to Queen Budur was called Prince Amjad, and the younger, born to Queen Hayat an-Nufus, was named Prince As'ad, and he was handsomer than his brother, Amjad.

The two boys were reared with good breeding and were spoiled with affection. They learned writing, science, government, and horsemanship, and they grew to perfection, possessing extraordinary beauty and grace, so that men and women everywhere were bewitched by them and they were the envy of everyone. Until they reached the age of seventeen years, they were always together, eating and drinking together, and were never separated from each other for as much as a single hour's time.

When they reached man's estate, their father began to take them with him when he traveled, letting them each in turn sit in the place of judgment, administering justice a day at a time.

Then it happened by inexorable destiny and foreordained fate that Queen Budur fell in love with As'ad, the son of Queen Hayat an-Nufus, and Queen Hayat an-Nufus fell in love with Amjad, the son of Queen Budur. Each of the two women began to play with the son of the other, to kiss him and press him to her bosom. When each mother saw this, she assumed that it stemmed merely from the other's affection and maternal love towards her son. But this love grew strong in the hearts of both women so that they were both completely infatuated with the boys. Each one, whenever the other's son came in, would clasp him to her bosom and not want to let him leave her.

When time passed and neither of them found a way to bring about a lovers' union, they abstained from eating and drinking and gave up the delights of sleep.

One day King Qamar az-Zaman went out hunting and commanded his sons to sit in his place to rule, each of them one day in turn, as was their custom.

On the first day Amjad, the son of Queen Budur, sat on the throne to administer the affairs of state. He issued commands, appointed and removed officials, and granted and denied petitions. Queen Hayat an-Nufus wrote a letter to him, seeking his compassion, and explaining that she was attached to him and enamoured of him. She revealed everything, telling him that she wanted a lovers' tryst with him. Taking a piece of paper she wrote these lines:

From the wretched lover, the sad and lonely one, whose youth is lost for love of you, whose torment is long because of you. If I described to you my long suffering, and the grief with which I am tormented, the passion in my heart, my weeping and mourning, the rending of my sad heart, the succession of my cares, and the sequence of my worries, this lonely separation, and the sadness and burning in my bosom, the description would be too long for this letter, for there are not sufficient numbers to count them all. Earth and heaven have become too strait for me; I have no hope for the future in any-one save you; I am at the point of death and I am suffering from fear of perdition. This burning inside me has increased, as has the pain of separation. If I tried to describe my desire, there would not be enough paper to do so.

After this, she wrote these two verses:

Wrote I of all my cares, my passion, and my pain,
On earth nor pens nor ink nor paper would remain.

Then Queen Hayat an-Nufus wrapped the paper in a piece of precious silk perfumed with musk and amber. In it she also placed some of her hair-fillets, which were more precious than wealth untold. She wrapped it in a handkerchief and gave it to her eunuch, bidding him deliver it to Prince Amjad.

The eunuch went to Prince Amjad, not knowing what was in store for him, for the Knower of the Unknown disposes matters as it pleases Him. When he went in to Prince Amjad, the eunuch kissed the ground before his feet and handed him the kerchief with the missive. The Prince took the kerchief from the eunuch and, unfolding it, he saw the paper, which he opened and read. When he understood its import, he realized that the wife of his father contemplated betrayal and that she had already betrayed his father, King Qamar az-Zaman, in her soul. He grew angry beyond measure and blamed women for their deeds, saying: "God curse women who are treacherous and lacking in intellect and religion!"

Then he drew his sword and said to the eunuch: "Woe to you, wicked slave! Do you dare to deliver a treacherous missive from the wife of your master? By God, there is no good in you, O black of complexion and countenance, ugly of aspect and vile-natured one that you are!" With this, he struck the eunuch on the neck with his sword, severing his head from his body. Then, refolding the kerchief, he put it into his pocket and, going to his mother, he told her what had happened, and heaped insults and reproaches on her.

"Each one of you is viler than the next, by God Almighty. If I did not fear behaving offensively to my father, Qamar az-Zaman, and my brother, As'ad, I would go to her and cut off her head just as I did her eunuch's!" Then he left his mother, Queen Budur, still in a paroxysm of rage.

When Queen Hayat an-Nufus, his father's wife, learned what he had done to her eunuch, she reviled and cursed him, and began to plot against him.

Amjad spent that night weak with anger and oppressed by his thoughts, enjoying neither food, nor drink, nor sleep.

When morning came, his brother Prince As'ad came out and sat in the hall of his father, Qamar az-Zaman, to deal with the affairs of state. His mother, Hayat an-Nufus, had become ill on hearing that Amjad had slain her eunuch. As'ad sat in his father's place, administering justice, making appointments and dismissals, issuing commands, granting petitions and presents until it was almost evening. At this time, Queen Budur sent for a cunning old woman whom she knew, and revealed to her what was in her heart. She took a piece of paper to write a letter to Prince As'ad, her husband's son, to complain to him of her great love and passion for him, and she wrote the following lines:

> From one destroyed by passion and desire, to the handsomest of men both in form and character, who is proud in his beauty, haughty in his attractive-ness, who turns from whoever seeks union with him, who has no need to come near one humbled and subdued; to him who treats others unkindly and irksomely, to Prince As'ad of superior grace and pure beauty, the moonlike face, and the shining forehead and the brilliant radiance. This letter of mine is to one who has melted my body and torn my flesh and bones. Know that my patience is exhausted, my state is in confusion, desire and separation have filled me with anxiety; patience and sleep have shunned me; sadness and wakefulness have clung to me, and I am overcome by emaciation and illness. My life be your ransom, if your lover's death will please. May God grant you a long life, and preserve you from all evil.

After these words, she added the following verses:

> I must love thee!—This is fate's decree—
> Thou, whose beauty like the moon doth rise.
> Thou hast all eloquence and grace in thee,
> Thy radiance not of earth, but paradise.
> I am content thy torments to endure,
> If one glance as alms fall to my lot;
> Happy the one who dies for love of thee,
> But no good comes to him who loveth not.

Then Queen Budur perfumed the paper with fine musk, and tied round it her hair-fillets which were of Iraqi silk and had little rod-shaped pendants of green emerald and were encrusted with pearls and precious gems. Hand-ing it to the old woman, she bade her deliver it to Prince As'ad, the son of her husband, Qamar az-Zaman.

In deference to her, the old woman went immediately to Prince As'ad, who was alone when she came in. She delivered the note to him and stood waiting for a reply. When As'ad read the letter and understood its import, he tied it with the fillets and, putting it into his pocket, he fell into a paroxysm of rage, which could not have been more intense. He cursed all treacherous women and, drawing his sword from its scabbard, he struck the old woman on the neck and severed her head from her body.

Then he went at once to his mother, Hayat an-Nufus, and found her lying in bed, ill from what had occurred between her and Prince Amjad. Prince As'ad cursed her and upbraided her and then went out to meet with his brother, Amjad. He told him everything that had befallen him with Queen Budur and that he had slain the old woman who had brought him the message.

"By Allah, my brother," he concluded, "if I had not been ashamed to do so before you, I would have gone in to your mother at the same time and cut her head from her shoulders!"

"By Allah, O brother," cried Prince Amjad, "the same thing happened to me yesterday, when I was sitting on the throne that happened to you today! Your mother sent me a message saying much the same thing."

Then he related to him everything that had befallen him with Queen Hayat an-Nufus. "My brother," he concluded, "if I had not been ashamed before you, I would have gone in to her and dealt with her as I dealt with the eunuch."

They spent the remainder of the night together talking and cursing treacherous women. They furthermore agreed together to conceal the affair lest it should reach the ears of their father, who would surely slay both women. Thus they remained, passing the night sorrowfully together, till it was morning.

When morning came, King Qamar az-Zaman returned from hunting. He went up to the palace and, after sending the emirs about their business, he entered and found that his two wives were lying in bed seriously ill. The women had plotted against their sons and had agreed to cause them to be done to death, for they had disgraced themselves with them and feared to be at their mercy.

When the King saw them in this state, he asked what the matter was. Whereupon they arose and kissing his hand, they related the whole affair to him in reverse, saying: "Know, O King, that your sons who were raised in your favor have betrayed you with your wives and have disgraced you."

When Qamar az-Zaman heard his wives speak these words, the light of his face grew dark and he fell into a dreadful rage, in the intensity of which he very nearly went out of his mind. Then he commanded his wives to explain the matter fully.

"Know, O King of the Age," replied Queen Budur, "that your son As'ad has for some days been corresponding with me, writing me notes, trying to seduce me into adultery. I forbade him, but he did not stop and, when you left, he burst in upon me, drunk, with sword in hand. I feared that he would slay me if I refused him, just as he slew my eunuch, so he had his way with me by force. If you do not give him his just deserts, O King, I will slay myself with my own hand, for I have no wish to live in this world after this monstrous deed."

Queen Hayat an-Nufus likewise told him the same sort of story as Budur had related, saying: "I too experienced the same thing from your son Amjad." She cried and moaned, and swore that if he did not deal justly with his son on her behalf she would tell her father, King Armanus. Then they both wept long and loud before their husband, King Qamar az-Zaman.

The King believed they had spoken the truth and became even angrier with his sons. He was on his way to attack his sons and kill them when he was met by his father-in-law, King Armanus, who had come in to greet him, having heard that he had returned from hunting. He saw him sword in hand, with blood pouring from his nose from the excess of his wrath, and asked what was wrong.

Qamar az-Zaman related to him the whole story of his sons, Amjad and As'ad and added: "Now I am going to slay them in the worst manner possible and make of them a horrible example."

King Armanus was also incensed against them, but he said: "What you are going to do is excellent, my son; may God not bless them nor any sons who do such things to their father. But my son, the proverb says: 'He who does not consider consequences, will not be favored by fate.' They are, after all, your sons, so do not slay them with your own hand, lest you see their death-agony and feel remorse after slaying them, when remorse will do no good. Send them rather with one of your slaves to kill them in the desert where they will be out of sight."

When King Qamar az-Zaman heard his father-in-law, King Armanus, say these words, he considered them good advice, so he sheathed his sword, and went and sat on his royal throne. He then summoned his Treasurer, who was an old man knowledgeable in affairs and familiar with the vicissitudes of fate.

"Go in to my sons, Amjad and As'ad," he commanded, "and bind them securely. Put them each in a chest and load them onto mules. Then ride out and take them into the middle of the desert and slay them there. Afterwards, fill two bottles with their blood and bring them to me at once."

"I hear and obey," replied the Treasurer. He arose at once and went to find Amjad and As'ad, whom he met as they were coming into the entrance hall of the palace. They had put on their most splendid garments with the intention of going to greet their father and felicitate him on his safe return from the hunt.

When the Treasurer saw them, he stopped them, and said: "My sons, know that I am only a slave under orders, and that your father has given me a command. Will you obey his command?"

"Yes," they replied, and thereupon the Treasurer had them bound and placed in two chests, which he loaded on the backs of mules. He brought them out of the city and continued on into the desert till it was almost noon, when he dismounted in a lonely and deserted spot. Taking the chests down from the mules and opening them, he took Amjad and As'ad out.

As he gazed at them, the Treasurer wept bitterly because of their grace and beauty, but at last he drew his sword, and said: "By Allah, my masters, it is hard for me to do you an evil turn, but I have an excuse in this affair since I am only a slave under orders. Your father, King Qamar az-Zaman, has commanded me to cut off your heads."

"O Emir," they replied, "do as the King commanded you. We will endure patiently what God—He is exalted and mighty—has decreed for us, and you shall be innocent of our blood." So speaking, they embraced each other and said farewell.

Then Prince As'ad said to the Treasurer: "I beg you, for God's sake, O uncle, do not force me to witness the death-agony of my brother, and do not afflict me with his loss, but rather slay me before him, so that it will be easier for me."

Amjad spoke to the Treasurer in the same fashion, trying to induce him to kill him before his brother, As'ad.

"My brother is younger than I," he said. "Do not make me taste the agony of his death."

They both wept bitterly and the Treasurer wept with them. They embraced and said farewell once again, and one said to the other: "All this is the result of the guile of our treacherous mothers. This is the outcome of what happened between my mother and you, and your mother and me. There is no power or strength save in God the Exalted, the Almighty. Verily we are God's, and to Him we return." Thereupon both brothers wept and sighed and embraced each other again.

"I beg you," said Amjad to the Treasurer once more, "for the sake of the One, the All-Conquering, the Ruler, and the Protector, to slay me before my brother, As'ad; thus my heart's fire will be extinguished, so let it burn no longer."

And As'ad wept, saying: "It is I who must be slain first."

"The best idea," said Amjad finally, "is for us to embrace one another so that the sword will descend on us and slay us at one stroke."

So they embraced face to face and clung together, while the Treasurer tied and bound them together with ropes, weeping all the while. Then, drawing his sword, he asked: "By Allah, my masters, it is hard for me to slay you. Do you have any need that I can fulfill, or last request that I can carry out, or a message I can deliver?"

"We need nothing," replied Amjad, "but I request that you place As'ad beneath me and me above, so that the stroke will fall on me first. And when you have killed us and have come to our father and he asks you what you heard us say before dying, say to him; 'Your sons send you greetings and say to you that you do not know whether they are innocent or guilty, for you have slain them without making sure of their guilt and without examining their case.' Then recite to him these verses:

> Women were created imps of hell;
> From their wicked guile God guard us well!
> Of all the trials that pious men dismay—
> And worldly men as well—the cause are they.

Our only request is that you convey these verses which you have just heard to our father."

When the Treasurer heard Amjad say these things, he wept until his beard was soaked.

The brothers then embraced once more until they were like a single person. The Treasurer raised his sword to strike. Then suddenly his horse bolted and ran off into the desert. Now, this horse was worth a thousand dinars and had on a saddle that was worth much money. The Treasurer at once threw down his sword and went off after his horse. His heart was enflamed, and he kept running after the horse, trying to catch it, until it went into a wood, and he followed after. The horse ran into the middle of the wood, stamping the ground with its hooves and stirring up a great cloud of dust which rose and spread as the horse whinnied and neighed and snorted and raged.

There was in this wood a dangerous lion, ugly of aspect, whose eyes cast sparks. It had a forbidding visage and an appearance that would strike terror to the soul. The Treasurer happened to turn and saw the lion coming towards him, but he could find no way to escape its claws for he did not have his sword.

"There is no power or strength save in God the Exalted, the Almighty," he said to himself. "I have come to these dire straits because of the guilt of Amjad and As'ad. This journey was ill-omened from the start."

In the meantime, Amjad and As'ad were becoming oppressed by the heat, and they grew so thirsty that their tongues hung out. They cried out for help against their thirst but no help came.

"Would that we were slain and were relieved of this!" they said. "Where can the horse have bolted to, which the Treasurer followed, leaving us bound together like this? If he returned and slew us, it would be easier than suffering this torture."

"Be patient, my brother," said As'ad, "for God—He is praised and exalted—will deliver us. Surely the horse bolted only because of God's graciousness to us, and all we have suffered is thirst."

Then he shook himself and moved right and left, so that his bonds were loosened. Then he arose and undid the bonds of his brother. Taking the emir's sword, he addressed his brother, saying: "By Allah, we will not leave this place till we discover what has befallen him." So they began to follow the tracks which led them to the wood.

"The horse and the Treasurer cannot have gone far into this wood," they said.

"Wait here," said As'ad, "while I go into the wood and search it."

"I will not let you go in by yourself," replied Amjad. "We shall not enter except together, and if we perish, we shall perish together."

So the two of them went into the wood together and found that the lion had attacked the Treasurer, who was lying beneath its paws like a sparrow, sending up prayers to God and crying out to heaven.

When Amjad saw him, he seized the sword and rushing upon the lion, smote it between the eyes and slew it. The lion collapsed on the ground and the emir, getting up in amazement, saw Amjad and As'ad, the sons of his master, standing there. Throwing himself at their feet, he exclaimed: "It was wrong of me to wish to slay you unjustly; may the man never be who would slay you; my life shall be your ransom!" Then he arose and embraced them and asked how they had broken their bonds and had come to him. They told him how they had grown thirsty, how the bonds had been loosed from one of them, who had then freed the other out of true affection, and how they had followed his tracks till they reached him.

When he heard their tale, he thanked them for what they had done, and went out with them to the edge of the wood. When they came out, they said to him: "O uncle, do now what our father commanded you."

"God forbid that I should do you any harm!" he exclaimed. "I wish to remove your clothes and dress you in my own. Then I shall fill two bottles with the lion's blood, and go to your father and tell him I have slain you. But as for you, you must travel to distant lands, for God's earth is wide; and know, O my masters, that it is hard for me to leave you."

Then the Treasurer and the two youths wept together. They removed their clothes, and he clad them in his own. The Treasurer then tied up their clothes each in a bundle, and filled the two bottles with the lion's blood and placed the two bundles on the back of his horse. Then bidding them farewell, he departed, returning to the city.

As soon as he arrived, he went to the King, kissing the ground before him. The King saw that his face had altered—which was the result of his encounter with the lion—but Qamar az-Zaman thought it was from having slain his sons, and he rejoiced.

"Have you done the deed?" he asked.

"Yes, master," he replied, and he handed him the two bundles of clothes and the two bottles filled with blood.

"How did they act? Did they give you any last instructions?"

"I found them patient and hopeful of recompense in the hereafter for what had befallen them. They said, 'Our father is to be excused, so give him our greetings and tell him you are innocent of killing us and guiltless of our blood. But we direct you to recite to him these two verses:

> Women were created imps of hell;
> From their wicked guile God guard us well!
> Of all the trials that pious men dismay—
> And worldly men as well—the cause are they.' "

When the King had heard the Treasurer's story, he hung his head for a long time, for he recognized that the words of his sons indicated that they had been slain unjustly. Then he reflected on the guile of women and the calamities they cause and, taking the two bundles, he opened them and began turning the clothes over in his hands.

When he opened the clothing of his son As'ad, he found in the pocket a note written in the hand of his wife Budur, enclosed with which were her hair-fillets. He unfolded the paper and having read it and understood its import, he realized that his son Asʿad had been wronged.

When he examined the clothes of Amjad, he found in the pocket a paper written in the hand of his wife Hayat an-Nufus, in which were her hair-fillets. He opened the note and read it, realizing then that Amjad had been wronged.

Then King Qamar az-Zaman struck his hands together, and cried out: "There is no power or strength save in God the Exalted, the Almighty! I have slain my sons unjustly!"

He beat himself on the face, crying: "Alas, my sons! Alas, I shall grieve forever!" And he commanded that two graves be dug and a house be built over them, which he called the "House of Grief." Over the graves he wrote the names of his two sons, and threw himself upon them alternately, weeping, and lamenting, and reciting elegies to their memory.

He abandoned his friends and companions, his women and his intimates, and, retiring to the House of Grief, he passed all his time there, weeping over his sons.

In the meantime, Amjad and Asʿad kept on traveling through the desert for a whole month, eating from the plants of the earth and drinking what rainwater they could find, till finally they came to a mountain of black granite, the extent of which could not be ascertained. Here the road divided, one branch cutting through the mountain and the other going upward towards the summit. They followed the road over the top of the mountain and continued on it for five days without coming to the end. Both were exhausted with fatigue, for neither was accustomed to walking in the mountains, or anywhere else.

When they despaired of reaching the top, they came back and followed the way which led through the mountains. They traveled all that day until night, by which time Asʿad had grown tired from much walking.

"O my brother," he said, "I cannot walk any farther, for I am very weak."

"Take courage, brother," replied Amjad, "perhaps God will deliver us."

They continued walking an hour after nightfall, until Asʿad was completely exhausted.

"My brother," he cried, "I am weary and fatigued from walking." Then he fell on the ground and wept.

His brother Amjad picked him up and carried him, walking an hour and resting an hour, till the dawn grew light, at which time he sought repose. He and his brother went up the mountain and discovered a spring with water gushing forth, near which was a pomegranate tree and a prayer niche. Scarcely believing their eyes, they sat down at the spring and drank of its water and ate some of the pomegranates from the tree. Then they slept in that place till the sun rose high. When they awoke, they washed themselves in the spring, ate more of the pomegranates that were on the tree, and slept again until evening. They wished to go on, but Asʿad was unable to walk because his feet had become swollen, so they remained there for three days refreshing themselves.

Then they traveled on for several days over the mountain, suffering severely from thirst, until finally a city appeared in the distance. They rejoiced and kept going till they reached it. When they drew near, they gave thanks to God—He is exalted.

Then Amjad said to As'ad: "My brother, sit here while I go into the city to see what it is like and ask about it, so that we may know where in God's wide world we are, and what country we have traversed in crossing this mountain. If we had not cut through the mountains, we would not have reached this city in a whole year. Praise be to God for our safety!"

"O my brother," As'ad replied, "no one but me shall go to the city, may I be your ransom. For if you leave me and go down and vanish from sight, I shall be overwhelmed with worries for you, for I have not the strength to endure being separated from you."

"Go then," said Amjad, "and do not delay."

So As'ad came down the mountain, and entered the city. As he was walking along its streets, he met a man, an old man advanced in years, who had a forked beard which came down to his breast. In his hand was a staff; he was wearing splendid clothes, and on his head was a large red turban. When As'ad saw him, he was amazed at his clothing and his appearance, and advancing towards him, he greeted him and asked the way to the market.

The old man smiled and answered: "My son, you seem to be a stranger here."

"Yes, uncle," replied As'ad, "I am a stranger here."

"Your visit to our country is most kind," said the old man, "and your own people must surely miss you. What is it that you want from the market?"

"O my uncle," explained As'ad, "I have a brother whom I left in the mountains. We have traveled from a far country and have already been three months on the way. When we drew near this city, I came in to buy food to bring back to my brother, so that we may have some nourishment."

"Rejoice in your good fortune, my son," said the old man, "for today I am giving a banquet for many guests, and I have brought together the finest and best foods that anyone could wish for. Would you like to come with me to my house? I will give you all that you want and not require you to pay anything. Moreover, I will give you information about this city. God be praised that it was I who met you and no one else."

"Do as you see fit," replied As'ad, "but let us make haste, for my brother awaits me and I must consider his feelings."

Taking As'ad by the hand, the old man led him to a narrow street, smiling all the while and exclaiming: "Praise God, who saved you from the people of this city!" They walked on and finally entered a spacious house with a large hall, in which were seated forty old men well on in years. They were ranged in a circle, in the middle of which a fire was burning. The old men were sitting around the fire, worshipping it, and prostrating themselves before it.

When As'ad saw that, his whole body trembled and he did not know what to think. Then the old man called out to the assembly: "O elders of the fire, what a blessed day is this!" He then called out the name "Ghadban," and a black slave came in, with a stern face and a flat nose, a crooked body and a fearsome aspect. He made a sign to the slave, who bound As'ad securely. Then the old man said: "Take him down to the chamber beneath the ground and leave him there. Tell the slave girl to torture him day and night."

The slave took him and, bringing him down into the chamber, handed him over to a slave girl who proceeded to torment him. She gave him one loaf of bread at the beginning of the day and another at the end, and one pitcher of water in the morning and another at evening.

The old man said to some of those present: "When the time of the festival comes, we shall sacrifice him on the mountain, and thereby come near the god of the fire."

The slave girl came down to him and beat him painfully until the blood flowed from all his members and he lost consciousness. Then she placed a loaf and a pitcher of brackish water at his head and left him. As'ad awoke in the middle of the night and found that he was in chains. He was in pain from the beating he had received, and he wept and sighed bitterly, recalling his former state of high rank and happiness, and power and authority. When he noticed the bread and the pitcher of brackish water at his head, he ate a little to still the pangs of hunger and drank a little of the water. He passed the remainder of the night awake, unable to sleep because of the many bugs and lice that infested the place.

When morning came, the slave girl came down again and stripped off his clothes. They had been drenched with blood and had stuck to his skin, so that parts of his skin were torn away with his shirt. He cried out and moaned, saying: "O my Lord, if this pleases Thee, then let me have more! My Lord, Thou wilt not forget those who mistreat me, so take vengeance on them!" He sighed and wept, and the slave girl beat him again till he lost consciousness. Throwing him a loaf and setting down a pitcher of brackish water, she left him, sad and alone, with the blood flowing from his limbs, chained in iron fetters, and far from his friends. He called to mind his brother and the honor that had been his. He moaned and wept and poured forth his tears, groaning and complaining, and bitterly lamenting the separation from his brother.

In the meantime, his brother, Amjad, remained waiting until midday, and when As'ad did not return, his heart became troubled, and the pain of separation grew strong. He began to weep copiously, crying out: "Alas for my loss! How fearful I am at this separation!"

Then, with the tears still flowing down his cheeks, he descended the mountain and went into the city. He kept on walking till he came to the market, where he asked the people the name of the city and the nature of its people. He was told that the city was called the City of the Magians and that its inhabitants were worshippers of the fire instead of the King Almighty. Then he asked about the City of Ebony, and was told that it was a year's journey away by land and six months by sea. Its king was called Armanus, and he had recently taken as his son-in-law and set in his own place another king named Qamar az-Zaman, who was just, generous, magnanimous, and trustworthy. When Amjad heard his father's name mentioned, he was seized with longing, and he wept and complained, and wandered away not knowing where he was heading. He had bought something to eat, and he went to a place where he could not be observed and sat down to eat. He thought about his brother and wept, and ate only enough to keep body and soul together. Then he arose and walked about the city to find out what it was like.

At last, he happened upon a Moslem tailor in a shop and, sitting down with him, he told him what had happened.

"If your brother has fallen into the hands of one of the Magians," said the tailor, "you are not likely to see him again, but perhaps God will bring you together."

Then he invited Amjad to lodge with him. Amjad accepted, and the tailor was overjoyed. Amjad remained with him many days, during which time the tailor comforted him, urged him to patience, and instructed him in the tailor's art until he became expert at it.

One day, Amjad went down to the sea shore and washed his clothes. Then, after going to the baths, he put on the clean clothes and, coming out of the baths, he strolled around looking at the town. On his way he met a woman of grace and beauty and pleasing form and symmetry, the like of which he had never seen. When she saw him, she raised the veil from her face and, making signs to him with her eyebrows and eyes, she flirted with him by glances.

When Amjad saw this, his heart was delighted with her, and his body yearned for her, for he was already in the grip of passion. So he responded to her with a gesture in turn, and she sighed deeply and made further signs to him.

"Will you come with me, or shall I come with you?" asked Amjad.

She bowed her head in modesty and recited from the Koran: " 'Men are the guardians of women since God has preferred one above the other.' " Amjad understood by this hint that she wanted to go with him wherever he went and that it was up to him to find the place. He was ashamed, however, to take her to the tailor's house where he dwelt, so they walked along from street to street, he leading the way and she following behind. Finally the maiden became tired.

"Sir," she asked, "where is your house?"

"Only a little way ahead," he replied. Then he turned into a fine street along which he proceeded with her following after. When he came to the end of the street, he found that there was no way out.

"There is no power or strength save in God the Exalted, the Mighty!" he exclaimed. He looked around and found at the head of the street a great door with a stone bench on either side. The door was locked, however, so he sat down on one bench and she sat on the other.

"My lord," she asked, "what is it that you are waiting for?"

He stared at the ground for a long time, then, raising his head, he replied: "I am waiting for my slave, for he has the keys. I told him to prepare food

and drink, and to set out the wine, for when I should come out of the baths."
To himself he said: "Perhaps the time will pass too slowly for her, and she
will go away and leave me here in this place."

But when she grew tired of waiting, she said: "My lord, the slave is very
late and here we are sitting in the street." Then she picked up a stone and
went over to the door.

"Do not be hasty," begged Amjad, "but be patient till the slave comes."

She paid no attention to what he said, but pounded on the lock with the
stone till she broke it in two and the door came open.

"What possessed you to do that?" cried Amjad.

"What is the matter, master?" she replied. "Is this not your house?"

"Yes," said he, "but there was no need to break the lock."

The maiden then entered the house, and Amjad was dismayed. He was
afraid of the owner of the house, and he did not know what to do.

"Why don't you come in, light of my eyes, and heart of my heart?" she
asked.

"I hear and obey," said Amjad. "But the slave is late and I do not know
whether he has carried out my orders or not."

He entered with her, extremely worried and fearful of the owner of the
house, and found himself in a large chamber with four raised daises facing
each other around the sides. In it were cupboards and divans upholstered in
silk and brocade, and in the center was a precious fountain. Beside the fountain stood a table heaped with plates set with gems, full of fruits and flowers.
Along with these were drinking vessels and a candlestick with a candle set
therein. The place was full of precious stuffs. There were chests and chairs;
on each of the latter was a bundle of clothing and a purse full of dinars. The
house itself bore witness to the opulence of its owner, since the floors were
paved with marble.

When Amjad saw all this he became even more confused, and said to himself: "I am lost! Verily we are God's and to Him we shall return!"

But the maiden was overjoyed at the sight, and exclaimed: "My lord, your
slave has not been remiss, for he has swept the place, cooked the food and
prepared the fruit! I have come at the best possible time!"

Amjad paid no heed to her, for his heart was still occupied by his fear of
the owner of the place.

"My lord," she asked, "what is the matter? Why are you standing there
like that?"

Then she sighed deeply and gave Amjad a kiss which sounded like the
cracking of an almond. "My lord," she said, "if you have made an appointment with someone else, I will tie up my skirts and serve her."

Amjad laughed, his heart full of wrath, and came and sat down, puffing
with anger. "Death and damnation," he said to himself, "if the owner of the
house comes—"

The maiden sat down beside him and began to laugh and play, but Amjad
was frowning worriedly and turning over a thousand thoughts in his mind.

"The owner of this place must surely come, and what shall I say then?"
he asked himself. "He will kill me without a doubt."

The maiden arose and set to work; she drew up a table and, setting a tray on it, began to eat. "Eat, my lord," she said. And Amjad came forward and began to eat, but the food did not taste good to him, for he was continually glancing toward the door.

When the maiden had eaten her fill, she removed the table and brought a plate of fruit and served the dessert. Then she brought the wine and, opening the flagon, she filled a cup and presented it to Amjad.

Taking it from her, Amjad sighed: "Woe is me, if the owner comes and sees me here!" His eyes wandered to the entry way, while the cup was still in his hand, and at that very moment the owner of the house returned.

The owner was one of the great mamelukes of the city, for he was Master of the Horse to the King. He had had this chamber made for his own pleasure, so that he might make merry and retire with whomever he wished. On this day he had sent for a lover of his to come and had gotten things ready for him. The name of this mameluke was Bahadur, and he was generous, magnanimous, and charitable, and was in the habit of doing good deeds and bestowing favors.

When he came near the chamber, he found the door open, so he entered stealthily and, peering around the door, he saw Amjad and the maiden with the plate of fruit and the drinking vessels in front of them. At that moment Amjad, with the cup in his hand, was looking fixedly at the door. When their eyes met, he grew pale and trembled with fear. Bahadur also turned pale and his countenance changed. He placed his finger over his lips as a sign to Amjad to keep silent, and beckoned him to come.

Amjad set the cup down and got up to go to him. The maiden asked him where he was going, and he indicated to her that he had to relieve himself. Then, full of fear, he went out to the entrance hall. He at once realized that Bahadur was owner of the house, and he hastily kissed his hands, saying: "I beg you, for God's sake, before you harm me, listen to what I have to say." Then he told the whole story from beginning to end, how he had left his own country and kingdom, and that he had not entered the chamber by choice, but that it was the maiden who, breaking the lock, had opened the door and done these things.

When Bahadur had heard Amjad's story and learned that he was a king's son, he felt compassion and sympathy for him.

"Listen to me, Amjad," he said, "and do what I say, and I will guarantee your safety, but if you disobey me, I will slay you."

"Command me as you will," replied Amjad, "and I will never disobey you, for I am the freedman of your generosity."

"Go back into the chamber then," said Bahadur, "and sit down where you were and be at ease. My name is Bahadur, and when I come in to you, revile me and upbraid me. Ask me why I have delayed for so long, and do not accept any excuses, but get up and beat me. If you show any sympathy for me, I will destroy your life. Go in now, and be merry; whatever you ask me for, you will find served up to you immediately. Pass this night as you please, and tomorrow you will go your way honored as a stranger should be, for I love strangers and feel myself obliged to honor them."

Amjad kissed his hand and went in, his pallor now changed to his usual red and white.

"My lady," he said, on entering, "you have made this place a delight, and tonight is surely a blessed night."

"How strange of you," she replied, "to show me any friendliness."

"My lady, I had thought that my slave Bahadur had taken some necklaces of precious gems belonging to me, each one of which is worth ten thousand dinars. When I went out just now, they weighed heavily on my mind, so I searched and found them in their place. I do not know why my slave is so late, but he surely will be punished for it."

The maiden was relieved at these words and the two of them played and drank and delighted themselves until it was almost evening. Then Bahadur came in to them. He had changed his clothes and put on a girdle and shoes in the manner of a servant. He greeted them, kissed the ground, and stood with his arms folded behind his back, his eyes fixed on the ground like one confessing a fault.

Amjad looked at him angrily, and said: "Why are you so late, you wicked slave?"

"My lord," he answered, "I was busy washing my clothes, and I did not know that you were here. Your appointment was for this evening and not during the day."

"You lie, wicked slave!" shouted Amjad. "By God, I am going to beat you!" So speaking, he jumped up and flung Bahadur to the floor. Seizing a stick, he proceeded to beat him but not too hard. At this, the maiden sprang up and, snatching the stick from Amjad's hand, she fell upon Bahadur and beat him so hard that he grit his teeth in pain, and wept, and cried out for help.

"Do not do this," Amjad said. But she replied: "Let me still my rage on him!" Finally, Amjad snatched the stick from her hand and pushed her away. Then Bahadur, wiping the tears from his face, arose and stayed to serve them for a while. Then he swept the chamber and lit the candles. Each time Bahadur passed to or fro, the maiden reviled and cursed him. Amjad grew angry and said: "By Allah, you must leave my slave alone, for he is not accustomed to this sort of thing!"

They continued eating and drinking, with Bahadur still serving them, till midnight when, weary from waiting on them and from the beating, he fell asleep in the middle of the hall, snorting and snoring.

The girl, who by now had become drunk, said to Amjad: "Take that sword hanging there and cut off this slave's head; if you do not, I will be the death of you."

"What has possessed you to kill my slave?" cried Amjad.

"My pleasure will not be complete unless he is slain," she said, "and if you do not do it, I will kill him myself."

"Don't do it, for God's sake!" exclaimed Amjad.

"I will," she insisted. Taking the sword, she drew it from the scabbard, and was on the point of killing Bahadur.

"This man has dealt kindly with us," said Amjad to himself, "and has overlooked our offense and has treated us well. He has made himself my slave. How can we reward him for this by killing him? May this never be!"

"If my slave must be slain," he said to the maiden, "it is better for me to do it than you."

He took the sword from her hand and, raising it, he struck her a blow on the neck, sending her head flying from her body. The head fell upon the owner of the house, who awoke and sat up. When he opened his eyes, he saw Amjad standing with the bloody sword in his hands. Then he looked at the girl and saw that she had been slain. He asked Amjad what had happened, and he repeated to him what she had said.

"She would not be content unless you were slain, and this is her reward," said Amjad.

Bahadur arose and kissed Amjad on the head. "O master," he said, "would that you had spared her. Now the only thing to be done is to take her away before sunrise." Thereupon, Bahadur got busy and, taking the girl, he wrapped her in a cloak. He placed the bundle in a large basket and picked it up to carry it away. "You are a stranger," he said, "and you do not know anyone, so stay here and wait for me until the sun rises. If I return, I will surely do well by you and make every effort to find out about your brother. But if I have not returned by sunrise, then you can be sure that all is over with me. In that case, farewell, and this house and all the money and stuffs that it contains are yours."

Then he left the house, carrying the basket, and made his way through the markets along the road to the salt sea in order to throw her in. When he approached the ocean, he looked up suddenly and saw that the Governor and his deputies had surrounded him. When they recognized him, they were surprised, so they opened the basket and found the slain girl. They, of course, arrested him and kept him in chains till morning, at which time they took him and the basket before the King. When the King was informed of what had happened, he grew very angry, and said: "Woe to you. You are always doing this sort of thing, killing people, throwing them into the sea, and taking all their money! How many murders have you committed before this?"

Bahadur hung his head before the King and said nothing.

"Woe to you," said the King. "Who killed this maiden?"

"My lord, I killed her," replied Bahadur. "There is no strength or power save in God the Exalted, the Mighty!"

Angrily, the King ordered that he be hanged. When the King had given the command, the executioner took him down to the town, and the Governor came down with a herald who announced the coming spectacle of Bahadur's execution in the streets of the city. Together they paraded Bahadur through the streets and market places.

As for Amjad, when day came and the sun arose, and Bahadur had not returned, he said: "There is no strength or power save in God the Exalted, the Mighty! I wonder what has befallen him."

While he was deliberating, he suddenly heard the herald announcing the impending execution of Bahadur, who was to be hanged at midday.

When Amjad heard the announcement, he wept, exclaiming: "Verily we are God's and to Him we shall return! He wishes to die for my sake, for I am the one who killed her. May this never be!"

Then he left the house, locking it behind him, and walked to the center of the city, and came to the place where Bahadur was being held. Stopping before the Governor of the town, he said: "O my lord, do not slay Bahadur, for he is innocent. By Allah, it was I who killed the girl."

When the Governor heard this, he took Amjad together with Bahadur up to the King and told him what Amjad had said.

The King looked at Amjad and asked: "Was it you who killed the maid?" When Amjad admitted that it was he, the King said: "What was your reason for slaying her? Tell me the truth."

"O King," said Amjad, "a strange and amazing adventure has befallen me. If it were written with needles in the corners of the eye, it would be an admonition to whoever would take heed."

Then he told the King his story, including all that had happened to him and his brother from beginning to end.

The King was greatly amazed, and said: "I know now that you are to be excused. O young man, would you like to become my Vizier?"

"I hear and obey," said Amjad, and the King bestowed splendid robes of honor on him and on Bahadur, and gave him a fine house with slaves and a retinue. He favored him with everything he required, appointing for him salaries and stipends, and commanded him to seek for his brother. In his post as Vizier, Amjad ruled and administered justice, invested and deposed officials, and gave and took. He likewise sent a herald through the streets of the city, to give notice to all and sundry about his brother, As'ad. The herald spent several days crying the announcement in the streets and market places, but no trace of As'ad was found.

In the meantime, As'ad remained in the hands of the Magians, who tormented him day and night, morning and evening, for the period of a whole year, until the time for the festival approached. Bahram, the Magian, made preparations for the journey and fitted out a ship. He then placed As'ad in a chest, which he locked and transported to the ship. At the very moment that Bahram was transporting the chest in which As'ad was concealed, Amjad, by a chance stroke of fate, happened to be standing looking out to sea, and he saw the cargo as it was being loaded into the ship. His heart gave a leap, and he commanded his servants to bring his horse. He mounted, and with a group of his retainers rode down to the shore, stopped before the Magian's ship, and ordered those with him to go down into the ship and search it. The men went down and searched the whole ship but found nothing, so they came up again and informed Amjad. He mounted and, returning home, he entered the palace, cast down and in low spirits, and wept while thinking of his brother.

After Amjad had departed, the Magian went down into the ship and, shouting at the crew, ordered them to make haste and set the sails. The sailors quickly made sail, and the ship stood out to sea. They sailed for many days and nights and, every other day, the Magian would remove As'ad from the chest and give him a little food to eat and a little water to drink. As they drew near the Mountain of Fire, a high wind blew up and the sea began to rage, so that the ship was blown off its course. Following a false course, they finally came to a city built on the shore of the sea and ruled by a woman named Marjanah.

The ship-captain spoke to Bahram, saying: "We have wandered from our course and we must go into this city to rest and, afterwards, let God do as he will."

"This is a good idea," replied Bahram. "Do as you think best."

"Suppose the Queen sends and asks us about ourselves, what will our answer be?"

"I have with me a Moslem," said Bahram. "Let us dress him as a slave and take him with us, and if the Queen sees him, she will think he is a slave. I will tell her that I am a buyer and seller of slaves and that I had many slaves with me, but I have sold them all except this one."

The ship-captain agreed that this was a good story.

They went on towards the city and, entering the anchorage, they lowered the sails and the ship came to a stop. Immediately, Queen Marjanah came down to them with her army and, halting before the ship, she called to the captain. He came up to her and kissed the ground before her.

"What do you have in your ship and who is with you?" she asked.

"O Queen of the Age," he replied, "there is a merchant with me who sells slaves."

"Bring him to me," she commanded.

Bahram came up at once, with As'ad walking behind him in the manner of a slave. Bahram approached her and kissed the ground before her. The Queen asked him what his business was, and he replied that he was a slave dealer.

She then looked at As'ad and, thinking him a slave, she asked: "What is your name?"

Choked with tears, he replied: "My name is As'ad."

Feeling sympathy for him in her heart, she asked him if he could write. When he replied that he could, she handed him an inkwell, pen, and paper, saying: "Write something so I can see your handwriting." So he wrote for her these verses:

> How can a slave escape the wicked snares
> That cruel fates in league for him have set?
> Into the sea he's thrown, bound hand and foot,
> And grimly warned: "Take care lest you get wet."

When she read the verses, she felt compassion for him, and said to Bahram: "Sell me this slave." But he replied: "My lady, I cannot sell him, because I have sold all my slaves, and he is the only one I have left."

"I must have him from you," insisted the Queen, "either by sale or as a gift."

"I will neither sell him nor give him away," replied Bahram.

So she laid hold of As'ad and took him up with her to the palace, and sent word to Bahram, saying: "If you do not set sail from our land this very night, I will take all your goods and smash your ship."

When the message reached him, he was greatly worried, and said: "This voyage has resulted in nothing worthwhile." He made ready and got together everything he required, and then waited for the night in order to depart. To the sailors, he gave orders, saying: "Make ready, fill your water-skins full, and see that we sail before the end of night." The sailors proceeded to carry out their duties.

In the meantime, Queen Marjanah, having brought As'ad into the palace, opened the windows which overlooked the sea, and commanded her slave girls to bring food. She and As'ad ate together, after which she ordered the wine brought in. As she drank with him, God—He is praised and exalted—inspired love for As'ad into her heart, so she kept filling his cup and giving him to drink until his wits were befuddled. He arose to answer a call of nature and, going down from the palace, he observed an open door, which he entered. He walked on till he came at last to a great garden in which were all sorts of fruit and flowers.

Sitting down under a tree, he satisfied his need, and then went over to the pool that was in the middle of the garden. He flung himself down on his back, with his clothes loosened so that the breeze blew on him, and slept there till nightfall.

At the same time, Bahram, seeing the approach of night, shouted to the sailors, saying: "Hoist the sails and depart!"

"We hear and obey," they replied, "but be patient till we have filled our water-skins." They went up from the ship, carrying their water-skins, and walked around the palace, but found only the walls of the garden. So they climbed over, descending into the garden, and, following the footpath leading to the pool, they came and found As'ad lying on his back asleep. They recognized him and were overjoyed. After filling their water-skins, they picked him up and, jumping down from the wall, they carried him quickly to Bahram, the Magian.

"Rejoice at the attainment of your desire and the easing of your heart," they said, "and beat your drums and play your pipes, for we have found and brought back your prisoner whom Queen Marjanah took away from you by force!" Then they threw As'ad down before him.

When Bahram saw him, his heart leaped for joy, and he rejoiced and was delighted. He bestowed presents upon them and bade them make sail. The sails were raised and they departed, directing their course towards the Mountain of Fire. They sailed on till morning came.

In the meantime, Queen Marjanah, after As'ad had gone down, waited for him a while, but he did not return. She arose and searched for him and, when she did not find him, she lit candles and commanded her slave girls to look, too. Then she went down herself and, finding that the garden was opened, she realized that he had gone in there. Entering the garden, she found his sandals beside the pool and proceeded to search the whole garden, but she found no trace of him, even though she searched in all corners of the garden till morning came.

Then she asked about the ship, and was told that it had sailed during the first watch of the night. She realized then that they had taken him with them. This was hard for her to endure; she grew incensed, and commanded that ten ships be made ready for battle at once. She went aboard one of the ten herself and took her army, splendidly equipped with the accoutrements and implements of war. As they set sail, she said to the captains: "When you catch up with the ship of the Magians, you will receive from me robes of honor and presents of money, but if you fail to overtake them, I will slay you to the last man." The sailors were thus inspired by a tremendous dread. The ships sailed on all through that day and night, and then the second and third day. At last, on the fourth day, the ship of Bahram, the Magian, came in sight, and the day had not yet ended when the Queen's ships surrounded that of the Magian.

At this very moment, Bahram had brought As'ad out and was beating and torturing him. As'ad, in great pain, was calling for help and crying out for protection, but found no helper or protector among those people. While Bahram was torturing him, he happened to glance up and saw that the ships of the Queen had surrounded his ship as the white of an eye surrounds the iris. He was certain that he was a dead man, without any doubt.

"Woe to you," he said to As'ad in despair. "This is all your fault." Then he seized him by the hand and ordered the sailors to throw him into the sea, saying: "By Allah, I will kill you before my death!" The sailors picked him up by his hands and feet and threw him into the sea. But God—He is praised and exalted—because He willed his safety and continuance in life, permitted him to go down and rise again. As'ad struck out with his feet and hands, till God made things easy for him and granted him deliverance. The waves buffeted him and carried him far from the Magian's ship, until, finally reaching land, he came out on the shore, scarcely believing that he was saved. On reaching land, he took off his clothes, wrung them out and spread them out to dry, and sat down naked, weeping over his misfortunes and the captivity that he had undergone.

Finally he arose and put on his clothes, but he did not know which way to turn. Walking along aimlessly, he ate of the plants of the earth, the fruit of the trees, and drank of the water of rivers. He traveled by night and day, until at length he approached a city, at the sight of which he rejoiced. He walked hurriedly towards the city, but by the time he reached it, night had fallen, and the gates had been closed. Now, this city was the one where he had been held prisoner, and in which his brother, Amjad, was Vizier. When he saw that the gates were locked, he turned aside and went into the cemetery, which was outside the walls. Finding a tomb without a door, he crept into it and fell asleep there, his head in the hollow of his arm.

When Queen Marjanah with her fleet overtook Bahram, the Magian, he was able by his powers of magic to elude her ships and escape. He set out at once, overjoyed, returning to his home. It so happened by fate's decree that, as he came up from the ship, he passed by the cemetery and walked among the graves. He happened to see that the tomb in which As'ad was sleeping was open. Amazed at this, he said to himself: "I must look into this tomb." When he looked in, he saw As'ad lying there asleep with his head on his arm. On looking at his face, Bahram recognized him, and exclaimed: "Are you still alive?"

Then seizing As'ad, Bahram carried him off to his house again. He loaded his feet with heavy fetters, and put him down in the underground chamber which he kept in his house for the torture of Moslems.

Bahram had a daughter, who was named Bustan, and her he charged with torturing As'ad to death. Then he gave As'ad a painful beating and, locking the trap door on him, he entrusted the keys to his daughter.

When his daughter, Bustan, went down to beat As'ad, she found that he was a youth of handsome features and pleasing aspect, with eyebrows arched like bows and eyes black as kohl, and she fell in love with him at first sight. She asked him his name, and he replied that it was As'ad.

"May you be happy and may all your days be happy," she said. "You do not deserve to be tortured. I realize now that you have been wronged."

Then she asked him about the religion of Islam, and he told her that it was the true and right religion, and that our master, Muhammad, had performed splendid wonders and manifest miracles, that the fires of hell are harmful and do not benefit, and he taught her the fundamentals of Islam. She yielded to his suasion; the love of the true faith entered her heart, and God compounded love for As'ad in her soul. She pronounced the confession of faith and became one of the people of felicity.

She fed him, gave him to drink, and talked to him, and the two of them prayed together. She prepared chicken broth for him until his illness left him and he returned to his former state of health. One day, Bustan, the daughter of Bahram, had gone out of the house and was standing at the door when the herald passed by, crying: "Whoever has a handsome young man whose description is so-and-so and discloses him will receive all the money that he asks; but he who has him and denies it will be hanged at the door of his own house, his wealth will be plundered, and his blood can be shed with impunity."

As'ad had already told Bustan all that happened to him, so when she heard what the herald said she knew that he was the one sought for and at once went down to him and told him the news. Then she let him out of the house secretly, and he made his way to the abode of the Vizier. When he entered the palace, he caught sight of the Vizier, and exclaimed: "This Vizier is none other than my brother, Amjad!" He rushed forward and threw himself upon his brother. Amjad at once recognized him. They embraced each other, surrounded by the mamelukes, and both fainted from the excess of their joy.

When they recovered, Amjad took his brother and, bringing him to the King, he related all that had happened to him.

The King then commanded Amjad to plunder the house of Bahram, so he sent a company of men for that purpose. They went to his house and plundered it. Taking his daughter, they brought her to the Vizier, who honored her greatly, for As'ad had told his brother of the tortures he had endured and of the kindness that she had shown him.

Amjad also told As'ad all that had happened to him with the girl and how he had escaped hanging and had become Vizier. Each of them recounted the pain he had felt at being separated from his brother.

Then the King ordered Bahram brought into his presence and commanded that his head be cut off.

"O great King," asked Bahram, "are you determined to slay me?"

"Yes," replied the King.

"Bear with me a little while," said Bahram, and lowered his head to the ground. Then he raised his eyes and repeated the confession of faith, and became a Moslem at the hand of the Sultan.

They all rejoiced at his becoming a Moslem, and Amjad and As'ad told him all that had happened to them. Then Bahram spoke, saying: "My lords, prepare for a journey, and I will bring you back to your father's kingdom."

They had rejoiced at his becoming a Moslem, but now they wept at being reminded of their estrangement from their father.

"Weep not, my lords," said Bahram, "for your return will unite you with those you love."

When morning came, Amjad and As'ad rode to the King's palace and asked permission to enter and, when this was granted, went in to the presence of the King, who showed them great honor. They were sitting talking with one another, when suddenly the populace of the city began to shout and cry out to one another, appealing for help. The Chamberlain came in to the King, and informed him that a king accompanied by a great army with weapons ready was descending on the city, and that no one knew what they wanted. The King told his Vizier, Amjad, and his brother, As'ad, what the Chamberlain had said.

"I will go out to him," said Amjad, "and find out who he is and what he wants."

Leaving the city, Amjad went out and encountered the king with his many soldiers and mounted mamelukes. When they saw that he was a messenger from the king of the city, they took him into the presence of their ruler. He kissed the ground before him, and suddenly saw that king was a woman with a veil over the lower part of her face.

"Know," she said, "that my only purpose in this city is to find a beardless slaveboy. If I find him among you, you will suffer no harm, but if I do not, that will mean war between us, for he is the only reason for my coming here."

"O Queen," said Amjad, "what about this slave? What is his name and what does he look like?"

"His name is As'ad, and I am the Queen Marjanah. This slave came to me in company with Bahram, the Magian, who would not consent to sell him to me, so I took him by force, but Bahram seized him and stole him from me by night. As for his looks, his description is so-and-so."

When he heard this, Amjad knew that it was his brother.

"O Queen of the Age," he exclaimed, "praise be to God, who has brought us deliverance! This slave is none other my brother, As'ad."

Then he related to her the whole story of what had happened to them in foreign lands, and told her of the reason for their leaving the Ebony Isles. Queen Marjanah was amazed and overjoyed at finding As'ad again, and she bestowed a robe of honor on his brother, Amjad.

When Amjad returned to the King and told him what had taken place, they rejoiced, and the King, together with Amjad and As'ad, went out to the Queen, who received them. While they were sitting talking with one another, suddenly a great cloud of dust arose covering the whole countryside. After a while it dispersed, revealing an immense army like the billowing sea, well-equipped and well-armed. They made for the city and, with drawn swords, encircled it as a ring encircles the little finger.

"Verily we are God's and to Him we shall return!" exclaimed Amjad and As'ad. "What is this great army? Surely they must be enemies, and if we do not agree with Queen Marjanah to fight them together, they will take the city from us and put us to the sword. There is nothing for us to do but go out to them and find out who they are."

Amjad arose and went out. Passing through the forces of Queen Marjanah, he reached the strange army, which—as he was to find out—was the army of his grandfather, King Ghayur, lord of the Isles and Seas and the Seven Palaces, the father of his mother, Queen Budur.

When he came into his presence, he kissed the ground before him and delivered the message from his sovereign.

"My name is King Ghayur," the King replied, "and I am traveling this way because fate has dealt harshly with me regarding my daughter, Budur. She left me and did not return, and I have heard no news of her and her husband, Qamar az-Zaman. Do you know anything about them?"

Amjad remained deliberating for a while, his eyes fixed on the ground, until he realized that this was his grandfather, the father of his mother. Then he raised his head and, kissing the ground before him, he told him that he was his daughter's son.

When the King heard that he was the son of his daughter, Budur, he threw himself upon him and they both burst out weeping.

"Praise be to God, my son," exclaimed the king, "that I have met with you safe and sound!"

Then Amjad told him that his daughter, Budur, was well, and likewise his father, Qamar az-Zaman, informing him that they were in a city called the Ebony Isles. He also told him that his father was angry at him and his brother and had ordered them slain, but that the Treasurer had felt compassion for them and had spared their lives.

"I will take you and your brother back to your father and make peace between you, and remain among you," said King Ghayur. And Amjad kissed the ground before him. Then the King bestowed a robe of honor on his grandson, Amjad, who returned to the king of the city, smiling, and told him the story of King Ghayur.

The King was greatly amazed, and at once hospitably sent out to King Ghayur horses, camels, sheep, fodder and the like, and did the same for Queen Marjanah at the same time, telling her what had happened.

"I will take my army and come with you to work for the reconciliation," she said.

As they were talking, suddenly they saw another cloud of dust arise, covering the countryside so that the day became dark. In the midst of it, they heard shouts and cries and the neighing of horses, and saw swords flashing and lances leveled. When they drew near the city, they beat their drums and when the King observed this, he exclaimed: "This is indeed a blessed day! Praise be to God, who has made peace between us and these two armies. If God wills, He will make peace with this one too. Go, Amjad, you and your brother, As'ad, and find out who these soldiers are, for I have never seen an army mightier than this one."

So Amjad and his brother, As'ad, went out together, opening the gates of the city which had been closed for fear of the host surrounding it, and came to the army which had newly arrived. They discovered that it was the army of King Armanus, with which was their father, Qamar az-Zaman. When they saw him, they kissed the ground before him, weeping, and Qamar az-Zaman threw himself upon them and, weeping copiously, he begged their forgiveness and clutched them to his bosom. He told them of the great loneliness that he had suffered after their departure. Then Amjad and As'ad told him that King Ghayur had arrived, so Qamar az-Zaman mounted up with his escort and, taking his sons, Amjad and As'ad, he rode till he approached the camp of King Ghayur. One of them rode on ahead to King Ghayur and informed him that Qamar az-Zaman had arrived. The King came out to meet him, and they met together, amazed at how they had been reunited in this place.

The people of the city prepared banquets with all kinds of food and sweets. They presented them with horses, camels, and fodder, as well as other gifts, and provided everything that the armies required.

While they were thus engaged, suddenly another cloud of dust arose and covered the countryside. The earth trembled beneath the horses' hooves, the drums beat like a windstorm, and the whole force was clad in mail and fully armed. They were all wearing black and in their midst was an old man dressed in black clothes whose beard came down to his breast.

When the people of the city saw this great army, the Lord of the city said to the Kings: "Praise be to God, by whose permission you have joined together on the same day, and have found that you are all known to one another! What is this mighty army that covers the countryside?"

"Do not fear," the Kings said, "for we are three kings and each of us has his army. If they are enemies, we shall fight them with you, though they were thrice as many as they are."

While they were speaking, a messenger from the army reached the town and was taken before Qamar az-Zaman, King Ghayur, Queen Marjanah, and the ruler of the city. He kissed the ground and said: "This King is from the land of the Persians. Many years ago he lost his son and he is now traveling through all lands searching for him. If he finds him with you, you will come to no harm, but if he does not, it will mean war between you and him, and he will destroy your city."

"He will not succeed in that," said Qamar az-Zaman. "But what is this King called in the land of the Persians?"

"He is called King Shahriman, Lord of the Isles of Khalidan," replied the messenger, "and he has gathered this army from all the lands through which he has passed looking for his son."

On hearing this, Qamar az-Zaman uttered a loud cry and fell down in a faint. He remained unconscious for an hour. Then, when he recovered, he wept bitterly, and said to Amjad and As'ad and their followers: "Go with the messenger, my sons, and greet your grandfather, King Shahriman, and give him the glad tidings that he has found me, for he is grieving at having lost me and is dressed in black for my sake."

Then he related to the Kings present all that had happened to him during the days of his youth, at which they were all greatly amazed. Afterwards, they and Qamar az-Zaman went down and made their way to his father. Qamar az-Zaman greeted his father, and they embraced each other and fell into a faint from the intensity of their joy. When they returned to themselves, he told his father everything that had befallen him. Then the other Kings saluted him as well.

After some time had passed, they sent Queen Marjanah back to her own country, and charged her not to cease corresponding with them. Then they married Amjad to Bustan, the daughter of Bahram, and they all journeyed together to the City of Ebony, where Qamar az-Zaman retired with his father-in-law and told him everything that had befallen him and how he had been reunited with his sons. King Armanus was overjoyed and congratulated him on his safe return.

King Ghayur, the father of Queen Budur, went to visit his daughter. He greeted her, and satisfied his longing for the sight of her.

They stayed in the City of Ebony a whole month; then King Ghayur departed for his own country, taking his daughter and Amjad with him. After he had settled in his kingdom, Amjad was set to rule in his grandfather's place.

Meanwhile, Qamar az-Zaman set up his son As'ad to rule in his place in the city of Armanus with the latter's approval. Then he made ready and departed with his father, King Shahriman. When they reached the Isles of Khalidan, the city was decorated for him, and the glad tidings resounded without ceasing for a whole month. Qamar az-Zaman was elevated to the throne to rule in his father's stead.

And thus they all lived until overtaken by death, which severs all delights and sunders all bonds of union.

God knoweth all things best.

The Saga of Hrafnkel Priest of Frey

Translated by John C. McGalliard

Editor's Note

There is a certain fitness to our not being able to specify the author or date of "The Saga of Hrafnkel." For the very style in which prose sagas were written—impersonal, terse, unpsychological, as utterly "rendered" or "dramatized" as Henry James could have wished—turns the reader from considering the author as man or artist to contemplating the story, the work of art, itself. Moreover, although the history in which the writer pretends to embed his story is so detailed as to seem veracious, the geographical details and names are verifiable enough, and the genealogies go back to actual families, yet the important effect of all this is to surround the imagined characters and events not so much with actuality as with heroism, for already when the saga was being written (probably some time in the fourteenth century) the days of Hrafnkel were seen as heroic. King Harald, in whose reign the story begins, ruled in Norway at the end of the ninth and beginning of the tenth centuries, and it was then that independent Norsemen were first settling Iceland. The best sagas concern themselves with those early days of freedom, of heroic freedom, of much freedom and little law. When they were being written, three to five centuries later, the country was tearing itself apart for lack of government and was voluntarily giving itself over to the foreign rule of the king of Norway in preference to lawlessness.

At the time of the story the Icelanders were pagan. As priest of Frey, who was god of fertility and one of the three main Scandinavian deities, Hrafnkel served as chieftain in his community and as sacrificer in the local temple, which was owned by him; but he seemed to have no moral responsibility and to be no spiritual shepherd of his flock. In politics, such government as the Icelanders recognized consisted in the presenting of a grievance at the annual national assembly, called the Thing (or Althing), and the acquittal or sentencing of the accused. But there was no executive power, so that a weak plaintiff had to collect allies even to present his case physically at the Thing, and the execution of a sentence on a man who refused to recognize its validity rested on the plaintiff. The crime pled was usually murder; the punishment the law sought to impose was banishment or a money payment instead of private revenge. Except for the Thing, which met not far from the present Reykjavik, the main actions of the story take place on the east coast of Iceland.

"The Saga of Hrafnkel" is less cluttered with genealogies than most, but it has its full share of place-naming. To make entering the saga no more difficult than need be, two deletions have been made: in the first sentence, King Harald's genealogy, and the fifth sentence, which concerns the naming of a place not again mentioned in the saga.

The Saga of Hrafnkel Priest
of Frey

I T WAS IN THE DAYS OF KING HARALD THE FAIRHAIRED THAT A MAN NAMED Hallfred came with his ship to Broaddale in Iceland. This is below Fleet-dale District. On the ship were his wife and son, whose name was Hrafnkel. The son was then fifteen years old, promising and capable. Hall-fred set up housekeeping. In the spring Hallfred moved his household north across the heath and built a dwelling there called Goatdale. One night he dreamed that a man came to him and said: "There you are lying, all un-awares, Hallfred. Move your household away to the west, across Lakefleet; all your luck is there." After that he woke up. He moved his household out across the Crooked River to the Tongue, to a place which has since been called Hallfredstead, and he lived there till old age. He left behind a pair of goats. And the same day that Hallfred moved away a landslide struck the house and these animals perished, and hence it has since been called Goatdale.

Hrafnkel was in the habit of riding over the heath in the summer. At this time Glacierdale was settled as far up as the bridges. Hrafnkel rode up along Fleetdale District and saw where an unoccupied valley led off from Glacierdale. This valley seemed to Hrafnkel more habitable than the other valleys that he had seen before. When Hrafnkel came home he asked his father for his share of the property, and said that he wanted to build a homestead for himself. His father consented, and he set up his farm in that valley and called it Adalbol. Hrafnkel married Oddbjorg Skjolf's daughter from Salmon River Dale. They had two sons; the elder was named Thorir and the younger Asbjorn. At the time when Hrafnkel took up land at Adalbol he held a great sacrifice; and thereafter he maintained a large

Translated by John C. McGalliard. Reprinted, slightly revised, with omission of geneal-ogies and notes, from *World Masterpieces*, Vol. I, edited by Maynard Mack, General Editor. By Permission of W. W. Norton & Company, Inc. Copyright 1956 by W. W. Norton & Company, Inc.

temple. Hrafnkel loved no other god more than Frey, and gave him half of all his best possessions. Hrafnkel had the whole valley and gave land to men; but he wished to be their chief and took priestly authority over them. Because of this he was given a nickname and was called Frey's Priest; he was very headstrong, but very capable. He compelled the Glacierdale people to be his dependents; he was mild and easygoing with his own men but hard and strict with the Glacierdale men, and they got no equality from him. Hrafnkel often engaged in duels and compensated no one with money, so that no man got any recompense from him, no matter what Hrafnkel did. Fleetdale District is difficult to travel, very stony and swampy; nevertheless, father and son rode regularly to each other's places, for they were on good terms. The road seemed difficult to Hallfred and he sought a route over the peaks that rise in Fleetdale District; there he got a drier and a longer road, and it is called Hallfred's Way. Only those who are quite familiar with Fleetdale District take this road.

Bjarni was the name of a man who lived at the farm called Bathhouses. It is close to Hrafnkelsdale. He was married and had two sons by his wife; one was named Sám and the other Eyvind, both fine and able men. Eyvind was at home with his father, but Sám was married and lived in the northern part of the valley at the farm called Playsheds; and he had a great deal of property. Sám was very fond of litigation and keen in the law, but Eyvind became a voyager and went off to Norway and was there a year. From there he went on out to Constantinople and was honorably received by the king of the Greeks and was there for a time.

Among his possessions Hrafnkel had a treasure that seemed to him better than any other. This was a horse, dark gray with a black stripe down the back, whom he called Freyfaxi. To Frey, his friend, he gave half the horse. He had such great affection for that horse that he took an oath that he would slay the man who should ride it without his permission.

There was a man named Thorbjorn; he was a brother of Bjarni and lived at the farm in Hrafnkelsdale called Hill, opposite Adalbol to the east. Thorbjorn had little wealth, but many family dependents. His eldest son was named Einar; he was large and well built. It happened, one spring, that Thorbjorn told Einar that he should look for some kind of job: "Because I do not need more workmen than the crowd that is here; but it will be easy for you to get a good post, for you are well built. Lack of affection is not the cause of this separation, for you are the most useful of my children; rather, my poverty and lack of means is the cause of it; my other children will become farm workers, but you will fare better in getting a job than they." Einar answered: "You have told me this too late, for all the best jobs are now filled, and I don't like to take the leavings." One day Einar took his horse and rode to Adalbol. Hrafnkel was sitting in the hall. He greeted Einar cheerfully. Einar asked Hrafnkel for work. He answered: "Why did you look for this so late? For I should have taken you first. But now I have engaged all my staff, except for the one job for which you will have no inclination." Einar asked what that was.

Hrafnkel said that he had not employed a man for the sheep-herding but that he was in great need of one. Einar said that he did not care what he worked at, whether it was that or something else, but that he wanted food and lodging for two seasons: "I will make you a quick offer," said Hrafnkel; "you are to drive fifty ewes to the summer shed and bring home all the summer wood. You will do this for board and lodging for two seasons. But I wish to stipulate one thing with you as with my other shepherds. Freyfaxi goes about in the dales with his herd; you will look after him winter and summer. But I give you warning about one thing: I wish you never to get on his back, however strong the motive you have to do so, for I have taken a great oath to be the slayer of the man who rides him. Twelve mares trail after him; whichever of them you wish shall be yours to ride by night or day. Do now as I say; for there is an old proverb that 'he who warns another is not responsible.' Now you know what I have had to say." Einar said that he would not be so ill bent as to ride the horse that was forbidden him if there were many others available. Einar now went home for his clothes and took them to Adalbol. Later he moved up to the shed in Hrafnkelsdale which is called Rocky Strip Shed.

Einar got along nicely as the summer passed, so that no sheep were lost until midsummer. Then, one night, nearly thirty ewes were missing. Einar looked through all the pastures and did not find them. One morning, when they had been lost nearly a week, Einar went out early. The rain and mist from the south had cleared off. He took his staff, bridle, and saddle-blanket and went along across the Rocky Strip River, which ran directly in front of the shed. There, on the gravelly banks, lay the sheep that had been at home the evening before. He drove them back to the shed and went to look for those that had been missing all along. Now he saw the herd of horses on the banks ahead of him and decided to catch one to ride, thinking that he would get on more swiftly if he rode than if he walked. But when he came up and approached the horses they were all shy—except only Freyfaxi—not being used to riders. Freyfaxi was as quiet as if he had been rooted to the ground. Einar knew that the morning was advancing, and he believed that Hrafnkel would not know it if he should ride the stallion. Now he took the horse, bridled him, put the saddle-blanket on his back and rode up by Rocky River Gorge, then up to the glacier and west along it to where the Glacier River descends, and down the river to Hot Spring Shed. He asked all the shepherds at the sheds whether anyone had seen the sheep, and no one had. Einar rode Freyfaxi steadily from dawn till midafternoon. The horse carried him swiftly and far, for he was a good mount. Then it occurred to Einar that it was time to go back and drive in the flock that was at home, though he should not find the others. He rode then east over the ridge into Hrafnkelsdale, and when he came down by Rocky Strip he heard a bleating of sheep ahead in the ravine, which he had ridden past earlier. He turned in that direction and saw thirty ewes in front of him—the same ones that he had lost a week ago. He drove them home with the rest of the flock.

The horse was all wet with sweat, so that it dripped from every hair; he was badly spattered with mud and completely worn out. He rolled over about twelve times and after that set up a loud neighing. Then he took off at high speed down the road. Einar started after him, trying to catch him and take him back to his herd, but he was so wild that Einar got nowhere near him. The horse ran down the valley and did not stop until he came to Adalbol. At that moment Hrafnkel was sitting at the table. When the horse came to the door he neighed loudly. Hrafnkel told a woman who was serving the meal to go to the door, for a horse had neighed: "And it seemed to me like Freyfaxi's neigh." She went to the door and saw Freyfaxi in bad shape. She told Hrafnkel that Freyfaxi was outside the door, looking very filthy. "What does the fine fellow want—why has he come home?" said Hrafnkel. "No good will come of this." Then he went out and saw Freyfaxi and said to him: "I don't like it at all that you are treated this way, my fosterling; but you had your wits about you, for you have told me about it, and it shall be avenged. Go now to your herd." And the horse went at once up the valley to his herd of mares. Hrafnkel went to bed in the evening and slept through the night. Then in the morning he had his horse saddled and rode up to the shed. He was dressed in blue clothes and had an ax in his hand, but no other weapons. Einar had just finished driving the sheep into the milking pens. He was leaning on the railing, counting the sheep, and the women were busy milking. They all greeted Hrafnkel. He asked how things were going. Einar answered: "They haven't gone so well with me, for thirty ewes were missing for nearly a week; but they are found now." Hrafnkel said that he was not complaining about that: "But has there been nothing worse? —and in fact sheep have not been lost as often as was expected. But did you not ride Freyfaxi yesterday?" Einar said he could not deny it. Hrafnkel answered: "Why did you ride that horse, which was forbidden you, when there were enough others that you were allowed to ride? Yet I should have let you off the first time if I had not taken such an oath—though you have clearly admitted the act." And in the belief that no good comes to those who bring down a curse on their heads by breaking their oaths, he leaped from his horse's back to Einar and struck him a death blow. After this he rode home to Adalbol and reported the news. Then he sent another man to the shed to take care of the sheep. And he had Einar carried from the shed to the hillside and raised a beacon beside the burial mound. It is called Einar's Beacon, and marks midevening as seen from the shed.

Thorbjorn, over at Hill, heard of the slaying of Einar, his son. He was much distressed at the news. Now he took his horse and rode over to Adalbol and asked Hrafnkel for legal compensation for his son's slaying. Hrafnkel said that he had killed more men than this one: "It is not unknown to you that I am unwilling to pay compensation for any man, and people have to put up with that. Nevertheless, I grant that this deed appears among the worst of the slayings that I have committed. You have been my neighbor for a long time and you have pleased me well—indeed, each has pleased the other. No other small matter would have caused trouble between Einar and me, if he had not ridden the horse. But we often have this to regret, that we are too free-spoken; less often do we regret saying fewer words rather than more. I will now show you that this act of mine seems to me worse than the others that I have done. I will supply your household with milk cattle in the summer and with meat in the fall; I will do this for you every season, as long as you wish to keep up a house. We shall provide for your sons and daughters with my support and assist them so that they make good marriage settlements thereby; and as for anything that you know to be in my possession and that you have need of, you shall tell me of it and not go without anything that you need. You shall maintain your household as long as it pleases you and move over here when you get tired of it, and I will take care of you till you die. Thus we shall be reconciled; and I will venture the boast that many would say that this man is very expensive." "I will not accept that offer," said Thorbjorn. "What terms do you want, then?" said Hrafnkel. Then Thorbjorn said: "I wish us to choose men to arbitrate between us." Hrafnkel answered: "Then you consider yourself my equal, and we shall never be reconciled on that basis."

Then Thorbjorn rode away and down through the district. He came to Bathhouses and found Bjarni, his brother, told him the news, and asked him to take some part in the case. Bjarni said that he was not dealing with his match when Hrafnkel was involved: "And even though we had a great deal of money, still we couldn't contest a suit with Hrafnkel; and it is true that he is strong who knows himself. Hrafnkel has won out in lawsuits over many who had more backing than we. It seems to me that you have shown little sense if you have refused such good terms, and I will have nothing to do with the matter." Thorbjorn spoke many hard words to his brother, saying that the more important a thing was, the less he could be counted on. Thorbjorn then rode away and they said good-bye with little cordiality. He did not stop till he came down to Playsheds and knocked on the door. Someone came to the door and Thorbjorn asked Sám to come out. Sám greeted his kinsman cheerfully and invited him to stay. Thorbjorn was slow in his responses. Sám saw the dejection in his face and asked the news, and Thorbjorn told him of the slaying of Einar, his son. "It is no great news," and Sám, "that Hrafnkel is killing men." Thorbjorn asked whether Sám was willing to offer him some assistance, adding that: "This case is such that, although the slain man is closest to me, yet the blow has fallen not far from you." "Have you asked for any redress from Hrafnkel?" Thorbjorn told the truth about everything that had happened between him and Hrafnkel. "I have not been aware before," said Sám, "that Hrafnkel has made such offers to anyone as he has to you. Now I am willing to ride with you up to Adalbol, and then let us take up the matter politely with Hrafnkel and find out whether he will confirm the original offer; in any event, things will go well for him." "Two points," says Thorbjorn: "one is that Hrafnkel will not be willing to do it now; the other is that I am no more in favor of it now than when I rode away from there." Sám said: "I think it will be a hard job to oppose Hrafnkel in a lawsuit." Thorbjorn answered: "That is why you young men never get anywhere—everything looks too big to you. I think there can be nobody who has such shiftless fellows for kinsmen as I. It appears to me that men like you are in a bad way: you seem to be keen in law and active enough in petty suits, but you will not take over this case, which is so clear. It will be a disgrace to you, as is right, for you are the great braggart of our whole family. I see now how it will turn out." Sám answered: "How much better off are you if I should take over the case and then we should both be shamefully driven away from the court?" Thorbjorn answered: Nevertheless, it is a great consolation to me that you should take over the suit; let it end as it may." Sám answered: "I go into this thing against my will; I am doing it more for the sake of our kinship than anything else. But you shall know that, in aiding you, I feel that I am helping a foolish man." Then Sám reached out his hand and formally took over the case from Thorbjorn.

Sám got his horse and rode up the valley to a farmstead and gave legal notice of the slaying. He got men to aid him against Hrafnkel. Hrafnkel heard of this, and it appeared laughable to him that Sám had started a suit against him. Winter came on now. Then, in the spring, when the summons-days came along, Sám rode from his home up to Adalbol and summoned Hrafnkel in the case of the slaying of Einar. After this Sám rode down through the dales and summoned householders to go to the Thing. Then he let matters rest until the time when people got ready for the trip to the Thing. Hrafnkel then sent men down through the dales and summoned *his* jurors. With his company of seventy Thingmen he rode east across Fleetdale District and around the end of the lake, over the ridge to Screeddale, up through the valley and south at Ax Heath to She-Bear Firth, reaching Thingmen's Road at Side. South from Fleetdale it is seventeen days' journey to Thingfield. Then after Hrafnkel had ridden out of the district Sám summoned men. For his company he got mostly men without land and those whom he had called up; he supplied these men with weapons and clothes and provisions. Sám took a different route from the valley; he went north to the bridge, across it, and thence over Madderdale Heath, stopping in Madderdale for the night. From there the company rode to Broadshoulder Tongue, then down Blue Fells and from there into Crookdale and on south to Sand. Then they came down to Sheepfells and went on from there to Thingfield.

Hrafnkel had not yet arrived; the journey had been slower for him since he had a longer route. Sám set up a booth for his men at a considerable distance from the place where the men of the East Firths were accustomed to lodge. Sometime afterward Hrafnkel came to the Thing and set up his booth in his usual place. He heard that Sám was at the Thing and thought that amusing. This Thing was very well attended, most of the chiefs in Iceland being on hand. Sám looked up all the chiefs and asked for help and support, but all answered the same way: no one said he had such obligation to Sám that he would be willing to oppose Hrafnkel Priest and thus endanger his own position. They said, too, that matters had turned out in just one way for most men who had engaged in a contest with Hrafnkel at the Thing, namely, that he had driven them all from the court in disgrace. Sám went back to his booth; he and his kinsman were heavy-hearted, fearing that their suit would fail, so that they would get nothing from it but shame and humiliation. They were so worried that they could not sleep or eat, for all the chiefs had refused to help them, including those from whom they had really expected assistance.

Old Thorbjorn woke up early one morning. He awakened Sám and asked him to get up, saying: "I can't sleep." Sám got up and put on his clothes. They went out and down to the Ax River below the bridge, and washed themselves. Thorbjorn said to Sám: "My advice is that you have our horses rounded up and we get ready to go home; it is clear now that we shall get nothing but disgrace." Sám answered: "That's fine, in view of the fact that you insisted on a suit against Hrafnkel and refused terms that many a man seeking compensation for a relative would have accepted gladly. You accused me of cowardice—and all the rest who were unwilling to go into the suit with you. Now, I shall not give it up until it seems to me beyond all expectation that I can get anything done." Thorbjorn was so moved by this that he wept. In a moment they saw five men walking away from a booth a little distance below the point on the river where they were sitting. The man who walked in front was tall but not thick; he wore a leaf-green kirtle and carried a sword in his hand. He was a man with regular features, a ruddy complexion, good looks, and thick blond hair. This man was easily recognized, for he had a light-colored lock of hair on the left side. Sám said: "Let's get up and go west across the river and see these men." Then they walked down the river; and the man who was in front of the group greeted them before they spoke to him; and he asked who they were. They told him, and Sám asked the man his name; he said he was Thorkel Thjostason. Sám asked what family he came from and where he lived. He said that he was a West Firther by birth and breeding and lived at Cod Firth. Sám said: "Are you a man of priestly rank?" He said definitely that he was not. "Have you an estate of your own?" said Sám. He said he did not. Sám said: "What is your situation, then?" He answered: "I am unattached; I came out here a year ago; I had been abroad seven years, having gone to Constantinople and joined the household of the king of the Greeks; but now I am living with my brother, whose name is Thorgeir." "Is he a man of priestly status?" said Sám. Thorkel answered: "Certainly, he has priestly authority around Cod Firth and elsewhere in the West Firths." "Is he here at the Thing?" said Sám. "Certainly, he is here." "How large a company has he?" "He has seventy men," said Thorkel. "Are there more brothers?" said Sám. "There is a third," said Thorkel. "Who is he?" said Sám. "His name is Thormod," said Thorkel, "and he lives at Garths in Swansness; he is married to Thordis, daughter of Thorolf Skallagrimsson of Borg." "Will you give us some assistance?" said Sám. "What do you need?" said Thorkel. "The help and support of chiefs," said Sám, "for we have a suit to carry on against Hrafnkel Priest in connection with the slaying of Einar Thorbjarnsson, and with your backing we can be sure of an opportunity to present the case properly." Thorkel answered: "As I said, I have no priestly authority." "Why are you excluded that way, when you are a chief's son like your brothers?" Thorkel said: "I didn't tell you that I had not had the rank; but I turned over my chief's authority to my brother Thorgeir before I went abroad. I have not taken it back since because I am satisfied as long as he has it in charge. Go and see him, ask him for help; he is of energetic nature, a good fellow, well endowed in every way, and a young man eager for honor; such men are the most likely to give you assistance." Sám said; "We shall get nothing from him unless you join us in asking for it." Thorkel said: "This I will promise, to be for you rather than against you, inasmuch as I think you have good cause to bring suit for the slaying of a close relative. Go ahead now to the booth, and inside it; people are sleeping there. You will see two pallets on the far side of the booth; I got up from one, and Thorgeir, my brother, is resting on the other. He has had a big boil on his foot, since he came to the Thing, and hence has slept little at night; but it burst last night and now the core is out and he has been sleeping since. He has his foot stuck out from under the footboard on account of the fever in the foot. Let this old man [Thorbjorn] go on inside the booth; he looks very feeble, both in eyesight and from old age in general. Then, fellow," said Thorkel to Thorbjorn, "when you come to the pallet you must stumble heavily and fall on the pallet, then take hold of the toe that is bound up and give it a jerk—and see how he takes it." Sám said: "You mean to give us good counsel, but this does not seem advisable to me." Thorkel answered, "You can take your choice; either do as I propose or do not look to me for help." Sám said to Thorbjorn: "You must do as he advises." Thorkel said he would come along later: "For I am waiting for my men."

Then Sám and Thorbjorn went along to the booth. Everybody was asleep there, and they saw at once where Thorgeir was lying. Old Thorbjorn stumbled badly as he walked, and when he came to the pallet he fell against the footboard, grasped the toe that had been inflamed, and pulled it toward him. Thorgeir awakened, jumped from the pallet, and asked who was moving about there so clumsily that he ran into people's feet that were already sore. Thorbjorn and Sám could think of nothing to say. Just then Thorkel slipped into the booth and said to his brother Thorgeir: "Don't be hasty or excited about this, kinsman, for nothing is going to harm you; things turn out worse for many people than they intend, and men are not always careful about everything when they have much on their minds. So it is an excuse for you that your foot is sore and has been very painful— that you know best yourself. Now it may be that for an old man his son's death is no less painful than to get no compensation and be lacking in everything himself. He will know his own feelings best; and it is to be expected that a man who has a great deal to worry about will not be careful about everything." Thorgeir said: "I should not have thought that he could be offended with me for that, for I did not kill his son and he cannot avenge the deed on me." "He did not mean to avenge it on you," said Thorkel; "instead, he came up to you more roughly than he intended, for which his dimness of sight is responsible; but he was expecting some assistance from you. It is a noble act, now, to aid an old and needy man. Necessity, and not avarice, leads him to bring suit for the slaying of his son. But now all the chiefs refuse support to this man and thereby show themselves very unheroic." Thorgeir said: "Against whom are these men bringing suit?" Thorkel answered: "Hrafnkel Priest has slain Thorbjorn's son without cause. He commits all kinds of misdeeds against others and will give no man redress for them." Thorgeir said: "It will be with me as with others—I do not know that I have such obligations to these men as to be willing to engage in contests with Hrafnkel. As it appears to me, the same thing happens every summer to those men who take part in suits against him: most of them get little or no honor when it is all over. I see that it goes that way for everybody, and hence I think most men would be reluctant about it, unless they are compelled by necessity." Thorkel said: "It may be that, if I were a chief, I should think it bad to oppose Hrafnkel; but actually it does not look that way to me. For it would appear to me as if one were going up against the most powerful kind of opponent, by whom all had hitherto been routed; and I should think my reputation, or that of any chief who might get the better of Hrafnkel, would be greatly increased. On the other hand, it would not be diminished if things should turn out for me as they have for the rest, for 'that may happen to me which has happened to others'; and also, 'nothing ventured, nothing gained.' " "I see how you are inclined," said Thorgeir; "you want to help these men. Now I will turn over to you my priestly authority over men; you take it, as I have had it hitherto, and henceforth let us both have it equally, and you help those you wish to help." "It seems to me," said Thorkel, "that our authority would be best managed if you should keep it as long as possible. There is no one to whom I am so willing to give it, for you have many qualifications beyond your two brothers, whereas I am uncertain what I shall do with myself at present. And you know, kinsman, that I have taken little part in affairs since I came to Iceland. I can see now how my advice is rated; and now I have said my say for the time being. It may be that Thorkel Lock will reach the point where his words are more highly valued." Thorgeir said: "Now I see what is happening, kinsman—you are displeased, and I cannot allow that; so let us go in with these men, however things turn out, if you wish it." Thorkel said: "I ask only for that which it seems to me best to grant." "How much of their suit do these men think they can handle effectively?" said Thorgeir. "As I told you to-day," said Sám, "we need backing from chiefs, but I will undertake the pleading of the case." Thorgeir said that would do well: "And now it is important to prepare the case as correctly as possible, and it seems to me, if Thorkel is willing, that you should go to see him before the court sits. In the end you will have some solace in return for your trouble, or else more humiliation than before, besides the worry and anxiety. Go along now and don't be downhearted, for if you are going to contest against Hrafnkel you will need to keep up your spirits in the meantime. But don't tell anyone that we have promised you assistance." Then they went back to their booth very cheerfully. Everybody wondered why they had had a change of mood so quickly, for they had been very gloomy when they left their booth. They remained there now until the court sat.

Then Sám called his men and went to the Law Rock, where the court was in session. Sám walked boldly up to the court. He began by naming his witnesses and then presented his case against Hrafnkel Priest without error and according to the correct statutes of the land, as well as with excellent delivery. Just then Thjosti's sons arrived with a great crowd of men. All the men from the western part of the country supported them, and it appeared that Thjosti's sons were fortunate in friends. Sám prosecuted his case to the point where Hrafnkel was invited to defend himself, unless there was someone present who wished to offer a defense in his behalf according to correct legal procedure. Great applause followed Sám's speech, and no one offered to speak for the defense. Men ran to Hrafnkel's booth and told him what was going on. He sprang up quickly, called his men, and went to the court, thinking there would be few to resist him. He intended to teach little men a lesson about bringing suits against him; he was going to break up the court in Sám's presence and thus force him to give up the case. But now there was no chance of that. There was such a crowd that Hrafnkel got nowhere near; he was pushed away by a much larger force, so that he did not hear the speeches of those who were suing him. Thus it was difficult for him to offer his defense. But Sám prosecuted the case to the limit of the law, with the result that Hrafnkel was declared a full outlaw at that Thing.

Hrafnkel went at once to his booth, had his horses brought up, and rode away from the Thing ill pleased with the ending of the case, for he had never had such a thing happen before. He rode east to Heatherdale Heath, then east to Side, and did not stop till he got back home to Hrafnkelsdale. There he settled down at Adalbol and acted as though nothing had happened. Sám remained at the Thing and went about with great self-confidence. Many men thought it good that the affair had turned out that way, so that Hrafnkel suffered disgrace; they remembered that he had shown unfairness to many. Sám stayed until the Thing closed and people prepared to go home. He thanked the brothers for their support, and Thorgeir laughingly asked Sám how things were going. When he said he was well pleased with the result, Thorgeir said: "Do you think you are any better off than before?" Sám said: "I think Hrafnkel has had a humiliation that will be talked about for a long time, and that is worth a great deal of money." "A man is not a full outlaw until a judgment of execution is carried out; and that must be done at his home, fourteen days after the

Taking Up of Weapons." The Taking Up of Weapons marks the time when everyone leaves the Thing. "But I think," said Thorgeir, "that Hrafnkel has gone home and expects to remain at Adalbol; I think he will keep his chief's authority in spite of you. You, however, may at best hope to ride home and settle down on your farm, if you can. I think you have this as the result of your suit: you can call him an outlaw. But I think he will keep most men as much intimidated as before unless you should take further steps." "I never had that in mind," said Sám. "You are a brave man," said Thorgeir, "and I believe my kinsman Thorkel is unwilling to let you down in the end. He wishes to stand by you until your quarrel with Hrafnkel is finally settled and you can live in peace. You will naturally think us the most suitable ones to assist you, since we have taken the most interest in the matter hitherto. We should go with you this once to the East Firths. Now, do you know any route to the East Firths other than the regular road?" Sám was delighted at this, and said that they would go by the same route that he had come on the way from the east.

Thorgeir chose his band of followers and took forty men with him; Sám also had forty. When they had been well equipped with weapons and horses, the whole company traveled by the same route till they reached Glacierdale one morning at dawn and crossed the bridge over the river. This was the day on which the judgment of execution had to be carried out. Thorgeir now asked Sám how they could approach in the least expected way, and Sám said that he would know how to manage that. Then he led them off the road, up to the knoll, and then along the ridge between Hrafnkelsdale and Glacierdale until they came to the lower slope of the mountain beneath which lies the farmstead of Adalbol. Grassy glens reached as far up as the heath, and there was a sharp descent into the dale; and there lay the farmstead below. Sám now dismounted and said: "Let us turn our horses loose, with twenty men to guard them; then sixty of us can make a dash for the house—and I think few people will be stirring." They did so, and the place has since been called Horse Glens. They ran quickly to the house; it was then six o'clock, and no one had got up. They broke in the door with a stick and rushed in. Hrafnkel was resting in his bed. They took him outside, along with all his armed servants; the women and children were driven into an outbuilding. In the yard was also a store-house; a clothes beam reached from this to the wall of the main house. They led Hrafnkel and his men to this spot. He made many offers for himself and for his men, and when that did no good, he entreated for the lives of the men: "For they have done no harm to you; but it is no dishonor to me, though you kill me; I will not ask to escape that. I do ask to be spared insult; there is no honor to you in that." Thorkel said: "We have heard that you have not been gentle with your enemies, and it is well that you should feel it to-day for yourself." Then they took Hrafnkel and his men and bound their hands behind their backs. Next they broke open the storehouse and took ropes from the hooks, got out their knives, and cut holes in the tendons of the captives. They pulled the ropes through the holes, tossed the men up over the beam, and then tied the eight of them together. Then Thorgeir said: "That has now happened to you, Hrafnkel, which is just; and you must have thought it unlikely that you would ever receive such shame from any man as has now been done to you. Which do you wish to do now, Thorkel: stay here beside Hrafnkel and guard these men or go with Sám outside the yard and away, within distance of a bow-shot from the house, to carry out the judgment of execution on some stony cliff or other, where there is neither plowed field nor meadow?" At that time this had to be done when the sun was due south. Thorkel said: "I will stay here by Hrafnkel, it seems like less work." Thorgeir and Sám then went and carried out the judgment of execution. When they came back, they took down Hrafnkel and his men and placed them in the yard; their eyes were now bloodshot. Then Thorgeir told Sám that he should do with Hrafnkel as he wished: "for he does not look hard to deal with now." Sám then answered: "I give you a choice of two things, Hrafnkel: one, you and such of your men as I wish shall be led out of the yard and killed; but inasmuch as you have many family dependents to care for, I am willing to allow you to make provision for them. On the other hand, if you choose life, then leave Adalbol together with all the members of your household and take only those possessions which I assign you—which will be very little. I shall take over your homestead and all your chief's authority; neither you nor your heirs shall ever lay claim to them; and you shall come nowhere nearer than the east side of Fleetdale District. Now you can be reconciled with me if you are willing to accept these terms." Hrafnkel said: "To many a quick death would seem better than such insults; but it will go with me as with many others— I will take life, if there is a choice. I do it mostly for the sake of my sons, for their prospects will be slight if I die." Then Hrafnkel was untied, and he granted Sám the right to settle things as he wished. Sám assigned Hrafnkel such of the property as he pleased, and it was little, indeed. Hrafnkel had his spear with him, but no other weapons. That day Hrafnkel and all his people moved away from Adalbol. Thorkel then said to Sám: "I do not know why you are doing this; you yourself will regret it most that you grant him life." Sám said that was the way it was to be.

Hrafnkel now moved his household east across Fleetdale District and beyond Fleetdale to the east of Lakefleet. At the end of the lake stood a little farmstead called Lockhill. Hrafnkel bought this land on credit, for he had no more capital than he needed for farm equipment. People talked a great deal about how his pride had fallen, and many recalled an old proverb, "Arrogance is short-lived." This property was a large forest land, of wide extent and poor in buildings, and for this reason he bought the land for a small price. Not worrying about the expense, he cut down the forest, for it was large, and built a splendid house, which has since been called Hrafnkelsstead. It has always been known as a good farmstead. For the first season Hrafnkel lived on the place with great inconvenience, but he did well with the fishing. While the house was under construction he worked very hard. Hrafnkel kept calves and kids through the winter that first season and took good care of them, so that nearly every one of his animals lived. One could almost say there were two heads to every living creature. In the summer of this year there was a great run of fish in Lakefleet. This was a great advantage for householders in the district, and it continued every summer.

Sám established his home at Adalbol as successor to Hrafnkel; soon after he made preparations for a noble feast and invited all those who had been Hrafnkel's liegemen. Sám planned to be their chief in his place. The men consented to this, although they thought it rather dubious. Thjosti's sons advised him that he should be kind, generous, and helpful to his men—a benefactor of those in need: "Then they are not men if they do not stand firmly by you whenever you need anything. We give you this advice because we should like you to succeed in everything, for we think you are a fine man. Be on your guard, now, and wary, for 'it is hard to watch out for the wicked.' " Thjosti's sons had Freyfaxi and his herd sent for, saying that they wished to see these prized possessions, about which there were such tales. The horses were brought to the house and the brothers looked them over. Thorgeir said: "These horses appear to me to be serviceable on the estate; my advice is that they do such useful work as they can until they are ready to die of old age. But this stallion looks no better to me than other stallions—worse, rather, in that much evil has come about because of him. I do not wish him to be the occasion of more slayings than have already occurred; it will be proper, now, that he who owns him should take charge of him." They then led the horse down through the valley. There was a cliff along the river there, directly above a deep place in the stream. They led the horse to this cliff, and Thjosti's sons pulled a bag over his head. They tied a stone around his neck, then took long sticks and pushed him off the cliff, and thus destroyed the horse. The place has since been called Freyfaxi's Cliff. Farther down the valley stood the temples which Hrafnkel had owned, and Thorkel wanted to go there. He gave directions to strip all the statues of the gods of their ornaments and then to set fire to the temples and burn up everything at once. Then the guests prepared to leave. Sám chose excellent presents for both brothers, and both parties promised each other loyal devotion, so they said good-bye in perfect friendship. The brothers then rode west by the regular route to the Firths and came home with honor to Cod Firth. Sám settled Thorbjorn down at Playsheds, where he was to live, and Sám and his wife moved to Adalbol and lived there for a time.

Hrafnkel, over in east Fleetdale, heard that Thjosti's sons had destroyed Freyfaxi and burned the temples. He remarked: "I think it foolishness to believe in gods," and said that henceforth he would never believe in them. He held to that, and never offered sacrifice afterward. Hrafnkel remained at Hrafnkelsstead and accumulated wealth. He soon got a great reputation in the district; everyone was eager to do as Hrafnkel wished. This was the time when the largest number of ships came from Norway to Iceland; people settled the largest part of the land in the district in Hrafnkel's day. No one could occupy land in peace unless he asked Hrafnkel's permission. They all had to promise him their support, and he promised them his protection; thus he got all the land east of Lakefleet under his control. This Thing-district soon became much bigger and more populous than the one which he had had earlier; it extended to Screeddale and all along Lakefleet. By now a change had come about in his nature; the man was much better liked than before. He had the same disposition to be useful and helpful, but he was more popular, as well as milder and more reasonable in everything. Often Sám and Hrafnkel encountered each other at public meetings, but they never brought up their previous relations. Thus seven years went by. Sám was well liked by his liegemen, for he was mild and quiet and ready in helping people—he remembered the advice those brothers had given him. Inciden-tally, he was a great dandy.

It was reported that a ship from abroad, whose captain was Eyvind Bjarnason, had arrived at Whale Firth. Eyvind had been away seven years and had enormously improved and developed, so that he had become a very gallant man. He was quickly told what had happened at home; but, being a man of great reserve, he had little to say about it. As soon as Sám learned of his arrival, he rode down to the ship and there was a very happy meeting of the brothers. Sám invited him to come west to his place and Eyvind agreed, but asked Sám to ride on ahead and send back horses to carry his goods. Meanwhile he hauled his ship on shore and took care of it, and Sám went home and rounded up horses to go and meet him. When Eyvind had his goods ready, he started on the journey to Hrafnkelsdale, going up along Whale Firth. There were five in Eyvind's party—and his servant made a sixth. This last was of Icelandic origin and related to Eyvind, who had rescued the boy from destitution and taken him abroad, looking out for him as carefully as for himself. This act was generally known, and it was universally agreed that there were few like Eyvind. The party rode up Thorisdale Heath, driving sixteen pack horses ahead. Two of the men were servants of Sám and three were from the ship; all were in bright clothes and had handsome shields. They rode across Screeddale and over the Ridge to the place called Bulungfields in Fleetdale, then down to Gorge River bank; this stream flows west to the lake between Hallormsstead and Hrafnkelsstead. They rode up along Lakefleet below the plain to Hrafnkelsstead, then around the end of the lake and across the Glacier River at Shed Ford. It was now about half past seven in the morning. There was a woman on the bank washing clothes, and she saw the travelers. This serving woman bundled up the laundry, ran home, threw the clothes down outside near a woodpile, and rushed inside. Hrafnkel had not yet got up, and some trusted men were lying in the hall. The working men, however, had gone to their tasks; it was the time of hay harvest. The woman began speaking as soon as she came in: "Very true it is, as was said long ago, that 'he gets slack who grows old.' The repute that was won early becomes little if a man shamefully lets himself get sluggish and has not the courage to set things right some time or other—and this is a great wonder in a man who was once brave.

Now it is otherwise with those who grow up with their father and seem to you of no esteem in comparison with you. But then, when they are grown, they go from land to land and appear to be of great repute wherever they go —and so come home and look better than chiefs. Eyvind Bjarnason rode across the river here at Shed Forth with a shield so bright that the light shone from it. He is such a man that vengeance on him would be fitting." Hrafnkel got up and answered her: "Maybe what you say is all too true— not because you intend it to be agreeable. It is well now that you should have more to do: go in a hurry to Willow Plains for Hallstein's sons, Sigvat and Snorri. Ask them to come quickly to me with the men there who bear arms." He sent another serving woman out to Hrolfsstead for Hrolf's sons, Thord and Halla, and the men who bore arms there. All these were valiant and very capable men. Hrafnkel also sent for his own servants; and the entire company amounted to eighteen.

Eyvind's party had now come up to the heath. Eyvind rode west till he came to a place in the middle of the heath called Bessi's Way. Here there is a marsh, with no grass at all, and it was like riding through nothing but mud that always came up to the knee or the mid-leg, sometimes to the belly. Underneath it was as hard as a stony field. There is a rocky, broken stretch to the west, and when they came to it the boy looked back and said to Eyvind: "Men are riding behind us, not less than eighteen; there is a tall man on horseback in blue clothes and he looks to me like Hrafnkel Priest, though I have not seen him for a long time." Eyvind answered: "What does it matter to us? I know of nothing to fear from Hrafnkel's riding; I have not done anything against him. Doubtless he has an appointment to meet his friends west in the Dale." The boy answered: "I still think it is you that he wants to meet." Eyvind said: "I don't know of anything that has happened between him and my brother Sám since they were reconciled." The boy answered: "I wish you would ride away west to the Dale; then you will be safe. I know Hrafnkel's nature; he will do nothing to us if he cannot get you. Everything is taken care of if you are, for then there is no animal in the trap; and it will be all right, whatever happens to us." Eyvind said he would not ride away in a hurry: "For I don't know who these men are, it would seem laughable to many a man if I ran away without finding out something." They rode west then from the rocky strip and there was another marsh in front of them, called Ox Marsh. It is covered with grass, but there are quicksands, so that it is almost impassable; that is why old Hallfred built the upper road, longer though it was. Eyvind rode west to the marsh, and the horses sank deep in the mire, which delayed them a good deal. Hrafnkel's party, without packs on their horses, followed rapidly and came along to the marsh. Eyvind's party had not got through the marsh; they could see Hrafnkel and both his sons. Eyvind's men then asked him to ride off: "All the bad spots are now passed; you can get to Adalbol while the marsh is between them and you." Eyvind answered: "I will not flee from these men, for I have done them no harm." His party rode then up to the ridge. Moderate-sized peaks rise from the ridge, and on one of the slopes

is a bit of turf, bare and windblown, surrounded by high banks. Eyvind rode
to the spot and dismounted to wait for the pursuers, remarking: "Now we
will soon know their business." Then he and his men walked up to the
turf and broke up some stones. Hrafnkel then turned south off the road toward the turf. He exchanged no words with Eyvind, but attacked at once,
Eyvind defended himself well and bravely. His servant, thinking himself
inadequate to the fight, got his horse, rode west over the ridge to Adalbol,
and told Sám what was going on. Sám got up quickly and sent for men. This
company numbered twenty men, well equipped. Sám rode east on the
heath to the site of the battle, which was now finished—and Hrafnkel had
ridden away east. Eyvind and all his men had fallen. First of all, Sám
looked for signs of life in his brother; but he was done for, and all five lay
dead together. Twelve of Hrafnkel's men had also fallen, but six survivors
had left the scene. Sám tarried only a little, and told his men to follow at
once. Hrafnkel's party had ridden away as fast as they could, and now their
horses would be tired. Sám declared: "We can catch them, for they have
tired horses but ours are all fresh; it will be a near thing whether we catch
them before they get off the heath." Hrafnkel had now gone east across Ox
Marsh, and both parties rode along until Sám came to the edge of the heath.
Then he saw that Hrafnkel had gone farther down into the slopes and
that he would make good his escape into the district below. Sám then said:
"Here we will turn back, for it will be easy for Hrafnkel to get men." In
this situation, then, Sám went back to the place where Eyvind lay and set
to work heaping up a burial mound over him and his fellows. These sites are
now called Eyvind's Knoll, Eyvind's Fells, and Eyvind's Dale. Sám then
took all Eyvind's goods home to Adalbol. When he arrived, he sent for his
liegemen to come there next morning about nine o'clock, planning to ride
west across the heath—"let the journey turn out as it may." In the evening
Sám went to bed, there being a number of men on hand.

Hrafnkel rode home and told the news. He ate a meal and then summoned
men, so that he got together a company of seventy. With these he rode west
across the heath, arrived unexpectedly at Adalbol, took Sám in his bed, and
led him out. Then Hrafnkel said: "Now something has happened to you,
Sám, that you must have thought unlikely for some time—I have your life in
my power. I shall not treat you worse than you did me. I offer you a choice
of two things: to be killed or to let me fix and settle the terms between
us." Sám said that he would choose to live; but he said he thought either
choice would be hard. Hrafnkel said that he could expect it: "For we have
that to pay you back. I should treat you twice as well if you deserved it.
You shall leave Adalbol and go down to Playsheds to live. You shall take
with you the property that Eyvind owned. You shall not remove from here
anything except that which you have brought—all of that you shall take with
you. I will take over my chief's authority, as well as the house and homestead. I see there has been a great increase in my property, and you shall not
have the benefit of that. No compensation shall be paid for your brother
Eyvind, because you ruthlessly prosecuted the case of Einar, your earlier

kinsman, and have had sufficient compensation in that you have had power and property for six years. The killing of Eyvind and his men does not appear to me worth more than the maiming of me and my men. You made me a fugitive from the district, but I shall be pleased to have you live at Playsheds; and that will do well, if you are not too arrogant for your own good. You shall be my subordinate as long as we both live. You may also expect to fare worse if there is any more trouble between us." Sám then left with his company for Playsheds and went to live there.

Hrafnkel then arranged the household at Adalbol with his own men. His son, Thorir, he established at Hrafnkelsstead. Hrafnkel now had chief's authority in all the settlements. His son Asbjorn remained with his father, for he was younger. Sám stayed at Playsheds that winter, glum and silent. Many discovered that he was little pleased with his lot. But in the course of the winter, when the days grew longer, Sám, with another man and three horses between them, went across the river, thence over Madderdale Heath, then across the Glacier River up on the mountain; then to Midge Lake, and from there across Fleet Heath and Clear Lake Pass. He did not stop till he reached Cod Firth in the west, where he was well received. Thorkel had just recently returned from his travels; he had been abroad four years. When Sám had rested for a week, he told the brothers of the affair with Hrafnkel and asked for their aid and support as before. This time Thorgeir did more of the talking for the brothers. He said it was out of the question: "We are far away. We thought we had put you in good shape before we left, so that it would be easy for you to maintain yourself. It has turned out as I anticipated at the time when you granted Hrafnkel life, namely, that you would regret it most. We urged you to take his life, but you wanted to have your way. It is easy to see now what difference in sense there has been between you and him—since he let you live in peace and waited for the time when he could dispose of the man that he thought bigger than you. We cannot meddle in this lucklessness of yours; and we have no incentive to oppose Hrafnkel great enough to make us risk our reputation a second time. But we will invite you to move here under our protection, with your entire household, if you think it less vexatious than living near Hrafnkel." Sám said he did not care for that, but wished to go back home. He asked them to swap horses with him, and this was readily arranged. The brothers wanted to give Sám good gifts, but he would accept none, saying that they were mean-spirited men. In this situation he rode home and lived on there till old age. He never got the advantage of Hrafnkel as long as he lived. Hrafnkel remained on his estate and kept up his repute. He died of illness, and his burial mound is in Hrafnkelsdale out from Adalbol; in the grave beside him was laid much money, along with all his armor and his good spear. His sons took over his chief's authority. Thorir lived at Hrafnkelsstead, Asbjorn at Adalbol; they held the priesthood together and both were considered important men. Thus ends the story of Hrafnkel.

Rameau's Nephew

BY

Denis Diderot

Translated by Arthur Knodel

Editor's Note

Denis Diderot was born at Langres in 1713, the son of a cutler. His father, a strong honest man whom Diderot never ceased to admire, entrusted the education of his son to the Jesuits, first at Langres and later in Paris. Relations between father and son were, for a time, strained, first by Diderot's refusal to study law seriously and later by his clandestine marriage, against his father's will, to a girl of obscure background and limited mentality. The marriage was, in fact, not to be a very happy one. Meanwhile, though, Diderot had to make ends meet, and he supported himself by doing every kind of hack work—tutoring, ghost-writing, translating, book-reviewing, pulp-writing. He read prodigiously and especially enjoyed that supreme eighteenth-century pastime—animated conversation.

In 1746 Diderot finally took on a permanent and gruelling job, namely, the organizing, compiling, and editing of a vast collaborative work, the *Encyclopedia*. This compendium of human knowledge began to appear in 1751, but the last of its thirty-five volumes of text and plates was not off the presses until 1772. Diderot saw the project through to the bitter end, in spite of every kind of official and unofficial harassment, including the desertion of his main collaborator, the mathematician d'Alembert, in 1759.

The *Encyclopedia* has become the very symbol of the Age of Reason, yet it is far less daring and revolutionary than literary manuals lead us to believe. Diderot was, in fact, a much more daring speculator than any of the hundreds of articles he wrote for the *Encyclopedia* indicate. But he reserved his dangerous thoughts for private letters, dialogues, novels, tales—and even a first-rate comedy—which remained in manuscript and were seen only by his friends and admirers.

Among the latter was the Empress Catherine of Russia who, on learning of Diderot's unhappy financial situation after a lifetime of toil on the *Encyclopedia*, bought at a handsome price the enormous library he had accumulated, with the stipulation that he remain custodian thereof until his death. Diderot died peacefully in 1784, at home with his wife, only a few years after he had made the arduous voyage to Saint Petersburg to thank his benefactress in person.

Rameau's Nephew is one of the most remarkable of the many works that remained in manuscript during Diderot's lifetime. The final publication of the authentic text is in itself an incredible tale. In brief, *Rameau's Nephew* first appeared in 1805 in a German translation made by Goethe from a manuscript now lost. It was not until 1891 that, quite by chance, a manuscript of the work in Diderot's own handwriting came to light. That manuscript served as the basis of the limited edition of 1891 and of the meticulously annotated edition published in 1950 by Jean Fabre.

This novel in dialogue is much more closely related to Diderot's work on the *Encyclopedia* than is usually recognized, for the household from which the title-character has just been ejected, and of which he gives so vivid and devastating an account, was a real one and is presented by Diderot as the gathering place of the most vocal enemies of the *Encyclopedia* group. Diderot is evening up old scores, and his dialogue therefore bristles with allusions to persons alive at the time. These constant contemporary references are a nuisance to the uninstructed reader, but hardly more. For the title-character, while he serves as a pretext for attacking a host of Diderot's enemies, at the same time reveals his own very complex nature. The title-character was himself an actual person, but the extent to which Diderot's tumultuous and disquieting portrait corresponds to the actual nephew of the famous composer is not known. What matters is that he comes to life for us as an independent and memorable entity.

Rameau's Nephew

Vertumnis, quotquot sunt, natus iniquis.
Horace *Book II, satire* 7

COME RAIN OR SHINE, I'M IN THE HABIT OF TAKING A STROLL AROUND FIVE in the afternoon in the Palais Royal gardens. I'm the fellow you always see sitting bemused and alone on Argenson's Bench. I argue with myself about politics, love, matters of taste, or philosophy. I let my mind wander off on any wanton tack it wants to take. I let it go after the first sensible or crazy idea that comes along, just the way you see our dissolute young blades in Foy's Alley go after a giddy courtesan with a laughing face, a come-hither glance, and a turned-up nose, only to give her the slip for the next one that comes along, chasing all of them but not sticking with any one. Well, my thoughts are my chippies. If it's too cold or rainy, I take refuge in the Regency Coffee House and while away the time watching the chess-players. In all the world Paris is the city, and the Regency Coffee House is the place in Paris, where the best chess is played. Rey's Regency is where Légal the Profound, Foxy Philidor, and Stout Mayot take each other on; and it's also where you see the most unexpected moves and hear the stupidest remarks. For, while it's possible to be a man of wit and a great chess-player like Légal, it's also possible to be a great chess-player and a fool, like Foubert and Mayot.

I was there one evening after dinner, watching intently, not saying much and trying to hear as little as possible, when I was accosted by one of the oddest characters in this land, where, God knows, there is certainly no dearth of odd characters. This one is compounded of pride and baseness, of good sense and madness. Notions of respectability and impropriety must be strangely mixed up in his head, because he unostentatiously lets you see the good qualities Nature has given him, while flaunting the bad ones. He is endowed, moreover, with the physique of an ox, a singularly overheated imagination, and a most uncommon lung-power. If ever you run into him and are not scared off by his originality, you'll either stick your fingers in your ears or take to your heels. Gad, what terrifying lungs!

The person he least resembles is himself. Sometimes he's skinny and gaunt as a patient in the last stages of consumption; you could count his teeth through the skin of his cheeks; you'd think he hadn't eaten for several days or that he's just come out of La Trappe. The next month he's so fat and paunchy that you'd say he'd been eating regularly at some banker's table or been holing up in a Bernardine monastery. Today his linen is dirty, his breeches torn; he's in rags and almost barefoot. He hangs his head and slinks off; you almost feel like calling after him just to give him a few cents. Tomorrow he'll be powdered, well shod, primped up, well dressed; he holds his head high, lets you know he's around; you'd almost take him for a gentleman. He lives from day to day, sad or gay, depending on his circumstances. His first concern when he gets up in the morning is to figure out where he'll dine. After dinner he thinks about where he'll find supper. And nighttime has its special worries for him. Either he walks back to the garret where he lives—unless the landlady is tired of waiting for her rent and asked him to give back his key—or he hides out in some local tavern until dawn over a piece of bread and a schooner of beer. When there isn't so much as a sixpence left in his pocket, as sometimes happens, he falls back either on some hack-driver he knows or on the coachman of some great lord who will let him bed down in the straw alongside the horses. The next morning he still has bits of his "mattress" in his hair. When the weather is mild, he wanders up and down the Cours-la-Reine or the Champs Elysées all night long. At dawn he shows up in town dressed for the day, and sometimes for the rest of the week, in last night's clothes.

I don't have much use for these eccentric fellows, though some folk strike up acquaintances with them and even become their friends. About once a year I give them a hearing when I run into them, because their character clashes so with all the others and relieves the tiresome uniformity resulting from our upbringing, social conventions, and normal good manners. If one of these fellows turns up in company, he's a bit of leaven that ferments and restores something of our natural individuality to each of us. He startles us, shakes us up, forces us to approve or condemn; he brings truth out of hiding, makes us recognize the really fine people and unmasks the rascals. That's the moment when a man of judgment listens and sizes everyone up.

I know this particular fellow from way back. He used to be a regular visitor in a household where his talent had gained him an entrée. There was an only daughter in the house. He would swear to the father and mother that he'd marry their daughter. The parents shrugged their shoulders, laughed in his face, told him he was crazy—but I saw it happen just as he said it would. He borrowed a few crowns from me, which I let him have. He had somehow wormed his way into a few respectable homes where there was always a place set for him at table, provided that he would not talk without first having got permission. He kept quiet and ate in a fury. It was quite a sight to see him under such restraint. When he couldn't hold in any longer and opened his mouth, at his first word all the guests would shout: "Oh, Rameau!" Rage would blaze in his eyes, and he'd set to eating again, more furious than ever. You've been curious to know the man's name, and now you know it. He's the nephew of the famous composer who delivered us from Lulli's plain-song that we've been droning out for the last hundred years and who has written so much visionary nonsense and so many apocalyptic "truths" about music theory that no one, not even himself, ever understood what it was all about. And he has given us a certain number of operas in which there are harmony, snatches of song, disconnected ideas, a great din, flights, triumphal processions, sallies, apotheoses, mutterings, endless victories, and dance-tunes that will last forever. Rameau, who, after himself burying the Florentine, will in his turn be buried by the new Italian virtuosi—a thing which he himself foresaw and which made him gloomy, sad, and cantankerous, because no one, not even a pretty woman who wakes up with a pimple on her nose, can be in a nastier mood than a composer or writer in danger of outliving his own reputation. Look at Marivaux and Crébillon the younger.

He comes up to me:

"Ah ha! So it's you, Mister Philosopher. And what are you doing here among all these idlers? Do you too waste your time pushing the wood around?" (That's the contemptuous way of referring to chess or checkers.)

I: No, but when I don't have anything better to do, I enjoy, at least for a little while, watching those who really know how to push it around.

He: In that case, you don't enjoy yourself very often. Except for Légal and Philidor, the rest don't know what it's all about.

I: Come, come—even de Bissy?

He: Well, he's to chess what Mademoiselle Clairon is to acting. They both know everything about their games that can be *learned.*

I: You're a hard man to please. I can see that only sheer genius meets with your approval.

He: Yes, in chess, checkers, poetry, eloquence, music, and similar child's play. Why put up with mediocrity in those areas?

I: Well, I almost agree with you. The trouble is that a whole lot of people have to try their hand for one genius to appear. He's one in a million. But let's forget about it. I haven't seen you for ages. I hardly give you a thought when I don't see you, but I always like to see you again. What are you doing these days?

He: What you, I, and everyone else are doing: good, bad, and nothing at all. And then, I've been hungry and eaten when there was a chance to eat, and when I finished eating, I got thirsty, so I drank once in a while. Meanwhile, my beard kept growing, and when it got too heavy, I had it shaved off.

I: That was a mistake. That's the only thing you lack to be a real sage.

He: How true, how true. I've a broad wrinkled forehead, a fiery eye, a prominent nose, full cheeks, black and bushy eyebrows, a well-shaped mouth, full lips, and a square jaw. Cover this imposing chin with a long beard and, you know, it would look fine in bronze or marble.

I: Right next to a Caesar, a Marcus Aurelius, a Socrates.

He: No, I'd like it better between Diogenes and Phryne. I'm as shameless as the one, and I'm not averse to the company of the other.

I: Do you keep feeling pretty well?

He: Yes, usually, but I'm not in top form today.

I: Why? You've got a belly like Silenus and a face—

He: —a face that you'd take for its counterpart behind. The spleen that's corroding my dear uncle's innards seems to fatten his dear nephew.

I: Well, now that you mention your uncle, do you see him once in a while?

He: Yes. I see him pass by in the street.

I: Doesn't he help you out at all?

He: If he helps anyone out, it's without his realizing it. He's a philosopher, in his way. He thinks only of himself; he doesn't give a rap for the rest of the world. His daughter and wife can die off any time they like; provided that the parish bells tolling for them go right on sounding the twelfth and seventeenth intervals, everything will be all right. That's fortunate for him, and that's what I especially like about men of genius. They're good for only one thing; beyond that they're a blank. They don't even know what it means to be a citizen, father, mother, brother, cousin, or friend. And just between us, we should try to be just like that, but without wanting geniuses to spring up everywhere. We need men, but not men of genius. No, no. No men of genius, please. They're the ones who change the face of the earth; and in even the smallest things, stupidity is so commonplace and so powerful that it can never be corrected without kicking up a terrible ruckus. Some things are partly changed by what the geniuses think up, but a good part stays just the way it was. That's how we come to have two gospels, a parti-colored Harlequin's outfit. The wisdom of Rabelais's monk is the true wisdom for his own peace of mind and for everybody else's: Do your duty, more or less, always speak well of the worthy Prior, and let the rest of the world do as it pleases. It must do pretty well, since the mass of humanity is satisfied with it. If I knew history, I'd prove to you that the evil here below has always been the work of some man of genius. But I don't know history, because I don't know anything. Devil take me if I ever learned anything, or if I'm any the worse off for it. One day I was dining at the table of one of the King's ministers who has brains enough for any four men. Well, he showed as clearly as two and two make four that nothing is more useful to the nations of the world than falsehood, and nothing is more harmful than truth. I can't quite recall his proof, but an obvious consequence was that men of genius are hateful and that, if a child at birth bore some mark on his brow that indicated the presence of this dangerous gift of nature, the child ought either to be smothered or thrown to the dogs.

I: Yet the people who are such declared enemies of genius always claim to be geniuses themselves.

He: Oh yes, I believe they think just that, way down inside, but I don't believe they'd dare admit it.

I: Out of modesty. So you developed a terrible hatred for genius from that moment on.

He: And I've hated them ever since.

I: But I remember a time when you despaired because you'd never be anything but a mediocrity. You'll never be happy if you want both the pro and the con. You'll have to make your choice and stick with it. Even though I agree that men of genius are usually very odd, or, as the saying goes, "No master mind without a grain of madness," the fact still remains that we'll always have contempt for periods of history that don't produce men of genius. They are the glory of the nations that produce them. Sooner or later, statues are erected to them, and they are looked upon as the benefactors of mankind. With all due respect for the minister you quoted, I'm of the opinion that, although falsehood may be temporarily expedient, it is necessarily harmful in the long run; and that truth, on the other hand, is profitable in the long run, even though it may be momentarily harmful. Whence I am tempted to conclude that the man of genius who discredits a widespread error or establishes some great truth is always a person worthy of veneration. It may happen that this person is the victim of prejudice and established law; but there are two sorts of laws: those which are absolutely fair and universally applicable, and those which are arbitrary and which only blindness or the necessity of circumstances makes operative. The latter sort bring only a momentary disgrace on those who break them, a disgrace that time will turn forever against the judges and nations who were responsible. Which is reviled today: Socrates or the magistrate who made him drink the hemlock?

He: A lot of good that did Socrates! Did it keep him from being condemned? Was he put to death any the less for it? Was he any less of a rabble-rouser? And by breaking a bad law, did he in any way discourage fools from breaking good ones? And was he, for all that, any less a foolhardy and peculiar individual? You yourself came close to making an unfavorable judgment on men of genius just a moment ago.

I: Just listen, my good man. A society should not have bad laws; and if it had only good ones, it would never have to persecute a man of genius. I never said that genius was inseparably bound up with evil, nor evil with genius. A fool is more apt to be a wicked man than a genius is. And even if a man of genius is usually of a harsh, difficult, thorny, and insufferable humor, even wicked, what would you conclude from that?

He: That he's fit to be drowned.

I: Easy, easy now, my good man. And tell me, do you think I'd take your uncle as an example? No. He's a hard man, brutal, without compassion, stingy, a bad father, a bad husband, a bad uncle. But it's not at all certain yet that he's a man of genius, that he has really contributed greatly to his art or that his works will still be discussed ten years from now. But what about Racine? Now there was a genius for you, and he didn't have the reputation of being a very good man. And what about Voltaire?

He: Don't press me too hard, because I'll follow through to the bitter end.

I: Which way would you rather have it?—that he should have been a good man, completely immersed in his business like Briasson, or a walking tape-measure like Barbier, who gets his wife with child regularly and legitimately every year—a good husband, a good father, a good uncle, a good neighbor, an honest merchant, but nothing more—or that he should have been a cheat, false, ambitious, envious, mean—but also the author of *Andromaque, Britannicus, Iphigénie, Phèdre,* and *Athalie?*

He: Well, in his case he might have been better off if he'd been the former.

I: That's infinitely truer than you realize.

He: Oh, that's just like you fellows! If we say something sensible, it's only as madmen or mystics do—by chance. You fellows are the only ones who really know what's what. Look here, Mister Philosopher, I know what I'm talking about, just as much as you know what you're talking about.

I: All right then, why would Racine have been better off the other way?

He: Because all his fine works didn't bring him in twenty thousand francs; whereas, if he'd been a good silk-merchant down in the rue Saint-Denis or the rue Saint-Honoré, a good wholesale grocer or a well-patronized apothecary, he'd have amassed a huge fortune. And while he was amassing it, there is no pleasure he wouldn't have enjoyed. He'd have given an occasional farthing to some poor devil of a clown like myself for making him laugh or for finding him an occasional young chit to break the monotony of eternally cohabiting with his wife. We'd have enjoyed excellent meals in his house, gambled for big stakes, drunk excellent wines, excellent liqueurs, excellent coffee, gone on outings in the country. So you see, I knew perfectly well what I was talking about. You laugh. But let me finish. It would even have been better for everybody around him.

I: Unquestionably. Provided he hadn't put the wealth he'd acquired through legitimate trade to some dishonest use, and provided he'd have sent all those gamblers, parasites, dull flatterers, ne'er-do-wells, and useless louts packing; and provided he had his shop-help beat up the busybody who consoles husbands for having to sleep with their wives all the time by offering a little variety.

He: Beat him up, sir, beat him up! No one is ever beaten up in a well-governed city. It's a respectable profession. Lots of people, even titled ones, indulge in it. And what in the devil's name do you think money is for, if not for a good table, good company, good wines, beautiful women, all sorts of pleasures and every kind of amusement? I'd just as soon be a beggar as have a huge fortune and not enjoy any of these pleasures. But getting back to Racine. He benefited only those who didn't know him, and that, long after he'd died.

I: Right. But weigh the evil and the good. A thousand years from now he will still make people cry; he'll be admired by men in every country on earth; he'll inspire compassion, commiseration, tenderness: People will ask who he was, where he came from, and France will be envied. He made a few people, who are no longer alive, suffer—people who have almost no interest for us. We have nothing to fear from either his vices or his faults.

It would undoubtedly have been better had he received from nature the virtues of a good man along with the talents of a great one. He was a tree that made some of the trees around him dry up, that choked off the plants growing at his foot. But the treetop reaches the clouds; its branches spread wide; it gives shade to all—past, present and future—who come to relax a moment near its majestic trunk. It has borne and continues to bear fruit that have an exquisite flavor. It would be nice if Voltaire also had the sweetness of Duclos, the artlessness of Abbé Trublet, the dignity of Abbé d'Olivet. But since that isn't possible, let's look at the matter from the really interesting angle. Let's forget for a moment the point we occupy in time and space, and turn our sights on the ages to come, on the remotest regions, and on nations yet unborn. Let's think of the good of mankind. Assuming we are not generous enough, let's at least pardon nature for knowing its business better than we do. If you throw cold water on Greuze's head, you may extinguish his talent along with his vanity. If you make Voltaire less touchy about criticism, he won't plumb the depths of Merope's soul; he won't move you any longer.

He: But if Nature is as powerful as she is wise, why didn't she make them as good as they are great?

I: But don't you see that in arguing this way you are overturning the general order of things, and that if everything here below were excellent, nothing would really be excellent?

He: You're right. The important point is that you and I shall exist, and that we shall be you and I. Beyond that, let everything get along as it can. The best order of things, to my way of thinking, is the order in which I have a place, and a fig for the most perfect of worlds, if I'm not in it. I prefer to be, and even to be an impertinent logic-chopper, than not to be at all.

I: Everybody thinks as you do and criticizes the order of things as they are, not realizing that a different order of things would cancel out his own existence.

He: That's true.

I: So let's accept things as they are. Let's try to find out their cost and their profit for us; and let's not bother with all the things that we don't know enough about, either to praise or criticize—things that may not be either good or bad, if they are all rigidly determined, as lots of honest people think.

He: I don't follow all the stuff you're peddling. I guess it's philosophy, but I warn you that I don't go much for it. All I know is that I'd like to be someone else, on the chance that I might be a genius or a great man. Yes, I have to admit that; something tells me it's so. I've never yet heard a genius or great man praised without feeling secretly furious. I'm envious. When I hear some little degrading thing about their private lives, I always listen with pleasure. It brings them down to my level. I can put up with my mediocrity more easily. I say to myself: "Well, you could never have written *Mahomet*, but then, you wouldn't have been guilty of praising

Maupeou either." I've been a mediocrity all along, and I hate being a mediocrity. Ah yes, I'm a mediocrity, and I hate it. I've never yet heard the overture to *Les Indes Galantes* played, or the "Profonds abîmes du Témare" or "Nuit, éternelle nuit" sung, without saying ruefully to myself: "There's something you'll never be able to produce." So I've been jealous of my uncle; and if there were a few good harpsichord pieces tucked away in his briefcase at the time of his death, I wouldn't hesitate for a moment being myself, and at the same time, being him.

I: If that's all that's worrying you, I assure you it's not worth the trouble.

He: It's nothing. Just a passing fit of depression.

And then he began to sing the overture to *Les Indes Galantes* and the aria, "Profonds abîmes," adding:

"The something inside that keeps talking to me says: 'Rameau, you wish you'd composed those two pieces. If you had composed those two pieces, you'd certainly compose two more; and when you'd have composed a certain number of them, you'd be played, you'd be sung everywhere. When you go for a walk, you'd hold your head high; you'd know in your own mind how great your merit was. People would point you out and say: "That's the fellow who wrote those charming gavottes." ' "

He sang the gavottes; and then, with the expression of a man who is deeply moved, who is delirious with joy, who weeps for joy, he added, rubbing his hands together:

". . . You'll have a fine big house."

And he measured it off with his arms.

". . . a good bed,"

And he stretched out nonchalantly in it.

". . . good wines,"

Which he tasted, clicking his tongue against his palate.

". . . a fine coach and four,"

And he raised his foot to climb into it.

". . . pretty women,"

Whose breasts he already fondled and whom he gazed at voluptuously.

". . . A hundred toadies would come to burn incense at my shrine each day."

And he saw them all around him; he saw Palissot, Poinsinet, Fréron senior and junior, La Porte. He heard them, strutted about, nodded agreement, smiled at them, ignored them, showed contempt for them, sent them packing, called them back. And then he went on:

". . . And that way they would tell you every morning that you are a great man. You would read in *Three Centuries of Our Literature* that you are a great man, and by nightfall you'd be convinced that you *are* a great man. And this great man, Rameau's nephew, would fall asleep to the soft murmur of praises sounding in his ear; he'd look self-satisfied even when he slept. His chest would expand, rise and fall with ease; he'd snore as a great man does."

And while he said all this, he sprawled out languidly on a bench, closed his eyes, and imitated the blissful sleep he had imagined. After enjoying a few minutes of sweet repose, he awoke, stretched his arms, yawned, rubbed his eyes, and looked around to see where his insipid flatterers were.

I: So you think that the happy man sleeps soundly?

He: Think? I *know.* Me, poor devil that I am, when I go back to my garret at night and stuff myself into my pallet, I'm all huddled together under my bedcover; my chest is tight and my breathing hard. You can just barely hear a kind of faint moan; whereas a financier makes the walls of his apartment reverberate and even causes people in the street to stop in amazement. But today it's not snoring and uneasy sleep that worry me.

I: Still, that's very unpleasant.

He: But what's happened to me is still more so.

I: And what could that be?

He: You've always taken a certain interest in me because I'm a pleasant sort of scamp whom you really despise but who amuses you.

I: That's true.

He: So I'll tell you what happened.

Before beginning, he heaves a big sigh and raises both hands to his forehead; then he recovers his composure and says to me:

"You know that I'm an ignoramus, a fool, a madman, a fresh guy, a lazybones, what our Burgundians call a bloody beggar, a swindler, a glutton . . ."

I: What a panegyric!

He: Every bit of it is true. Can't take back a word of it. Let's not argue about that, please. Nobody knows me better than I do, and I still haven't told all.

I: Well, I wouldn't want to irritate you; so I'll agree with everything you say.

He: Well, I was living with people who had taken a liking to me precisely because I was uncommonly endowed with all these qualities.

I: Strange, but up until now I've always thought that you hid such qualities, even from yourself, if you had them, or simply forgave yourself for having them and always condemned them in others.

He: Hide them from yourself? Who can do that? You can be sure that when Palissot is all alone and considers himself, he tells himself these things and a lot more. And you can also be sure that in private conversation with his collaborator, both parties frankly admit that they are nothing but a couple of prize scoundrels. Condemn these faults in others! The people I was talking about were a lot fairer, and their attitude made it possible for me to get along famously when I was around them. I was really sitting pretty. I was the fair-haired boy. I couldn't be away for a moment without their regretting it. I was their little Rameau, their pretty-boy Rameau, their madcap Rameau, their insolent, ignorant, lazy, piggish, clownish, dumb-ox of a Rameau. Not a single one of these epithets was said without a smile, a caress, a little tap on the shoulder, a kick, or, at table, a juicy piece that they tossed onto my plate. And when we weren't at table, I could take liberties without consequence, because I'm an inconsequential person. People do anything they want to me, with me, in front of me; I never take offense. And all the little presents they used to shower on me! Stupid ass that I am! I've lost it all! I lost it all because, for once, I had a little common sense, the only time in my life! Never, never will it happen again!

I: Well, what was it all about?

He: A piece of incredible folly—stupid, incomprehensible, unforgivable.

I: What folly?

He: Rameau, Rameau, is that what they expected of you? The folly of having a little good taste, a little wit, a little good sense. Rameau, my friend, this will teach you to stay what God made you and what your protectors wanted you to be. Instead, they grabbed you by the shoulders and showed you the door. They told you: "You dolt, get out and don't set foot here again. A dolt who wants to show good sense and reason, no less! Get out! We've got reason and sense, enough and to spare, around here." So you went off, biting your fingernails. What you should have done was to bite off your damned tongue first. Because you didn't think of doing that, here you are, on the pavement, penniless, and with nowhere to turn. You were fed all you could eat, now weren't you? And now you're on the way back to the leftover stall. You were well housed, and now you'll be only too happy if you can get your garret back. Well bedded, and now you can look forward to the straw between Monsieur de Soubise's coachman and friend Robbé. Instead of sleeping gently and peacefully, as you did, with one ear you'll hear the whinnying and pawing of horses, and with the other, the noise—which is a thousand times more unbearable—of verses that are dry, harsh, and barbarous. Miserable, stupid fellow, possessed of a thousand devils!

I: But isn't there some way you could get back into the good graces of your former host? Was your crime that unpardonable? If I were you, I'd go back to these people. You're really more necessary to them than you realize.

He: Oh, I'm sure that now they don't have me around to make them laugh, they're bored stiff.

I: Then I'd go back to them. I wouldn't give them time enough to get used to not having me around or to have recourse to some respectable amusement. Who knows what might happen?

He: That's not what I'm afraid of. That will never happen.

I: No matter how sublime you may be, there's always someone else who can take your place.

He: Not likely.

I: Granted. But just the same I'd go to them just as you are—with that hangdog face, those rolling eyes, that threadbare collar, that mussed-up hair—in short, in the really deplorable state you're in. I'd throw myself at the feet of the goddess; I'd touch the ground with my forehead, and without getting up, I'd say in a feeble and sobbing voice: "Forgiveness, madam, forgiveness! I am unworthy, vile. It was an off-moment; for you know that I'm not ordinarily subject to attacks of common sense, and I promise never to have another for the rest of my days."

What was really amusing was that, while I was holding forth, he supplied the pantomime for every word. He had prostrated himself, face to the floor, and looked exactly as if he were holding the tip of a slipper in his two hands. He wept, sobbed, and said: "Yes, yes, my dainty queen, I promise, I'll never have another attack of common sense again for the rest of my life, my whole life." Then, jumping up suddenly, he added in a perfectly serious tone:

He: Yes, you're right. That's probably the best thing to do. She's good-hearted. Monsieur Vieillard says that she is *so* good-hearted! And I'm faintly aware of the fact myself. But just the same—to go and humiliate yourself before the little bitch, to beg mercy at the feet of a miserable little ham-actress who is constantly hissed by the parterre! I, Rameau, son of Monsieur Rameau, apothecary of Dijon, who is a man of good standing and who has never bent his knee before anyone! I, Rameau, the nephew of the man known as the Great Rameau, who walks upright and gesticulates freely in the Palais Royal ever since Carmontelle drew him hunched over and with his hands behind his coat-tails! I who have composed pieces for the harpsichord that no one plays, but which may well be the only ones that will be handed down to posterity and played hereafter. I, I, I should go and . . . Really, sir, that just can't be.

And putting his right hand on his heart, he went on:

He: I feel something here, beating and saying to me: "Rameau, you'll do nothing of the sort." There must be a certain dignity inherent in man's nature that nothing can stifle. It is aroused, for example, when you consider boots. Yes, boots that have to be licked. Because there are some days when I have no trouble being as vile as you like. On those days, for a farthing, I'd kiss the ass of little Miss Hus.

I: Ho, ho! But, my friend, she's fair-skinned, pretty, young, gentle, dimpled, and chubby: and that's an act of humility that people a lot more particular than you would sometimes stoop to commit.

He: Let me make myself clear. The fact is that you can kiss an ass literally or figuratively. Just ask that fat Bergier who kisses Madame de la Marque's ass both literally and figuratively—a case, as a matter of fact, where both the literal and the figurative disgust me equally.

I: Well, if the expedient that I suggest doesn't suit you, at least have the courage to admit being a beggar.

He: It's hard to be a beggar, especially when there are so many wealthy fools you can live off of. And then, self-contempt is unbearable.

I: Have you ever experienced the feeling!?

He: Have I! How many times I've said to myself: "Rameau, there are ten thousand well-served tables in Paris, each with fifteen or twenty place-settings, and out of all of them, not one for you. There are purses full of money, overflowing to right and left, but not one penny rolls your way! A thousand witlings—untalented, worthless; a thousand little unattractive creatures; a thousand mean little schemers are well dressed, and you have to go around practically naked! Are you that imbecilic? Can't you flatter the way others do? Can't you lie, swear, commit perjury, promise, keep your word or go back on it the way others do? Can't you encourage this young fellow to speak to Mademoiselle and persuade Mademoiselle to give him a hearing the way others do? Can't you make the daughter of one of our respectable townspeople understand that she dresses badly, that fine earrings, a little rouge, laces, a dress in the Polish mode would suit her to a T? That her dainty little feet are not made to walk the streets? That there is a handsome gentleman, young and rich, who wears a gold-braided outfit, has a superb coach and six tall lackeys, and who saw her as he passed by and found her ravishing, and hasn't been able to eat, drink or sleep since and will die as a result? 'But what will daddy say?' 'Ah yes, your daddy. At first he'll be a little upset.' 'And mummy, who always keeps telling me to be a good girl and says that honor is the most important thing in the world?' 'Old stuff that doesn't mean a thing.' 'And my confessor?' 'Just don't see him any more, or if you persist in the silly notion of going to him with the tale of your amusements, it will cost you at most a few pounds of sugar and coffee.' 'He's a very strict man who has already refused me absolution for singing the song, "Come into my cell. . . ."' 'That was because you had nothing for him . . . but when you show up in laces . . .' 'I'll have laces?' 'Of course, of every kind, fastened with fine diamond pins.' 'I'll have fine diamond pins?' 'Yes.' 'Like the ones the marquise has who comes into our shop sometimes to buy gloves?' 'Exactly. In a fine coach, with dapple-grey horses, two strapping lackeys, a little nigger, an advance courier, rouge, beauty-spots, a train that will have to be carried.' 'To a ball?' 'To the ball, the Opera, the comic theater . . .' Her heart is already beginning to go pit-a-pat with joy. You play around with a piece of paper that you're holding in your hand. 'What's that?' 'Oh, nothing.' 'Oh no, it's something.' 'A note.' 'Who for?' 'For you, if you really want to know.' 'But I'm dying to know. Let me see it.' She reads it. 'A meeting?—that just can't be.' 'On the way to mass.' 'Mummy is always with me; but maybe if he came here, rather early. I always get up first, and I'm behind the counter before anyone else gets up . . .' He comes; she likes him. One fine day, under cover of darkness, the young thing disappears, and I'm paid my two thousand pounds . . .

"You have that talent and you've no bread to eat? Aren't you ashamed of yourself, you poor fool? I thought of a host of rascals who couldn't even hold a candle to me for resourcefulness and who wallowed in wealth. I wore a coarse cloth coat; they were swathed in velvet. They leaned on gold-pommelled, crutch-handled walking-sticks and wore cameos of Aristotle and Plato on their fingers. And yet, who were they, really? Miserable hack musicians, for the most part. And today they are lords, of a sort."

That thought gave me courage, uplifted my soul, made me feel sharp-witted, equal to any situation. But this elation didn't last long, apparently.

Because, up to now, I haven't really got anywhere. Anyhow, that's the content of my frequent soliloquies. You can play any variations you like on the theme, provided that you manage to understand that I do know what self-contempt is—that torment of the soul that comes from not being able to cash in on the gifts that Providence has bestowed on us. It's the cruellest of all torments. A man might better never have been born.

I kept listening to him, and as he played the scene of the procurer and the young girl being seduced, torn between conflicting impulses, I didn't know whether I should give way to laughter or to my mounting indignation. I was in pain. On twenty different occasions, a burst of laughter kept me from venting my rage. Twenty times, the rage that welled up from the bottom of my heart ended in a burst of laughter. I was dumbfounded by so much wisdom and so much baseness; by ideas that were alternately so right and so wrong; by so complete a perversion of feeling, and by such complete turpitude and such uncommon frankness. He noticed the conflict that was going on inside of me.

"What's wrong?" he said to me.

I: Nothing.

He: You look upset to me.

I: Well, I am upset.

He: But what do you advise me to do, then?

I: To talk about something else. You poor wretch, how meanly you were born, and how low you have fallen!

He: I admit it. But don't let my state bother you too much. I didn't confide in you to make you feel uncomfortable. I managed to save up a little while I was staying at that last place. You mustn't forget that I didn't have to pay for a thing, not for a blessed thing. And they gave me quite a bit just for pocket money.

Then he started in again, knocking his forehead with his fists, biting his fists, biting his lip, and rolling his eyes wildly toward the ceiling, adding: "But it's all over now. I've put a little aside; time has gone by, and so there's at least that much gained."

I: You mean lost.

He: No, no. Gained. Every minute we grow richer: one day less to live means one more pound to spend; it's the same thing either way. The important thing is to go to the toilet every night unconstipated, free and easy, copiously. *O stercus pretiosum!* That's the great end of life at every level. In the end, everybody is as rich as everybody else. Samuel Bernard, who, by dint of thievery, pillage, and bankruptcies, leaves behind a fortune of twenty-seven million in gold, and Rameau, who won't leave anything at all —Rameau, who'll have to depend on charity for the piece of canvas he'll be shrouded in. The dead man doesn't hear the bells toll. A hundred priests can yell at the top of their voices for him, he can have a long line of burning torches fore and aft—it all won't do any good, because his soul doesn't walk alongside the master of ceremonies. Whether you rot under marble or under bare dirt, you still rot. What difference does it make whether you have a bunch of orphans in red and blue attending your casket or no one at all? Take a look at this wrist. It was stiff as the devil. And these ten fingers were so many rods stuck in a metacarpus hard as wood. And these tendons—they were old gut-strings, drier, stiffer, more brittle than the strings they use on a turner's wheel. But I've given them such a workout, I've worn them down and broken them in so much: "You don't want to perform, but, by God, I say you *will* perform, and you do."

And while saying all that, he took the fingers and wrist of his left hand in his right and bent them far back and forward. His fingertips touched his arm; his joints cracked; I was afraid his bones would be dislocated.

"Be careful," I said, "you're going to hurt yourself permanently."

He: Don't worry. They're used to it; I've given them a lot worse beating than that these last ten years. No matter how they resented it, they had to get used to it, had to learn how to get over the keys and flit around on the strings. And they're pretty good at it now. Really pretty good.

Right off, he assumes the stance of a violinist. He hums an allegro by Locatelli. His right arm imitates the motion of bowing, and his left hand and fingers seem to be sliding along the strings. If he plays out of tune, he stops, tightens or loosens the string, plucks it with his fingernail to see that it's in tune. He starts the piece over at the point where he left off. He beats time with his foot. His head, feet, hands, arms—his whole body is in wild motion, just as you've sometimes seen Ferrari or Chibran or some other virtuoso at the sacred music concerts go through similar contortions, presenting the same picture of torture, and causing me just about as much real pain. (For isn't it really a painful thing to see in torment a person who is supposed to be giving you pleasure? Draw a curtain between that man and me if he has to present the spectacle of a victim being questioned on the rack.) If, in the midst of his agitations and cries, he comes across a hold—one of those harmonious moments when the bow is drawn slowly across several strings at the same time—his face takes on an ecstatic expression; his voice softens; he shows signs of rapturous astonishment. There is no doubt that the chords are sounding in his ears and mine. Then, tucking his instrument back under his left arm with the same hand that held it, and letting his right hand fall, still holding the bow: "Well," he said, "what do you think of that?"

I: Marvelous.

He: It strikes me as all right. It sounds as good as most of the others.

And right off he crouches like a musician taking his seat at the keyboard.

"Please, leave off, both for your sake and mine," I said to him.

He: No, no. Since I've got you cornered, you'll have to listen to me. I won't accept any approval that's given without due cause. You'll praise me in a more convincing way, and maybe I'll get a pupil or two as a result.

I: But I don't get around much, and you'll wear yourself out for nothing.

He: I never wear myself out.

I saw that taking pity on the fellow was pointless; even though the violin sonata had put him in a sweat, I decided to let him do as he wanted. So there he was, seated at the harpsichord, with his legs bent and his head stretched towards the ceiling where you'd have thought he was reading a musical score, singing, warming up, then performing a piece by Alberti or Galuppi— I don't recall which. His voice was like the wind, and his fingers flew over the keys, now leaving the treble for the bass, now leaving off the accompaniment to play the melody. The various passions succeeded one another in his face. You could make out tenderness, anger, pleasure, pain; you could tell when he was playing the soft or the loud passages. And I'm positive that someone who knew a little more about it than I do would have recognized the piece by its movement and general character and by his grimaces and the bits of song that he would give out with from time to time. But what was really curious was the way he would now and again fumble around and begin over, as if he'd missed a passage and was annoyed with himself for not having the piece at his fingertips.

"Well, you can see," he said as he straightened up and wiped away the beads of sweat that rolled down his cheeks, "that we too know how to place a tritone or an augmented fifth, and that we know a thing or two about dominant progressions. Those enharmonic passages, that our dear uncle has made so much of, aren't such insurmountable obstacles. We manage to get around them."

I: You've gone to a lot of trouble to show me that you're very clever, but I was quite ready to take your word for that.

He: Very clever? Oh no! I know my business, and that's really more than I need to know. Because in this country, do you really have to know what you claim to be able to do?

I: No more than you have to know what you teach.

He: That's right, by God, very right! And on that score, Master Philosopher, cross your heart and hope to die: Wasn't there a time when you weren't as well heeled as you are now?

I: I'm still not very well heeled.

He: But you wouldn't go walking in the Luxembourg Gardens in summer . . . Do you remember?

I: Let's skip that. Yes, I remember.

He: In a waistcoat of grey plush . . .

I: Yes, yes.

He: Threadbare on one side, cuffs torn, black woolen stockings darned in the back with white thread.

I: All right, all right, if it makes you any happier.

He: What kind of figure did you cut in Lovers' Lane then?

I: A pretty sad one.

He: And when you came out of Lovers' Lane you shambled along the pavement.

I: Right.

He: You gave math lessons.

I: And without knowing a thing about math. Isn't that what you're trying to get at?

He: Exactly.

I: I learned by teaching others, and I turned out a few good pupils.

He: That's possible; but music isn't like algebra or geometry. Now that you're an important personage . . .

I: Not that important.

He: Now that you've made your little pile . . .

I: A very little pile.

He: You hire tutors for your daughter.

I: Not yet. Her mother takes care of her education for the moment. After all, you have to have a little peace in the house.

He: Peace in the house? Good God! You have peace in the house only when you're the servant or the master; and you'd better be the master. I used to have a wife, God rest her soul! But when she'd get a bit fussy on occasion, I'd rear up on my hind legs and let the thunder roll; I'd say, like God himself: "Let there be light." And there was light. And the result was that for four whole years we didn't squabble more than ten times or so. How old is your child?

I: That's irrelevant.

He: How old is your child?

I: Devil take you! Let my child and her age be, and get back to the tutors she's eventually going to have.

He: I swear to God that I don't know of anything as bull-headed as a philosopher. Begging most humbly of you, might one not be able to ascertain from Milord Philosopher what might be the approximate age of Mademoiselle His Daughter?

I: Well, let's say about eight.

He: Eight! She should have had her fingers on the keys for the last four years already.

I: But maybe I don't care too much about including in her educational program a pursuit that is so time-consuming and of so little use.

He: So what will you teach her, if you please?

I: To think straight, if I can—something very uncommon among men, and even rarer among women.

He: Let her be as scatterbrained as she likes, provided she's pretty, lively, and a good dresser.

I: Since Nature has been unkind enough to give her a very delicate constitution and a very sensitive soul, and at the same time exposes that constitution to the same hardships as if she had a heart of bronze, I shall teach her, if I am able, to face all these hardships courageously.

He: Eh! Let her cry, suffer, whimper, have nerves as jumpy as the next female, provided she is pretty, lively, and a good dresser. And no dancing lessons?

I: No more than will be necessary to teach her to curtsy gracefully, have good posture, come into a room with poise, and walk properly.

He: No voice lessons?

I: No more than will be necessary to give her good pronunciation.

He: No music lessons?

I: If I could find a good teacher of harmony, I'd have her take lessons from him two hours a day for a couple of years, but no more than that.

He: And in place of all the essentials that you are eliminating . . .

I: I put grammar, mythology, history, geography, a little drawing, a great deal of moral precept.

He: How easy it would be for me to prove to you the uselessness of all this knowledge in a society like ours. Did I say uselessness? I might better say dangerousness. But for the moment, I'll just put one question: She'll need one or two tutors, won't she?

I: Of course.

He: Ah, then there we are! And you really expect these teachers to know grammar, mythology, history, geography, morals enough to give her lessons in them? Stuff and nonsense, my dear Master, stuff and nonsense. If a teacher really knew enough to teach those subjects, he wouldn't be teaching them.

I: And why not?

He: Because he'd have spent his whole life learning them. You have to study an art or a science very thoroughly before you can even really grasp the fundamentals. Classical works can actually be turned out only by people who've been hitched to the wagon for a lifetime. The middle and the end finally dispel the darkness of the beginnings. Just ask your friend Monsieur d'Alembert, the leading mathematician of the day, whether he's not too far along to be bothered with fundamentals. It took my uncle thirty to forty years of constant hard work to see the first real glimmer of musical theory.

"You madman, you arch-madman," I shouted. "How does it come about that in your crazy head such sound ideas are mixed up, pell-mell, with so many extravagant ones?"

He: Who the devil is to say? Chance throws them together in one's head, and there they stay mixed up. Which means that if you don't know everything, you really don't know anything worth while. We don't know where this thing's headed for or where that one comes from, or where this and that should be pigeon-holed, or what to put in first place and what in second. Can anyone teach well without a method? And where does one come by a method? Look, Mister Philosopher, it strikes me that physics will always be a poor science, a drop of water picked up on the point of a needle out of the vast ocean, a pebble broken loose from the Alps. And the causes of things? In truth, we might as well know nothing at all as to know so little, and that so badly. And that was what I'd concluded when I decided to be a teacher of accompaniment and composition. What are you thinking?

I: I'm thinking that all you've just said is more specious than solid. But let's skip that. You've taught, you say, accompaniment and composition.

He: Yes.

I: And you don't know anything about either?

He: Not a thing, upon my faith. And that's why there were worse teachers than me—the ones who thought they really knew something. At least I didn't spoil the youngsters' mind and hands. When they went on from me to a good teacher, since they hadn't learned a thing, at least there was nothing they had to unlearn. And that always meant a saving in time and money.

I: How did you actually go about things?

He: The way they all go about them. I arrive, throw myself into a chair. "What foul weather! How tiring it is to walk!" I'd dish up a little gossip: "Mademoiselle Lemierre was supposed to play the role of a vestal virgin in the new opera, but she's pregnant for the second time. They don't know who will take her place. Mademoiselle Arnould just broke with her little count. They say she's negotiating with Bertin. The little count, nevertheless, found Montamy's porcelain. At the last amateur concert, there was a young Italian girl who sang like an angel. Préville really is a rare sort, you simply must see him in *Mercure galant;* the puzzle-scene is priceless. But Dumesnil, poor thing, just doesn't know what she's saying or doing any more. Come now, Mademoiselle, go find your music-book." And while Mademoiselle takes her time looking for her book, which she's misplaced, and while they call a maid and scold her, I go right on: "La Clairon is really beyond the pale. They're talking about an absolutely ridiculous marriage; Mademoiselle What's-her-name?—you know, a little thing whom he was keeping, and who had two or three children by him, and who had been kept by so many other men." "Come, come, Rameau, that can't be; you're talking nonsense." "I am not talking nonsense. They say the thing is even signed and sealed already. And the rumor's going around that Voltaire is dead—which is all to the good . . ." "Why all to the good?" "Because it means he's about to come up with another good one. He usually dies about two weeks before he pulls the thing off." And what else all? I'd peddle a bit of dirt that I'd picked up in the other houses where I'd been, because we're all great dirt-peddlers. I'd play the clown, and they'd listen to me and laugh and exclaim: "He's always so amusing." Meanwhile Mademoiselle's book has been found—under an armchair where it had been dragged, chewed up, and torn to bits by a young bulldog or kitten. She sits down at her keyboard, at first making a few noises on it all by herself, and then I'd approach, after I'd nodded approval to her mother.

Mother: "It isn't going too badly. If she'd just make a little effort, but she won't. It's much more fun to waste time chattering, primping up, running around and doing I-don't-know-what-all. No sooner have you gone than she closes the music-book, not to open it again until your next visit. And then, you never scold her."

Meanwhile, since you have to do something, I take her hands and place them in a different position. I make a fuss, shout: "G, g, g, Mademoiselle, it's a *g!*"

Mother: "My dear, don't you have ears? Even I, who can't play and can't see your music-book, even I can sense that it has to be a *g*. You're making things terribly difficult for Monsieur Rameau. I don't see how he manages to be so patient. You don't retain a thing he tells you; you're not making any headway at all . . ."

Then I'd soften the blows a little and, shaking my head, I'd say: "Excuse me, Madame, excuse me. Things could be going much better if Mademoiselle would just practice a little, but things aren't going too badly."

Mother: "If I were you, I'd keep her a whole year on the same piece."

"Oh, don't worry. She won't be given another one until she's overcome all the difficulties of this one. That won't take as long as you think, Madame."

Mother: "Monsieur Rameau, you're flattering her. You're too kind. What you've just said is the only thing in the whole lesson she'll remember, and she'll be sure to repeat it to me at the appropriate moment."

The hour goes by; my pupil pays me my little fee with the graceful arm-movement and curtsy that she learned from her dancing master. I'm putting it in my pocket while mother says: "Very nice, my dear, very nice. If Javillier were here, he'd compliment you." So I'd chatter a little while longer, for politeness' sake, and then dodge out. That's what they used to call a lesson in accompaniment.

I: And is it any different today?

He: Good Lord, yes! I arrive; I'm serious; I hurriedly pull off my muff. I open the harpsichord and try the keys. I'm always in a hurry. If I'm kept waiting one instant, I yell as if they were robbing me. An hour from now I must be some place else. In two hours I'm due at the duchess what's-her-name's. I'm expected to dine at the home of a beautiful marquise, and after that, it's a concert at the Baron de Bagge's place in the rue Neuve-des-Petits-Champs.

I: When, as a matter of fact, you're not expected anywhere?

He: Right.

I: But why stoop to all these vile little ruses?

He: Vile? And why "vile," if you please? They're the stock-in-trade of my calling. I'm not vile just because I do what everyone else does. I'm not the one who invented these things, and I'd be queer and clumsy if I didn't conform to the common practice. Really, I know perfectly well that, if you apply certain general principles to the situation—principles of I-don't-know-what moral code that everyone pays lip-service to without ever practicing—it'll turn out that white is black and black is white. But, Mister Philosopher, there is a universal morality just as there is a universal grammar. And then, in every language there are exceptions which you call, I believe, you scholars . . . which you call . . . uh . . . uh . . . Help me out!

I: Idioms.

He: That's it. Well, every calling has its exceptions to universal morality, to which I would give the name of "trade-idioms."

I: I see what you're getting at. Fontenelle speaks well and writes well, even though his style teems with French idioms.

He: And the sovereign, the minister of state, the financier, the judge, the military man, the man of letters, the lawyer, the attorney general, the trades-man, the banker, the craftsman, the singing teacher, the dancing master are all very respectable people, even though their conduct departs in several particulars from universal morality and abounds in moral idioms. And the older the profession, the more idioms there are in it. And the harder the times are, the more these idioms proliferate. A calling is as good as the man who practices it; and, reciprocally, at least, any man is as good as his calling. So everyone gets all he can out of his particular profession.

I: The one thing that emerges clearly from all this round-about talk is that few professions are honestly practiced, and that there are few honest persons in the various professions.

He: In fact, there aren't any. But on the other hand, there are very few cheats outside their own shop, and things would go pretty well if it weren't for a number of people who are called industrious, reliable, conscientious, scrupulous in doing their duty, strict. Or what amounts to the same thing— people who stay in their shop all the time, at their business from morning till night, and never do anything else. And of course, they're the only ones who get rich and enjoy a fine reputation.

I: By sheer dint of idioms.

He: Right. I see that you've understood me. Well then, an idiom that you'll find in almost all callings (for there are idioms common to all countries and ages, just as there are widely-shared misconceptions)—a widespread idiom, I say, is to have as many customers as possible. A widespread misconception is the belief that the most skilled person is the one who has the most customers. There you have two exceptions to the universal morality that you simply have to accept. You have to extend a kind of credit. It's nothing in itself, but it takes on value through public opinion. They used to say that "a good name is more precious than gold." Yet many a person with a good reputation never has gold. And I note that nowadays gold almost always assures a good name. As far as it's possible, one should have both the good reputation and the gold. That's my aim when I put on a front by using what you call "vile tricks" and "unworthy, petty ruses." I give my lesson as it should be given; I follow the universal rule. I make people believe that I have more lessons to given than there are hours in the day. That's the idiom.

I: And do you really give a good lesson?

He: Yes, not bad, pretty good. My dear uncle's "fundamental bass" has simplified everything. I really used to steal my pupils' money—yes, actually steal it. But now I earn my money, at least as much as the next music teacher does.

I: And did you steal your money without a twinge of conscience?

He: Absolutely without a twinge. They say that "when one thief robs another, the devil laughs." My pupils' parents were loaded with ill-gotten gain. They were courtiers, tax-collectors, wholesale merchants, bankers, businessmen. I was simply helping them to restore their gain to the original possessors. I, and a bunch of other people they also employed. In Nature, all species prey on one another. In society, all classes prey on one another. We even up scores without dragging in the Law. The Prince used to get revenge on his tax collector by keeping Deschamps, the ballerina. Today

La Guimard has taken her place. And then the dress-designer, the jeweler, the upholsterer, the seamstress, the sharper, the chambermaid, the cook, the harness-maker even up scores with La Deschamps for the tax-collector. In all of this, only the imbecile or the idler gets hurt without having stepped on anyone else's toes; they get what they deserve. From this you can infer that these exceptions to the general morality, these moral idioms that cause such a hue and cry when they're referred to as "pulling a fast one," are really nothing. All things considered, it just means that you have to have a quick eye.

I: I really admire your way of looking at things.

He: And then there's poverty. The voice of conscience and honor is very weak when your guts cry out. But just let me get rich once and I'll do a little restoring of my own, and I'm determined to make restitution in every possible way: by wining, dining, gaming, and wenching.

I: But I'm afraid you'll never get rich.

He: Well, I suspect you're right.

I: But if it did turn out otherwise, what would you do?

He: I'd do like all the other beggars on horseback. I'd be the most insolent bully you've ever seen. That's when I'd remember what I'd been made to suffer, and I'd pay back generously all the insults I had to endure at their hands. I like to order people around, and I'd order them around. I like to be praised, and people would praise me. I'd have the whole Vilmorien clan at my beck and call, and I'd say to them, just the way they've said to me: "Go ahead, you rabble, make me laugh." And they'd make me laugh. "Let's hear some dirt about all the respectable people." And they'd dish it up—if there are still any respectable people around. And we'd have whores and slap each other on the back when we got drunk; and we'd drink and make up tall tales; we'd indulge every kind of whim and vice. It would be delightful. We'd prove that Voltaire had no genius and that Buffon, the big stuffed shirt, is just a windbag; and that Montesquieu is merely a drawing-room wit; we'd relegate d'Alembert to his mathematics; and we'd hail blows on the backside and paunch of all the little Catos like yourself who disdain us out of envy and whose modesty is the cloak of overweening pride, and whose sobriety is dictated by want. And as for music—Gad, how we'd make it!

I: I can see by the good use you'd make of your wealth what a shame it is that the likes of you are beggars. You'd be living in a style that would do honor to the human race, be useful to your fellowmen, and bring you fame.

He: Why, I think you're trying to make fun of me. Mister Philosopher, you don't realize whom you've taken on. You don't even seem to suspect that at this moment I am representing the most important part of the Town and Royal Court. Our well-to-do citizens of every rank may or may not have told themselves what I've just imparted to you. But the fact remains that the life I'd lead if I were in their shoes is exactly the life they are leading. You fellows still think that the same kind of happiness suits everyone. What a strange misconception! Your kind of happiness presupposes a certain sentimental turn of mind, an unusual temperament, a special kind of taste that we don't have. You even embellish this quirk with the name of "virtue"; you call it philosophy. But do virtue and philosophy suit everyone? Virtue is for the fellow who can afford it and who can afford to hang on to it. Just imagine a wise and philosophical universe. You have to admit it would be a devil of a dreary place. Well, I say, long live philosophy—the wisdom of Solomon, that is: drinking good wines, gorging yourself on delicate dishes, laying pretty women, sleeping in downy beds. Except for that, all the rest is vanity.

I: What, even fighting for the fatherland?

He: Vanity! There's no fatherland any more; from pole to pole I see only tyrants and slaves.

I: Even helping one's friends?

He: Vanity! Does anyone really have friends? And even if you did have, would you risk making ingrates of them? Look at the thing carefully, and you'll see that's what you almost always get for being helpful. Gratitude is a burden, and burdens are made to be shaken off.

I: And having a responsible position in society and filling it conscientiously?

He: Vanity! What difference does it make what position you hold in society provided that you're rich, since that's the only reason you seek a position in the first place. Fulfilling your obligations—what does that get you? Jealousy, worries, persecution. Is that the way to get ahead? The way to get ahead is to pay court, by Gad! Pay court, know the right people, study their tastes, serve their whims, cater to their vices, approve their misdeeds—that's the secret of success.

I: And what about looking after the education of one's children?

He: Vanity! That's their tutor's business.

I: But if the tutor, imbued with your principles, neglects his job—who will pay the penalty?

He: Well, not I, anyhow. But someday, maybe, my daughter's husband or my son's wife.

I: But if both sink into debauchery and vice?

He: That goes with their social position.

I: Even if they disgrace themselves?

He: No matter what you do, you can't disgrace yourself when you're rich.

I: If they ruin themselves financially?

He: So much the worse for them.

I: But it seems to me that if you don't take the trouble to look after the behavior of your wife, your children, your servants, you are very apt to neglect your own financial affairs.

He: Hold on. It's sometimes hard to find money; so it's wise to take measures far in advance.

I: Then you wouldn't look after your wife much?

He: Not at all, if you please. The best policy where one's better half is concerned is to do what she wants you to. Do you really think society would be very amusing if everyone did just what he was supposed to?

I: Why not? My happiest evening always comes when I've spent the morning in a worthy manner.

He: I'm that way too.

I: What makes society people so demanding about their amusements is their extreme idleness.

He: Don't believe it; they're always on the go.

I: Since they never really get tired, they can never genuinely relax.

He: Don't believe it; they're constantly wearing themselves out.

I: Pleasure is their only concern; they never feel a real need.

He: So much the better for them. Need is always painful.

I: Everything goes stale on them. Their spirit becomes jaded; boredom grips them. A person who would deprive them of life in the midst of their staggering abundance would be doing them a good turn. For the only aspect of happiness they know is the one that is quickest to lose its zest. I don't disdain sensual pleasures. I too have a palate, and it's tickled by a delicate dish or a delicious wine. I have a heart and eyes, and I like to look at a pretty woman; I like to feel the firmness and roundness of her bosom under my hand and to press her lips to mine, to drink bliss from her glances and swoon in her arms from it. And on occasion, when I'm with friends, a bit of debauchery, even rather rowdy debauchery, doesn't displease me. But I won't conceal from you the fact that I get a lot more pleasure from helping out some unfortunate person, or smoothing over some unpleasant affair, or giving salutary advice, or reading a good book, or taking a stroll with a man or woman dear to my heart, or spending a few instructive hours with my children, or writing a good page, or discharging the duties of my profession, or saying to the woman I love tender, gentle things that make her throw her arms around my neck. I know of a certain deed that I'd give up all my possessions to have done. *Mahomet* is a sublime work, but I'd rather have rehabilitated the memory of the Calas family. A man I know took refuge in Cartagena. He was the youngest son of a family in a country where custom transmits all the worldly goods to the older sons. In Cartagena he learns that his older brother, a spoiled child, had ruined his over-indulgent father and mother, driven them out of their mansion and left the worthy old folks to languish in a small provincial town. So what does the younger son do—the one whom his parents had treated harshly and who has gone to seek his fortune in a foreign land? He sends help; he makes haste to put his affairs in order; he comes back rich; he restores his father and mother to their home; he finds husbands for his sisters. Ah, my dear Rameau, that man looks on those days as the happiest of his life. There were tears in his eyes when he told me about it. And I myself, as I tell you about it, feel my heart swell and my speech falter from pleasure.

He: You fellows really are queer ones!

I: You fellows are really to be pitied if you can't understand that it's possible to rise above one's fate and that it's impossible to be unhappy when you've done a couple of deeds as splendid as the two I just told you about.

He: That's a kind of happiness I'd have a hard time getting familiar with, because you don't run across it very often. But then, according to your way of thinking, we really ought to be decent people?

I: In order to be happy? Most assuredly.

He: And yet I see a lot of decent people who are not happy, and a lot of people who are happy without being decent.

I: That's only the way it looks to you.

He: And isn't it precisely because I showed a little common sense and frankness for once that I don't know where I'll find supper tonight?

I: Of course not. It's because you haven't been sensible and frank all along, because you didn't learn soon enough that the first thing a person has to do is find a livelihood that in no way depends on servitude.

He: Servitude or no, my source of livelihood is at least the one that's easiest to come by.

I: And also the least certain and respectable.

He: But the best adapted to my loutish, stupid, and generally worthless personality.

I: Granted.

He: Since I can manage to find happiness through vices that are natural to me, acquired without labor and retained without effort—vices condoned by custom and congenial to my protectors—vices that are closer to their own little private needs than any virtues would be, because virtues, like so many reproaches, would make them uncomfortable the livelong day—it would be very strange if I tormented myself like a soul in hell just to turn myself inside out and be something that I am not, to acquire a character other than my own, full of praiseworthy qualities, no doubt—I'll agree, just to avoid argument—but qualities that it would cost me dearly to come by and put to use, and that would get me nowhere. Or perhaps worse than nowhere, since I'd be a living satire of the rich circles in which beggars like myself have to seek their livelihood. People praise virtue but really hate it and flee it. Virtue is always out in the cold, and in this world you have to keep your feet warm. And inevitably, it would make me testy. Why do we so often find devout people so harsh, edgy, and unsociable? Why, because they're forcing themselves to do a task that doesn't come naturally. They suffer, and when a person suffers he makes others suffer. That's not for me, nor for my patrons. I have to be gay, easy-going, amusing, clownish, funny. Virtue inspires respect, and respect is uncomfortable. Virtue commands admiration, and having to admire someone is no fun. I have to deal with people who are bored, and I have to make them laugh. Well, nonsense and madcap pranks are what provoke laughter; so I have to be nonsensical and madcap. And even if Nature hadn't made me that way, the best thing I could do in that case would be to act as if I were. Fortunately, I don't have to be a hypocrite; there are already so many around of every stripe, not even counting the people who are hypocritical with themselves. The Chevalier de La Morlière, who pulls the brim of his hat down over one ear, walks with his nose in the air, looks disdainfully over his shoulder at every passerby, and has a long sword slapping against his thigh, who has a ready insult for anyone who doesn't carry a sword, and who seems to challenge everyone who comes along—what does he really do? He does everything he can to persuade himself that he is a stout fellow. But he's a coward. Tweak his nose, and he'll take it without a murmur. Do you want to take him down a peg? Just go up a peg or two yourself. Brandish your cane or apply your foot between his buttocks. Surprised at finding himself a coward, he'll ask who let you in on the secret and where you found it out. Just the moment before, he didn't realize it himself. Putting on the daredevil act so long and constantly finally got him. He'd gone through the outward motions so much that he finally believed he was the real thing.

And what about that woman who mortifies her flesh, visits prisons, attends all the charity gatherings, who walks with lowered eyes and wouldn't dare look a man straight in the face, and who is forever on guard against the temptation of the senses? Does all that keep her heart from burning, or her sighs from escaping, or her lust from kindling, or her desires from obsessing her, or her imagination from rehearsing night and day the scenes of *Le Portier des Chartrains* or Aretino's *Positions?* What finally happens to her? What does her chambermaid think when she has to get out of bed in her nightgown and fly to the rescue of her suffocating mistress? Justine, go back to bed; you're not the one she's calling for in her delirium.

And friend Rameau, if he should one day decide to spurn wealth, women, good cheer, and idleness, if he should decide to go in for the Spartan life, what would he be? A hypocrite. Rameau has to be what he is: a happy thief among well-heeled thieves, and not a flaunter of virtue or even a really virtuous man nibbling his dry crust alone or among beggars. To settle the matter once and for all, I want none of your kind of felicity or of the happiness that a few dreamers like yourself propose.

I: I see, my dear fellow, that you don't have any idea what I'm really talking about and that you're constitutionally incapable of ever understanding it.

He: So much the better, by God, so much the better. If I understood, it would probably be the death of me through hunger, boredom, and maybe even remorse.

I: Well, that being the case, the only piece of advice I can give you is to get back as quickly as possible into the household you so foolishly managed to get yourself thrown out of.

He: And do what you don't seem to disapprove in the literal sense and what rather disgusts me in the figurative?

I: That's my advice.

He: Apart from the metaphor, which I don't like right now but which I may not dislike a moment later—

I: What a queer business!

He: There's nothing queer about that. I'm quite willing to be abject, but not when I'm forced to be. I'm quite willing to climb down off my dignity . . . You're laughing?

I: Yes, your dignity makes me laugh.

He: Every man to his own dignity. I'm quite willing to forget mine, but at my pleasure and not at somebody else's orders. Shall people say: "Crawl!" and I be automatically obliged to crawl? That's the worm's mode of locomotion, and mine, too. We both do it, when we're left alone; but both of us rear up when our tail is stepped on. I've been stepped on, and now I'll rear up. And then, you really don't know what kind of a loony-bin the place is.

Imagine a gloomy, sullen individual plagued with vapors, wrapped in two or three thicknesses of dressing-gown, who is bored with himself and everybody else; who can hardly manage a smile even when you put your weight and wit through a hundred different contortions; who looks with a fishy eye at the hilarious grimacing of my face and the even more hilarious grimacing of my wit. For, just between us, that ugly Benedictine monk who's so well known for his grimacing is—his successes at the King's Court notwithstanding (and I say it without vaunting either him or myself)—just a wooden puppet in comparison to me. I goad myself on to the sublimest lunacy; but it's no use. Nothing does any good. Will he or won't he laugh? That's what I have to keep asking myself in the midst of my contortions. You can easily imagine how this uncertainty spoils talent. My hypochondriac, with his head stuck far into a night-cap that covers his eyes, looks like a motionless Buddhist priest with a string attached to his chin and running down below his armchair. You wait for the string to be pulled, but it's never pulled. Or if the jaw happens to be open just a little, it's only to let a few chilling words escape—words that make it clear you haven't even been noticed and that all your monkeyshines have been for naught. The words are the answer to a question you put to him some four days ago. Once they are spoken, the mastoid process relaxes and the jaw snaps to.

(Then he did a take-off on his man. He'd planted himself in a chair, with his head held rigid, hat pulled down to his eyes, eyes half-closed, arms dangling, as he moved his jaw up and down like an automaton, saying: "Yes, you're right, Mademoiselle. We'll have to be very cagey about it.")

Because he makes decisions; he's always making decisions, and without appeal, morning, noon, and night, at the dressing-table, at dinner, at the coffee-house, at the gaming table, at the theater, at supper, on going to bed, and, so Heaven help me, even when he's in his mistress's arms. I'm not within earshot of the decisions that he makes while in the latter posture, but I'm fed up with hearing all the others. Brooding, gloomy, and final as Destiny—that's the old man.

Opposite him is a prude who acts important and whom you could reluctantly call pretty because she still is, even though there are already a few scabs on her face here and there, and even though she's a runner-up to Madame Bouvillon when it comes to avoirdupois. I like pleasing plumpness, but too much is too much; and then, motion is so essential to matter! *Item:* she's meaner, prouder, and stupider than a goose. *Item:* she thinks she's witty. *Item:* you have to persuade her that she's wittier than anyone else. *Item:* she's completely ignorant, but passes judgment on everything. *Item:* you have to applaud her decisions with hands and feet, jump for joy, swoon with admiration: "How wonderful, how delicate, how cleverly put, how finely observed and exquisitely felt! How *do* you women do it? Without study, by sheer intuition, by unaided natural lights. It's simply miraculous. And yet people persist in saying that experience, study, reflection, and education have something to do with it!" And similar nonsense proffered with tears of joy. You have to bow ten times a day, one knee bent in front and the other dragging behind; arms outstretched to the goddess, you try to read her wishes in her eyes. You hang on every word, awaiting her command and executing it in a flash. Who could bring himself to play such a part but a poor wretch who finds in it, two or three times a week, the means of calming the tribulation of his intestines? And what are we to think of the others, such as Palissot, Fréron, the Poinsinets, Baculard—none of whom is penniless—who can't even plead the rumblings of a tortured stomach as an excuse for their baseness?

I: I'd never have dreamed you were so fastidious.

He: I'm not. At the outset I saw what the others did and followed their example, even improving on it a little, because I'm more unabashedly impudent, a better actor, more starved, and possessed of better lungs. I must be a direct descendant of Stentor.

And to give me some idea of the strength of his viscera, he began coughing with a violence that rattled the plate-glass windows of the coffee-house, and momentarily diverted the attention of the chess-players.

I: But what's the use of such a talent?

He: Can't you guess?

I: No. I'm a little slow-witted.

He: Just suppose that there's an argument going on and the victory is in doubt. I rise, and loosing my thunder, I say: "It's just as Mademoiselle says it is. That's what you call sizing up a situation. Our bright young whipper-snappers wouldn't come near it in a hundred tries. The way she puts it is sheer genius." Of course, you can't always approve in the same way; that would be monotonous; you'd be unconvincing, you'd become stale. Your only chance of avoiding that pitfall is to have a fertile wit. You have to know just when to strike a major and peremptory key and seize the opportunity and the moment. When, for example, there's a difference of opinion, when the dispute has reached its highest pitch of violence, when the disputants can't even hear each other any more and everyone talks at the same time—

why then you have to be waiting on the sidelines, in the corner of the room farthest from the field of battle. You set the stage for your explosion by preceding it with a long silence, and then you hurtle suddenly like an exploding bomb into the midst of the fray. No one has ever mastered that art as I have. But where I'm really extraordinary is in the opposite approach. I have simpering tones that I underscore with a smile, an infinite variety of facial expression to convey approval—nose, mouth, forehead, eyes: all come into play. I have a rolling hip-movement, a way of twisting my spine and of shrugging my shoulders or letting them sag, of spreading my fingers and inclining my head, of closing my eyes and being thunderstruck as if I had just heard an angelic and celestial voice. That's what you call real flattery. I don't know whether you fully appreciate the effectiveness of that last pose. I didn't invent it, but no one has surpassed me in striking it. Just watch, just watch.

I: You're right. It's matchless.

He: Is there any normally vain woman with brainpower enough to resist it?

I: No, I'll have to admit that you've pushed the art of making a fool of people, and of debasing yourself, as far as it can go.

He: Try as hard as they will, all of them, they'll never manage that. The best of them, Palissot, for example, will never be more than a rank amateur. But even if the part is amusing at first, even if you take a certain pleasure at inwardly laughing at the stupidity of those you take in, in the long run it loses its zest. After a certain number of discoveries, you're forced to repeat yourself. Wit and art have their limits. Only God or a few rare geniuses ever manage to keep coming up with something new. Bouret the tax-farmer may be one of them. I've heard things about him that impress me—me, of all people—as being sublime. The lap-dog trick, the *Guide to Happiness,* the torches along the road to Versailles are things that confound and humiliate me; they're enough to make me want to give up my calling.

I: What do you mean by the lap-dog trick?

He: Where have you been, anyway? Do you really mean that you don't know how this amazing fellow went about getting his little dog to dislike him and to transfer its affection to the Keeper of the Seals who'd taken a fancy to the animal?

I: I admit I don't know a thing about it.

He: Well, then. It's one of the rarest things ever thought up. All Europe marvelled at it, and there isn't a courtier it didn't make green with envy. You're not wholly stupid; tell me how you'd have gone about the thing in his place. Bear in mind that Bouret was loved by his dog, that the Keeper of the Seals's strange ministerial uniform frightened the little animal, and that Bouret had only a week's time to surmount these obstacles. You have to know all the conditions of the problem to appreciate the full beauty of the solution. Well, then?

I: Well, I'll have to confess that, in this kind of business, the simplest things would nonplus me.

He: Listen— (He said to me, tapping me on the shoulder, because he doesn't mind being familiar.) —listen and marvel. He has a mask made for himself that looks like the Keeper of the Seals. From one of the Keeper's valets he borrows the capacious magistrate's robe. He covers his face with the mask and puts on the robe. He calls his dog, pets it, gives it a biscuit; then suddenly, changing his get-up, he's no longer the Keeper of the Seals. He's Bouret who calls his dog and whips it. In less than two or three days of this routine, carried on from morning till night, the dog learns to run away from Bouret the tax-farmer and run after Bouret the Keeper of the Seals. But I'm far too generous; you're not one of the clan, and you don't deserve to be in on the miracles that take place almost under your nose.

I: But please tell me about the book and the torches anyhow.

He: No, no. The very paving-stones could tell you about them; instead, make the most of the circumstance that has brought us together; find out things that nobody but me knows.

I: You're right.

He: Just think, he borrowed the robe and the *wig*—I forgot about the wig —of the Keeper of the Seals! Had a mask made that looks like him! It's the mask that really takes my breath away. And so he's now the most highly respected of men, and a millionaire, to boot. There are holders of the Cross of Saint Louis for bravery who go without bread. So why do everything to be awarded the Cross when you only run the risk of doing youself in? Why not go after a position that presents no risks and never fails to be rewarding? That's what you call going places. But examples like Bouret are discouraging; they make you feel sorry for yourself, and you get to feeling low. The mask, the mask! I'd give up one of my fingers to have hit on the mask.

I: But with this passion for the finer things in life and this fertile imagination of yours, haven't you invented anything on your own?

He: Well, of course. For example, there's that twist of the torso to express admiration that I told you about. I regard that as my own discovery, though there are envious persons who might dispute my claim. I'll admit it was used before me; but who before me fully realized how convenient the posture is for laughing covertly at the impertinent fool you're pretending to admire? And then there are the hundred ways I know to begin seducing a young girl right alongside her mother without mama's suspecting a thing, or even by making her my unwitting accomplice. I'd hardly begun that career when I began to disdain all the usual crude ways of slipping a lovenote to a girl. Why, I've ten ways of getting them to beg me for it, and I do think I can say that among the ten, there are a few new ones. I'm especially good at encouraging a timid young fellow. I've helped some succeed who had neither wit nor good looks. If all this were a matter of written record, I think people would grant that I have a touch of genius.

I: You mean, would do you a strange kind of honor?

He: No doubt about it.

I: If I were you, I'd jot these things down on paper. It would be a pity if they were lost to posterity.

He: That's true; but you've no idea how little I care for method and pre-cept. The person who has to have an instruction-book will never go far. Geniuses read very little, experiment a great deal, and are self-made. Look at Caesar, Turenne, Vauban, the Marquise de Tencin, her brother the Cardi-nal, and his secretary, the Abbé Trublet. And Bouret? Who ever gave Bouret lessons? No one. It's Nature who teaches these men of distinction. Do you think he found the dog-and-mask routine written in some book?

I: But in your spare moments, when the acute ache of your empty stomach or the sluggishness of your over-filled stomach keeps you from sleeping . . .

He: I'll think about it. It's better to write about great feats than to ac-complish insignificant ones. For that's what uplifts the soul, fires the imagina-tion and sets it running wild; whereas it contracts when you have to tell the little Hus woman about the applause that the stupid public insists on shower-ing on that mincing little Dangeville hussy and her flat-footed acting. She walks about the stage almost bent double and has the affectation of con-stantly gazing into the eyes of her leading man while quietly stealing the scene—Dangeville, who actually thinks these grimaces are clever and her mincing little steps graceful. Or that hammy Clairon female, who is skinnier, more made-up, studied, and starched than you can say. The imbecilic audi-ence claps for them until it splits your ears, and doesn't even notice that we are a veritable bundle of delights. (It's true that the bundle is getting a little bulgy, but anyhow . . .) Or that we have the finest skin, the most soulful eyes, the prettiest little nose. (Not much passion, it's true; and a walk that isn't airy, but not nearly as lumbering as they say.) And when it comes to emoting, there isn't anyone we can't outdo.

I: How do you mean all this to be taken? As irony or truth?

He: The trouble is that this confounded emotion is entirely within; not a glimmer of it shines through. But take it from me, the little Hus woman has it. Or if she doesn't, it's very close to the real thing in any case. You should see, when we're in a fit of bad humor, how we upbraid the valets and slap the chambermaids and kick around the Keeper of the Petty Cash if they fail in the slightest to pay us due respect. She's a little devil, I tell you, with lots of feeling and style . . . Oh, ho! You can't tell what's what by this time, can you?

I: I confess I can't figure out whether you're talking seriously or being funny. I'm a forthright man, so be kind enough to deal more forthrightly with me, and leave your art out of it.

He: That's what we tell little Hus about Dangeville and Clairon, though I threw in a few words here and there that would give you a hint or two at what I was up to. I'm quite willing for you to take me for a scoundrel, but not for a fool. And only a fool or a man head over heels in love could seriously rattle off such a lot of stuff and nonsense.

I: But where do you get the nerve to say it all?

He: You don't come by it just like that. But little by little you get used to doing it. *Ingenii largitor venter.*

I: You must really be driven by a cruel hunger.

He: Possibly. Nevertheless, no matter how insolent this stuff may seem to you, I assure you that the people it's intended for are far more used to hearing it than we are to giving out with it.

I: Is there any one of them honest enough to agree with you?

He: What do you mean, "anyone"? Why, all of society feels and talks that way.

I: The people in your set who aren't great rascals must be great fools.

He: Fools, in that company? I swear there's only one: the fellow who wines and dines us for taking him in the way we do.

I: But how can a person let himself be taken in so grossly? After all, the superior talents of Dangeville and Clairon are common knowledge.

He: We gulp down the flattering lie, but drink a bitter truth sip by sip. And then, we put on such a sincere, such a heart-rending act.

I: Yet you must have broken the rules of your art at least once and inadvertently let slip a few of those offensive bitter truths. For, in spite of the wretched, abject, vile, and abominable role that you play, I believe that you're basically a very sensitive soul.

He: I? Not a bit of it. Devil take me if I really know what I am. In general, my wit is as sound as a bowling-ball and my mood as open as wickerwork. I'm never two-faced when there's anything to be gained by being honest; and never honest when there's anything to be gained by being two-faced. I say whatever comes into my head. If it happens to be sensible—fine. If it's silly, no one minds. I always say what I like. I've never in my life thought a thing over either before, while, or after I say it. And so I don't really offend anyone.

I: But it did happen in the case of those fine people you were living with and who where so good to you.

He: Well, what can you expect? Accidents will happen. It was one of those bad breaks that we all have at times. No one can be forever happy. I was too well off; it was too good to last. As you know, the company there was of the most numerous and select. A real school of civilized living, a revival of classical, old-time hospitality.

If a writer produces a flop, we come to the rescue. We had Palissot after his *Zarès*, Bret after *Le Faux Généreux*. We also go in for all the composers who never get performed, all the unread authors, all the actors and actresses that are hissed off the stage. In short, we're a bunch of poor, shameful wretches and dull parasites at whose head I have the honor of being—the brave leader of fainthearted troops. I'm the one who urges them to eat the first time they show up. I'm the one who asks for their glasses to be refilled. They're such timid souls. A few ragged young fellows, good-looking enough, but who don't know their way around at all; a real scoundrel or two to cajole the old man and put him off guard in order to glean the old lady's field once he's finished. We seem gay, but inside we're consumed by a foul humor and a fierce appetite. Wolves aren't more voracious nor tigers any crueller. We attack the food as wolves do when the ground has been snow-covered for a long time; and, like tigers, we rend everything that is successful. Sometimes the Bertin, Monsauge, and Vilmorien packs all join forces, and then there's really a fine din in the menagerie. You've never seen such a collection of sullen, snarling, evil-intentioned, enraged beasts. You hear nothing but the names of Buffon, Duclos, Montesquieu, Rousseau, Voltaire, d'Alembert, and Diderot; and Lord only knows what epithets are tacked on to each of them. No one must be deemed a man of parts unless he is as stupid as we are. That's where we thought up the *Philosophes* comedy. I'm the fellow who supplied the peddler scene, which I stole from *Distaff Theology*. You don't come off any better than the rest of them in it.

I: So much the better! Maybe they do me more honor than I deserve. I'd be very humiliated if people who malign able honest folk took it into their heads to speak well of me.

He: There are a lot of us, and each one has to make his contribution. After the sacrifice of the big game, we offer up the left-overs.

I: Insulting knowledge and virtue for a living! I'd say you pay dearly for your bread.

He: But I've already told you that we don't really count. We insult everyone and don't really hurt anyone. Sometimes we have with us that heavy-handed Abbé d'Olivet, fat Abbé LeBlanc, and that hypocrite Batteux. The fat abbé is really nasty only before dinner. Once he's had his coffee, he plumps himself into an armchair, puts his feet up on the mantelpiece, and goes to sleep like an old parrot on its perch. If the shouting gets too loud, he yawns, stretches his arms, rubs his eyes and says: "Well, what's up? what's up?" "We're trying to decide whether Piron has more wit than Voltaire." "Well, let's clear up one point. Are you really talking about wit? Don't you really mean taste? Because your Piron fellow hasn't the slightest idea what taste is." "Not the slightest idea?" "None whatever."

And so, off we go into a discussion of taste. At this point, the old man signals with his hand that he wants to be heard, because he particularly prides himself on having taste. "Taste," he says, "taste is . . ." Well, I don't know any more what he said it was. And neither does he.

Sometimes we have friend Robbé with us. He regales us with his cynical stories, with the miracles of the convulsionaries, which he's actually seen, with a few cantos of a poem of his on a subject he knows inside out. I hate his verse, but I like to hear him recite. He really throws a fit, and everybody around him shouts: "Now that's what you call a poet!" Just between you and me, his poetry is nothing but wild clatter, the original gibberish of the Tower of Babel.

Then we're joined on occasion by a certain simpleton who seems dull and stupid but who really is sharp as a demon and more mischievous than an old monkey. He has one of those faces that just seems to call for jokes and snubs but that God has created for the express purpose of teaching people not to judge by appearances. Their own mirror should already have taught them that it's just as easy to be a man of wit and look stupid as it is to hide a fool under a bright-looking exterior. To do in a good man just to amuse others is a common failing, and people always light on this particular fellow.

It's a trap we set for newcomers, and I have scarcely seen a single one who hasn't fallen right into it.

(At times I was really surprised at the justness of this madman's remarks on men and their humors, and I told him so.)

"Well," says he, "bad company is as much of an education as debauchery is. Loss of innocence is made up for by the loss of one's prejudices. In the company of really bad men, where vice is unashamedly flaunted, one learns how to recognize it. And then, I've done a little reading."

I: What have you read?

He: I have read, and continue to read and reread, Theophrastus, La Bruyère, and Molière.

I: Excellent books.

He: Even better than you think. But who really knows how to read them?

I: Everyone, to the extent that we're capable.

He: Almost no one. Could you tell me what people usually look for in these books?

I: Entertainment and instruction.

He: But what kind of instruction? That's the important point.

I: Knowledge of one's duties, love of virtue, hatred of vice.

He: Now, what I find in them is a manual of everything that one must do and of everything that one must not say. I say to myself: "Be as miserly as you like, but don't talk like a miser." When I read *Tartuffe,* I say to myself: "Be a hypocrite if you want to, but don't talk like a hypocrite. Hang on to vices that are profitable, but don't acquire the tone or appearances that go with them and that would make you look ridiculous." In order to avoid them, you have to know what they are. Well, these authors have portrayed them marvelously. I am myself; and I remain what I am; but I act and talk as one should. I'm not one to despise the moralists. There's a lot to be had from them, especially from those who show us morals in action. Vice offends men only now and then; but we take offense at the outward signs of vice from dawn to dusk. It's probably safer to be really insolent than to seem insolent. The genuinely insolent person insults you only now and then; but an insolent look insults you all the time. And don't think for a minute that I'm the only reader of my kind. My sole merit is that I have done systematically, out of clearsightedness and a reasonable and just view of things, what most other people do gropingly, by instinct. That's why their reading doesn't make them any better than me, and they remain ridiculous in spite of their efforts; whereas I'm ridiculous only when I want to be—in which case I surpass them all by far. Because the same skill that enables me to keep from being ridiculous on one occasion permits me on another to be ridiculous in a superior way. Then I recall everything that others have said, everything I've read, and I add to it my own contribution—which, in this case, is surprisingly rich.

I: You were wise to reveal all these mysteries to me, otherwise I might have thought you were contradicting yourself.

He: Not at all. Because, for every single time one must avoid being ridiculous, there are a hundred where you must be as ridiculous as possible. There's no better role around important people than the jester's role. For a long time there was an officially-appointed king's jester, but never has there been an official title like "The King's Wiseman." As for myself, I'm Bertin's jester, and the jester of a lot of other people—maybe yours, at the moment. Or maybe you're mine. Now the fellow who has a jester is not himself a wiseman. And if he's not a wiseman, he's a jester. And perhaps, if the fellow happened to be king, his jester's jester. Furthermore, remember that in an area as variable as morals, there is nothing that is absolutely, basically, generally true or false, unless it's the precept that one must be what self-interest requires: good or bad, wise or mad, dignified or ridiculous, respectable or vicious. If, by chance, virtue led to fortune, I'd have been virtuous or at least simulated virtue the way the next fellow does. But people want me to be ridiculous, so I act that way. As for my vices, Nature alone took care of them. Though when I say "vices," it's merely because I'm talking your language. For, if we really thrashed the thing out, it could well be that what you call vice, I call virtue, and vice-versa.

And then we have writers from the Opéra Comique, along with their actors and actresses, and even more often their managers, like Corby and Moette. All people of wealth and superior merit!

And I forgot the literary critics: The *Forerunner*, the *Little Announcements*, the *Literary Year*, the *Literary Observer*, the *Weekly Censor*, the whole gang of hack-reviewers.

I: The *Literary Year* and the *Literary Observer?* That can't be. They hate each other.

He: That's true. But all beggars get along when they line up for mess. That damned *Literary Observer!* The Devil take him—him and his sheet! It's that stingy, stinking, usurious dog of a petty priest who's the cause of my fall from grace. He hove into view yesterday for the first time. He arrived at the moment that flushes all of us out of our lairs: the dinner hour. When the weather's bad, happy is the fellow among us who has a few cents in his pocket! Sometimes one of us makes fun of a confrère in the morning for arriving covered with mud and drenched to the bone, only to go back to our lair that night in the same condition. One fellow, I forget which one, had a violent quarrel a few months ago with the Savoyard porter who had posted himself at our door. Debts were involved; the creditor wanted the debtor to pay up, and the debtor wasn't in funds.

Dinner is served; the abbé is given the place of honor at the head of the table. I come in and see him there. "Well, well, abbé," I say to him, "are you presiding? That's all right for today; but tomorrow, if you please, you'll move down a place-setting, and the day after tomorrow, still one more. And so from plate to plate, either to the left or the right, until, from the place that I once occupied before you (and Fréron once after me, and Dorat once after Fréron, and Palissot once after Dorat), you will become a stationary fixture next to me, another poor insignificant bugger like you, *qui siedo sempre come un maestoso cazzo fra duoi coglioni.* The abbé, who's good-natured and doesn't take offense at things, began to laugh. Mademoiselle, struck by the justness of my observation and the accuracy of my comparison, began to laugh. All those seated to the right and left of the abbé, and whom he'd forced to move down a notch, began to laugh. Everybody laughs except the old man, who gets angry and says a few things that would have been of no consequence had we been alone:

"Rameau, you're an impertinent scoundrel."

"Yes, I know. That's the footing on which I was admitted here."

"A rascal."

"Like other rascals."

"A beggar."

"Would I be here if I were anything else?"

"I'll have you thrown out."

"After dinner I'll go of my own accord."

"You'd better."

We dined. I didn't miss a bite. After I'd eaten and drunk my fill—for, after all, no matter what the circumstances, Sir Belly is a person I've always accommodated with good grace—I made up my mind and got ready to leave. I'd given my word in the presence of so many people that I couldn't go back on it. I took quite a bit of time poking around the apartment, looking for my cane and hat where I knew they weren't, figuring that the old man would again break out in a torrent of abuse, that someone would intercede for me, and that we'd finish by patching things up when we'd argued ourselves out. I kept circling around, since nothing was really eating me; but the old man, gloomier than Homer's Apollo when he let his arrows fly on the Greek army, and with his nightcap pulled down on his brow even lower than usual, kept pacing back and forth with his fist under his chin. Mademoiselle comes up to me: "But Mademoiselle, what is so out of the ordinary? Have I been any different today from what I usually am?"

"I want him to clear out."

"I'm clearing out, but I haven't been disrespectful."

"I beg your pardon! We invite Monsieur l'Abbé, and . . ."

"He's the one at fault, because he invited the abbé and me and all the rest of the ne'er-do-wells along with me."

"Come, Monsieur Rameau, you have only to ask the abbé's pardon."

"I'll have none of his pardon . . ."

"Come, come. All this will blow over."

She takes me by the hand, leads me to the abbé's armchair. I stretch out my arms; I look at the abbé with a certain astonishment—for who ever begged an abbé's pardon?

"Abbé," I say, "abbé, this is all pretty ridiculous, isn't it?"

And then I burst out laughing, and so does the abbé. So everything was set right, at least in that quarter; but I had to deal with the old man too, and what I had to say to him was a horse of another color. I can't remember just how I phrased my excuse.

"Sir, behold a madman . . ."

"I've put up with him too long; I don't want to hear another word about him."

"He's very sorry about the whole business . . ."

"Yes, I'm very sorry . . ."

"It won't happen again . . ."

"Until the next scoundrel comes along . . ."

I don't know whether he was having one of his bad days when Mademoiselle is afraid to approach him and can't even touch him with kid gloves, or whether he didn't hear what I was saying very well, or whether I didn't speak clearly; anyhow, things were worse than ever. Devil take him! Doesn't he know me for what I am? Doesn't he realize that I'm like a child and that there are times when I can't hold in any longer? And I really believe, so help me God, that I wouldn't have a moment's peace. Even a steel puppet would wear out if its strings were pulled from morning to night and night to morning. I have to dispel their boredom—that's the condition laid down. But once in a while I have to have a little fun of my own. In the midst of this mess, I was suddenly struck by a thought that made me overweeningly arrogant, really proud and insolent: it was that they couldn't get along without me, that I was an indispensable man.

I: Yes, I suppose they do really need you, but you need them even more. You won't find as good a house as that at just a moment's notice. But if they're short one jester, they can easily find a hundred others.

He: A hundred others like me! No, Mister Philosopher, they're not that plentiful. Dull jokesters, yes. But people are much harder to please when it comes to nonsense than when it's a matter of talent or virtue. I'm a rare specimen, yes, very rare. Now that they don't have me around any more, what do they do? They're absolutely hangdog. I'm an inexhaustible bag of nonsense. For every moment I had a joke that made them laugh till the tears came to their eyes. I was a one-man crazy-house to them.

I: And that got you bed and board, waistcoat, vest and breeches, shoes, and pocket money.

He: That was the plus side, the profit; but you didn't mention the minus side. To begin with, if there was talk of a new play, no matter what the weather, I had to ferret around in all the attics of Paris until I found its author, manage to read the thing somehow, adroitly hint that there was a part in it that was just cut out for someone of my acquaintance:

"And who might that be, if you please?"

"Who, indeed! The very embodiment of all grace, charm, and delicacy."

"You mean Mademoiselle Dangeville? Do you happen to know her?"

"Yes, slightly, but she's not the one I mean."

I'd whisper her name.

"You don't mean . . .?"

"Yes, her," I'd echo, blushing a little, because I sometimes do feel a twinge of decency. And when the name is repeated, you should see the long face the playwright pulls—that is, when he doesn't laugh right in my face. But no matter how he felt about it, I *had* to get my man to that dinner. He's afraid to commit himself, keeps making excuses and thanking me effusively. You should have seen how I was treated when I didn't succeed in my mission. I was a lout, a fool, a bungler. I was good for nothing, not even worth the glass of water they let me have. It was even worse when the play was put on and I had to brave the hoots and catcalls of a public which, in spite of everything they say about it, is a pretty good judge. I had to be a one-man claque, with everybody staring at me, so that sometimes the catcalls were diverted from the actress to me. And someone next to you whispers: "He's a valet in disguise, a servant of the fellow she's sleeping with. When will the bastard stop that racket?" People can't imagine what might bring a man to do this. They mistake it for ineptness, when it's done for the best reason in the world.

I: Even to the point of breaking laws?

He: Finally, though, they got to know me, and they'd say: "Oh, it's just Rameau." To make up for the ridiculous plight of applauding all alone, all I could do was drop a few ironic comments, which everyone misinterpreted. You'll have to admit that a man must be really determined, to brave the assembled public that way. And admit, too, that each miserable job was worth more than a measly écu.

I: Why didn't you get someone to help along?

He: I would, now and then, and I'd make a little from it. Before going into the torture-chamber you had to load your memory with the purple passages that you were supposed to get applauded. When I'd happen to forget them and get mixed up, I'd tremble with fear when I got back to the house. There'd be a hue and cry such as you can't imagine. And then, at the house there was a pack of hounds I had to look after. It's true I was fool enough to bring that on myself by first offering to do it. And there was a bunch of cats I had to care for, too. I considered myself lucky when Micou would do no more than favor me with a swipe of the paw that would rip open my sleeve or my hand. Criquette is subject to colics; I'm the one who has to rub her belly. And then, Mademoiselle used to have vapors, but now it's nerves— not to mention the other slight indispositions that no one ever bothered to conceal from me. But as far as that's concerned, let it pass. I was never one to stand on ceremony. I once read—I can't remember where—that a prince who was referred to as "The Great . . ." would sometimes lean on the back of his mistress's toilet-chair when she was on it. Familiarity breeds contempt, and on those occasions they were more familiar with me than anyone else. Well, I'm all for familiarity and casualness. I'd preach them by setting the example, without anyone ever objecting. They just let me do as I liked.

Well, I've sketched in the old man for you. Mademoiselle is beginning to put on weight. You should hear the stories they made out of that.

I: You didn't join in, I hope?

He: Why not?

I: Well, it's unbecoming, to say the least, to make fun of your benefactors.

He: But isn't it even worse to use the benefits you bestow as an excuse to debase your protégé?

I: But if the protégé weren't vile to begin with, nothing would lead his protector to act that way.

He: But if these people weren't really ridiculous themselves, they wouldn't be a natural subject for malicious tales. And then, is it my fault that they're getting more and more vulgar? Is it my fault, once they've gone bad, that they're taken advantage of and scoffed at? A fellow who decides to hobnob with people like us, if he has any common sense at all, has to expect every conceivable kind of treachery. When they invite us in, don't they know us for what we are?—that is, for self-seeking, vile, and treacherous souls? Since they know what we are, they can't complain. There's a sort of tacit agreement that they'll give us a handout, and that, sooner or later, we'll bite the hand that feeds us. Isn't that the kind of agreement that exists between a man and his pet monkey or his parrot? Brun protests loudly because Palissot, his guest and friend, has made up comic verses about him. Palissot had to write those verses, and Brun is in the wrong. Poinsinet protests loudly because Palissot attributes to him the verses that Palissot himself wrote against Brun. Palissot had to say that Poinsinet is responsible for the verses that he himself wrote against Brun, and Poinsinet is the one who's in the wrong. Little Abbé Rey protests loudly because Palissot has stolen his mistress, to whom the abbé himself had introduced Palissot. Well, he should never have introduced Palissot to his mistress in the first place, or else he should have been resigned to losing her right from the start. Palissot did his duty, and Abbé Rey is in the wrong. David the bookseller protests loudly because his partner, Palissot, has slept or tried to sleep with his wife. The bookseller's wife protests because Palissot has let anyone who wants to listen believe that he *had* slept with her. (Whether Palissot did or did not sleep with the bookseller's wife is hard to say, because the wife would have had to deny what might actually have happened, and Palissot may very well have let people believe what didn't happen at all.) However that may be, Palissot played his part properly, and David and his wife are in the wrong. Helvétius may protest loudly because Palissot lampoons him in a play as a dishonest person, though he still owes Helvétius money lent to him for medical expenses and for food and clothing. But did Helvétius have any business expecting any other kind of treatment from a man who is already besmirched with every kind of infamy, who—just to kill time—gets a friend to abjure his religion, cheats his business associates, and himself knows neither faith nor law nor decent feeling, who hunts fortune *per fas et nefas*, who remembers each day in terms of the villainies he committed on it, and who has even depicted himself on the stage as the most dangerous rotter—a piece of effrontery, I believe, without example and not likely to be equalled in the near future—? No, it's not Palissot, but Helvétius who is in the wrong. If you take a youngster from the provinces to the zoo at Versailles and he foolishly takes it into his head to put his hand in between the bars of the tiger's or panther's cage, and if the kid leaves his arm behind in the wild animal's maw, who's in the wrong? All this is written down in the tacit agreement. It's just too bad for the man who hasn't studied it or forgets it. How many people there are that I could exonerate on the basis of this universal and sacred compact! People who are accused of wickedness, when it's the others who should be accused of stupidity!

Yes, my fat countess, you're the one who is wrong when you gather around you people who are known in your circle as "trash." You're in the wrong when this trash plays dirty tricks on you or gets you to play them on others and then turns respectable people against you. Respectable people do what they must, and so does the trash. And you're the one who is in the wrong to take them in in the first place. If Bertinhus lived quietly and peacefully with his mistress, if he and she had, by their dignified behavior, acquired a few respectable friends; if they had gathered about them men of talent and people known to society for their virtue; and if they had reserved their leisure hours—those hours stolen from the pleasure of being together, loving each other and telling each other so in quiet retreat—do you think anyone would have made them the subject of either good or bad stories? But what did they get? Just what they deserved. They've been punished for their imprudence; and we're the ones that Providence since time immemorial has predestined to even up scores with all the Bertins of the moment. And it's the likes of us among our descendants that Providence has predestined to even up scores with the Monsauges and Bertins of the future. But while we carry out these just decrees against stupidity, you who depict us as we really are, you are executing the just decrees of Providence against us. What would you think of us if we, with our shameful ways, sought to acquire public esteem? You'd think we were out of our heads. And those who expect honest dealings from people who are born vicious and have a vile and base character, are they sensible? Everything in the world gets what's coming to it. There are two attorneys general: the one is at your door and punishes offenses against society; the other one is Nature. It takes care of all the vices that escape the law. If you give yourself over to debauchery with women, you'll become dropsical; go in for fast living, and you'll be consumptive; open your door to riffraff and live with them, and you'll be betrayed, jeered at, and despised. The simplest thing to do is to concede the correctness of these judgments and say to yourself: "That's as it should be." Take yourself by the scruff of the neck and reform, or stay what you are, but under the stipulations prescribed by the compact.

I: You're right.

He: And as far as that goes, I myself don't make up evil gossip; I'm content just to peddle what I hear. They say that, a few days ago around five in the morning, a terrible ruckus broke out; all the bells in the house rang furiously, mingled with the interrupted and muffled cries of a man who was suffocating: "Help, help, I'm suffocating! I'm dying!" The cries came from the old man's rooms. Everyone comes running to the rescue. Our great fat creature, who had lost her head, didn't know what she was doing and couldn't see what she was doing—as is usually the case at that moment—and she kept speeding up her movements, raised herself up on two hands as high as she could and came down on the old man's delicate parts with a weight of two or three hundred pounds, with all the momentum imparted by the fury of desire. They had a terrible time prying him loose. But what the devil was the idea of putting such a little hammer under such a heavy anvil anyway?

I: You've a dirty mind. Let's talk about something else. I've had a question on the tip of my tongue ever since we started to chat.

He: Why did you keep it waiting there so long?

I: Well, I was afraid it might be indiscreet.

He: After all I've told you, I can't conceive what I'd want to hide from you.

I: You are in no doubt as to my opinion of your character?

He: None at all. In your eyes I'm a very abject and contemptible creature, and sometimes I'm that way in my own eyes, but not very often. I congratulate myself on my vices more often than I blame myself for them. Your contempt is much more unrelenting.

I: That's true. But why do you reveal the full extent of your turpitude to me?

He: First, because a good part of it is already known to you; and second, because I saw there was more to be gained than lost by admitting the rest.

I: Now I ask you, how can that be?

He: If there's one sphere in which it's indispensable to be sublime, it's in the sphere of evil-doing. We spit on a petty pickpocket, but we can't deny a certain esteem to a great criminal. We're amazed by his courage and awe-struck by his ferocity. People admire consistency of character in any field.

I: But you yourself don't yet have this fine consistency of character. Now and again I find you vacillating in your principles. I can't decide whether your meanness comes naturally or is acquired by study, or even whether you achieved anything through such study.

He: I grant you that; but I've done my best. Haven't I had the modesty to point out examples far more perfect than myself? Didn't I tell you about Bouret with the sincerest ring of admiration? Bouret is the greatest man on earth, to my way of thinking.

I: And you come right after Bouret?

He: No.

I: Who then? Palissot?

He: Yes, Palissot; but not just Palissot.

I: And who would be worthy of sharing second place with him?

He: The Renegade of Avignon.

I: I've never heard of the Renegade of Avignon. He must be quite a remarkable fellow.

He: He certainly is.

I: The lives of great men have always interested me.

He: I should hope so. This particular one lived in the home of a good and honest member of the tribe of Abraham, that father of all True Believers, whose offspring were to equal the stars in number.

I: A Jew?

He: A Jew. The fellow first managed to arouse the Jew's pity, then his good will, and finally he won his complete confidence. For that's the way it always goes: We count so heavily on the benefits we bestow on others that we hardly ever hide our secrets from such people. How do you expect to get rid of ingrates when we expose men to the temptation of being ungrateful with impunity? This sound reflection our Jew failed to make. So he confided to the Renegade that, in good conscience, he couldn't eat pork. You'll see how completely a fertile mind was able to exploit this avowal. For a few months our Renegade grew more and more attached to his host. When he felt sure that he had completely won over the Jew's affections and, through his obligingness, convinced the Jew that he didn't have a better friend among all the tribes of Israel . . . Just think of the man's extraordinary circumspection! He doesn't rush things; he lets the pear ripen before he shakes the branch. Too much eagerness would have spoiled his plan. Greatness of character, you see, is usually the result of a natural state of equilibrium between several conflicting qualities.

I: Please, spare me your reflections and get on with your story.

He: Impossible. There are days when I can't help being reflective. It's a malady that you have to let run its course. Where was I?

I: At the close friendship between the Jew and the Renegade.

He: Ah yes, the pear was finally ripe . . . But you're not listening. What's struck you?

I: I was struck by the contrasts in your way of talking. Sometimes it's elevated, sometimes vulgar.

He: Can a fellow who exploits his vices always talk the same way? . . . One night he comes home to his good friend. He looks aghast; he stammers haltingly; his face is as pale as death; he trembles all over.

"What's wrong?"

"We're ruined."

"Ruined? How's that?"

"Ruined, hoplessly ruined, I tell you!"

"Explain yourself . . ."

"Just a minute; let me get hold of myself."

"That's right, do calm down," says the Jew, instead of saying: "You're a barefaced blackguard; I don't know what you're going to tell me, but I do know you're a barefaced blackguard. Your fright is just an act you're putting on."

I: And why should he have talked that way?

He: Because the Renegade was lying in his teeth and overplaying the act. It's perfectly clear to me. And don't keep interrupting me.

"We're ruined, hopelessly ruined!" Can't you sense how bogus that repeated *ruined* is?

"A stool-pigeon has betrayed us to the Holy Inquisition—you as a Jew, me as a renegade, a vile renegade." Note how the traitor doesn't blush at using the foulest terms. It takes more courage than you think to call yourself a name like that. You have no idea what it takes to achieve that.

I: No, I certainly don't. But what about this vile Renegade?

He: A damn liar, but very clever in his lying. The Jew is beside himself with fright. He plucks his beard; he rolls on the floor; he sees the Inquisition agents at his door; he already pictures himself decked out in the sanbenito. He sees his *auto-da-fe* being readied. "My dear, dear friend, my only friend, what's to be done?"

"What to do? Why, show ourselves everywhere, act as if we lived in the greatest security, behave as usual. The court procedure is secret but slow. You must take advantage of the delays to sell everything you own. I'll go charter a ship, or have it chartered by a third party. Yes, by a third party— that will be better. We'll put your money aboard, because that's what they're really after, and then together we'll sail, you and I, to other climes, to seek the freedom of worshipping our God, and observing the law of Abraham and our conscience in peace. The main thing in the perilous circumstances we're in is not to do anything rash."

No sooner said than done. The boat is chartered, stocked with provisions, manned. The Jew's fortune is put aboard. The next day at early dawn, they'll set sail. They sup gaily and sleep soundly. Tomorrow they will be out of reach of their persecutors. During the night the Renegade gets up, steals the Jew's wallet, purse, and jewels, boards the ship, and off he sails. You think that's the whole story? Well, you're way off. When I was told this story, I managed to guess what was coming—the part I haven't yet told you, just to see how sharp you really are. It's good you decided to be an honest man, because you'd have been a pretty sad scoundrel. Up to this point, the Renegade isn't much more than that: a contemptible rascal that no one would want to emulate. The sheer genius of his evil-doing resides in the fact that he himself was the stool-pigeon who turned in his good Israelite friend, who was seized by the Holy Inquisition on waking up and who made a fine bonfire for them a few days later. And that's how the Renegade came to enjoy, with utmost security, the fortune of that accursed descendant of those who crucified Our Lord.

I: It's hard to say which revolts me more, the dastardliness of your renegade or the way you tell about him.

He: But that's just what I was saying: the atrociousness of the deed carries you beyond contempt. That's why I'm being perfectly honest with you. I wanted you to know the full extent of my artistic achievements, to wring from you the admission that at least I was original in my vileness. I wanted you to rank me in your mind with the truly great scoundrels. I could shout: "*Vivat Mascarillus, fourbum Imperator!*" Come now, be gay, Mister Philosopher. All together: "*Vivat Mascarillus, fourbum Imperator!*"

And thereupon he begins to sing a truly remarkable song in fugal form. Now the melody was grave and majestic, now light and frolicking. One minute he imitated the bass, the next minute it was the treble parts. With his arm and outstretched neck he indicated to me the places where there were holds. He composed and performed a song of triumph in his own honor, demonstrating clearly that he knew more about good music than about good morals.

I hardly knew whether I should stay or run off, laugh or express indignation. I stayed, hoping to turn the conversation to a subject that would dispel the horror that filled my soul. It was becoming almost unbearable to put up with the presence of a man who discussed a horrible deed, a heinous crime, in the same way a connoisseur of painting or poetry examines the beauties of a work of art, or the way a moralist or historian points out and brings to light all the aspects of a heroic deed. I felt gloom settling over me in spite of my effort to shake it off. He noticed this and said:

He: What's wrong? Do you feel sick?

I: A little. But it will pass.

He: You have the worried look of a man plagued by dark thoughts.

I: That's just it.

After a few moments during which neither of us spoke, though he walked up and down, whistling and singing, I said to him, in the hope of getting him back on the subject of his talent: "What are you doing in music these days?"

He: Nothing.

I: Sounds tiring.

He: I was pretty stupid right from the start. I went to hear the music of Duni and the rest of our young composers, and that did it.

I: So you like this new style of music?

He: Certainly do.

I: And you find beauty in these new-fangled songs?

He: Do I find beauty in them? Good God! I should say I do. How well it's all declaimed. How true it rings! What expression!

I: Every imitative art finds its model in nature. What's the musician's model when he composes a melody?

He: Why not go one step farther and ask: "What is melody?"

I: I admit that the question is beyond me. We're all alike. All we remember is words that we think we understand through frequent—and even correct—use. But we have only vague notions in our head. When I say the word *melody*, I have no clearer idea about it than you and your cronies when you say *reputation, blame, honor, vice, virtue, modesty, respectability, shame, ridicule.*

He: Melody is an imitation, either vocal or instrumental, using the sounds of a scale invented by art or inspired by nature, as you prefer—an imitation of physical noises or the accents of passion. You can see that, by changing a term here and there, this definition would exactly fit painting, eloquence, sculpture, or poetry. Now, to come back to your question— what is the model of the musician or of his melody? It's declamation, if the model is alive and a thinking being; it's noise, if the model is inanimate. You have to consider declamation as a line and melody as another line that weaves in and around it. The firmer and truer the declamation (which guides the melody) is, the more will the melody fitted to it intersect it at many points. The truer the melody, the more beautiful it will be. And that's what our young musicians have so thoroughly grasped. When you hear the song, "I'm a Poor Devil," you really think you're hearing a miser's complaint. If he didn't sing, he'd use the same tones when he talks to the ground where he buries his gold, saying: "O earth, receive my treasure." And the little girl who feels her heart palpitate, who blushes, who gets confused and begs monsieur to let her go, would she express herself in any other way? There are characters of every sort in these compositions, an infinite variety of declamation. I'm here to tell you, it's sublime. Go, just go and hear the piece where the young man who feels close to death cries out: "My heart expires!" Listen to the singing, listen to the orchestra, and then tell me what difference there is between the real accents of a dying man and the turn of the song. You'll see how the melodic line coincides exactly with the spoken word. I'm not talking about rhythm, which is another determining factor in melody. I'm talking only about expressiveness. There's nothing more self-evident than the phrase I read somewhere: *Musices seminarium accentus;* that is: "Accent is the breeding ground of melody." From this you see how difficult and important it is to know how to handle a good recitative. There is no beautiful air out of which you can't make a good recitative, and no beautiful recitative that won't provide a good composer with a fine air. I won't go so far as to say that the person who recites well will sing well; but I'd be surprised if the person who sings well didn't know how to recite well. And take my word for everything I've been telling you, because it's all true.

I: I'd like nothing better than to believe you, if it weren't for a small difficulty that prevents me.

He: What difficulty is that?

I: Only this: If the music you talk about is sublime, the divine Lulli's, Campra's, Destouches's, de Mouret's—and even, just between you and me, your dear uncle's—must be rather flat.

He: (Coming close to my ear.) I wouldn't want to be overheard, because there are a lot of people hereabouts who know me, but, as a matter of fact, it *is* flat. It's not that I give a rap about dear uncle, since you make him *dear*. He's a heart of stone. If he saw my tongue hanging out a foot long, he wouldn't give me a glass of water. But try as he will, with his octave and his seventh—ho, ho, heh, heh, tu, tu, tu turelututu—with a devil of an uproar, the people who are beginning to catch on and no longer take racket for music will never take to that. There ought to be a police ordinance prohibiting anyone of any quality or rank whatsoever from having Pergolesi's *Stabat* performed. That *Stabat* ought to have been burned by the public executioner. I swear, these damned Italian buffoons, with their *Serva padrona*, their *Tracollo*, have certainly straightened our backs by giving us a real kick in the ass. In the old days, a *Tancrède*, an *Issé*, a *Europe galante*, the *Indies* and *Castor*, the *Talents lyriques* would run for four, five, six months, and there was no end to the performances of *Armide*. But today they all fall flat, like a row of dominoes. And Rebel and Francoeur, the Opera directors, are yelling bloody murder. They say all is lost, that they're ruined, and that if we allow these riff-raff carnival musicians to go on, our national music will go to the devil and the Opera

—the Royal Dead End Academy—may just as well close up shop. And there's a modicum of truth in it. The old stuffed shirts that have been going there every Friday for nigh on thirty or forty years, instead of having a good time the way they used to, are bored and keep yawning without knowing exactly why. They ask themselves why but can't find the answer. Why don't they ask me? Duni's prophecy will come true, and at the rate things are going, I'm a dead duck if, four or five years after the *Painter in Love with his Model*, there's even so much as an alley-cat left in the famous Dead End Street where our Academy is. Ah, the simple souls! They've given up their own French symphonies to play Italian ones. They thought their ears could get used to this new instrumental music without their taste in vocal music being affected—as if instrumental music weren't in the same relation to song (except for the greater freedom afforded by instruments and the mobility of the fingers) as song is to oral declamation. As if the violin didn't ape the singer, who in his turn will ape the violin when vocal acrobatics finally replace real beauty. The first musician to play Locatelli was the apostle of the new music. And now others will have their turn. We'll get accustomed to the imitation of the accents of passion or natural phenomena, by song and voice, by instruments, because that's really the whole object of music. And will we still go on liking flights and sallies, glories, triumphs, and victories? I should live to see the day! They somehow imagined that they'd still be admirers of *Ragonde* and *Platée* after they had wept and laughed at real tragic or comic scenes set to music, after their ears had heard the true accents of fury, hate, and jealousy, real love-laments, the ironies and pleasantries of the French or Italian theater. Well, guess again, my little wren! They imagined that they could constantly be made to feel how the ease, flexibility, softness, and harmony of Italian, how its prosody, ellipses, and inversions all are naturally adapted to art, movement, expression, to the turns of song and the quantitative value of sounds—and still not notice how stiff, harsh, heavy, lumbering, and pedantic their own language is. Ah yes, yes. They were convinced that, after they had mingled their tears with those of a mother lamenting the death of her son, after they had shuddered at the decree of a tyrant commanding a murder to be committed, they thought they could still go on not being bored with their fairy-tales, their insipid mythology, their sickly-sweet little madrigals that show the poet's bad taste as much as they do the bankruptcy of the musical art that accomodates them. The simple souls! That's not the case and never can be. The true, the good, and the beautiful will be heard. They are challenged, but in the end they command admiration. What is counterfeit can be admired for a time, but people finally end up yawning at it. So go ahead and yawn, gentlemen, yawn to your hearts' content, don't mind us. The sovereign power of Nature and my trinity, against which the gates of hell cannot prevail—the true, which is the engendering Father; the good, which is the Son; whence proceeds the beautiful, which is the Holy Spirit. Well, their sovereign power is quietly taking over. The foreign god takes his place

humbly on the altar alongside the native idol; little by little he becomes a fixture; and one fine day he elbows his fellow-god off the altar. And there goes
your idol, tumbling to the ground. They say that's how the Jesuits implanted
Christianity in China and India. And the Jansenists can say what they like,
this politic method that moves towards its goal quietly, without bloodshed
or martyrdom, without a tuft of hair pulled out, strikes me as the best
method.

I: There's a good deal of sense, give and take a little, in everything
you've just said.

He: Sense? Well and good. But devil take me if I'm really working at it.
It all comes out willy-nilly. I'm like the Dead End composers were when
my uncle appeared on the scene. If I happen to hit things right, it only
goes to show that a coal-hauler will always be able to talk more intelligently
about coal than a whole Academy or all the Duhamels in the world.

And with that he begins pacing back and forth, humming way back in his
throat a few of the arias from *The Isle of Madmen, The Painter in Love
with his Model, The Blacksmith, The Pretty Plaintiff.* Occasionally he
would cry out, raising hands and eyes to heaven: "Now if that isn't
beautiful, by God! if that isn't beautiful! How can a man have a pair of
ears attached to his head and ask such a question?" He began to warm up
and sing softly. He sang louder and louder as he warmed up more and
more. Then came the gestures, the facial grimaces, and the body contortions. I said to myself: "Good. He's losing his head again and working up
to another scene." And sure enough, with a sudden whoop he begins: "I'm
a poor miserable wretch . . ." "Milord, milord, I beg you, let me go . . ."
"O earth, receive my gold, guard well my treasure . . ." "My soul, my soul,
my life! Oh earth! . . ." "There he goes, my little sweetheart . . ." "*Aspet-
tare e non venire . . .*" "*A Zerbina penserete . . .*" "*Sempre in contrasti con te
si sta . . .*"

He jumbled together some thirty different arias—Italian, French, tragic,
comic, of every conceivable character. Now he descends to the depths of
hell in a basso profondo voice. Then, screeching in a falsetto, he'd tear apart
the high notes, imitating the various gait, posture, gestures, of the characters
whose songs he sang—successively furious, calm, imperious, and sneering.
Now it's a weepy young girl, and he goes through all her simperings. Then
he's a priest, a king, a tyrant; he threatens, commands, rages. Now he's a
slave, an obedient slave. He calms down, laments bitterly, complains, laughs;
never off-key or off-beat, and never missing the meaning of the words and
character of the aria.

All the wood-pushers had left their chessboards and gathered round. Outside, the coffee-house windows were lined with people, passers-by who had
stopped on hearing the commotion. There were bursts of laughter fit to
raise the roof. He didn't notice anything. He went right on, seized by a
sort of frenzy, an enthusiasm so close to insanity that you're not sure he'll
come out of it, and you wonder whether he shouldn't be thrown into a

carriage and taken straight to the madhouse. When he sang a snatch of Jomelli's *Lamentations*, he reproduced the finest passages of each piece in it with an unbelievable precision, fidelity, and warmth. That beautiful obbligato recitative in which the prophet describes the desolation of Jerusalem—he watered it with a flood of tears, and not a listener's eye remained dry. It had everything: delicacy of voice, forcefulness of expression, genuine grief. He brought out those passages where the composer had particularly proved himself to be a great master. When he stopped singing the vocal part, it was only to take up the instrumental parts, which he'd suddenly leave off to go back to the voice, combining the two in a way that preserved all the transitions and unity of the whole, gripping our very souls and keeping us suspended in the most singular way that I've ever experienced . . . Did I feel admiration? Yes, I did. Was I moved to pity? I was. But a tinge of ridicule had colored these feelings and spoiled them.

But you too would have burst into peals of laughter at the way he imitated the various instruments. With swollen, puffed-out cheeks and an ominous throaty sound he would be the horns and bassoons. He'd affect a shrill, nasal tone for the oboes, and then make sounds at an unbelievable speed for the strings in an attempt to find the tones most like them. He whistled the piccolos and warbled the flutes, shouting, singing, carrying on like a madman, being the male dancer and the ballerina, the tenor and the prima donna, a whole orchestra, a whole operatic company, all rolled into one, taking on twenty different roles, running about, stopping like an energumen with eyes flashing and mouth frothing. It was stiflingly hot, and the sweat that ran along the wrinkles of his brow and down his cheeks got mixed with the powder in his hair, streamed off him, wilted the upper part of his coat. What all didn't I see him do? He wept, shouted, sighed. He looked about, dewy-eyed, or tranquil, or furious. He was a woman swooning with grief, a poor wretch plunged in despair. A temple being erected, birds singing their last notes at sundown, water murmuring in a cool, lonely spot or cascading in torrents from the mountain heights. A storm, a typhoon, the cries of men about to perish mingled with the howling of the winds and claps of thunder. He was night with its gloom; he was shade and silence—for even silence may be expressed in sound. He'd completely lost his head.

Exhausted with fatigue, like a man emerging from a very deep sleep or coma, he stood motionless, stunned, amazed. He kept looking around like a man who's lost his way and tries to make out where he is. He waited for his strength and spirits to revive; he wiped his face mechanically. Then, like a man waking up and finding his bed surrounded by a great number of people, having completely forgotten or remaining completely unaware of what he's done, he began by shouting: "Well, gentlemen, what's wrong? Why are you laughing? And why do you look so astonished? What's wrong?" Then he added: "Now that's what I call music, and by a real composer. And yet, gentlemen, certain pieces by Lulli should not be scorned. I defy anyone to improve on the scene. Ah, I shall wait . . ." without changing the words. And certain passages in Campra should not be scorned. And the violin pieces by my uncle: his gavottes, his processional music for

soldiers and priests: "Pale torches, night more dreadful that Stygian darkness . . ." "Gods of Tartarus, gods of oblivion . . ." He suddenly bellowed
out, holding each note. The neighbors all came running to their windows.
We plugged our fingers in our ears. He added: "For that bit you have to
have lungs, a tremendous vocal organ, real air capacity. But before long the
Feast of Assumption will be here; Lent and Twelfth Night are over. People
still don't know what should be set to music, and consequently what will
really suit the composer. Really great operatic lyrics are yet to be written,
but they'll get around to it. By listening to Pergolesi, the Saxon, Terradeglias, Traetta, and the rest, by dint of reading Metastasio, they'll get
there sooner or later."

I: Do you mean to say that Quinault, La Motte, and Fontenelle didn't
know what they were about?

He: No, not in the new style. There aren't a half a dozen consecutive
verses in all their pretty poems that you can set to music. They're ingenious
little epigrams or madrigals, light, sweet, delicate. But to understand how
little all this has to offer our art—which is the most physically exhausting of
all of them, not excepting the art of Demosthenes—why just get someone
to recite their libretti for you. How cold, dull, and monotonous they'll
seem! I'd just as soon put La Rochefoucauld's *Maxims* or Pascal's *Pensées*
to music. The melodic line we seek must be dictated by the animal cry of
passion. These moments of passion must come tumbling out pell-mell. The
phrases in each verse must be short, the meaning broken off and suspended.
The composer must be able to dispose of each and every part as he sees fit,
omitting or repeating a word, adding one that he needs, turning the phrase
inside out, the way you can a polyp, without destroying it. All of which
makes operatic lyrics much harder to write in French than in languages
where inversions are usual—languages which by their very nature have
all the advantages I'm talking about: "Oh cruel barbarian, plunge your
dagger in my breast. I stand ready to receive the fatal blow. Strike, dare
strike . . . Ah, I languish, I die . . . A secret fire seethes in all my senses . . .
Cruel love, what would you from me? Leave me that sweet peace I have
enjoyed . . . Give back my reason . . ." The passions must be strong; the
tenderness of the composer and the lyric writer must be extreme. In any
scene, the aria is almost always the peroration. Give us exclamations, inter-
jections, suspensions, interruptions, affirmations, negations. We call out,
invoke, shout, moan, weep, laugh openly. No more witticisms, no more
epigrams, no more neatly-turned little thoughts—all that is too far from
real nature. And don't think for a moment that the gestures and declamation of stage-actors can serve us as models. Perish the thought! It has to be
more energetic, less mannered, more real. Simple speeches, the natural terms
of passion, will be all the more necessary, since our native French tongue
is more monotonous and has less accent. The cry of the animal or of a man
in the throes of passion will give the speeches their needed accent.

While he talked to me this way, the crowd that had gathered around us
either could not hear or had lost interest in what we were saying and

wandered off, because man and child alike would rather be amused than instructed. Everyone had gone back to his game, and we were left alone in our corner. Seated on a bench with his head against the wall, his arms dangling, and his eyes half-closed, he said to me: "I don't know what's come over me. When I came in here I was feeling rested and in good form, and now I'm worn out and dog-tired as if I'd walked ten leagues. It came over me all of a sudden."

I: Do you want something refreshing to drink?

He: Gladly. My throat's scratchy; I'm a little faint, and my chest aches. It happens to me almost every day, and I can't understand why.

I: What will you have?

He: Anything you say. I'm not hard to please. Poverty has taught me not to be choosy.

They bring us beer and lemon soda, with which he refills a large glass that he empties two or three times without stopping. Then, like a man who's come to life again, he coughs loudly, flails about, and continues where he left off: "Now to your way of thinking, Milord Philosopher, isn't it a very, very strange thing that a foreigner, an Italian, a man named Duni, should be the one to teach us how to give the proper accent to our music, to adapt our singing to every kind of movement, rhythm, and declamation, without doing violence to prosody? Yet it really wasn't a Herculean job. Anyone who has ever heard a beggar ask for alms in the street, a man in a rage, a jealous and infuriated woman, a desperate lover, a flatterer—yes, a flatterer softening his tone, drawing out honeyed syllables—in short, any passion whatever, provided that it has force enough to supply the musician with a real model—anyone who has ever done that ought to have noticed two things: First, that the long and short syllables have no fixed values, or even a fixed relation between values; and second, that passion does just about as it likes with prosody, bridging the widest intervals. The person who cries out at the height of his grief: 'Ah, miserable creature that I am!' raises his voice to the highest and shrillest register on the exclamation and reduces the rest to the gloomiest, lowest register, spanning an octave or even greater interval, and giving each note the value that the melodic phrase requires without the least offending the ear, and yet without preserving the long or short values that the syllables have in ordinary speech. What a long way we've come since the days when we used to cite the parenthetical aside from *Armide*, 'Rinaldo's conqueror, if such there be,' or the 'Let us obey without hesitation,' from the *Indes galantes*, as marvels of musical declamation! Nowadays theses marvels make me shrug with pity. At the rate the art of music is progressing, I don't know where it will finally lead. Meanwhile, let's have another drink."

He has two or three without really noticing them. He would have unwittingly drowned himself, just the way he had worn himself out without realizing it, if I hadn't moved away the bottle that he distractedly kept reaching for. Then I said to him:

I: How does it come about that with such sureness of touch, with so great a sensitivity to the beauties of music, you are so blind to moral beauty and so insensitive to the charms of virtue?

He: Well, it must be that others have a sense that I lack, a fiber that I was not endowed with, or one that's gone slack and been plucked to death and won't vibrate any more. Or maybe it's that I've spent my life around good musicians and bad people, which has resulted in a very fine ear and a very deaf heart. And then heredity has something to do with it. My father's blood is the same as my uncle's; my blood is the same as my father's. The paternal molecule was hard and obtuse, and that damned first molecule infected all the rest.

I: Do you love your boy?

He: Do I love the little savage? I'm crazy about him.

I: Don't you ever think seriously about counteracting the effect of that accursed paternal molecule in him?

He: It would be wasted effort, I'm afraid. If he's fated to be a good man, I won't do him any harm. But if the molecule dictates that he should be a worthless fellow like his father, the trouble that I'd take to make him an honest man would do more harm than good. If his upbringing constantly went counter to the molecule's natural tendency, it would be as if he were tugged at by two opposing forces and go walking lop-sided down the road of life—like a lot of people I know, who are as inept in doing good as in doing harm. They're what we call *nobodies*—the most dreaded of all names because it indicates mediocrity and the utmost contempt. A great scoundrel is a great scoundrel but isn't a nobody. So, before the paternal molecule finally gained the upper hand again and brought my son to the state of complete abjectness that I've achieved, it would take an endless amount of time. He'd waste his best years. So I'm not doing anything about him at the moment. I'm letting him develop; I'm observing him. He's already gluttonous, devious, thieving, lazy, and lying; so I'm afraid he's a chip off the old block.

I: And you're going to make him a musician so that the resemblance will be complete?

He: A musician? A musician! Sometimes I look at him and grind my teeth and mutter to myself: "If you ever learn a note, I think I'll wring your little neck."

I: Why, if I may ask?

He: Because music doesn't lead anywhere.

I: It leads everywhere.

He: Yes, if you're first-rate. But who can ever be sure that his child will turn out first-rate? The odds are ten thousand to one that he'll be a miserable catgut-scraper like me. I tell you it would probably be easier to bring up a child to govern a nation and be a great king than it would be to make him a great violinist!

I: It seems to me that pleasing talents, even mediocre ones, speed a man along the road to fortune in an immoral society corrupted with debauchery and luxury. I personally heard the following conversation between a patron of sorts and a would-be protégé. The latter had been sent to the former on the assumption that the former was an obliging person who could be of service.

"Sir, what do you know how to do?"

"I know mathematics fairly well."

"All right, go ahead teaching mathematics, and after you've slogged through the filth of Paris streets for ten or twelve years, you'll have an income of three or four hundred pounds at most."

"I've also studied law and am versed in its practice."

"If Puffendorf and Grotius came back to life today, they would die of starvation at the side of the road."

"I am very well versed in history and geography."

"If there were any parents who really cared about the education of their children, your fortune would be made; but there aren't any such parents."

"I'm a fairly good musician."

"Well, why didn't you tell me that right off? Just to show you what profit you can draw from that talent: I have a daughter. Come around every day from seven thirty in the evening until nine and give her music lessons. I'll give you twenty-five gold louis a year. You'll have lunch, tea, dinner, and supper with us. The rest of the day will be your own to dispose of as you like."

He: And what became of the fellow?

I: If he'd had any sense, he'd have made a fortune—which, I gather, is all you care about.

He: Right. Gold, gold. Gold is everything. Everything else without gold is nothing. As a matter of fact, instead of stuffing my son's head with fine maxims that he'd have to forget if he is to avoid being a pauper, why, whenever I have a gold louis (which isn't often), I plant myself in front of him; I pull the goldpiece out of my pocket, show it to him admiringly, raise my eyes to heaven and kiss the goldpiece. And just to make him understand the importance of the sacred coin still more clearly, I tell him with voice and gesture of everything that he can buy with it: a fine outfit, a fine cap, a tasty muffin. Then I put the goldpiece back in my pocket, strut about proudly, lift my coat-tails, slap my coin-pocket. That's how I make him understand that it's the goldpiece inside it that gives me this unaccustomed assurance.

I: You couldn't find a better way. But suppose that some day, because he is so deeply impressed with the value of the goldpiece that . . .

He: I know what you are going to say. You just have to close your eyes to that. There is no principle of conduct without its handicap. At worst, you're upset for a little while, and then it's all over.

I: But even in spite of such wise and courageous precepts, I persist in believing that it would be a good thing to make a musician out of your son. I don't know any easier way of getting next to important people, catering to their vices, and profiting from one's own.

He: That's true. But I have plans for even a quicker and surer success. Ah, if he were only a girl! But since we can't always have things our way, we have to take them as they come and make the best of it. And to do that, you have to avoid doing what most fathers stupidly do—and they couldn't do worse if they purposely set out to make their children unhappy—I mean, giving a Spartan education to a child who is destined to live in Paris. If such an education is bad for them, that's not my fault, but the fault of the morals and manners of my country. And you tell me whose fault *they* are . . . I want my son to be happy or, what amounts to the same thing, honored, rich, and powerful. I have an idea or two about the easiest way to achieve that goal, and I'll teach them to him while he's still young. If you wiseacres blame me for that, the great majority of people, and success itself, will absolve me. He'll have gold; I'm telling you, he'll have gold. And if he has a lot of it, he won't be deprived of anything, not even of your own esteem and respect.

I: You might be mistaken.

He: Well, then he'll manage to get along without them, the way so many others do.

There was in all of this much of what we think and act on but never say aloud. That was, in fact, the outstanding difference between my man and most of the rest of us. He frankly admitted the vices which he had, and which he shared with others; but he wasn't hypocritical. He was neither more nor less hateful than the rest of us. He was simply franker, more consistent; and on occasion, he combined insight with depravity. I shuddered at the thought of what his boy would become with such a master. It was a certainty that, if the boy were raised according to principles that conform so strictly to our actual *mores*, he would go far, unless he were prematurely stopped along the way.

He: Oh, never fear. The important point, the difficult point that a good father has to concentrate on is not to give his children vices that will make him rich or eccentricities that will make him sought after by important people. Everybody does that, if not systematically as I do, at least by example and precept. No, the important point is to teach him just how far he can go, to teach him the art of avoiding shame, dishonor, and the law. Those things are dissonances in the social harmony that you have to know how to place, prepare, and resolve. There's nothing as dull as a progression of perfect chords. There has to be something to keep our anticipation alive, to split up the beam of light and reveal the component spectrum.

I: Fine. That comparison brings me back from morals to music, which I'd digressed from, in spite of myself, and I thank you for it. Because, to be perfectly frank, I like you better as a musician than as a moralist.

He: Yet I'm just a second-rater in music, whereas I'm really first-rate when it comes to morals.

I: I doubt that; but even if it were so, I'm an honest man and your principles are not mine.

He: So much the worse for you. Ah, if only I had your talent!

I: Let's forget about my talent and get back to yours.

He: If I knew how to express myself the way you do! I talk a hell of a ridiculous kind of jargon, partly from the drawing-room, partly from the gutter.

I: I'm not a good talker. All I can do is tell the truth, and that doesn't always go over well, as you know.

He: But it's not for telling the truth that I envy you your talent. On the contrary, it's because I could lie more convincingly. If I knew how to write, to throw together a book, to turn out a dedicatory epistle, make a fool drunk with his own importance, wheedle my way into women's graces!

I: But you know how to do all that a thousand times better than I do. Why, I'm not even fit to be your pupil.

He: What wasted talents! And you don't begin to realize their value!

I: I get back what I put in.

He: If that were so, you wouldn't be wearing that coarse suit, that muslin jacket, those woolen stockings, those heavy shoes, and that old-fashioned wig.

I: Granted. Yet you must be very maladroit, since you'll descend to anything to get rich and yet still aren't rich. But, you see, there are a few people like me who don't regard wealth as the most important thing in the world—queer people.

He: Very queer. No one is born with that turn of mind. It's acquired, because it isn't in nature.

I: In human nature?

He: In human nature. Every living thing, without excepting man, seeks its well-being at the expense of what is likely to dominate it. And I'm sure that if I let my young savage grow up without telling him anything, he'd say of his own accord that he wanted to be richly dressed, spendidly fed, liked by men, loved by women, that he wanted to live surrounded by all the good things in life.

I: If your little savage were left entirely to himself, if his native uncouthness were left untouched, if he had had the rudimentary mind of the infant but the violent passions of a thirty-year-old man, he would wring his father's neck and go to bed with his mother.

He: Which proves the necessity of a good education. But who's denying that? And what's a good education anyway, if not one that leads to all sorts of pleasures without risks and inconvenience?

I: I'm almost in agreement with you on that point, but let's not go into it.

He: Why not?

I: Because I'm afraid that we're only superficially in agreement, and that, were we to go into the risks and inconveniences to be avoided, we'd no longer agree.

He: And what difference does that make?

I: Let's forget about it, I say. What I know about it I could never teach you. It would be a lot easier for you to teach me what you know—and I don't—about music. My dear Rameau, let's talk music. Tell me how it happens that with your facility at understanding, remembering, and performing the most beautiful passages of the great masters, with your enthusiasm for them and your ability to make that enthusiasm contagious, you've never done anything worth while.

Instead of answering me, he began nodding his head and, pointing his finger towards heaven, he added: "It's my star! My star! When Nature made Leo, Vinci, Pergolesi, Duni—she smiled. She assumed an imposing and serious air when she formed dear Uncle Rameau, who has been referred to as the Great Rameau for ten years or so now, but will soon be forgotten. But when she threw his nephew together, she made a wry face, several wry faces, in fact."

And while he said these words, he made every kind of grimace. He expressed contempt, disdain, irony, and he seemed to be kneading a bit of clay between his fingers and smiling at the ridiculous shapes he gave it. That done, he tossed the misshapen idol away and said: "That's how Nature made me and threw me on the heap with all the other misshapen idols— some with fat wrinkled bellies, some with short necks, others with eyes bulging out of their heads, apoplectic-looking, and still others with necks awry. There were dried-up ones with bright eyes and hooked noses. All of them burst out laughing and kept right on laughing when they caught sight of me. And I held my sides and almost died laughing when I saw them, for fools and madmen find each other amusing; they seek each other out; they attract one another.

"When I was thrown on the heap, if the proverb, 'The fools' money is the patrimony of the man of wit,' hadn't already existed, I'd have invented it. I felt that Nature had put my legitimate heritage in the purse of these misshapen idols, and I devised a thousand ways of getting it back."

I: I know those ways; you've told me about them, and I was properly impressed. But with so wide a choice at your disposal, why didn't you ever try composing a musical masterpiece?

He: That's just what a man of the world said to the Abbé Le Blanc. The abbé had said: "Madame de Pompadour takes me by the hand, leads me to the threshold of the Academy. Then she let's go of my hand. I fall down and break both my legs . . ." The man of the world answered: "Well, abbé, what you have to do is get up and knock down the door; use your head . . ." The abbé replied: "I tried that, and do you know what I got for my pains? A huge bump on my noggin."

After that little tale, my man began pacing up and down, head lowered, pensive and downcast. He sighed and wept and groaned, threw up his hands and raised his eyes, pounded himself on the forehead hard enough to break either his skull or his knuckles, and then went on: "And yet I'm sure there's something here; but it doesn't do any good to knock or shake it. Nothing ever comes out." Then he began shaking his head again and knocking still harder on his forehead, saying: "Either there's nobody home, or they won't answer."

The next minute he assumed a very proud attitude, threw his head back, put his right hand over his heart, stepped forward and said: "But I have feelings; I do have feelings." He acted the part of a man getting irritated or indignant, or who is moved, who commands and implores. He improvised angry tirades, words of commiseration, hatred, or love. He caught the accents of each passion with an astonishing subtlety and accuracy. Then he went on: "Well, that's it, I guess. It's coming. That's what you call finding an obstetrician who knows the right irritants to hurry up the labor-pains and make the baby come out. But when I'm alone, I take quill in hand; I want to write. I bite my fingernails; I rack my brains. But all I get is a 'Sorry, sir, the god is not in.' I'm convinced I'm a genius. But I reread the first line I've written and it says that I'm a fool, a fool, a fool. But how can a man really feel things, rise to the heights, think, have bold conceptions when he has to frequent the kind of people that I have to see every day just to keep going? And hear on every side idle chatter: 'The boulevard was delightful today. Have you heard the little minx?—she's really priceless in her role. Mister So-and-so had the most beautiful team of dapple-grays you ever saw. The gorgeous Mrs. What's-her-name isn't exactly holding her own these days. Really, at forty-five, why *will* she still wear a hair-do like that? Young So-and-so is covered with diamonds that cost her practi-cally nothing. —You mean, that really cost her *very* dearly? —Why no. —Where did you see her? —At the performance of Goldoni's *Harlequin's Baby Lost and Found*. The desperation scene was played as never before. The Punchinello at the Fair has a good voice but no training, no soul. Madame So-and-so gave birth to two children simultaneously—one for each father.' Do you think hearing this kind of stuff over and over again, day after day, kindles the imagination and spurs one to great things?

I: No. You'd do better to shut yourself up in an attic, drink plain water, eat dry bread, and try to find yourself.

He: Maybe so, but I don't have the courage it takes. Then there's the risk of sacrificing well-being for an uncertain success! And what about the name I bear? Rameau! It's a drawback to be named Rameau. Talent isn't like nobility, which is transmitted and becomes more illustrious as it passes from grandfather to father, father to son, son to grandson, without grandpa's setting any embarrassing example of real ability that his descendants would have to live up to. The old trunk branches out into an enormous crown of fools. But what's the difference? That's not true of talent, though. Merely to have a reputation equal to your father's, you have to be a lot cleverer than he was. You have to inherit his fiber. Well, I lack the fiber, even though my wrist is limber, the bow scrapes, and the pot boils. It isn't fame, but at least it's a bowl of soup.

I: If I were in your shoes, I wouldn't take all this for granted. I'd give things a try.

He: You think I haven't tried? I was hardly fifteen when I said to myself for the first time: "What's wrong with you, Rameau? You're dreaming. And what are you dreaming of? Of composing or wanting to compose something that the whole world will marvel at. Ah yes, all you have to do is blow hard and wiggle your fingers. Just stick a feather in your cap and you're a peacock." A little later I said the same thing to myself. I still say it—and I'm still in the crowd around the statue of Memnon.

I: What's this about the statue of Memnon?

He: I should think it's clear enough. Around the statue of Memnon there was a host of other statues, all struck by the sun's rays. But Memnon was the only one that gave out a sound. Our poets? There's Voltaire. And who else? Voltaire. And in third place, Voltaire. And in fourth, Voltaire. Our composers? Rinaldo da Capua, Hasse, Pergolesi, Alberti, Tartini, Locatelli, Terradeglias, my uncle, and little Duni, who looks like nothing at all, but feels deeply, by God, and knows what melody and expressiveness are. All the others clustered around these few Memnons are just so many pairs of donkey-ears stuck on a stick. And we're all beggars, such miserable beggars that it's pitiful. Ah, Mister Philosopher, Poverty is a terrible thing. I see Her squatting, open-mouthed, hoping to catch a few drops of the cool water that pours through the Danaïds' barrel. Yet we're only too happy if we can find a place under it! I had a place under it, but I couldn't hold out. I've done the fool trick once before already. I was travelling in Bohemia, Germany, Switzerland, Holland, Flanders—wandering all over the place.

I: Under the bottomless barrel?

He: Under the bottomless barrel. He was a rich and free-spending Jew who liked music and my monkeyshines. I made music just any old way, and I played the fool. I had everything I could ask for. My Jew was a man who knew the precepts of his faith and lived up to them strictly, sometimes even among friends, and always among strangers. This got him into a tight spot, which I'll have to tell you about, because it's quite funny. There was a charming courtesan in Utrecht. The Jew was tempted by the Christian wench, and secretly dispatched a messenger to her with a letter of credit for a tidy sum. The bizarre creature refused his offer. The Jew was in despair. The messenger said: "Why be so upset? You want to sleep with a pretty woman? Nothing is simpler, even with a lot prettier woman than the one you're after. I mean my wife. I'll let you take over for the same price." No sooner said than done. The messenger keeps the letter of credit, and my Jew goes to bed with the messenger's wife. The letter of credit reaches maturity. The Jew lets it lapse and be brought up in court, where he declares it to be a forgery. "The fellow will never dare to say how he comes to possess my letter, and I'll never have to pay up." At the hearing, he cross-examines the messenger:

"Who gave you this letter of credit?"

"You did."

"For money lent to me?"

"No."

"For goods supplied by you?"

"No."

"For services rendered?"

"No. But that's all beside the point. I hold the letter; you signed it; and you'll pay it."

"I did not sign it."

"So I'm a forger?"

"Either you or someone you're an agent for."

"I'm a coward, but you're a swindler. Don't push me too far, or I'll tell everything. I'll go down to ruin, but you'll go down with me."

The Jew paid no attention to the threat, and the messenger exposed the whole affair at the next court-session. Both men were castigated, and the Jew was sentenced to pay up on the letter of credit, but the sum was used for charitable purposes. That's when I left him and came back here. What was I to do? It meant either perishing from poverty or finding something to do. All kinds of projects went through my head. One day I was for joining up with a troupe of travelling players. I was ready to perform on the stage or in the orchestra, since I was about equally good, or bad, at both. The next day I'd think about having a set of those pictures painted that you fasten on the end of a long pole and plant in a town square, where I'd have shouted at the top of my voice: "This is his birthplace; here he's leaving his father, the apothecary. Now he arrives in the capital looking for his uncle's house. Here he is on his knees before his uncle, who sends him away. So here he has to take up with a Jew, etcetera, etcetera." The day after, I'd get up firmly resolved to join a band of street-singers. There are a lot worse things I could have done. We could have gone serenading under my uncle's windows and made him seethe with rage. But finally I came to a decision.

At that point he stopped, successively assuming the attitudes of a man holding a violin and tightening the strings with all his might, then of a poor devil dead with fatigue, all his strength gone and teetering on his legs, ready to collapse if someone doesn't throw him a piece of bread. He indicated his pressing need by pointing a finger at his half-open mouth. Then he added: "Everybody understands that. They'd throw me a crust, and three or four of us starvelings would fight over it. Well, have fine ideas and do wonders on that kind of fare!"

I: It's difficult, all right.

He: Well, knocking about from pillar to post, I finally landed at this last place. I had it good. I got thrown out. I'll have to start scraping the cat-gut again and resort to the gesture of the finger at the gaping mouth. Nothing is stable in this world. Today you're at the top of the heap; tomorrow you're at the bottom. Accursed circumstance leads on, or, more usually, leads us astray.

Then taking a swallow of what was left in the bottom of the bottle and turning to his neighbor: "Sir, for kindness' sake, a pinch of snuff. You have a handsome snuffbox there. Aren't you a musician?"

"No . . ."

"Good for you. Because musicians are poor bastards that should be pitied. Fate has decreed that I should be one, while in mills on Montmartre there is probably a miller or his helper who'll never hear anything but the click of the ratchet, but might have been able to come up with the most beautiful melodies! To the mill, Rameau! To the mill! That's where you belong."

I: Whatever a man really applies himself to doing is what Nature intended him to do.

He: Then she makes strange blunders. My outlook isn't so lofty that the man pruning a tree and the caterpillar gnawing its leaves are just a blur and simply look like two different insects, each one going about his business. Perch yourself on the epicycle of Mercury, and from that vantage point, if you feel like it, classify men the way Réaumur classifies flies into cutters, loopers, harvesters; divide up the human species into woodturners, carpenters, runners, dancers, singers. That's your affair and not mine. I'm here on the ground, and that's where I'm staying. But if it's natural to be hungry (I always get back to hunger—an ever present sensation to me), I find that things aren't well-ordered if one doesn't always have something to eat. What the devil kind of an economy is that? Some men who have more than they need of everything, while others who have just as importunate a stomach as theirs, and whose hunger is just as recurrent as theirs, haven't a crust to nibble. The worst of it is the constrained posture in which hunger keeps us. The needy man doesn't walk the way others do. He jumps, crawls, twists about, drags his feet. He spends his life assuming and executing positions.

I: What do you mean by "positions"?

He: Go ask Noverre. The world counts more different positions than his dancer's art can imitate.

I: There you go, to use your expression or Montaigne's, *perching on the epicycle of Mercury*, and considering the various pantomimes of the human species.

He: No, I tell you, no. I'm too awkward to get up that high. I'll leave their cloudy haunts to the cranes. I stick to the ground. I look around me and assume my positions or amuse myself watching the positions others assume. I'm an excellent mimic, as you'll see.

He begins to smile, to imitate a man admiring, a man imploring, an obsequious man. He has his right foot forward, his left hand behind, his back arched, his head thrown back, his glance as if gazing into someone else's eyes. His lips are parted, his arms outstretched towards some object. He waits for a command; he receives it; he takes off like an arrow; he comes back. The command has been carried out; he reports on it. He's attentive to everything; he picks up what is dropped; he puts a cushion or a tabouret under people's feet, holds a saucer, brings a chair. He shuts a window, draws the curtains, observes the master and mistress. He is motionless, arms dangling, legs parallel. He's listening. He tries to read what is written in their faces. He finally says: "There you have a pantomime of myself. It's about the same for flatterers, courtiers, flunkies, and beggars."

This man's foibles, the Abbé Galiani's tales, and the wild exaggerations of Rabelais have sometimes made me wonder a great deal. They are three storehouses from which I've supplied myself with absurd-looking masks that I project onto the faces of the gravest personages. I see Pantaloon in a prelate, a satyr in a magistrate, a pig in a cenobite, an ostrich in a government minister, a goose in place of his first secretary.

I: But the way you look at it, there are plenty of beggars in the world, for there's almost no one, to my knowledge, who doesn't know at least a step or two of your dance.

He: You're right. In a whole kingdom there's only one man who walks upright, and that's the sovereign himself. All the others assume positions.

I: The sovereign? But one could even say something about him. Don't you suppose there are times when he finds himself next to a dainty foot, a pert hairdo, a little nose that makes him indulge in a bit of pantomime? Whoever is in need of others is indigent to a certain extent and assumes a position. The king assumes a position before his mistress and before God; he does a step or two of pantomime. The minister does the courtier's, flatterer's, valet's or beggar's step before his king. The crowd of ambitious climbers dance all your positions, each a hundred ways viler than the next. The abbé of noble birth with his bands of fur and black cloak does it at least once a week before the official in charge of benefices. Good heavens, what you call the beggar's pantomime is what makes the world go round. Every man has his pretty little Hus and his Bertin.

He: That consoles me.

But while I spoke, he killingly mimicked the positions of the persons I enumerated. For the little abbé, for example, he held his hat under his arm and his breviary in his left hand. With the right, he lifted his coat-tails, and stepped forward with his head slightly tilted to one side, eyes lowered, doing such a perfect imitation of a hypocrite that I could just see the author of the *Refutations* petitioning the Bishop of Orleans before my very eyes. When he came to the flatterers and social-climbers, he crawled like a worm—the picture of Bouret before the Chief Auditor.

I: Brilliantly done. But there is, nevertheless, one being exempt from putting on a pantomime: the philosopher, who has nothing and asks for nothing.

He: And where did you ever see such an animal? If he has nothing, he must be suffering. If he asks for nothing, he'll get nothing, and so he'll go on suffering.

I: No. Diogenes made sport of his wants.

He: But a man has to have clothes.

I: No, he went about stark naked.

He: But sometimes it was cold in Athens.

I: Less than here.

He: And a man had to eat there.

I: No doubt.

He: At whose expense?

I: At Nature's. What does the savage do? He turns to the earth, to animals, fishes, to the trees, herbs and roots, to the streams.

He: An unappetizing board.

I: But copious.

He: And badly served.

I: Yet we plunder it to furnish our own.

He: You must admit, though, that the industry of our cooks, pastrymen, roastmen, caterers, and confectioners helps along considerably. With the austere diet that your Diogenes kept, he mustn't have had very demanding organs.

I: You're wrong. The Cynic's garb was the same as that of our monks and just as virtuous. The Cynics were the Carmelites and Franciscan friars of Athens.

He: But there I've got you. Because, in that case, Diogenes also danced the pantomime, if not before Pericles, at least before Lais or Phryne.

I: Wrong again. The others had to pay dearly for the favors of the courtesan who gave herself to Diogenes simply for the pleasure of it.

He: But suppose the courtesan happened to be busy and the Cynic in a hurry?

I: He went back into his tub and did without her.

He: And you would advise me to follow his example?

I: I swear on my life that it would be better than crawling, better than debasing and prostituting yourself.

He: But I have to have a good bed and good board, warm clothes in winter, cool in summer, leisure, money, and a lot of other things that I'd rather owe to someone's benevolence than acquire through work.

I: That's because you're a lazy lout, a glutton, a coward, and rotten to the core.

He: That's just what I've been trying to tell you.

I: The so-called good things in life are worth having, no doubt. But you don't seem to realize the price of the sacrifice you make to obtain them. You dance, you have danced, and you'll go on dancing the vilest pantomine.

He: That's true. But it hasn't cost me very much and won't cost me very much more. That's why I'd be ill-advised to adopt a different stance that would be painful to hold and that I couldn't keep up. But I can see now, from what you've been telling me, that my poor dear wife was something of a philosopher. She was courageous as a lion. Sometimes we were without bread and hadn't a penny to our name, and most of our gladrags had already been pawned. I'd throw myself across the foot of the bed and rack my brains trying to think of someone who would lend me a few francs that I'd never pay back. She, gay as a lark, would sit down at the harpsichord and sing to her own accompaniment. She had the throat of a nightingale. I'm sorry you never heard her. When I had to take part in some concert, I'd take her with me. On the way, I'd say to her: "Go ahead, my lady, make them admire you; turn on your talent and charms; take them by storm, bowl them over." We'd arrive; she'd sing; take them by storm, bowl them over. Alas, I lost her, the poor little thing! Beside her talent, she had such a delicate little mouth that you could hardly get your little finger into it. And teeth— a row of pearls. And eyes, feet, skin, cheeks, tits, legs like a doe, thighs and buttocks for a sculptor to model. Sooner or later she'd have snagged a tax-farmer, at the very least. And her walk, her rump, oh God! what a rump!

And off he goes, imitating his wife's walk. He took little steps, tilted his nose in the air, fluttered his fan, waggled his behind. It was a perfect take-off of the come-hither act of our little flirts.

Then, picking up the thread of his conversation, he added: "I used to take her everywhere—to the Tuileries Gardens, the Palais Royal, on the boulevards. It was just too good to last. When she crossed the street in the mornings, bareheaded and wearing a short jacket, you'd have stopped just to look at her. And you could have held her waist in one hand without squeezing her. The men who followed her and watched her trot along on her little feet and sized up that ample rump molded by her thin petticoats— well, they doubled their pace. She let them catch up with her. Then she'd suddenly turn her big, black, shiny eyes on them and stop them cold in their tracks. Because the obverse of the medal was as good as the underside. But alas, I lost her, and along with her all my hopes of making a fortune. That's the only reason I married her. I'd told her all my plans. She was far too sensible not to realize that they were sure-fire, and she had too much judgment not to approve of them."

And all at once he was sobbing and crying and saying: "No, no, I'll never get over it. Ever since, I've been wearing the cleric's collar and brimmed skull-cap."

I: Out of grief?

He: If you like. But really just so I could always have my porringer on my head . . . But let's see what time it is, because I have to go to the Opera.

I: What are they putting on?

He: The Dauvergne thing. There's some pretty good stuff in his music. Too bad he wasn't the first to think it up. Among the dead there are always a few to come back and haunt the living. What can you expect? *Quisque suos non patimur manes.*

But it's five thirty. I can hear the bell at the Opera ticket-window— the bell that calls me and the Abbé de Canaye to vespers. Goodbye, Mister Philosopher. Isn't it true that I'm the same as ever?

I: Alas, yes—unfortunately.

He: All I ask is that this misfortune will go on for another forty years or so. He who laughs last, laughs best.

Michael Kohlhaas

FROM AN
OLD CHRONICLE

BY

Heinrich von Kleist

Translated by Sigurd Burckhardt

Editor's Note

Heinrich von Kleist was born in 1777 in Frankfort on the Oder, the son of a retired major. In 1792 he entered the Prussian army; he served in the Rhine campaign in 1794; he retired, a lieutenant, at the age of 22. He studied law and philosophy, and in 1800 entered the Ministry of Finance at Berlin. Shortly thereafter, although betrothed, he went traveling with his sister, visiting especially Paris, and settled in Switzerland for a while, where he began writing; he broke off his engagement when his fiancée hesitated to join him. He turned restlessly from one study, place, occupation, to another. In 1807 he was arrested by the French as a spy and imprisoned for six months. In 1808 he published a literary journal, and the last two years of his life he edited a newspaper in Berlin. In 1811 on the shore of the Wannsee near Potsdam, he carried out a suicide pact between himself and the incurably ill wife of a friend.

Kleist's writing consists chiefly of a handful of plays, none of which he saw produced in his lifetime but which are now in the repertory of all German theaters, and a handful of stories, which were also a long time in assuming their rightful place even in Germany. Kleist's themes and style alike were uncongenial to his age; he dedicated one of his major poetic tragedies, *Penthesilea*, to Goethe "on the knees of his heart," and Goethe—the arbiter of literary taste and the influential director of the Weimar theater—rejected it coldly.

Of Kleist's prose style, extraordinarily complex even for German, Professor Burckhardt has written:

His syntax is atonal, so to speak; it refuses to take for granted, as normal syntax does, a commonly held rational order within which the parts will readily fall into place. Ordinary sentences, like tonal melodies, satisfy the whistling impulse of our reason; Kleist's periods frustrate it. They thrust up detail—the picking up of a glove, the emptying of a chamber pot—so as to remind us that normal syntax begs the question of intelligibility by refusing to accommodate what does not fit its order.

Michael Kohlhaas

FROM AN

OLD CHRONICLE

TOWARD THE MIDDLE OF THE SIXTEENTH CENTURY, THERE LIVED ON the banks of the Havel a horsedealer named Michael Kohlhaas, a schoolmaster's son, one of the most upright and, at the same time, most terrible men of his day. Until the age of thirty, this extraordinary man would have been judged the model of a good citizen. In the village which still bears his name, he owned a farm on which he earned a quiet competence by his trade; the children his wife had borne him he reared to be godfearing, industrious, and honest; not one of his neighbors but had benefited from his liberality and just dealing. In short, the world would have had cause to bless his memory had he not carried one virtue to excess: His sense of justice made him a robber and murderer.

I

One day he rode abroad with a string of young horses, all sleek and well-fed, and was calculating how he would spend the profit he hoped to make from them at various fairs—partly, in the way of good managers, on reinvestment for further profit, but in part also on present enjoyment—when he reached the Elbe and found himself, near an imposing castle on Saxon territory, halted by a toll gate which he had never encountered on this road before. In the heavy rain which was just then falling, he stopped his horses and called for the tollkeeper, who presently stuck his surly face out of the window. The horsedealer told him to raise the gate. "What's happened here?" he asked when the tollkeeper, having taken his time about it, emerged from the house. "Seignorial privilege," the man answered as he opened the gate, "granted to the Squire Wenzel von Tronka." "So," said Kohlhaas, "Wenzel is the Squire's name?" and he gazed at the castle whose shining battlements overlooked the countryside. "Is the old lord dead?" "Died of an apoplexy," replied the tollkeeper, and raised the gate. "A pity!" Kohlhaas said; "he was a worthy old gentleman, who took pleasure in seeing people, and furthered trade and traffic wherever he could. Once, because one of my mares broke a leg, he had the road paved, down there where it enters the village. Well, what do I owe you?" And he had some trouble fetching the required coins from beneath his wind-whipped cloak. "All right, old man," he added when the other mumbled: "Hurry! Hurry!" and cursed the weather; "if that piece of timber had been left standing in the woods, we would be better off, both of us." With that, he handed over the money and started to ride on.

But he had not yet passed the gate when another voice rang out from the tower behind him: "Hold there, horsedealer!" and he saw the castellan slam the window shut and hurry down to him. "Well, what is it now?" Kohlhaas asked himself, and halted the horses. Buttoning his waistcoat over his expansive middle and leaning into the wind, the castellan came up and asked him for his pass. "My pass?" said Kohlhaas. Disconcerted, he went on to explain that so far as he knew he had none, but if they would tell him what manner of thing it was, perhaps he might happen to carry one. The castellan gave him an unpleasant look and answered that without a permit from the Elector no horsedealer with horses was allowed to cross the border. Kohlhaas assured him that he had crossed it seventeen times, always without a permit; he kept himself exactly informed of all Electoral ordinances bearing on his trade; surely this was some mistake which he begged they would reconsider and not needlessly detain him, since he had a long day's ride before him. But the castellan replied that he would not sneak past them the eighteenth time; the ordinance had recently been issued for just that purpose; and he would either have to purchase the pass right here or go back where he came from. After a moment's reflection, the horsedealer, whom these illegal extortions were beginning to exasperate, dismounted, handed the reins to his groom, and said that he would talk to the Squire von Tronka himself about the matter.

He went up to the castle; the castellan followed, mumbling about skinflint money-grubbers and wholesome blood-letting; and the two of them, glaring at each other, entered the great hall. It happened that the Squire was sitting over wine with some boon companions, and all of them happened to be roaring over some jest when Kohlhaas approached to present his grievance. The Squire asked what he wanted; the other knights fell silent at the sight of the stranger; but no sooner had the latter begun his request concerning the horses than the whole crew shouted: "Horses? Where are they?" and rushed to the window for a look at them. When they saw the glossy animals, they eagerly took up the Squire's suggestion and hurried down to the yard; the rain had stopped; castellan, steward, and stablehands gathered, and all fell to judging the horses. One praised a bay with a white blaze, another preferred the chestnut, a third patted the piebald with brown spots; and all were agreed that these were horses like deer, as good as the best raised in the country. Kohlhaas cheerfully responded that the horses were no better than the knights that were to ride them, and encouraged them to buy. The Squire, who was much tempted by the powerful bay stallion, inquired after the price; his steward, being short of draft horses and thinking that he could use them, pressed him to buy a team of blacks; but when the dealer named his prices, the knights thought them too high, and the Squire remarked that at that rate he had better find the Round Table and apply to King Arthur. Kohlhaas, who noticed how the castellan and the bailiff whispered with each other and cast ominous glances at the blacks, did what he could to sell the horses. He said to the Squire: "Sir, I bought the blacks six months ago for 25 gold florins; give me 30, and they are yours." Two knights who were standing near left little doubt that they thought the horses were easily worth that much; but the Squire decided that while he might be willing to spend money for the bay, he did not much care to do so for the blacks. He got ready to return to the hall; whereupon Kohlhaas, saying that perhaps they could strike a bargain the next time he should pass through, took his leave and reached for the reins of his horse, ready to ride on.

At that moment, the castellan stepped forward to say: the horsedealer had been told that he could not go on without a pass. Kohlhaas turned around and asked the Squire whether this regulation, which would be ruinous to his trade, was actually in force. With an embarrassed air, the Squire, as he walked away, replied: "Yes, Kohlhaas, you have to get a pass. Settle it with the castellan, and you can go on." Kohlhaas assured him that he had no intention of circumventing rules that might have been issued governing the export of horses; he promised to obtain the pass at the Privy Chancery in Dresden on his way through there, and asked only to be let off this once, since he had known absolutely nothing of the requirement. "Oh well," said the Squire, since the storm was starting up again and the wind was whistling through his skinny bones, "let the beggar through. Come." He turned to his companions and wanted to go indoors. But the castellan, addressing the Squire, said that at least Kohlhaas must leave a security against his obtaining the paper. The Squire stopped once more. Kohlhaas asked how much, in money or goods, he should deposit for the blacks. The bailiff mumbled that he might leave the blacks themselves. "Quite so," said the castellan, "that is the best way; once he has the pass, he can fetch them whenever he pleases." Taken aback by so brazen a demand, Kohlhaas explained to the Squire, who stood by shivering and with his coattails wrapped about him, that it was the blacks he wanted to sell; but, a blast of wind just then driving a shower of rain and hail into the doorway, the Squire, to put an end to the dispute, cried: "If he won't leave the horses, throw him back beyond the gate!" The horsedealer, aware that he had no choice but to yield to force, decided to do what they demanded; he unhitched the blacks and led them to a stable which the castellan pointed out to him. With them he left his groom, supplied him with money, and warned him to watch the horses carefully until his return. Then, doubtful whether the regulation in question had not perhaps after all been issued as a protection against an incipient epidemic, he continued with the remainder of his string toward Leipzig, where he meant to attend the fair.

Arrived in Dresden, in a suburb of which he owned a house and some stables for use as a depot in his trade at the small-town fairs of the region, he promptly went to the Chancery and was informed by the councillors, some of whom he knew, that he had been quite correct in his initial conviction: the story of the pass was a fairy-tale. Kohlhaas, having asked the annoyed councillors for a written statement to this effect, smiled at the skinny Squire's joke, although its point still escaped him; and when within a few weeks he had sold the horses he had brought at satisfactory prices, he returned to Tronka Castle, with no resentment beyond what the common distresses of life inspire. When he showed the chancery statement to the castellan, the latter made no comment; and when he asked if he could now have his horses back, he was told that he was free to go and fetch them. Even as he crossed the courtyard, however, he had the disagreeable experience of being informed that his groom, allegedly for insolent conduct, had been whipped and chased from the Castle only a few days after being left there. The horsedealer asked the boy who told him this what the groom had done, and who, since then, had cared for the horses; his heart swelled with misgivings when the boy replied that he did not know and led him to the stable. But how great was his astonishment when, instead of his two sleek blacks, he beheld a pair of skinny, run-down nags, their bones protruding like pegs to hang things on, their manes and hair matted for lack of care and currying: the very image of misery in the animal kingdom! Kohlhaas, whom the horses greeted by neighing and stirring feebly, was outraged, and asked what had been done to them. The boy answered that they had met with no particular mishap; they had even been properly fed; but, it being harvest time and draft animals in short supply, they had been used for a little field work. Kohlhaas cursed such shameful, deliberate abuse; but, aware that he was powerless, he forced back his anger and, having no other choice, prepared to get out of this robbers' lair with his horses. Just then the castellan appeared, attracted by the sound of argument, and asked what the matter was. "The matter!" Kohlhaas retorted. "Who gave the Squire von Tronka and his men leave to use my blacks for field work?" He asked if that was a humane thing to do, tried to rouse the enfeebled beasts with a flick of the whip, and showed that they did not even stir. The castellan fixed him defiantly for a moment and said: "Look at the ruffian! Shouldn't the lout be thanking God that the horses are still alive?" Who, he asked, was supposed to take care of them after the groom's running off; and was it not reasonable to make the horses earn their feed by working a little in the fields? He concluded that Kohlhaas had better not make trouble, else he would call out the dogs and restore order in the courtyard.

The horsedealer's heart beat against his doublet. He yearned to throw the potbellied parasite into the mud and grind his heel in that copper-colored face. He was still standing there, combing tangles out of the blacks' manes and considering what he ought to do, when the scene suddenly changed and Squire Wenzel von Tronka, come home from coursing hares, galloped into the yard with a swarm of knights, grooms, and dogs. When he asked what had happened, the castellan quickly spoke up; with the dogs on one side barking murderously at the sight of the stranger and the knights on the other side trying to quiet them, he proceeded by vicious distortions to show what a storm the horsedealer was raising simply because his blacks had been put to some use; adding with a sneer that now he refused to recognize the horses as his own. Kohlhaas cried: "These are not my horses, your worship! These are not the horses that were worth 30 gold florins! I want my well-fed, healthy horses back!" The Squire paled slightly, and said in dismounting: "If the bastard doesn't want to take his horses back, he can leave them. Come, Günther!" he called; "Hans, come along!" brushing dust off his breeches. And from the doorway, as he entered, he called: "Fetch wine!" Kohlhaas said that he would sooner call the knacker and have the horses thrown into the carrion pit than put them into his stable in Kohlhaasenbrück in their present state. Bothering no further with them, he left them standing in the yard, mounted his bay and, declaring that he would know how to get justice, rode away.

He was going full tilt toward Dresden when the thought of his groom and the castellan's charges against him caused him to slow down and, before he had gone a thousand paces, to turn his horse about and head it toward Kohlhaasenbrück, since he thought it both prudent and just first to question the groom. For notwithstanding the insults he had suffered, a sure sense of the world's fragility disposed him to bear, as a just consequence, the loss of his horses, provided the groom were in any degree culpable. But on the other hand, a feeling just as sure—and which became more deeply rooted as he went on and heard, wherever he stopped, reports of the injustices travellers had daily to suffer at Tronka Castle—told him that if, as seemed most likely, the whole incident proved a piece of calculated trickery, he was pledged and bound to the world to devote all his being to obtaining satisfaction for the injury he had sustained and security against future injuries for his fellow citizens.

On his arrival in Kohlhaasenbrück, as soon as he had embraced his loyal wife Lisbeth and kissed his children, who were shouting happily about his knees, he straightway inquired after Herse, the chief groom: had there been news of him? Lisbeth said: "Ah, dearest Michael, this Herse! Only think: About two weeks ago he came here, miserably beaten; so badly, in fact, that he could not breathe freely. We put him to bed, where he coughed up blood; and when we kept questioning him, he told us an unintelligible tale: about how you had left him behind at Tronka Castle with some horses that were not permitted to pass through; how they had forced him by the vilest maltreatment to leave the Castle; and how it had been impossible for him to bring along the horses." "Oh?" said Kohlhaas, taking off his coat, "is he well again?" "More or less," she answered, "except for spitting blood. I meant to send a stablehand to Tronka right away, to take care of the horses until your return. For since Herse has always been truthful and the most devoted of all our people, it would have been wrong of me to doubt his story, borne out as it was by such visible marks, and to suspect that he had lost the horses in some other manner. But he implored me not to send anyone else into that robbers' lair, and rather to give up the beasts than to sacrifice another human being for them." "Is he still in bed?" Kohlhaas asked as he took off his neckerchief. "For the last few days he has been up a little. You'll see," she continued, "that he told the truth, and that this is one of the outrages which have lately been practiced on strangers by the Tronka folk." "I'll have to look into it first," Kohlhaas replied. "If he is up, Lisbeth, call him in." With that, he sat down, and his wife, glad to see him so calm, went to fetch the groom.

"What did you do at the Castle?" Kohlhaas asked as Herse followed Lisbeth into the room. "I am not very pleased with you."

The man, whose pale face turned a spotty red at these words, was silent a while; then he answered: "You are in the right of it, master; because by chance I had a sulphur wick in my pocket, with which I meant to set fire to that robbers' nest after they threw me out; but when I heard a child crying inside, I threw the wick into the Elbe, and thought: 'Let God's lightning set it afire; I won't.'"

Taken aback, Kohlhaas asked: "But how did you have yourself chased out of the Castle?"

Herse wiped the sweat from his forehead: "By a nasty trick. But what's done can't be undone. I didn't want to see the horses ruined by field work, and said they were still young and had never been in harness."

Kohlhaas, trying to cover his confusion, said that in this he had not told the exact truth, since the blacks had been in harness for a little early that spring. "Considering that you were, in a sense, a guest at the Castle, you might have helped out once or twice, if there was need to bring in the crop in a hurry."

"So I did, Master," said Herse. "When they began to look sulky, I thought: 'Surely it won't kill the horses.' The third morning I hitched them up and brought in three wagon-loads of grain."

His heart swelling, Kohlhaas looked to the floor and said: "They didn't mention that, Herse."

Herse assured him that it was so. "My not being helpful," he went on, "was in refusing to hitch up again at noon, when the horses had barely finished feeding; and later, when the castellan and the steward offered to let me have the fodder free if I would do it, so that I could pocket the money you had left with me, I told them they knew what they could do with it, turned around, and went off."

"But surely that was not why you were driven off?"

"God forbid!" cried the groom. "No, it was for something devilishly wicked! That evening the horses of two visiting knights were put into the stable, while mine were to be tied to the door. When I took them away from the castellan, who was just tying them, and asked him where I was to put them, he pointed to a pigsty, a rickety lean-to by the castle wall."

"You mean," Kohlhaas interrupted him, "a shelter so miserable that it was more like a pigsty than a stable."

"It was a pigsty, master," Herse insisted, "literally a pigsty, with pigs running in and out, and so low that I couldn't stand up in it."

"Perhaps no other shelter was available," Kohlhaas suggested; "in a sense, the knights' horses took precedence."

"It *was* a little crowded," Herse said, his voice sinking. "In all there were seven knights staying at the Castle. Had it been you, you would have moved the horses a little closer together. I said I would look in the village for a stable I might rent; but the castellan replied he had to keep an eye on the beasts and I wasn't to dare take them out of the yard."

"Hm!" said Kohlhaas. "What did you say to that?"

"Since the steward told me that the knights were staying only one night and would ride on the next morning, I moved the horses into the pigsty. But nothing happened the next day; and the morning after, the word was that the gentlemen would stay a few weeks longer."

"All in all, Herse, perhaps things weren't as bad in the pigsty as they seemed when you first stuck your nose into it."

"True enough," the groom said. "After I cleaned the place up a bit, it was bearable. I gave sixpence to a maid, so that she would move the pigs somewhere else. And I even managed it so that the horses could stand up during the day; at dawn I would take some boards off the top, and at night I would put them back. The beasts gawked out of the roof like geese and looked around for Kohlhaasenbrück or wherever else life might be better."

"Well, then," Kohlhaas demanded, "why for heaven's sake were you chased out?"

"I'll tell you, master," Herse answered. "Because they wanted to be rid of me. Because they couldn't ruin the horses as long as I was there. Everywhere, in the yard and in the servants' quarters, I was given dirty looks; but since, for all I cared, they could make faces till they were cross-eyed, finally they picked a quarrel and threw me out."

"But the occasion!" Kohlhaas cried. "Surely they must have had some occasion."

"Indeed they did," answered Herse; "as just as can be. After two days in the pigsty, I took the horses out to ride them to the horse pond, since after all they had got dirty in there. No sooner am I at the gate and about to turn, when I hear castellan, steward, and all the hands, with sticks and dogs, rush after me and shout: 'Stop that thief! Stop that jailbird!' as if they were possessed. The gatekeeper blocks my way, and when I ask him and that mad mob at my heels what the matter is, the castellan takes hold of the reins and says: 'The matter?! Where are you going with these horses?'—and then he takes me by my shirt. I say: 'Where am I going? To the horse pond, damn

it! Do you think I—?' 'To the horse pond!' the castellan shouts. 'You rogue,
I'll pound you down the highway all the way to Kohlhaasenbrück!' At that,
he and the steward, with a mean, vicious jerk on my leg, pulled me off the
horse, so that I measured my full length in the mud. 'Hell and damnation!'
I yelled. 'The breast-straps and blankets are still in the stable, as well as my
bundle of clothing!' But while the steward led the horses off, the rest fell on
me with whips, sticks, and boots, leaving me half-dead outside the gate.
And when I said: 'Those thieving dogs! Where are they taking my horses?'
and stumbled to my feet again, the castellan yelled: 'Get out of here! Sick
'em, Caesar! Sick 'em, Spitz!' A pack of twelve dogs or more jumped at me.
I tore off a fence picket or something—I don't know what—and laid out
three of them dead at my feet; but when I finally had to give way,
miserably torn and bleeding, there was a shrill whistle: the dogs were called
back, the gate slammed shut, the bolt shot home; and I collapsed on the
road in a dead faint."

Kohlhaas, pale but with forced jocularity, said: "Perhaps you did mean to
make off, eh, Herse?" and when the man flushed deeply and looked down,
he went on: "Admit it! You didn't like it in the pigsty; you thought things
would be better in the stable back in Kohlhaasenbrück."

"Blast it!" cried Herse. "Didn't I leave the breast-straps and blankets and
my bundle in the pigsty? Wouldn't I have tucked away the three florins I
had hidden behind the manger in my red-silk kerchief? Hell and damnation!
When you talk that way, I wish I could light the wick again that I threw in
the river."

"All right, all right," said the horsedealer. "No offense meant. Look, I
believe what you've told me, every word of it; I am ready to take Holy
Communion on it when it comes up. I am sorry you haven't fared better
in my service; now go to bed, Herse, have them give you a bottle of wine
and console yourself: you shall have justice!" With that, he stood up, made
a list of the things the groom had left in the pigsty, noted down the value of
each, asked him how high he set the cost of his treatment, shook his hand,
and dismissed him.

Then he told his wife Lisbeth the full story, its cause and effects, and
explained to her that he was resolved to seek public justice; he rejoiced to
find that she supported him wholeheartedly in this resolution. For she said
that many more travellers, perhaps less patient than he had been, would pass
by the Castle; that it was doing God's work to put a stop to disorders of
this sort; and that somehow she could save whatever the lawsuit would cost
him. Kohlhaas called her his stouthearted wife, and spent that day and the
next happily with her and his children. But as soon as his affairs permitted, he
set out for Dresden again, in order to lay his suit before the court.

II

In Dresden, with the help of an advocate known to him, Kohlhaas drew up
a complaint in which, having given a circumstantial account of the outrage

committed against him and his groom Herse by the Squire Wenzel von
Tronka, he petitioned for lawful punishment of the latter, restoration of the
horses to their original condition and payment of damages to himself and his
groom. His claim was, indeed, clear beyond cavil. The fact that his horses
had been detained contrary to law cast an unambiguous light on everything
else; even on the assumption that they had sickened by mere chance, the
horsedealer's demand to have them returned in a healthy state would still
have been just. Nor did Kohlhaas, when he looked about in the capital, lack
friends who promised to support his case vigorously; his far-flung trade with
horses and the honesty of his dealing had won him not merely the acquaintance but the goodwill of the foremost men in the country. Several times, and
in fine spirits, he dined with his advocate—also a man of some standing—
deposited a sum of money with him to cover the legal expenses, and after a
few weeks, confident of the success of his suit, returned to Kohlhaasenbrück
and his wife Lisbeth.

Nevertheless, months passed, and the year was drawing to its close before he received from Saxony as much as an acknowledgment of the suit he
had instituted there, not to mention a final judgment. After several applica-
tions to the court, Kohlhaas finally asked his lawyer, in a confidential letter,
about the reason for this undue delay; he was answered that, at the instance
of higher authorities, the complaint had been dismissed. His puzzled inquiry
as to the cause drew this further explanation: the Squire Wenzel von Tronka
was related to two noblemen, Hinz and Kunz von Tronka, of whom one was
Cupbearer to the sovereign, and the other, Chamberlain. The advocate advised him to desist from any further effort to obtain legal redress and rather
to try to recover the horses from Tronka Castle; the Squire, who was just
then staying in the capital, had apparently instructed his people to hand over
the horses. The advocate's letter closed with the request that, if Kohlhaas
found this advice unacceptable, he would at least not trouble him with
further commissions in the matter.

At the time, Kohlhaas chanced to be in Brandenburg, where the city commandant, Heinrich von Geusau, whose jurisdiction also included Kohlhaasenbrück, was engaged in establishing several charitable institutions for the poor
and sick, out of a considerable fund that had fallen to the city. The commandant was especially interested in fitting up, for the benefit of the infirm, a
mineral spring which ran in a nearby village and which was thought to have
greater healing powers than it subsequently proved to possess. Since Kohlhaas was known to him from dealings during a former stay at court, he had
allowed Herse, who since that evil day at Tronka Castle had been suffering
pains in breathing, to try the effects of the little spring, which meanwhile had
been enclosed and roofed over. It happened that the commandant, busy with
giving instructions, was standing by the basin into which Herse had been put,
when Kohlhaas was handed his advocate's last, discouraging letter by a messenger his wife had sent after him. While talking to a physician, the commandant noticed Kohlhaas's dropping a tear on the letter he had just opened; he
went over to him and, in a warm and cordial manner, asked what mischance

had befallen him. And when Kohlhaas silently handed him the letter, this worthy man, who knew of the abominable injustice committed at Tronka Castle and the possibly permanent infirmity Herse suffered from as a result, clapped him on the shoulder and told him not to lose heart; he himself would help him get satisfaction. The same evening, he advised Kohlhaas, who at his bidding presented himself at the castle, simply to draw up a petition to the Elector of Brandenburg, containing a brief account of the incident, the advocate's reply, and an invocation of the sovereign's protection against the violence done him on Saxon territory. He promised to deliver the petition, with some other papers ready for submission, into the Elector's hands; the Elector for his part would, if conditions permitted, certainly remonstrate with the Elector of Saxony; and no more would be required to obtain justice from the Dresden courts, whatever intrigues the Squire and his kind might engage in. Full of joy, Kohlhaas thanked the commandant warmly for this new proof of his goodwill; his only regret was, he said, that he had not immediately taken his case to Berlin, without any proceedings in Dresden. And as soon as he had drawn up his petition in the city Chancery, exactly according to the suggestions, and given it to the commandant, he returned to Kohlhaasenbrück, more confident than ever of the outcome.

But only a few weeks later, a magistrate, who passed through the village on business from the commandant to Potsdam, brought the grievous news that the Elector had transmitted the petition to his Chancellor, Count Kallheim, who in turn had not, as would have seemed proper, applied directly to the court in Dresden for investigation and punishment of the outrage, but instead had asked for additional preliminary information from the Squire von Tronka. The magistrate—who had evidently been instructed to broach this news to Kohlhaas, since he had stopped his carriage outside Kohlhaas's gate— had no satisfactory answer to the puzzled question why such a procedure had been followed. He merely added that the commandant counselled patience. He seemed in a hurry to drive on, and only at the end of the brief exchange did Kohlhaas gather from some by-the-way remarks that Count Kallheim was related by marriage to the Tronka family.

Filled with foreboding, Kohlhaas, who no longer took joy in his house and farm and horses—indeed, hardly even in his wife and children—passed a month in waiting; when, much as he expected, Herse returned from Brandenburg, somewhat improved in health, but with a letter from the commandant to this purpose: he was sorry not to be able to do anything in the matter at issue; he enclosed a resolution sent him by the State Chancery, and advised Kohlhaas to fetch the horses he had left behind at Tronka Castle and then to let the case rest. The resolution read as follows: "That Kohlhaas was, according to the report of the court in Dresden, an idle troublemaker; the Squire with whom the horses had been left was perfectly willing to hand them over; Kohlhaas was to send to the Castle and have them fetched or at least let the Squire know where they were to be taken; in any event, however, he was to refrain from plaguing the Chancery with suchlike mischievous and petty quarrels."

Kohlhaas, who was not concerned about the horses—he would have been as grieved had it been a pair of dogs—foamed with rage when he read this letter. Every time there was a noise in the courtyard, he looked toward the gate with the most disagreeable feeling he had ever experienced; for he feared that the Squire's men might appear and deliver the horses, starved and emaciated, with perhaps, to top it all, an apology. That was the only eventuality to which his soul, well disciplined by life though it was, was unprepared to respond with anything appropriate to his feelings. But presently he heard from an acquaintance, who had come past Tronka Castle, that his nags were still being used in the fields there, like the Squire's other horses; and from the core of the pain of seeing the world in such monstrous disorder there rose up in him the deep satisfaction of knowing that now there was order within his own soul.

He asked over his neighbor, a bailiff, who had for some time considered enlarging his holdings by the purchase of adjoining properties, and as soon as he was seated, asked him what he would pay for his, Kohlhaas's, possessions —land and houses, movables and immovables in a lump, both in Brandenburg and Saxony. Lisbeth, his wife, grew pale at these words. She turned and took up her youngest child, who had been playing on the floor behind her; past the red cheeks of the boy, who now played with her kerchief, she cast a look of deadly fear at the horsedealer and the papers in his hand. The bailiff also gave him a startled glance and asked what had suddenly given him so strange an idea; whereupon Kohlhaas, with as much gaiety as he could muster, said: the notion of selling his farm by the Havel was not a very new one; they had talked of it before; compared to it, his house in the Dresden suburbs was a mere annex, not worth considering; in short, if the bailiff would fall in with his idea and take over the two properties, he was prepared to close the bargain. With somewhat forced humor, he added that, after all, Kohlhaasenbrück wasn't the world; there might be aims compared to which being a respectable householder was secondary and unimportant; in short, he must tell him that he had set his mind on great things, which perhaps would soon make a noise in the world. Reassured by these words, the bailiff said jokingly to the wife, who kept kissing the child: "Surely he won't ask cash on the barrelhead"; and putting his hat and stick, which he had held on his knees, on the table, he took the paper Kohlhaas was holding to read it through. Kohlhaas moved his chair up and explained that it was a contingent contract of sale he had drawn up himself, revocable within the next four weeks. He showed the bailiff that nothing was lacking except the signatures and the figures both of the purchase price and of the forfeit which he, Kohlhaas, agreed to pay if he should withdraw from the contract within the four weeks period; and he encouraged him to make an offer, assuring him that he would be reasonable and easy in his conditions. Lisbeth paced back and forth in the room, her bosom heaving so violently that the kerchief at which her boy had tugged threatened to slide completely off her shoulders. The bailiff remarked that he had no way of judging the value of the property in Dresden; whereupon Kohlhaas, pushing forward letters dealing with

his purchase of it, said that he valued it at a hundred gold florins, even
though the letters showed that it had cost him half again as much. The bailiff
read through the paper again; and finding in it an unusual clause under which
he likewise could withdraw from the contract, he said, his mind already half
made up, that he would have no use for the stud horses in the stables. But
when Kohlhaas replied that he did not mean to sell the horses nor, for that
matter, some weapons that were hanging in the armory, the other became
hesitant again and finally repeated an offer which he had made once during
a stroll, more in jest than in earnest, and which was trifling compared to the
real value of the property. Kohlhaas pushed over pen and ink for him to fill
in the sum; and after the bailiff, hardly trusting his senses, had asked him
once more if he was serious, and was asked in reply, somewhat heatedly, if
he thought he were being made sport of, he reluctantly and with a doubtful
expression took up the pen and wrote; but he scored out the clause concerning the seller's forfeit in case of withdrawal, assumed a mortgage of one hundred gold florins on the Dresden property, which he refused to purchase
outright, and gave Kohlhaas full liberty to withdraw, without forfeit, within
the next two months. Moved by such generosity, the horsedealer shook his
hand with much warmth; a major point—that one fourth of the purchase
price was to be paid immediately and in cash, the balance to be deposited
within three months in the Bank of Hamburg—having then been agreed on,
he called for wine to celebrate the happy conclusion of the business. He told
the maid who brought the bottles that Sternbald, one of his men, was to
saddle the chestnut; he claimed that he had to ride to the capital, where he
had matters to attend to, and hinted that upon his return he would speak
more openly of things which, for the time being, he had to keep to himself. Then, as he filled the glasses, he inquired about the Poles and the Turks,
who were then at war, involved the bailiff in all kinds of political conjectures
concerning them, once again drank to the prosperous bargain they had
struck, and bade him farewell.

When the bailiff had left the room, Lisbeth fell to her knees before her
husband. "If you have any love for me," she cried, "and for the children I
have borne you—if you have not already, for reasons I know nothing of,
banished us from your heart—tell me the meaning of these frightful preparations!"

Kohlhaas said: "Dear wife, as things stand at present, it is nothing you
need feel distressed over. I have received a resolution saying that my complaint against the Squire Wenzel von Tronka is mischievous troublemaking.
And since clearly there must be some misunderstanding, I have decided to
submit my complaint once more, this time in person, to the sovereign."

"Why then do you want to sell your house?" she cried, getting to her feet
with a distracted look. The horsedealer embraced her gently and answered:
"Because, dearest Lisbeth, I do not care to remain in a country which does
not give me the protection of the laws. If I am to be kicked, I'd rather be a
dog than a man! I am sure that on this point my wife thinks as I do."

"How do you know," she asked softly, "that your rights will not be protected? If you approach the sovereign with your petition, modestly as befits you, how do you know that it will be cast aside or answered with a refusal to hear your case?'

"Very well," Kohlhaas replied, "if my misgivings are unfounded, neither is my house sold as yet. I know the sovereign himself is just; if only I can contrive to get past the men that surround him and to speak to him in person, I do not doubt but that I shall have justice and come happily back to you and to my trade, before the week is out. And I wish nothing better," he added as he kissed her, "than to spend the rest of my life by your side. But it is advisable," he continued, "to be prepared for every eventuality; that is why, for a little space, I should like you to go away from here, if possible, and to take the children to your aunt in Schwerin, whom in any case you have long wanted to visit."

"What?" cried Lisbeth. "I am to go to Schwerin? Across the border with the children, to my aunt in Schwerin?" Fright choked off her words.

"Certainly," Kohlhaas said, "and right now, if possible, so that I am not hindered in whatever steps I mean to take."

"Oh, I understand!" she cried. "You need nothing now but horses and weapons; let who will take the rest!" With that she turned away, threw herself down on a chair and wept.

Taken aback, Kohlhaas said: "Dearest Lisbeth, what are you saying? God has blessed me with a wife, children, and possessions; am I to wish for the first time now that it were otherwise?" He gently sat down by her, while she blushed and threw her arms about his neck. "Tell me," he said, brushing the curls from her forehead, "what am I to do? Shall I go to Tronka Castle and ask the Squire to give me back my horses, and mount them and ride them back to you?"

Lisbeth did not dare say: "Yes! Yes! Yes!" Tearfully, she shook her head, pressed him to her and covered his chest with burning kisses. "Well then," Kohlhaas exclaimed, "if you feel that, in order to continue in my trade, I must have justice, then do not deny me the freedom of action I need to obtain it!"

With that, he rose and told the servant, who came to announce that the chestnut was saddled, to see that the bays were hitched up the next day to take the mistress to Schwerin. Lisbeth got up, dried her tears, and asked her husband, who had sat down at the desk, if he would give her the petition and let her go to Berlin in his stead to deliver it to the sovereign. For more than one reason, Kohlhaas was touched by this request; he drew her down on his knees and said: "Dearest wife, that can hardly be! The sovereign is surrounded by many people, and whoever would approach him exposes himself to all kinds of annoyances."

Lisbeth retorted that in a thousand instances a woman found the approach easier than a man. "Let me have the petition," she insisted. "If all you want is to be sure that it gets into the sovereign's hands, I pledge my life that he shall receive it." Kohlhaas, who had many proofs of both her courage and her astuteness, asked how she intended to go about it; whereupon she answered, a little shame-faced, that the castellan of the Elector's palace had at one time, while he was in service in Schwerin, courted her; to be sure, he was married now and had several children, but he had not altogether forgotten her; in short, Kohlhaas could leave it to her to make the most of this circumstance, as well as of others, which it would take too long to explain. Kohlhaas kissed her joyfully, said that he agreed to her plan, advised her that, to encounter the sovereign in the palace itself, she need only take lodgings with the castellan's wife, handed her the petition, had the bays hitched, and sent her off, well wrapped and escorted by his faithful servant, Sternbald.

But of all the futile steps he had taken in his cause, this proved the most unfortunate. Only a few days later, Sternbald returned to the farm, leading the horses at a walk, with his mistress, prostrate with a dangerous contusion of the chest, lying inside the wagon. Kohlhaas, paling as he stepped up to the vehicle, could get no coherent information about the cause of the accident. As the man told it, the castellan had not been at home, so that they had to put up at a nearby inn. The following morning, Lisbeth had left, ordering Sternbald to stay behind with the horses; when she was brought back late that evening, she was in her present condition. It seemed that she had been too importunate in trying to get close to the sovereign; without his knowledge, one of the guards surrounding him had, with rough zeal, pushed the shaft of his halberd against her chest. So, at any rate, the people said who had carried her unconscious to the inn that evening; she herself could hardly speak because of the blood flowing from her mouth. The petition had been taken from her afterwards by some knight. Sternbald said he had meant to ride off immediately to inform Kohlhaas of the mishap; but in the face even of the representations of the surgeon that had been called in, the mistress had insisted that no word be sent ahead, but that she be taken back to her husband in Kohlhaasenbrück.

Barely alive after the journey, she was carried by Kohlhaas to her bed, where she lingered on a few days, painfully laboring to breathe. Attempts to recall her to consciousness, so that she might provide some clue to what had happened to her, were unavailing; she lay with staring, almost glassy eyes, and did not answer. Only once, shortly before she died, did she regain consciousness. For when a pastor of the Lutheran faith—which, following her husband's example, she had embraced almost from its inception—was standing by her bed and in a loud, solemn, and moving voice reading a chapter from the Bible, of a sudden she looked at him somberly, took the Bible from his hands as though she did not need to be read to, and turned page after page, apparently to find a certain place; finally her index finger pointed out to Kohlhaas, who was sitting at her bedside, the verse: "Forgive your enemies; do good to them who hate you." As she did so, she pressed his hand, looked at him with deep feeling, and died.

Kohlhaas thought: "May God never forgive me as I forgive the Squire!" his tears running freely, he kissed her, closed her eyes, and left the room. He took the hundred gold florins the bailiff had already paid him for the

property in Dresden and ordered a funeral more befitting a princess than a
burgher's wife: an oak coffin with heavy brass mountings, silken cushions
with gold and silver tassels, and a grave eight yards deep, lined with field-
stone and lime. He himself stood by the tomb, his youngest child on his arm,
and watched the work. On the day of the funeral, the body, white as snow,
was laid out in a hall he had had hung in black cloth. Hardly had the pastor
finished a pathetic address by her bier when Kohlhaas was handed the
sovereign's reply to the petition the dead woman had carried: he was
ordered to fetch his horses from Tronka Castle and to take no further action
in the matter, on pain of imprisonment. As soon as the mound was raised, a
cross planted on it, and the funeral guests gone, he threw himself down once
more by her now empty bed and then took up the business of vengeance.

III

He sat down and drew up a decree in which, by innate authority, he condemned the Squire Wenzel von Tronka, within three days of receipt
thereof, to return the blacks he had seized and ruined in fieldwork, and in
person to feed them back to health in Kohlhaas's stables. He sent the decree
by mounted messenger, whom he instructed to hurry back to Kohlhaasenbrück as soon as he had delivered the document. When three days had passed
without the horses having been returned, he called in Herse; he made known
to him what he had ordered the Squire to do by way of restoring the horses,
and asked him two things: was he willing to ride with him to Tronka Castle
and fetch the Squire, and would he wield the whip in Kohlhaas's stables, in
case the Squire should prove sluggish in fulfilling the terms of the decree.
And when Herse, as soon as he understood, shouted jubilantly: "This very
day, Sir!" threw his cap into the air, and promised to get a leather tong with
ten knots in it to teach the Squire how to curry a horse, Kohlhaas sold the
house, sent his children by wagon over the border, at nightfall called together his other hands, seven in number and everyone true as gold, armed
and mounted them, and set out for Tronka Castle.
    With this little troop, at dusk of the third day, he descended upon the
Castle, riding down the tollkeeper and gatekeeper where they stood talking
in the gate. Sheds and stables were put to the torch; and while Herse ran
through the castle yard, up the winding stairs into the castellan's tower, and
with blows and thrusts fell upon the castellan and the steward where they
were sitting, half-dressed, over cards, Kohlhaas rushed into the castle to find
the Squire. He was like the Angel of Judgment descending from Heaven.
The Squire, who was just reading the horsedealer's decree, amidst huge
laughter, to a crowd of young companions, no sooner heard Kohlhaas's voice
in the yard than he turned pale as a corpse, shouted: "Friends, save yourselves!" to the gentlemen, and vanished. Upon entering the hall, Kohlhaas
took by the doublet a certain Hans von Tronka, who was charging him,
and threw him with such force into a corner of the room that his brains
splattered on the masonry. And while the other gentlemen, who had drawn

their swords, were overpowered and driven off by his men, he asked where the Squire Wenzel von Tronka was. Seeing that the stunned guests knew nothing, and finding no one himself, though he kicked down two doors leading into the wings of the Castle and searched the vast building in every direction, he at last went cursing back down into the yard and ordered all exits to be watched. Meanwhile, the Castle and its wings had caught fire from the outbuildings and were sending heavy smoke clouds skyward. Sternbald, with three of the men, was gathering everything movable and throwing it down among the horses as legitimate booty; from the open windows of the castellan's quarters the bodies of the castellan and the steward, followed by those of their wives and children, were flung into the yard to the triumphant shouting of Herse. As Kohlhaas came down the castle stairs, he was stopped by the Squire's gouty old housekeeper, who threw herself down at his feet; when he asked her where the Squire Wenzel von Tronka was, and she, in a weak, trembling voice, replied that she believed he had sought refuge in the chapel, he called two of his men with their torches, had the chapel doors, for lack of keys, broken down with crowbars and axes, knocked over pews and altars, but to his fury and distress failed to discover the Squire.

A young castle servant happened to run past as Kohlhaas emerged from the chapel, meaning to lead the Squire's chargers out of a large, stone-built stable that was threatened by the flames. Kohlhaas, who at that moment noticed his blacks standing in a small thatch-roofed shed, asked the servant why he did not save those. When the boy, putting the key in the stable door, answered that the shed was already afire, Kohlhaas tore the key violently out of the lock, flung it over the wall, drove the boy with a hail of blows into the burning shed and, amid the horrible laughter of his men, forced him to save the blacks. But a few moments later, when the terrified fellow led the horses out of the shed, which promptly collapsed behind him, Kohlhaas had left; and when he joined the men in the yard and repeatedly asked what he was to do with the animals, Kohlhaas, after first turning his back on him, suddenly and with fearsome violence raised his foot, so that, had he actually delivered the kick, it would have been the boy's death. Then, without a word, he mounted his bay, stationed himself beneath the gate and, while his men continued their pillage, waited for the breaking of day.

By dawn the Castle had burned down to the walls; no one was left in it but Kohlhaas and his seven men. He dismounted and once again, by the sun which now lit up every corner, searched the ruins; and when, much against his will, he had to admit to himself that his enterprise had failed, with a heavy heart he sent out Herse and some men to gather intelligence about the direction in which the Squire had fled. He was especially disturbed over a rich convent, called Erlabrunn, which stood on the banks of the Mulde River and whose abbess, Antonia von Tronka, was known throughout the region as a pious, charitable, and saintly woman; for it appeared only too probable to the unfortunate Kohlhaas that the Squire, stripped as he was of all necessities, had fled to this convent, since the abbess was his aunt and had had charge of him during his childhood. Having learned all this, Kohlhaas climbed the castellan's tower, in which there still was a habitable room, and composed a so-called "Kohlhaas Mandate," warning the country not to aid, in any manner soever, the Squire Wenzel von Tronka, with whom he was engaged in a just war, and charging every inhabitant, Tronka's friends and relatives not excepted, to surrender the Squire to him, on pain of death and destruction by fire of whatever they called their own. This declaration he broadcast throughout the countryside by means of travellers and strangers; one copy of it he gave to his man Waldmann, with explicit instructions to deliver it into the hands of Lady Antonia in Erlabrunn. Then he engaged some of the Tronka servants, who were dissatisfied with their master and, attracted by the prospect of booty, wished to enter his service; he armed them, like foot-soldiers, with crossbows and daggers and taught them to ride behind the mounted men; and after he had sold all that his men had plundered for ready money and had distributed it among them, he took, again beneath the castle gate, a few hours' respite from his sorry labors.

Toward noon Herse returned and confirmed what Kohlhaas, always fearing the worst, had suspected: the Squire was at Erlabrunn with his aunt, Lady Antonia von Tronka. He had, it seemed, escaped by a door that opened through the castle's rear wall and onto a flight of narrow stone steps, lightly roofed over, which ran down to some boats on the Elbe River. However it was, Herse reported that about midnight the Squire had landed at a downriver village, in a boat without oars or rudder, much to the astonishment of the villagers, who were assembled to watch the fire in Tronka Castle; a farmer's cart had taken him on to Erlabrunn. At this news, Kohlhaas sighed deeply; he asked if the horses had been baited and, being answered that they were, had the troop mount and within three hours stood before Erlabrunn.

A distant storm rumbled on the horizon; he and his men, carrying torches they had lit in the village, had just entered the convent courtyard and Waldmann, meeting him, had reported that he had properly delivered the Mandate, when they saw the abbess and the warden, in agitated conversation, step out under the portal. While the warden, a little old man with snow-white hair who looked at Kohlhaas in grim defiance, had his armor put on and boldly ordered the men about him to ring the alarm bell, the abbess, white as her linen and carrying a silver image of Christ Crucified, came down the ramp and, with all her nuns, knelt down in front of Kohlhaas's horse. Herse and Waldmann overpowered the warden, who had no sword, and led him off among the horses, while Kohlhaas asked the abbess where the Squire von Tronka was.

"In Wittenberg, worthy Kohlhaas," she answered, unfastening from her girdle a large bundle of keys, and tremulously added: "Fear God and do no evil!" Kohlhaas, thrust back into the hell of unslaked vengeance, wheeled his horse about and was on the point of shouting: "Put the place to the torch!" when a terrible thunderbolt struck the ground close by. He turned back and asked the lady if she had received his Mandate; to which she replied, in a feeble, scarcely audible voice: "Only a moment ago." "When?" "Two hours after the Squire, my nephew, left, so help me God." When Waldmann, stammering under Kohlhaas's lowering glance, confirmed this, and explained that the Mulde, swollen by rains, had prevented his arriving sooner, Kohlhaas checked his wrath. A sudden, heavy downpour, which fell on the courtyard pavement and put out the torches, also helped to ease the anguish in his unhappy breast; he curtly saluted the abbess, swung around again, and saying: "Follow me, comrades; the Squire is in Wittenberg!" he spurred his horse and left the convent grounds.

At nightfall he put up at a roadside inn, where he had to stop for a day to rest his weary horses; and since he realized that with a troop of ten men (that being his present strength) he could not challenge a place as strong as Wittenberg, he composed a second Mandate, in which he briefly set forth how he had been treated in Saxony and summoned "every good Christian"— as he put it—"to take up his cause against the Squire von Tronka as the common enemy of all Christians," promising wages and other emoluments of war. In a further Mandate, which appeared soon after, he styled himself "a free and independent noble of the Empire and the world, subject only to God"—a form of mad and monstrous fanaticism which, nevertheless, backed by the promise of money and the prospect of plunder, gained him many recruits among the rabble whom the peace with Poland had left without a livelihood; so that, when he returned to the right bank of the Elbe, purposing to burn down Wittenberg, he commanded some thirty-odd men. With these he camped beneath the roof of an old, abandoned brick kiln, in the solitude of a dark forest then enclosing the town; and as soon as he learned from Waldmann (whom he had sent, disguised, into the town to post the Mandate) that the Mandate was already known there, he set out with his men on Whitsuntide Eve and, the townspeople being sound asleep, started fires in several different places at once. While his men plundered the suburbs, he fastened a notice to the door post of one of the churches, saying that "he, Kohlhaas, had set fire to the town, and if the Squire were not surrendered to him, he would burn it down so utterly that"—as he put it—"he would not need to look behind walls to find him."

The townsmen's terror at this unheard-of outrage was indescribable. At daybreak, after the flames—which had gutted only nineteen buildings (one of them a church), the night luckily having been still and summery—had been brought under control, the old Governor, Otto von Gorgas, sent out a squadron of fifty men to capture the maniac. But the captain in command, Gerstenberg by name, conducted himself so badly that the sortie, instead of subduing Kohlhaas, gained him a most dangerous military reputation. For while the Captain, thinking to encircle and crush Kohlhaas, split up his command into several detachments, Kohlhaas kept his men together, attacked, and routed the enemy piece-meal; so that by the next following evening not a man of the force on which the hope of the province rested was left to oppose him. The morning after, Kohlhaas, who had lost only a few men in these skirmishes, again set fire to the town; on this occasion his murderous measures were so well taken that a great many houses, and almost all the barns outside the city walls, were burned down. Again he posted the afore-mentioned Mandate, this time on the corners of the City Hall itself, adding a report on the defeat of Captain von Gerstenberg, whom the Governor had sent against him.

Furious at this defiance, the Governor placed himself, with several knights, at the head of a force of a hundred and fifty men. He also furnished the Squire von Tronka, at his request, with a watch to protect him against the violence of the populace, who flatly demanded his removal from the city; and after having posted guards in all the neighboring villages and manned the city walls to guard against a surprise attack, he set out in person on St. Jervis's Day to vanquish the dragon that laid waste the country. The horsedealer was clever enough to avoid this force; when, by skilful move-ments, he had lured the Governor five leagues away from the town and through various feints had induced him to believe that, yielding to superior strength, he was withdrawing into Brandenburg, he quickly wheeled about three nights later, made a forced march back to Wittenberg, and for the third time set the town afire. It was Herse who, slipping into the city in dis-guise, executed the gruesome feat; and with a brisk north wind blowing, the fire was so destructive and devouring that within less than three hours forty-two houses, several churches and schools, and even the gubernatorial building were reduced to ashes.

When the Governor, who believed his opponent in Brandenburg territory, was informed of what had happened, he returned in frantic marches to Wittenberg, which he found in a state of general rebellion. People by the thousands had gathered before the Squire's house, which had been barricaded with heavy timbers, and were wildly clamoring for his deportation. Two burgomasters named Jenkens and Otto, in their official dress and at the head of the entire City Council, tried in vain to persuade the crowd that they must await the return of a courier who had been dispatched to the president of the State Chancery with an urgent request that the Squire be removed to Dresden, where he himself, for various reasons, desired to go. The irra-tional mob, armed with pikes and poles, paid no heed, began to manhandle some of the councillors who called for forceful measures, and was about to storm and tear down the Squire's house, when Otto von Gorgas, the Gov-ernor, appeared in the city at the head of his force. This dignified old gentle-man, whose mere presence usually inspired reverence and obedience, had luckily—in compensation, as it were, for the ill success of the enterprise from which he returned—caught three stray members of the incendiary's crew just outside the city walls. These he ordered put in chains before the eyes of the crowd; and by assuring the councillors, in a shrewd speech, that he was on Kohlhaas's track and expected shortly to bring him in a prisoner, he succeeded in disarming the fears of the people and in temporarily recon-ciling them to the Squire's presence until the courier's return from Dresden. He dismounted, had the barricades removed and, accompanied by some knights, went into the house, where he found the Squire falling from one faint into another and being cared for by two physicians, who tried to revive him with stimulants and aromatic essences. Gorgas, aware that this was not the time to begin a dispute over the Squire's former misconduct, merely looked at him with quiet contempt, and desired him to get dressed and, for his own safety, to follow him to the rooms of the knights' prison. When the Squire, in a doublet and helmet they had put on him and with his shirt half unbuttoned to ease his breathing, appeared on the street, led by the Governor and his brother-in-law, Count von Gerschau, a chorus of blasphemies and horrid curses rose against him. The people, barely kept in bounds by the soldiers, called him a bloodsucker, a miserable tormentor of country and people, the curse of Wittenberg and the perdition of Saxony; and after a sorry progress through the ravaged town, during which he repeatedly lost his helmet nor would have missed it if a knight had not kept clapping it back on his head from behind, he finally reached the prison and disappeared in a heavily guarded tower.

Presently the town took new alarm from the return of the courier bearing the Elector's decison. The Saxon Government, pressed by an urgent petition of the citizens of Dresden, would not hear of the Squire's coming to the capital before the incendiary had been put down; rather, since the Squire had to be somewhere, the Governor was ordered to keep him where he was now and to protect him with whatever forces he had available. However, the Government, to quiet the fears of the loyal citizens of Wittenberg, made known to them that a force of five hundred soldiers, commanded by Prince Friedrich of Meissen, was on its way to defend them from further depradations. The Governor saw clearly that a decision of this kind could nowise satisfy the people. For not only had several minor successes outside the city walls given currency to highly disturbing rumors about the strength of the horsedealer's band; his mode of warfare—under cover of darkness, with disguised bandits, and by straw, pitch, and sulfur—was so unheard of and novel that even a stronger force than that approaching under the Prince of Meissen might well be ineffective against him. After brief reflection, therefore, the Governor decided to suppress the order he had received. He merely posted throughout the town a letter in which the Prince of Meissen announced his arrival; a covered wagon emerged at daybreak from the yard of the knights' prison and took the highway to Leipzig, escorted by four heavily armed horsemen, who let it be understood that they were bound for the Pleissenburg, the citadel of Leipzig. The people thus having been appeased in the point of the disastrous Squire, whose mere presence seemed to bring visitations by fire and sword, the Governor set out with three hundred men to join the Prince of Meissen.

Kohlhaas's force meanwhile, owing to the strange position he had assumed in the world, had in fact grown to a hundred and nine men; and since in Jessen he had managed to seize a store of arms sufficient fully to equip his troop, he decided to meet the two storm clouds moving toward him and, with the speed of the wind, to scatter them before they could join and destroy him. Accordingly, within twenty-four hours, he attacked the Prince

of Meissen at night near Mühlberg. In this encounter he was deeply grieved
to lose Herse, who fell by his side in the first exchange of shots; but, embittered by this loss, in three hours' fighting he so severely mauled the
Prince, who was unable to collect his forces in the town, that by daybreak
the latter, himself badly wounded and with his troops in total disorder, was
compelled to withdraw to Dresden. Heady with this success, Kohlhaas
turned on the governor before news of the first battle had reached him,
attacked him at high noon near the village of Damerow and fought him until
nightfall, suffering murderous losses, to be sure, but inflicting losses just as
heavy. He would, in fact, have renewed the attack with the remainder of his
men the following morning, except that the Governor, entrenched for the
night in the Damerow churchyard, had meanwhile learned from a scout of
the Prince's defeat at Mühlberg and so had thought it wiser to withdraw and
wait in Wittenberg for a more propitious occasion. Five days after the dis-
persal of these two forces, Kohlhaas stood before the gates of Leipzig and
set fire to the city on three sides.

In the Mandate which he broadcast on this occasion, he styled himself "a
viceregent of the Archangel Michael, come to punish with fire and sword
all those who in this quarrel should take the Squire's side, for the false
dealing into which the whole world had fallen." From Lützen Castle, which
he had taken by surprise and where he had established himself, he called
upon the people to join his cause of setting up a better order of things and,
in a kind of ecstasy, signed the Mandate: "Given at the Seat of our
Provisional World Government, the Arch-Palace at Lützen." Luckily for
the citizens of Leipzig, a steady rain kept the fires from spreading, so that, the
fire watch working with great expedition, only a few small shops near
the Pleissenburg were burned down. All the same, the mad incendiary's
presence, joined with his conviction that the Squire was in the city, caused
unspeakable consternation; and after a detachment of one hundred and eighty
horse sent forth against him returned in a rout, the Council, who did not
want to endanger the city's wealth, had no choice but to bar the gates completely and to make the citizens stand twenty-four-hour watch outside the
walls. It was in vain that the Council posted declarations in the villages of
the district, giving positive assurances that the Squire was not in the
Pleissenburg; the horsedealer, in similar notices, maintained that he *was*
there, and that if he were not, he, Kohlhaas, would nevertheless proceed as
though he were, until they had informed him of the place, by name, where
he was to be found. The Elector, notified by courier of the city's plight,
declared that he was assembling an army of two thousand men and would
lead it in person to capture Kohlhaas. Otto von Gorgas received a severe rep-
rimand for the ill-considered and ambiguous device he had used to rid
Wittenberg of the incendiary; and it is impossible to describe the confusion
in all of Saxony, but especially in the capital, when it became known that
someone, nobody knew who, had posted a notice in the villages around
Leipzig to the effect that Squire Wenzel was with his cousins Hinz and Kunz
in Dresden.

IV

At this juncture, Doctor Martin Luther undertook the office of trying whether the power of persuasion, aided by the moral authority which his place in the world gave him, would force Kohlhaas back within the confines of ordered society. Relying upon an element of goodness within the incendiary's heart, Luther issued a letter to him, which was placarded in all the villages and cities of the Electorate and read as follows:

> Kohlhaas, you who claim to have been chosen to wield the sword of justice, how dare you, presumptuous man, act in the rage of purblind passion—you, who are yourself filled head to foot with injustice? Because the sovereign, whose subject you are, has denied you your right—your right in a quarrel over a paltry possession—you rise up, godless wretch, and with fire and sword, like the wolf of the desert, break into the peaceful herd that is under his protection. You, who lead men astray with this your claim full of falsehood and deceit: do you, sinner, hope to maintain it before God, on that day which will lay bare the last recesses of the heart? How can you maintain that your right has been denied you—you, who in the wrath of your soul, lusting for a base private revenge, have after the first half-hearted and unavailing attempts ceased all further efforts to obtain satisfaction? Are a bench of constables and beadles, who suppress a petition entrusted to them or withhold a ruling they are charged to deliver—are these your supreme authority? Need I tell you, godforsaken man, that your sovereign knows nothing of your case—nay more, that he against whom you rebel knows not even your name; so that when, on the last of days, you come before God's throne thinking to accuse him, he will be able to say with a serene countenance: 'This man, Lord, was never wronged by me, for my soul is a stranger to his existence'? Know that the sword you wield is the sword of rapine and murder; you are a rebel, not a warrior of the just Lord. Your destiny on earth is the wheel and the gallows, and in the beyond that damnation which is visited upon crime and godlessness.
>
> Wittenberg, etc.   Martin Luther.

At the castle in Lützen, Kohlhaas was turning his ravaged mind to a new plan for burning down Leipzig—for he gave no credence to the posted report of the Squire's being in Dresden, since it was signed by no one, let alone the Council, as he had demanded—when Sternbald and Waldmann, to their consternation, noticed Luther's placard, which during the night had been fastened to the castle gate. Reluctant to call Kohlhaas's attention to it, for several days they hoped that he would see it himself—but in vain; though in the evening he came out, gloomy and self-absorbed, to issue his daily orders, he did not see the placard. Finally, on a morning when he planned to have two of his men, who against his orders had looted in the vicinity, executed by hanging, they decided to bring him to notice it. He was returning from the place of execution, with the ceremony which, since his last Mandate, had become his custom: a large archangel's sword was carried before him on a red leather cushion adorned with gold tassels, and twelve servants with burning torches followed him. As the crowd on both sides timidly gave way, Sternbald and Waldmann, their swords under their arms, stepped out from behind the placarded pillar in such a way that it was sure to attract Kohlhaas's attention. Walking toward the portal with his hands clasped behind his back and deep in thought, he looked up and stopped short; and when the two men stepped respectfully aside, he glanced at them absentmindedly and with a few quick steps approached the pillar. But who can describe what passed through his soul when he saw there the letter charging him with injustice—signed by the most beloved and revered name known to him, Martin Luther! He flushed darkly; taking off his helmet, he read a second time; then, with an uncertain look, he turned back to his men, as though he meant to say something, but said nothing; finally he took down the placard, read it once again, called out: "Waldmann, have my horse saddled!" and: "Sternbald, follow me inside!" and disappeared. No more than Luther's few words were needed to disarm him instantly, though he was then at the height of his power and destructive rage. He disguised himself as a Thuringian tenant farmer; told Sternbald that business of great weight made it necessary for him to ride to Wittenberg; entrusted him, in the presence of some of the leading men, with the command of the band, under orders to remain in Lützen; and, promising to be back within three days, during which time there was no danger of an attack, he rode off.

In Wittenberg he put up at an inn under an assumed name; by nightfall, wrapped in his cloak and armed with a brace of pistols he had taken from Tronka Castle, he stepped into Luther's study. When Luther, who was sitting at his desk amid books and papers, saw the stranger enter the door and then bolt it behind him, he asked who he was and what he wanted. But no sooner had the invader, respectfully holding his hat in his hand and diffidently conscious of the fright he would cause, replied that he was Michael Kohlhaas the horsedealer, than Luther cried: "Away from me!" rose from his desk and hurried toward the bell, adding: "Your breath is pestilence and your presence destruction!" Without moving from where he stood, Kohlhaas drew his pistol and said: "Reverend sir, if you touch the bell, this pistol will drop me lifeless at your feet. Sit down and hear me; you are as safe with me as among the angels whose psalms you are writing down." Luther sat down and asked: "What do you want?" Kohlhass replied: "I want to refute your judgment that I am an unjust man. In your notice you told me that my sovereign knows nothing of my case; well then, procure me a safe-conduct, and I shall go to Dresden to submit my case to him."

"Impious and terrible man!" Luther cried, confused and at the same time encouraged by these words. "Who gave you the right to render a verdict on your private, arbitrary authority, to execute it by attacking the Squire von Tronka, and, when you did not find him in his castle, to visit fire and sword on the entire community that shelters him?"

Kohlhaas answered: "No one did, Reverend sir—as things stand now! Information I had from Dresden has deceived and misled me! The war I am waging against human society is criminal if, as you have now assured me, I was not cast out from it."

"Cast out!" Luther exclaimed, looking at him. "What madness possessed you? Who could have cast you out of the community of the state in which you lived? Indeed, as long as there have been states, has there ever been a case of someone's—anyone's—being so cast out?"

Kohlhaas clenched his fist. "Cast out," he said, "I call the man who is denied the protection of the laws! For this protection I need, if my peaceful trade is to prosper. More: it is the reason why I seek shelter in ordered society for myself and for what I have gained. Whoever denies it to me casts me out among the savages of the desert; he puts into my hand—how can you deny that?—the club of self-protection."

"Who denied you the protection of the laws?" Luther cried. "Did I not tell you that the complaint you submitted is unknown to the sovereign? If his servants suppress lawsuits behind his back or otherwise make a mockery of his sacred name without his knowledge—who but God may hold him to account for his choice of such servants? And are you, accursed and dreadful man, entitled to sit in judgment on him?"

"Very well," Kohlhaas retorted, "if the sovereign does not cast me out, I for my part return to the community whose protector he is. I repeat: Procure me a safe-conduct to Dresden, and I shall dismiss the force I have collected in Lützen and once more lay before the courts the suit they previously rejected."

Luther looked annoyed, shuffled the papers on his desk and was silent. The defiant posture this man assumed in the state vexed him. Pondering the verdict Kohlhaas had issued against the Squire from Kohlhaasenbrück, he finally asked what the horsedealer meant to sue for in Dresden. Kohlhaas answered: "Punishment of the Squire according to law; restoration of the horses to their former condition; and compensation for the damages sustained both by myself and by the late Herse, my groom, since killed at Mühlberg, in consequence of the outrages committed against us."

Luther cried: "Compensation for damages! You have borrowed money by the thousands, from Jews and Christians, on notes and mortgages, to pay for your mad vengeance! Do you mean to put all that on the bill, if it comes to the reckoning?"

"God forbid!" Kohlhaas answered. "I do not ask restitution of my house and farm and of my former wealth, nor even the cost of my wife's burial! Herse's old mother will present an account of the medical expenses and a list of the things her son lost at Tronka Castle; a court expert can estimate the damage I suffered by not selling the blacks."

"Mad, incomprehensible and dreadful man!" Luther said, fixing him. "After your sword has brought upon the Squire the most ferocious vengeance conceivable, why will you insist on a judgement which, if ultimately it is rendered,will touch him so lightly?"

A tear rolled down Kohlhaas's cheek as he answered: "Reverend sir, it has cost my wife! Kohlhaas means to show the world that she died in no unrighteous cause. Yield to my wishes on these points and let the court speak; on all other disputed points I will yield to you."

Luther said: "Look: what you demand—if in truth the circumstances are

as public report has them—is just; and if, before taking the law into your
own hands, you had known how to bring the dispute before the sovereign
for his decision, I do not doubt but your demands would have been granted
in every particular. But all things weighed, would you not have done better
to have forgiven the Squire for your Saviour's sake, taken your blacks however feeble and starved, mounted them and ridden back to your stables in
Kohlhaasenbrück to fatten them up again?"

Kohlhaas said: "Maybe!" and stepped to the window. "And maybe not!
If I had known that it would cost my dear wife's blood to put them back on
their feet, perhaps I would have done as you say, Reverend sir, and not
grudged a bushel of oats! But since, as things stand, they have cost me so
dear, I think that the matter should run its course; let judgment be rendered,
as is my due, and let the Squire fatten my blacks."

Beset by the most various ideas, Luther took up his papers again and said
he would negotiate with the Elector on Kohlhaas's behalf. Kohlhaas, meanwhile, was to remain quietly in Lützen; if the Elector should grant him a
safe-conduct, he would be informed by public notice. "Of course," Luther
continued as Kohlhaas bent down to kiss his hand, "I do not know if the
Elector will let mercy prevail over justice; I hear that he is gathering an
army and ready to capture you in the castle at Lützen. But in the meantime,
as I told you, I shall do what I can." With that he stood up to dismiss him.

Kohlhaas said that, with Luther interceding for him, he had no fear of the
result; but when Luther made a gesture of farewell, he suddenly got down
on one knee and said he had one more request. On Whitsunday, when it
was his custom to take Holy Communion, he had failed to attend church,
being engaged in this warlike undertaking; would Luther have the kindness
to hear his confession, without further preparation, and in return grant him
the blessing of the Holy Sacrament? Luther looked at him keenly and,
after brief thought, replied: "Yes, Kohlhaas, I am willing! But the Lord
Whose body you desire forgave His enemies. Will you likewise," he added,
as the other gave him a disturbed look, "forgive the Squire who has offended
you, go to Tronka Castle, mount your blacks and ride them back to Kohlhaasenbrück to feed them to health?"

"Reverend sir," Kohlhaas said, flushing and seizing Luther's hand. "Well?"
"The Lord also did not forgive all His enemies. Let me forgive the Electors,
my two sovereigns, as well as the castellan and the steward, the lords Hinz
and Kunz, and whoever else may have injured me in this matter; but as for
the Squire, let me, if I can, compel him to fatten my blacks again!"

At this, Luther looked displeased, turned his back on him and rang the
bell. When the servant thus summoned came into the anteroom with a
light, Kohlhaas, disconcerted, rose from the floor and wiped his eyes; and
as the servant tried vainly to open the bolted door, he opened it for him,
Luther having sat down again at his desk. With a curt glance at the stranger,
Luther ordered the servant: "Light the way!" Whereupon the latter, somewhat puzzled to see a visitor, took the house key from the wall and went
back to the half-open door, waiting for Kohlhaas to leave.

Shaken, Kohlhaas took his hat, and said: "Then I cannot, Reverend sir, have the blessing of reconciliation which I asked of you?" Luther answered curtly: "With your Saviour, no; with your sovereign—that depends on the success of the attempt I promised you to undertake." Then he motioned to the servant to do, without more delay, the business he had been called for. With a look of painful feeling, Kohlhaas pressed both hands to his chest, followed the man who was lighting him downstairs, and disappeared.

The next morning, Luther dispatched a formal letter to the Elector of Saxony. After a bitter allusion to the lords Hinz and Kunz von Tronka, who, as the Chamberlain and Cupbearer attending upon his Grace's person, had, as everyone knew, suppressed the complaint, he told him, with characteristic frankness, that under these circumstances there was no choice but to accept the horsedealer's proposal and to grant him an amnesty for what had happened, so that he could resume his lawsuit. Public opinion, Luther noted, had sided with this man in a most dangerous degree, so that even in Wittenberg, thrice set afire by him though it had been, people were unanimous in taking his part. And since Kohlhaas, if his offer should be rejected, would without fail make it public, furnished with partisan comments, the people might easily be led astray to the point where the Government would be powerless against him. He concluded that, in this extraordinary case, the danger of entering into negotiations with a subject who had taken arms against the State must be disregarded; for Kohlhaas, by the treatment accorded him, had indeed been placed outside the confines of the social order. In short, to extricate itself from its embarrassments, the Government, instead of treating him as a rebellious subject, must rather consider him as a foreign, invading power, which, not being a citizen of Saxony, in a sense he was.

When the Elector received this letter, there were present at court: Prince Christiern of Meissen, Generalissimo of the Empire and uncle of the Prince Friedrich who had been defeated at Mühlberg and was still laid up with his wounds; Count Wrede, the Lord Chancellor; Count Kallheim, President of the State Chancery; and the lords Hinz and Kunz von Tronka, confidants and boyhood friends of the sovereign, one the Cupbearer and the other, Chamberlain. The Chamberlain, Kunz, who in his capacity as privy councillor attended to his master's private correspondence and was authorized to use the Elector's name and seal, was the first to speak. Having once more and at great length protested that he would never, on his own authority, have suppressed the charges preferred by the horse dealer against his cousin the Squire if he had not, misled by false evidence, considered them entirely baseless, idle, and mischievous, he then addressed himself to the present situation. He noted that neither divine nor human law justified the horsedealer's wreaking, for this mistake, so horrendous a vengeance as he had permitted himself; he pictured the splendor and dignity which would accrue to this damnable rebel from being negotiated with as with a power entitled to wage war; and the ignominy thereby cast upon the sacred person of the Elector seemed to him so insupportable that, in the heat of his eloquence, he wanted rather to bear the worst—see the mad rebel's verdict made good and his cousin the Squire led off to Kohlhaasenbrück to feed the horses—than to have Dr. Luther's proposal accepted.

The Lord Chancellor, Count Wrede, half turning toward Sir Kunz, expressed regret that the tender concern for the sovereign's reputation which the Chamberlain was showing in the settling of this very awkward business had not animated him at its inception. He explained to the Elector his misgivings at employing the sovereign power in the enforcing of a measure manifestly unjust. Pointedly alluding to the great following the horsedealer had in the country, he noted that the web of injustice was likely to be spun out indefinitely, and that nothing but plain just dealing, prompt and uncompromising amends for the misconduct the Government had been guilty of, could cut the thread and extricate them from this ugly affair.

Prince Christiern of Meissen, asked by the Elector for his opinion, turned toward the Chancellor and said that, of course, the latter's way of thinking inspired him with the utmost respect; but in wishing to secure justice for Kohlhaas, the Chancellor failed to consider that it would be at the expense of Wittenberg's, Leipzig's and, indeed, the entire ravaged country's just claims to restitution or, at least, punishment. The order of the State, he thought, was so entirely out of joint in its relation to this man that more than an axiom of jurisprudence would be required to set it right. For his part, therefore, he joined the Chamberlain in proposing that the means designed for such cases be employed, i.e., that an army of adequate strength be collected and the horsedealer, in his fastness in Lützen, be either captured or crushed.

The Chamberlain fetched two chairs from the wall and politely placed them for the Elector and the Prince. He was pleased, he said, to find himself in agreement with a man of such integrity and penetration on the means of settling this ambiguous business. The Prince looked at him and, holding the chair but not sitting down, replied that the gentleman had little cause to be pleased, a necessary condition of the proposal being that a warrant be issued for his arrest and he be tried for abuse of the sovereign's name. For though necessity might compel the covering of a series of crimes, because the countless progeny could no longer find room before the throne of justice, that principle did not apply to the parent offense from which all the others had sprung; hence only Sir Kunz's trial on a capital charge could give the State the authority to crush the horsedealer, whose cause was well known to be a just one and who was wielding a sword they themselves had put into his hand.

Taken aback, the Chamberlain looked anxiously at the Elector, who turned away, his face reddening, and stepped to the window. After a general, embarrassed silence, Count Kallheim said that in this way they would never get out of the magic circle in which they were caught. With equal justice, Prince Friedrich, the old Prince's nephew, might be tried; for in the strange expedition he had led against Kohlhaas, he had gone beyond his instructions on several points; so that if they were now to search for the multitude of those who had caused the present predicament, he too would have to be numbered among them and be held accountable by the sovereign for what happened at Mühlberg.

The Elector looked perplexed and walked back to the table; and Hinz von Tronka, the Cupbearer, spoke up. He could not understand how men of such wisdom as those here gathered failed to see the policy that ought to be adopted. As far as he knew, the horsedealer had promised to dismiss the band with which he had invaded the country, in return for a mere safe-conduct and a renewed investigation of his case. But from this it did not follow that he must be granted an amnesty for his criminal pursuit of a private revenge; these were two distinct legal concepts, which both Dr. Luther and the councillors seemed to confuse. "Once," he continued, with his finger alongside his nose, "the court in Dresden has ruled on the blacks, no matter how, there is nothing to prevent us from imprisoning Kohlhaas for his crimes of arson and robbery—a politic solution, which combines the advantages of the views of both these gentlemen and is sure to win the applause of present and future generations." Since the Prince as well as the Chancellor responded to Sir Hinz's speech with no more than a look and the discussion therefore seemed ended, the Elector said that he would think over their various opinions until the next meeting of the Council of State.

In view of the corollary measure demanded by the Prince, the Elector, who was very receptive to the feelings of friendship, seemed to have lost all desire to proceed with the expedition against Kohlhaas, though it was already fully prepared. At any rate, he detained the Chancellor, Count Wrede, whose counsel he found most to the purpose; and when the Chancellor showed him letters indicating that the horsedealer's force had grown to four hundred men and that, owing to the popular discontent over the Chamberlain's malfeasance, this strength was likely to double or triple within a short time, the Elector decided, without further consultations, to follow the advice given him by Dr. Luther. Accordingly, he placed Count Wrede in charge of the Kohlhaas affair; and a few days later a public notice was posted, the main points of which we cite:

> We, etc., etc., Elector of Saxony, with most gracious regard to the intercession made with us by Dr. Martin Luther, grant to Michael Kohlhaas, horsedealer, of Brandenburg, a safe-conduct to Dresden for the renewing of his lawsuit, on condition that within three days after sight of this notice, he will lay down his arms; it being further understood that if, as is not likely, his complaint concerning the blacks should be rejected by the Dresden courts, he will be prosecuted with the full severity of the law for his wilful presumption in taking the law into his own hands; but in the contrary event, that he, with his entire band, will be treated with mercy rather than justice, being granted a full amnesty for the acts of violence committed by him on Saxon territory.

As soon as Kohlhaas had received, from Dr. Luther, a copy of this notice, which was also posted in every town and village of the land, he called his men together and, disregarding the declaration's conditional phrasing, dismissed them with presents, expressions of gratitude, and suitable admonitions. All monies, weapons, and implements left to him he deposited with the Lützen courts as Electoral property; and after he had sent Waldmann to Kohlhaasenbrück with letters to the bailiff concerning the repurchase, if possible, of his farm, and Sternbald to Schwerin to fetch his children, whom he wished to have with him again, he left the castle at Lützen, carrying the remainder of his little wealth in notes, and made his way unrecognized to Dresden.

v

Day was breaking and the city still asleep when Kohlhaas knocked on the door of the small house in the suburb of Pirna, which, thanks to the bailiff's honest dealing, had remained in his possession. He asked Thomas, the caretaker, who opened with startled alarm, to report to the Prince of Meissen, at the Government House, that Kohlhaas the horse-dealer had arrived. The Prince, so informed, thought it proper to find out promptly, and in person, on what footing they would be with this man; when he appeared soon afterwards, attended by knights and guards, he found an immense crowd already gathered in the streets that led to Kohlhaas's house. The news of the arrival of the avenging angel who had punished the oppressors of the people with fire and sword had aroused all of Dresden, city as well as suburbs; the front door had to be bolted against the press of the curious mob, and boys were climbing up to the windows to catch a glimpse of the incendiary, who was breakfasting inside. When the Prince, aided by the guards, had made his way into the house and had entered the room where Kohlhaas, half-dressed, was standing by a table, he asked if he were Kohlhaas the horsedealer; whereupon Kohlhaas answered: "yes," took from his belt a wallet with several papers concerning his affairs, and respectfully handed it to the Prince. He went on to say that, having dissolved his band, he had now, in accordance with the sovereign's safe-conduct, come to Dresden to lay his complaint against the Squire Wenzel von Tronka before the courts. The Prince leafed through the papers, took in Kohlhaas from head to foot with a quick glance, and had him explain the meaning of the receipt the Lützen court had made out for the money and goods deposited in favor of the Electoral treasury. After he had probed Kohlhaas's character with various questions concerning his children, his property, and his plans, and had satisfied himself that there was no reason for apprehension, he returned the papers and said there were no further obstacles in the way of the lawsuit; to have it instituted, Kohlhaas should apply directly to the Lord Chancellor, Count Wrede. "Meanwhile," the Prince continued as he stepped to the window and beheld the crowd before the house, "you will have to accept a guard for the first few days, for your protection at home and abroad."

Kohlhaas lowered his eyes in dismay and said nothing. The Prince stepped back, saying: "As you wish. If anything happens, you will have no one to blame but yourself." With that, he turned toward the door, intending to leave. Kohlhaas, having collected his thoughts, said: "My

Lord, do as you please! If you give me your word that the guards will be dismissed as soon as I demand it, I have no objection to this measure." The Prince replied that that was understood; he had three soldiers, selected for this duty, brought before him and instructed them that the man at whose house they were being left was entirely free and that they were to follow him solely for his protection whenever he went abroad. Then he saluted the horsedealer with a gracious wave of the hand and left.

Toward noon, Kohlhaas, accompanied by his three soldiers and followed by a vast crowd—which, warned as it had been by the police, offered him no harm—went to see Count Wrede, the Chancellor. The Count received him with great kindness in his antechamber, talked with him for two full hours and, having informed himself of the entire course of events from beginning to end, referred him to an eminent advocate who was attached to the court and would assist him in the prompt drawing up and submission of the complaint. Without delay, Kohlhaas went to the advocate's chambers: and after the complaint had been made out, exactly like the earlier, suppressed one—asking appropriate punishment of the Squire, restoration of the horses to their former condition, and damages for himself and for his groom, Herse, who had fallen at Mühlberg, the last to be paid to Herse's old mother—he returned home, still followed by the gawking multitude and determined not to go out except on necessary business.

Meanwhile, the Squire had been released from custody in Wittenberg. After he had recovered from a dangerous inflammation of the foot, he had been peremptorily summoned by the High Court to present himself in Dresden to answer the charge made against him by the horsedealer Kohlhaas concerning a pair of blacks unlawfully seized and ruined by overwork. The Chamberlain and the Cupbearer, at whose house he put up, received him with the utmost bitterness and contempt; they called him a worthless wretch who was bringing disgrace upon the entire family, predicted that he was sure to lose the suit, and suggested that he had best arrange for the finding of the blacks, whom he would be condemned to feed to health, a spectacle of scorn and laughter for the entire world. In a weak and trembling voice, the Squire professed himself the most pitiable of men. He swore that he had known little of the whole cursed business that was plunging him into misery, and that the castellan and steward were to blame for everything, since it was they who had, without his remotest knowledge or consent, used the horses for harvesting and ruined them by overwork, part of it even in their own fields. Saying this, he sat down and begged they would not wantonly, by their insults and abuse, bring on again the disease from which he had barely recovered.

The following day, the lords Hinz and Kunz, at their cousin's request and having no other choice, wrote to the stewards and tenants of estates they owned near burned-down Tronka Castle, in order to obtain information about the blacks, who on that evil day had disappeared and had not been heard of since. But the place having been utterly destroyed and almost all of its inhabitants massacred, all they could discover was that a stable boy, under blows from the incendiary's sword, had rescued the horses from the burning shed they were in, but had been answered with a kick when he asked what he was to do with them. The Squire's gouty old housekeeper, who had fled to Meissen, responded to a written inquiry by reporting that on the morning after that dreadful night the stable boy had taken the horses toward the Brandenburg border; but all further inquiries in that direction proved fruitless, and, indeed, the report seemed mistaken, since none of the Squire's men came from Brandenburg or even from places on the road to Brandenburg. Some Dresdeners, who a few days after the burning of Tronka Castle had been in Wilsdruf, said that at that time a stablehand had appeared there leading two horses so run down and exhausted that he had to leave them behind in the stable of a cowherd, who was ready to try to do what he could for them. For several reasons it seemed highly probable that these were the blacks in question; but according to people from Wilsdruf, the cowherd had already sold them to someone else, nobody knew whom. And a third rumor of undetermined source even had it that the creatures had already given up the ghost and were buried in the Wilsdruf boneyard.

The lords Hinz and Kunz were understandably eager to credit this rumor, since, their cousin no longer having stables of his own, it would have relieved them of the necessity of taking the blacks into theirs and feeding them. Nevertheless, to make quite sure of the matter and to confirm the rumor, Squire Wenzel, as hereditary liege lord and chief magistrate, sent a letter to the Wilsdruf court giving a full description of the horses—entrusted to him, he said, and accidentally lost—and requesting that they be searched for and their present owner, whoever he might be, be urged to deliver them to the stables of the Lord Chamberlain Kunz von Tronka in Dresden, where he would be amply reimbursed. A few days later, the man to whom the Wilsdruf cowherd had sold the horses did in fact appear and led the emaciated and stumbling beasts, tied to his cart, onto the Dresden market square. But as the ill luck of Squire Wenzel, and still more of the honest Kohlhaas, would have it, this man happened to be the knacker of Döbbeln.

As soon as Sir Wenzel, in the Chamberlain's presence, was told that a man with two black horses said to have been saved from the Tronka Castle fire had arrived in town, the two gentlemen, escorted by a few hurriedly summoned domestics, went to the square, meaning, if the horses proved to be Kohlhaas's, to pay the fellow for them and take them home. But to their annoyed surprise they found the two-wheel cart and the horses that were tied to it engulfed by a rapidly growing mob, who had turned out to watch the spectacle and were laughing uproariously, shouting that the animals on whose account the State was tottering were in the hands of a knacker! The Squire went around the cart to inspect the miserable beasts, who looked as though at any moment they might breathe their last; whereupon he stammered that those were not the horses he had taken from Kohlhaas. But Sir Kunz, the Chamberlain, casting at him a glance of speechless fury which, had it been iron, must have crushed him, threw back his cloak so as to reveal his orders and chain of office, stepped up to the knacker and asked him: were these the blacks which the Wilsdruf cowherd had taken over and which Squire Wenzel von Tronka had asked the Wilsdruf court to send to Dresden as belonging to him?

The knacker, who was carrying a pail to water his own horse, a fat, big-bellied nag, said: "The blacks?" He put the pail down, took the bit out of the horse's mouth, and went on: the blacks that were tied to his cart had been sold to him by the swineherd in Hainichen. Where the swineherd had got them, or whether they came from the Wilsdruf cowherd, he had no idea. The Wilsdruf beadle, he added as he picked up the pail again and propped it between his knee and the shaft—the Wilsdruf beadle had told him to take them to the house of the Tronkas in Dresden: but the gentleman he was supposed to deal with was named Kunz. At this, he turned his back on the Chamberlain and poured the water the nag had left in the pail onto the pavement. Surrounded by the jeering mob and unable to make the fellow, who with complete unconcern went about his business, look at him, the Chamberlain said: he was Kunz von Tronka; but the blacks he was looking for had to be horses belonging to his cousin, Squire Wenzel; they had passed from a stablehand, who had fled from the Tronka Castle fire, to the Wilsdruf cowherd and had originally belonged to the horsedealer Kohlhaas. Did he know anything about them? he asked the knacker, who now stood with his legs apart, hitching up his pants; and most importantly, hadn't perhaps the Hainichen swineherd bought them from the Wilsdruf cowherd, or else from a third party who for his part had got them from the cowherd?

The knacker, after having stepped to the cart and made water, said he had been sent with the blacks to Dresden, to be paid for them at the house of the Tronkas. He didn't understand what the other was talking about; since he hadn't stolen them, it was no affair of his whether formerly they had belonged to Tom, Dick, or Harry. Then, feeling hungry, he started off, his whip across his shoulders, intending to get breakfast at a public house across the square.

The Chamberlain, who was at a loss what to do with the horses whom the Hainichen swineherd had sold to the Döbbeln knacker, unless they were the ones whom the Devil was riding through Saxony, asked the Squire for a decision. But when the Squire, with pale and trembling lips, replied that they had best buy the horses, whether or not they were Kohlhaas's, the Chamberlain, cursing his cousin's parents for having brought him into the world and knowing neither what to do nor what not to do, drew his cloak about him and stepped back from the crowd. He called to the Baron von Wenk, an acquaintance of his, who happened to be riding by; stubbornly determined not to yield ground to the mob— who, with mocking looks and handkerchiefs crammed into their mouths, seemed merely to be waiting for his retreat to break into open laughter—he asked the Baron to stop at the house of the Chancellor, Count Wrede, and have him arrange for Kohlhaas's coming and inspecting the blacks.

It happened that when the Baron entered the Chancellor's room, Kohlhaas was present to furnish some required explanation concerning the things deposited in Lützen; as the Chancellor rose from his chair with an annoyed look, leaving Kohlhaas standing to one side with the papers, the Baron, who did not know Kohlhaas by sight, reported the embarrassment in which the von Tronka family found themselves. In response to a defective order from the Wilsdruf court, he explained, the Döbbeln knacker had turned up with horses so hopelessly run down that Squire Wenzel had doubts about identifying them as Kohlhaas's; so that a direct identification by Kohlhaas was required to resolve the doubt, before they could be bought from the knacker and taken to the gentlemen's stables, there, if it were still possible, to be restored. "Be good enough, therefore," he concluded, "to have a guard fetch Kohlhaas from his house and bring him to the market square, where they are now standing."

The Chancellor took the spectacles off his nose and told the Baron that he was under a twofold misapprehension: first, in thinking that the matter could not be settled by some means other than Kohlhaas's direct identification; and secondly, in assuming that he, the Chancellor, was empowered to have a guard take Kohlhaas to wherever the Squire might think fit. Then he introduced the horsedealer, who was standing behind him, sat down again, put his spectacles back on, and requested the Baron to address himself to Kohlhaas in person. Kohlhaas gave no hint of what he felt; he said he was ready to go to the square and look at the horses the knacker had brought in, went back to the Chancellor's desk to conclude the explanation of the Lützen documents, and then asked to be excused. The Baron, who had been visibly disconcerted in confronting him and then, flushing, had turned to the window, now likewise took his leave; and the two men, escorted by the Prince of Meissen's three soldiers and followed by a large crowd, made their way to the square.

Sir Kunz, the Chamberlain, meanwhile had disregarded the advice of several friends who had joined him and was standing his ground among the mob and opposite the knacker. As soon as the Baron appeared with Kohlhaas, he approched the latter, his sword haughtily under his arm, and asked him if the horses standing by the cart were his. The horsedealer turned modestly toward the unfamiliar gentleman who was putting the question, lifted his hat, and then, without answering the question, went to the cart, followed by all the noblemen. At a distance of twelve feet, he took a brief look at the creatures, where they stood, heads drooping and legs trembling, over a bundle of hay the knacker had thrown them but which they did not touch. Then he turned back to the Chamberlain: "My lord, the knacker is quite right; the horses tied to the cart are mine." With that and a final look at the group of gentlemen, he once more lifted his hat and with his guard left the square.

So rapidly that the plumes of his hat were shaking, the Chamberlain went up to the knacker and tossed him a purse; then, as the knacker, the purse in his hand, combed back his hair with a leaden comb, Sir Kunz ordered one of his servants to untie the horses and lead them home. Obedient to his master's call, the servant left a group of friends and relatives he had found in the crowd and, blushing, stepped across a large puddle the horses had made, to untie them; but he had barely touched the halter when his cousin, Master Himboldt, took him by the arm and flung him away from the cart, crying: "Don't you touch those knacker's beasts!" Then he stepped cautiously back across the puddle, turned to the Chamberlain, who stood by speechlessly, and continued: for that sort of service he would have to get a knacker's man! Foaming with rage, the Chamberlain fixed Himboldt for a moment, then turned his back and over the heads of the gentlemen surrounding him called for the guard; as soon as an officer with a few Electoral halberdiers had been summoned by Baron von Wenk and appeared on the scene, Sir Kunz gave a brief account of the citizens' shameful insolence in fomenting rebellion and demanded that their ringleader, Master Himboldt, be arrested. He seized Himboldt by the shirt and accused him of having pushed and manhandled the servant who had been ordered to untie the blacks. With a skilful motion Himboldt twisted free of the Chamberlain's grasp and said: "My lord! Making clear to a twenty-year-old fellow what is the proper thing for him to do is not the same as inciting him to rebellion. Ask him if, against custom and decency, he is willing to meddle with the horses tied to that cart; if he is, after what I have said, so be it! For all I care, he can then skin them right here."

At this, the Chamberlain turned to the servant to ask if he had any objection to untying Kohlhaas's horses and leading them home. And when the fellow retreated into the crowd and timidly answered: before that was expected of him, the horses had first to be made honest again, the Chamberlain came after him, tore off his livery hat and trampled it underfoot, drew and with angry blows of his sword drove him from the square and out of his service. Master Himboldt shouted: "Throw the bloody madman down!" and while the enraged citizens pressed close and blocked off the guards, he threw the Chamberlain to the ground from behind, tore off his cloak, collar, and plumed hat, wrenched the sword from his hand and with a mighty heave hurled it across the square. Squire Wenzel, scurrying away from the melee, called in vain on the gentlemen to come to his cousin's aid; before they could get a step closer, they were scattered by the rush of the crowd; so that the Chamberlain, who in falling had injured his head, was entirely at the furious mob's mercy. He was saved only by the appearance of a troop of mounted soldiers who happened to cross the square and were called by the officer in command of the halberdiers.

That was the disastrous outcome of the sincere and well-intentioned effort to give the horsedealer satisfaction for the injustices he had suffered. The Döbbeln knacker, his business finished, did not want to lose any more time; when the crowd began to disperse, he tied the horses to a lantern post, where they stood for the rest of the day, a source of fun for street urchins and idlers; until finally, in the absence of anyone willing to care for them, the police had to take them in charge. At nightfall, the Dresden knacker was called to take them to his place outside the city and, pending further disposition, to see to them.

The incident, little though the horsedealer was to blame for it, nevertheless aroused throughout the country, even among moderate and well-disposed people, a feeling very threatening to the success of his suit. His position in relation to the legal order was felt to be intolerable; in private as well as in public, the opinion gained ground that it was better to commit a manifest injustice and to dismiss the entire case than on so trivial a point to do justice extorted by violence merely to satisfy one man's insane obstinacy. To complete poor Kohlhaas's ruin, the Chancellor himself, overly scrupulous in his sense of right and hence confirmed in his hatred of the Tronka clan, contributed to the spreading and hardening of this mood. It was most unlikely that the horses, now in the care of the Dresden knacker, could ever be restored to the condition in which they had left their stable in Kohlhaasenbrück; but even if the possibility were assumed, the disgrace which would in that case befall the Squire's family was so great that, considering its importance as one of the oldest and noblest in the country, by far the most appropriate and equitable settlement appeared to be the paying of a compensation in money. Nevertheless, when a few days later the Chancellor received a letter from the President, Count Kallheim, proposing such a settlement on behalf of the still bedridden Chamberlain, the Chancellor—though indeed he wrote to Kohlhaas and advised him not to reject such an offer if it were extended— returned a curt and disobliging answer to the President, requesting him not to burden the Chancellor's Office with such private business but to apply directly to the horsedealer, whom he described as a very reasonable and modest man. Kohlhaas, whose determination had in fact been shaken by the riot on the market square, was only waiting for the Squire and his relatives to take the first step, in which case he was ready to follow the Chancellor's advice, forgive the past and fall in with their wishes. But it was just this first step the proud noblemen found it too humiliating to take; deeply embittered, they showed the Chancellor's letter to the Elector when, two days later, he visited the Chamberlain, who was still laid up with his injuries. His voice weak and pathetic from his illness, the Chamberlain asked the Elector whether, having risked his life to settle the matter according to the sovereign's wishes, he was now expected to expose his good name to the world's contempt and to beg indulgence and more favorable terms from a man who had brought every imaginable disgrace upon him. The Elector read the letter and in an embarrassed manner asked Count Kallheim if the courts did not have authority, without consulting Kohlhaas and on the grounds that the horses were irrecoverable, to rule that they were to be treated as dead and hence to be paid for in money. The Count replied: "Your Highness, they are judicially dead now, since they are valueless, and will be physically so before they can be transferred from the knacker's yard to the Tronka stables." At that, the Elector, putting away the letter, said that he himself would talk with the Chancellor and spoke reassuringly to the Chamberlain, who half raised himself and gratefully kissed his hand; then he asked him to be careful of his health, rose, and with a gracious farewell left the room.

VI

Thus matters stood in Dresden, when from Lützen there gathered another, still more threatening storm, whose bolt the crafty noblemen were able to direct against the unfortunate Kohlhaas. For Johann Nagelschmidt, one of the band assembled by the horsedealer and, after the granting of the Electoral amnesty, dismissed again, had seen fit, a few weeks later, to gather part of this lawless and ruthless crew near the Bohemian border and on his own initiative to carry on the trade Kohlhaas had taught him. Partly to frighten the constables who were at his heels, and partly to induce the peasantry to aid him in his rascalities as before, this scoundrel called himself Kohlhaas's deputy; with a skill he had learned from his erstwhile master, he spread the rumor that in the case of several men the promise of amnesty had been broken upon their return home, and that Kohlhaas himself was the victim of an outrageous breach of faith, having been arrested and put under guard as soon as he arrived in Dresden. In this fashion, through placards very similar to Kohlhaas's, he made it appear that his crew of bandits was a host of warriors fighting for God's glory and devoted to enforcing the Elector's amnesty—whereas in truth, as mentioned before, it was not God's glory that prompted him, nor any attachment to Kohlhaas, to whose fate he was utterly indifferent, but simply, under the cover of such pretenses, the wish to loot with greater ease and less danger.

When news of this first reached Dresden, the noblemen could not conceal their delight at a turn of events which promised to cast a different light on the entire affair. With sage and critical comments, they expatiated on the ill-advised decision, taken over their repeated and urgent warnings, to grant an amnesty to Kohlhaas, as though the intention were to encourage all sorts of malefactors to follow his example. Nor did they stop at accepting at face value Nagelschmidt's pretense of fighting for the cause and safety of his oppressed leader; they were sure, they said, that Nagelschmidt's doings were nothing but a plot of Kohlhaas's to intimidate the Government and to extort a verdict which in every point would satisfy his mad self-will. Indeed, Sir Hinz, the Cupbearer, in the presence of some courtiers who, after dinner, had gathered about him in the Elector's antechamber, did not scruple to picture the dissolution of the band in Lützen as no more than a damnable feint; ridiculing the Chancellor's great love of justice, he proved by a clever combination of various facts that the band was still in being, hidden in the forests of the Electorate, and waiting only for Kohlhaas's signal to break forth again with fire and sword.

Prince Christiern of Meissen, much perturbed by this turn of events and the threat it held of staining his master's good name, immediately went to the palace to see the Elector; well aware of the noblemen's interest in exploiting the new crimes to bring Kohlhaas to ruin, he asked permission to start a prompt inquiry into the horsedealer's conduct. Kohlhaas, to his alarm, found himself escorted by a constable to the Government House; he appeared carrying his two little boys, Heinrich and Leopold, on his arms. (His man Sternbald had arrived from Mecklenburg the day before, bringing his five children, who had been staying there; and various considerations, not necessary to enumerate, led Kohlhaas to yield to the two boys' tearful pleading, pick them up, and take them along to the interrogation.) The Prince, after a kind look at the children, whom their father had set down beside him, and friendly inquiries about their names and ages, informed Kohlhaas of the liberties his former follower, Nagelschmidt, was taking with his name in the valleys of the Ore Mountains; and showing him the man's so-called "mandates," he asked him what he could say in his own defense. The horsedealer was deeply upset at the sight of these vile and treacherous notices; however, he had little difficulty in satisfying a man of the Prince's honesty that the accusations raised against him were baseless. He not only remarked that, as matters were going, he needed no aid from a third party to bring his case to a satisfactory conclusion; he was also able to show, from some letters he had with him and laid before the Prince, how improbable it was that Nagelschmidt, of all people, should wish to render such aid, since just before disbanding he had meant to have the fellow hanged for rape and other rascalities committed in the countryside. Only the publication of the Elector's amnesty had saved Nagelschmidt's life, since it severed their connection; but they had parted mortal enemies. With the Prince's assent, Kohlhaas sat down and drew up a public letter to Nagelschmidt, condemning the latter's claim to have taken up arms in order to enforce the amnesty as a shameless and criminal pretense, proclaiming that during his stay in Dresden he had been neither imprisoned nor put under guard, and that his case was progressing just as he wished, and finally abandoning Nagelschmidt to the full severity of the law for the acts of arson and murder he had committed since the amnesty. To this letter there were attached a few excerpts from the proceedings Kohlhaas had begun against Nagelschmidt in Lützen, so as to inform the public of the crimes of this scoundrel, who had already been destined for the gallows and had been saved solely by the Elector's proclamation. That done, the Prince reassured Kohlhaas concerning the suspicions which, under the circumstances, he had been compelled to voice during the interrogation. He pledged that, as long as he was in Dresden, the amnesty would not be violated in a single point, then gave the boys some fruit from his table and shook their hands, and dismissed Kohlhaas with a friendly salute.

The Chancellor, conscious of the danger which nevertheless still hung over Kohlhaas's head, did his utmost to close the case before it should be complicated by more such events; but to complicate it was precisely the aim of the shrewd noblemen. No longer content, as hitherto they had been, with silently admitting their culpability and seeking to obtain a milder verdict, they now began, by insidious and hairsplitting arguments, to deny culpability altogether. At one time, they pretended that Kohlhaas's blacks had been kept at Tronka Castle by the arbitrary action of the castellan and steward, the Squire having known nothing of the matter; then again, they protested that the animals had suffered from a dangerous catarrh even at their arrival, in support of which they cited witnesses whom they claimed they could produce. And when, after protracted investigations, these arguments were refuted, they quoted an Electoral edict, issued twelve years earlier, which had in fact prohibited the import of horses from Brandenburg to Saxony because of a cattle pest: clear proof, they claimed, not merely of the Squire's right but of his duty to hold up the horses Kohlhaas was taking across the border.

Kohlhaas, who in the meantime had repurchased his farm in Kohlhaasenbrück by paying a small indemnity to the honest bailiff, wished to leave Dresden for a few days and visit his hometown—less, perhaps, to settle the legal transfer of the property (though that also was urgent, if the winter crops were to be put in) than, in a situation so ambiguous and strange, to test his position—and possibly for still other reasons, which those who know their own hearts will readily divine. Accordingly, leaving his guard at home, he went to the Chancellor, showed him the bailiff's letters, and informed him that if, as seemed to be the case, his presence in court was not required for the moment, he meant to leave the city and go to Brandenburg for eight to twelve days, within which time he promised to return. Troubled, the Chancellor lowered his eyes and replied that in his view Kohlhaas's presence seemed more necessary now than ever before, since the court might need his testimony and explanations on innumerable unforeseeable points to counter the clever dodges of the defendants. But when Kohlhaas reminded him of his lawyer, who was thoroughly conversant with the case, modestly insisted on his request, and promised to return within a week, the Chancellor thought briefly, said that he expected Kohlhaas would apply to the Prince of Meissen for a passport, and dismissed him.

Kohlhaas, who knew well how to read the Chancellor's face, felt the more confirmed in his resolve; he immediately, and without giving reasons, wrote to the Prince of Meissen, as chief of the administration, to request a passport for a week to Kohlhaasenbrück and back. In answer, he received an official notice, signed by the Governor of the Palace, Baron Siegfried von Wenk, to the effect that his request would be put before his Serene Highness, the Elector, upon whose consent, as soon as it was received, the passport would be issued. When Kohlhaas asked his lawyer how it was that the notice was signed by a Baron von Wenk and not by Prince Christiern of Meissen, to whom he had written, he was told that the Prince had left three days earlier for his estates and that during his absence the affairs of his office had been entrusted to Baron Siegfried von Wenk, a cousin of the gentleman of like name previously mentioned.

Amid all these difficulties, Kohlhaas's heart began to beat uneasily. For several days he waited for a decision on his request, so oddly submitted to the sovereign in person; but more than a week passed without his receiving a reply or, for that matter, a judgment in his suit, definitely though the last had been promised. On the twelfth day, finally determined to force the Government to reveal its intentions toward him, whatever they might be, he sat down and composed a second, urgent petition for his passport. But the next evening, when he, still without an answer and pondering the amnesty obtained for him by Luther and his situation in general, stepped to the window of his back room, he was greatly perturbed not to see the guards whom the Prince of Meissen had assigned him and who had been quartered in a small outbuilding across the courtyard. His old caretaker, Thomas, whom he called and asked what this meant, answered with a sigh: "Master, things are not as they should be; there are more halberdiers than usual tonight, and at dusk they took positions all around the house. Two of them, armed, are standing at the street door, two more at the back door, and another two are lying on a bundle of straw in the hall, saying they will sleep there." Kohlhaas paled, turned away and said it was no matter, as long as they were there; Thomas, on his way through the hall, was to put a light there for them to see by. Then, on the pretense of emptying a chamberpot, he opened the front shutters to verify the servant's report and was just in time to see a silent relief of the watch—a measure never yet taken as long as the guards had been there. Though little inclined to sleep, Kohlhaas went to bed, instantly resolving what he would do the next day. One thing above all he was determined to prevent: that the Government he had to deal with should preserve the appearance of legality, when in truth it was breaking the amnesty promised him. If he was in fact a prisoner, as he could no longer doubt, he would force the authorities to own to the fact, positively and without evasion.

At daybreak, therefore, he had his man Sternbald hitch up the wagon and bring it to the gate, his announced intention being to drive to Lockwitz and visit the steward there, an old acquaintance who had talked with him in Dresden a few days before and invited him and his children for a visit. The guards, noticing the stir of these preparations, put their heads together and sent one of their number into town; whereupon a government official with several constables appeared a few minutes later and went into the house opposite, as though he had business there. While dressing his boys, Kohlhaas for his part took note of these movements, and having purposely kept the wagon waiting somewhat longer than necessary, he emerged from his house with his children the moment the police had taken their measures. In passing, he told the halberdiers by the door that they need not accompany him, lifted the boys into the wagon, and consoled the weeping little girls, whom he had ordered to stay behind with the caretaker's daughter. He had barely mounted the wagon himself when the official with his retinue of constables came out of the house opposite, approached him, and asked where he was going. When Kohlhaas answered that he was driving to Lockwitz at the invitation of his friend, the steward, to visit there for a few days, the official replied that in that case he must wait a few minutes, since upon orders of the

Prince of Meissen a few mounted men would escort him. Kohlhaas smiled down from the wagon and asked: did the gentleman think him in danger at the house of a friend who had offered to entertain him for a day? In an agreeable and easy manner, the official responded that, to be sure, the danger was not great; nor, he added, would the men in any way trouble him. Kohlhaas, now serious, said that at his arrival in Dresden the Prince had left him free to decide whether or not he would make use of the guards; and when the official expressed surprise and diplomatically referred to their uninterrupted presence throughout his stay in Dresden, Kohlhaas explained the circumstances that had led to the detailing of the watch. The official assured him that, according to the orders he had from Baron von Schenk, who at the moment was chief of police, it was his duty to protect Kohlhaas at all times; if he was unwilling to be escorted, would he be so good as to go to the Government House and there to clear up what was evidently a misunderstanding? Kohlhaas looked at him keenly and, determined to bring the matter to a head, said he would do so; tensely he dismounted, asked the caretaker to carry the boys back into the house and Sternbald to remain with the wagon in front, and together with the official and the guards went to the Government House.

It happened that when Kohlhaas entered the room of Baron von Wenk, the latter was engaged in inspecting a group of Nagelschmidt's men who had been caught near Leipzig and brought to Dresden the evening before, and who were now being interrogated by several noblemen in the hope of eliciting testimony damaging to the horsedealer. When they saw Kohlhaas, the noblemen fell silent and the Baron came forward and asked him what he wanted. In a respectful manner, Kohlhaas told him of his plan to have dinner with the steward in Lockwitz and of his wish to go without the halberdiers, of whom he had no need. The Baron, paling and evidently suppressing an angry retort, answered that Kohlhaas would do well to stay home and to postpone the feast in Lockwitz for the time being; whereupon he broke off the exchange, turned to the official and told him that his orders stood as before, and that this man was not to leave the city unless escorted by six mounted guards. When Kohlhaas asked if he was to conclude that he was a prisoner and that the amnesty, solemnly and publicly pledged, was now broken, the Baron reddened with fury, went up close to him and, looking straight into his face, said: "Yes! Yes! Yes!"—then turned his back on him and resumed the questioning of Nagelschmidt's men.

Kohlhaas left the room, and though he was aware that by this step he had greatly lessened his sole remaining chance of saving himself—namely flight—he nevertheless did not regret his conduct, since he now found himself released from any obligation to abide by the conditions of amnesty. Returned home, he had the wagon unhitched and went to his room in great distress; and while the official, who had followed him, kept protesting, to Kohlhaas's disgust, that it must all be a misunderstanding and soon everything would be set right, the constables at his orders bolted all doors except the front door—which, he insisted, Kohlhaas was free to use when and as he pleased.

In the forests of the Ore Mountains, meanwhile, Nagelschmidt was so hard pressed by constables and soldiers and so lacking in resources for the enterprise he had undertaken that he thought of actually enlisting Kohlhaas' support. Having obtained exact information from a traveller about the latest developments in Kohlhaas's situation, he hoped that he might induce him to a new alliance, the manifest enmity between them notwithstanding. Accordingly, he dispatched one of his men to him, with a letter in barely intelligible German, saying that if Kohlhaas would come to the Altenburg region and resume command of the remnants of the band who had gathered there, he, Nagelschmidt, stood ready to aid his escape from Dresden with horses, men, and money; moreover, he promised to be more obedient, and generally to conduct himself better in the future than he had formerly, and, in proof of his loyalty and affection, to come in person to the vicinity of Dresden to help in Kohlhaas's liberation. But the fellow entrusted with this letter had the misfortune, in a village near Dresden, to be taken with an ugly fit of a kind he had suffered since childhood; people who came to his aid found the letter inside his jerkin, whereupon, when he had recovered, he was arrested and, a crowd following him, taken under guard to the Government House. As soon as Baron von Wenk had read the letter, he went to the palace, where he found the Elector attended by Kunz and Hinz von Tronka (the former recovered from his injuries) and the President of the Chancery, Count Kallheim. The gentlemen were of the opinion that Kohlhaas should be immediately arrested and tried on the charge of conspiring with Nagelschmidt; they argued that such a letter could not have been written except in answer to a prior one from Kohlhaas and as part of a plan to establish a wicked and criminal alliance for the committing of further outrages. The Elector steadfastly refused to break the safe-conduct he had pledged Kohlhaas on no more evidence than this letter; in his view, the letter showed, rather, that in all probability there had been no prior arrangements between the two men. All he would agree to, by way of clearing up the question, was a proposal by the President, which after much hesitation he accepted: that Nagelschmidt's man be set free and induced to deliver the letter, so that they could discover whether and how Kohlhaas would respond to it.

Accordingly, the fellow, after a night in prison, was taken to the Government House, where the Baron returned the letter to him and promised to let him go free and unpunished, provided he delivered it to Kohlhaas as though nothing had happened. The man promptly agreed to lend himself to this sordid maneuver; with pretended secrecy, under the guise of selling crabs (which a police officer had bought for him at the market), he entered Kohlhaas's room. While the children played with the crabs, Kohlhaas read the letter. Under different circumstances, he would certainly have collared the rascal and handed him over to the halberdiers outside; but since, as things now stood, even that act would have been liable to misconstruction, and since he was convinced that there was no chance of openly extricating himself from the web he was caught in, he looked sadly into the fellow's familiar face, asked him where he was staying, and ordered him to return in a few hours, at which time he would let him know what he had decided regarding his master's proposal. He had Sternbald, who happened to enter, buy some of the crabs; this done, the two men left the room without recognizing each other, while Kohlhaas sat down and wrote a letter to Nagelschmidt, saying: first, that he accepted the proposal to take over the leadership of the band in the Altenburg area; that Nagelschmidt, therefore, was to send a wagon with two horses to Neustadt near Dresden to free him and his five children from the arrest recently imposed on them; that moreover, to speed his flight, he would require a further team of horses to be stationed on the road to Wittenberg, where, though it meant a detour, he had to go before coming to Altenburg, for reasons too complicated to explain; that he expected to be able to bribe the halberdiers who guarded him, but that, in case force had to be used, he desired the presence in Neustadt of a few stouthearted, intelligent, and well-armed men; that, to defray the expenses of all these preparations, he was sending him, by the messenger, twenty gold crowns and would settle with him when the affair was concluded; and that, finally, he did not wish Nagelschmidt himself to come to Dresden for the rescue, but on the contrary, ordered him explicitly to remain in Altenburg in temporary charge of the band, which must not be left without a leader. When the messenger returned in the evening, Kohlhaas gave him the letter, rewarded him liberally, and instructed him to use the utmost care. His real intention, however, was to make his way to Hamburg with his five children and there to take ship for the Levant, or the East Indies, or wherever else the sun might shine on people different from those he knew; for, aside from his revulsion at the thought of making common cause with Nagelschmidt, he had, bowed as he was by his grief, given up the goal of compelling the restoration of his blacks.

Hardly had the fellow delivered Kohlhaas's answer to Baron von Wenk when the Chancellor was dismissed, Count Kallheim, the President, was appointed in his place to head the tribunal, and an Electoral order was issued to arrest Kohlhaas, put him in chains, and throw him in the city dungeon. On the evidence of the letter, copies of which were posted on all street corners, Kohlhaas was tried; and when, before the bar, he was shown the letter, and answered: "Yes!" to the question whether he acknowledged it as written by him, and, his eyes lowered: "No!" to the question whether he had anything to say in his own defense, he was condemned to be torn with redhot pincers by knacker's men, quartered, and his body burned between the wheel and the gallows.

VII

Thus matters stood with poor Kohlhaas in Dresden, when the Elector of Brandenburg rescued him from the grasp of arbitrary power by sending a note to the Saxon State Chancery and claiming jurisdiction over him as a subject of Brandenburg. For Heinrich von Geusau, the honest Governor, had informed the Elector, during a walk along the Spree, of the story of this strange and far from damnable man; in his story, pressed by his master's surprised inquiries, he had been compelled to mention the responsibility the Elector himself had incurred through the misconduct of his Chancellor, Count Siegfried von Kallheim; whereupon the Elector had indignantly summoned the Chancellor, questioned him, and, finding that the Count's kinship with the Tronkas was at the root of the matter, had promptly dismissed him in disgrace and appointed Heinrich von Geusau Chancellor in his stead.

At just this time, the Polish Crown chanced to be involved in a dispute with the House of Saxony—over what point we do not know—and had repeatedly and urgently pressed the Elector of Brandenburg to join its cause against the Saxons; so that Chancellor von Geusau, who was a diplomat of some skill, had every hope of satisfying his master's wish to help Kohlhaas to justice, whatever the cost—indeed, of doing so without endangering the commonweal more grievously than the interest of a single citizen warrants. In view of the Saxon Government's wholly arbitrary procedure, offensive both to divine and to human law, the Chancellor demanded not only Kohlhaas's prompt and unconditional extradition, so that, if he was guilty, he could be judged by the laws of Brandenburg on whatever charges the Saxon court might wish to press against him; he even demanded a passport for an attorney whom his master desired to send to Dresden, to obtain redress for the unlawful seizure of Kohlhaas's horses on Saxon soil and for other outrageous acts of violence committed against him. Kunz von Tronka, the Chamberlain, who in the change of offices in Dresden had assumed the presidency of the Chancery, had various reasons for not offending the court in Berlin at this troubled time; in the name of his much disheartened master, he replied that Dresden was surprised at the hostility and unfairness of being denied jurisdiction in the crimes Kohlhaas had committed in Saxony, it being well known that he held considerable property in the capital and did not even himself disclaim his Saxon citizenship. But since Poland was already assembling an army of 5000 men on the Saxon border to enforce its claims, and since Chancellor von Geusau declared that Kohlhaasenbrück, the town from which Kohlhaas derived his name, was located in Brandenburg, so that he would be bound to view the carrying out of the death sentence as a breach of the law of nations, the Chamberlain preferred to withdraw from the affair, and advised the Elector to recall Prince Christiern of Meissen; a few words from this wise nobleman were sufficient to persuade the Elector to yield to Berlin's demands and surrender Kohlhaas.

At the hard-pressed sovereign's request, the Prince, though he was far from pleased with the improprieties committed during his absence, agreed to take over the management of the case and inquired on what charges he should proceed against Kohlhaas before the courts in Berlin. But as the case could not be based on Kohlhaas's unfortunate letter to Nagelschmidt, the circumstances under which it had been written being in the highest degree ambiguous and doubtful, and as the amnesty made it impossible to charge him with his earlier acts of arson and robbery, the Elector decided to lay a report of Kohlhaas's invasion of Saxony before the Emperor in Vienna, to complain of the breach of the Imperial peace thereby committed, and to request the Emperor, as a party not bound by the amnesty, to have an Imperial prosecutor arraign Kohlhaas on this charge before the High Court in Berlin. A week later Friedrich von Malzahn, a knight whom the Elector of Brandenburg had sent to Dresden with six mounted men to fetch Kohlhaas, put the chained horsedealer on a wagon, together with his five children, who at his plea had been collected from various orphanages and foundling homes, and set off for Berlin.

It happened that the Elector of Saxony—at the invitation of the High Bailiff, Count Aloysius von Kallheim, who at that time held considerable estates along the Saxon border, and in the company of Sir Kunz the Chamberlain and his wife, Lady Heloise, daughter of the High Bailiff and sister of the President, as well as a brilliant entourage of lords and ladies, courtiers and hunting pages—had gone to a great stag hunt that had been got up for his entertainment at the village of Dahme. Beneath gaily pennanted tents that had been pitched on a hill on both sides of the highway, the entire company, still dusty from the hunt, sat at table, served by pages and entertained by gay music coming from beneath an oak tree—when Kohlhaas's wagon came slowly along the road from Dresden, escorted by mounted men. The illness of one of Kohlhaas's small and delicate children had forced Sir Friedrich von Malzahn to stop for three days in Herzberg; being answerable only to his master, he had not thought it necessary to inform Dresden of this delay. The Elector, his shirt open at the throat and his hat adorned with sprigs of fir in hunter's fashion, was sitting beside Lady Heloise, who had been the first love of his youth; caught in the gay and festive charm of the occasion, he said: "Let us go and present this cup of wine to that unfortunate, whoever he may be!" Lady Heloise gave him a divine look, rose quickly and ransacked the table of fruit, cakes, and bread, which she piled onto a silver dish handed her by a page; the rest of the company followed her example, and all were crowding out of the tent when the High Bailiff met them, deeply embarrassed, and asked them to stay where they were. Puzzled, the Elector asked him what had happened to upset him so; whereupon the High Bailiff half turned toward the Chamberlain and stammered that the man in the wagon was Kohlhaas. At this news, which none could understand, since it was generally known that Kohlhaas had left six days before, Sir Kunz took his cup, turned toward the tent and poured the wine into the sand. The Elector flushed deeply and put his cup on a tray which a page, at a sign from the Chamberlain, held before him; and while Sir Friedrich, ignorant of whom he was passing, but with a respectful salute, made his way slowly through the tent lines and on toward Dahme, the company took no further note of him but followed the High Bailiff back into the tent. When the Elector was seated again, the High Bailiff secretly dispatched a messenger to Dahme to induce the town magistrate to send Kohlhaas on without delay; but when Sir Friedrich, in view of the late hour, declared positively that he meant to stop for the night, there was nothing for it but to put him up at one of the magistrate's farms, which lay off the road and hidden in a copse.

Toward evening, when the Elector's company had forgotten the entire incident over wine and rich desserts, the High Bailiff suggested that they go out again to hunt a herd of deer which had just been spotted—a proposal they all were delighted to follow, so that they took their guns and hurried off in pairs, cross-field, to the nearby forest. Thus it came about that the startled Elector and Lady Heloise, who clung to his arm to watch the chase, found themselves taken by their guide directly through the yard of the farm where Kohlhaas and the horsemen from Brandenburg had been quartered. When the lady discovered this, she said: "Come, your Highness, come!" playfully hid the chain the Elector was wearing inside his silken shirt, and went on: "Let us slip inside the farmhouse before the others get here, and take a look at the strange man in there." The Elector reddened, took her hand, and said: "Heloise! What are you saying?" But she looked at him displeased, saying that after all no one would know him in his hunting costume, and pulled him on. And when just then a few pages, who had satisfied their curiosity, came out of the house and reported that, thanks to the High Bailiff's care, neither Kohlhaas nor the knight with him knew who the company outside Dahme had been, he pulled his hat down over his face, smiled and said: "Folly, it's you who rule the world, and your throne is a pretty woman's lips."

When the noble visitors entered the house, Kohlhaas was sitting on a bundle of straw, leaning against the wall, and feeding milk and white bread to the child that had been taken ill in Herzberg. The lady, to start the conversation, asked who he was, what ailed the child, what he had done, and where he was being taken under such heavy guard; at which he lifted his leather cap and, while he continued the feeding, answered all her questions briefly, but adequately. For lack of something better to say, the Elector, who, standing behind some pages, had noticed a small leaden locket hanging from Kohlhaas's neck by a silk string, asked what it meant and what it contained. Kohlhaas answered: "Ah yes, your Worship, this locket"—saying which he slipped it off, opened it and took from it a small piece of paper sealed with gum—"there is a strange tale connected with this locket. It's about seven months now, the very day after my wife's burial; as perhaps you know, I had set out from Kohlhaasenbrück to seize the Squire von Tronka, who had done me great injury, when my way led me through Jüterbok, a market town, where just then the Electors of Brandenburg and Saxony were meeting for some negotiations, I don't know about what. In the evening, after they had come to an agreement, they walked through the town, talking amiably, to watch the merrymaking at the fair then being held. There they came upon a gypsy woman who sat on a stool telling the fortunes of the people surrounding her; in jest, they asked her if she could not tell them, too, something they might be pleased to hear. Having just put up with my men at an inn, I was present on the square where this took place; but since I was standing behind a crowd of people at the portals of a church, I could not hear what the strange woman said to the two gentlemen; so that when the people laughed and whispered that she would not share her knowledge with just anybody, and pressed closer to see the show that seemed to be in the making, I climbed onto a bench cut into the church entrance, less to satisfy my curiosity than to make room for the curious. Hardly had I taken this position, with a clear view of the two lords and the woman who sat there on a stool before them and seemed to be scribbling something, when suddenly she stood leaning on her crutches, looked over the crowd, focussed on me who had never exchanged a word with her nor at any time of my life wished to traffic in her science, came up to me and said: 'There! If the gentleman wants to know, let him ask it of you.' And with that, your Worship, her withered, bony hand extended this piece of paper toward me. And when, startled and stared at by those around me, I said: 'But Granny, what is it you are giving me?' she mumbled a good deal of unintelligible stuff—containing, however, my name, much to my surprise—and ended: 'An amulet, Kohlhaas the horsedealer! Take good care of it; it will save your life yet!'—and vanished. Well," Kohlhaas went on goodnaturedly, "to tell the truth, I didn't lose my life in Dresden, though it was a close thing; how I will fare in Berlin and whether the amulet will see me through there also, the future must show."

At these words, the Elector sat down on a bench; and although, to Lady Heloise's worried inquiries, he answered: "It's nothing;" he fell to the ground in a faint before she had time to come to his aid or catch him in her arms. Sir Friedrich von Malzahn, entering just then on some errand, cried: "Good God, what is the matter with the gentleman?" The lady cried: "Fetch water!" The pages lifted him up and carried him to a bed in the adjoining chamber; the confusion reached its height when the Chamberlain, called by a page, after several vain attempts to restore him to consciousness, declared that all signs pointed to an apoplexy. The Cupbearer sent a mounted messenger to Luckau for a physician, while the High Bailiff, when the Elector opened his eyes, had him placed in a carriage and very slowly driven to a hunting lodge he owned nearby; but even so, this trip brought on two further fainting spells, so that it was only the next morning, after the physician had arrived, that there were definite signs of recovery, though with clear symptoms of an approaching nervous fever.

As soon as the Elector was in possession of his faculties again, he half rose in his bed, and his first question was: Where was Kohlhaas? The Chamberlain misconstrued the question and, taking his master's hand, begged him to be easy on the score of that horrible man, who, after the strange and unaccountable seizure, had remained in the farm at Dahme, well guarded by the Brandenburg horsemen. He assured the Elector of his most lively concern, told him that he had bitterly reproached his wife for her unpardonable frivolity in bringing him together with this man, and asked what it was that, during his talk with him, had affected him so fearfully. The Elector said he had to confess that the cause of the whole disagreeable incident was nothing more than the sight of a piece of paper which this man carried in a leaden locket. He added some further explanations, none of which the Chamberlain understood, suddenly pressed the latter's hand between his and assured him that it was of the utmost importance for him to gain possession of the paper; he ended by begging Sir Kunz to ride back to Dahme that very moment and to purchase the paper from the horsedealer, whatever the price. The Chamberlain, who found it difficult to hide his embarrassment, told him that if he valued the paper, nothing was more essential than to conceal this fact from Kohlhaas, since if he should discover it through some unguarded remark, all the Elector's riches would not be enough to still the man's ferocious and insatiable vindictiveness. To calm him, he added that they must think of another way, and that since the piece of paper was of such value to him, while that devil of a man probably set no great store by it in itself, it might be possible to trick him into surrendering it to some third person who knew nothing of the entire matter. The Elector wiped the perspiration from his face and asked if they could not immediately send someone to Dahme to prevent Kohlhaas's being taken across the border until they had, by whatever means, got possession of the paper. The Chamberlain could hardly trust his ears, but replied that unfortunately it was most probable that the horsedealer had already left Dahme and was by now across the border and in Brandenburg territory, where any attempt to interfere with his transport, let alone to bring him back to Saxony, would have the most far-reaching and disagreeable consequences, and might, indeed, cause unmanageable complications. And when the Elector lay back in silence with a gesture of utter hopelessness, the Chamberlain asked him what the paper contained and by what inexplicable chance he had discovered that the contents had to do with him. But to this the Elector did not respond, except by looking doubtfully at Sir Kunz, whose readiness to help him in this affair he mistrusted; stiffly he lay there, his heart beating restlessly and his eyes fixed abstractedly on the corner of the handkerchief he held, until suddenly, pretending to have some other business to settle, he asked him to send in the Junker vom Stein.

The Junker was a young, energetic, and clever gentleman, whom the Elector had on several occasions employed in secret affairs. Having explained the matter to him and impressed on him the importance of the paper in Kohlhaas's possession, the Elector asked him if he would earn an everlasting claim to his friendship by obtaining the paper before it got to Berlin. And when the Junker, as soon as he had formed some notion of this very odd business, assured him that he was entirely at his service, the Elector instructed him to ride after Kohlhaas and, since money would hardly win him, to offer him life and liberty in return for the paper; indeed, if Kohlhaas demanded it, the Junker, with all due caution, was to aid him with men, money, and horses in effecting his escape from the Brandenburg guards.

Having obtained credentials in the Elector's own hand, the Junker immediately set out with a few men and, by not sparing the horses, succeeded in overtaking Kohlhaas in a border village, where the horsedealer, his five children, and Sir Friedrich were taking their midday meal in the open in front of a house. Sir Friedrich, to whom the Junker presented himself as a stranger passing through and wishing to get a look at their remarkable captive, obligingly introduced him to Kohlhaas and invited him to join their table; a little later, while Sir Friedrich went back and forth arranging for their departure and the horsemen were still eating at a table on the other side of the house, the Junker found an opportunity to reveal to the horse-dealer who he was and what special business he came charged with. Kohlhaas had in the meantime learned the name and station of the man who on seeing the locket had fainted in the Dahme farmhouse, and his sense of intoxicating triumph over this discovery lacked nothing for its fulfillment but the knowledge of the paper's secrets, which for a number of reasons he was determined not to pry into from mere curiosity; now, mindful of the ignoble and unprincely treatment he had suffered in Dresden despite his readiness to make every possible concession, he said that he meant to keep the paper. And when the Junker asked what prompted him to this strange refusal, since no less than life and liberty were offered him in return, Kohlhaas answered: "Sir, if your master should come and say: 'I am willing to destroy myself and with me the entire crew of those who assist me'—destroy himself, you understand, and thus satisfy my most cherished wish—even then I should refuse him this paper, which is worth more to him than his life. I would say: 'You can send me to the scaffold, but I can hurt you, and I shall!' " With that, his mien deadly, he called over a horseman and offered him an ample helping of food that was left in the dish; for the rest of the hour they stayed in the village, he treated the Junker, who remained at the table, as though he did not exist, turning to give him a parting nod only as he mounted the wagon.

At this news, the Elector grew so much worse that for three critical days the physician greatly feared for his life. Nevertheless, owing to his naturally sound constitution, and in spite of attacks upon his health from many quarters at once, he recovered after a few painful weeks in bed—sufficiently at any rate to be placed in a well-cushioned coach and taken back to Dresden and the affairs of state. Immediately upon his arrival, he summoned Prince Christiern of Meissen and inquired what arrangements had been made for the dispatch of Councillor Eibenmayer, the attorney who was to be sent to Vienna to lay before the Emperor the charges against Kohlhaas, pleading breach of the Imperial peace. The Prince replied that, in accordance with the instructions the Elector had left at his departure for Dahme, the councillor had gone to Vienna directly after the arrival in Dresden of Dr. Zäuner, the jurist whom the Elector of Brandenburg had sent to press charges against the Squire Wenzel von Tronka concerning the blacks. The Elector flushed, walked to his desk, and expressed surprise at this haste: he felt sure his orders had been that, because of necessary prior consultations with Dr. Luther, who had procured the amnesty, Eibenmayer's departure was to wait until he himself should issue more specific and definite instructions. As he said this, he tossed about letters and papers on his desk, giving evidence of barely suppressed anger. The Prince, after staring at him a moment in surprise, said he was sorry if he had failed to give satisfaction in this matter; however, he was prepared to produce the decision of the Council of State, which had ordered him to dispatch the attorney at the time indicated. There had been no mention, he added, of any consultation with Dr. Luther; such a regard for the reverend gentleman who had interceded for Kohlhaas might have been very appropriate at an earlier point, but hardly now, when they had, before the eyes of the entire world, violated the amnesty they had pledged the horsedealer, arrested him, and surrendered him to the courts of Brandenburg to be convicted and executed.

The Elector remarked that the oversight of having sent Eibenmayer was, after all, no great matter; however, it was his wish that, for the time being and until further orders, no proceedings should be instituted in Vienna; would the Prince be good enough to send an express courier to the councillor with corresponding instructions. The Prince replied that unhappily this order came a day late; a report received this very day indicated that Eibenmayer had presented himself in his legal capacity and had started proceedings in the Imperial Chancery. To the Elector's dismayed question how this could have been done in so short a time, he answered that three weeks had passed since the man's departure, and that he had been instructed to take up the business without delay, as soon as he arrived in Vienna. A delay, the Prince continued, would have been especially improper in this case, since Zäuner, the attorney from Brandenburg, was proceeding against the Squire with the most stubborn insistence; already he had applied to the courts for a provisional removal of the blacks from the knacker, with a view to their eventual restoration, and had persuaded the judges so to rule, all the defendant's objections notwithstanding. The Elector pulled the bell rope and said it was no matter; after he had addressed a few indifferent questions to the Prince concerning conditions in Dresden and events during his absence, he made a gesture of dismissal, quite unable to conceal the real state of his feelings.

Before the day was out, he sent the Prince a note asking for the entire dossier on Kohlhaas, on the pretense that, in view of the political importance of the case, he intended to deal with it in person. And since he could not bear the thought of destroying the man who alone could reveal to him the secrets of the mysterious paper, he wrote in his own hand a letter to the Emperor, warmly imploring him to permit the withdrawal of Eibenmayer's charges against Kohlhaas, until he himself could, for reasons he hoped soon to explain more precisely, reconsider this decision. The Emperor replied with a note prepared by the Chancery: he was astonished by this sudden change of the Elector's mind; the report submitted to him by Saxony had made the Kohlhaas affair the concern of the entire Holy Roman Empire; accordingly, he, the Emperor, had considered it his duty to appear as plaintiff in the case before the Brandenburg courts; so that, his councillor, Franz Müller, having already gone to Berlin to act as attorney in Kohlhaas's trial for breach of the public peace, there no longer was any possibility for withdrawing the charges: the case would have to run its course according to law.

This reply left the Elector utterly disheartened; and when presently he received letters from Berlin reporting the opening of the trial and noting the probability of Kohlhaas's ending on the scaffold, despite all the efforts of the lawyer assigned to him, the unhappy prince resolved to make one more attempt: in a personal letter, he entreated the Elector of Brandenburg to spare Kohlhaas's life. He pretended that the amnesty he had pledged was a legal barrier to this man's execution; he protested that, for all the appearance of severity with which Saxony had proceeded against him, it had never been his own intention to let him die; and finally he described how disconsolate he would be if the protection which Berlin had claimed to extend to Kohlhaas should, by this unexpected turn of events, cause him harm far greater than he would have suffered if he had remained in Saxony and his case had been decided under Saxon law. To the Elector of Brandenburg, this plea appeared evasive and ambiguous; he answered that the energy with which the Emperor's attorney was pursuing the case made it quite impossible to yield to these wishes and depart from the strict letter of the law. His Saxon cousin's solicitude, he remarked, really went too far, since the charges against Kohlhaas were now pressed, not by him, who had granted an amnesty for the crimes in question, but by his Imperial Majesty, who was in no wise bound by that amnesty. Finally, he showed how necessary it was, in view of Nagel-schmidt's continuing outrages, which he had had the audacity to carry even into Brandenburg territory, to make an example of Kohlhaas; but if none of these arguments convinced his cousin of Saxony, he would have to apply directly to the Emperor, since if there were to be a pardon for Kohlhaas, only an Imperial declaration could bring it about.

Vexation and grief over all these miscarried efforts plunged the Elector back into his illness; and one morning when the Chamberlain was with him, he showed him the letters he had sent to Berlin and Vienna to obtain a reprieve for Kohlhaas, and thereby at least to gain time for getting hold of the paper in Kohlhaas's possession. The Chamberlain fell to his knees and implored his master, by all he held dear, to tell him the contents of the paper. The Elector asked him to bolt the door and sit on his bed; then he seized the other's hand, pressed it to his heart with a sigh, and spoke as follows:

"Your wife, I hear, has already told you that the Elector of Brandenburg and I met with a gypsy woman, the third day of our meeting in Jüterbok. The Elector, with his native liveliness of mind, decided on a jest to expose this weird woman before all the people, the more so because her skill had been unduly talked up at our dinner table. Hence, his arms folded, he walked up to her stall and demanded that, before she told his fortune, she furnish him with a sign that could be put to the proof immediately; otherwise, he could not believe her words, though she were the Roman Sibyl in person. The woman briefly looked us up and down and said the sign would be this: the big, horned roebuck which the gardener's son had been raising in the park would come to meet us in the market square where we then were, before we should have left it. Now this buck, you must know, was intended for the kitchen in Dresden and was locked in an oak-shaded enclosure of high palings; moreover, the park and the garden leading to it were kept carefully locked to guard various smaller game and fowl; so that it was impossible to see how the animal could, as predicted, come to meet us on the square. All the same, the Elector, suspecting possible trickery and determined to play out the jest and to discredit all the woman would say, consulted with me and then sent orders to the palace to have the buck killed immediately and prepared for the table a few days hence. Then he turned back to the woman, who had heard these orders being given, and said: 'Well then, what kind of future can you discover to me?' The woman looked at his hand and replied: 'Hail to my master, the Elector! Your Grace will have a long reign, the house from which you spring will endure for many years, and your descendants will rise to greatness and glory, and gain power beyond all the world's princes and rulers!' For a space, the Elector looked thoughtfully at the woman and then turned to me, saying softly that he was almost sorry now to have sent the order which would bring such a prophecy to nought. Then, as the knights attending him shouted their approval and showered coins in the woman's lap, he added a gold coin from his own pocket and asked if the salute she had in store for me was of a like silvery sound. The woman opened a box by her side, with deliberate slowness sorted the coins into it by kind and value, locked the box again, shaded her eyes with her hand as though the sunlight annoyed her, and looked at me; and when I repeated the question, saying jokingly to the Elector, while she read my hand: 'To me, it seems, she has nothing pleasant to reveal,' she grasped her crutches, slowly raised herself from her stool, leaned very close to me and, with her hands held mysteriously before her, whispered audibly into my ear: 'No!'

" 'No?' I said in confusion and stepped back, while she lowered herself onto the stool behind her, her eyes, cold and lifeless as marble, fixed on mine. 'From where is my house threatened?' The woman took up a piece of charcoal and some paper, asking if she should write it down for me; and when, having no choice under the circumstances, I answered with some embarrassment: 'Yes, do that!' she said: 'Well then, I shall put down three things: The name of the last ruler of your house, the date on which he will lose his realm, and the name of him who will conquer it by force of arms!' Having done so before the entire crowd, she rose, sealed the paper with gum which she moistened in her withered mouth, and imprinted on it a leaden signet ring she wore on her middle finger. But when I—more curious than I can describe, as you may well imagine—reached for the paper, she said: 'By no means, your Highness!' turned about and pointed with one of her crutches: 'If you wish, you may redeem the paper from the man over there, with the plumed hat, who is standing behind the people by the church door.' With that, she left me standing, speechless with surprise; and before I had quite grasped her meaning, she had closed her box, shouldered it, and lost herself amidst the surrounding crowd, without my noticing what became of her. To my truly great relief, the knight whom the Elector had sent to the palace returned just then to report, with a smile, that he himself had watched the buck being killed and taken to the kitchen by two hunters. The Elector jovially put his arm into mine to lead me off the square and said: 'So you see, her prophesying was a common swindle, not worth the time and money it cost us.' But what was our surprise when, at this moment, a great shouting arose from all over the square and everyone turned to stare at a huge butcher's dog who had grabbed the buck in the kitchen and was now carrying his booty from the palace yard toward us, with the servants running after him. Three paces in front of us the dog dropped the carcass, so that in truth the woman's prediction, warranty of all her other prophecies, had been fulfilled: the buck, though dead, had met us on the square. Lightning in winter is no more devastating than this sight was to me. As soon as I could excuse myself from the company, I did what I could to find the man with the plumed hat whom the woman had pointed to; but none of the men whom, for three days, I had out to look for him was able to discover even a trace. And now, dear Kunz, I have seen the man with my own eyes, a few weeks back, in the farmhouse at Dahme." With that he let go of the Chamberlain's hand, wiped his perspiring face, and fell back on his pillows.

Thinking it futile to try to contradict the Elector's view of this incident or to correct it by stating his own, the Chamberlain urged him to use every means to possess himself of the paper, and afterwards leave the fellow to his fate. But the Elector answered that he saw no way whatever of doing so, even though he was close to despair at the thought of having to do without this knowledge and seeing it perish with the horsedealer. When Sir Kunz asked if attempts had been made to trace the gypsy woman, he replied that he had ordered the police authorities, under a false pretense, to scour the entire Electorate for her, but that so far the search had been in vain; nor did he believe, for reasons he refused to go into, that she was to be found in Saxony at all. Now it happened that the Chamberlain planned to go to Berlin to settle an inheritance of several considerable estates which had come to his wife by the death of Count Kallheim, the recently dismissed and since deceased Chancellor of Brandenburg. Sincerely devoted to his master as he was, he now asked if he might have a free hand in the matter of the paper; and since the Elector warmly pressed his hand and said: "Put yourself in my place and get it for me!" the Chamberlain delegated the duties of his office, advanced his departure by several days and, leaving his wife behind, hurried off to Berlin accompanied only by a few servants.

VIII

Kohlhaas meanwhile, as we have said, had arrived in Berlin and, on special orders from the Elector, had been taken to the knights' prison, where he was lodged with his five children as commodiously as circumstances permitted. Upon the appearance of the Emperor's counsel, he had been summoned before the bar of the High Court and charged with breach of the public and

Imperial peace; and though he pleaded that, by virtue of the agreement made between him and the Elector of Saxony at Lützen, he could not be held chargeable for his armed invasion of Saxony and the acts of violence thereby committed, he was instructed that his Imperial Majesty, as here represented by counsel, could not regard this as a valid objection. And when this was fully explained to him, and he was told that, on the other hand, he would get full satisfaction from Dresden in his case against the Squire von Tronka, he was content.

It happened that the verdict was rendered on the day when the Chamberlain arrived from Dresden; Kohlhaas was sentenced to die by the sword— a sentence which, lenient though it was, no one believed would be carried out, partly because of the complicating circumstances of the case, but even more because the entire city, knowing of the Elector's good-will toward Kohlhaas, was unshakeably hopeful that there would be a decree commuting the punishment to a term, possibly long and severe, of imprisonment. The Chamberlain, who nevertheless realized that he had best not lose time if he expected to fulfill his master's wish, began his scheme by showing himself, fully and in his normal court dress, one morning on the street below Kohlhaas's prison window, from which the condemned man was innocently gazing at the passers-by; and he had the satisfaction of seeing how the horse-dealer, the moment a sudden motion of his head betrayed that he had noticed him, involuntarily put his hand to the part of his chest where the locket hung. This the Chamberlain thought preparation sufficient to take the next step in his plan to get possession of the paper. He sent for an old huckster woman whom he had noticed on the streets of Berlin hobbling about on crutches among a crew of other rag-pickers, and who seemed to him to answer closely, in age and dress, to the Elector's description of the gypsy woman; assuming that Kohlhaas could not have retained a clear memory of the gypsy who in one fleeting encounter had handed him the note, he decided to substitute this woman for her and, if possible, to have her play the gypsy's role with Kohlhaas. Accordingly, he prepared her by informing her minutely of everything that had occurred between the gypsy and the Elector at Jüterbok; nor did he neglect to impress on her the three mysterious points in the note, since he could not be sure how much the gypsy had revealed to Kohlhaas. Next, he instructed her what dark and disconnected hints she was to drop concerning certain stratagems to get hold, by force or trickery, of a paper so important to the Saxon court; and finally, he charged her to ask Kohlhaas to leave the paper in her keeping for a few critical days, on the pretense that it was no longer safe with him. On the promise of a substantial reward, part of which she demanded in advance, the huckster woman readily agreed to undertake the business; and since some months before she had come to know the mother of Herse, Kohlhaas's late groom, who had official permission to visit him occasionally, it was an easy matter for her, with the aid of a small present to the jailer, to gain access to Kohlhaas only a few days afterwards.

When Kohlhaas saw the woman enter, he thought he recognized in her, by the signet ring on her hand and a chain of coral beads around her neck, the old gypsy woman who in Jüterbok had given him the paper. And as probability and truth do not always coincide, something had in fact chanced to happen which we are bound to report, but which we must also leave every reader who is so inclined at liberty to doubt. By a colossal error, the Chamberlain, in choosing the huckster woman to imitate the mysterious gypsy, had seized upon the very woman whom he meant to be imitated. At any rate, the woman, leaning on her crutches and patting the cheeks of the children, who, rather frightened by her strange appearance, clung to their father, told this story: some time ago, she had returned from Saxony to Brandenburg; when the Chamberlain had incautiously inquired in the streets of Berlin after the gypsy woman who during the spring of the preceding year had been in Jüterbok, she had immediately approached him under a false name and made herself available for the business he wanted done. The horsedealer found a strange similarity between her and his late wife, Lisbeth, so striking that he felt tempted to ask her if she were his wife's grandmother; for not only did the features of her face, her still beautifully formed hands and especially the use she made of them in gesturing remind him vividly of Lisbeth; he even noticed a birthmark on her neck, identical with one his wife had borne. Beset by strange and confused thoughts, he made her sit down on a chair and asked what in the world the Chamberlain's business with him might be. The woman scratched the head of Kohlhaas's old dog, who sniffed at her and waved his tail, and replied that her charge from the Chamberlain was threefold: to tell him to what three questions, of grave importance to the court of Saxony, the paper held the answers; to warn him against an emissary who was in Berlin to obtain possession of the paper; and to demand the paper from him, on the pretense that with him it was no longer safe. But her real intention in coming was, so she explained, to let Kohlhaas know that the plot to rob him of the paper by force or trickery was a witless and empty delusion; that, guarded and protected as he was by the Elector of Brandenburg, he had nothing to fear in this respect; indeed, that the paper was far safer with him than it would be with her, and that he must take good care not to surrender it to anyone on any pretense whatever.

All the same, she concluded by advising him to use the paper to the end for which she had given it to him at the Jüterbok fair: which was to accept the proposal made him at the border by the Junker vom Stein and to trade the paper, which could be of no further benefit to him, for life and liberty. Kohlhaas, triumphant at the thought that he had the power mortally to bruise his enemy's heel at the very moment when it crushed his head, replied: "Not for the world, granny, not for the world!" The woman lifted the youngest child, who had squatted down by her feet, onto her lap and said: "Perhaps not for the world, Kohlhaas the horsedealer, but for this pretty little blond boy!"—at which she smiled at the child, hugged and kissed him and, as he looked at her wide-eyed, handed him with withered hands an apple she carried in her bag. Confused, Kohlhaas said that the children themselves, once they were grown, would praise his decision, and that he could bestow no greater benefit on them or their children than to keep the paper. Moreover, he asked, who, after his prior experiences, would secure him against further betrayals? Would he not end by surrendering the paper to the Elector for nothing, just as he had the band of soldiers whom he had collected at Lützen? "I will not trade promises again with someone who has once broken his promise to me," he said; "nothing except a definite and unequivocal demand from *you* will make me part with this paper, which has procured me so miraculous a satisfaction for all the wrongs I have suffered." To which the woman, putting the child down, replied that in many respects he was right and must act as he thought best.

Kohlhaas repeated his question about the paper's contents; and when she carelessly replied that he was free, after all, to open it, even if it were from mere curiosity, he passed on to other things he wanted her to tell him before she left: who really was she? how had she come by the secret intelligence she possessed? why had she refused the paper to the Elector, for whom she had written it, and given it to him, of all people, who had never desired her knowledge? But just then there was a noise, made by some police officials who were mounting the stairs; so that the woman, suddenly fearful of being caught by them in this room, answered: "Farewell, Kohlhaas, farewell! When we meet again, you shall not be denied understanding of all these things!" With that she went to the door, cried: "Good-bye, little ones, good-bye!" kissed the little tribe one after the other, and left.

Meanwhile, the Elector of Saxony, at the mercy of his grieved imaginings, had called in two astrologers, Oldenholm and Olearius, at that time of great repute in Saxony, and had consulted them about the contents of this mysterious paper, of such consequence to him and to all his descendants. But the two men, after spending several days of profound investigation in the Dresden palace tower, could not agree whether the prophecy related to future centuries or to the present, nor even whether it did not perhaps refer to the still very warlike posture of the Polish Crown; so that the Elector's disquiet, not to say despair, was aggravated rather than allayed by this learned dispute and, in the end, rose to an insupportable intensity. To make matters worse, the Chamberlain had asked his wife, who was about to follow him to Berlin, not to leave before she had gently broken the news to the Elector that there was now little hope of getting the paper away from Kohlhaas: his attempt to do so had miscarried, an old woman whom he had employed to this end not having been seen since; and the sentence of death had, after a careful study of the entire record, been signed by the Elector of Brandenburg, with the date of execution set for the Monday after Palm Sunday. At this news, the Elector, consumed with grief and regrets, locked himself in his room like a man lost and sick of life, for two days refused all food and suddenly, on the third, sent word to the Government House that he was going away to hunt with the Prince of Dessau, whereupon he disappeared from Dresden. Where he really went, and whether he took the road to Dessau, we leave open, since the chronicles on which we base our report strangely contradict and cancel each other on this point. It is certain, however, that the Prince of Dessau lay at this time ill in Braunschweig, at the residence of his uncle Duke Heinrich, and hence was quite unfit to be hunting; while Lady Heloise arrived the next evening in Berlin at her husband the Chamberlain's lodgings, accompanied by a certain Count Königstein, whom she passed off as her cousin.

The Elector of Brandenburg, meanwhile, ordered that the death sentence be read to Kohlhaas, his chains be struck off, and the property deeds, of which the Dresden court had ruled him dispossessed, be restored to him. When the court officials asked Kohlhaas what he wanted done with his possessions after his death, he drew up a testament with the aid of a notary, naming his children as his heirs and appointing his honest friend, the bailiff in Kohlhaasenbrück, to be their guardian. That done, his remaining days were of incomparable peace and contentment, the more so because, by an extraordinary privilege granted him by the Elector, his prison rooms were opened to all the many friends he had in the city, who were free to visit him at any time of day or night. Indeed, he had the particular satisfaction of a visit from the theologian, Jacob Freising, who came to him as an emissary of Dr. Luther, bearing a letter in Luther's own hand (which beyond doubt must have been a noteworthy document but is now lost), and from whom, assisted by two clergymen from Brandenburg, the horsedealer received the blessing of Holy Communion.

Amidst general excitement among the citizens, who still had not relinquished all hope of a decree of pardon, the fateful Monday after Palm Sunday arrived on which Kohlhaas was to atone to the world for his too direct effort to wrest justice from it. He emerged from the gate of his prison, escorted by a strong guard, the theologian, Jacob Freising, by his side, and on his arms his two boys—a favor he had expressly requested before the bar of the court. At that moment, from among a press of acquaintances who shook his hand and bade him farewell, the castellan of the palace stepped up to him, visibly disturbed, and handed him a note he said he had received from an old woman. Kohlhaas gave the man, whom he scarcely knew, a puzzled look, broke the seal which bore an imprint reminding him of the old gypsy, and opened the note. To his great astonishment he read as follows: "Kohlhaas, the Elector of Saxony is in Berlin; he has gone to the place of execution and can be recognized, if it matters to you, by a hat with white and blue plumes. I need not tell you his intentions; he means to exhume the locket as soon as you are under ground, and open the paper inside it.—Your Elizabeth." Deeply shaken, Kohlhaas turned to the castellan and asked him if he knew the woman who had given him the note. But since the castellan began: "Kohlhaas, the woman . . ." and then broke off strangely in midsentence, seeming to tremble in every limb, Kohlhaas, carried forward by the procession which just then resumed its march, was unable to hear what the man was trying to bring out.

When he arrived at the place of execution, he beheld, surrounded by an immense mass of people, the Elector of Brandenburg and his entourage on horseback, among them the Chancellor Heinrich von Geusau; at the Elector's right was the Imperial Councillor, Franz Müller, holding a copy of the death sentence, and at his left, his own attorney, the jurist, Anton Zäuner, with the final decree of the court in Dresden, while in the center of the semicircle thus formed there was a herald with a bundle of personal belongings and holding the two blacks, glossy with health and zestfully pawing the ground. For the Chancellor had gained every last point of the claim which, in his master's name, he had presented in Dresden against Squire Wenzel von Tronka; in consequence of which, the horses, having been rendered honest again by having a banner waved over their heads and being redeemed from the knacker who had taken care of them, had been fed back to health by the Squire's men and, in the presence of a commission set up especially for this purpose, been handed over to Councillor Zäuner on the Dresden market square. As Kohlhaas, flanked by guards, walked up the hill toward the Elector, the sovereign spoke: "This, Kohlhaas the horsedealer, is the day on which justice will be done to you! Look! Here I return to you all that was violently taken from you at Tronka Castle, and which I, your sovereign, was duty-bound to restore to you: blacks, neckerchief, gold florins, linen, not forgetting the costs of the treatment of your man Herse, lately killed at Mühlberg. Are you satisfied with me?"

Kohlhaas put his boys down on the ground beside him, and with gleaming eyes read through the final decree from Dresden, which had been handed to him at a sign from the Chancellor; and when he saw in it one clause sentencing Squire Wenzel to two years' imprisonment, his feelings overcame him and, his hands crossed over his chest, he knelt down before the Elector. He rose again and joyfully assured the Chancellor that his dearest worldly wish had been fulfilled, stepped over to the horses to inspect them and pat their sleek necks, and then turned back to the Chancellor, telling him gaily that he would leave them to his two sons, Heinrich and Leopold. The Chancellor, looking benignly down to him from his mount, promised in the Elector's name that his last wishes would be held sacred and asked him to dispose of the things in the bundle as he thought proper. Kohlhaas called Herse's mother from the surrounding crowd where he had seen her and said: "Here, mother, these are yours!" giving her the bundle and the money and adding, as a present from him for the ease and comfort of her old age, the money he himself had been awarded for damages.

The Elector called: "And now, Kohlhaas the horsedealer, having thus received satisfaction, make ready on your part to give satisfaction to his Imperial Majesty, represented here by his counsel, for the breach of his peace!" Taking off his hat and dropping it to the ground, Kohlhaas replied that he was ready; he lifted up his children once more, embraced them, and gave them to the bailiff of Kohlhaasenbrück, who, weeping quietly, led them away from the place of execution. Then he walked toward the block. He was just undoing his kerchief and shirt when, glancing over the encircling crowd, he saw not far away, between two knights who half concealed him, the familiar face of the man with white and blue plumes. With a sudden motion which left the startled guards behind, Kohlhaas stepped close up to the man, untied the locket on his chest, took out the paper, unsealed and read it; then, looking fixedly at the man, who was beginning to nourish fond hopes, he put the paper in his mouth and swallowed it. Seeing this, the man with the white and blue plumes collapsed in a convulsive fit. While his terrified companions bent down and lifted him from the ground, Kohlhaas turned back to the scaffold, where his head fell under the executioner's axe.

Thus ends the story of Kohlhaas. Amidst general lament, his body was laid in a coffin; and while the bearers carried it off to a decent burial in a churchyard in the suburbs, the Elector called the dead man's sons to him and dubbed them knights, instructing the Chancellor that they were to be educated at his school for young noblemen. The Elector of Saxony soon afterwards came back to Dresden, shattered in body and soul; his further fate can be read in history books. As late as the last century, on the other hand, some of Kohlhaas's descendants were still living in Mecklenburg, blessed with health and happiness.

The Vicar of Tours

BY

Honoré de Balzac

Translated by Nora Elliott and George P. Elliott

Editor's Note

Honoré de Balzac was born in 1799 in Tours. His father, born a peasant, had risen to the ranks of the prosperous bourgeoisie and was something of a *philosophe*. (In our usage, an eighteenth century *philosophe* was closer to an "intellectual" than to a "philosopher." Diderot was the supreme *philosophe*.) When Balzac was eight, he was sent away to school and stayed there for the next six years; he rarely went home, and his mother, who preferred his younger brother, never visited him. All his life he was unable either to break with his mother or to forgive her for this neglect. At eighteen he went to Paris and studied law for two years at the Sorbonne, working in the offices of two of his father's friends. At twenty he dropped his studies and, with the assistance of a meager allowance from his father, made a two-year trial of the life of letters.

Balzac did not abandon letters, as his parents had hoped, but for ten years wrote pot-boilers, novels he did not publish under his own name. Also, in 1825 he entered into the first of a long series of business ventures, all of them failures, some of them expensive ones. This first venture collapsed in 1828, leaving him far in debt. Though Balzac later earned large sums from his novels, which were numerous and popular, he was never out of debt again, thanks to his personal extravagance and his rash business enterprises.

Aside from his difficult mother and from his sister, for whom his love was undisturbed, there were three principal women in Balzac's life, all of the nobility. The third, Mme. Hanska, a Polish woman of tempestuous character, became his mistress not long after their first meeting in 1833; her husband died in 1841; she married Balzac a few months before his death.

Balzac thought of himself as a Catholic, though thirty-five of his novels (not including *The Vicar of Tours*) were put on the *Index of Prohibited Books;* as a Royalist, though Marx and Engels saw in him an acute and congenial social commentator; and as a scientist of society, though at most, in this respect, he was a journalist whose observations survive by reason of the power of his art.

In 1829 he published the first of his serious novels. (Following his father's example, he added to his name a *de* to which he had no title.) In 1842 he began calling his fiction *The Human Comedy* and arranging the stories in thematic clusters. His productivity was stupendous. In 1831, for example, he published *La Peau de Chagrin*, twelve *contes philosophiques*, and about a hundred articles. He wrote fast and not always carefully, but he revised endlessly, even in proof right up to the time of publication; there are sixteen beginnings to *The Vicar of Tours* (1832).

Balzac's grand intention in *The Human Comedy* was to give a sociological picture of French society, and especially of Paris where half the stories are principally located; he projected some three or four thousand characters from all walks of life, especially from that money-minded bourgeoisie which had risen to power in France after the Revolution. Despite his prodigious accomplishment (there are some two thousand characters realized in *The Human Comedy*), he left his design incomplete when he died, exhausted, in 1850.

The Vicar of Tours

IN THE EARLY AUTUMN OF 1826 WHILE RETURNING HOME FROM THE HOUSE where he had spent the evening, Abbé Birotteau, the main character of this story, was overtaken by a shower. So, as quickly as his plumpness allowed, he crossed the small deserted square, called the Close, which lies behind the apse of the Cathedral of Saint-Gatien, in Tours.

Abbé Birotteau, a short little man of apoplectic constitution, then about sixty years old, had already suffered several attacks of gout. Now, of all the little miseries of human life, the one which the good priest disliked the most was to get his silver-buckled shoes rained on and the soles soaked. Indeed, even though he scrupulously kept his feet protected by flannel socks with the care that clergymen take of themselves, they always got a little damp; and then, the next day infallibly, his gout would give him proof of its constancy. Nevertheless, since the pavement of the Close is commonly dry and since Abbé Birotteau had won three francs ten sous playing whist at Mme. de Listomère's, he resigned himself to the rain, which had started to come down in earnest when he reached the middle of the archbishopric square. Besides, at this moment, he was fondling his idle fancy, a wish already more than twelve years old—a priest's wish!—one which he dreamed about every evening and which seemed at that instant near to being fulfilled; in short, he was too well wrapped in a canon's fur robes to mind the foul weather. During the evening, the people who usually gathered at Mme. de Listomère's had almost guaranteed his appointment to the post of canon—then vacant in the metropolitan chapter of Saint-Gatien—by proving to him that no one deserved it more than he, whose rights had gone too long unrecognized but were incontestable. If he had lost the game, if he had known that Abbé Poirel, his rival, had been promoted to the canonship, then the good man would have found the rain quite cold. Perhaps he would have cursed life. But he was in one of those rare moods where agreeable thoughts make one forget everything. He quickened his step as if obeying a mechanical impulse, and it must be mentioned, since truth is so essential to a story of manners, that he was thinking neither about the downpour nor his gout.

Formerly on the Grand'Rue side of the Close, there were several houses, joined by a fence, which belonged to the cathedral and in which a few of the chapter's dignitaries lived. After the confiscation of the property of the clergy, the city turned the passageway dividing these houses into a street, the name of which was Choir School Street, joining the Close to the Grand'Rue; as the name clearly indicates, the precentor, his schools, and those in his charge used to reside here. On the left side of the street there is but one house. Saint-Gatien's flying buttresses cross over its walls and are so implanted in its small, narrow garden as to make one wonder whether the cathedral were built before or after this antique dwelling. But, if an archaeologist were to examine the arabesques, the shape of the window, the arch of the door, and the darkened exterior, he would see that it has always been part of the great monument to which it is joined. If there had been an antiquary in Tours (culturally one of the least literate cities in France), he would even have been able to recognize, at the entrance to the passageway to the Close, a few vestiges of the arcade which formerly made up the front gate of these ecclesiastical dwellings and which must once have been in harmony with the building's general appearance. Lying to the north of Saint-Gatien, this house is continually shaded by the great cathedral, on which the years have thrown their black mantel, imprinted their lines, and sown their damp chill, their mosses, and tall weeds. Thus it is always wrapped in a deep silence, interrupted only by the noise of bells, by the chanting that drifts over the church walls when services are being performed, or by the cries of jackdaws nesting in the belltowers. This spot is a desert of stones, a solitude with a character of its own, in which there can live only those who have become total ciphers or those who are graced with a remarkable strength of soul.

The house we are speaking of had always been occupied by priests, and belonged to a spinister named Mlle. Gamard. Her father had acquired this property from the nation during the Reign of Terror; but, since she had let rooms to priests for twenty years, no one took it into his head to find fault with a devout woman's keeping a national property under the Restoration. Perhaps religious people assumed she would bequeathe it to the chapter, and worldly people noticed no change in the use to which it was being put.

Abbé Birotteau was headed for this house, where he had lived for two years. His apartment had been, as the canonship still was, the object of his longing and his *hoc erat in votis* for a dozen years. To be Mlle. Gamard's lodger and to become a canon, these were the two great concerns of his life. Perhaps they accurately sum up the ambition of a priest: conceiving himself as on the highroad to eternity, he can wish in this world for no more than good quarters, good meals, clean clothes, silver-buckled shoes, enough to satisfy the needs of the flesh, and a canonship to gratify his sense of his own importance, that ineffable sense which will cling to us, they say, even in God's presence, since there are degrees among the saints. But the abbé's craving for the apartment he now lived in, a trifling sentiment in secular eyes, had been a consuming passion for him, a passion full of obstacles, and like the most criminal passions, full of hopes, pleasures, and remorse.

The size and lay-out of the house did not allow Mlle. Gamard to have more than two lodgers at the same time. Now, about twelve years before the day Birotteau became the spinster's lodger, she had undertaken to maintain in joy and good health M. l'Abbé Troubert and M. l'Abbé Chapeloud. Abbé Troubert was still alive. Abbé Chapeloud had died, and Birotteau had immediately taken his place.

The late Abbé Chapeloud, in his lifetime a canon of Saint-Gatien, had been the intimate friend of Abbé Birotteau. Every time the priest had come to see the canon, he would admire his apartment, furniture, and library. One day, out of this admiration, there was born the craving to own these handsome things. He could not stifle this desire, although it often made him suffer horribly to think that only the death of his best friend could satisfy this hidden but unrelenting cupidity. Abbé Chapeloud and his friend Birotteau were not rich. Both sons of peasants, they had nothing more than the small salaries granted priests, and their scanty savings had all been used up during the troubled times of the Revolution. When Napoleon re-established the Catholic religion, Abbé Chapeloud was appointed canon of Saint-Gatien and Birotteau became vicar of the cathedral. At this time, Chapeloud took lodgings at Mlle. Gamard's. When Birotteau came to visit the canon at his new home, he found the apartment quite well laid out, but he noticed nothing else about it. The onset of his lust for possessions was similar to that of a genuine passion, which, in a young man, sometimes begins with a cold respect for the woman he will later love forever.

The apartment, reached by a stone staircase, was in a part of the building exposed to the noon sun. Abbé Troubert lived on the ground floor and Mlle. Gamard in the second story on the street side. When Chapeloud first moved in, the rooms were bare and the ceilings black with smoke. The rather poorly-cut stone of the chimney piece had never been painted. All the furnishings the poor canon could at first install were a bed, a table, some chairs, and the few books he owned. His apartment was like a beautiful woman in rags. But two or three years later, when an elderly lady left him two thousand francs, Abbé Chapeloud used the money to purchase an oak bookcase—with carvings worthy of an artist's admiration—which had been rescued from a demolished château torn down by a company of speculators called the Black Band. The abbé made this purchase less because he was seduced by the bargain than because the dimensions of the piece made it suitable for his gallery. His savings permitted him at that time to renovate the rundown gallery completely. The parquet flooring was carefully scrubbed, the ceiling whitened, and the wainscots painted to imitate the tints and knots of oak wood. A marble fireplace took the place of the old one. The canon had enough taste to look for and find old arm chairs of carved walnut. A long ebony table and two Boulle cabinets put the finishing touches on the gallery, which now had a certain distinction. Within two years, the generosity of several devout people and some bequests from penitents, small though they were, filled up the empty shelves with books. Finally, one of Chapeloud's uncles bequeathed him his folio collection of the Church Fathers and several other great works of value to a clergyman.

Birotteau, more and more astonished by the changes wrought on this once bare gallery, became slowly and involuntarily covetous. He wished to possess the study, so suitable to the gravity of clerical ways. This passion grew daily. Spending entire days working in this refuge, the priest learned to appreciate its silence and peace, after first having admired its convenient arrangement. During the following years, Abbé Chapeloud turned the study into a private chapel which his devout friends enjoyed decorating. Later on, a lady offered the canon a piece of furniture for his bedroom, the tapestry cover of which she had been working on for a long time right under his nose without his having guessed for whom it was intended. Then Birotteau was as dazzled by the bedroom as he had been by the gallery. As the last touch to the comfort of this apartment, Abbé Chapeloud, three years before he died, decorated the drawing-room. Though modestly trimmed in Utrecht red velvet, the furniture seduced Birotteau. From the moment the canon's friend saw the red silk damask curtains, the mahogany furniture, and the Aubusson carpet adorning the large and newly painted room, Chapeloud's apartment became the object of his secret obsession. To live there, to sleep in the bed hung with long silk curtains, to be surrounded with all these comforts as Chapeloud was surrounded by them—this was Birotteau's idea of utter happiness: he saw nothing beyond it. All the envy and ambition which worldly things give rise to in other men was in Birotteau concentrated in the deep, secret desire to have a home such as Chapeloud had made. When his friend fell sick, he of course came to see him out of sincere affection; but, when he learned that the canon was indisposed or while he was keeping him company, in spite of himself there rose from the depths of his heart a thousand thoughts which could be reduced to the simple formula: "If Chapeloud died, I could have his lodgings." Yet, since he had a good heart, narrow ideas, and a limited intelligence, he did not go so far as to think up ways to get his friend to leave him his library and furniture.

Abbé Chapeloud, an amiable and indulgent egoist, guessed his friend's passion, which was not hard to do, and pardoned him for it, which might seem easy for a priest to do. But then, the vicar, whose friendship remained constant, did not fail to take a walk with his friend every day along the same path in the Mall at Tours, without begrudging him a moment of the time consecrated to this walk by the usage of twenty years. Because Birotteau thought of his involuntary wishes as sins, he could have performed the greatest sacrifice for his friends out of contrition. A few days before his death, Abbé Chapeloud paid his debt to this sincere and artless brotherly affection by saying to the vicar, who was reading him the daily paper, the *Quotidienne:* "This time you will get the apartment. I feel that it's all over with me."

In fact, in his will Abbé Chapeloud bequeathed his library and the rest of his belongings to Birotteau. The possession of these desired objects and the anticipation of living at Mlle. Gamard's considerably softened the blow of his friend's death: Birotteau would not have resurrected him, perhaps, but he mourned for him. For a few days, he was like Gargantua, who, when his wife died, giving birth to Pantagruel, did not know whether to rejoice at his son's birth or weep at his good Badbec's funeral and, in his confusion, rejoiced at the burial of his wife and bemoaned the birth of Pantagruel. Abbé Birotteau spent the first few days of his mourning looking over the works of *his* library, and using and examining *his* furniture, saying in a tone which unfortunately cannot be suggested: "Poor Chapeloud!" In short, his joy and woe kept him so busy that it cost him not even a pang to see that someone else was given the canonship which Chapeloud had intended for him.

Mlle. Gamard welcomed the vicar warmly as a lodger, and from that time on he enjoyed those material pleasures which the late canon had extolled to him. Incalculable benefits! To hear the late Abbé Chapeloud, not one of all the priests in Tours, not excepting the archbishop, could be the object of such delicate, meticulous care as Mlle. Gamard lavished on her two lodgers. The first thing the late canon would mention on their walks on the Mall had almost always been the delicious dinner he had just eaten, and during the seven walks of the week he rarely failed to remark at least fourteen times: "That excellent woman certainly has a vocation for looking after priests."

"Just think of it," he went on. "For twelve whole years, clean linen, albs, surplices, collars: nothing has been overlooked. I never run short of anything, and I always find everything in its place, scented with orrisroot. My furniture is polished and so well dusted that for a long time I haven't known what dust is. Have you ever seen a speck of it in my rooms? Never! What's more, the firewood is carefully selected, the slightest details are looked after; in a word, she always seems to have an eye on my rooms. I can't remember ringing twice in ten years for anything I wanted. That's what I call living! Not to have to look for anything, not even your slippers. Always to have a good fire, a good meal. For example, I was having trouble with my bellows—the nozzle was clogged. I only mentioned it once. Poof! The next day, Mlle. Gamard give me a very pretty pair, and these small tongs you see me poking the fire with."

For answer, Birotteau could only repeat: "Scented with orrisroot!"

This *scented with orrisroot* always struck him. The canon's words suggested fantastic happiness to the poor vicar, whose collars and albs were never quite up to par; for he was not well organized and often forgot even to order dinner. So, whether he was taking up the collection or saying the mass, whenever he saw Mlle. Gamard at Saint-Gatien he did not fail to cast at her a look as tender and benevolent as any Saint Theresa could have cast towards heaven.

Now, although the well-being which is desired by every creature, and which Birotteau had dreamed of so often, had finally become his, it is difficult for anyone, even a priest, to live without a hobby, and for eighteen months the abbé's two satisfied passions had been replaced by the desire for a canonship. The title of canon became for him what a peerage must be to a public servant of lower class extraction. Thus it was that speculation on his chances for getting the appointment, added to the hopes which had recently been pumped into him at Mme. de Listomère's, so distracted him that he did not even remember having left his umbrella at her house till he arrived home. He would probably not have remembered it at all if the rain had not started to fall in torrents, for he was absorbed in repeating to himself everything that had been said about his promotion at the house of the old lady whom he visited on Wednesday evening, Mme. de Listomère.

The priest rang the doorbell briskly, as if to tell the servant not to keep him waiting. Then he squeezed himself into the corner of the doorway, to keep as dry as he could; but the water ran from the roof unerringly onto the tips of his shoes, and every so often the wind blew gusts of rain on him like a shower-bath. When he thought he had waited long enough for someone to come from the kitchen and pull the latch-string, he rang again in such a way as to produce a very noticeable peal. "They can't have gone out," he thought when he still could not hear anyone inside. When he rang for the third time, the noise resounded sharply through the house and was caught up by the echoes of the cathedral: no one could have slept through the racket. So it was not without considerable satisfaction, mingled with ill-humor, that he heard the maid's shoes a few minutes later clicking across the cobblestones. Nevertheless, the gouty old fellow's discomfort did not end as soon as he had expected. Instead of pulling the cord, Marianne had to unlock the door with the big key and undo the bolts.

"How could you let me ring three times in such weather?" he said to her.

"But, sir, you can see for yourself that the door was locked. Everyone went to bed a long time ago; it struck a quarter to eleven a while ago. Mademoiselle must have thought you hadn't gone out."

"But you yourself saw me go out! Besides, Mademoiselle knows perfectly well that I go to Mme. de Listomère's every Wednesday."

"Good heavens, sir, I only did what she told me to do," answered Marianne, and closed the door.

Her words hit him all the harder because his revery had been making him so happy. He said nothing more and followed Marianne to the kitchen to get his candlestick, which he assumed would be there. But instead of going into the kitchen, she led him to his apartment; on the stair landing, they passed through a sort of antechamber which the late canon had enclosed by having windows installed, and Birotteau saw the candlestick on a table near the door of the red parlor. Speechless with surprise, he hastily went into his bedroom, only to see that there was no fire in the fireplace. He called Marianne back before she had time to go downstairs again.

"I see you haven't lit the fire," he said.

"Excuse me, sir," she said, "but it must have gone out."

He looked again at the fireplace, and was convinced that the fire had not been touched since morning.

"I need to dry my feet," he said. "Make the fire."

Marianne obeyed with the alacrity of one who wants to sleep. As he hunted around for his slippers, which were not on the rug by his bed where they should have been, he observed from the way Marianne was dressed that she could not have just got out of bed as she had said. He realized then that for about two weeks he had been deprived of all those little attentions which had been making his life so sweet for eighteen months. Narrow-minded people naturally conjecture about the meaning of the smallest trifles. He suddenly gave himself over to great reflections on these four events which would have been imperceptible to anyone else, but which for him constituted four catastrophes. In the neglect of his slippers, Marianne's lie about the fire, the unusual placing of his candlestick on the table in the antechamber, and the enforced wait on the doorstep in the rain, he saw himself threatened by the complete loss of his happiness.

When the fire was burning on the hearth and the night lamp had been lit, when Marianne had left without asking as she used to, "Do you need anything else, sir?", then Abbé Birotteau slowly lowered himself into the large easy chair of his late friend; but in the way he sank into it there was something sad. The worthy man was oppressed by forebodings of a dreadful misfortune. His eyes wandered from the fine panels on the chest of drawers, to the seats, curtains, rugs, the four-poster, the font, the crucifix, to a *Virgin* by Valentin, to a *Christ* by Lebrun—in fact, to every furnishing in the room; and his face expressed all the grief of the tenderest farewell ever made by a lover to his first mistress or by an old man to the last trees he will ever plant. The priest had just recognized, a bit late to be sure, the signs of a sly persecution which Mlle. Gamard had been carrying on against him for three months; a clever man would undoubtedly have guessed her unkind intentions much sooner. Old maids have a certain talent for stressing actions and words inspired by their hatred. They claw like cats. Not only do they wound, but they enjoy wounding and letting their victim know that it was they who wounded him. Where a man of the world would not let himself be scratched twice, the good Birotteau needed to be clawed in the face several times before he would believe the act had been intentionally malicious.

Immediately, with the inquisitorial shrewdness that priests acquire in directing consciences and extracting trifles from the depths of the confessional, Abbé Birotteau—as if the affair were a religious controversy—developed the following argument: "Let us suppose that Mlle. Gamard had forgotten about Mme. de Listomère's Wednesday evenings, that Marianne had simply neglected to make the fire, that they thought I had come home; considering that this morning I myself, I my own self, took down my *candlestick!* Mlle. Gamard certainly could not have thought I was out when she saw it in her living room! *Ergo*, Mlle. Gamard wanted to leave me at the door in the rain; and by having my candlestick sent up to my room, she intended to let me know. . . . What?" he said aloud, carried away by the gravity of the situation. He stood up to get out of his wet clothes and prepare for bed.

He paced back and forth between the bed and the fireplace, gesticulating, delivering the following phrases in various tones, but ending them all in a falsetto voice as if to indicate the exclamation mark: "What in the world have I done to her? What does she have against me? Marianne could not have forgotten my fire! Mlle. Gamard herself must have told her not to light it! Considering the tone she is taking with me, I'd have to be a child not to see that I've had the bad luck to offend her. Nothing like this ever happened to Chapeloud! I won't be able to live in the middle of these torments which . . . At my age! . . ."

He went to bed hoping that the morning would shed some light on the cause of her hatred—a hatred which was about to annihilate the happiness he had enjoyed for a year and a half, after having yearned so long for it. Alas! The secret motives of the grudge that Mlle. Gamard bore against him were to be forever unknown to him, not because they were hard to guess, but because the poor man did not have the candor with which great minds and scoundrels can confront and judge themselves. Only a man of genius or a schemer can tell himself: "I was wrong." Self-interest and talent are the only conscientious, clear-sighted advisers. Now, Abbé Birotteau, whose kindliness in some respects bordered on foolishness, whose education was a veneer put on with hard work, who had no experience of the world or its ways, and who lived between the mass and the confessional, mainly occupied in deciding the most trivial matters of conscience as confessor of the boarding-schools in town and of a few other good souls who appreciated him—Abbé Birotteau could be thought of as a big baby, for most social customs were completely alien to him. However, that egoism natural to all human beings, reinforced by the egoism special to priests and by the egocentric narrowness of provincial life, had imperceptibly grown in his heart without his knowing it.

If someone had been interested enough to pry into the priest's soul to show him that, in the infinitely small details of his existence and in the tiniest duties of his private life, he was essentially lacking in that devotion which he thought he professed, he would have punished and mortified himself in all good faith. But those whom we offend, even without knowing it, care little for our innocence; they want and know how to get revenge. So Birotteau, weak though he was, had to submit to that great, distributive Justice which always entrusts the world with putting its judgments into effect, judgments which some fools call "the misfortunes of life."

There was this difference between the late Abbé Chapeloud and the vicar: one was a clever and ingenious egoist; the other, an artless and bumbling one. When Abbé Chapeloud came to board with Mlle. Gamard, he sized up his landlady perfectly. The confessional had taught him to recognize the bitterness in the heart of an old maid excluded from society; so he shrewdly calculated how to conduct himself with Mlle. Gamard. The landlady, who at that time had just turned thirty-eight, still hung onto a few pretentions which eventually developed into a very high self-esteem, as they do in discreet people. The canon understood that, in order to get along with Mlle. Gamard, he must be more infallible than the Pope, must offer her unfailing attention and consideration. With this in mind, he made sure that they should have only such contacts as are strictly required by politeness and such as necessarily come about between people living under the same roof. Therefore, though both he and Abbé Troubert took three meals a day, he did not share his breakfast with the other two, but had a cup of coffee with cream sent up to him in bed. Moreover, he avoided the bother of supper by taking tea at the houses where he spent the evenings. In this way, he rarely saw his landlady at any time other than the noon meal; but for this meal he always came a few minutes before the appointed time. During this, as it were, courtesy call, he had made the same inquiries and received the same answers from her for the twelve years he lived there. How Mlle. Gamard had slept the night before, her breakfast, small household events, her appearance, her health, the weather, the length of the Cathedral service, any small happening at mass, and finally, the health of such and such a priest—these matters made up the small change of their daily conversation. During the dinner, he proceeded, by indirect flatteries, from the merits of the fish, the delicacy of a seasoning, or the virtues of a sauce, to Mlle. Gamard's own merits and virtues as mistress of the house. He was sure to tickle her spinster's vanity by extolling her preserves, pickles, jams, pâtés, and other epicurean concoctions. To cap it off, the artful canon never left her yellow drawing room without saying that in no other house in Tours could there be coffee as good as that which he had just tasted. Thanks to his perfect understanding of Mlle. Gamard's character and to the science of living he applied for twelve years, there had never been occasion for them to discuss the smallest detail of household management. Abbé Chapeloud had immediately perceived the angularity, the thorniness, the irascibility of this old maid and had so smoothed down the inevitable points of friction between them as to get all the concessions necessary to his quiet and happiness. Consequently, Mlle. Gamard said that Abbé Chapeloud was a very amiable man, extremely easy to live with, and highly intelligent.

As for Abbé Troubert, she said absolutely nothing about him. He was completely caught up in the movements of her life, like a satellite orbiting a planet; he seemed to her to be a creature of a race somewhere between the human and the canine; in her heart, he occupied a position just in front of the place intended for friends and filled by a fat asthmatic pug which she loved tenderly; she governed him absolutely. The indiscriminate mingling of their interests grew so obvious that many of Mlle. Gamard's acquaintances and friends thought that Troubert had an eye on the old maid's fortune, that he was patiently and imperceptibly tightening the bonds between them, and that, without seeming to have the slightest desire to lead her, he controlled her the better by seeming to obey her.

When Abbé Chapeloud died, the old maid, wanting a well-mannered boarder, naturally thought of the vicar. The canon's will had not been read before she began making plans to give his rooms to her good Abbé Troubert, whom she thought poorly lodged on the ground floor. But when

Abbé Birotteau came to draw up the agreement about his future lodgings with Mlle. Gamard, she saw that he was so taken with the former canon's lodgings, for which he could now openly express his desire, that she did not dare mention an exchange, but had to make affection yield to the demands of self-interest. To console her beloved canon, she had a smoking chimney overhauled and had parquet flooring in a herring-bone pattern installed in place of the large white Château Renault tiles with which the floor had been paved.

Abbé Birotteau had seen his friend regularly for a dozen years without once wondering about the motive for his extreme circumspection in his relations with Mlle. Gamard. When he himself came to live in the holy spinster's establishment, he was in the frame of mind of a lover about to be made happy. Now, even if he had not been naturally unobservant, his eyes were too dazzled by this impending happiness for him possibly to have sized up Mlle. Gamard or have decided what limits to set in his daily conduct with her. Seen from a distance and through the prism of material joys which the priest had dreamt of enjoying beneath her roof, Mlle. Gamard appeared to be a perfect creature, an accomplished Christian, a basically charitable person, the woman of the Gospel, the wise virgin adorned with those humble and modest virtues which exhale a celestial fragrance upon life. Accordingly, with all the enthusiasm of a man who achieves a long-desired goal, with both the frankness of a child and the heedlessness of an unsophisticated old man, he went into Mlle. Gamard's life like a fly getting caught in a spider's web.

The first day he dined and slept there, he was detained in the drawing room by the desire to become acquainted with her, and also by that inexplicable discomfort which often afflicts timid people so that fear of being impolite keeps them from interrupting a conversation to take their leave. He had stayed there all evening. Another spinster, a friend of his named Mlle. Salomon de Villenoix, came that evening. Mlle. Gamard then had the pleasure of organizing a game of boston. That night as he was going to bed, the priest found he had spent a very agreeable evening. He knew Mlle. Gamard and Abbé Troubert only slightly as yet; he saw only the surface of their characters. Few people bare their faults to public view right at first. Generally, everyone tries to give himself an attractive shell. Abbé Birotteau, then, conceived the charming plan of devoting his evenings to Mlle. Gamard instead of going to spend them elsewhere.

For some years, Mlle. Gamard had been cherishing a desire which had daily grown stronger. This desire, which old people and even pretty women indulge in, had become in her a passion like Birotteau's passion for his friend's apartment, and was bound to her spinsterish heart by those vain, selfish, envious feelings which are common among worldly people. This is a timeless story: one need only enlarge a bit the narrow circle in which these characters move to find an adequate explanation of events which happen in the highest spheres of society.

Mlle. Gamard spent her evenings in six or eight different houses in turn.

Whether she suffered at having to go out and look for company and felt that at her age she had the right to demand some sort of recompense; whether her self-esteem had been wounded by the lack of society at her house; or, finally, whether her vanity needed those compliments and benefits which she saw her friends enjoy—her whole ambition was to make her drawing room the center of a gathering towards which a certain number of people would turn their steps each evening *with pleasure*. After Birotteau and his friend Mlle. Salomon had spent a few evenings at her house, along with the faithful and patient Troubert, one evening when she was coming out of Saint-Gatien Mlle. Gamard mentioned to some good friends, ladies whose slaves she had considered herself up till then, that people who wished to see her should kindly come once a week to her house, where enough people would be gathered to have a game of boston; she could not leave Abbé Birotteau, her new boarder, alone; Mlle. Salomon had not missed an evening that week; she was at the service of these friends, and that . . . and that . . . etc., etc. Her words were all the more humbly haughty and fulsomely sweet since Mlle. Salomon de Villenoix belonged to the most aristocratic society in Tours. Even though Mlle. Salomon only came out of friendship for the vicar, Mlle. Gamard felt triumphant at having her in her drawing room and saw herself, thanks to Abbé Birotteau, about to succeed in her great plan of forming a circle which could become as large and as agreeable as those of Mme. de Listomère, Mlle. Merlin de la Blottière, and other devout ladies whose position permitted them to receive religious society in Tours. But alas! Abbé Birotteau dashed her hopes.

Now, if those who have attained the enjoyment of some long-sought happiness have understood Birotteau's joy at sleeping in Chapeloud's bed, they must also have some slight idea of Mlle. Gamard's chagrin when her cherished plan fell through. After accepting his good fortune patiently enough for six months, Birotteau deserted her drawing room, taking Mlle. Salomon with him. Despite herculean efforts, the ambitious Gamard had been able to recruit scarcely five or six people, whose constancy was very doubtful, and she had to have at least four faithful ones to make up a game of boston. So she was forced to make suitable apologies and go back to visiting old friends, for old maids find themselves such poor company that they can not resist looking for the equivocal pleasures of society.

The cause of this desertion is easily understood. Although the priest was one of those to whom heaven will one day belong by virtue of the decree, *Blessed are the poor in spirit*, he, like many fools, could not bear the boredom inflicted on him by other fools. Dull-witted people are like weeds which thrive in good soil, and the more they bore themselves, the more they like to be amused. The boredom of which they are at once the embodiment and the victims, added to the need they feel to be taken out of themselves, produces their characteristic passion for being on the go, their urgency for always being somewhere else; this is the same passion which characterizes people who are deficient in feeling, or those who have no future, or those who have brought their sufferings upon themselves. Without really fathoming Mlle. Gamard's emptiness, her nullity, or pondering the shallowness of her ideas, poor Birotteau became aware, a little too late for his own good, both of those faults she shared with all old maids and also of those which belonged just to her. Other people's faults so outshine their good points that we usually see them before they hurt us. This moral phenomenon would justify, if justification is needed, our being more or less inclined to say ill of others. Socially speaking, it is so natural to make fun of other people's imperfections that we should pardon the bantering gossip which our own absurdities warrant, and only be surprised by downright slander. But the good priest's eyesight had not quite achieved that acuity which permits a man of the world to detect and avoid his neighbor's rough edges. Consequently, in order to recognize his landlady's faults, he had to receive the warning which nature gives to all her creatures, pain!

Now, old maids, not having molded their character and their life to another life and other characters, as a woman is destined to do, usually have a mania for making everything around them adapt itself to them. In Mlle. Gamard, this tendency was degenerating into despotism, but this despotism could make itself felt only in small matters. One example among a thousand: Abbé Birotteau's basket of counters and pegs had to stay at the precise spot on the boston table where she had put it; the abbé, by moving it a little as he did nearly every evening, vexed her terribly. What caused this irritation which could be aroused by such trifles? What was its purpose? No one could have said; Mlle. Gamard herself did not know.

Though sheep-like by nature, the new lodger did not like the feel of the crook any better than most sheep, especially when it bristled with barbs. Without thinking about Abbé Troubert's great patience, Birotteau decided to withdraw from the happiness which his landlady aspired to flavor for him in her own style, as though happiness could be prepared like jam; but in his naïveté, the poor vicar went about it rather awkwardly. The separation was not accomplished without many squabbles and prickles, which he forced himself to pretend not to notice.

By the end of his first year under Mlle. Gamard's roof, the abbé had gone back to his previous custom of spending two evenings a week at Mme. de Listomère's house, three with Mlle. Salomon, and the other two with Mlle. Merlin de la Blottière. These ladies belonged to the aristocratic society of Tours, to which Mlle. Gamard had not been admitted. The landlady was deeply outraged at the abbé's defection, which made her feel how little she was worth: every choice implies contempt for the thing refused.

"M. Birotteau did not find us pleasant enough," Abbé Troubert said to Mlle. Gamard's friends when she was forced to give up her evenings. "He's a man of parts, a gourmet! He must have the fashionable world, luxuries, sparkling conversation, the gossip of the city."

These words always led Mlle. Gamard to a comparison of the two abbés, at the expense of Birotteau.

"He's not so clever as all that," she would say. "Without Abbé Chapeloud, he would never have been received at Mme. de Listomère's. Oh, what a loss I suffered in Abbé Chapeloud! How pleasant he was, how easy to live with! For twelve whole years, I never had the slightest difficulty or disagreement with him."

Mlle. Gamard painted such an unflattering picture of Abbé Birotteau that in her bourgeois circle, which secretly was an enemy to aristocratic society, he was taken for a man essentially hard to please and very trying to live with. For a few weeks, the old maid had the pleasure of hearing her friends pity her, those friends who, without believing a word they said, would forever be saying: "Good lord, you are so kind and sweet—how could it be that he dislikes you?" or, "Console yourself, my dear Mlle. Gamard, everyone knows you too well to . . ." etc. But, overjoyed at escaping the one evening a week in the Close, the darkest and most deserted place in Tours and the one farthest from the center of town, they all blessed the vicar.

When two people are constantly thrown together, the hate and love between them never stops growing: each moment gives them a reason to hate more or love more. So it came about that Abbé Birotteau became unbearable to Mlle. Gamard. Eighteen months after she had taken him as a lodger, just when the good man thought it was the peace of contentment that he saw in the silence of her hate and was congratulating himself on having "shaped things up so well," to use his own expression, he became the victim of her sly persecution and coldly calculated revenge. It took nothing less than those four capital events—the closed door, his forgotten slippers, no fire in the fireplace, and the candlestick taken to his room—finally to reveal her frightful enmity; and its momentous consequences were not to strike him until the damage was irreparable.

As he fell asleep, the good priest cudgeled his brains (and he must have worn them out quickly) for some explanation of her singularly impolite behavior, but in vain. Indeed, since he had acted so logically upon premises dictated by his selfishness, it was impossible for him to guess how he had transgressed against his landlady.

Though great matters may be easy to understand and to explain, the small ones of life call for many details. These incidents constitute, as it were, the prologue to this bourgeois drama, but the passions are as violent as if they had been inspired by great interests. For such reasons, this story has needed a long introduction, and a scrupulous historian could hardly have abridged it by even the smallest developments.

The next morning when he woke up, Birotteau was so occupied with his canonship that the four events which he had seen as sinister omens of an unhappy future the night before did not even enter his mind. The vicar was not a man to get up without a fire; he rang to let Marianne know he was awake and ready for her to come up. Then, as was his wont, he sank back into a morning nap, in the course of which the servant would usually make the fire, pulling him gently from this last snooze with the buzz of her questions and bustling, a type of music which he found pleasing. A half hour went by and Marianne did not appear. The vicar, already half a canon, was about to ring again but let the bell-cord go when he heard the sound of a man's footsteps on the stairway.

It was Abbé Troubert. After knocking discreetly at the door, he came in at Birotteau's invitation. This visit, which the two abbés paid each other regularly once a month, did not surprise the vicar. The canon immediately expressed astonishment that Marianne had not yet lighted his fellow-priest's fire. He opened a window, called her in a sharp voice, and told her to come immediately to Birotteau's quarters; then, turning to his brother, he said: "If Mlle. Gamard found out that you had no fire, she would scold Marianne." After this remark, he inquired after Birotteau's health, and asked him in a soft voice if he had any recent news which would give him reason to hope he might be made canon. The vicar detailed the steps he had taken and guilelessly told him which people Mlle. de Listomère was going to work on in his behalf, not knowing that Troubert had never been able to forgive this lady for never having received him in her house—him, Abbé Troubert, who had twice been suggested as vicar-general of the diocese.

It would be impossible to come upon two people more dissimilar in appearance than these two abbés. Troubert was tall and gaunt, with a yellow, bilious complexion, while the vicar was what is familiarly called chubby. Round and reddish, Birotteau's face bespoke a good nature devoid of ideas; while Troubert's, which was long and creased with deep wrinkles, at certain times had an expression full of irony or disdain, though it was necessary to look closely to discover these two sentiments. The canon gave the impression of perfect calm; this he did by keeping his lids almost always lowered over his eyes, from which he could at will cast clear and penetrating glances. Auburn hair completes the picture of this somber face, which was always darkened by a veil of grave meditation. The first impression he made on many people was that he was absorbed by a profound ambition, but those who claimed to know him best had in the end demolished this opinion, painting him as stultified by Mlle. Gamard's despotism or worn out by excessive fasting. He rarely spoke and never laughed. When he happened to be agreeably moved, a weak smile would escape and lose itself in the lines of his face. Birotteau, on the contrary, was expansiveness and frankness itself, loved good things, and trifled away his time with the simplicity of a man without rancor or malice. Abbé Troubert inspired at first sight an involuntary terror, while the vicar provoked a gentle smile from everyone who saw him. When the tall canon, his head bowed, his eyes severe, paced solemnly through the arcades and aisles of Saint-Gatien, he inspired respect: his bent figure was harmonious with the yellowed vaulting of the cathedral, the folds of his cassock had something monumental to them, worthy of sculpture. But the good vicar went around without dignity, trotted and jogged about, and seemed sometimes to be rolling along. Nevertheless, these two had one point of resemblance. Just as Troubert's air of ambitiousness, by giving people reason to dread him, had perhaps contributed to condemning him to the insignificant post of mere canon, Birotteau's character and appearance seemed to destine him permanently to be no more than vicar of the cathedral.

However, Abbé Troubert, by his judicious conduct, by the semblance of total lack of ambition, and by his saintly life, had completely dissipated the anxieties aroused in his superiors by his alarming exterior and suspected ability. Since his health had seriously declined in the past year—he was now fifty—his early elevation to the rank of vicar-general of the archbishopric seemed probable. Even his competitors hoped for his appointment, so as the better to consolidate their own positions during the brief span left him by his chronic illness. Far from offering the same hopes, Birotteau's triple chin presented his rivals to the canonship with all the symptoms of a flourishing health, and his gout seemed to be, as the saying goes, the sign of a long and merry life.

Abbé Chapeloud, a man of good sense, whose affability had made him much sought after by people in good society and by the various leaders of the diocese, had always opposed Abbé Troubert's elevation—albeit secretly and with discretion. He had even adroitly managed to have entry to the best drawing rooms of Tours forbidden Troubert, though in his lifetime Troubert had always treated him with great respect, on every occasion displaying the highest deference to him. This constant submission had not been able to change the late canon's opinion, and he was still saying to Birotteau on their last walk together: "Watch out for that cold fish Troubert! He's Sixtus the Fifth on a diocesan scale."

Such was Mlle. Gamard's friend, the boarder who came to visit Birotteau and show him signs of friendship the very morning after she had, so to speak, declared war on him.

"We must pardon Marianne," the canon said when he saw her come in. "I think she must have begun by doing my room first. My quarters are very damp, and I coughed a great deal during the night. You are lodged very healthily here," he added, looking at the cornices.

"Oh, I live like a canon," Birotteau answered with a smile.

"And I like a vicar," answered the humble canon.

"Yes, but you'll soon be living in the archbishop's palace," said the good priest, who wanted everyone to be happy.

"Oh, or in a cemetery. But God's will be done!" And Troubert raised his eyes to heaven in resignation. "I came to ask if you would lend me your *Register of Bishops*. You're the only one in Tours who has a copy."

"Certainly, it is there on the bookshelf," answered Birotteau. Troubert's last words had recalled to him the delights of his life.

The tall canon went into the library, and stayed there while the vicar dressed. Presently the bell for breakfast rang, and the gouty priest, thinking that without Troubert's visit, he would have had no fire to get up to, said to himself: "He's a good man."

The two went down together, each armed with an enormous folio which they placed on one of the side-tables in the dining room.

"What's that?" Mlle. Gamard asked Birotteau sharply. "I hope you're not going to clutter up my dining room with your old books."

"They're some books I need," Abbé Troubert answered. "M. Birotteau has been so kind as to lend them to me."

"I should have guessed that," she said, letting a smile of disdain escape. "M. Birotteau seldom opens those big books."

"How are you today, Mademoiselle?" her lodger asked in a piping voice.

"Not too well," she answered drily. "Because of you, I was wakened during my first sleep last night, and I felt the effects of it all night long." Taking her seat, she added: "Gentlemen, the milk is getting cold."

Astounded at being welcomed so acidly by his landlady when he expected excuses, but terrified by the prospect of an argument, as timid people are especially when they themselves are the point at issue, the poor abbé sat down in silence. Then, recognizing obvious symptoms of bad temper in Mlle. Gamard's face, he sat there at war with himself: his good sense bade him not put up with his landlady's lack of respect, while his natural inclination prompted him to steer clear of a quarrel. A prey to this inner anguish, Birotteau began carefully to examine the broad green stripes on the oil cloth which from time immemorial Mlle. Gamard had put on the table during breakfast, unconcerned about its worn edges or many splits. The two lodgers were seated facing one another on opposite sides of the large square table, each one in a cane chair, and between them, back to the dining room stove, sat Mlle. Gamard, dominating the meal from the heights of the chair, which was raised on casters and padded with cushions. This room and the common living room were on the ground floor, under Birotteau's bedroom and parlor.

When the vicar had received his cup of sweetened coffee from Mlle. Gamard, he was frozen by the absolute silence during which he was about to perform the usually cheerful function of taking his breakfast. He did not dare look at Troubert's expressionless face or the old maid's threatening one. Not knowing what to do, he turned to the big fat pug, which never budged from its cushion near the stove, since it always found a little plate full of fried tidbits to the left and a bowl of fresh water to the right.

"Well, my pet," he said, "so you're waiting for your coffee."

This personage—one of the most important members of the household, though not very annoying since he never barked anymore and left conversation to his mistress—looked up at Birotteau with little eyes buried in folds of fat, and then slyly shut them again. To understand Birotteau's suffering, it must be said that, gifted as he was with a sonorous loquacity as empty as the resonance of a soccer ball, he claimed that conversation aided digestion, though he had never been able to give a doctor one sound reason for his opinion. Mlle. Gamard, who shared this hygienic doctrine, had never yet failed, despite their disagreements, to chat through the meals; but for several mornings the vicar had been wasting his efforts in trying to pose artful questions which might loosen her tongue.

If the narrow limits of this story permitted the reporting of even one of these conversations, which nearly always provoked a bitter, sardonic smile from Abbé Troubert, it would have presented a perfect picture of the Boeotian life of the provinces. Some people with a lively turn of mind might enjoy following the strange turns and twists which Abbé Birotteau and Mlle. Gamard took in expounding their personal opinions on such subjects as politics, religion, and literature. There was certainly something comical about the reasons for which they both doubted, in 1826, that Napoleon was dead or the conjectures which led them to believe that Louis XVII had survived by escaping in a hollow log. Who would not have laughed to hear them establishing, by a process of reasoning all their own, that the king of France alone disposed of all the money collected in taxes, that the Chambers had assembled to destroy the clergy, or that more than thirteen hundred thousand people had died on the scaffold during the Revolution? And then, they would talk about the press without being acquainted with the various newspapers or even having the least conception what this modern instrument was all about. M. Birotteau listened attentively while Mlle. Gamard asserted that a man who ate an egg every morning would undoubtedly die at the end of a year and that it had been known to happen; that eating a soft roll, without drinking anything for a few days, would cure sciatica; that all the workers who had worked on the demolition of Saint-Martin Abbey had died within six months; that a certain prefect under Bonaparte had done all he could to have the towers of Saint-Gatien demolished; and a thousand other absurd tales.

But, on this occasion, Birotteau, feeling tongue-tied, resigned himself to eating with no attempt at conversation. Presently, however, he thought that the silence was perilous for his digestion, and said heartily: "This is excellent coffee!" This act of courage was utterly useless. After looking at the bit of sky visible above the garden between two of Saint-Gatien's dark flying buttresses, he had enough courage left to say: "It will be nicer today than yesterday."

At this remark, Mlle. Gamard bestowed the most gracious of her glances on Abbé Troubert, and then turned her eyes with terrible severity on Birotteau, who had fortunately lowered his.

In no human being of the gentler sex was the mournful nature of old maids reduced to a formula more perfectly than in Sophie Gamard. But, the better to paint a person whose character lends a great interest to the small events of this drama and to the previous life of its dramatis personae, perhaps it would be well to recapitulate here the ideas which express themselves in old maids. Habit shapes the soul, and the soul shapes the face.

If everyone in society as in the world at large must have a purpose, there are certainly on the earth some lives whose purpose and use are inexplicable. Ethical and political theory alike reject anyone who consumes without producing, who has a place in the sun yet spreads neither good nor evil around him—for evil is doubtless good in a form such that the results are not immediately manifest. It is rare that old maids do not place themselves in the class of the unproductive. Now, if consciousness of work accomplished gives one a feeling of satisfaction which helps him to bear life, the certain knowledge of being a burden to others or even of being useless must produce a contrary effect, causing him to feel for himself the same contempt which others feel for him. This harsh social reprobation is one of the causes which, without her knowing it, helps to fill an old maid's soul with the bitterness which her face expresses.

A prejudice which probably has something to it looks with great disfavor on women with whom no one has wanted to share the good things and bear the evils of life; this is even more the case in France than elsewhere. Now, these spinsters reach an age at which the world, rightly or wrongly, condemns them for the very rejection of which they are victims. If they are ugly, their goodness of heart should have made up for the imperfections of nature; if they are pretty, their misfortune must have had serious causes. It is hard to say which of the two types is more deserving of scorn. If their spinisterhood has been deliberate, if they have vowed independence, neither men nor mothers pardon them for having been untrue to the ideal of womanly self-sacrifice; they have refused to yield to the passions which make their sex so touching, and to renounce those sorrows is to do away with poetry and no longer to be worthy of the sweet consolations to which a mother has incontestable rights. Moreover, the generous sentiments and exquisite qualities of a woman develop only with constant excercise. By remaining single, a creature of the feminine sex is reduced to nonsense: selfish and cold, she inspires horror.

This implacable judgment is unfortunately too true for old maids to be unaware of the reasons for it. These ideas sprout in their hearts as naturally as the effects of their sad lives appear in their features. Therefore they wither, for the constant ripening, the happiness which causes a woman's face to bloom and fills her movements with such softness, has never existed for them. They become bitter and peevish; anyone who has missed his vocation is discontented, for he suffers, and suffering engenders spite. Long before blaming herself for her isolation, an old maid blames the world for it, and from blame to the desire for vengeance is only a step. Again, the lack of charm, the gracelessness of their persons is the necessary result of their life: never having felt impelled to please, they remain strangers to elegance and good taste. In themselves they see only themselves. This attitude leads them imperceptibly to choosing things which suit their own convenience instead of things which might be pleasing to others. Without really understanding how they differ from other women, they finally perceive that they do, and suffer for it. Jealousy is an indelible sentiment in a woman. Old maids are jealous in a vacuum, for they know only the miseries of the one passion which men find pardonable in the fair sex, pardonable because it flatters them.

Thus, frustrated in all their wishes, forced to deny their nature its full growth, old maids feel an inner uneasiness which they never get used to. Is it not hard at any age, especially for a woman, to read on people's faces an expression of repulsion, when it is her true destiny to awaken in the hearts around only gracious emotions? If old maids are always casting sidelong glances, it is less from modesty than from fear and shame. They do not forgive society for their false position because they do not forgive themselves. A woman perpetually at war with herself or at odds with life cannot possibly refrain from envying other people their happiness, and leave them in peace.

This whole array of sad ideas loomed there behind Mlle. Gamard's dull grey eyes, and the dark circles around them betrayed the long battles of her solitary life. Her face was wrinkled in straight lines. The structure of her forehead, skull, and cheek-bones suggested rigidity and dryness. On the moles scattered about on her chin she permitted once-brown hairs to grow unheeded. Her thin lips barely covered her teeth, which were overlong though they were white enough. She had formerly been a brunette, but frightful sick headaches had turned her hair white. This disaster compelled her to wear a patch of false hair in front, but not knowing how to wear it so as to hide its real function, she often left slight gaps between the edge of her cap and the black ribbon which held the badly-curled half-wig in place. Her dress, taffeta in summer and merino in winter but always carmelite brown, was always a bit tight for her angular frame and thin arms. Forever wilted, her collar exposed a neck whose reddish skin was lined as artistically as an oak leaf in full light. Her origins help account for the defects of her disposition. She was the daughter of a wood merchant, a peasant who had come up in the world. At eighteen, she might have been fresh and plump, but not a trace was left of the whiteness of skin or the high coloring she bragged of having had. Her flesh had acquired the pasty tone which is so common among zealous church-goers. Her aquiline nose, more than any other feature, expressed the despotism of her nature, just as her flat forehead betrayed the narrowness of her mind. Her movements had a curious jerkiness which precluded any kind of grace; and one would only need to see her pull her handkerchief from her purse and blow her nose with a mighty honk to guess her character and habits. Being rather tall, she held herself erect, and justified the observation of some naturalist who explained the gait of old maids physiologically by claiming that their joints had fused together. She walked without distributing her movement equally throughout her body so as to produce those graceful undulations so attractive in women; she went, so to speak, all of a piece, seeming to rise at each step like the statue of the Commendatore. In her good moods, she let it be understood, as old maids do, that she could very easily have got married, but that luckily she had perceived in time her suitor's ulterior motive; thus, without knowing it, she indicted her heart in favor of her shrewdness.

This typical member of the species *old maid* was well framed by the grotesque pattern, supposed to represent Turkish landscapes, on the varnished wall-paper which decorated the dining room. Mlle. Gamard usually occupied this room, which was embellished with two console tables and a barometer. On each abbé's chair, there was a small cushion covered with faded tapestry. The drawing room in which she received guests was worthy of her. It is adequately suggested by its name, *the yellow room:* the drapes were yellow, the furniture and wall-paper yellow; on the mantelpiece, over which hung a mirror with a gilded frame, crystal candlesticks and a crystal clock glinted so brightly as to be hard on the eyes. As for her own apartment, no one had ever been allowed to enter it. One could only guess that it was full of the odds and ends, broken-down furniture, and scraps of material which old maids surround themselves with and cling to so hard.

Such was the person destined to exert the greatest influence over Abbé Birotteau's last days.

Failing to use her feminine energy as nature intended and having to use it up somehow, this old maid had transferred it to the shabby intrigues, the provincial cabals, the selfish stratagems which all old maids end up devoting themselves to. Birotteau, to his undoing, had inspired in Sophie Gamard the only emotion she could feel, hatred. Till then, it had remained latent because of the calm and monotony of provincial life—her horizons were especially narrow—but now it proved to be the more intense for being turned loose upon petty things and in a limited sphere. Birotteau was one of those predestined to suffer everything: since they can't see what's right in front of them, they can't avoid it, and the worst happens.

"Yes, it's going to be fine today," the canon answered after a moment. He seemed to be coming out of a revery, wanting to follow the rules of politeness.

Birotteau, dismayed at the length of time which had lapsed between the question and the answer (for the first time in his life he had drunk his coffee without talking), left the dining room, where his heart was being squeezed as if in a vise. Feeling his coffee lying heavily on his stomach, he went out in the garden in a gloomy frame of mind, and walked along the narrow, box-boarded pathways laid out in the shape of a star. But, as he turned after his first round, he saw Mlle. Gamard and Abbé Troubert standing silently in the drawing-room doorway: he, with arms crossed and as motionless as a statue on a tomb; she, leaning on the shuttered door. Both of them seemed to be counting his steps as they watched. Nothing is more troubling to a naturally timid creature than to be the object of scrutiny; and when the inspection is made with the eyes of hatred, the suffering it causes turns into intolerable martyrdom. Before long, Abbé Birotteau fancied that he was hindering Mlle. Gamard and the canon from taking a walk. This idea, generated both by fear and by kindness, grew to such proportions that he abandoned the place. He was so absorbed by the old maid's desperate tyranny that when he left he was no longer thinking about his canonship. Luckily for him, there chanced to be a good deal of work at Saint-Gatien—several funerals, a marriage and two baptisms. He could forget his sorrows.

When his stomach told him it was dinner-time, he pulled out his watch and saw, not without a qualm, that it was a few minutes after four. He knew Mlle. Gamard's punctuality; he hurried to get home. In the kitchen, he noticed that the dishes from the first course had already been cleared from the table. And when he entered the dining room, the old maid said to him in a voice at once bitter with reproach and joyful at finding her lodger at fault: "It is four-thirty, M. Birotteau. You know we must not be kept waiting."

The vicar looked at the dining room clock, and the position of the gauze dust-cover convinced him that his landlady had rewound it that morning, and had treated herself to setting it ahead of the cathedral clock. No comment was possible. The merest hint of his suspicion would have provoked the most terrible and best justified of those eloquent explosions which Mlle. Gamard, like all women of her sort, was ready to burst out with on an occasion like this.

The thousand and one vexations a servant can subject his master to, or a woman her husband in the course of daily life, were divined by Mlle. Gamard, who overwhelmed her lodger with them. The way she relished plotting against the poor priest's domestic happiness bore the mark of a profoundly malicious spirit. She so contrived things as never to appear to be in the wrong.

A week after the time when this story begins, the atmosphere in the house and Birotteau's relations with Mlle. Gamard finally made him aware of a plot which had been six months in the hatching. As long as the old maid had taken her vengeance covertly, and as long as the vicar could persist in his error by refusing to believe in the malevolence of her intentions, the evil made little headway in his mind. But, since the business of the candle taken to his room and the clock's hands put forward, Birotteau could no longer doubt that he was living under the sway of an ever-watchful hatred. From then on, he rapidly descended to despair, and he saw that Mlle. Gamard's hooked, talon-like fingers were always ready to sink into his heart. Tickled to death to be having so rich an emotion as vengeance, the old maid relished hovering and brooding over the vicar as a bird of prey hovers and broods over a field mouse before seizing and devouring it. The dazed priest could hardly have guessed it, but for a long time she had been nursing a scheme which she now did not delay putting into effect. Lonely people whose souls are so unused to the grandeur of true religious feeling that they throw themselves into the trivialities of religious observances display something like genius for this sort of scheming.

Birotteau was an expansive man who loved to be pitied and consoled, and the last twist of the knife was that the nature of his troubles deprived him of the comfort of telling his friends about them. His modicum of tact, which he owed to his timidity, made him afraid that he would appear ridiculous for worrying about such petty, simple-minded things. And yet these were the things that made up his whole life, his dear life so busy about nothing, so nothing in its business; a grey, dull existence in which it was a misfortune for feelings to become too strong and in which the absence of all emotion was a blessing. So, the poor abbé's paradise suddenly changed to a hell. His suffering finally became intolerable. His terror at the prospect of having matters out with Mlle. Gamard grew daily, and the secret distress which was blighting his declining years had a bad effect on his health. One morning, as he was putting on his mottled blue socks, he noticed that his calf had shrunk quite perceptibly. Stunned by this cruelly undeniable evidence, he decided to approach Abbé Troubert and ask him to be so obliging as to mediate between Mlle. Gamard and himself.

In order to receive him in an uncluttered room, the canon promptly left the inner study, crammed with papers, where he was always at work and where no one was admitted. Finding himself in this imposing presence, the vicar was almost ashamed to speak of petty annoyances to a man who seemed so terribly busy. But, after going through all the torments of inner deliberations which humble, undecided, or weak people go through even in matters of no importance, he decided, though not without palpitations of the heart, to explain his position to Abbé Troubert. The canon listened gravely and coldly, trying in vain to repress certain little smiles which perhaps would have revealed a private satisfaction to sharper eyes. A flame sparkled from under his eyelids as Birotteau described, with the eloquence of real feeling, the cup of bitterness he was being made to drink; but Troubert put his hand over his eyes in the thinker's favorite gesture, and preserved the dignified demeanor which was habitual with him. When the vicar had finished speaking, he would have been quite puzzled if he had tried to read on Troubert's face any sign of the feelings he must have inspired in this mysterious priest, for that face was now mottled with spots even yellower than its usual bilious hue.

After a moment of silence, the canon made one of those answers every word of which had to be studied for a long time for the whole meaning to come clear, but which afterwards provided thoughtful people with proof of the surprising depth of his soul and the strength of his intellect. He overwhelmed Birotteau by saying that these things astonished him, all the more since he would never have noticed them without his brother's confession; he attributed this lack of observation to his serious preoccupation, to his labors, and to the tyranny of certain lofty thoughts which did not allow him to take due notice of the petty details of life. He pointed out, seemingly not wanting to censure the conduct of a man whose age and knowledge deserved his respect, that, formerly, recluses seldom worried about their food or shelter, dedicated as they were to saintly contemplation in the depths of the wilderness, and that nowadays a priest can by meditation make a wilderness for himself anywhere. Then, returning to the present matter, he added that these disagreements were entirely new to him. For twelve years, nothing like this had taken place between Mlle. Gamard and the venerable Abbé Chapeloud. As for himself, he went on, doubtless he could serve as mediator between the vicar and their landlady, because his friendship with her did not overstep the limits which church laws imposed on her faithful servants; but then again, justice demanded that he also listen to Mlle. Gamard. Furthermore, he found nothing about her changed; she was as he had always known her; he had voluntarily put up with a few of her eccentricities, knowing that this respectable maiden lady was kindness and sweetness itself; the slight changes in her disposition should be attributed to a lung trouble which she never spoke of and to which she had resigned herself like a true Christian. . . . He ended by telling the vicar that, if he meant to stay a few more years with Mlle. Gamard, he would learn to understand her better and to recognize the riches of her excellent character.

Abbé Birotteau left confounded. Since he was absolutely obliged to consult no one but himself, he judged Mlle. Gamard by his own standards. The good man fancied that, if he left for a few days, her hatred might be extinguished for want of fuel. He therefore resolved to go, as he used to do, and spend a few days in the country house where Mme. de Listomère went toward the end of autumn, when the air is usually clear and soft in Touraine. Poor man! He was doing precisely what his terrible enemy wanted; her plans could only have been baffled by the patience of a monk. But, guessing nothing, not even knowing how to take care of his own affairs, the vicar was doomed to fall like a lamb under the butcher's first blow.

Mme. de Listomère's estate offered the delights of the country and the pleasures of the city; it was situated on the embankment between Tours and and the heights of Saint-Georges, with a southern exposure and in the shelter of rocky cliffs. It took less than ten minutes to go from the Tours bridge to the front door of this house, called The Lark—a precious advantage in a place where no one wants to put himself out about anything, not even to go looking for amusement.

Abbé Birotteau had been at The Lark for about ten days when, one morning at breakfast time, the doorman came to tell him that M. Caron wished to speak to him. M. Caron was a lawyer in charge of Mlle. Gamard's affairs. Birotteau, not remembering this, and knowing no reason why he might be entangled in litigation with anyone on earth, left the table in considerable agitation. He found the lawyer modestly sitting on the balustrade of a terrace.

"Inasmuch as your intention of no longer lodging at Mlle. Gamard's has become clear . . ." the man of affairs began.

"But, Monsieur," interrupted Birotteau, "I never thought of leaving!"

"However, Monsieur," the lawyer continued, "you must have expressed yourself in some such way to Mlle. Gamard, since she has sent me to find out how long you will be staying in the country. The case of a prolonged absence not having been foreseen in your agreement, this could give occasion for dispute. Now, Mlle. Gamard understands that your board . . ."

"Monsieur," Birotteau interrupted again, "it doesn't seem to me necessary to use almost legal means to . . ."

"Mlle. Gamard, who wishes to avoid any difficulty," said M. Caron, "sent me to come to an understanding with you."

"Very well, if you would be so kind as to come back tomorrow," answered Birotteau, "I shall have taken advice on the matter."

"Agreed." And the paper-pusher withdrew.

The poor vicar, appalled at the persistence with which Mlle. Gamard was persecuting him, returned to the dining room, his face so woebegone that at the mere sight of him, everyone asked: "Why, M. Birotteau, what has happened?"

Desolated, the abbé sat down without answering, so stricken was he by vague visions of misfortune. But after breakfast, when several of his friends had gathered in the drawing room before a good fire, Birotteau artlessly told them his story to the last detail. His audience, beginning to be bored with the long stay in the country, was greatly interested in a plot so characteristic of provincial life. Everyone took the abbé's part against the old maid.

"Why," Mme. de Listomére said to him, "don't you see—it's obvious that Abbé Troubert wants your apartment?"

At this point, the narrator ought properly to sketch this lady; but it occurred to him that even those unacquainted with Sterne's system of *cognomology* could not pronounce these three words, *Madame de Listomère*, without imagining her to be noble, worthy, tempering the rigors of piety with polished manners, with the old, classical elegance of life under the monarchy; good, but rather stiff; tending to speak through her nose; permitting herself to read *La Nouvelle Héloïse* and to go to the theater; not yet wearing a cap.

"Abbé Birotteau mustn't give an inch to that old trouble-maker!" exclaimed M. de Listomère, a lieutenant in the navy who was spending his leave with his aunt. "If the vicar has any pluck and takes my advice, he'll soon have his peace of mind back again."

In a word, everybody began to analyze Mlle. Gamard's conduct with the perspicacity of people who live in the country; it cannot be denied that they have the knack of exposing the most hidden motives of human conduct.

"You haven't quite hit it yet," said an old landowner who knew Touraine well. "There is something important here that I haven't got hold of yet. Abbé Troubert is too deep to be understood so fast. Our dear Birotteau is only at the beginning of his troubles. First of all, will he be happy and undisturbed, even if he gives up his rooms to Troubert? I doubt it. If Caron has come to tell you," he added, turning towards the dumbfounded priest, "that you intend to leave Mlle. Gamard's, doubtless she intends to turn you out. Well then, you'll have to leave whether you want to or not. People of this sort never take a risk, they only play when they're sure to win."

This old gentleman, M. de Bourbonne, embodied provincial ideas as thoroughly as Voltaire embodied the spirit of his age. In matters of dress, this dry, thin old man displayed all the indifference of a landowner the value of whose holdings is speculated on and talked about throughout the Department. His face, tanned by the Touraine sun, was not so much wise as shrewd. He was used to weighing his words and planning every action, and he hid his profound cautiousness beneath a deceptive bluntness. One could tell at a glance that, like a Normandy peasant, he always came out ahead in business deals. He excelled in the science of wine-making, the favorite branch of learning in Touraine. He had managed to extend the meadow lands of one of his estates by appropriating some of the alluvial soil deposited by the Loire River, and to do it without getting involved in a suit with the Government. For this achievement, he was taken as a man of ability. Suppose you had been interested enough by M. de Bourbonne's conversation to have asked some native Tourainian to tell you about him. "Oh, he's a sly old fox," would have been the conventional answer of all those who envied him, and there were many. In Touraine, as in most provinces, envy lies at the root of the tongue.

M. de Bourbonne's observation produced a momentary silence, during which the people who made up this little committee seemed to be meditating. In this interval, Mlle. Salomon de Villenoix was announced. The wish to help Birotteau had brought her from Tours, and her news put a whole new light on the matter. When she came in, everyone except the landowner was advising Birotteau to wage war on Troubert and Gamard, under the auspices of the aristocratic party, which would protect him.

"The vicar-general, who is in charge of appointments and promotions," said Mlle. Salomon, "has just fallen sick, and the Archbishop has put M. l'Abbé Troubert in his place. So now the appointment to the canonship depends entirely on him. And yesterday at Mlle. de la Blottière's, Abbé Poirel talked of the difficulties Abbé Birotteau was giving Mlle. Gamard, as if to justify the disgrace which is to befall our good Abbé. 'Abbé Birotteau had much need of Abbé Chapeloud,' he said 'and since the death of that venerable canon, it has been proved that . . .' Then came hints, guesses, slanders! You see what's coming?"

"Troubert will be vicar-general," M. de Bourbonne said solemnly.

"All right!" exclaimed Mme. de Listomère looking at Birotteau. "Which would you prefer, to become a canon or to stay at Mlle. Gamard's?"

"To be a canon!" was the general cry.

"Well then," she continued, "we must let Abbé Troubert and Mlle. Gamard have their way. Aren't they letting you know indirectly, by Caron's visit, that if you agree to leave you'll be made canon? Tit for tat!"

Everyone exclaimed over Mme. de Listomère's acumen, her sagacity, except the Baron de Listomère, her nephew, who said to M. de Bourbonne comically: "I'd have liked a good fight—Gamard versus Birotteau."

But, unhappily for the abbé, the power of his supporters was not equal to that of the old maid backed by Troubert. The time soon came when battle lines were drawn and the combat grew till it assumed enormous proportions. On the advice of Mme. de Listomère and most of her adherents, who were beginning to take a partisan interest in this intrigue that had been tossed into the vacuum of their provincial lives, a servant was dispatched to M. Caron. The lawyer returned with remarkable promptness, a fact which frightened no one but M. de Bourbonne.

"Let's don't decide anything till we know more about it," was the advice of this Fabius in a dressing gown, whose profound meditations revealed to him the master strategies of the Tourainian chessboard. He wanted to enlighten Birotteau on the dangers of his position, but the wisdom of the sly old fox did not serve the passions of the moment, so that he got scant attention.

The conference between the lawyer and Birotteau lasted only a short while. The vicar came back rather haggard, saying: "He's asking me for a written statement affirming my *relinquishment*."

"That's a formidable word," said the lieutenant.

"What does it mean?" cried Mme. de Listomère.

"It simply means," answered M. de Bourbonne, taking a pinch of snuff, "that the abbé must declare he wants to leave Mlle. Gamard's house."

"Is that all? Sign it," Mme. de Listomère said, her eyes on Birotteau. "If you are serious about leaving her house, there is no harm in stating that it is your will to do so."

Birotteau's *will!*

"That's true enough," said M. de Bourbonne, closing his snuff box with a dry gesture whose meaning cannot be put into words for it was a language to itself. "But it is always dangerous to put things in writing," he added while putting the box on the mantel in such a way as to make the priest tremble.

Birotteau was so stunned by the upsetting of all his ideas, by the speed with which events kept catching him defenseless, and by the casual way in which his friends treated the matters closest and dearest to him in his solitary life, that he stood motionless, as if lost on the moon, thinking of nothing, but listening and trying to make sense out of the words everyone was firing back and forth. He took M. Caron's document, and read it as if he was going to give his attention to the wording of the lawyer's document, but it was a mechanical gesture. And he signed the paper, and, by doing so, he acknowledged that he was voluntarily relinquishing room and board at Mlle. Gamard's according to the agreement made between them.

When he had signed, M. Caron took the paper and asked him where his client should send the vicar's belongings. Birotteau named Mme. de Listomère's. With a nod, this lady consented to put the abbé up for a few days, never doubting he would soon be appointed canon.

The old landowner wanted to see this deed of relinquishment, and M. Caron brought it him.

"So, then," he asked the vicar after reading it, "there is a written agreement between you and Mlle. Gamard? Where is it? What does it stipulate?"

The landowner turned to the lawyer: "Do you know what is in it?"

"No, Monsieur," said M. Caron, holding out his hand for the fatal paper.

"Ah ha!" the old landowner said to himself. "You know every clause in that contract all right, my friend, but you aren't being paid to tell us." And M. de Bourbonne returned the paper to the lawyer.

"Where am I going to put all my furniture?" cried Birotteau. "And my books, my beautiful bookcase, my beautiful paintings, my red furnishings—everything I own?"

The poor man's despair on finding himself uprooted, so to speak, was so naïve, it showed so clearly the innocent purity of his way of living and his ignorance of worldly things, that Mme. de Listomère and Mlle. Salomon consoled him in the tone of mothers promising a toy to their children, saying: "You're not going to worry about those silly things now, are you? We'll certainly find you a house which is not so cold and dark as Mlle. Gamard's. If we don't come across a place that suits you, well then, one of us will take you in as a boarder. Come on, let's have a game of backgammon. Tomorrow you'll go and see M. l'Abbé Troubert to ask for his support, and you'll see how cordially he will receive you!"

Weak people are as easily reassured as they are frightened. So poor Birotteau, dazzled by the prospect of living at Mme. de Listomère's, forgot the irreparable destruction of the happiness he had so long desired and so delectably enjoyed. But that evening before falling asleep, with the distress of a man for whom the confusion of moving and of forming new habits was the end of the world, he racked his brain trying to think where he could find another place for his bookcase as convenient as his gallery. Imagining his books strewn about, his furniture dispersed, all his household arrangements disordered, he asked himself for the thousandth time why his first year at Mlle. Gamard's had been so sweet and his second so cruel. And always this perplexity was a bottomless well into which his reason, floundering, sank. The canonship no longer seemed adequate compensation for so many misfortunes, and he compared his life to a stocking, in which one loose thread can unravel the whole weave. Mlle. Salomon was left him, but, in losing his old illusions, the poor priest no longer dared put much trust in so recent a friendship.

In the *città dolente* of old maids, one meets many, especially in France, whose life is a sacrifice nobly and daily offered to noble principles. Some remain proudly faithful to a soul too early torn from them by death; martyrs to love, it is by the spirit that they find the secret of being women. Others are obedient to family loyalty, which, to our shame, decays day by day, and devote themselves to the welfare of a brother or some orphaned nephews: they become mothers without ceasing to be virgins. These spinsters attain the highest heroism of their sex by consecrating all their feminine feeling to the sacred service of misfortune. They idealize the image of woman by refusing the rewards of her destiny and accepting only her sorrows. They live encompassed in the splendor of their self-sacrifice, and before their wan, lined faces, men bow their heads in respect. Mlle. de Sombreuil was neither wife nor maid; she was and always will be a living poem. Mlle. Salomon de Villenoix belonged to this heroic breed. Her self-sacrifice was, in the true religious sense, sublime, in that it would have to go unrecognized though it had meant long-drawn suffering. Beautiful, young, she had loved and been loved; her future husband lost his mind. With loving courage, for five years she had devoted herself to the material welfare of this unhappy man, with whose madness she was so intimate that she did not even think him mad. Moreover, she was a person simple of manner and straightforward in speech; her pale face was not lacking in character, though the features were regular. She never talked about what had happened to her. Only, sometimes when listening to an account of something frightening or sad, she would make a sudden start, and there would be revealed in her those beautiful qualities engendered by great suffering. She had come to live in Tours after losing the companion of her life. There, she could not be appreciated at her true worth, and was taken for a *good-hearted person*. She did much good and, by preference, attached herself to the weak. For this reason, the poor vicar had naturally aroused her deep interest.

Mlle. de Villenoix, who was going to town early in the morning, took Birotteau along with her; she dropped him off on the quay of the cathedral, and left him determined to save at least the canonship from the wreckage and to superintend the moving of his belongings. It was not without many palpitations that he rang at the door of this house to which for fourteen years he had had the habit of coming, where he had lived, and from which he was now exiled forever, though he had dreamed of dying there in peace like his friend Chapeloud.

Marianne seemed surprised to see him. He told her he had come to speak with Abbé Troubert, and started towards the canon's apartment on the ground floor. But Marianne called out: "Abbé Troubert isn't there any more, M. l'Abbé. He's in your old rooms."

Her words gave him a dreadful shock. And finally he came to understand Troubert's character and the depth of his long-planned vengeance, when he found him ensconced in Chapeloud's library, seated in Chapeloud's handsome gothic armchair, no doubt sleeping in Chapeloud's bed, enjoying Chapeloud's furniture, living in Chapeloud's very heart, annulling Chapeloud's will, and finally disinheriting the friend of that same Chapeloud who had penned him in at Mlle. Gamard's for so long by making any advancement impossible and closing the drawing rooms of Tours against him. What magic wand brought about this metamorphosis? Didn't these things belong to Birotteau any more? Indeed, when he saw the sardonic air with which Troubert looked at the bookcase, poor Birotteau realized that the future vicar-general was certain of owning forever the spoils of those he had hated so cruelly, Chapeloud as an enemy and Birotteau because something of Chapeloud survived in him. When he saw Troubert's face, a swarm of thoughts rose in the good vicar's heart and enveloped him in a sort of dream. He stood motionless, as if spellbound by Troubert's fixed gaze.

"I don't suppose, Monsieur," Birotteau finally said, "that you would want to deprive me of the things which rightfully belong to me. If Mlle. Gamard was in a hurry to give you better quarters, she still ought to be considerate enough to leave me time to pack my books and have my furniture moved."

"Monsieur," Abbé Troubert answered coldly, letting no sign of emotion show on his face, "Mlle. Gamard informed me yesterday of your departure, the cause of which is as yet unknown to me. If she installed me here, it was from necessity. M. l'Abbé Poirel has taken my apartment. I have no idea whether the things in this apartment belong to Mlle. Gamard or not; but, if they are yours, you know she will be fair: the saintliness of her life is a guarantee of her uprightness. As for me, you are not unaware of the simplicity of my ways. For fifteen years, I have slept in a bare room, without regard for the dampness which has been killing me by inches. However, if you want to live in this apartment again, I am willing to give it up to you."

Hearing these terrible words, Birotteau forgot the canonship. He ran back downstairs as fast as a young man to look for Mlle. Gamard, and met her at the foot of the staircase on the large flagstone landing that joined the two parts of the building.

"Mademoiselle," he said bowing and heeding neither the sourly scornful smile on her lips nor the extraordinary flame making her eyes bright as a tiger's, "I cannot account for the fact that you have not waited till I moved my furniture to . . ."

"What!" she interrupted him. "Haven't all your things been sent to Mme. de Listomère's?"

"But my furniture?"

"You haven't read your agreement then?" said the old maid in a tone which would have to be written in musical notation to suggest the subtlety with which her hatred inflected each word.

And Mlle. Gamard seemed to grow larger, and her eyes shone more brilliantly, and her face opened up, and her whole body quivered with pleasure. Abbé Troubert opened a window so that he could read his folio the better. Birotteau stood as if thunderstruck. Mlle. Gamard blared in his ears, in a voice as shrill as the sound of a trumpet:

"Wasn't it agreed that if you left my house your furniture would belong to me, to indemnify me for the difference between what you paid for board and room and what the venerable Abbé Chapeloud paid? Now, since M. l'Abbé Poirel has been appointed canon . . ."

Hearing these last words, Birotteau made a feeble bow, as if taking leave of the old maid; then he rushed out of the house. He was afraid that if he stayed any longer he would break down completely, and so give his implacable enemies too great a triumph. Walking like a drunk man, he got to Mme. de Listomère's house, where, in a little back room, he found a trunk containing his linen, clothes, and papers. At the sight of all that was left of his belongings, the unfortunate priest sat down and hid his face in his hands to conceal his tears from the servants. Abbé Poirel was canon! And he, Birotteau, found himself without home, fortune, or possessions!

Fortunately, Mlle. Salomon happened to be passing by in her carriage. The doorkeeper, understanding the poor priest's despair, signalled the coachman. Then, after the old maid and the doorkeeper had exchanged a few words, the vicar let himself be led half-dead to the side of his faithful friend, to whom he could speak only incoherently. Mlle. Salomon, alarmed by the temporary derangement of a mind none too strong in the first place, took him directly out to The Lark, supposing that Poirel's appointment had brought about these symptoms of mental disturbance. She knew nothing about the agreement between the priest and Mlle. Gamard, for the excellent reason that he himself did not know its ramifications. And as it is in the nature of things for something of the comic to mingle even with the pathetic, Birotteau's odd responses almost made Mlle. Salomon smile.

"Chapeloud was right," he said. "He's a monster!"

"Who is?" she said.

"Chapeloud. He's taken everything!"

"You mean Poirel?"

"No, Troubert."

At last they arrived at The Lark, where the priest's friends lavished such heart-felt solicitude on him that, towards evening, they had managed to calm him down and were able to get from him a straight account of what had happened that morning.

The phlegmatic landowner naturally asked to see the agreement, which, since the previous evening, had seemed to him to hold the key to the riddle. Birotteau pulled the fatal piece of stamped paper from his pocket and handed it to M. de Bourbonne, who read through it quickly, soon arriving at a clause drawn up as follows:

"Whereas there is a difference of eight hundred francs a year between the rent paid by the late M. Chapeloud and that which said Sophie Gamard agrees to charge, under the terms hereinbefore stated, the aforesaid François Birotteau; and whereas the undersigned François Birotteau fully acknowledges that for several years to come he will be unable to pay the full price paid by Mlle. Gamard's other lodgers and, more especially, by Abbé Troubert; and whereas, finally, in consideration of the various pecuniary advances made by the undersigned Sophie Gamard, said Birotteau promises to leave her, as indemnity, the furniture of which he may be possessed at the time of his decease or at such time as he might for whatever cause quit voluntarily the premises at this time rented to him, and no longer to avail himself of the benefits stipulated in the agreement drawn up between Mlle. Gamard and himself, hereinbefore . . ."

"My God, what a contract!" the landowner exclaimed. "And what claws the said Sophie Gamard is armed with!"

Poor Birotteau's infantile mind had never imagined that anything might some day separate him from Mlle. Gamard; he had counted on dying in her house. He had no memory of this clause, whose terms had seemed so fair to him at the time that he had not even discussed them, for then, in his eagerness to belong to the old maid's establishment, he would have signed any legal paper put before him. This innocence was so worthy of respect and Mlle. Gamard's conduct was so atrocious, there was something so deplorable in the poor old man's fate and his weakness made him so touching, that in the first flush of indignation Mme. de Listomère exclaimed:

"I am the reason you signed that document and ruined yourself. I must restore the happiness I deprived you of."

"But," the old gentleman said, "the contract constitutes a fraud, and provides ground for legal action . . ."

"Fine!" cried the Baron de Listomère. "Birotteau will take it to court. If he loses in Tours, he'll win in Orléans. If he loses in Orléans, he'll win in Paris."

"If he wants to sue," M. de Bourbonne replied coldly, "I advise him first of all to resign his benefice at the cathedral."

"We'll consult lawyers," said Mme. de Listomère, "and we'll bring suit if we have to. But this business is so disgraceful for Mlle. Gamard and could turn out to be so injurious to Abbé Troubert, that we'll surely be able to reach some sort of compromise."

After mature consideration, everyone there promised to assist Abbé Birotteau in the battle about to be joined between him and his antagonists with all their partisans. A sound instinct, an indefinable provincial apprehensiveness, forced everyone to link the names of Gamard and Troubert. But none of them at Mme. de Listomère's, except the old fox, had a very accurate notion of the importance of such a conflict. M. de Bourbonne drew the poor abbé into a corner.

"Of the fourteen people who are here," he said in a low voice, "there won't be one on your side in two weeks. If you need to call on someone for help, you may not find anyone but myself daring enough to come to your defense, because I know the district, the people, the issues, and, above all, the interests involved. But your friends—though they may all be full of good intentions, they're steering you the wrong way, and you won't be able to turn back once you're started. Follow my advice. If you want to live in peace, leave the vicarage of Saint-Gatien, leave Tours. Don't say where you're going, and find some parish a good distance off, where Troubert can't get hold of you."

"Leave Tours!" the vicar exclaimed with an indescribable dismay.

That was a kind of death for him. Did it not mean tearing up all the roots by which he was attached to the world? Bachelors replace feelings with habits, and when weakness of character is added to the moral system that makes them go through rather than live life, the external world gains an astonishing ascendancy over them. Thus Birotteau had come to resemble a plant: to transplant him would be to imperil his innocent flowering and fruit. Just as a tree must daily absorb the same juices in order to live, and always have the hairs of its roots in the same soil, so Birotteau was meant forever to patter about Saint-Gatien, forever to trot along on the Mall where he took his daily walk, always to traverse the same streets, and night after night to go to the three drawing rooms where he played whist or backgammon.

"Ah, I hadn't thought of that," M. de Bourbonne answered, looking at the priest with a kind of pity.

Before long, everybody in Tours knew that Mme. la Baronne de Listomère, widow of a lieutenant-general, was harboring Abbé Birotteau, the vicar of Saint-Gatien. This fact, which a good many people were dubious about accepting, cut short further discussion and defined the factions, especially when Mlle. Salomon, the first to dare do so, spoke of fraud and legal action. With the subtle vanity and fanatical self-concern characterizing old maids, Mlle. Gamard felt terribly wounded by the course Mme. de Listomère had taken. The Baroness was a woman of high rank, elegant in her way of life, whose good taste, polished manners, and piety were beyond challenge. By harboring Birotteau, she formally and flatly contradicted all Mlle. Gamard's assertions, indirectly censured her conduct, and appeared to sanction the abbé's complaints against his former landlady.

For the better comprehension of this story, it is necessary at this point to explain how the discernment and spirit of analysis with which old maids dissect the actions of others gave strength to Mlle. Gamard, and what the resources of her faction were. Escorted by the taciturn Abbé Troubert, she spent her evenings in four or five houses where a dozen people gathered, all linked by the same tastes and the similarity of their situation. There were one or two old men whose chief interest was their servants' passions and chatter, and five or six spinsters who spent their days sifting every word and scrutinizing every action of their neighbors and of people somewhat above or below them in the social scale; and finally, there were several old women exclusively engaged in distilling scandal, keeping an exact account of everyone's fortunes and a double check on other people's actions—they foretold marriages, and they censured the conduct of their friends as harshly as that of their enemies. Living all together in the same town and forming a network of capillary vessels like a plant's, they drank in, thirsty as a leaf for the dew, the secrets of every household, sucked in the news and transmitted it to Abbé Troubert as automatically as leaves transmit to the stem the fresh moisture they have absorbed. So, every evening of the week, urged on by the need for excitement which everyone has, these good churchgoers drew up an exact balance sheet of the state of the city, with a shrewdness worthy of the Council of Ten, and armed with that faculty for unerring espionage which passion begets, they constituted a police force. Then, when they had ferreted out the secret reason for some event, their conceit led each of them to appropriate to his own use the collective wisdom of the sanhedrin so as to set the key for the gossip in their respective zones. This congregation, idle yet busy, invisible yet all-seeing, taciturn yet endlessly talking, had an influence which the nonentity of its members made apparently harmless, but which all the same could become terrible when concerned with matters of consequence.

Now, for a long time nothing had entered the sphere of their lives so serious and generally important to them all as the struggle between Birotteau, backed by Mme. de Listomère, and Abbé Troubert and Mlle. Gamard. In fact, since the drawing rooms of Mme. de Listomère and Mlles. Merlin de la Blottière and de Villenoix were considered as enemy territory by Mlle. Gamard's followers, there lay at the heart of this quarrel a sort of *esprit de corps*, with all its vanities. It was the Roman people and Senate struggling on a mole-hill, or a tempest in a glass of water, as Montesquieu said of the Republic of San Marino where the term of public office lasted only a day, so easy was it to seize despotic power. Nevertheless, this tempest developed as many passions in the souls of these people as would have been needed to conduct the greatest social enterprises.

It would be a great mistake to think that time passes quickly only for those whose hearts are consumed by vast projects that keep their life in a seething turmoil. Abbé Troubert's hours rushed just as fast, flew laden with thoughts as anxious, were harassed by despairs and hopes as profound, as the hours of an ambitious man, a gambler, or a lover could ever have fled. God alone knows the secret of the energy we expend in triumphs over men, things, and ourselves. If we cannot always be sure where we are going, we well know the hardships of the journey. Yet, if the narrator may for a moment turn from the drama he is telling and take a critic's stance, if he may invite you to take a glance at the lives of these old maids and the abbés, so as to seek in those lives the cause of the sadness which corrupted their very essence, it will perhaps be proved to you that man must feel certain passions, if there are to blossom in him those qualities which give life nobility, broaden its horizons, and quell the egoism natural to all creatures.

Mme. de Listomère returned to town without knowing that for five or six days several of her friends had been forced to combat a rumor being spread about her (she would have laughed at it if she had known of it) which implied that her affection for her nephew was of an almost criminal nature. She took Abbé Birotteau to her lawyer, to whom the lawsuit looked anything but easy. The vicar's friends, who were confident in the knowledge that their cause was just, or else were not overly concerned with a law suit which would not affect them personally, had postponed initiating the suit till they were all back in Tours. Mlle. Gamard's friends had thus been able to steal a march on them, and had been telling the story in such a way as to cast little credit on Abbé Birotteau. So the man of law, whose clientele was made up exclusively of the churchgoing people of the city, greatly astonished Mme. de Listomère by advising her not to embark on such an affair. Furthermore, he closed their conference by saying that he would not take the case because, according to the terms of the contract, Mlle. Gamard was legally in the right; that in equity, that is to say, over and above legal justice, Abbé Birotteau would seem, in the eyes of the court and all good citizens, to lack the spirit of peace, conciliation, and forbearance he had been assumed up till then to possess; that Mlle. Gamard, known as a kindly person and one easy to live with, had obliged Birotteau by lending him the money necessary to pay the inheritance tax on Chapeloud's legacy without asking him for a receipt; that Birotteau was neither of an age nor a character to sign a document without knowing its contents or realizing their significance; and that if he had left Mlle. Gamard's after living there two years, when his friend Chapeloud had stayed twelve years and Troubert fifteen, it could only be with some intent plain to himself; that the suit would be considered an act of ingratitude, etc. After letting Birotteau walk ahead towards the staircase, the attorney took Mme. de Listomère aside as he was showing her out, and urged her in the name of her peace of mind to have nothing to do with the whole business.

However, that evening the poor vicar, in the torments of a man in the condemned cell at Bicêtre waiting for the result of his appeal, could not resist telling his friends about the result of his visit, as the group was gathered before Mme. de Listomère's fireplace before breaking up into groups to play cards.

"Except for the Liberal attorney," exclaimed M. de Bourbonne, "I don't know a shyster in Tours who would take this case on without intending to lose it for you. My advice to you is: stay out of it."

"Well, it's a damned outrage!" said the lieutenant in the navy. "I'll take the abbé to this lawyer myself."

"Go after dark," M. de Bourbonne interrupted.

"Yes? Why?"

"I've just learned that Abbé Troubert has been named vicar-general, to take the place of the former one, who died day before yesterday."

"I don't give a damn for Abbé Troubert!"

Unfortunately, the Baron de Listomère, a man of thirty-six, did not see the signal M. de Bourbonne made; trying to warn him to weigh his words, he was pointing at a city councillor who was a friend of Troubert. So the lieutenant went on:

"If M. l'Abbé Troubert is a scoundrel . . ."

"Come now," M. de Bourbonne interrupted again, "why drag Abbé Troubert into a mess he has nothing to do with?"

"But," said the Baron, "doesn't he have Abbé Birotteau's furniture? I remember calling on Chapeloud and seeing two quite valuable paintings there. Suppose they're worth ten thousand francs. Do you really think M. Birotteau meant to give ten thousand francs for two years board and room at Mlle. Gamard's when the library and furniture are worth that much again?"

Abbé Birotteau opened his eyes wide when he learned what an enormous capital he had possessed.

The Baron went on heatedly: "By God! M. Salmon, the former art expert who used to be with the Paris Museum, is here visiting his mother-in-law. I'm going there this very evening, with Abbé Birotteau, to ask him to give an estimate on the paintings. From there, I'll take him to that lawyer."

Two days after this conversation, the lawsuit had taken shape. The Liberal attorney, now Birotteau's, cast much discredit on the vicar's cause. Those who opposed the Government and those who were known to dislike priests or religion, two attitudes which many people confused, eagerly seized on the business, and the whole city talked about it. The former Museum expert had put a value of eleven thousand francs on Valentin's *Virgin* and Lebrun's *Christ*—very choice items. As for the bookcase and gothic furniture, the growing fashion for this sort of thing in Paris gave them, for the moment at least, a value of twelve thousand francs. After due examination, the expert evaluated the Abbé's possessions at thirty thousand francs all told. Now it was obvious that, since Birotteau had not intended to give Mlle. Gamard this enormous sum for the small amount he might owe her under the stipulations in the agreement, there were legal grounds for changing the contract; otherwise, the old maid would have been guilty of deliberate fraud. So the Liberal attorney instituted proceedings by serving a preliminary writ on Mlle. Gamard. Though very peremptory, the document, supported by citations from Supreme Court decisions and corroborated by certain articles of the Code, was nonetheless a masterpiece of legalistic logic and condemned the old maid so unquestionably that thirty or forty copies were spitefully distributed through the city by the party opposed to her.

A few days after the commencement of hostilities between the old maid and Birotteau, the Baron de Listomère, who had hopes of being appointed captain of a corvette in a coming promotion which for some time had been promised by the Ministry of the Navy, received a letter in which one of his friends told him that the board was considering taking him off the active list. Greatly surprised by this news, he immediately left for Paris and called on the Minister the very first evening His Excellency was receiving. This official appeared quite astonished by what the Baron told him of his fears and laughed at them. The next day, in spite of His Excellency's word, the Baron inquired at the Ministry. With an indiscretion that heads of departments often commit for their friends, a secretary showed him a report which would already have been submitted to the Minister had it not been for the illness of one of the directors and which confirmed the fatal news.

The Baron de Listomère went directly to one of his uncles who, in his capacity as deputy, could see the Minister of the Navy at the Chamber at any time, and begged him to find out what His Excellency had in mind, for his whole future was at stake. Sitting in his uncle's carriage, he waited with the keenest anxiety for the end of the session. The deputy came out long before the Chamber adjourned, and said to his nephew on their drive back to the house:

"Why the devil are you waging war on the clergy? The Minister began by telling me you'd put yourself at the head of the Liberals in Tours! You have detestable opinions, you don't follow the Government line, and so on and so forth. His sentences got as involved as when he's speaking to the House. So I said to him, 'Come on, let's come to the point.' His Excellency ended by admitting that you were in bad with the hierarchy of the Church. In short, after I asked my colleagues a few questions, I found out that you've been speaking quite slightingly of a certain Abbé Troubert, a simple vicar-general but the most important personage in the province, where he is the representative of the Congregation. I made myself answerable for you to the Minister, body and soul. My dear nephew, if you want to get ahead, don't make an enemy of the clergy. Go right back to Tours and make your peace with this devil of a vicar-general. Let me tell you, a vicar-general is to be left strictly alone. Good lord, when everyone's working to reëstablish the Church, it's stupid for a naval lieutenant who wants to be a captain to speak against priests. If you don't patch things up with Abbé Troubert, don't count on me: I'll wash my hands of the whole business. The Minister of Ecclesiastical Affairs spoke to me of this man just now as a future bishop. If Troubert were to take a dislike to our family, he might be able to keep me from being included on the next list of peers. Do you understand?"

These words illuminated for the lieutenant the nature of Troubert's secret occupations, about which Birotteau had foolishly remarked: "I can't imagine what good it does him to stay up so late at night."

The canon's position at the center of the female cabal which so subtly policed the province, as well as his personal capacity, had made the Congregation choose him from all the clergy in the city to be the unacknowledged proconsul of Tours. Archbishop, general, prefect—high and low alike were under his secret dominion.

The Baron de Listomère had soon made up his mind. "I don't want to get another ecclesiastical broadside below my water-line," he told his uncle.

Three days after this diplomatic conference between uncle and nephew, the sailor hurried back to Tours by the mail coach, and that same evening informed his aunt of the dangers the Listomère family would be running if he and she both persisted in backing that *imbecile of a Birotteau*. The Baron had detained M. de Bourbonne just as the old gentleman was getting his cane and hat to leave after the whist game. He needed the sly old fox's shrewdness to shed light on the perils among which the Listomères found themselves making their way, and the old fox had prematurely gone for his cane and hat just in order to have it whispered in his ear: "Stay a while, we want to talk with you."

The Baron's quick return, together with the contrast between his air of satisfaction and the expression of gravity appearing on his face at certain moments, had more or less suggested to M. de Bourbonne that the lieutenant might have suffered some checks in his expedition against Gamard and Troubert. He showed no surprise when he heard the Baron expatiate upon the secret power of the vicar-general as representative of the Congregation.

"I knew that," he said.

"Is that so?" the Baroness exclaimed. "Then why didn't you warn us?"

"Madame," he answered quickly, "forget that I guessed the invisible influence of this priest, and I'll forget that you know about it, too. If we don't keep this secret, we'll be taken for his accomplices; we'll be feared and hated. Do as I do, pretend to be a dupe. But watch your step. I said more than enough, but you didn't understand me, and I didn't want to compromise myself."

"Where do we go from here?" said the Baron.

Deserting Birotteau was not even brought up for discussion; it was a major premise taken for granted by the council of three.

"To beat a retreat without loss of military honor has always been the masterstroke of the ablest generals," answered M. de Bourbonne. "Give way to Troubert: if his spite is weaker than his vanity, you'll make him your ally; but if you give way too far, he'll trample all over you. Make him think you're leaving the service, and you'll escape his clutches, M. le Baron. Send the vicar away, Madame; let this Gamard woman win her case. Go to the Archbishop's party and ask Troubert if he knows how to play whist. He'll say yes. Invite him for a rubber in this drawing room, where he wants to be received; he'll certainly come. You are a woman; find out how to use him to your own advantage. When the Baron is the captain of a vessel, his uncle a peer of France, and Troubert a bishop, you can easily make Birotteau a canon. Until then, yield; but yield with grace and somewhat threateningly.

Your family can lend Troubert as much support as he will give you: you'll get along famously. One last point, sailor: take soundings as you go!"

"Poor Birotteau!" said the Baroness.

"Break with him right away," replied the landowner as he went out. "If some clever Liberal gets hold of that featherbrain, he may cause you a lot of trouble. After all, the court would decide in his favor, and Troubert must be afraid of the verdict. He can still forgive you for having started the fight, but after a defeat, he'd be implacable. I've had my say."

He clicked his snuff box shut, put on his galoshes, and left.

The next morning after breakfast, the Baroness stayed behind with the vicar and said to him, not without visible embarrassment: "My dear M. Birotteau, you're going to find my request very unjust and very inconsistent; but it is necessary, both for your sake and for ours, to drop the case against Mlle. Gamard by your withdrawing your claims, and then you must leave my house."

At these words, the poor priest grew pale.

"I am the innocent cause of your misfortune," she continued, "and I know that were it not for my nephew you wouldn't have started this suit which is so troubling for all of us now. But listen!"

In a few words she laid out before him the wide expanse of the affair and explained the seriousness of its consequences. Her meditations during the night had led her to form an idea of what Troubert's past history had been. Thus she could unerringly show Birotteau the web in which the machinations of vengeance had enveloped him; she could reveal to him his enemy's enormous capacity and power by unveiling that hatred, teaching him its causes, and showing him how his enemy had crouched to Chapeloud for a dozen years, had then devoured Chapeloud, and was persecuting him still in the person of this friend. The innocent Birotteau clasped his hands as if to pray, and wept for sorrow at the thought of such human enormities as his pure soul had never suspected. As horrified as if he were on the brink of a bottomless pit, eyes fixed and moist, but saying nothing, he listened to what his benefactress said.

She finished with these words: "I know how wrong it is to abandon you, my dear abbé, but the claims of family come before those of friendship. Bend before this storm as I am doing; I will give you proof of my gratitude. I won't mention your personal interests; I will look after them myself. You won't need to worry about your livelihood. Thanks to Bourbonne, who'll be able to save appearances, I shall arrange that you lack for nothing. My friend, give me the right to betray you. I shall remain your friend, and at the same time conform to the maxims of worldly prudence. Decide."

The poor, stupefied abbé exclaimed: "So Chapeloud was right when he said that if Troubert could come pull him by the heels out of the grave he'd do it! He sleeps in Chapeloud's bed."

"It's not the time to complain," said Mme. de Listomère. "We haven't much time to spare. Now then!"

At times of great crisis, Birotteau was too good-hearted not to obey the first, unreflecting impulse towards self-sacrifice. And after all, his life was now just one long misery. Looking at his benefactress with a despair that wrung her heart, he said: "I put myself in your hands. I'm nothing but a straw in the street now."

The word he used, *bourrier*, is a Tourainian word for which there is no equivalent but *straw*. But there are pretty little bits of straw, yellow and shiny, which delight children; whereas the *bourrier* is discolored, muddy, tumbled in the gutter, whipped by the wind, and crushed by the feet of passers-by.

"But Madame, I don't want to let Abbé Troubert have Chapeloud's portrait. It was made for me; it belongs to me. Make sure I get that, and I'll give up everything else."

"Very well, I'll go see Mlle. Gamard."

She said this in a tone which revealed the enormous effort it cost the Baroness de Listomère to humble herself in order to flatter the old maid's pride. "I'll try my best to arrange things," she added, "though I have hardly any hope. Go see M. de Bourbonne so he can draft your order of discontinuance in the proper form, and bring me the document when it's in order. Then, with the help of the archbishop, perhaps we'll be able to get the thing settled."

Birotteau left appalled. In his eyes, Troubert had taken on the dimension of an Egyptian pyramid: his hands were in Paris and his elbows in the close of Saint-Gatien. "That man," he said to himself, "to think that *he* could prevent the Marquis de Listomère from becoming a peer of France! *And perhaps, with the archbishop's help, we can get the thing settled!*"

In the presence of such momentous doings, Birotteau felt like a worm: he did himself justice.

The news that Birotteau was moving out was all the more astonishing in that its cause was unfathomable. Mme. de Listomère said that, since her nephew wanted to get married and leave the service, she needed to enlarge his apartment by adding the vicar's room to it. No one yet knew the suit was being discontinued. Thus M. de Bourbonne's instructions were discreetly carried out.

These two pieces of news were bound to flatter the vicar-general's vanity when they reached his ears: though the Listomères didn't capitulate, they were at least staying neutral, and tacitly recognizing the Congregation's secret power. And was not that as much as to submit to it? But for the suit to remain *sub judice*—wasn't this complying and menacing at the same time?

The Listomères had thus taken an attitude exactly like the vicar-general's in this fight: they kept outside and could direct everything.

But something of importance happened which made it even more difficult for M. de Bourbonne and the Listomères ever to appease the Gamard-Troubert faction. The day before, Mlle. Gamard had caught a chill as she left the cathedral, had taken to bed, and was said to be dangerously ill. The whole town resounded with sham sympathy. "Mlle. Gamard's sensitive constitution could not endure the scandal of this lawsuit. Even though she was in the right, she was going to die of grief. Birotteau has been killing his benefactress . . ." Such was the substance of the comments poured out by the capillary vessels of the great female organization and repeated by the whole city of Tours.

Mme. de Listomère had the mortification of calling on the old maid without reaping the fruit of her visit. Very politely, she asked to speak with the vicar-general.

Perhaps Troubert was flattered to be receiving a woman who had slighted him, and to be receiving her in Chapeloud's very library before the chimney-piece adorned by the two famous, disputed paintings: he made the Baroness wait a moment, and then consented to give her an audience. Never did courtier or diplomat, discussing their personal interests or negotiating an international deal, use more adroitness, dissimulation, and deep calculation than did Baroness and priest at the moment they found themselves face to face.

The sly old fox, like the sponsor who in the Middle Ages armed the champion and fortified his valor with useful counsel when he was about to enter the lists, had told the Baroness: "Don't forget your role: you're there as a conciliator, not as an interested party. Troubert is a mediator as well. Weigh your words carefully. Study the inflexions of the vicar-general's voice. If he strokes his chin, you've won him over."

Certain caricaturists amuse themselves by sketching the contrast frequently to be found between *what one says* and *what one thinks*. At this point, really to appreciate the verbal duel between the priest and the great lady, we must reveal the thoughts they both hid under apparently insignificant sentences.

Mme. de Listomère began by expressing the regret she felt over Birotteau's lawsuit; she then spoke of her wish to see the affair settled to the satisfaction of both parties.

"The harm is done, Madame," said the abbé solemnly. "The good Mlle. Gamard is dying." (*I don't care any more about the stupid old maid than I do about Prester John*, he thought, *but I'd like to saddle you with her death and burden your conscience with it, in case you're simple-minded enough to worry about it.*)

"When I heard about her illness, Monsieur," the Baroness answered, "I asked the vicar for a discontinuance, which I was just bringing to this holy woman." (*I've got your number, you sly rascal*, she thought, *but now we're protected from your slanders. As for you, if you accept the discontinuance, you'll fall right into the trap; you'll be admitting your complicity.*)

There was a moment of silence.

"The temporal affairs of Mlle. Gamard do not concern me," the priest said finally, and lowered the heavy lids over his eagle eyes to veil his emotions. (*Oh ho, you won't compromise me! But God be praised, those damned lawyers won't be pleading a case which might sully my reputation. But what do the Listomères want, that they should come fawning on me this way?*)

"Monsieur," the Baroness answered, "I know as little about M. Birotteau's affairs as you do about Mlle. Gamard's; but unfortunately, religion may suffer from their disputes. It is to you as peace-maker that I come, I who also seek to make peace." (*Neither one of us will fool the other*, she thought. *Did you catch the epigrammatic twist of my answer?*)

"Religion suffer, Madame!" said the vicar-general. "Religion is far too high for men to be able to injure it." (*I am religion*, he thought.) "God will judge us infallibly, Madame. I recognize no other court but His."

"Well then, Monsieur," she answered, "let's try to bring men's judgements into accord with God's." (*Yes, you are religion, all right.*)

Abbé Troubert's tone changed: "Didn't your nephew go to Paris?" (*You discovered something about me there. I can crush you, you who have despised me. You have come to capitulate.*)

"Yes, Monsieur, and I thank you for the interest you take in him. He's returning to Paris this evening. He has been sent for by the Minister, who is kindness itself to us and doesn't want to see him leave the service." (*Jesuit, you shall not crush us. I see through your civility.*) A moment of silence. "I don't think his conduct was proper in this affair," she continued, "but a sailor may be pardoned for not knowing his way around in the law." (*Let's make an alliance. We shall gain nothing by fighting.*)

A faint smile lost itself in the folds of the abbé's face. "He has done us the service of letting us know the value of these two paintings," he said looking at the pictures. "They will be noble ornaments to the Chapel of the Virgin." (*You shot me an epigram*, he thought. *There are two for you. We're even Madame.*)

"If you are going to donate them to Saint-Gatien, I beg you to allow me to offer the church frames worthy of the place and paintings." (*How I would like to make you admit you covet Birotteau's belongings.*)

"They are not mine to give," said the priest, still on guard.

"But here is a document," said Mme. de Listomère, "which ends all discussion and makes them Mlle. Gamard's." She put the order of discontinuance on the table. (*Note, Monsieur, what confidence I have in you.*) "It is worthy of you, Monsieur, worthy of your fine character, to reconcile two Christians; though now M. Birotteau's affairs have little interest for me . . ."

"But he lives in your house," he interrupted.

"No, Monsieur, not any longer." (*What mean actions my brother-in-law's peerage and nephew's rank are making me commit!*)

The abbé remained impassive, but the calmness of his expression was indicative of the most violent emotions. Only M. de Bourbonne had guessed the secret of that apparent serenity. The priest was triumphant!

"Then why did you undertake to deliver his discontinuance?" he asked, prompted by a feeling similar to that which makes a woman fish for compliments.

"I couldn't help feeling sorry for him. Birotteau—you know the weakness of his character—entreated me to see Mlle. Gamard in order to obtain, in exchange for his renunciation . . ."

The abbé frowned.

". . . of *rights* recognized by distinguished lawyers, the portrait . . ."

The priest watched Mme. de Listomère.

". . . the portrait of Chapeloud," she continued. "I leave you to be judge of his claim." (*You'd lose if you fought the case*, she thought.)

The emphasis the Baroness put on the words *distinguished lawyers* let the priest see that she knew the enemy's weakness as well as his strength. In the course of their conversation, which maintained this tone for a long time, Mme. de Listomère made her skill so plain to this experienced connoisseur that he went downstairs to obtain Mlle. Gamard's answer to the proposed transaction.

Troubert returned shortly. "Madame, here is what the poor dying woman says: 'M. l'Abbé Chapeloud showed me too much friendship,' she told me, 'for me to part with his portrait.' As for myself," he went on, "if it were mine, I wouldn't give it up to anyone. My feelings for the dear late canon have remained too strong for me not to think I have the right to fight for his likeness against anyone whatever."

"Monsieur, let us not have a falling out over a bad painting." (*I care as little about it as you.*) "Keep it, we'll have a copy made. I rejoice at having brought this unfortunate lawsuit to a quiet end, and through it I personally have had the good fortune to become acquainted with you. I've heard talk of your talent at whist. You must excuse a woman's curiosity," she said smiling. "If you would like to come to my house for a game sometime, you may be sure you would be most welcome."

Troubert stroked his chin. (*He's caught! Bourbonne was right*, she thought. *He has his share of vanity!*)

Indeed, at that moment the vicar-general was feeling that delicious sensation which Mirabeau could not resist when, in the days of his power, he saw the gates of a mansion formerly closed to him open before his carriage.

"Madame," he answered, "my affairs are too pressing to allow me the time to go into society. But for you, what wouldn't one do?" (*The old maid is going to cork out. I'll make friends with the Listomères, and be useful to them if they will be useful to me. Better to have them as friends than enemies.*)

Mme. de Listomère went home hoping that the archbishop would finish a job of peacemaking so propitiously begun. But Birotteau was not even to profit by his discontinuance. The following day Mme. de Listomère learned of Mlle. Gamard's death. When her will was opened, no one was surprised to hear she had made the Abbé Troubert her sole legatee. Her fortune was appraised at three hundred thousand francs. The vicar-general sent two invitations for his friend's funeral service to Mme. de Listomère: one for her, the other for her nephew.

"We have to go," she said.

"There's nothing else you can do!" exclaimed M. de Bourbonne. "It's obviously Monseigneur Troubert's way of testing you. Baron, you must go clear to the cemetery," he added, turning to the naval lieutenant, who, unluckily for him, had not left Tours.

The service was of great ecclesiastical magnificence. Only one person wept. This was Birotteau, who, alone and unseen in a secluded chapel, felt guilty for this death, and prayed sincerely for the dead woman's soul, bitterly regretting not having gained her pardon for the wrong he had done her.

Abbé Troubert attended his friend's corpse up to the grave where she was to be interred. At the graveside, he delivered a speech of such eloquence that the picture of the narrow life led by the woman who had bequeathed him her worldly goods took on monumental proportions. The spectators especially noticed these words in the peroration:

"This life made up of days devoted to God and to religion, this life adorned by so many good deeds performed in silence, so many modest and unknown virtues, has been shattered by a grief we might call unmerited, if, on the edge of eternity, it were possible for us to forget that all our afflictions are sent to us from God. The many friends of this holy woman, knowing the nobility and candor of her soul, foresaw that she could bear anything save the suspicions which were robbing her whole life of joy. And so it may be that Providence carried her away to the bosom of God to spare her our miseries. Fortunate are those who can rest in peace with themselves here on earth, as Sophie now rests in the abode of the blessed, robed in her gown of innocence."

"When he'd finished this pompous speech," continued M. de Bourbonne— as soon as the other guests had left, the doors had been closed, and they were alone with the Baron, he described the burial in detail to Mme. de Listomère —"just imagine, if you can, this Louis XI in a cassock giving the last shake to the aspergil full of holy water—like this." The sly old fox took the tongs and imitated Troubert's movement so well that the Baron and his aunt couldn't help smiling. "Only then did he give himself away. Up till then his demeanor had been perfect; but no doubt it was impossible for him to seal the old maid up for good without letting his joy betray itself in a gesture. For he had heartily despised her, perhaps he had even hated her as much as she had detested Chapeloud."

The next morning, Mlle. Salomon came to lunch at Mme. de Listomère's, and, when she arrived, told her in great agitation: "Our poor Abbé Birotteau has just now received a terrible blow, and it is obviously the result of the careful calculations of hatred. He's been appointed vicar of Saint-Symphorien."

Saint-Symphorien is a suburb of Tours, on the other side of the bridge. This bridge, one of the handsomest monuments of French architecture, is nineteen hundred feet long, and the squares at either end are exactly alike.

"Don't you understand?" she asked after a pause, completely astonished at the coolness with which Mme. de Listomère received this news. "For Abbé Birotteau, to be there will be like being a hundred leagues from Tours, from his friends, from everything. Don't you see that his exile will be all the worse because he's being torn from a city he will see every day, but can hardly ever visit? Ever since his misfortunes, he has just barely been able to walk, and here he will have to come two and a half miles to see us! At this very moment, the unfortunate man is in bed with a fever. The vicarage of Saint-

Symphorien is cold and damp, and the parish isn't rich enough to repair it. So the poor old man is going to find himself buried in a veritable tomb. What a villainous plot!"

Now to finish this story, it will be enough for us to report certain events and sketch a final scene.

Five months later, the vicar-general was made a bishop. Mme. de Listomère had died, leaving in her will fifteen hundred francs a year to Birotteau. The day the Baroness's will became known, Mgr. Hyacinthe, bishop of Troyes, was just about to leave Tours to return to his diocese, but he delayed his departure. Furious at having been the dupe of a woman to whom he'd extended his hand while she was secretly holding that of a man he thought of as his enemy, Troubert again threatened the Baron's future and the Marquis de Listomère's peerage. He uttered in public, in the archbishop's parlor, one of those ecclesiastical phrases heavy with vengeance and full of honeyed meekness. The ambitious sailor went to see the implacable priest, who no doubt dictated harsh conditions, for the Baron's conduct bore witness to his utter submission to the will of the terrible representative of the Congregation.

By a deed of gift, the new bishop turned over Mlle. Gamard's house to the cathedral chapter; he gave Chapeloud's bookcase and books to the small seminary; he dedicated the two disputed paintings to the Chapel of the Virgin. But he kept Chapeloud's portrait. No one could account for this almost total relinquishment of Mlle. Gamard's bequest. M. de Bourbonne concluded that the bishop was secretly retaining the liquid assets so he could maintain his position with honor if he were called to the Bench of Bishops in the Upper Chamber. Finally, on the eve of Mgr. Troubert's departure, the sly old fox could fathom the ultimate calculation behind this action, the final blow administered by the most persistent of vengeances to the feeblest of victims. Mme. de Listomère's legacy to Birotteau was contested by the Baron de Listomère on the ground of undue influence! A few days after the preliminary writ, the Baron was given command of a vessel. By a disciplinary order, the vicar of Saint-Symphorien was placed under an interdict, his priestly functions suspended. The ecclesiastical superiors were prejudging the issue. So the late Sophie Gamard's assassin was a swindler too! If Mgr. Troubert had kept his bequest from the old maid, he would have been in a difficult position to censure Birotteau.

As Mgr. Hyacinthe, bishop of Troyes, was going in his post chaise along the Saint-Symphorien quay en route to Paris, the poor Abbé Birotteau had been put out in the sun in an armchair at the edge of a terrace. The poor priest, smitten by his archbishop, was pale and thin. The grief imprinted on all his features completely altered that face which had formerly shone with such gentle gaiety. Over his eyes, which had once been naïvely lit up at the pleasures of good living and undimmed by serious thoughts, illness cast a veil which gave him the appearance of pensiveness. This was only the skeleton of that Birotteau who a year before had rolled across the Close empty-headed but content. The bishop cast a contemptuous, pitying glance on his victim; then he deigned to forget him, and passed on.

No doubt in other days Troubert would have been a Hildebrand or an Alexander VI. Today, the Church is no longer a political power and no longer absorbs the energies of solitary people. So then, celibacy offers this capital vice: it concentrates all of a man's faculties on a single passion, egoism, and renders celibates either harmful or useless. We live in a time when the fault of governments is to make the man fit society rather than society fit the man. There is a perpetual conflict between the individual and the system which is arranged to exploit him and which he attempts to exploit for his own profit; whereas, formerly, man, in reality freer, proved to be more generous in matters of public welfare.

The circle in which each man moves about has imperceptibly grown larger; the mind which can embrace it as one whole will always be the magnificent exception, for, commonly in the moral as well as in the physical sphere, motion loses in intensity what it gains in scope. Society can not be based on exceptions. First, man was purely and simply a father, and his heart beat warmly, concentrated in his family circle. Later, he lived for a clan or for a small republic: hence the great, historic instances of devotion in Greece or Rome. Then he was a man belonging to a caste or religion, for the glory of which he often proved himself sublime; but there, the extent of his interests was increased by all the realms of the intellect. Today, his life is attached to that of an immense fatherland; soon, his family will be, so they say, the whole world.

But is not this moral cosmopolitanism, the hope of Christian Rome, a sublime error? It is so natural to believe in the realization of a noble vision, in the brotherhood of men, but, alas, the human machine does not have such divine proportions. Souls large enough to embrace a range of sentiments which only great men can feel will never belong to simple citizens or fathers of families.

Certain physiologists think that, when the brain grows larger like this, the heart must contract. A fallacy! Is not the obvious egoism of men who carry a science, a nation, or a system of laws in their breast the noblest of passions and, in some way, the maternity of the masses? To give birth to new peoples or to produce new ideas, they must unite in their mighty heads the breasts of a woman with the power of God. The history of the Innocent IIIs, the Peter the Greats, and all the great leaders of a century or a nation would, if need be, testify on a very high level to that enormous mental activity which Troubert represented in the depths of the Close of Saint-Gatien.

The Duel

BY

Anton Chekhov

Translated by Constance Garnett

Editor's Note

Anton Chekhov was born in 1860 in Taganrog, a small city on the Black Sea. Anton's grandfather, a serf, had managed to buy his freedom, and Anton's father, raised a serf, owned a grocery store at the time of Anton's birth. When a railroad was built to nearby Rostov and failed to stop at Taganrog, the city rapidly declined. In 1876 the store failed and Anton's father avoided debtor's prison by fleeing with the family to Moscow. Anton stayed behind, earning his living by tutoring. Three years later he went to Moscow and enrolled in the university, where he studied medicine. In 1880 he began publishing the humorous sketches which he wrote for some years and with which he helped support his family. In 1884, finishing his studies, he began the practice of medicine. He wrote increasingly serious stories, which were well received, and after a few years left medicine almost entirely for literature. In 1886 he recognized alarming symptoms of tuberculosis in himself, but refused for many years to be examined by another physician or to follow treatment.

During the next dozen years, Chekhov moved about restlessly, wrote many stories (over 800 in all) and two plays, and acquired a considerable reputation. "The Duel" (1891) was written at a time when he was reacting against the influence of Tolstoy's religious philosophy, which had dominated him for a while; he returned to the humane faith based on liberal trust in the beneficence of science which for the most part he had embraced since his childhood in the Orthodox Church. In 1898 the new Moscow Art Theatre, under Stanislavsky, put on *The Sea Gull*, and Chekhov was famous. In 1901 he married the actress who had originally played one of *The Three Sisters*, though by this time his lungs were so bad that the couple passed their honeymoon in a sanatorium. His last play, *The Cherry Orchard*, was first presented on his forty-fifth birthday, January 17, 1905, and he died the following July.

The Duel

I

IT WAS EIGHT O'CLOCK IN THE MORNING—THE TIME WHEN THE OFFICERS, the local officials, and the visitors usually took their morning dip in the sea after the hot, stifling night, and then went into the pavilion to drink tea or coffee. Ivan Andreitch Laevsky, a thin, fair young man of twenty-eight, wearing the cap of a clerk in the Ministry of Finance and with slippers on his feet, coming down to bathe, found a number of acquaintances on the beach, and among them his friend Samoylenko, the army doctor.

With his big cropped head, short neck, his red face, his big nose, his shaggy black eyebrows and grey whiskers, his stout puffy figure and his hoarse military bass, this Samoylenko made on every newcomer the unpleasant impression of a gruff bully; but two or three days after making his acquaintance, one began to think his face extraordinarily good-natured, kind, and even handsome. In spite of his clumsiness and rough manner, he was a peaceable man, of infinite kindliness and goodness of heart, always ready to be of use. He was on familiar terms with everyone in the town, lent everyone money, doctored everyone, made matches, patched up quarrels, arranged picnics at which he cooked *Shashlik* and an awfully good soup of grey mullets. He was always looking after other people's affairs and trying to interest someone on their behalf, and was always delighted about something. The general opinion about him was that he was without faults of character. He had only two weaknesses: he was ashamed of his own good nature, and tried to disguise it by a surly expression and an assumed gruffness; and he liked his assistants and his soldiers to call him "Your Excellency," although he was only a civil councillor.

"Answer one question for me, Alexandr Daviditch," Laevsky began, when both he and Samoylenko were in the water up to their shoulders. "Suppose

Translated by Constance Garnett, in *The Duel and Other Stories* (New York, The Macmillan Company) and in *Select Tales of Tchehov*, Vol. 2 (London, Chatto & Windus Ltd.). Reprinted by permission of The Macmillan Company and of Chatto & Windus.

you had loved a woman and had been living with her for two or three years, and then left off caring for her, as one does, and began to feel that you had nothing in common with her. How would you behave in that case?"

"It's very simple. 'You go where you please, madam'—and that would be the end of it."

"It's easy to say that! But if she has nowhere to go? A woman with no friends or relations, without a farthing, who can't work . . ."

"Well? Five hundred roubles down or an allowance of twenty-five roubles a month—and nothing more. It's very simple."

"Even supposing you have five hundred roubles and can pay twenty-five roubles a month, the woman I am speaking of is an educated woman and proud. Could you really bring yourself to offer her money? And how would you do it?"

Samoylenko was going to answer, but at that moment a big wave covered them both, then broke on the beach and rolled back noisily over the shingle. The friends got out and began dressing.

"Of course, it is difficult to live with a woman if you don't love her," said Samoylenko, shaking the sand out of his boots. "But one must look at the thing humanely, Vanya. If it were my case, I should never show a sign that I did not love her, and I should go on living with her till I died."

He was at once ashamed of his own words; he pulled himself up and said:

"But for aught I care, there might be no females at all. Let them all go to the devil!"

The friends dressed and went into the pavilion. There Samoylenko was quite at home, and even had a special cup and saucer. Every morning they brought him on a tray a cup of coffee, a tall cut glass of iced water, and a tiny glass of brandy. He would first drink the brandy, then the hot coffee, then the iced water, and this must have been very nice, for after drinking it his eyes looked moist with pleasure, he would stroke his whiskers with both hands, and say, looking at the sea:

"A wonderfully magnificent view!"

After a long night spent in cheerless, unprofitable thoughts which prevented him from sleeping, and seemed to intensify the darkness and sultriness of the night, Laevsky felt listless and shattered. He felt no better for the bathe and the coffee.

"Let us go on with our talk, Alexandr Daviditch," he said. "I won't make a secret of it; I'll speak to you openly as to a friend. Things are in a bad way with Nadyezhda Fyodorovna and me . . . a very bad way! Forgive me for forcing my private affairs upon you, but I must speak out."

Samoylenko, who had a misgiving of what he was going to speak about, dropped his eyes and drummed with his fingers on the table.

"I've lived with her for two years and have ceased to love her," Laevsky went on; "or, rather, I realized that I never had felt any love for her. . . . These two years have been a mistake."

It was Laevsky's habit as he talked to gaze attentively at the pink palms of his hands, to bite his nails, or to pinch his cuffs. And he did so now.

"I know very well you can't help me," he said. "But I tell you, because unsuccessful and superfluous people like me find their salvation in talking. I have to generalize about everything I do. I'm bound to look for an explanation and justification of my absurd existence in somebody else's theories, in literary types—in the idea that we, upper-class Russians, are degenerating, for instance, and so on. Last night, for example, I comforted myself by thinking all the time: 'Ah, how true Tolstoy is, how mercilessly true!' And that did me good. Yes, really, brother, he is a great writer, say what you like!"

Samoylenko, who had never read Tolstoy and was intending to do so every day of his life, was a little embarrassed, and said:

"Yes, all other authors write from imagination, but he writes straight from nature."

"My God!" sighed Laevsky; "how distorted we all are by civilization! I fell in love with a married woman and she with me. . . . To begin with, we had kisses, and calm evenings, and vows, and Spencer, and ideals, and interests in common. . . . What a deception! We really ran away from her husband, but we lied to ourselves and made out that we ran away from the emptiness of the life of the educated class. We pictured our future like this: to begin with, in the Caucasus, while we were getting to know the people and the place, I would put on the Government uniform and enter the service; then at our leisure we would pick out a plot of ground, would toil in the sweat of our brow, would have a vineyard and a field, and so on. If you were in my place, or that zoologist of yours, Von Koren, you might live with Nadyezhda Fyodorovna for thirty years, perhaps, and might leave your heirs a rich vineyard and three thousand acres of maize; but I felt like a bankrupt from the first day. In the town you have insufferable heat, boredom, and no society; if you go out into the country, you fancy poisonous spiders, scorpions, or snakes lurking under every stone and behind every bush, and beyond the fields—mountains and the desert. Alien people, an alien country, a wretched form of civilization—all that is not so easy, brother, as walking on the Nevsky Prospect in one's fur coat, arm-in-arm with Nadyezhda Fyodorvna, dreaming of the sunny South. What is needed here is a life and death struggle, and I'm not a fighting man. A wretched neurasthenic, an idle gentleman. . . . From the first day I knew that my dreams of a life of labour and of a vineyard were worthless. As for love, I ought to tell you that living with a woman who has read Spencer and has followed you to the ends of the earth is no more interesting than living with any Anfissa or Akulina. There's the same smell of ironing, of powder, and of medicines, the same curl-papers every morning, the same self-deception."

"You can't get on in the house without an iron," said Samoylenko, blushing at Laevsky's speaking to him so openly of a lady he knew. "You are out of humour to-day, Vanya, I notice. Nadyezhda Fyodorovna is a splendid woman, highly educated, and you are a man of the highest intellect. Of course, you are not married," Samoylenko went on, glancing round at the adjacent tables, "but that's not your fault; and besides . . . one ought to be above conventional prejudices and rise to the level of modern ideas. I believe in free love myself, yes. . . . But to my thinking, once you have settled together, you ought to go on living together all your life."

"Without love?"

"I will tell you directly," said Samoylenko. "Eight years ago there was an old fellow, an agent, here—a man of very great intelligence. Well, he used to say that the great thing in married life was patience. Do you hear, Vanya? Not love, but patience. Love cannot last long. You have lived two years in love, and now evidently your married life has reached the period when, in order to preserve equilibrium, so to speak, you ought to exercise all your patience. . . ."

"You believe in your old agent; to me his words are meaningless. Your old man could be a hypocrite; he could exercise himself in the virtue of patience, and, as he did so, look upon a person he did not love as an object indispensable for his moral exercises; but I have not yet fallen so low. If I want to exercise myself in patience, I will buy dumb-bells or a frisky horse, but I'll leave human beings alone."

Samoylenko asked for some white wine with ice. When they had drunk a glass each, Laevsky suddenly asked:

"Tell me, please, what is the meaning of softening of the brain?"

"How can I explain it to you? . . . It's a disease in which the brain becomes softer . . . as it were, dissolves."

"Is it curable?"

"Yes, if the disease is not neglected. Cold douches, blisters. . . . Something internal, too."

"Oh! . . . Well, you see my position; I can't live with her: it is more than I can do. While I'm with you I can be philosophical about it and smile, but at home I lose heart completely; I am so utterly miserable, that if I were told, for instance, that I should have to live another month with her, I should blow out my brains. At the same time, parting with her is out of the question. She has no friends or relations; she cannot work, and neither she nor I has any money. . . . What could become of her? To whom could she go? There is nothing one can think of. . . . Come, tell me, what am I to do?"

"H'm! . . ." growled Samoylenko, not knowing what to answer. "Does she love you?"

"Yes, she loves me in so far as at her age and with her temperament she wants a man. It would be as difficult for her to do without me as to do without her powder or her curl-papers. I am for her an indispensable, integral part of her boudoir."

Samoylenko was embarrassed.

"You are out of humour to-day, Vanya," he said. "You must have had a bad night."

"Yes, I slept badly. . . . Altogether, I feel horribly out of sorts, brother. My head feels empty; there's a sinking at my heart, a weakness. . . . I must run away."

"Run where?"

"There, to the North. To the pines and the mushrooms, to people and ideas. . . . I'd give half my life to bathe now in some little stream in the province of Moscow or Tula; to feel chilly, you know, and then to stroll for three hours even with the feeblest student, and to talk and talk endlessly. . . . And the scent of the hay! Do you remember it? And in the evening, when one walks in the garden, sounds of the piano float from the house; one hears the train passing. . . ."

Laevsky laughed with pleasure; tears came into his eyes, and to cover them, without getting up, he stretched across the next table for the matches.

"I have not been in Russia for eighteen years," said Samoylenko. "I've forgotten what it is like. To my mind, there is not a country more splendid than the Caucasus."

"Vereshtchagin has a picture in which some men condemned to death are languishing at the bottom of a very deep well. Your magnificent Caucasus strikes me as just like that well. If I were offered the choice of a chimney-sweep in Petersburg or a prince in the Caucasus, I should choose the job of chimney-sweep."

Laevsky grew pensive. Looking at his stooping figure, at his eyes fixed dreamily on one spot, at his pale, perspiring face and sunken temples, at his bitten nails, at the slipper which had dropped off his heel, displaying a badly darned sock, Samoylenko was moved to pity, and probably because Laevsky reminded him of a helpless child, he asked: "Is your mother living?"

"Yes, but we are on bad terms. She could not forgive me for this affair."

Samoylenko was fond of his friend. He looked upon Laevsky as a good-natured fellow, a student, a man with no nonsense about him, with whom one could drink, and laugh, and talk without reserve. What he understood in him he disliked extremely. Laevsky drank a great deal and at unsuitable times; he played cards, despised his work, lived beyond his means, frequently made use of unseemly expressions in conversation, walked about the streets in his slippers, and quarrelled with Nadyezhda Fyodorovna before other people—and Samoylenko did not like this. But the fact that Laevsky had once been a student in the Faculty of Arts, subscribed to two fat reviews, often talked so cleverly that only a few people understood him, was living with a well-educated woman—all this Samoylenko did not understand, and he liked this and respected Laevsky, thinking him superior to himself.

"There is another point," said Laevsky, shaking his head. "Only it is between ourselves. I'm concealing it from Nadyezhda Fyodorovna for the the time. . . . Don't let it out before her. . . . I got a letter the day before yesterday, telling me that her husband has died from softening of the brain."

"The Kingdom of Heaven be his!" sighed Samoylenko. "Why are you concealing it from her?"

"To show her that letter would be equivalent to 'Come to church to be married.' And we should first have to make our relations clear. When she understands that we can't go on living together, I will show her the letter. Then there will be no danger in it."

"Do you know what, Vanya," said Samoylenko, and a sad and imploring expression came into his face, as though he were going to ask him about something very touching and were afraid of being refused. "Marry her, my dear boy!"

"Why?"

"Do your duty to that splendid woman! Her husband is dead, and so Providence itself shows you what to do!"

"But do understand, you queer fellow, that it is impossible. To marry without love is as base and unworthy of a man as to perform mass without believing in it."

"But it's your duty to."

"Why is it my duty?" Laevsky asked irritably.

"Because you took her away from her husband and made yourself responsible for her."

"But now I tell you in plain Russian, I don't love her!"

"Well, if you've no love, show her proper respect, consider her wishes. . . ."

" 'Show her respect, consider her wishes,' " Laevsky mimicked him. "As though she were some Mother Superior! . . . You are a poor psychologist and physiologist if you think that living with a woman one can get off with nothing but respect and consideration. What a woman thinks most of is her bedroom."

"Vanya, Vanya!" said Samoylenko, overcome with confusion.

"You are an elderly child, a theorist, while I am an old man in spite of my years, and practical, and we shall never understand one another. We had better drop this conversation. Mustapha!" Laevsky shouted to the waiter. "What's our bill?"

"No, no . . ." the doctor cried in dismay, clutching Laevsky's arm. "It is for me to pay. I ordered it. Make it out to me," he cried to Mustapha.

The friends got up and walked in silence along the sea-front. When they reached the boulevard, they stopped and shook hands at parting.

"You are awfully spoilt, my friend!" Samoylenko sighed. "Fate has sent you a young, beautiful, cultured woman, and you refuse the gift, while if God were to give me a crooked old woman, how pleased I should be if only she were kind and affectionate! I would live with her in my vineyard and . . ."

Samoylenko caught himself up and said: "And she might get the samovar ready for me there, the old hag."

After parting with Laevsky he walked along the boulevard. When, bulky and majestic, with a stern expression on his face, he walked along the boulevard in his snow-white tunic and superbly polished boots, squaring his chest, decorated with the Vladimir cross on a ribbon, he was very much pleased with himself, and it seemed as though the whole world were looking at him with pleasure. Without turning his head, he looked to each side and thought that the boulevard was extremely well laid out; that the young cypress-trees, the eucalyptuses, and the ugly, anæmic palm-trees were very handsome and would in time give abundant shade; that the Circassians were an honest and hospitable people.

"It's strange that Laevsky does not like the Caucasus," he thought, "very strange."

Five soldiers, carrying rifles, met him and saluted him. On the right side of the boulevard the wife of a local official was walking along the pavement with her son, a schoolboy.

"Good-morning, Marya Konstantinovna," Samoylenko shouted to her with a pleasant smile.

"Have you been to bathe? Ha, ha, ha! . . . My respects to Nikodim Alexandritch!"

And he went on, still smiling pleasantly, but seeing an assistant of the military hospital coming towards him, he suddenly frowned, stopped him, and asked:

"Is there anyone in the hospital?"

"No one, Your Excellency."

"Eh?"

"No one, Your Excellency."

"Very well, run along. . . ."

Swaying majestically, he made for the lemonade stall, where sat a full-bosomed old Jewess, who gave herself out to be a Georgian, and said to her as loudly as though he were giving the word of command to a regiment:

"Be so good as to give me some soda-water!"

II

Laevsky's not loving Nadyezhda Fyodorovna showed itself chiefly in the fact that everything she said or did seemed to him a lie, or equivalent to a lie, and everything he read against women and love seemed to him to apply perfectly to himself, to Nadyezhda Fyodorovna and her husband. When he returned home, she was sitting at the window, dressed and with her hair done, and with a preoccupied face was drinking coffee and turning over the leaves of a fat magazine; and he thought the drinking of coffee was not such a remarkable event that she need put on a preoccupied expression over it, and that she had been wasting her time doing her hair in a fashionable style, as there was no one here to attract and no need to be attractive. And in the magazine he saw nothing but falsity. He thought she had dressed and done her hair so as to look handsomer, and was reading in order to seem clever.

"Will it be all right for me to go to bathe to-day?" she said.

"Why? There won't be an earthquake whether you go or not, I suppose. . . ."

"No, I only ask in case the doctor should be vexed."

"Well, ask the doctor, then; I'm not a doctor."

On this occasion what displeased Laevsky most in Nadyezhda Fyodorovna was her white open neck and the little curls at the back of her head. And he remembered that when Anna Karenin got tired of her husband, what she disliked most of all was his ears, and thought: "How true it is, how true!"

Feeling weak and as though his head were perfectly empty, he went into his study, lay down on his sofa, and covered his face with a handkerchief that he might not be bothered by the flies. Despondent and oppressive thoughts always about the same thing trailed slowly across his brain like a long string of waggons on a gloomy autumn evening, and he sank into a state of drowsy oppression. It seemed to him that he had wronged Nadyezhda Fyodorovna and her husband, and that it was through his fault that her husband had died. It seemed to him that he had sinned against his own life, which he had ruined, against the world of lofty ideas, of learning, and of work, and he conceived that wonderful world as real and possible, not on this sea-front with hungry Turks and lazy mountaineers sauntering upon it, but there in the North, where there were operas, theatres, newspapers, and all kinds of intellectual activity. One could only there—not here—be honest, intelligent, lofty, and pure. He accused himself of having no ideal, no guiding principle in life, though he had a dim understanding now what it meant. Two years before, when he fell in love with Nadyezhda Fyodorovna, it seemed to him that he had only to go with her as wife to the Caucasus, and he would be saved from vulgarity and emptiness; in the same way now, he was convinced that he had only to part from Nadyezhda Fyodorovna and to go to Petersburg, and he would get everything he wanted.

"Run away," he muttered to himself, sitting up and biting his nails. "Run away!"

He pictured in his imagination how he would go aboard the steamer and then would have some lunch, would drink some cold beer, would talk on deck with ladies, then would get into the train at Sevastopol and set off. Hurrah for freedom! One station after another would flash by, the air would keep growing colder and keener, then the birches and the fir-trees, then Kursk, Moscow. . . . In the restaurants cabbage soup, mutton with kasha, sturgeon, beer, no more Asiaticism, but Russia, real Russia. The passengers in the train would talk about trade, new singers, the Franco-Russian *entente;* on all sides there would be the feeling of keen, cultured, intellectual, eager life. . . . Hasten on, on! At last Nevsky Prospect, and Great Morskaya Street, and then Kovensky Place, where he used to live at one time when he was a student, the dear grey sky, the drizzling rain, the drenched cabmen. . . .

"Ivan Andreitch!" someone called from the next room. "Are you at home?"

"I'm here," Laevsky responded. "What do you want?"

"Papers."

Laevsky got up languidly, feeling giddy, walked into the other room, yawning and shuffling with his slippers. There, at the open window that looked into the street, stood one of the young fellow-clerks, laying out some government documents on the window-sill.

"One minute, my dear fellow," Laevsky said softly, and he went to look for the ink; returning to the window, he signed the papers without looking at them, and said: "It's hot!"

"Yes. Are you coming to-day?"

"I don't think so. . . . I'm not quite well. Tell Sheshkovsky that I will come and see him after dinner."

The clerk went away. Laevsky lay down on his sofa again and began thinking:

"And so I must weigh all the circumstances and reflect on them. Before I go away from here I ought to pay up my debts. I owe about two thousand roubles. I have no money. . . . Of course, that's not important; I shall pay part now, somehow, and I shall send the rest, later, from Petersburg. The chief point is Nadyezhda Fyodorovna. . . . First of all we must define our relations. . . . Yes."

A little later he was considering whether it would not be better to go to Samoylenko for advice.

"I might go," he thought, "but what use would there be in it? I shall only say something inappropriate about boudoirs, about women, about what is honest or dishonest. What's the use of talking about what is honest or dishonest, if I must make haste to save my life, if I am suffocating in this cursed slavery and am killing myself? . . . One must realize at last that to go on leading the life I do is something so base and so cruel that everything else seems petty and trivial beside it. To run away," he muttered, sitting down, "to run away."

The deserted seashore, the insatiable heat, and the monotony of the smoky lilac mountains, ever the same and silent, everlastingly solitary, overwhelmed him with depression, and, as it were, made him drowsy and sapped his energy. He was perhaps very clever, talented, remarkably honest; perhaps if the sea and the mountains had not closed him in on all sides, he might have become an excellent Zemstvo leader, a statesman, an orator, a political writer, a saint. Who knows? If so, was it not stupid to argue whether it were honest or dishonest when a gifted and useful man—an artist or musician, for instance—to escape from prison, breaks a wall and deceives his jailers? Anything is honest when a man is in such a position.

At two o'clock Laevsky and Nadyezhda Fyodorovna sat down to dinner. When the cook gave them rice and tomato soup, Laevsky said:

"The same thing every day. Why not have cabbage soup?"

"There are no cabbages."

"It's strange. Samoylenko has cabbage soup and Marya Konstantinovna has cabbage soup, and only I obliged to eat this mawkish mess. We can't go on like this, darling."

As is common with the vast majority of husbands and wives, not a single dinner had in earlier days passed without scenes and fault-finding between Nadyezhda Fyodorovna and Laevsky; but ever since Laevsky had made up his mind that he did not love her, he had tried to give way to Nadyezhda Fyodorovna in everything, spoke to her gently and politely, smiled, and called her "darling."

"This soup tastes like liquorice," he said, smiling; he made an effort to control himself and seem amiable, but could not refrain from saying: "Nobody looks after the housekeeping. . . . If you are too ill or busy with reading, let me look after the cooking."

In earlier days she would have said to him. "Do by all means," or, "I see you want to turn me into a cook"; but now she only looked at him timidly and flushed crimson.

"Well, how do you feel to-day?" he asked kindly.

"I am all right to-day. There is nothing but a little weakness."

"You must take care of yourself, darling. I am awfully anxious about you."

Nadyezhda Fyodorovna was ill in some way. Samoylenko said she had intermittent fever, and gave her quinine; the other doctor, Ustimovitch, a tall, lean, unsociable man, who used to sit at home in the daytime, and in the evenings walk slowly up and down on the sea-front coughing, with his hands folded behind him and a cane stretched along his back, was of opinion that she had a female complaint, and prescribed warm compresses. In old days, when Laevsky loved her, Nadyezhda Fyodorovna's illness had excited his pity and terror; now he saw falsity even in her illness. Her yellow, sleepy face, her lustreless eyes, her apathetic expression, and the yawning that always followed her attacks of fever, and the fact that during them she lay under a shawl and looked more like a boy than a woman, and that it was close and stuffy in her room—all this, in his opinion, destroyed the illusion and was an argument against love and marriage.

The next dish given him was spinach with hard-boiled eggs, while Nadyezhda Fyodorovna, as an invalid, had jelly and milk. When with a preoccupied face she touched the jelly with a spoon and then began languidly eating it, sipping milk, and he heard her swallowing, he was possessed by such an overwhelming aversion that it made his head tingle. He recognized that such a feeling would be an insult even to a dog, but he was angry, not with himself but with Nadyezhda Fyodorovna, for arousing such a feeling, and he understood why lovers sometimes murder their mistresses. He would not murder her, of course, but if he had been on a jury now, he would have acquitted the murderer.

"*Merci*, darling," he said after dinner, and kissed Nadyezhda Fyodorovna on the forehead.

Going back into his study, he spent five minutes in walking to and fro, looking at his boots; then he sat down on his sofa and muttered:

"Run away, run away! We must define the position and run away!"

He lay down on the sofa and recalled again that Nadyezhda Fyodorovna's husband had died, perhaps, by his fault.

"To blame a man for loving a woman, or ceasing to love a woman, is stupid," he persuaded himself, lying down and raising his legs in order to put on his high boots. "Love and hatred are not under our control. As for her husband, maybe I was in an indirect way one of the causes of his death; but again, is it my fault that I fell in love with his wife and she with me?"

Then he got up, and finding his cap, set off to the lodgings of his colleague, Sheshkovsky, where the Government clerks met every day to play *vint* and drink beer.

"My indecision reminds me of Hamlet," thought Laevsky on the way. "How truly Shakespeare describes it! Ah, how truly!"

III

For the sake of sociability and from sympathy for the hard plight of new-comers without families, who, as there was not an hotel in the town, had nowhere to dine, Dr. Samoylenko kept a sort of table d'hôte. At this time there were only two men who habitually dined with him: a young zoologist called Von Koren, who had come for the summer to the Black Sea to study the embryology of the medusa, and a deacon called Pobyedov, who had only just left the seminary and been sent to the town to take the duty of the old deacon who had gone away for a cure. Each of them paid twelve roubles a month for their dinner and supper, and Samoylenko made them promise to turn up at two o'clock punctually.

Von Koren was usually the first to appear. He sat down in the drawing-room in silence, and taking an album from the table, began attentively scrutinizing the faded photographs of unknown men in full trousers and top-hats, and ladies in crinolines and caps. Samoylenko only remembered a few of them by name, and of those whom he had forgotten he said with a sigh: "A very fine fellow, remarkably intelligent!" When he had finished with the album, Von Koren took a pistol from the whatnot, and screwing up his left eye, took deliberate aim at the portrait of Prince Vorontsov, or stood still at the looking-glass and gazed a long time at his swarthy face, his big forehead, and his black hair, which curled like a Negro's, and his shirt of dull-coloured cotton with big flowers on it like a Persian rug, and the broad leather belt he wore instead of a waistcoat. The contemplation of his own image seemed to afford him almost more satisfaction than look-ing at photographs or playing with the pistols. He was very well satisfied with his face, and his becomingly clipped beard, and the broad shoulders, which were unmistakable evidence of his excellent health and physical strength. He was satisfied, too, with his stylish get-up, from the cravat, which matched the colour of his shirt, down to his brown boots.

While he was looking at the album and standing before the glass, at that moment, in the kitchen and in the passage near, Samoylenko, without his coat and waistcoat, with his neck bare, excited and bathed in perspiration, was bustling about the tables, mixing the salad, or making some sauce, or preparing meat, cucumbers, and onion for the cold soup, while he glared fiercely at the orderly who was helping him, and brandished first a knife and then a spoon at him.

"Give me the vinegar!" he said. "That's not the vinegar—it's the salad oil!" he shouted, stamping. "Where are you off to, you brute?"

"To get the butter, Your Excellency," answered the flustered orderly in a cracked voice.

"Make haste; it's in the cupboard! And tell Daria to put some fennel in the jar with the cucumbers! Fennel! Cover the cream up, gaping laggard, or the flies will get into it!"

And the whole house seemed resounding with his shouts. When it was ten or fifteen minutes to two the deacon would come in; he was a lanky young man of twenty-two, with long hair, with no beard and a hardly perceptible moustache. Going into the drawing-room, he crossed himself before the ikon, smiled, and held out his hand to Von Koren.

"Good-morning," the zoologist said coldly. "Where have you been?"

"I've been catching sea-gudgeon in the harbour."

"Oh, of course. . . . Evidently, deacon, you will never be busy with work."

"Why not? Work is not like a bear; it doesn't run off into the woods," said the deacon, smiling and thrusting his hands into the very deep pockets of his white cassock.

"There's no one to whip you!" sighed the zoologist.

Another fifteen or twenty minutes passed and they were not called to dinner, and they could still hear the orderly running into the kitchen and back again, noisily treading with his boots, and Samoylenko shouting:

"Put it on the table! Where are your wits? Wash it first."

The famished deacon and Von Koren began tapping on the floor with their heels, expressing in this way their impatience like the audience at a theatre. At last the door opened and the harassed orderly announced that dinner was ready! In the dining-room they were met by Samoylenko, crimson in the face, wrathful, perspiring from the heat of the kitchen; he looked at them furiously, and with an expression of horror, took the lid off the soup tureen and helped each of them to a plateful; and only when he was convinced that they were eating it with relish and liked it, he gave a sigh of relief and settled himself in his deep arm-chair. His face looked blissful and his eyes grew moist. . . . He deliberately poured himself out a glass of vodka and said:

"To the health of the younger generation."

After his conversation with Laevsky, from early morning till dinner Samoylenko had been conscious of a load at his heart, although he was in the best of humours; he felt sorry for Laevsky and wanted to help him. After drinking a glass of vodka before the soup, he heaved a sigh and said:

"I saw Vanya Laevsky to-day. He is having a hard time of it, poor fellow! The material side of life is not encouraging for him, and the worst of it is all this psychology is too much for him. I'm sorry for the lad."

"Well, that is a person I am not sorry for," said Von Koren. "If that charming individual were drowning, I would push him under with a stick and say, 'Drown, brother, drown away.' . . ."

"That's untrue. You wouldn't do it."

"Why do you think that?" The zoologist shrugged his shoulders. "I'm just as capable of a good action as you are."

"Is drowning a man a good action?" asked the deacon, and he laughed.

"Laevsky? Yes."

"I think there is something amiss with the soup . . ." said Samoylenko, anxious to change the conversation.

"Laevsky is absolutely pernicious and is as dangerous to society as the cholera microbe," Von Koren went on. "To drown him would be a service."

"It does not do you credit to talk like that about your neighbour. Tell us: what do you hate him for?"

"Don't talk nonsense, doctor. To hate and despise a microbe is stupid, but to look upon everybody one meets without distinction as one's neighbour, whatever happens—thanks very much, that is equivalent to giving up criticism, renouncing a straightforward attitude to people, washing one's hands of responsibility, in fact! I consider your Laevsky a blackguard; I do not conceal it, and I am perfectly conscientious in treating him as such. Well, you look upon him as your neighbour—and you may kiss him if you like: you look upon him as your neighbour, and that means that your attitude to him is the same as to me and to the deacon; that is no attitude at all. You are equally indifferent to all."

"To call a man a blackguard!" muttered Samoylenko, frowning with distaste—"that is so wrong that I can't find words for it!"

"People are judged by their actions," Von Koren continued. "Now you decide, deacon. . . . I am going to talk to you, deacon. Mr. Laevsky's career lies open before you, like a long Chinese puzzle, and you can read it from beginning to end. What has he been doing these two years that he has been living here? We will reckon his doings on our fingers. First, he has taught the inhabitants of the town to play *vint:* two years ago that game was unknown here! now they all play it from morning till late at night, even the women and the boys. Secondly, he has taught the residents to drink beer, which was not known here either; the inhabitants are indebted to him for the knowledge of various sorts of spirits, so that now they can distinguish Kospelov's vodka from Smirnov's No. 21, blindfold. Thirdly, in former days, people here made love to other men's wives in secret, from the same motives as thieves steal in secret and not openly; adultery was considered something they were ashamed to make a public display of. Laevsky has come as a pioneer in that line; he lives with another man's wife openly. . . . Fourthly. . . ."

Von Koren hurriedly ate up his soup and gave his plate to the orderly.

"I understood Laevsky from the first month of our acquaintance," he went on, addressing the deacon. "We arrived here at the same time. Men like him are very fond of friendship, intimacy, solidarity, and all the rest of it, because they always want company for *vint,* drinking, and eating; besides, they are talkative and must have listeners. We made friends—that is, he turned up every day, hindered me working, and indulged in confidences in regard to his mistress. From the first he struck me by his exceptional falsity, which simply made me sick. As a friend I pitched into him, asking him why he drank too much, why he lived beyond his means and got into debt, why he did nothing and read nothing, why he had so little culture and so little knowledge; and in answer to all my questions he used to smile bitterly, sigh, and say: 'I am a failure, a superfluous man'; or: 'What do you expect, my dear fellow, from us, the débris of the serf-owning class?' or: 'We are degenerate. . . .' Or he would begin a long rigmarole about Onyegin, Petchorin, Byron's Cain, and Bazarov, of whom he would say: 'They are our fathers in flesh and in spirit.' So we are to understand that it was not his fault that Government envelopes lay unopened in his office for weeks together, and that he drank and taught others to drink, but Onyegin, Petchorin, and Turgenev, who had invented the failure and the superfluous man, were responsible for it. The cause of his extreme dissoluteness and unseemliness lies, do you see, not in himself, but somewhere outside in space. And so—an ingenious idea!—it is not only he who is dissolute, false, and disgusting, but we . . . 'we men of the eighties,' 'we the spiritless, nervous offspring of the serf-owning class'; 'civilization has crippled us' . . . in fact, we are to understand that such a great man as Laevsky is great even in his fall: that his dissoluteness, his lack of culture and of moral purity, is a phenomenon of natural history, sanctified by inevitability; that the causes of it are world-wide, elemental; and that we ought to hang up a lamp before Laevsky, since he is the fated victim of the age, of influences, of heredity, and so on. All the officials and their ladies were in ecstasies when they listened to him, and I could not make out for a long time what sort of man I had to deal with, a cynic or a clever rogue. Such types as he, on the surface intellectual with a smattering of education and a great deal of talk about their own nobility, are very clever in posing as exceptionally complex natures."

"Hold your tongue!" Samoylenko flared up. "I will not allow a splendid fellow to be spoken ill of in my presence!"

"Don't interrupt, Alexandr Daviditch," said Von Koren coldly; "I am just finishing. Laevsky is by no means a complex organism. Here is his moral skeleton: in the morning, slippers, a bathe, and coffee; then till dinner-time, slippers, a constitutional, and conversation; at two o'clock slippers, dinner, and wine; at five o'clock a bathe, tea and wine, then *vint* and lying; at ten o'clock supper and wine; and after midnight sleep and *la femme*. His existence is confined within this narrow programme like an egg within its shell. Whether he walks or sits, is angry, writes, rejoices, it may all be reduced to wine, cards, slippers, and women. Woman plays a fatal, overwhelming part in his life. He tells us himself that at thirteen he was in love; that when he was a student in his first year he was living with a lady who had a good influence over him, and to whom he was indebted for his musical education. In his second year he bought a prostitute from a brothel and raised her to his level—that is, took her as his kept mistress, and she lived with him for six months and then ran away back to the brothel-keeper, and her flight caused him much spiritual suffering. Alas! his sufferings were so great that he had to leave the university and spend two years at home doing nothing. But this was all for the best. At home he made friends with a widow who advised him to leave the Faculty of Jurisprudence and go into the Faculty of Arts. And so he did. When he had taken his degree, he fell passionately in love with his present . . . what's her name? . . . married lady, and was obliged to flee with her here to the Caucasus for the sake of his ideals, he would have us believe, seeing that . . . to-morrow, if not to-day, he will be tired of her and flee back again to Petersburg, and that, too, will be for the sake of his ideals."

"How do you know?" growled Samoylenko, looking angrily at the zoologist. "You had better eat your dinner."

The next course consisted of boiled mullet with Polish sauce. Samoylenko helped each of his companions to a whole mullet and poured out the sauce with his own hand. Two minutes passed in silence.

"Woman plays an essential part in the life of every man," said the deacon. "You can't help that."

"Yes, but to what degree? For each of us woman means mother, sister, wife, friend. To Laevsky she is everything, and at the same time nothing but a mistress. She—that is, cohabitation with her—is the happiness and object of his life; he is gay, sad, bored, disenchanted—on account of woman; his life grows disagreeable—woman is to blame; the dawn of a new life begins to glow, ideals turn up—and again look for the woman. . . . He only derives enjoyment from books and pictures in which there is woman. Our age is, to his thinking, poor and inferior to the forties and the sixties only because we do not know how to abandon ourselves obliviously to the passion and ecstasy of love. These voluptuaries must have in their brains a special growth of the nature of sarcoma, which stifles the brain and directs their whole psychology. Watch Laevsky when he is sitting anywhere in company. You notice: when one raises any general question in his presence, for instance, about the cell or instinct, he sits apart, and neither speaks nor listens; he looks languid and disillusioned; nothing has any interest for him, everything is vulgar and trivial. But as soon as you speak of male and female—for instance, of the fact that the female spider, after fertilization, devours the male—his eyes glow with curiosity, his face brightens, and the man revives, in fact. All his thoughts, however noble, lofty, or neutral they may be, they all have one point of resemblance. You walk along the street with him and meet a donkey, for instance. . . . 'Tell me, please,' he asks, 'what would happen if you mated a donkey with a camel?' And his dreams! Has he told you of his dreams? It is magnificent! First, he dreams that he is married to the moon, then that he is summoned before the police and ordered to live with a guitar . . ."

The deacon burst into resounding laughter; Samoylenko frowned and wrinkled up his face angrily so as not to laugh, but could not restrain himself, and laughed.

"And it's all nonsense!" he said, wiping his tears. "Yes, by Jove, it's nonsense!"

IV

The deacon was very easily amused, and laughed at every trifle till he got a stitch in his side, till he was helpless. It seemed as though he only liked to be in people's company because there was a ridiculous side to them, and because they might be given ridiculous nicknames. He had nicknamed

Samoylenko "the tarantula," his orderly "the drake," and was in ecstasies when on one occasion Von Koren spoke of Laevsky and Nadyezhda Fyodorovna as "Japanese monkeys." He watched people's faces greedily, listened without blinking, and it could be seen that his eyes filled with laughter and his face was tense with expectation of the moment when he could let himself go and burst into laughter.

"He is a corrupt and depraved type," the zoologist continued, while the deacon kept his eyes riveted on his face, expecting he would say something funny. "It is not often one can meet with such a nonentity. In body he is inert, feeble, prematurely old, while in intellect he differs in no respect from a fat shopkeeper's wife who does nothing but eat, drink, and sleep on a feather-bed, and who keeps her coachman as a lover."

The deacon began guffawing again.

"Don't laugh, deacon," said Von Koren. "It grows stupid, at last. I should not have paid attention to his insignificance," he went on, after waiting till the deacon had left off laughing; "I should have passed him by if he were not so noxious and dangerous. His noxiousness lies first of all in the fact that he has great success with women, and so threatens to leave descendants—that is, to present the world with a dozen Laevskys as feeble and as depraved as himself. Secondly, he is in the highest degree contaminating. I have spoken to you already of *vint* and beer. In another year or two he will dominate the whole Caucasian coast. You know how the mass, especially its middle stratum, believe in intellectuality, in a university education, in gentlemanly manners, and in literary language. Whatever filthy thing he did, they would all believe that it was as it should be, since he is an intellectual man, of liberal ideas and university education. What is more, he is a failure, a superfluous man, a neurasthenic, a victim of the age, and that means he can do anything. He is a charming fellow, a regular good sort, he is so genuinely indulgent to human weaknesses; he is compliant, accommodating, easy, and not proud; one can drink with him and gossip and talk evil of people. . . . The masses, always inclined to anthropomorphism in religion and morals, like best of all the little gods who have the same weaknesses as themselves. Only think what a wide field he has for contamination! Besides, he is not a bad actor and is a clever hypocrite, and knows very well how to twist things round. Only take his little shifts and dodges, his attitude to civilization, for instance. He has scarcely sniffed at civilization, yet: 'Ah, how we have been crippled by civilization! Ah, how I envy those savages, those children of nature, who know nothing of civilization!' We are to understand, you see, that at one time, in ancient days, he has been devoted to civilization with his whole soul, has served it, has sounded it to its depths, but it has exhausted him, disillusioned him, deceived him; he is a Faust, do you see?—a second Tolstoy. . . . As for Schopenhauer and Spencer, he treats them like small boys and slaps them on the shoulder in a fatherly way: 'Well, what do you say, old Spencer?' He has not read Spencer, of course, but how charming he is when with light, careless irony he says of his lady friend: 'She has read Spencer!' And they all listen to him, and no one cares to understand that this charlatan has not the right to kiss the sole of Spencer's foot, let alone speak about him in that tone! Sapping the foundations of civilization, of authority, of other people's altars, spattering them with filth, winking jocosely at them only to justify and conceal one's own rottenness and moral poverty is only possible for a very vain, base, and nasty creature."

"I don't know what it is you expect of him, Kolya," said Samoylenko, looking at the zoologist, not with anger now, but with a guilty air. "He is a man the same as everyone else. Of course, he has his weaknesses, but he is abreast of modern ideas, is in the service, is of use to his country. Ten years ago there was an old fellow serving as agent here, a man of the greatest intelligence . . . and he used to say . . ."

"Nonsense, nonsense!" the zoologist interrupted. "You say he is in the service; but how does he serve? Do you mean to tell me that things have been done better because he is here, and the officials are more punctual, honest, and civil? On the contrary, he has only sanctioned their slackness by his prestige as an intellectual university man. He is only punctual on the 20th of the month, when he gets his salary; on the other days he lounges about at home in slippers and tries to look as if he were doing the Government a great service by living in the Caucasus. No, Alexandr Daviditch, don't stick up for him. You are insincere from beginning to end. If you really loved him and considered him your neighbour, you would above all not be indifferent to his weaknesses, you would not be indulgent to them, but for his own sake would try to make him innocuous."

"That is?"

"Innocuous. Since he is incorrigible, he can only be made innocuous in one way. . . ." Von Koren passed his finger round his throat. "Or he might be drowned . . . ," he added. "In the interests of humanity and in their own interests, such people ought to be destroyed. They certainly ought."

"What are you saying?" muttered Samoylenko, getting up and looking with amazement at the zoologist's calm, cold face. "Deacon, what is he saying? Why—are you in your senses?"

"I don't insist on the death penalty," said Von Koren. "If it is proved that it is pernicious, devise something else. If we can't destroy Laevsky, why then, isolate him, make him harmless, send him to hard labour."

"What are you saying!" said Samoylenko in horror. "With pepper, with pepper," he cried in a voice of despair, seeing that the deacon was eating stuffed aubergines without pepper. "You with your great intellect, what are you saying! Send our friend, a proud intellectual man, to penal servitude!"

"Well, if he is proud and tries to resist, put him in fetters!"

Samoylenko could not utter a word, and only twiddled his fingers; the deacon looked at his flabbergasted and really absurd face, and laughed.

"Let us leave off talking of that," said the zoologist. "Only remember one thing, Alexandr Daviditch: primitive man was preserved from such as Laevsky by the struggle for existence and by natural selection; now our civilization has considerably weakened the struggle and the selection, and we ought to look after the destruction of the rotten and worthless for ourselves;

otherwise, when the Laevskys multiply, civilization will perish and mankind will degenerate utterly. It will be our fault."

"If it depends on drowning and hanging," said Samoylenko, "damnation take your civilization, damnation take your humanity! Damnation take it! I tell you what: you are a very learned and intelligent man and the pride of your country, but the Germans have ruined you. Yes, the Germans! The Germans!"

Since Samoylenko had left Dorpat, where he had studied medicine, he had rarely seen a German and had not read a single German book, but, in his opinion, every harmful idea in politics or science was due to the Germans. Where he had got this notion he could not have said himself, but he held it firmly.

"Yes, the Germans!" he repeated once more. "Come and have some tea."

All three stood up, and putting on their hats, went out into the little garden, and sat there under the shade of the light green maples, the pear-trees, and a chestnut-tree. The zoologist and the deacon sat on a bench by the table, while Samoylenko sank into a deep wicker chair with a sloping back. The orderly handed them tea, jam, and a bottle of syrup.

It was very hot, thirty degrees Réaumur in the shade. The sultry air was stagnant and motionless, and a long spider-web, stretching from the chestnut-tree to the ground, hung limply and did not stir.

The deacon took up the guitar, which was constantly lying on the ground near the table, tuned it, and began singing softly in a thin voice:

"Gathered round the tavern were the seminary lads,"

but instantly subsided, overcome by the heat, mopped his brow and glanced upwards at the blazing blue sky. Samoylenko grew drowsy; the sultry heat, the stillness and the delicious afterdinner languor, which quickly pervaded all his limbs, made him feel heavy and sleepy; his arms dropped at his sides, his eyes grew small, his head sank on his breast. He looked with almost tearful tenderness at Von Koren and the deacon, and muttered:

"The younger generation. . . . A scientific star and a luminary of the Church. . . . I shouldn't wonder if the long-skirted alleluia will be shooting up into a bishop; I dare say I may come to kissing his hand. . . . Well . . . please God. . . ."

Soon a snore was heard. Von Koren and the deacon finished their tea and went out into the street.

"Are you going to the harbour again to catch sea-gudgeon?" asked the zoologist.

"No, it's too hot."

"Come and see me. You can pack up a parcel and copy something for me. By the way, we must have a talk about what you are to do. You must work, deacon. You can't go on like this."

"Your words are just and logical," said the deacon. "But my laziness finds an excuse in the circumstances of my present life. You know yourself that an uncertain position has a great tendency to make people apathetic. God only knows whether I have been sent here for a time or permanently. I am living here in uncertainty, while my wife is vegetating at her father's and is missing me. And I must confess my brain is melting with the heat."

"That's all nonsense," said the zoologist. "You can get used to the heat, and you can get used to being without the deaconess. You mustn't be slack; you must pull yourself together."

v

Nadyezhda Fyodorovna went to bathe in the morning, and her cook, Olga, followed her with a jug, a copper basin, towels, and a sponge. In the bay stood two unknown steamers with dirty white funnels, obviously foreign cargo vessels. Some men dressed in white and wearing white shoes were walking along the harbour, shouting loudly in French, and were answered from the steamers. The bells were ringing briskly in the little church of the town.

"To-day is Sunday!" Nadyezhda Fyodorovna remembered with pleasure.

She felt perfectly well, and was in a gay holiday humour. In a new loose-fitting dress of coarse thick tussore silk, and a big wide-brimmed straw hat which was bent down over her ears, so that her face looked out as though from a basket, she fancied she looked very charming. She thought that in the whole town there was only one young, pretty, intellectual woman, and that was herself, and that she was the only one who knew how to dress herself cheaply, elegantly, and with taste. That dress, for example, cost only twenty-two roubles, and yet how charming it was! In the whole town she was the only one who could be attractive, while there were numbers of men, so they must all, whether they would or not, be envious of Laevsky.

She was glad that of late Laevsky had been cold to her, reserved and polite, and at times even harsh and rude; in the past she had met all his outbursts, all his contemptuous, cold or strange incomprehensible glances, with tears, reproaches, and threats to leave him or to starve herself to death; now she only blushed, looked guiltily at him, and was glad he was not affectionate to her. If he had abused her, or threatened her, it would have been better and pleasanter, since she felt hopelessly guilty towards him. She felt she was to blame, in the first place, for not sympathizing with the dreams of a life of hard work, for the sake of which he had given up Petersburg and had come here to the Caucasus, and she was convinced that he had been angry with her of late for precisely that. When she was travelling to the Caucasus, it seemed that she would find here on the first day a cosy nook by the sea, a snug little garden with shade, with birds, with little brooks, where she could grow flowers and vegetables, rear ducks and hens, entertain her neighbours, doctor poor peasants and distribute little books amongst them. It had turned out that the Caucasus was nothing but bare mountains, forests, and huge valleys, where it took a long time and a great deal of effort to find anything and settle down; that there were no neighbours of any sort; that it was very hot and one might be robbed.

Laevsky had been in no hurry to obtain a piece of land; she was glad of it, and they seemed to be in a tacit compact never to allude to a life of hard work. He was silent about it, she thought, because he was angry with her for being silent about it.

In the second place, she had without his knowledge during those two years bought various trifles to the value of three hundred roubles at Atchmianov's shop. She had bought the things by degrees, at one time materials, at another time silk or a parasol, and the debt had grown imperceptibly.

"I will tell him about it to-day . . . ," she used to decide, but at once reflected that in Laevsky's present mood it would hardly be convenient to talk to him of debts.

Thirdly, she had on two occasions in Laevsky's absence received a visit from Kirilin, the police captain: once in the morning when Laevsky had gone to bathe, and another time at midnight when he was playing cards. Remembering this, Nadyezhda Fyodorovna flushed crimson, and looked round at the cook as though she might overhear her thoughts. The long, insufferably hot, wearisome days, beautiful languorous evenings and stifling nights, and the whole manner of living, when from morning to night one is at a loss to fill up the useless hours, and the persistent thought that she was the prettiest young woman in the town, and that her youth was passing and being wasted, and Laevsky himself, though honest and idealistic, always the same, always lounging about in his slippers, biting his nails, and wearying her with his caprices, led by degrees to her becoming possessed by desire, and as though she were mad, she thought of nothing else day and night. Breathing, looking, walking, she felt nothing but desire. The sound of the sea told her she must love; the darkness of evening—the same; the mountains—the same. . . . And when Kirilin began paying her attentions, she had neither the power nor the wish to resist, and surrendered to him. . . .

Now the foreign steamers and the men in white reminded her for some reason of a huge hall; together with the shouts of French she heard the strains of a waltz, and her bosom heaved with unaccountable delight. She longed to dance and talk French.

She reflected joyfully that there was nothing terrible about her infidelity. Her soul had no part in her infidelity; she still loved Laevsky, and that was proved by the fact that she was jealous of him, was sorry for him, and missed him when he was away. Kirilin had turned out to be very mediocre, rather coarse though handsome; everything was broken off with him already and there would never be anything more. What had happened was over; it had nothing to do with anyone, and if Laevsky found it out he would not believe in it.

There was only one bathing-house for ladies on the seafront; men bathed under the open sky. Going into the bathing-house, Nadyezhda Fyodorovna found there an elderly lady, Marya Konstantinovna Bityugov, and her daughter Katya, a schoolgirl of fifteen; both of them were sitting on a bench undressing. Marya Konstantinovna was a good-natured, enthusiastic, and genteel person, who talked in a drawling and pathetic voice. She had been a governess until she was thirty-two, and then had married Bityugov, a Government official—a bald little man with his hair combed on to his temples and with a very meek disposition. She was still in love with him, was jealous, blushed at the word "love," and told everyone she was very happy.

"My dear," she cried enthusiastically, on seeing Nadyezhda Fyodorovna, assuming an expression which all her acquaintances called "almond-oily." "My dear, how delightful that you have come! We'll bathe together— that's enchanting!"

Olga quickly flung off her dress and chemise, and began undressing her mistress.

"It's not quite so hot to-day as yesterday?" said Nadyezhda Fyodorovna, shrinking at the coarse touch of the naked cook. "Yesterday I almost died of the heat."

"Oh yes, my dear; I could hardly breathe myself. Would you believe it? I bathed yesterday three times! Just imagine, my dear, three times! Nikodim Alexandritch was quite uneasy."

"Is it possible to be so ugly?" thought Nadyezhda Fyodorovna, looking at Olga and the official's wife; she glanced at Katya and thought: "The little girl's not badly made."

"Your Nikodim Alexandritch is very charming!" she said. "I'm simply in love with him."

"Ha, ha, ha!" cried Marya Konstantinovna, with a forced laugh; "that's quite enchanting."

Free from her clothes, Nadyezhda Fyodorovna felt a desire to fly. And it seemed to her that if she were to wave her hands she would fly upwards. When she was undressed, she noticed that Olga looked scornfully at her white body. Olga, a young soldier's wife, was living with her lawful husband, and so considered herself superior to her mistress. Marya Konstantinovna and Katya were afraid of her, and did not respect her. This was disagreeable, and to raise herself in their opinion, Nadyezhda Fyodorovna said:

"At home, in Petersburg summer villa life is at its height now. My husband and I have so many friends! We ought to go and see them."

"I believe your husband is an engineer?" said Marya Konstantinovna timidly.

"I am speaking of Laevsky. He has a great many acquaintances. But unfortunately his mother is a proud aristocrat, not very intelligent. . . ."

Nadyezhda Fyodorovna threw herself into the water without finishing; Marya Konstantinovna and Katya made their way in after her.

"There are so many conventional ideas in the world," Nadyezhda Fyodorovna went on, "and life is not so easy as it seems."

Marya Konstantinovna, who had been a governess in aristocratic families and who was an authority on social matters, said:

"Oh yes! Would you believe me, my dear, at the Garatynskys' I was expected to dress for lunch as well as for dinner, so that, like an actress, I received a special allowance for my wardrobe in addition to my salary."

She stood between Nadyezhda Fyodorovna and Katya as though to screen her daughter from the water that washed the former.

Through the open doors looking out to the sea they could see someone swimming a hundred paces from their bathing-place.

"Mother, it's our Kostya," said Katya.

"Ach, ach!" Marya Konstantinovna cackled in her dismay. "Ach, Kostya!" she shouted. "Come back! Kostya, come back!"

Kostya, a boy of fourteen, to show off his prowess before his mother and sister, dived and swam farther, but began to be exhausted and hurried back, and from his strained and serious face it could be seen that he could not trust his own strength.

"The trouble one has with these boys, my dear!" said Marya Konstantinovna, growing calmer. "Before you can turn round, he will break his neck. Ah, my dear, how sweet it is, and yet at the same time how difficult, to be a mother! One's afraid of everything."

Nadyezhda Fyodorovna put on her straw hat and dashed out into the open sea. She swam some thirty feet and then turned on her back. She could see the sea to the horizon, the steamers, the people on the sea-front, the town; and all this, together with the sultry heat and the soft, transparent waves, excited her and whispered that she must live, live. . . . A sailing-boat darted by her rapidly and vigorously, cleaving the waves and the air; the man sitting at the helm looked at her, and she liked being looked at. . . .

After bathing, the ladies dressed and went away together.

"I have fever every alternate day, and yet I don't get thin," said Nadyezhda Fyodorovna, licking her lips, which were salt from the bathe, and responding with a smile to the bows of her acquaintances. "I've always been plump, and now I believe I'm plumper than ever."

"That, my dear, is constitutional. If, like me, one has no constitutional tendency to stoutness, no diet is of any use. . . . But you've wetted your hat, my dear."

"It doesn't matter; it will dry."

Nadyezhda Fyodorovna saw again the men in white who were walking on the sea-front and talking French; and again she felt a sudden thrill of joy, and had a vague memory of some big hall in which she had once danced, or of which, perhaps, she had once dreamed. And something at the bottom of her soul dimly and obscurely whispered to her that she was a petty, common, miserable, worthless woman. . . .

Marya Konstantinovna stopped at her gate and asked her to come in and sit down for a little while.

"Come in, my dear," she said in an imploring voice, and at the same time she looked at Nadyezhda Fyodorovna with anxiety and hope; perhaps she would refuse and not come in!

"With pleasure," said Nadyezhda Fyodorovna, accepting. "You know how I love being with you!"

And she went into the house. Marya Konstantinovna sat her down and gave her coffee, regaled her with milk rolls, then showed her photographs of her former pupils, the Garatynskys, who were by now married. She showed her, too, the examination reports of Kostya and Katya. The reports were very good, but to make them seem even better, she complained, with a sigh, how difficult the lessons at school were now. . . . She made much of her visitor, and was sorry for her, though at the same time she was harassed by the thought that Nadyezhda Fyodorovna might have a corrupting influence on the morals of Kostya and Katya, and was glad that her Nikodim Alexandritch was not at home. Seeing that in her opinion all men are fond of "women like that," Nadyezhda Fyodorovna might have a bad effect on Nikodim Alexandritch too.

As she talked to her visitor, Marya Konstantinovna kept remembering that they were to have a picnic that evening, and that Von Koren had particularly begged her to say nothing about it to the "Japanese monkeys" —that is, Laevsky and Nadyezhda Fyodorovna; but she dropped a word about it unawares, crimsoned, and said in confusion:

"I hope you will come too!"

VI

It was agreed to drive about five miles out of town on the road to the south, to stop near a *duhan* at the junction of two streams—the Black River and the Yellow River—and to cook fish soup. They started out soon after five. Foremost of the party in a char-à-banc drove Samoylenko and Laevsky; they were followed by Marya Konstantinovna, Nadyezhda Fyodorovna, Katya and Kostya, in a coach with three horses, carrying with them the crockery and a basket with provisions. In the next carriage came the police captain, Kirilin, and the young Atchmianov, the son of the shopkeeper to whom Nadyezhda Fyodorovna owed three hundred roubles; opposite them, huddled up on the little seat with his feet tucked under him, sat Nikodim Alexandritch, a neat little man with hair combed on to his temples. Last of all came Von Koren and the deacon; at the deacon's feet stood a basket of fish.

"R-r-right!" Samoylenko shouted at the top of his voice when he met a cart or a mountaineer riding on a donkey.

"In two years' time, when I shall have the means and the people ready, I shall set off on an expedition," Von Koren was telling the deacon. "I shall go by the sea-coast from Vladivostok to the Behring Straits, and then from the Straits to the mouth of the Yenisei. We shall make the map, study the fauna and the flora, and make detailed geological, anthropological, and ethnographical researches. It depends upon you to go with me or not."

"It's impossible," said the deacon.

"Why?"

"I'm a man with ties and a family."

"Your wife will let you go; we will provide for her. Better still if you were to persuade her for the public benefit to go into a nunnery; that would make it possible for you to become a monk, too, and join the expedition as a priest. I can arrange it for you."

The deacon was silent.

"Do you know your theology well?" asked the zoologist.

"No rather badly."

"H'm! . . . I can't give you any advice on that score, because I don't know much about theology myself. You give me a list of books you need, and I will send them to you from Petersburg in the winter. It will be necessary for you to read the notes of religious travellers, too; among them are some good ethnologists and Oriental scholars. When you are familiar with their methods, it will be easier for you to set to work. And you needn't waste your time till you get the books; come to me, and we will study the compass and go through a course of meteorology. All that's indispensable."

"To be sure . . ." muttered the deacon, and he laughed. "I was trying to get a place in Central Russia, and my uncle, the head priest, promised to help me. If I go with you I shall have troubled them for nothing."

"I don't understand your hesitation. If you go on being an ordinary deacon, who is only obliged to hold a service on holidays, and on the other days can rest from work, you will be exactly the same as you are now in ten years' time, and will have gained nothing but a beard and moustache; while on returning from this expedition in ten years' time you will be a different man, you will be enriched by the consciousness that something has been done by you."

From the ladies' carriage came shrieks of terror and delight. The carriages were driving along a road hollowed in a literally overhanging precipitous cliff, and it seemed to everyone that they were galloping along a shelf on a steep wall, and that in a moment the carriages would drop into the abyss. On the right stretched the sea; on the left was a rough brown wall with black blotches and red veins and with climbing roots; while on the summit stood shaggy fir-trees bent over, as though looking down in terror and curiosity. A minute later there were shrieks and laughter again: they had to drive under a huge overhanging rock.

"I don't know why the devil I'm coming with you," said Laevsky. "How stupid and vulgar it is! I want to go to the North, to run away, to escape; but here I am, for some reason, going to this stupid picnic."

"But look, what a view!" said Samoylenko as the horses turned to the left, and the valley of the Yellow River came into sight and the stream itself gleamed in the sunlight, yellow, turbid, frantic.

"I see nothing fine in that, Sasha," answered Laevsky. "To be in continual ecstasies over nature shows poverty of imagination. In comparison with what my imagination can give me, all these streams and rocks are trash, and nothing else."

The carriages now were by the bank of the stream. The high mountain banks gradually grew closer, the valley shrank together and ended in a gorge; the rocky mountain round which they were driving had been piled together by nature out of huge rocks, pressing upon each other with such terrible weight, that Samoylenko could not help gasping every time he looked at them. The dark and beautiful mountain was cleft in places by narrow fissures and gorges from which came a breath of dewy moisture and mystery: through the gorges could be seen other mountains, brown, pink, lilac, smoky, or bathed in vivid sunlight. From time to time as they passed a gorge they caught the sound of water falling from the heights and splashing on the stones.

"Ach, the damned mountains!" sighed Laevsky. "How sick I am of them!"

At the place where the Black River falls into the Yellow, and the water black as ink stains the yellow and struggles with it, stood the Tatar Kerbalay's *duhan*, with the Russian flag on the roof and with an inscription written in chalk: "The Pleasant Duhan." Near it was a little garden, enclosed in a hurdle fence, with tables and chairs set out in it, and in the midst of a thicket of wretched thorn-bushes stood a single solitary cypress, dark and beautiful.

Kerbalay, a nimble little Tatar in a blue shirt and a white apron, was standing in the road, and, holding his stomach, he bowed low to welcome the carriages, and smiled, showing his glistening white teeth.

"Good-evening, Kerbalay," shouted Samoylenko. "We are driving on a little further, and you take along the samovar and chairs! Look sharp!"

Kerbalay nodded his shaven head and muttered something, and only those sitting in the last carriage could hear: "We've got trout, your Excellency."

"Bring them, bring them!" said Von Koren.

Five hundred paces from the *duhan* the carriages stopped. Samoylenko selected a small meadow round which there were scattered stones convenient for sitting on, and a fallen tree blown down by the storm with roots overgrown by moss and dry yellow needles. Here there was a fragile wooden bridge over the stream, and just opposite on the other bank there was a little barn for drying maize, standing on four low piles, and looking like the hut on hen's legs in the fairy tale; a little ladder sloped from its door.

The first impression in all was a feeling that they would never get out of that place again. On all sides, wherever they looked, the mountains rose up and towered above them, and the shadows of evening were stealing rapidly, rapidly from the *duhan* and dark cypress, making the narrow winding valley of the Black River narrower and the mountains higher. They could hear the river murmuring and the unceasing chirrup of the grasshoppers.

"Enchanting!" said Marya Konstantinovna, heaving deep sighs of ecstasy. "Children, look how fine! What peace!"

"Yes, it really is fine," assented Laevsky, who liked the view, and for some reason felt sad as he looked at the sky and then at the blue smoke rising from the chimney of the *duhan*. "Yes, it is fine," he repeated.

"Ivan Andreitch, describe this view," Marya Konstantinovna said tearfully.

"Why?" asked Laevsky. "The impression is better than any description. The wealth of sights and sounds which everyone receives from nature by direct impression is ranted about by authors in a hideous and unrecognizable way."

"Really?" Von Koren asked coldly, choosing the biggest stone by the side of the water, and trying to clamber up and sit upon it. "Really?" he repeated looking directly at Laevsky. "What of 'Romeo and Juliet'? Or, for instance, Pushkin's 'Night in the Ukraine'? Nature ought to come and bow down at their feet."

"Perhaps," said Laevsky, who was too lazy to think and oppose him. "Though what is 'Romeo and Juliet' after all?" he added after a short pause. "The beauty of poetry and holiness of love are simply the roses under which they try to hide its rottenness. Romeo is just the same sort of animal as all the rest of us."

"Whatever one talks to you about, you always bring it round to . . ." Von Koren glanced round at Katya and broke off.

"What do I bring it round to?" asked Laevsky.

"One tells you, for instance, how beautiful a bunch of grapes is, and you answer: 'Yes, but how ugly it is when it is chewed and digested in one's stomach!' Why say that? It's not new, and . . . altogether it is a queer habit."

Laevsky knew that Von Koren did not like him, and so was afraid of him, and felt in his presence as though everyone were constrained and someone were standing behind his back. He made no answer and walked away, feeling sorry he had come.

"Gentlemen, quick march for brush wood for the fire!" commanded Samoylenko.

They all wandered off in different directions, and no one was left but Kirilin, Atchmianov, and Nikodim Alexandritch. Kerbalay brought chairs, spread a rug on the ground, and set a few bottles of wine.

The police captain, Kirilin, a tall, good-looking man, who in all weathers wore his great-coat over his tunic, with his haughty deportment, stately carriage, and thick, rather hoarse voice, looked like a young provincial chief of police; his expression was mournful and sleepy, as though he had just been waked against his will.

"What have you brought this for, you brute?" he asked Kerbalay, deliberately articulating each word. "I ordered you to give us *kvarel*, and what have you brought, you ugly Tatar? Eh? What?"

"We have plenty of wine of our own, Yegor Alekseitch," Nikodim Alexandritch observed, timidly and politely.

"What? But I want us to have my wine, too; I'm taking part in the picnic and I imagine I have full right to contribute my share. I im-ma-gine so! Bring ten bottles of *kvarel*."

"Why so many?" asked Nikodim Alexandritch, in wonder, knowing Kirilin had no money.

"Twenty bottles! Thirty!" shouted Kirilin.

"Never mind, let him," Atchmianov whispered to Nikodim Alexandritch; "I'll pay."

Nadyezhda Fyodorovna was in a light-hearted, mischievous mood; she wanted to skip and jump, to laugh, to shout, to tease, to flirt. In her cheap cotton dress with blue pansies on it, in her red shoes and the same straw hat, she seemed to herself little, simple, light, ethereal as a butterfly. She ran over the rickety bridge and looked for a minute into the water, in order to feel giddy; then, shrieking and laughing, ran to the other side to the drying-shed, and she fancied that all the men were admiring her, even Kerbalay. When in the rapidly falling darkness the trees began to melt into the mountains and the horses into the carriages, and a light gleamed in the windows of the *duhan,* she climbed up the mountain by the little path which zigzagged between stones and thorn-bushes and sat on a stone. Down below, the camp-fire was burning. Near the fire, with his sleeves tucked up, the deacon was moving to and fro, and his long black shadow kept describing a circle round it; he put on wood, and with a spoon tied to a long stick he stirred the cauldron. Samoylenko, with a copper-red face, was fussing round the fire just as though he were in his own kitchen, shouting furiously:

"Where's the salt, gentlemen? I bet you've forgotten it. Why are you all sitting about like lords while I do all the work?"

Laevsky and Nikodim Alexandritch were sitting side by side on the fallen tree looking pensively at the fire. Marya Konstantinovna, Katya, and Kostya were taking the cups, saucers, and plates out of the baskets. Von Koren, with his arms folded and one foot on a stone, was standing on a bank at the very edge of the water, thinking about something. Patches of red light from the fire moved together with the shadows over the ground near the dark human figures, and quivered on the mountain, on the trees, on the bridge, on the drying-shed; on the other side the steep, scooped-out bank was all lighted up and glimmering in the stream, and the rushing turbid water broke its reflection into little bits.

The deacon went for the fish which Kerbalay was cleaning and washing on the bank, but he stood still half-way and looked about him.

"My God, how nice it is!" he thought. "People, rocks, the fire, the twilight, a monstrous tree—nothing more, and yet how fine it is!"

On the further bank some unknown persons made their appearance near the drying-shed. The flickering light and the smoke from the campfire puffing in that direction made it impossible to get a full view of them all at once, but glimpses were caught now of a shaggy hat and a grey beard, now of a blue shirt, now of a figure, ragged from shoulder to knee, with a dagger across the body; then a swarthy young face with black eyebrows, as thick and bold as though they had been drawn in charcoal. Five of them sat in a circle on the ground, and the other five went into the drying-shed. One was standing at the door with his back to the fire, and with his hands behind his back was telling something, which must have been very interesting, for when Samoylenko threw on twigs and the fire flared up, and scattered sparks and threw a glaring light on the shed, two calm countenances with an expression on them of deep attention could be seen, looking out of the door, while those who were sitting in a circle turned round and began listening to the speaker. Soon after, those sitting in a circle began softly singing something slow and melodious, that sounded like

Lenten Church music. . . . Listening to them, the deacon imagined how it would be with him in ten years' time, when he would come back from the expedition: he would be a young priest and monk, an author with a name and a splendid past; he would be consecrated an archimandrite, then a bishop; and he would serve mass in the cathedral; in a golden mitre he would come out into the body of the church with the ikon on his breast, and blessing the mass of the people with the triple and the double candelabra, would proclaim: "Look down from Heaven, O God, behold and visit this vineyard which Thy Hand has planted," and the children with their angel voices would sing in response: "Holy God. . . ."

"Deacon, where is that fish?" he heard Samoylenko's voice.

As he went back to the fire, the deacon imagined the Church procession going along a dusty road on a hot July day; in front the peasants carrying the banners and the women and children the ikons, then the boy choristers and the sacristan with his face tied up and a straw in his hair, then in due order himself, the deacon, and behind him the priest wearing his *calotte* and carrying a cross, and behind them, tramping in the dust, a crowd of peasants—men, women, and children; in the crowd his wife and the priest's wife with kerchiefs on their heads. The choristers sing, the babies cry, the corncrakes call, the lark carols. . . . Then they make a stand and sprinkle the herd with holy water. . . . They go on again, and then kneeling pray for rain. Then lunch and talk. . . .

"And that's nice too . . ." thought the deacon.

VII

Kirilin and Atchmianov climbed up the mountain by the path. Atchmianov dropped behind and stopped, while Kirilin went up to Nadyezhda Fyodorovna.

"Good-evening," he said, touching his cap.

"Good-evening."

"Yes!" said Kirilin, looking at the sky and pondering.

"Why 'yes'?" asked Nadyezhda Fyodorovna after a brief pause, noticing that Atchmianov was watching them both.

"And so it seems," said the officer, slowly, "that our love has withered before it has blossomed, so to speak. How do you wish me to understand it? Is it a sort of coquetry on your part, or do you look upon me as a nincompoop who can be treated as you choose?"

"It was a mistake! Leave me alone!" Nadyezhda Fyodorovna said sharply, on that beautiful, marvellous evening, looking at him with terror and asking herself with bewilderment, could there really have been a moment when that man attracted her and had been near to her?

"So that's it!" said Kirilin; he thought in silence for a few minutes and said: "Well, I'll wait till you are in a better humour, and meanwhile I venture to assure you I am a gentleman, and I don't allow anyone to doubt it. Adieu!"

He touched his cap again and walked off, making his way between the bushes. After a short interval Atchmianov approached hesitatingly.

"What a fine evening!" he said with a slight Armenian accent.

He was nice-looking, fashionably dressed, and behaved unaffectedly like a well-bred youth, but Nadyezhda Fyodorovna did not like him because she owed his father three hundred roubles; it was displeasing to her, too, that a shopkeeper had been asked to the picnic, and she was vexed at his coming up to her that evening when her heart felt so pure.

"The picnic is a success altogether," he said, after a pause.

"Yes," she agreed, and as though suddenly remembering her debt, she said carelessly: "Oh, tell them in your shop that Ivan Andreitch will come round in a day or two and will pay three hundred roubles. . . . I don't remember exactly what it is."

"I would give another three hundred if you would not mention that debt every day. Why be prosaic?"

Nadyezhda Fyodorovna laughed; the amusing idea occurred to her that if she had been willing and sufficiently immoral she might in one minute be free from her debt. If she, for instance, were to turn the head of this handsome young fool! How amusing, absurd, wild it would be really! And she suddenly felt a longing to make him love her, to plunder him, throw him over, and then to see what would come of it.

"Allow me to give you one piece of advice," Atchmianov said timidly. "I beg you to beware of Kirilin. He says horrible things about you everywhere."

"It doesn't interest me to know what every fool says of me," Nadyezhda Fyodorovna said coldly, and the amusing thought of playing with handsome young Atchmianov suddenly lost its charm.

"We must go down," she said; "they're calling us."

The fish soup was ready by now. They were ladling it out by platefuls, and eating it with the religious solemnity with which this is only done at a picnic; and everyone thought the fish soup very good, and thought that at home they had never eaten anything so nice. As is always the case at picnics, in the mass of dinner napkins, parcels, useless greasy papers fluttering in the wind, no one knew where was his glass or where his bread. They poured the wine on the carpet and on their own knees, spilt the salt, while it was dark all round them and the fire burnt more dimly, and everyone was too lazy to get up and put wood on. They all drank wine, and even gave Kostya and Katya half a glass each. Nadyezhda Fyodorovna drank one glass and then another, got a litttle drunk and forgot about Kirilin.

"A splendid picnic, an enchanting evening," said Laevsky, growing lively with the wine. "But I should prefer a fine winter to all this. 'His beaver collar is silver with hoar-frost.' "

"Everyone to his taste," observed Von Koren.

Laevsky felt uncomfortable; the heat of the camp-fire was beating upon his back, and the hatred of Von Koren upon his breast and face: this hatred on the part of a decent, clever man, a feeling in which there probably lay hid a well-grounded reason, humiliated him and enervated him, and unable to stand up against it, he said in a propitiatory tone:

"I am passionately fond of nature, and I regret that I'm not a naturalist. I envy you."

"Well, I don't envy you, and don't regret it," said Nadyezhda Fyodorovna. "I don't understand how anyone can seriously interest himself in beetles and ladybirds while the people are suffering."

Laevsky shared her opinion. He was absolutely ignorant of natural science, and so could never reconcile himself to the authoritative tone and the learned and profound air of the people who devoted themselves to the whiskers of ants and the claws of beetles, and he always felt vexed that these people, relying on these whiskers, claws, and something they called protoplasm (he always imagined it in the form of an oyster), should undertake to decide questions involving the orgin and life of man. But in Nadyezhda Fydorovna's words he heard a note of falsity, and simply to contradict her he said: "The point is not the ladybirds, but the deductions made from them."

VIII

It was late, eleven o'clock, when they began to get into the carriages to go home. They took their seats, and the only ones missing were Nadyezhda Fyodorovna and Atchmianov, who were running after one another, laughing, the other side of the stream.

"Make haste, my friends," shouted Samoylenko.

"You oughtn't to give ladies wine," said Von Koren in a low voice.

Laevsky, exhausted by the pinic, by the hatred of Von Koren, and by his own thoughts, went to meet Nadyezhda Fyodorovna, and when, gay and happy, feeling light as a feather, breathless and laughing, she took him by both hands and laid her head on his breast, he stepped back and said dryly:

"You are behaving like a . . . cocotte."

It sounded horribly coarse, so that he felt sorry for her at once. On his angry, exhausted face she read hatred, pity and vexation with himself, and her heart sank at once. She realized instantly that she had gone too far, had been too free and easy in her behavior, and overcome with misery, feeling herself heavy, stout, coarse, and drunk, she got into the first empty carriage together with Atchmianov. Laevsky got in with Kirilin, the zoologist with Samoylenko, the deacon with the ladies, and the party set off.

"You see what the Japanese monkeys are like," Von Koren began, rolling himself up in his cloak and shutting his eyes. "You heard she doesn't care to take an interest in beetles and ladybirds because the people are suffering. That's how all the Japanese monkeys look upon people like us. They're a slavish, cunning race, terrified by the whip and fist for ten generations; they tremble and burn incense only before violence; but let the monkey into a free state where there's no one to take it by the collar, and it relaxes at once and shows itself in its true colours. Look how bold they are in picture galleries, in museums, in theatres, or when they talk of science: they puff themselves out and get excited, they are abusive and critical . . . they are bound to criticize—it's the sign of the slave. You listen: men of the liberal professions are more often sworn at than pickpockets—that's because three-quarters of society are made up of slaves, of just such monkeys. It never happens that a slave holds out his hand to you and sincerely says 'Thank you' to you for your work."

"I don't know what you want," said Samoylenko, yawning; "the poor thing, in the simplicity of her heart, wanted to talk to you of scientific subjects, and you draw a conclusion from that. You're cross with him for something or other, and with her, too, to keep him company. She's a splendid woman."

"Ah, nonsense! An ordinary kept woman, depraved and vulgar. Listen Alexandr Daviditch; when you meet a simple peasant woman, who isn't living with her husband, who does nothing but giggle, you tell her to go and work. Why are you timid in this case and afraid to tell the truth? Simply because Nadyezhda Fyodorovna is kept, not by a sailor, but by an official."

"What am I to do with her?" said Samoylenko, getting angry. "Beat her or what?"

"Not flatter vice. We curse vice only behind its back, and that's like making a long nose at it round a corner. I am a zoologist or a sociologist, which is the same thing; you are a doctor; society believes in us; we ought to point out the terrible harm which threatens it and the next generation from the existence of ladies like Nadyezhda Ivanovna."

"Fyodorovna," Samoylenko corrected. "But what ought society to do?"

"Society? That's its affair. To my thinking the surest and most direct method is—compulsion *Manu militari* she ought to be returned to her husband; and if her husband won't take her in, then she ought to be sent to penal servitude or some house of correction."

"Ouf!" sighed Samoylenko. He paused and asked quietly: "You said the other day that people like Laevsky ought to be destroyed. . . . Tell me, if you . . . if the State or society commissioned you to destroy him, could you . . . bring yourself to it?"

"My hand would not tremble."

IX

When they got home, Laevsky and Nadyezhda Fyodorovna went into their dark, stuffy, dull rooms. Both were silent. Laevsky lighted a candle, while Nadyezhda Fyodorovna sat down and, without taking off her cloak and hat, lifted her melancholy, guilty eyes to him.

He knew that she expected an explanation from him, but an explanation would be wearisome, useless and exhausting, and his heart was heavy because he had lost control over himself and been rude to her. He chanced to feel in his pocket the letter which he had been intending every day to read to her, and thought if he were to show her that letter now, it would turn her thoughts in another direction.

"It is time to define our relations," he thought. "I will give it her; what is to be will be."

He took out the letter and gave it her.

"Read it. It concerns you."

Saying this, he went into his own room and lay down on the sofa in the dark without a pillow. Nadyezhda Fyodorovna read the letter, and it seemed to her as though the ceiling were falling and the walls were closing in on her. It seemed suddenly dark and shut in and terrible. She crossed herself quickly three times and said:

"Give him peace, O Lord . . . give him peace. . . ."

And she began crying.

"Vanya," she called, "Ivan Andreitch!"

There was no answer. Thinking that Laevsky had come in and was standing behind her chair, she sobbed like a child, and said:

"Why did you not tell me before that he was dead? I wouldn't have gone to the picnic; I shouldn't have laughed so horribly. . . . The men said horrid things to me. What a sin, what a sin! Save me, Vanya, save me. . . . I have been mad. . . . I am lost. . . ."

Laevsky heard her sobs. He felt stifled and his heart was beating violently. In his misery he got up, stood in the middle of the room, groped his way in the dark to an easy-chair by the table, and sat down.

"This is a prison . . ." he thought. "I must get away. . . . I can't bear it."

It was too late to go and play cards; there were no restaurants in the town. He lay down again and covered his ears that he might not hear her sobbing, and he suddenly remembered that he could go to Samoylenko. To avoid going near Nadyezhda Fyodorovna, he got out of the window into the garden, climbed over the garden fence, and went along the street. It was dark. A steamer, judging by its lights, a big passenger one, had just come in. . . . He heard the clank of the anchor chain. A red light was moving rapidly from the shore in the direction of the steamer: it was the Customs boat going out to it.

"The passengers are asleep in their cabins . . ." thought Laevsky, and he envied the peace of mind of other people.

The windows in Samoylenko's house were open. Laevsky looked in at one of them, then in at another; it was dark and still in the rooms.

"Alexandr Daviditch, are you asleep?" he called. "Alexandr Daviditch!"

He heard a cough and an uneasy shout:

"Who's there? What the devil?"

"It is I, Alexandr Daviditch; excuse me."

A little later the door opened; there was a glow of soft light from the lamp, and Samoylenko's huge figure appeared, all in white, with a white nightcap on his head.

"What now?" he asked, scratching himself and breathing hard from sleepiness. "Wait a minute; I'll open the door directly."

"Don't trouble; I'll get in at the window. . . ."

Laevsky climbed in at the window, and when he reached Samoylenko, seized him by the hand.

"Alexandr Daviditch," he said in a shaking voice, "save me! I beseech you, I implore you. Understand me! My position is agonizing. If it goes on for another two days I shall strangle myself like . . . like a dog."

"Wait a bit. . . . What are you talking about exactly?"

"Light a candle."

"Oh . . . oh! . . ." sighed Samoylenko, lighting a candle. "My God! My God! . . . Why, it's past one, brother."

"Excuse me, but I can't stay at home," said Laevsky, feeling great comfort from the light and the presence of Samoylenko. "You are my best, my only friend, Alexandr Daviditch. . . . You are my only hope. For God's sake, come to my rescue, whether you want to or not. I must get away from here, come what may! . . . Lend me the money!"

"Oh, my God, my God! . . ." sighed Samoylenko, scratching himself. "I was dropping asleep and I hear the whistle of the steamer, and now you . . . Do you want much?"

"Three hundred roubles at least. I must leave her a hundred, and I need two hundred for the journey. . . . I owe you about four hundred already, but I will send it you all . . . all. . . ."

Samoylenko took hold of both his whiskers in one hand, and standing with his legs wide apart, pondered.

"Yes . . ." he muttered, musing. "Three hundred. . . . Yes. . . . But I haven't got so much. I shall have to borrow it from someone."

"Borrow it, for God's sake!" said Laevsky, seeing from Samoylenko's face that he wanted to lend him the money and certainly would lend it. "Borrow it, and I'll be sure to pay you back. I will send it from Petersburg as soon as I get there. You can set your mind at rest about that. I'll tell you what, Sasha," he said, growing more animated; "let us have some wine."

"Yes . . . we can have some wine, too."

They both went into the dining-room.

"And how about Nadyezhda Fyodorovna?" asked Samoylenko, setting three bottles and a plate of peaches on the table. "Surely she's not remaining?"

"I will arrange it all, I will arrange it all," said Laevsky, feeling an unexpected rush of joy. "I will send her the money afterwards and she will join me. . . . Then we will define our relations. To your health, friend."

"Wait a bit," said Samoylenko. "Drink this first. . . . This is from my vineyard. This bottle is from Navaridze's vineyard and this one is from Ahatulov's. . . . Try all three kind and tell me candidly. . . . There seems a little acidity about mine. Eh? Don't you taste it?"

"Yes. You have comforted me, Alexandr Daviditch. Thank you. . . . I feel better."

"Is there any acidity?"

"Goodness only knows, I don't know. But you are a splendid, wonderful man!"

Looking at his pale, excited, good-natured face, Samoylenko remembered Von Koren's view that men like that ought to be destroyed, and Laevsky seemed to him a weak, defenceless child, whom any one could injure and destroy.

"And when you go, make it up with your mother," he said. "It's not right."

"Yes, yes; I certainly shall."

They were silent for a while. When they had emptied the first bottle, Samoylenko said:

"You ought to make it up with Von Koren too. You are both such splendid, clever fellows, and you glare at each other like wolves."

"Yes, he's a fine, very intelligent fellow," Laevsky assented, ready now to praise and forgive everyone. "He's a remarkable man, but it's impossible for me to get on with him. No! Our natures are too different. I'm an indolent, weak, submissive nature. Perhaps in a good minute I might hold out my hand to him, but he would turn away from me . . . with contempt."

Laevsky took a sip of wine, walked from corner to corner and went on, standing in the middle of the room:

"I understand Von Koren very well. His is a resolute, strong, despotic nature. You have heard him continually talking of 'the expedition,' and it's not mere talk. He wants the wilderness, the moonlit night: all around in little tents, under the open sky, lie sleeping his sick and hungry Cossacks, guides, porters, doctor, priest, all exhausted with their weary marches, while only he is awake, sitting like Stanley on a camp-stool, feeling himself the monarch of the desert and the master of these men. He goes on and on and on, his men groan and die, one after another, and he goes on and on, and in the end perishes himself, but still is monarch and ruler of the desert, since the cross upon his tomb can be seen by the caravans for thirty or forty miles over the desert. I am sorry the man is not in the army. He would have made a splendid military genius. He would not have hesitated to drown his cavalry in the river and make a bridge out of dead bodies. And such hardihood is more needed in war than any kind of fortification or strategy. Oh, I understand him perfectly! Tell me: why is he wasting his substance here? What does he want here?"

"He is studying the marine fauna."

"No, no, brother, no!" Leavsky sighed. "A scientific man who was on the steamer told me the Black Sea was poor in animal life, and that in its depths, thanks to the abundance of sulphuric hydrogen, organic life was impossible. All the serious zoologists work at the biological station at Naples or Villefranche. But Von Koren is independent and obstinate: he works on the Black Sea because nobody else is working there; he is at loggerheads with the university, does not care to know his comrades and other scientific men because he is first of all a despot and only secondly a zoologist. And you'll see he'll do something. He is already dreaming that when he comes back from his expedition he will purify our universities from intrigue and mediocrity, and will make the scientific men mind their p's and q's.

Despotism is just as strong in science as in the army. And he is spending his second summer in this stinking little town because he would rather be first in a village than second in a town. Here he is a king and an eagle; he keeps all the inhabitants under his thumb and oppresses them with his authority. He has appropriated everyone, he meddles in other people's affairs; everything is of use to him, and everyone is afraid of him. I am slipping out of his clutches, he feels that and hates me. Hasn't he told you that I ought to be destroyed or sent to hard labour?"

"Yes," laughed Samoylenko.

Laevsky laughed too, and drank some wine.

"His ideals are despotic too," he said, laughing, and biting a peach. "Ordinary mortals think of their neighbour—me, you, man in fact—if they work for the common weal. To Von Koren men are puppets and nonentities, too trivial to be the object of his life. He works, will go for his expedition and break his neck there, not for the sake of love for his neighbour, but for the sake of such abstractions as humanity, future generations, an ideal race of men. He exerts himself for the improvement of the human race, and we are in his eyes only slaves, food for the cannon, beasts of burden; some he would destroy or stow away in Siberia, others he would break by discipline, would, like Araktcheev, force them to get up and go to bed to the sound of the drum; would appoint eunuchs to preserve our chastity and morality, would order them to fire at anyone who steps out of the circle of our narrow conservative morality; and all this in the name of the improvement of the human race. . . . And what is the human race? Illusion, mirage . . . despots have always been illusionists. I understand him very well, brother. I appreciate him and don't deny his importance; this world rests on men like him, and if the world were left only to such men as us, for all our good-nature and good intentions, we should make as great a mess of it as the flies have of that picture. Yes."

Laevsky sat down beside Samoylenko, and said with genuine feeling: "I'm a foolish, worthless, depraved man. The air I breathe, this wine, love, life in fact—for all that, I have given nothing in exchange so far but lying, idleness, and cowardice. Till now I have deceived myself and other people; I have been miserable about it, and my misery was cheap and common. I bow my back humbly before Von Koren's hatred because at times I hate and despise myself."

Laevsky began again pacing from one end of the room to the other in excitement, and said:

"I'm glad I see my faults clearly and am conscious of them. That will help me to reform and become a different man. My dear fellow, if only you knew how passionately, with what anguish, I long for such a change. And I swear to you I'll be a man! I will! I don't know whether it is the wine that is speaking in me, or whether it really is so, but it seems to me that it is long since I have spent such pure and lucid moments as I have just now with you."

"It's time to sleep, brother," said Samoylenko.

"Yes, yes. . . . Excuse me; I'll go directly."

Laevsky moved hurriedly about the furniture and windows, looking for his cap.

"Thank you," he muttered, sighing. "Thank you. . . . Kind and friendly words are better than charity. You have given me new life."

He found his cap, stopped, and looked guiltily at Samoylenko.

"Alexandr Daviditch," he said in an imploring voice.

"What is it?"

"Let me stay the night with you, my dear fellow!"

"Certainly. . . . Why not?"

Laevsky lay down on the sofa, and went on talking to the doctor for a long time.

X

Three days after the picnic, Marya Konstantinovna unexpectedly called on Nadyezhda Fyodorovna, and without greeting her or taking off her hat, seized her by both hands, pressed them to her breast and said in great excitement:

"My dear, I am deeply touched and moved: our dear kind-hearted doctor told my Nikodim Alexandritch yesterday that your husband was dead. Tell me, my dear . . . tell me, is it true?"

"Yes, it's true; he is dead," answered Nadyezhda Fyodorovna.

"That is awful, awful, my dear! But there's no evil without some compensation; your husband was no doubt a noble, wonderful, holy man, and such are more needed in Heaven than on earth."

Every line and feature in Marya Konstantinovna's face began quivering as though little needles were jumping up and down under her skin; she gave an almond-oily smile and said, breathlessly, enthusiastically:

"And so you are free, my dear. You can hold your head high now, and look people boldly in the face. Henceforth God and man will bless your union with Ivan Andreitch. It's enchanting. I am trembling with joy, I can find no words. My dear, I will give you away. . . . Nikodim Alexandritch and I have been so fond of you, you will allow us to give our blessing to your pure, lawful union. When, when do you think of being married?"

"I haven't thought of it," said Nadyezhda Fyodorovna, freeing her hands.

"That's impossible, my dear. You have thought of it, you have."

"Upon my word, I haven't," said Nadyezhda Fyodorovna, laughing. "What should we be married for? I see no necessity for it. We'll go on living as we have lived."

"What are you saying!" cried Marya Konstantinovna in horror. "For God's sake, what are you saying!"

"Our getting married won't make things any better. On the contrary, it will make them even worse. We shall lose our freedom."

"My dear, my dear, what are you saying!" exclaimed Marya Konstantinovna, stepping back and flinging up her hands. "You are talking wildly! Think what you are saying. You must settle down!"

" 'Settle down.' How do you mean? I have not lived yet, and you tell me to settle down."

Nadyezhda Fyodorovna reflected that she really had not lived. She had finished her studies in a boarding-school and had been married to a man she did not love; then she had thrown in her lot with Laevsky, and had spent all her time with him on this empty, desolate coast, always expecting something better. Was that life?

"I ought to be married though," she thought, but remembering Kirilin and Atchmianov she flushed and said:

"No, it's impossible. Even if Ivan Andreitch begged me to on his knees— even then I would refuse."

Marya Konstantinovna sat on the sofa for a minute in silence, grave and mournful, gazing fixedly into space; then she got up and said coldly:

"Good-bye, my dear! Forgive me for having troubled you. Though it's not easy for me, it's my duty to tell you that from this day all is over between us, and, in spite of my profound respect for Ivan Andreitch, the door of my house is closed to you henceforth."

She uttered these words with great solemnity and was herself overwhelmed by her solemn tone. Her face began quivering again; it assumed a soft almond-oily expression. She held out both hands to Nadyezhda Fyodorovna, who was overcome with alarm and confusion, and said in an imploring voice:

"My dear, allow me if only for a moment to be a mother or an elder sister to you! I will be as frank with you as a mother."

Nadyezhda Fyodorovna felt in her bosom warmth, gladness, and pity for herself, as though her own mother had really risen up and were standing before her. She impulsively embraced Marya Konstantinovna and pressed her face to her shoulder. Both of them shed tears. They sat down on the sofa and for a few minutes sobbed without looking at one another or being able to utter a word.

"My dear child," began Marya Konstantinovna, "I will tell you some harsh truths, without sparing you."

"For God's sake, for God's sake, do!"

"Trust me, my dear. You remember of all the ladies here, I was the only one to receive you. You horrified me from the very first day, but I had not the heart to treat you with disdain like all the rest. I grieved over dear, good Ivan Andreitch as though he were my son—a young man in a strange place, inexperienced, weak, with no mother; and I was worried, dreadfully worried. . . . My husband was opposed to our making his acquaintance, but I talked him over . . . persuaded him. . . . We began receiving Ivan Andreitch, and with him, of course, you. If we had not, he would have been insulted. I have a daughter, a son. . . . You understand the tender mind, the pure heart of childhood . . . 'whoso offendeth one of these little ones.' . . . I received you into my house and trembled for my children. Oh, when you become a mother, you will understand my fears. And everyone was surprised at my receiving you, excuse my saying so, as a respectable woman, and hinted to me . . . well, of course, slanders, suppositions. . . . At the bottom of my heart I blamed you, but you were unhappy, flighty, to be pitied, and my heart was wrung with pity for you."

"But why, why?" asked Nadyezhda Fyodorovna, trembling all over. "What harm have I done anyone?"

"You are a terrible sinner. You broke the vow you made your husband at the altar. You seduced a fine young man, who perhaps had he not met you might have taken a lawful partner for life from a good family in his own circle, and would have been like everyone else now. You have ruined his youth. Don't speak, don't speak, my dear! I never believe that man is to blame for our sins. It is always the woman's fault. Men are frivolous in domestic life; they are guided by their minds, and not by their hearts. There's a great deal they don't understand; woman understands it all. Everything depends on her. To her much is given and from her much will be required. Oh, my dear, if she had been more foolish or weaker than man on that side, God would not have entrusted her with the education of boys and girls. And then, my dear, you entered on the path of vice, forgetting all modesty; any other woman in your place would have hidden herself from people, would have sat shut up at home, and would only have been seen in the temple of God, pale, dressed all in black and weeping, and everyone would have said in genuine compassion: 'O Lord, this erring angel is coming back again to Thee. . . .' But you, my dear, have forgotten all discretion; have lived openly, extravagantly; have seemed to be proud of your sin; you have been gay and laughing, and I, looking at you, shuddered with horror, and have been afraid that thunder from Heaven would strike our home while you were sitting with us. My dear, don't speak, don't speak," cried Marya Konstantinovna, observing that Nadyezhda Fyodorovna wanted to speak. "Trust me, I will not deceive you, I will not hide one truth from the eyes of your soul. Listen to me, my dear. . . . God marks great sinners, and you have been marked out: only think—your costumes have always been appalling."

Nadyezhda Fyodorovna, who had always had the highest opinion of her costumes, left off crying and looked at her with surprise.

"Yes, appalling," Marya Konstantinovna went on. "Anyone could judge of your behaviour from the elaboration and gaudiness of your attire. People laughed and shrugged their shoulders as they looked at you, and I grieved, I grieved. . . . And forgive me, my dear; you are not nice in your person! When we met in the bathing-place, you made me tremble. Your outer clothing was decent enough, but your petticoat, your chemise. . . . My dear, I blushed! Poor Ivan Andreitch! No one ever ties his cravat properly, and from his linen and his boots, poor fellow! one can see he has no one at home to look after him. And he is always hungry, my darling, and of course, if there is no one at home to think of the samovar and the coffee, one is forced to spend half one's salary at the pavilion. And it's simply awful, awful in your home! No one else in the town has flies, but there's no getting rid of them in your rooms: all the plates and dishes are black with them. If you look at the windows and the chairs, there's nothing but dust, dead flies, and glasses. . . . What do you want glasses standing about for? And, my dear, the table's not cleared till this time in the day. And one's ashamed to go into your bedroom: underclothes flung about everywhere, india-rubber tubes hanging on the walls, pails and basins standing about. . . . My dear! A husband ought to know nothing, and his wife ought to be as neat as a little angel in his presence. I wake up every morning before it is light, and wash my face with cold water that my Nikodim Alexandritch may not see me looking drowsy."

"That's all nonsense," Nadyezhda Fyodorovna sobbed. "If only I were happy, but I am so unhappy!"

"Yes, yes; you are very unhappy!" Marya Konstantinovna sighed, hardly able to restrain herself from weeping. "And there's terrible grief in store for you in the future! A solitary old age, ill-health; and then you will have to answer at the dread judgment seat. . . . It's awful, awful. Now fate itself holds out to you a helping hand, and you madly thrust it from you. Be married, make haste and be married!"

"Yes, we must, we must," said Nadyezhda Fyodorovna; "but it's impossible!"

"Why?"

"It's impossible. Oh, if only you knew!"

Nadyezhda Fyodorovna had an impulse to tell her about Kirilin, and how the evening before she had met handsome young Atchmianov at the harbour, and how the mad, ridiculous idea had occurred to her of cancelling her debt for three hundred; it had amused her very much, and she returned home late in the evening feeling that she had sold herself and was irrevocably lost. She did not know herself how it had happened. And she longed to swear to Marya Konstantinovna that she would certainly pay that debt, but sobs and shame prevented her from speaking. "I am going away," she said. "Ivan Andreitch may stay, but I am going."

"Where?"

"To Russia."

"But how will you live there? Why, you have nothing."

"I will do translation, or . . . or I will open a library. . . ."

"Don't let your fancy run away with you, my dear. You must have money for a library. Well, I will leave you now, and you calm yourself and think things over, and to-morrow come and see me, bright and happy. That will be enchanting! Well, good-bye, my angel. Let me kiss you."

Marya Konstantinovna kissed Nadyezhda Fyodorovna on the forehead, made the sign of the cross over her, and softly withdrew. It was getting dark, and Olga lighted up in the kitchen. Still crying, Nadyezhda Fyodorovna went into the bedroom and lay down on the bed. She began to be very feverish. She undressed without getting up, crumpled up her clothes at her feet, and curled herself up under the bedclothes. She was thirsty, and there was no one to give her something to drink.

"I'll pay it back!" she said to herself, and it seemed to her in delirium that she was sitting beside some sick woman, and recognized her as herself. "I'll pay it back. It would be stupid to imagine that it was for money I . . . I will go away and send him the money from Petersburg. At first a hundred . . . then another hundred . . . and then the third hundred. . . ."

It was late at night when Laevsky came in.

"At first a hundred . . ." Nadyezhda Fyodorovna said to him, "then another hundred . . ."

"You ought to take some quinine," he said, and thought, "To-morrow is Wednesday; the steamer goes and I am not going in it. So I shall have to go on living here till Saturday."

Nadyezhda Fyodorovna knelt up in bed.

"I didn't say anything just now, did I?" she asked, smiling and screwing up her eyes at the light.

"No, nothing. We shall have to send for the doctor to-morrow morning. Go to sleep."

He took his pillow and went to the door. Even since he had finally made up his mind to go away and leave Nadyezhda Fyodorovna, she had begun to raise in him pity and a sense of guilt; he felt a little ashamed in her presence, as though in the presence of a sick or old horse whom one has decided to kill. He stopped in the doorway and looked round at her.

"I was out of humour at the picnic and said something rude to you. For-give me, for God's sake!"

Saying this, he went off to his study, lay down, and for a long while could not get to sleep.

Next morning when Samoylenko, attired, as it was a holiday, in full-dress uniform with epaulettes on his shoulders and decorations on his breast, came out of the bedroom after feeling Nadyezhda Fyodorovna's pulse and looking at her tongue, Laevsky, who was standing in the doorway, asked him anxiously: "Well? Well?"

There was an expression of terror, of extreme uneasiness, and of hope on his face.

"Don't worry yourself; there's nothing dangerous," said Samoylenko, "it's the usual fever."

"I don't mean that." Laevsky frowned impatiently. "Have you got the money?"

"My dear soul, forgive me," he whispered, looking round at the door and overcome with confusion. "For God's sake, forgive me! No one has any-thing to spare, and I've only been able to collect by five- and by ten-rouble notes. . . . Only a hundred and ten in all. To-day I'll speak to someone else. Have patience."

"But Saturday is the latest date," whispered Laevsky, trembling with im-patience. "By all that's sacred, get it by Saturday! If I don't get away by Saturday, nothing's any use, nothing! I can't understand how a doctor can be without money!"

"Lord have mercy on us!" Samoylenko whispered rapidly and intensely, and there was positively a breaking note in his throat. "I've been stripped of everything; I am owed seven thousand, and I'm in debt all round. Is it my fault?"

"Then you'll get it by Saturday? Yes?"

"I'll try."

"I implore you, my dear fellow! So that the money may be in my hands by Friday morning!"

Samoylenko sat down and prescribed solution of quinine and *kalii bromati* and tincture of rhubarb, *tincturæ gentianæ, aquæ fœniculi*—all in one mixture, added some pink syrup to sweeten it, and went away.

XI

"You look as though you were coming to arrest me," said Von Koren, seeing Samoylenko coming in, in his full-dress uniform.

"I was passing by and thought: 'Suppose I go in and pay my respects to zoology,' " said Samoylenko, sitting down at the big table, knocked together by the zoologist himself out of plain boards. "Good-morning, holy father," he said to the deacon, who was sitting in the window, copying something. "I'll stay a minute and then run home to see about dinner. It's time. . . . I'm not hindering you?"

"Not in the least," answered the zoologist, laying out over the table slips of paper covered with small writing. "We are busy copying."

"Ah! . . . Oh, my goodness, my goodness! . . ." sighed Samoylenko. He cautiously took up from the table a dusty book on which there was lying a dead dried spider, and said: "Only fancy, though; some little green beetle is going about its business, when suddenly a monster like this swoops down upon it. I can fancy its terror."

"Yes, I suppose so."

"Is poison given it to protect it from its enemies?"

"Yes, to protect it and enable it to attack."

"To be sure, to be sure. . . . And everything in nature, my dear fellows, is consistent and can be explained," sighed Samoylenko; "only I tell you what I don't understand. You're a man of very great intellect, so explain it to me, please. There are, you know, little beasts no bigger than rats, rather handsome to look at, but nasty and immoral in the extreme, let me tell you. Suppose such a little beast is running in the woods. He sees a bird; he catches it and devours it. He goes on and sees in the grass a nest of eggs; he does not want to eat them—he is not hungry, but yet he tastes one egg and scatters the others out of the nest with his paw. Then he meets a frog and begins to play with it; when he has tormented the frog he goes on licking himself and meets a beetle; he crushes the beetle with his paw . . . and so he spoils and destroys everything on his way. . . . He creeps into other beasts' holes, tears up the anthills, cracks the snail's shell. If he meets a rat, he fights with it; if he meets a snake or a mouse, he must strangle it; and so the whole day long. Come, tell me: what is the use of a beast like that? Why was he created?"

"I don't know what animal you are talking of," said Von Koren; "most likely one of the insectivora. Well, he got hold of the bird because it was incautious; he broke the nest of eggs because the bird was not skilful, had made the nest badly and did not know how to conceal it. The frog probably had some defect in its colouring or he would not have seen it, and so on. Your little beast only destroys the weak, the unskilful, the careless—in fact, those who have defects which nature does not think fit to hand on to posterity. Only the cleverer, the stronger, the more careful and developed survive; and so your little beast, without suspecting it, is serving the great ends of perfecting creation."

"Yes, yes, yes. . . . By the way, brother," said Samoylenko carelessly, "lend me a hundred roubles."

"Very good. There are some very interesting types among the insectivorous mammals. For instance, the mole is said to be useful because he devours noxious insects. There is a story that some German sent William I a fur coat made of moleskins, and the Emperor ordered him to be reproved for having destroyed so great a number of useful animals. And yet the mole is not a bit less cruel than your little beast, and is very mischievous besides, as he spoils meadows terribly."

Von Koren opened a box and took out a hundred-rouble note.

"The mole has a powerful thorax, just like the bat," he went on, shutting the box; "the bones and muscles are tremendously developed, the mouth is extraordinarily powerfully furnished. If it had the proportions of an elephant, it would be an all-destructive, invincible animal. It is interesting when two moles meet underground; they begin at once as though by agreement digging a little platform; they need the platform in order to have a battle more conveniently. When they have made it they enter upon a ferocious struggle and fight till the weaker one falls. Take the hundred roubles," said Von Koren, dropping his voice, "but only on condition that you're not borrowing it for Laevsky."

"And if it were for Laevsky," cried Samoylenko, flaring up, "what is that to you?"

"I can't give it to you for Laevsky. I know you like lending people money. You would give it to Kerim, the brigand, if he were to ask you; but, excuse me, I can't assist you in that direction."

"Yes, it is for Laevsky I am asking it," said Samoylenko, standing up and waving his right arm. "Yes! For Laevsky! And no one, fiend or devil, has a right to dictate to me how to dispose of my own money. It doesn't suit you to lend it me? No?"

The deacon began laughing.

"Don't get excited, but be reasonable," said the zoologist. "To shower benefits on Mr. Laevsky is, to my thinking, as senseless as to water weeds or to feed locusts."

"To my thinking, it is our duty to help our neighbours!" cried Samoylenko.

"In that case, help that hungry Turk who is lying under the fence! He is a workman and more useful and indispensable than your Laevsky. Give him that hundred-rouble note! Or subscribe a hundred roubles to my expedition!"

"Will you give me the money or not? I ask you!"

"Tell me openly: what does he want money for?"

"It's not a secret; he wants to go to Petersburg on Saturday."

"So that is it!" Von Koren drawled out. "Aha! . . . We understand. And is she going with him, or how is it to be?"

"She's staying here for the time. He'll arrange his affairs in Petersburg and send her the money, and then she'll go."

"That's smart!" said the zoologist, and he gave a short tenor laugh. "Smart, well planned."

He went rapidly up to Samoylenko, and standing face to face with him, and looking him in the eyes, asked: "Tell me now honestly: is he tired of her? Yes? tell me: is he tired of her? Yes?"

"Yes," Samoylenko articulated, beginning to perspire.

"How repulsive it is!" said Von Koren, and from his face it could be seen that he felt repulsion. "One of two things, Alexander Daviditch: either you are in the plot with him, or, excuse my saying so, you are a simpleton. Surely you must see that he is taking you in like a child in the most shameless way? Why, it's as clear as day that he wants to get rid of her and abandon her here. She'll be left a burden on you. It is as clear as day that you will have to send her to Petersburg at your expense. Surely your fine friend can't have so blinded you by his dazzling qualities that you can't see the simplest thing?"

"That's all supposition," said Samoylenko, sitting down.

"Supposition? But why is he going alone instead of taking her with him? And ask him why he doesn't send her off first. The sly beast!"

Overcome with sudden doubts and suspicions about his friend, Samoylenko weakened and took a humbler tone.

"But it's impossible," he said, recalling the night Laevsky had spent at his house. "He is so unhappy!"

"What of that? Thieves and incendiaries are unhappy too!"

"Even supposing you are right . . ." said Samoylenko, hesitating. "Let us admit it. . . . Still, he's a young man in a strange place . . . a student. We have been students, too, and there is no one but us to come to his assistance."

"To help him to do abominable things, because he and you at different times have been at universities, and neither of you did anything there! What nonsense!"

"Stop; let us talk it over coolly. I imagine it will be possible to make some arrangement. . . ." Samoylenko reflected, twiddling his fingers. "I'll give him the money, you see, but make him promise on his honour that within a week he'll send Nadyezhda Fyodorovna the money for the journey."

"And he'll give you his word of honour—in fact, he'll shed tears and believe in it himself; but what's his word of honour worth? He won't keep it, and when in a year or two you meet him on the Nevsky Prospect with a new mistress on his arm, he'll excuse himself on the ground that he has been crippled by civilization, and that he is made after the pattern of Rudin. Drop him, for God's sake! Keep away from the filth; don't stir it up with both hands!"

Samoylenko thought for a minute and said resolutely:

"But I shall give him the money all the same. As you please. I can't bring myself to refuse a man simply on an assumption."

"Very fine, too. You can kiss him if you like."

"Give me the hundred roubles, then," Samoylenko asked timidly.

"I won't."

A silence followed. Samoylenko was quite crushed; his face wore a guilty, abashed, and ingratiating expression, and it was strange to see this pitiful, childish, shamefaced countenance on a huge man wearing epaulettes and orders of merit.

"The bishop here goes the round of his diocese on horseback instead of in a carriage," said the deacon, laying down his pen. "It's extremely touching to see him sit on his horse. His simplicity and humility are full of Biblical grandeur."

"Is he a good man?" asked Von Koren, who was glad to change the conversation.

"Of course! If he hadn't been a good man, do you suppose he would have been consecrated a bishop?"

"Among the bishops are to be found good and gifted men," said Von Koren. "The only drawback is that some of them have the weakness to imagine themselves statesmen. One busies himself with Russification, another criticizes the sciences. That's not their business. They had much better look into their consistory a little."

"A layman cannot judge of bishops."

"Why so, deacon? A bishop is a man just the same as you or I."

"The same, but not the same." The deacon was offended and took up his pen. "If you had been the same, the Divine Grace would have rested upon you, and you would have been bishop yourself; and since you are not bishop, it follows you are not the same."

"Don't talk nonsense, deacon," said Samoylenko dejectedly. "Listen to what I suggest," he said, turning to Von Koren. "Don't give me that hundred roubles. You'll be having your dinners with me for three months before the winter, so let me have the money beforehand for three months."

"I won't."

Samoylenko blinked and turned crimson; he mechanically drew towards him the book with the spider on it and looked at it, then he got up and took his hat.

Von Koren felt sorry for him.

"What it is to have to live and do with people like this," said the zoologist, and he kicked a paper into the corner with indignation. "You must understand that this is not kindness, it is not love, but cowardice, slackness, poison! What's gained by reason is lost by your flabby good-for-nothing hearts! When I was ill with typhoid as a schoolboy, my aunt in her sympathy gave me pickled mushrooms to eat, and I very nearly died. You, and my aunt too, must understand that love for man is not to be found in the heart or the stomach or the bowels, but here!"

Von Koren slapped himself on the forehead.

"Take it," he said, and thrust a hundred-rouble note into his hand.

"You've no need to be angry, Kolya," said Samoylenko mildly, folding up the note. "I quite understand you, but . . . you must put yourself in my place."

"You are an old woman, that's what you are."

The deacon burst out laughing.

"Hear my last request, Alexandr Daviditch," said Von Koren hotly. "When you give that scoundrel the money, make it a condition that he takes his lady with him, or sends her on ahead, and don't give it him without. There's no need to stand on ceremony with him. Tell him so, or, if you don't, I give you my word I'll go to his office and kick him downstairs, and I'll break off all acquaintance with you. So you'd better know it."

"Well! To go with her or send her on beforehand will be more convenient for him," said Samoylenko. "He'll be delighted indeed. Well, good-bye."

He said good-bye affectionately and went out, but before shutting the door after him, he looked round at Von Koren and, with a ferocious face, said:

"It's the Germans who have ruined you, brother! Yes! The Germans!"

XII

Next day, Thursday, Marya Konstantinovna was celebrating the birthday of her Kostya. All were invited to come at midday and eat pies, and in the evening to drink chocolate. When Laevsky and Nadyezhda Fyodorovna arrived in the evening, the zoologist, who was already sitting in the drawing-room, drinking chocolate, asked Samoylenko:

"Have you talked to him?"

"Not yet."

"Mind now, don't stand on ceremony. I can't understand the insolence of these people! Why, they know perfectly well the view taken by this family of their cohabitation, and yet they force themselves in here."

"If one is to pay attention to every prejudice," said Samoylenko, "one could go nowhere."

"Do you mean to say that the repugnance felt by the masses for illicit love and moral laxity is a prejudice?"

"Of course it is. It's prejudice and hate. When the soldiers see a girl of light behaviour, they laugh and whistle; but just ask them what they are themselves."

"It's not for nothing they whistle. The fact that girls strangle their illegitimate children and go to prison for it, and that Anna Karenin flung herself under the train, and that in the villages they smear the gates with tar, and that you and I, without knowing why, are pleased by Katya's purity, and that every one of us feels a vague craving for pure love, though he knows there is no such love—is all that prejudice? That is the one thing, brother, which has survived intact from natural selection, and, if it were not for that obscure force regulating the relations of the sexes, the Laevskys would have it all their own way, and mankind would degenerate in two years."

Laevsky came into the drawing-room, greeted everyone, and shaking hands with Von Koren, smiled ingratiatingly. He waited for a favourable moment and said to Samoylenko:

"Excuse me, Alexandr Daviditch, I must say two words to you."

Samoylenko got up, put his arm round Laevsky's waist, and both of them went into Nikodim Alexandritch's study.

"To-morrow's Friday," said Laevsky, biting his nails. "Have you got what you promised?"

"I've only got two hundred. I'll get the rest to-day or to-morrow. Don't worry yourself."

"Thank God . . ." sighed Laevsky, and his hands began trembling with joy. "You are saving me, Alexandr Daviditch, and I swear to you by God, by my happiness and anything you like, I'll send you the money as soon as I arrive. And I'll send you my old debt too."

"Look here, Vanya . . ." said Samoylenko, turning crimson and taking him by the button. "You must forgive my meddling in your private affairs, but . . . why shouldn't you take Nadyezhda Fyodorovna with you?"

"You queer fellow. How is that possible? One of us must stay, or our creditors will raise an outcry. You see, I owe seven hundred or more to the shops. Only wait, and I will send them the money. I'll stop their mouths, and then she can come away."

"I see. . . . But why shouldn't you send her on first?"

"My goodness, as though that were possible!" Laevsky was horrified. "Why, she's a woman; what would she do there alone? What does she know about it? That would only be a loss of time and a useless waste of money."

"That's reasonable . . ." thought Samoylenko, but remembering his conversation with Von Koren, he looked down and said sullenly: "I can't agree with you. Either go with her or send her first; otherwise . . . otherwise I won't give you the money. Those are my last words. . . ."

He staggered back, lurched backwards against the door, and went into the drawing room, crimson, and overcome with confusion.

"Friday . . . Friday," thought Laevsky, going back into the drawing-room. "Friday. . . ."

He was handed a cup of chocolate; he burnt his lips and tongue with the scalding chocolate and thought: "Friday . . . Friday. . . ."

For some reason he could not get the word "Friday" out of his head; he could think of nothing but Friday, and the only thing that was clear to him, not in his brain but somewhere in his heart, was that he would not get off on Saturday. Before him stood Nikodim Alexandritch, very neat, with his hair combed over his temples, saying:

"Please take something to eat. . . ."

Marya Konstantinovna showed the visitors Katya's school report and said, drawling:

"It's very, very difficult to do well at school nowadays! So much is expected . . ."

"Mamma!" groaned Katya, not knowing where to hide her confusion at the praises of the company.

Laevsky, too, looked at the report and praised it. Scripture, Russian language, conduct, fives and fours, danced before his eyes, and all this, mixed with the haunting refrain of "Friday," with the carefully combed locks of Nikodim Alexandritch and the red cheeks of Katya, produced on him a sensation of such immense overwhelming boredom that he almost shrieked with despair and asked himself: "Is it possible, is it possible I shall not get away?"

They put two card tables side by side and sat down to play post. Laevsky sat down too.

"Friday . . . Friday . . ." he kept thinking, as he smiled and took a pencil out of his pocket. "Friday. . . ."

He wanted to think over his position, and was afraid to think. It was terrible to him to realize that the doctor had detected him in the deception which he had so long and carefully concealed from himself. Every time he thought of his future he would not let his thoughts have full rein. He would get into the train and set off, and thereby the problem of his life would be solved, and he did not let his thoughts go farther. Like a far-away dim light in the fields, the thought sometimes flickered in his mind that in one of the side-streets of Petersburg, in the remote future, he would have to have recourse to a tiny lie in order to get rid of Nadyezhda Fyodorovna and pay his debts; he would tell a lie only once, and then a completely new life would begin. And that was right: at the price of a small lie he would win so much truth.

Now when by his blunt refusal the doctor had crudely hinted at his deception, he began to understand that he would need deception not only in the remote future, but to-day, and to-morrow, and in a month's time, and perhaps up to the very end of his life. In fact, in order to get away he would have to lie to Nadyezhda Fyodorovna, to his creditors, and to his superiors in the Service; then, in order to get money in Petersburg, he would have to lie to his mother, to tell her that he had already broken with Nadyezhda Fyodorovna; and his mother would not give him more than five hundred roubles, so he had already deceived the doctor, as he would not be in a position to pay him back the money within a short time. Afterwards when Nadyezhda Fyodorovna came to Petersburg, he would have to resort to a regular series of deceptions, little and big, in order to get free of her; and again there would be tears, boredom, a disgusting existence, remorse, and so there would be no new life. Deception and nothing more. A whole mountain of lies rose before Laevsky's imagination. To leap over it at one bound and not to do his lying piecemeal, he would have to bring himself to stern, uncompromising action; for instance, to getting up without saying a word, putting on his hat, and at once setting off without money and without explanation. But Laevsky felt that was impossible for him.

"Friday, Friday . . ." he thought. "Friday. . . ."

They wrote little notes, folded them in two, and put them in Nikodim Alexandritch's old top-hat. When there were a sufficient heap of notes, Kostya, who acted the part of postman, walked round the table and delivered them. The deacon, Katya, and Kostya, who received amusing notes and tried to write as funnily as they could, were highly delighted.

"We must have a little talk," Nadyezhda Fyodorovna read in a little note; she glanced at Marya Konstantinovna, who gave her an almond-oily smile and nodded.

"Talk of what?" thought Nadyezhda Fyodorovna. "If one can't tell the whole, it's no use talking."

Before going out for the evening she had tied Laevsky's cravat for him, and that simple action filled her soul with tenderness and sorrow. The anxiety in his face, his absent-minded looks, his pallor, and the incomprehensible change that had taken place in him of late, and the fact that she had a terrible revolting secret from him, and the fact that her hands trembled when she tied his cravat—all this seemed to tell her that they had not long left to be together. She looked at him as though he were an ikon, with terror and penitence, and thought: "Forgive, forgive."

Opposite her was sitting Atchmianov, and he never took his black, love-sick eyes off her. She was stirred by passion; she was ashamed of herself, and afraid that even her misery and sorrow would not prevent her from yielding to impure desire to-morrow, if not to-day—and that, like a drunkard, she would not have the strength to stop herself.

She made up her mind to go away that she might not continue this life, shameful for herself, and humiliating for Laevsky. She would beseech him with tears to let her go; and if he opposed her, she would go away secretly. She would not tell him what had happened; let him keep a pure memory of her.

"I love you, I love you, I love you," she read. It was from Atchmianov.

She would live in some far remote place, would work and send Laevsky, "anonymously," money, embroidered shirts, and tobacco, and would return to him only in old age or if he were dangerously ill and needed a nurse. When in his old age he learned what were her reasons for leaving him and refusing to be his wife, he would appreciate her sacrifice and forgive.

"You've got a long nose." That must be from the deacon or Kostya.

Nadyezhda Fyodorovna imagined how, parting from Laevsky, she would embrace him warmly, would kiss his hand, and would swear to love him all her life, all her life, and then, living in obscurity among strangers, she would every day think that somewhere she had a friend, someone she loved—a pure, noble, lofty man who kept a pure memory of her.

"If you don't give me an interview to-day, I shall take measures, I assure you on my word of honour. You can't treat decent people like this; you must understand that." That was from Kirilin.

XIII

Laevsky received two notes; he opened one and read: "Don't go away, my darling."

"Who could have written that?" he thought. "Not Samoylenko, of course. And not the deacon, for he doesn't know I want to go away. Von Koren, perhaps?"

The zoologist bent over the table and drew a pyramid. Laevsky fancied that his eyes were smiling.

"Most likely Samoylenko . . . has been gossiping," thought Laevsky.

In the other note, in the same disguised angular handwriting with long tails to the letters, was written: "Somebody won't go away on Saturday."

"A stupid gibe," thought Laevsky. "Friday, Friday. . . ."

Something rose in his throat. He touched his collar and coughed, but instead of a cough a laugh broke from his throat.

"Ha-ha-ha!" he laughed. "Ha-ha-ha! What am I laughing at? Ha-ha-ha!"

He tried to restrain himself, covered his mouth with his hand, but the laugh choked his chest and throat, and his hand could not cover his mouth.

"How stupid it is!" he thought, rolling with laughter. "Have I gone out of my mind?"

The laugh grew shriller and shriller, and became something like the bark of a lap-dog. Laevsky tried to get up from the table, but his legs would not obey him and his right hand was strangely, without his volition, dancing on the table, convulsively clutching and crumpling up the bits of paper. He saw looks of wonder, Samoylenko's grave, frightened face, and the eyes of the zoologist full of cold irony and disgust, and realized that he was in hysterics.

"How hideous, how shameful!" he thought, feeling the warmth of tears on his face. ". . . Oh, oh, what a disgrace! It has never happened to me. . . ."

They took him under his arms, and supporting his head from behind, led him away; a glass gleamed before his eyes and knocked against his teeth, and the water was spilt on his breast; he was in a little room, with two beds in the middle, side by side, covered by two snow-white quilts. He dropped on one of the beds and sobbed.

"It's nothing, it's nothing," Samoylenko kept saying; "it does happen . . . it does happen. . . ."

Chill with horror, trembling all over and dreading something awful, Nadyezhda Fyodorovna stood by the bedside and kept asking:

"What is it? What is it? For God's sake, tell me."

"Can Kirilin have written him something?" she thought.

"It's nothing," said Laevsky, laughing and crying; "go away, darling."

His face expressed neither hatred nor repulsion: so he knew nothing; Nadyezhda Fyodorovna was somewhat reassured, and she went into the drawing-room.

"Don't agitate yourself, my dear!" said Marya Konstantinovna, sitting down beside her and taking her hand. "It will pass. Men are just as weak as we poor sinners. You are both going through a crisis. . . . One can so well understand it! Well, my dear, I am waiting for an answer. Let us have a little talk."

"No, we are not going to talk," said Nadyezhda Fyodorovna, listening to Laevsky's sobs. "I feel depressed. . . . You must allow me to go home."

"What do you mean, what do you mean, my dear?" cried Marya Konstantinovna in alarm. "Do you think I could let you go without supper? We will have something to eat, and then you may go with my blessing."

"I feel miserable . . ." whispered Nadyezhda Fyodorovna, and she caught at the arm of the chair with both hands to avoid falling.

"He's got a touch of hysterics," said Von Koren gaily, coming into the drawing-room, but seeing Nadyezhda Fyodorovna, he was taken aback and retreated.

When the attack was over, Laevsky sat on the strange bed and thought.

"Disgraceful! I've been howling like some wretched girl! I must have been absurd and disgusting. I will go away by the back stairs. . . . But that would seem as though I took my hysterics too seriously. I ought to take it as a joke. . . ."

He looked in the looking-glass, sat there for some time, and went back into the drawing-room.

"Here I am," he said, smiling; he felt agonizingly ashamed, and he felt others were ashamed in his presence. "Fancy such a thing happening," he said, sitting down. "I was sitting here, and all of a sudden, do you know, I felt a terrible piercing pain in my side . . . unendurable, my nerves could not stand it, and . . . and it led to this silly performance. This is the age of nerves; there is no help for it."

At supper he drank some wine, and, from time to time, with an abrupt sigh rubbed his side as though to suggest that he still felt the pain. And no one, except Nadyezhda Fyodorovna, believed him, and he saw that.

After nine o'clock they went for a walk on the boulevard. Nadyezhda Fyodorovna, afraid that Kirilin would speak to her, did her best to keep all the time beside Marya Konstantinovna and the children. She felt weak with fear and misery, and felt she was going to be feverish; she was exhausted and her legs would hardly move, but she did not go home, because she felt sure that she would be followed by Kirilin or Atchmianov or both at once. Kirilin walked behind her with Nikodim Alexandritch, and kept humming in an undertone:

"I don't al-low people to play with me: I don't al-low it."

From the boulevard they went back to the pavilion and walked along the beach, and looked for a long time at the phosphorescence on the water. Von Koren began telling them why it looked phosphorescent.

XIV

"It's time I went to my *vint*. . . . They will be waiting for me," said Laevsky. "Good-bye, my friends."

"I'll come with you; wait a minute," said Nadyezhda Fyodorovna, and she took his arm.

They said good-bye to the company and went away. Kirilin took leave too, and saying that he was going the same way, went along beside them.

"What will be, will be," thought Nadyezhda Fyodorovna. "So be it. . . ."

And it seemed to her that all the evil memories in her head had taken shape and were walking beside her in the darkness, breathing heavily, while she, like a fly that had fallen into the inkpot, was crawling painfully along the pavement and smirching Laevsky's side and arm with blackness.

If Kirilin should do anything horrid, she thought, not he but she would be to blame for it. There was a time when no man would have talked to her as Kirilin had done, and she had torn up her security like a thread and destroyed it irrevocably—who was to blame for it? Intoxicated by her passions she had smiled at a complete stranger, probably just because he was tall and a fine figure. After two meetings she was weary of him, had thrown him over, and did not that, she thought now, give him the right to treat her as he chose?

"Here I'll say good-bye to you, darling," said Laevsky. "Ilya Mihalitch will see you home."

He nodded to Kirilin, and, quickly crossing the boulevard, walked along the street to Sheshkovsky's, where there were lights in the windows, and then they heard the gate bang as he went in.

"Allow me to have an explanation with you," said Kirilin. "I'm not a boy, not some Atchkasov or Latchkasov, Zatchkasov. . . . I demand serious attention."

Nadyezhda Fyodorovna's heart began beating violently. She made no reply.

"The abrupt change in your behaviour to me I put down at first to coquetry," Kirilin went on; "now I see that you don't know how to behave with gentlemanly people. You simply wanted to play with me, as you are playing with that wretched Armenian boy; but I'm a gentleman and I insist on being treated like a gentleman. And so I am at your service. . . ."

"I'm miserable," said Nadyezhda Fyodorovna beginning to cry, and to hide her tears she turned away.

"I'm miserable too," said Kirilin, "but what of that?"

Kirilin was silent for a space, then he said distinctly and emphatically:

"I repeat, madam, that if you do not give me an interview this evening, I'll make a scandal this very evening."

"Let me off this evening," said Nadyezhda Fyodorovna, and she did not recognize her own voice, it was so weak and pitiful.

"I must give you a lesson. . . . Excuse me for the roughness of my tone, but it's necessary to give you a lesson. Yes, I regret to say I must give you a lesson. I insist on two interviews—to-day and to-morrow. After to-morrow you are perfectly free and can go wherever you like with anyone you choose. To-day and to-morrow."

Nadyezhda Fyodorovna went up to her gate and stopped.

"Let me go," she murmured, trembling all over and seeing nothing before her in the darkness but his white tunic. "You're right: I'm a horrible woman. . . . I'm to blame, but let me go . . . I beg you." She touched his cold hand and shuddered. "I beseech you. . . ."

"Alas!" sighed Kirilin, "alas! it's not part of my plan to let you go; I only mean to give you a lesson and make you realize. And what's more, madam, I've too little faith in women."

"I'm miserable. . . ."

Nadyezhda Fyodorovna listened to the even splash of the sea, looked at the sky studded with stars, and longed to make haste and end it all, and get away from the cursed sensation of life, with its sea, stars, men, fever.

"Only not in my home," she said coldly. "Take me somewhere else."

"Come to Muridov's. That's better."

"Where's that?"

"Near the old wall."

She walked quickly along the street and then turned into the side-street that led towards the mountains. It was dark. There were pale streaks of light here and there on the pavement, from the lighted windows, and it seemed to her that, like a fly, she kept falling into the ink and crawling out into the light again. At one point he stumbled, almost fell down and burst out laughing.

"He's drunk," thought Nadyezhda Fyodorovna. "Never mind. . . . Never mind. . . . So be it."

Atchmianov, too, soon took leave of the party and followed Nadyezhda Fyodorovna to ask her to go for a row. He went to her house and looked over the fence: the windows were wide open, there were no lights.

"Nadyezhda Fyodorovna!" he called.

A moment passed, he called again.

"Who's there?" he heard Olga's voice.

"Is Nadyezhda Fyodorovna at home?"

"No, she has not come in yet."

"Strange . . . very strange," thought Atchmianov, feeling very uneasy. "She went home. . . ."

He walked along the boulevard, then along the street, and glanced in at the windows of Sheshkovsky's. Laevsky was sitting at the table without his coat on, looking attentively at his cards.

"Strange, strange," muttered Atchmianov, and remembering Laevsky's hysterics, he felt ashamed. "If she is not at home, where is she?"

He went to Nadyezhda Fyodorovna's lodgings again, and looked at the dark windows.

"It's a cheat, a cheat . . ." he thought, remembering that, meeting him at midday at Marya Konstantinovna's, she had promised to go in a boat with him that evening.

The windows of the house where Kirilin lived were dark, and there was a policeman sitting asleep on a little bench at the gate. Everything was clear to Atchmianov when he looked at the windows and the policeman. He made up his mind to go home, and set off in that direction, but somehow found himself near Nadyezhda Fyodorovna's lodgings again. He sat down on the bench near the gate and took off his hat, feeling that his head was burning with jealousy and resentment.

The clock in the town church only struck twice in the twenty-four hours —at midday and midnight. Soon after it struck midnight he heard hurried footsteps.

"To-morrow evening then, again at Muridov's," Atchmianov heard, and he recognized Kirilin's voice. "At eight o'clock; good-bye!"

Nadyezhda Fyodorovna made her appearance near the garden. Without noticing that Atchmianov was sitting on the bench, she passed beside him like a shadow, opened the gate, and leaving it open, went into the house. In her own room she lighted the candle and quickly undressed, but instead of getting into bed, she sank on her knees before a chair, flung her arms round it, and rested her head on it.

It was past two when Laevsky came home.

XV

Having made up his mind to lie, not all at once but piecemeal, Laevsky went soon after one o'clock next day to Samoylenko to ask for the money that he might be sure to get off on Saturday. After his hysterical attack, which had added an acute feeling of shame to his depressed state of mind, it was unthinkable to remain in the town. If Samoylenko should insist on his conditions, he thought it would be possible to agree to them and take the money, and next day, just as he was starting, to say that Nadyezhda Fyodorovna refused to go. He would be able to persuade her that evening that the whole arrangement would be for her benefit. If Samoylenko, who was obviously under the influence of Von Koren, should refuse the money altogether or make fresh conditions, then he, Laevsky, would go off that very evening in a cargo vessel, or even in a sailing-boat, to Novy Athon or Novorossiisk, would send from there an humiliating telegram, and would stay there till his mother sent him the money for the journey.

When he went into Samoylenko's, he found Von Koren in the drawing-room. The zoologist had just arrived for dinner, and, as usual, was turning over the album and scrutinizing the gentlemen in top-hats and the ladies in caps.

"How very unlucky!" thought Laevsky, seeing him. "He may be in the way. Good-morning."

"Good-morning," answered Von Koren, without looking at him.

"Is Alexandr Daviditch at home?"

"Yes, in the kitchen."

Laevsky went into the kitchen, but seeing from the door that Samoylenko was busy over the salad, he went back into the drawing-room and sat down. He always had a feeling of awkwardness in the zoologist's presence, and now he was afraid there would be talk about his attack of hysterics. There was more than a minute of silence. Von Koren suddenly raised his eyes to Laevsky and asked:

"How do you feel after yesterday?"

"Very well indeed," said Laevsky, flushing. "It really was nothing much. . . ."

"Until yesterday I thought it was only ladies who had hysterics, and so at first I thought you had St. Vitus's dance."

Laevsky smiled ingratiatingly, and thought:

"How indelicate on his part! He knows quite well how unpleasant it is for me. . . ."

"Yes, it was a ridiculous performance," he said, still smiling. "I've been laughing over it the whole morning. What's so curious in an attack of hysterics is that you know it is absurd, and are laughing at it in your heart, and at the same time you sob. In our neurotic age we are the slaves of our nerves; they are our masters and do as they like with us. Civilization has done us a bad turn in that way. . . ."

As Laevsky talked, he felt it disagreeable that Von Koren listened to him gravely, and looked at him steadily and attentively as though studying him; and he was vexed with himself that in spite of his dislike of Von Koren, he could not banish the ingratiating smile from his face.

"I must admit, though," he added, "that there were immediate causes for the attack, and quite sufficient ones too. My health has been terribly shaky of late. To which one must add boredom, constantly being hard up . . . the absence of people and general interests. . . . My position is worse than a governor's."

"Yes, your position is a hopeless one," answered Von Koren.

These calm, cold words, implying something between a jeer and an uninvited prediction, offended Laevsky. He recalled the zoologist's eyes the evening before, full of mockery and disgust. He was silent for a space and then asked, no longer smiling:

"How do you know anything of my position?"

"You were only just speaking of it yourself. Besides, your friends take such a warm interest in you, that I am hearing about you all day long."

"What friends? Samoylenko, I suppose?"

"Yes, he too."

"I would ask Alexandr Daviditch and my friends in general not to trouble so much about me."

"Here is Samoylenko; you had better ask him not to trouble so much about you."

"I don't understand your tone," Laevsky muttered, suddenly feeling as though he had only just realized that the zoologist hated and despised him, and was jeering at him, and was his bitterest and most inveterate enemy.

"Keep that tone for someone else," he said softly, unable to speak aloud for the hatred with which his chest and throat were choking, as they had been the night before with laughter.

Samoylenko came in in his shirt-sleeves, crimson and perspiring from the stifling kitchen.

"Ah, you here?" he said. "Good-morning, my dear boy. Have you had dinner? Don't stand on ceremony. Have you had dinner?"

"Alexandr Daviditch," said Laevsky, standing up, "though I did appeal to you to help me in a private matter, it did not follow that I released you from the obligation of discretion and respect for other people's private affairs."

"What's this?" asked Samoylenko, in astonishment.

"If you have no money," Laevsky went on, raising his voice and shifting from one foot to the other in his excitement, "don't give it; refuse it. But why spread abroad in every back street that my position is hopeless, and all the rest of it? I can't endure such benevolence and friend's assistance where there's a shillings-worth of talk for a ha'p'orth of help! You can boast of your benevolence as much as you please, but no one has given you the right to gossip about my private affairs!"

"What private affairs?" asked Samoylenko, puzzled and beginning to be angry. "If you've come here to be abusive, you had better clear out. You can come again afterwards!"

He remembered the rule that when one is angry with one's neighbour, one must begin to count a hundred, and one will grow calm again; and he began rapidly counting.

"I beg you not to trouble yourself about me," Laevsky went on. "Don't pay any attention to me, and whose business is it what I do and how I live? Yes, I want to go away. Yes, I get into debt, I drink, I am living with another man's wife, I'm hysterical, I'm ordinary. I am not so profound as some people, but whose business is that? Respect other people's privacy."

"Excuse me, brother," said Samoylenko, who had counted up to thirty-five, "but . . ."

"Respect other people's individuality!" interrupted Laevsky. "This continual gossip about other people's affairs, this sighing and groaning and everlasting prying, this eavesdropping, this friendly sympathy . . . damn it all! They lend me money and make conditions as though I were a schoolboy! I am treated as the devil knows what! I don't want anything," shouted Laevsky, staggering with excitement and afraid that it might end in another attack of hysterics. "I shan't get away on Saturday, then," flashed through his mind. "I want nothing. All I ask of you is to spare me your protecting care. I'm not a boy, and I'm not mad, and I beg you to leave off looking after me."

The deacon came in, and seeing Laevsky pale and gesticulating, addressing his strange speech to the portrait of Prince Vorontsov, stood still by the door as though petrified.

"This continual prying into my soul," Laevsky went on, "is insulting to my human dignity, and I beg these volunteer detectives to give up their spying! Enough!"

"What's that . . . what did you say?" said Samoylenko, who had counted up to a hundred. He turned crimson and went up to Laevsky.

"It's enough," said Laevsky, breathing hard and snatching up his cap.

"I'm a Russian doctor, a nobleman by birth, and a civil councillor," said

Samoylenko emphatically. "I've never been a spy, and I allow no one to insult me!" he shouted in a breaking voice, emphasizing the last word. "Hold your tongue!"

The deacon, who had never seen the doctor so majestic, so swelling with dignity, so crimson and so ferocious, shut his mouth, ran out into the entry and there exploded with laughter.

As though through a fog, Laevsky saw Von Koren get up and, putting his hands in his trouser-pockets, stand still in an attitude of expectancy, as though waiting to see what would happen. This calm attitude struck Laevsky as insolent and insulting to the last degree.

"Kindly take back your words," shouted Samoylenko.

Laevsky, who did not by now remember what his words were, answered:

"Leave me alone! I ask for nothing. All I ask is that you and German upstarts of Jewish origin should let me alone! Or I shall take steps to make you! I will fight you!"

"Now we understand," said Von Koren, coming from behind the table. "Mr. Laevsky wants to amuse himself with a duel before he goes away. I can give him that pleasure. Mr. Laevsky, I accept your challenge."

"A challenge," said Laevsky, in a low voice, going up to the zoologist and looking with hatred at his swarthy brow and curly hair. "A challenge? By all means! I hate you! I hate you!"

"Delighted. To-morrow morning early near Kerbalay's. I leave all details to your taste. And now, clear out!"

"I hate you," Laevsky said softly, breathing hard. "I have hated you a long while! A duel! Yes!"

"Get rid of him, Alexandr Daviditch, or else I'm going," said Von Koren. "He'll bite me."

Von Koren's cool tone calmed the doctor; he seemed suddenly to come to himself, to recover his reason; he put both arms round Laevsky's waist, and, leading him away from the zoologist, muttered in a friendly voice that shook with emotion:

"My friends . . . dear, good . . . you've lost your tempers and that's enough . . . and that's enough, my friends."

Hearing his soft, friendly voice, Laevsky felt that something unheard of, monstrous, had just happened to him, as though he had been nearly run over by a train; he almost burst into tears, waved his hand, and ran out of the room.

"To feel that one is hated, to expose oneself before the man who hates one, in the most pitiful, contemptible, helpless state. My God, how hard it is!" he thought a little while afterwards as he sat in the pavilion, feeling as though his body were scarred by the hatred of which he had just been the object.

"How coarse it is, my God!"

Cold water with brandy in it revived him. He vividly pictured Von Koren's calm, haughty face; his eyes the day before, his shirt like a rug, his voice, his white hand; and heavy, passionate, hungry hatred rankled in his

breast and clamoured for satisfaction. In his thoughts he felled Von Koren
to the ground, and trampled him underfoot. He remembered to the minutest
detail all that had happened, and wondered how he could have smiled ingratiatingly to that insignificant man, and how he could care for the opinion
of wretched petty people whom nobody knew, living in a miserable little
town which was not, it seemed, even on the map, and of which not one
decent person in Petersburg had heard. If this wretched little town suddenly
fell into ruins or caught fire, the telegram with the news would be read in
Russia with no more interest than an advertisement of the sale of second-
hand furniture. Whether he killed Von Koren next day or left him alive, it
would be just the same, equally useless and uninteresting. Better to shoot
him in the leg or hand, wound him, then laugh at him, and let him, like an
insect with a broken leg lost in the grass—let him be lost with his obscure
sufferings in the crowd of insignificant people like himself.

Laevsky went to Sheshkovsky, told him all about it, and asked him to be
his second; then they both went to the superintendent of the postal telegraph
department, and asked him, too, to be a second, and stayed to dinner with
him. At dinner there was a great deal of joking and laughing. Laevsky made
jests at his own expense, saying he hardly know how to fire off a pistol,
calling himself a royal archer and William Tell.

"We must give this gentleman a lesson . . ." he said.

After dinner they sat down to cards. Laevsky played, drank wine, and
thought that duelling was stupid and senseless, as it did not decide the question but only complicated it, but that it was sometimes impossible to get
on without it. In the given case, for instance, one could not, of course, bring
an action against Von Koren. And this duel was so far good in that it made
it impossible for Laevsky to remain in the town afterwards. He got a little
drunk and interested in the game, and felt at ease.

But when the sun had set and it grew dark, he was possessed by a feeling
of uneasiness. It was not fear at the thought of death, because while he was
dining and playing cards, he had for some reason a confident belief that
the duel would end in nothing; it was dread at the thought of something
unknown which was was to happen next morning for the first time in his
life, and dread of the coming night. . . . He knew that the night would be
long and sleepless, and that he would have to think not only of Von Koren
and his hatred, but also of the mountain of lies which he had to get through,
and which he had not strength or ability to dispense with. It was as though
he had been taken suddenly ill; all at once he lost all interest in the cards and
in people, grew restless, and began asking them to let him go home. He was
eager to get into bed, to lie without moving, and to prepare his thoughts
for the night. Sheshkovsky and the postal superintendent saw him home and
went on to Von Koren's to arrange about the duel.

Near his lodgings Laevsky met Atchmianov. The young man was breathless and excited.

"I am looking for you, Ivan Andreitch," he said. "I beg you to come
quickly. . . ."

"Where?"

"Someone wants to see you, someone you don't know, about very important business; he earnestly begs you to come for a minute. He wants to speak to you of something. . . . For him it's a question of life and death. . . ."

In his excitement Atchmianov spoke in a strong Armenian accent.

"Who is it?" asked Laevsky.

"He asked me not to tell you his name."

"Tell him I'm busy; to-morrow, if he likes. . . ."

"How can you!" Atchmianov was aghast. "He wants to tell you something very important for you . . . very important! If you don't come something dreadful will happen."

"Strange . . ." muttered Laevsky, unable to understand why Atchmianov was so excited and what mysteries there could be in this dull, useless little town.

"Strange," he repeated in hesitation. "Come along, though; I don't care."

Atchmianov walked rapidly on ahead and Laevsky followed him. They walked down a street, then turned into an alley.

"What a bore this is!" said Laevsky.

"One minute, one minute . . . it's near."

Near the old rampart they went down a narrow alley between two empty enclosures, then they came into a sort of large yard and went towards a small house.

"That's Muridov's, isn't it?" asked Laevsky.

"Yes."

"But why we've come by the back yards I don't understand. We might have come by the street; it's nearer. . . ."

"Never mind, never mind. . . ."

It struck Laevsky as strange, too, that Atchmianov led him to a back entrance, and motioned to him as though bidding him go quietly and hold his tongue.

"This way, this way . . ." said Atchmianov, cautiously opening the door and going into the passage on tiptoe. "Quietly, quietly, I beg you . . . they may hear."

He listened, drew a deep breath and said in a whisper:

"Open that door, and go in . . . don't be afraid."

Laevsky, puzzled, opened the door and went into a room with a low ceiling and curtained windows.

There was a candle on the table.

"What do you want?" asked someone in the next room. "Is it you, Muridov?"

Laevsky turned into that room and saw Kirilin, and beside him Nadyezhda Fyodorovna.

He didn't hear what was said to him; he staggered back, and did not know how he found himself on the street. His hatred for Von Koren and his uneasiness—all had vanished from his soul. As he went home he waved his right arm awkwardly and looked carefully at the ground under his feet,

trying to step where it was smooth. At home in his study he walked backwards and forwards, rubbing his hands, and awkwardly shrugging his shoulders and neck, as though his jacket and shirt were too tight; then he lighted
a candle and sat down to the table. . . .

XVI

"The 'humane studies' of which you speak will only satisfy human thought
when, as they advance, they meet the exact sciences and progress side by
side with them. Whether they will meet under a new microscope, or in the
monologues of a new Hamlet, or in a new religion, I do not know, but I
expect the earth will be covered with a crust of ice before it comes to pass.
Of all humane learning the most durable and living is, of course, the
teaching of Christ; but look how differently even that is interpreted! Some
teach that we must love all our neighbours but make an exception of
soldiers, criminals, and lunatics. They allow the first to be killed in war, the
second to be isolated or executed, and the third they forbid to marry.
Other interpreters teach that we must love all our neighbours without
exception, with no distinction of *plus* or *minus*. According to their teaching, if a consumptive or a murderer or an epileptic asks your daughter in
marriage, you must let him have her. If *crétins* go to war against the
physically and mentally healthy, don't defend yourselves. This advocacy of
love for love's sake, like art for art's sake, if it could have power, would
bring mankind in the long run to complete extinction, and so would
become the vastest crime that has ever been committed upon earth. There
are very many interpretations, and since there are many of them, serious
thought is not satisfied by any one of them, and hastens to add its own
individual interpretation to the mass. For that reason you should never put a
question on a philosophical or so-called Christian basis; by so doing you only
remove the question further from solution."

The deacon listened to the zoologist attentively, thought a little, and
asked:

"Have the philosophers invented the moral law which is innate in every
man, or did God create it together with the body?"

"I don't know. But that law is so universal among all peoples and all ages
that I fancy we ought to recognize it as organically connected with man. It
is not invented, but exists and will exist. I don't tell you that one day it will
be seen under the microscope, but its organic connection is shown, indeed,
by evidence: serious affections of the brain and all so-called mental diseases,
to the best of my belief, show themselves first of all in the perversion of the
moral law."

"Good. So then, just as our stomach bids us eat, our moral sense bids us
love our neighbours. Is that it? But our natural man through self-love
opposes the voice of conscience and reason, and this gives rise to many brain-
racking questions. To whom ought we to turn for the solution of those
questions if you forbid us to put them on the philosophic basis?"

"Turn to what little exact science we have. Trust to evidence and the logic of facts. It is true it is but little, but, on the other hand, it is less fluid and shifting than philosophy. The moral law, let us suppose, demands that you love your neighbour. Well? Love ought to show itself in the removal of everything which in one way or another is injurious to men and threatens them with danger in the present or in the future. Our knowledge and the evidence tells us that the morally and physically abnormal are a menace to humanity. If so you must struggle against the abnormal; if you are not able to raise them to the normal standard, you must have strength and ability to render them harmless—that is, to destroy them."

"So love consists in the strong overcoming the weak."

"Undoubtedly."

"But you know the strong crucified our Lord Jesus Christ," said the deacon hotly.

"The fact is that those who crucified Him were not the strong but the weak. Human culture weakens and strives to nullify the struggle for existence and natural selection; hence the rapid advancement of the weak and their predominance over the strong. Imagine that you succeeded in instilling into bees humanitarian ideas in their crude and elementary form. What would come of it? The drones who ought to be killed would remain alive, would devour the honey, would corrupt and stifle the bees, resulting in the predominance of the weak over the strong and the degeneration of the latter. The same process is taking place now with humanity; the weak are oppressing the strong. Among savages untouched by civilization the strongest, cleverest, and most moral takes the lead; he is the chief and the master. But we civilized men have crucified Christ, and we go on crucifying Him, so there is something lacking in us. . . . And that something one ought to raise up in ourselves, or there will be no end to these errors."

"But what criterion have you to distinguish the strong from the weak?"

"Knowledge and evidence. The tuberculous and the scrofulous are recognized by their diseases, and the insane and the immoral by their actions."

"But mistakes may be made!"

"Yes, but it's no use to be afraid of getting your feet wet when you are threatened with the deluge!"

"That's philosophy," laughed the deacon.

"Not a bit of it. You are so corrupted by your seminary philosophy that you want to see nothing but fog in everything. The abstract studies with which your youthful head is stuffed are called abstract just because they abstract your minds from what is obvious. Look the devil straight in the eye, and if he's the devil, tell him he's the devil, and don't go calling to Kant or Hegel for explanations."

The zoologist paused and went on:

"Twice two's four, and a stone's a stone. Here to-morrow we have a duel. You and I will say it's stupid and absurd, that the duel is out of date, that there is no real difference between the aristocratic duel and the drunken brawl in the pot-house, and yet we shall not stop, we shall go there and fight. So there is some force stronger than our reasoning. We shout that war is plunder, robbery, atrocity, fratricide; we cannot look upon blood without fainting; but the French or the Germans have only to insult us for us to feel at once an exaltation of spirit; in the most genuine way we shout 'Hurrah!' and rush to attack the foe. You will invoke the blessing of God on our weapons, and our valour will arouse universal and general enthusiasm. Again it follows that there is a force, if not higher, at any rate stronger, than us and our philosophy. We can no more stop it than that cloud which is moving upwards over the sea. Don't be hypocritical, don't make a long nose at it on the sly; and don't say, 'Ah, old-fashioned, stupid! Ah, it's inconsistent with Scripture!' but look it straight in the face, recognize its rational lawfulness, and when, for instance, it wants to destroy a rotten, scrofulous, corrupt race, don't hinder it with your pilules and misunderstood quotations from the Gospel. Leskov has a story of a conscientious Danila who found a leper outside the town and fed and warmed him in the name of love and of Christ. If that Danila had really loved humanity, he would have dragged the leper as far as possible from the town, and would have flung him in a pit, and would have gone to save the healthy. Christ, I hope, taught us a rational, intelligent, practical love."

"What a fellow you are!" laughed the deacon. "You don't believe in Christ. Why do you mention His name so often?"

"Yes, I do believe in Him. Only, of course, in my own way, not in yours. Oh, deacon, deacon!" laughed the zoologist; he put his arm round the deacon's waist, and said gaily: "Well? Are you coming with us to the duel to-morrow?"

"My orders don't allow it, or else I should come."

"What do you mean by 'orders'?"

"I have been consecrated. I am in a state of grace."

"Oh, deacon, deacon," repeated Von Koren, laughing, "I love talking to you."

"You say you have faith," said the deacon. "What sort of faith is it? Why, I have an uncle, a priest, and he believes so that when in time of drought he goes out into the fields to pray for rain, he takes his umbrella and leather overcoat for fear of getting wet through on his way home. That's faith! When he speaks of Christ, his face is full of radiance, and all the peasants, men and women, weep floods of tears. He would stop that cloud and put all those forces you talk about to flight. Yes . . . faith moves mountains."

The deacon laughed and slapped the zoologist on the shoulder.

"Yes . . ." he went on; "here you are teaching all the time, fathoming the depths of the ocean, dividing the weak and the strong, writing books and challenging to duels—and everything remains as it is; but, behold! some feeble old man will mutter just one word with a holy spirit, or a new Mahomet, with a sword, will gallop from Arabia, and everything will be topsy-turvy, and in Europe not one stone will be left standing upon another."

"Well, deacon, that's on the knees of the gods."

"Faith without works is dead, but works without faith are worse still—mere waste of time and nothing more."

The doctor came into sight on the sea-front. He saw the deacon and the zoologist, and went up to them.

"I believe everything is ready," he said, breathing hard. "Govorovsky and Boyko will be the seconds. They will start at five o'clock in the morning. How it has clouded over," he said, looking at the sky. "One can see nothing; there will be rain directly."

"I hope you are coming with us?" said the zoologist.

"No, God preserve me; I'm worried enough as it is. Ustimovitch is going instead of me. I've spoken to him already."

Far over the sea was a flash of lightning, followed by a hollow roll of thunder.

"How stifling it is before a storm!" said Von Koren. "I bet you've been to Laevsky already and have been weeping on his bosom."

"Why should I go to him?" answered the doctor in confusion. "What next?"

Before sunset he had walked several times along the boulevard and the street in the hope of meeting Laevsky. He was ashamed of his hastiness and the sudden outburst of friendliness which had followed it. He wanted to apologize to Laevsky in a joking tone, to give him a good talking to, to soothe him and to tell him that the duel was a survival of medieval barbarism, but that Providence itself had brought them to the duel as a means of reconciliation; that the next day, both being splendid and highly intelligent people, they would, after exchanging shots, appreciate each other's noble qualities and would become friends. But he could not come across Laevsky.

"What should I go and see him for?" repeated Samoylenko. "I did not insult him; he insulted me. Tell me, please, why he attacked me. What harm had I done him? I go into the drawing-room, and, all of a sudden, without the least provocation: 'Spy!' There's a nice thing! Tell me, how did it begin? What did you say to him?"

"I told him his position was hopeless. And I was right. It is only honest men or scoundrels who can find an escape from any position, but one who wants to be at the same time an honest man and a scoundrel—it is a hopeless position. But it's eleven o'clock, gentlemen, and we have to be up early to-morrow."

There was a sudden gust of wind; it blew up the dust on the sea-front, whirled it round in eddies, with a howl that drowned the roar of the sea.

"A squall," said the deacon. "We must go in, our eyes are getting full of dust."

As they went, Samoylenko sighed and, holding his hat, said:

"I suppose I shan't sleep to-night."

"Don't you agitate yourself," laughed the zoologist. "You can set your mind at rest; the duel will end in nothing. Laevsky will magnanimously fire into the air—he can do nothing else; and I dare say I shall not fire at all. To be arrested and lose my time on Laevsky's account—the game's not worth the candle. By the way, what is the punishment for duelling?"

"Arrest, and in the case of the death of your opponent a maximum of three years' imprisonment in the fortress."

"The fortress of St. Peter and St. Paul?"

"No, in a military fortress, I believe."

"Though this fine gentleman ought to have a lesson!"

Behind them on the sea, there was a flash of lightning, which for an instant lighted up the roofs of the houses and the mountains. The friends parted near the boulevard. When the doctor disappeared in the darkness and his steps had died away, Von Koren shouted to him:

"I only hope the weather won't interfere with us to-morrow!"

"Very likely it will! Please God it may!"

"Good-night!"

"What about the night? What do you say?"

In the roar of the wind and the sea and the crashes of thunder, it was difficult to hear.

"It's nothing," shouted the zoologist, and hurried home.

XVII

> "Upon my mind, weighed down with woe,
> Crowd thoughts, a heavy multitude:
> In silence memory unfolds
> Her long, long scroll before my eyes.
> Loathing and shuddering I curse
> And bitterly lament in vain,
> And bitter though the tears I weep
> I do not wash those lines away."
>
> —PUSHKIN.

Whether they killed him next morning, or mocked at him—that is, left him his life—he was ruined, anyway. Whether this disgraced woman killed herself in her shame and despair, or dragged on her pitiful existence, she was ruined, anyway.

So thought Laevsky as he sat at the table late in the evening, still rubbing his hands. The windows suddenly blew open with a bang; a violent gust of wind burst into the room, and the papers fluttered from the table. Laevsky closed the windows and bent down to pick up the papers. He was aware of something new in his body, a sort of awkwardness he had not felt before, and his movements were strange to him. He moved timidly, jerking with his elbows and shrugging his shoulders; and when he sat down to the table again, he again began rubbing his hands. His body had lost its suppleness.

On the eve of death one ought to write to one's nearest relation. Laevsky thought of this. He took a pen and wrote with a tremulous hand:

"Mother!"

He wanted to write to beg his mother, for the sake of the merciful God in whom she believed, that she would give shelter and bring a little warmth and kindness into the life of the unhappy woman who, by his doing, had been disgraced and was in solitude, poverty, and weakness, that she would forgive and forget everything, everything, everything, and by her sacrifice atone to some extent for her son's terrible sin. But he remembered how his mother, a stout, heavily-built old woman in a lace cap, used to go out into the garden in the morning, followed by her companion with the lap-dog; how she used to shout in a peremptory way to the gardener and the servants, and how proud and haughty her face was—he remembered all this and scratched out the word he had written.

There was a vivid flash of lightning at all three windows, and it was followed by a prolonged, deafening roll of thunder, beginning with a hollow rumble and ending with a crash so violent that all the window-panes rattled. Laevsky got up, went to the window, and pressed his forehead against the pane. There was a fierce, magnificent storm. On the horizon lightning-flashes were flung in white streams from the storm-clouds into the sea, lighting up the high, dark waves over the far-away expanse. And to right and to left, and, no doubt, over the house too, the lightning flashed.

"The storm!" whispered Laevsky; he had a longing to pray to someone or to something, if only to the lightning or the storm-clouds. "Dear storm!"

He remembered how as a boy he used to run out into the garden without a hat on when there was a storm, and how two fair-haired girls with blue eyes used to run after him, and how they got wet through with the rain; they laughed with delight, but when there was a loud peal of thunder, the girls used to nestle up to the boy confidingly, while he crossed himself and made haste to repeat: "Holy, holy, holy. . . ." Oh, where had they vanished to! In what sea were they drowned, those dawning days of pure, fair life? He had no fear of the storm, no love of nature now; he had no God. All the confiding girls he had ever known had by now been ruined by him and those like him. All his life he had not planted one tree in his own garden, nor grown one blade of grass; and living among the living, he had not saved one fly; he had done nothing but destroy and ruin, and lie, lie. . . .

"What in my past was not vice?" he asked himself, trying to clutch at some bright memory as a man falling down a precipice clutches at the bushes.

School? The university? But that was a sham. He had neglected his work and forgotten what he had learnt. The service of his country? That, too, was a sham, for he did nothing in the Service, took a salary for doing nothing, and it was an abominable swindling of the State for which one was not punished.

He had no craving for truth, and had not sought it; spellbound by vice and lying, his conscience had slept or been silent. Like a stranger, like an alien from another planet, he had taken no part in the common life of men, had been indifferent to their sufferings, their ideas, their religion, their sciences, their strivings, and their struggles. He had not said one good word, not written one line that was not useless and vulgar; he had not done his fellows one ha'p'orth of service, but had eaten their bread, drunk their wine, seduced their wives, lived on their thoughts, and to justify his contemptible, parasitic life in their eyes and in his own, he had always tried to assume an air of being higher and better than they. Lies, lies, lies. . . .

He vividly remembered what he had seen that evening at Muridov's, and he was in an insufferable anguish of loathing and misery. Kirilin and Atchmianov were loathsome, but they were only continuing what he had begun; they were his accomplices and his disciples. This young weak woman had trusted him more than a brother, and he had deprived her of her husband, of her friends and of her country, and had brought her here—to the heat, to fever, and to boredom; and from day to day she was bound to reflect, like a mirror, his idleness, his viciousness and falsity—and that was all she had had to fill her weak, listless, pitiable life. Then he had grown sick of her, had begun to hate her, but had not had the pluck to abandon her, and he had tried to entangle her more and more closely in a web of lies. . . . These men had done the rest.

Laevsky sat at the table, then got up and went to the window; at one minute he put out the candle and then he lighted it again. He cursed himself aloud, wept and wailed, and asked forgiveness; several times he ran to the table in despair, and wrote:

"Mother!"

Except his mother, he had no relations or near friends; but how could his mother help him? And where was she? He had an impulse to run to Nadyezhda Fyodorovna, to fall at her feet, to kiss her hands and feet, to beg her forgiveness; but she was his victim, and he was afraid of her as though she were dead.

"My life is ruined," he repeated, rubbing his hands. "Why am I still alive, my God! . . ."

He had cast out of heaven his dim star; it had fallen, and its track was lost in the darkness of night. It would never return to the sky again, because life was given only once and never came a second time. If he could have turned back the days and years of the past, he would have replaced the falsity with truth, the idleness with work, the boredom with happiness; he would have given back purity to those whom he had robbed of it. He would have found God and goodness, but that was as impossible as to put back the fallen star into the sky, and because it was impossible he was in despair.

When the storm was over, he sat by the open window and thought calmly of what was before him. Von Koren would most likely kill him. The man's clear, cold theory of life justified the destruction of the rotten and the useless; if it changed at the crucial moment, it would be the hatred and the repugnance that Laevsky inspired in him that would save him. If he missed his aim or, in mockery of his hated opponent, only wounded him, or fired in the air, what could he do then? Where could he go?

"Go to Petersburg?" Laevsky asked himself. But that would mean beginning over again the old life which he cursed. And the man who seeks salvation in change of place like a migrating bird would find nothing any-where, for all the world is alike to him. Seek salvation in men? In whom and how? Samoylenko's kindness and generosity could no more save him than the deacon's laughter or Von Koren's hatred. He must look for salvation in himself alone, and if there were no finding it, why waste time? He must kill himself, that was all. . . .

He heard the sound of a carriage. It was getting light. The carriage passed by, turned, and crunching on the wet sand, stopped near the house. There were two men in the carriage.

"Wait a minute; I'm coming directly," Laevsky said to them out of the window. "I'm not asleep. Surely it's not time yet?"

"Yes, it's four o'clock. By the time we get there . . ."

Laevsky put on his overcoat and cap, put some cigarettes in his pocket, and stood still hesitating. He felt as though there was something else he must do. In the street the seconds talked in low voices and the horses snorted, and this sound in the damp, early morning, when everybody was asleep and light was hardly dawning in the sky, filled Laevsky's soul with a disconsolate feeling which was like a presentiment of evil. He stood for a little, hesitating, and went into the bedroom.

Nadyezhda Fyodorovna was lying stretched out on the bed, wrapped from head to foot in a rug. She did not stir, and her whole appearance, especially her head, suggested an Egyptian mummy. Looking at her in silence, Laevsky mentally asked her forgiveness, and thought that if the heavens were not empty and there really were a God, then He would save her; if there were no God, then she had better perish—there was nothing for her to live for.

All at once she jumped up, and sat up in bed. Lifting her pale face and looking with horror at Laevsky, she asked:

"Is it you? Is the storm over?"

"Yes."

She remembered; put both her hands to her head and shuddered all over.

"How miserable I am!" she said. "If only you knew how miserable I am! I expected," she went on, half closing her eyes, "that you would kill me or turn me out of the house into the rain and storm, but you delay . . . delay . . ."

Warmly and impulsively he put his arms round her and covered her knees and hands with kisses. Then when she muttered something and shuddered with the thought of the past, he stroked her hair, and looking into her face, realized that this unhappy, sinful woman was the one creature near and dear to him, whom no one could replace.

When he went out of the house and got into the carriage he wanted to return home alive.

XVIII

The deacon got up, dressed, took his thick gnarled stick and slipped quietly out of the house. It was dark, and for the first minute when he went into the street, he could not even see his white stick. There was not a single star in the sky, and it looked as though there would be rain again. There was a smell of wet sand and sea.

"It's to be hoped that the mountaineers won't attack us," thought the deacon, hearing the tap of the stick on the pavement, and noticing how loud and lonely the taps sounded in the stillness of the night.

When he got out of town, he began to see both the road and his stick. Here and there in the black sky there were dark cloudy patches, and soon a star peeped out and timidly blinked its one eye. The deacon walked along the high rocky coast and did not see the sea; it was slumbering below, and its unseen waves broke languidly and heavily on the shore, as though sighing "Ouf!" and how slowly! One wave broke—the deacon had time to count eight steps; then another broke, and six steps; later a third. As before, nothing could be seen, and in the darkness one could hear the languid, drowsy drone of the sea. One could hear the infinitely far-away, inconceivable time when God moved above chaos.

The deacon felt uncanny. He hoped God would not punish him for keeping company with infidels, and even going to look at their duels. The duel would be nonsensical, bloodless, absurd, but however that might be, it was a heathen spectacle, and it was altogether unseemly for an ecclesiastical person to be present at it. He stopped and wondered—should he go back? But an intense, restless curiosity triumphed over his doubts, and he went on.

"Though they are infidels, they are good people, and will be saved," he assured himself. "They are sure to be saved," he said aloud, lighting a cigarette.

By what standard must one measure men's qualities, to judge rightly of them? The deacon remembered his enemy, the inspector of the clerical school, who believed in God, lived in chastity, and did not fight duels; but he used to feed the deacon on bread with sand in it, and on one occasion almost pulled off the deacon's ear. If human life was so artlessly constructed that everyone respected this cruel and dishonest inspector who stole the Government flour, and his health and salvation were prayed for in the schools, was it just to shun such men as Von Koren and Laevsky, simply because they were unbelievers? The deacon was weighing this question, but he recalled how absurd Samoylenko had looked yesterday, and that broke the thread of his ideas. What fun they would have next day! The deacon imagined how he would sit under a bush and look on, and when Von Koren began boasting next day at dinner, he, the deacon, would begin laughing and telling him all the details of the duel.

"How do you know all about it?" the zoologist would ask.

"Well, there you are! I stayed at home, but I know all about it."

It would be nice to write a comic description of the duel. His father-in-law would read it and laugh. A good story, told or written, was more than meat and drink to his father-in-law.

The valley of the Yellow River opened before him. The stream was broader and fiercer for the rain, and instead of murmuring as before, it was raging. It began to get light. The grey, dingy morning, and the clouds racing towards the west to overtake the storm-clouds, the mountains girt with mist, and the wet trees, all struck the deacon as ugly and sinister. He washed at the brook, repeated his morning prayer, and felt a longing for tea and hot rolls, with sour cream, which were served every morning at his father-in-law's. He remembered his wife and the "Days Past Recall," which she played on the piano. What sort of woman was she? His wife had been introduced, betrothed, and married to him all in one week: he had lived with her less than a month when he was ordered here, so that he had not had time to find out what she was like. All the same, he rather missed her.

"I must write her a nice letter . . ." he thought. The flag on the *duhan* hung limp, soaked by the rain, and the *duhan* itself with its wet roof seemed darker and lower than it had been before. Near the door was standing a cart; Kerbalay, with two mountaineers and a young Tatar woman in trousers—no doubt Kerbalay's wife or daughter—were bringing sacks of something out of the *duhan*, and putting them on maize straw in the cart.

Near the cart stood a pair of asses hanging their heads. When they had put in all the sacks, the mountaineers and the Tatar woman began covering them over with straw, while Kerbalay began hurriedly harnessing the asses.

"Smuggling, perhaps," thought the deacon.

Here was the fallen tree with the dried pine-needles, here was the blackened patch from the fire. He remembered the picnic and all its incidents, the fire, the singing of the mountaineers, his sweet dreams of becoming a bishop, and of the Church procession. . . . The Black River had grown blacker and broader with the rain. The deacon walked cautiously over the narrow bridge, which by now was reached by the topmost crests of the dirty water, and went up through the little copse to the drying-shed.

"A splendid head," he thought, stretching himself on the straw, and thinking of Von Koren. "A fine head—God grant him health; only there is cruelty in him. . . ."

Why did he hate Laevsky and Laevsky hate him? Why were they going to fight a duel? If from their childhood they had known poverty as the deacon had; if they had been brought up among ignorant, hard-hearted, grasping, coarse and ill-mannered people who grudged you a crust of bread, who spat on the floor and hiccoughed at dinner and at prayers; if they had not been spoilt from childhood by the pleasant surroundings and the select circle of friends they lived in—how they would have rushed at each other, how readily they would have overlooked each other's shortcomings and would have prized each other's strong points! Why, how few even outwardly decent people there were in the world! It was true that Laevsky was flighty, dissipated, queer, but he did not steal, did not spit loudly on the floor; he did not abuse his wife and say, "You'll eat till you burst, but you don't want to work"; he would not beat a child with reins, or give his servants stinking meat to eat—surely this was reason enough to be indulgent to him? Besides, he was the chief sufferer from his failings, like a sick man from his sores. Instead of being lead by boredom and some sort of misunderstanding to look for degeneracy, extinction, heredity, and other such incomprehensible things in each other, would they not do better to stoop a little lower and turn their hatred and anger where whole streets resounded with moanings from coarse ignorance, greed, scolding, impurity, swearing, the shrieks of women. . . .

The sound of a carriage interrupted the deacon's thoughts. He glanced out of the door and saw a carriage and in it three persons: Laevsky, Sheshkovsky, and the superintendent of the post-office.

"Stop!" said Sheshkovsky.

All three got out of the carriage and looked at one another.

"They are not here yet," said Sheshkovsky, shaking the mud off. "Well? Till the show begins, let us go and find a suitable spot; there's not room to turn round here."

They went further up the river and soon vanished from sight. The Tatar driver sat in the carriage with his head resting on his shoulder and fell asleep. After waiting ten minutes the deacon came out of the drying-shed, and taking off his black hat that he might not be noticed, he began threading his way among the bushes and strips of maize along the bank, crouching and looking about him. The grass and maize were wet, and big drops fell on his head from the trees and bushes. "Disgraceful!" he muttered, picking up his wet and muddy skirt. "Had I realized it, I would not have come."

Soon he heard voices and caught sight of them. Laevsky was walking rapidly to and fro in the small glade with bowed back and hands thrust in his sleeves; his seconds were standing at the water's edge, rolling cigarettes.

"Strange," thought the deacon, not recognizing Laevsky's walk; "he looks like an old man. . . ."

"How rude it is of them!" said the superintendent of the post-office, looking at his watch. "It may be learned manners to be late, but to my thinking it's hoggish."

Sheshkovsky, a stout man with a black beard, listened and said:

"They're coming!"

XIX

"It's the first time in my life I've seen it! How glorious!" said Von Koren, pointing to the glade and stretching out his hands to the east. "Look: green rays!"

In the east behind the mountains rose two green streaks of light, and it really was beautiful. The sun was rising.

"Good-morning!" the zoologist went on, nodding to Laevsky's seconds. "I'm not late, am I?"

He was followed by his seconds, Boyko and Govorovsky, two very young officers of the same height, wearing white tunics, and Ustimovitch, the thin, unsociable doctor; in one hand he had a bag of some sort, and in the other had, as usual, a cane which he held behind him. Laying the bag on the ground and greeting no one, he put the other hand, too, behind his back and began pacing up and down the glade.

Laevsky felt the exhaustion and awkwardness of a man who is soon perhaps to die, and is for that reason an object of general attention. He wanted to be killed as soon as possible or taken home. He saw the sunrise now for the first time in his life; the early morning, the green rays of light, the dampness, and the men in wet boots, seemed to him to have nothing to do with his life, to be superfluous and embarrassing. All these had no connection with the night he had been through, with his thoughts and his feeling of guilt, and so he would have gladly gone away without waiting for the duel.

Von Koren was noticeably excited and tried to conceal it, pretending that he was more interested in the green light than anything. The seconds were confused, and looked at one another as though wondering why they were here and what they were to do.

"I imagine, gentlemen, there is no need for us to go further," said Sheshkovsky. "This place will do."

"Yes, of course," Von Koren agreed.

A silence followed. Ustimovitch, pacing to and fro, suddenly turned sharply to Laevsky and said in a low voice, breathing into his face:

"They have very likely not told you my terms yet. Each side is to pay me fifteen roubles, and in the case of the death of one party, the survivor is to pay thirty."

Laevsky was already acquainted with the man, but now for the first time he had a distinct view of his lustreless eyes, his stiff moustaches, and wasted, consumptive neck; he was a money-grubber, not a doctor; his breath had an unpleasant smell of beef.

"What people there are in the world!" thought Laevsky, and answered: "Very good."

The doctor nodded and began pacing to and fro again, and it was evident he did not need the money at all, but simply asked for it from hatred. Everyone felt it was time to begin, or to end what had been begun, but instead of beginning or ending, they stood about, moved to and fro and smoked. The young officers, who were present at a duel for the first time in their lives, and even now hardly believed in this civilian and to their thinking, unnecessary duel, looked critically at their tunics and stroked their sleeves. Sheshkovsky went up to them and said softly: "Gentlemen, we must use every effort to prevent this duel; they ought to be reconciled."

He flushed crimson and added:

"Kirilin was at my rooms last night complaining that Laevsky had found him with Nadyezhda Fyodorovna, and all that sort of thing."

"Yes, we know that too," said Boyko.

"Well, you see, then . . . Laevsky's hands are trembling and all that sort of thing . . . he can scarcely hold a pistol now. To fight with him is as inhuman as to fight a man who is drunk or who has typhoid. If a reconciliation cannot be arranged, we ought to put off the duel, gentlemen, or something. . . . It's such a sickening business, I can't bear to see it."

"Talk to Von Koren."

"I don't know the rules of duelling, damnation take them, and I don't want to either; perhaps he'll imagine Laevsky funks it and has sent me to him, but he can think what he likes—I'll speak to him."

Sheshkovsky hesitatingly walked up to Von Koren with a slight limp, as though his leg had gone to sleep; and as he went towards him, clearing his throat, his whole figure was a picture of indolence.

"There's something I must say to you, sir," he began, carefully scrutinizing the flowers on the zoologist's shirt. "It's confidential. I don't know the rules of duelling, damnation take them, and I don't want to, and I look on the matter not as a second and that sort of thing, but as a man, and that's all about it."

"Yes. Well?"

"When seconds suggest reconciliation they are usually not listened to; it is looked upon as a formality. *Amour propre* and all that. But I humbly beg you to look carefully at Ivan Andreitch. He's not in a normal state, so to speak, to-day—not in his right mind, and a pitiable object. He has had a misfortune. I can't endure gossip. . . ."

Sheshkovsky flushed crimson and looked round.

"But in view of the duel, I think it necessary to inform you, Laevsky found his madam last night at Muridov's with . . . another gentleman."

"How disgusting!" muttered the zoologist; he turned pale, frowned, and spat loudly. "Tfoo!"

His lower lip quivered, he walked away from Sheshkovsky, unwilling to hear more, and as though he had accidentally tasted something bitter, spat loudly again, and for the first time that morning looked with hatred at Laevsky. His excitement and awkwardness passed off; he tossed his head and said aloud:

"Gentlemen, what are we waiting for, I should like to know? Why don't we begin?"

Sheshkovsky glanced at the officers and shrugged his shoulders.

"Gentlemen," he said aloud, addressing no one in particular. "Gentlemen, we propose that you should be reconciled."

"Let us make haste and get the formalities over," said Von Koren. "Reconciliation has been discussed already. What is the next formality? Make haste, gentlemen, time won't wait for us."

"But we insist on reconciliation all the same," said Sheshkovsky in a guilty voice, as a man compelled to interfere in another man's business; he flushed, laid his hand on his heart, and went on: "Gentlemen, we see no grounds for associating the offence with the duel. There's nothing in common between duelling and offences against one another of which we are sometimes guilty through human weakness. You are university men and men of culture, and no doubt you see in the duel nothing but a foolish and out-of-date formality, and all that sort of thing. That's how we look at it ourselves, or we shouldn't have come, for we cannot allow that in our presence men should fire at one another, and all that." Sheshkovsky wiped the perspiration off his face and went on: "Make an end to your misunderstanding, gentlemen; shake hands, and let us go home and drink to peace. Upon my honour, gentlemen!"

Von Koren did not speak. Laevsky, seeing that they were looking at him, said:

"I have nothing against Nikolay Vassilitch; if he considers I'm to blame, I'm ready to apologize to him."

Von Koren was offended.

"It is evident, gentlemen," he said, "you want Mr. Laevsky to return home a magnanimous and chivalrous figure, but I cannot give you and him that satisfaction. And there is no need to get up early and drive eight miles out of town simply to drink to peace, to have breakfast, and to explain to me that the duel is an out-of-date formality. A duel is a duel, and there is no need to make it more false and stupid than it is in reality. I want to fight!"

A silence followed. Boyko took a pair of pistols out of a box; one was given to Von Koren and one to Laevsky, and then there followed a difficulty which afforded a brief amusement to the zoologist and the seconds. It appeared that of all the people present not one had ever in his life been at a duel, and no one knew precisely how they ought to stand, and what the seconds ought to say and do. But then Boyko remembered and began, with a smile, to explain.

"Gentlemen, who remembers the description in Lermontov?" asked Von Koren, laughing. "In Turgenev, too, Bazarov had a duel with someone. . . ."

"There's no need to remember," said Ustimovitch impatiently. "Measure the distance, that's all."

And he took three steps as though to show how to measure it. Boyko counted out the steps while his companion drew his sabre and scratched the earth at the extreme points to mark the barrier. In complete silence the opponents took their places.

"Moles," the deacon thought, sitting in the bushes.

Sheshkovsky said something, Boyko explained something again, but Laevsky did not hear—or rather heard, but did not understand. He cocked his pistol when the time came to do so, and raised the cold, heavy weapon with the barrel upwards. He forgot to unbutton his overcoat, and it felt very tight over his shoulder and under his arm, and his arm rose as awkwardly as though the sleeve had been cut out of tin. He remembered the hatred he had felt the night before for the swarthy brow and curly hair, and felt that even yesterday at the moment of intense hatred and anger he could not have shot a man. Fearing that the bullet might somehow hit Von Koren by accident, he raised the pistol higher and higher, and felt that this too obvious magnanimity was indelicate and anything but magnanimous, but he did not know how else to do and could do nothing else. Looking at the pale, ironically smiling face of Von Koren, who evidently had been convinced from the beginning that his opponent would fire in the air, Laevsky thought that, thank God, everything would be over directly, and all that he had to do was to press the trigger rather hard. . . .

He felt a violent shock on the shoulder; there was the sound of a shot and an answering echo in the mountains: ping-ting!

Von Koren cocked his pistol and looked at Ustimovitch, who was pacing as before with his hands behind his back, taking no notice of anyone.

"Doctor," said the zoologist, "be so good as not to move to and fro like a pendulum. You make me dizzy."

The doctor stood still. Von Koren began to take aim at Laevsky.

"It's all over!" thought Laevsky.

The barrel of the pistol aimed straight at his face, the expression of hatred and contempt in Von Koren's attitude and whole figure, and the murder just about to be committed by a decent man in broad daylight, in the presence of decent men, and the stillness and the unknown force that compelled Laevsky to stand still and not to run—how mysterious it all was, how incomprehensible and terrible!

The moment while Von Koren was taking aim seemed to Laevsky longer than a night: he glanced imploringly at the seconds; they were pale and did not stir.

"Make haste and fire," thought Laevsky, and felt that his pale, quivering, and pitiful face must arouse even greater hatred in Von Koren.

"I'll kill him directly," thought Von Koren, aiming at his forehead, with his finger already on the catch. "Yes, of course I'll kill him. . . ."

"He'll kill him!" A despairing shout was suddenly heard somewhere very close at hand.

A shot rang out at once. Seeing that Laevsky remained standing where he was and did not fall, they all looked in the direction from which the shout had come, and saw the deacon. With pale face and wet hair sticking to his forehead and his cheeks, wet through and muddy, he was standing in the maize on the further bank, smiling rather queerly and waving his wet hat. Sheshkovsky laughed with joy, burst into tears, and moved away. . . .

XX

A little while afterwards, Von Koren and the deacon met near the little bridge. The deacon was excited; he breathed hard, and avoided looking in people's faces. He felt ashamed both of his terror and his muddy, wet garments.

"I thought you meant to kill him . . ." he muttered. "How contrary to human nature it is! How utterly unnatural it is!"

"But how did you come here?" asked the zoologist.

"Don't ask," said the deacon, waving his hand. "The evil one tempted me, saying: 'Go, go. . . .' So I went and almost died of fright in the maize. But now, thank God, thank God. . . . I am awfully pleased with you," muttered the deacon. "Old Grandad Tarantula will be glad. . . . It's funny, it's too funny! Only I beg of you most earnestly don't tell anybody I was there, or I may get into hot water with the authorities. They will say: 'The deacon was a second.' "

"Gentlemen," said Von Koren, "the deacon asks you not to tell anyone you've seen him here. He might get into trouble."

"How contrary to human nature it is!" sighed the deacon. "Excuse my saying so, but your face was so dreadful that I thought you were going to kill him."

"I was very much tempted to put an end to that scoundrel," said Von Koren, "but you shouted close by, and I missed my aim. The whole procedure is revolting to anyone who is not used to it, and it has exhausted me, deacon. I feel awfully tired. Come along. . . ."

"No, you must let me walk back. I must get dry, for I am wet and cold."

"Well, as you like," said the zoologist, in a weary tone, feeling dispirited, and, getting into the carriage, he closed his eyes. "As you like. . . ."

While they were moving about the carriages and taking their seats, Kerbalay stood in the road, and, laying his hands on his stomach, he bowed low, showing his teeth; he imagined that the gentry had come to enjoy the beauties of nature and drink tea, and could not understand why they were getting into the carriages. The party set off in complete silence and only the deacon was left by the *duhan*.

"Come to the *duhan*, drink tea," he said to Kerbalay. "Me wants to eat."

Kerbalay spoke good Russian, but the deacon imagined that the Tatar would understand him better if he talked to him in broken Russian. "Cook omelette, give cheese. . . ."

"Come, come, father," said Kerbalay, bowing. "I'll give you everything. . . . I've cheese and wine. . . . Eat what you like."

"What is 'God' in Tatar?" asked the deacon, going into the *duhan*.

"Your God and my God are the same," said Kerbalay, not understanding him. "God is the same for all men, only men are different. Some are Russian, some are Turks, some are English—there are many sorts of men, but God is one."

"Very good. If all men worship the same God, why do you Mahommedans look upon Christians as your everlasting enemies?"

"Why are you angry?" said Kerbalay, laying both hands on his stomach. "You are a priest; I am a Mussulman: you say, 'I want to eat'—I give it you. . . . Only the rich man distinguishes your God from my God; for the poor man it is all the same. If you please, it is ready."

While this theological conversation was taking place at the *duhan*, Laevsky was driving home thinking how dreadful it had been driving there at daybreak, when the roads, the rocks, and the mountains were wet and dark, and the uncertain future seemed like a terrible abyss, of which one could not see the bottom; while now the raindrops hanging on the grass and on the stones were sparkling in the sun like diamonds, nature was smiling joyfully, and the terrible future was left behind. He looked at Sheshkovsky's sullen, tear-stained face, and at the two carriages ahead of them in which Von Koren, his seconds, and the doctor were sitting, and it seemed to him as though they were all coming back from a graveyard in which a wearisome, insufferable man who was a burden to others had just been buried.

"Everything is over," he thought of his past, cautiously touching his neck with his fingers.

On the right side of his neck was a small swelling, of the length and breadth of his little finger, and he felt a pain, as though someone had passed a hot iron over his neck. The bullet had bruised it.

Afterwards, when he got home, a strange, long, sweet day began for him, misty as forgetfulness. Like a man released from prison or from hospital, he stared at the long-familiar objects and wondered that the tables, the windows, the chairs, the light, and the sea stirred in him a keen, childish delight such as he had not known for long, long years. Nadyezhda Fyodorovna, pale and haggard, could not understand his gentle voice and strange movements; she made haste to tell him everything that had happened to her. . . . It seemed to her that very likely he scarcely heard and did not understand her, and that if he did know everything he would curse her and kill her, but he listened to her, stroked her face and hair, looked into her eyes and said:

"I have nobody but you. . . ."

Then they sat a long while in the garden, huddled close together, saying nothing, or dreaming aloud of their happy life in the future, in brief, broken sentences, while it seemed to him that he had never spoken at such length or so eloquently.

XXI

More than three months had passed.

The day came that Von Koren had fixed on for his departure. A cold, heavy rain had been falling from early morning, a north-east wind was blowing, and the waves were high on the sea. It was said that the steamer would hardly be able to come into the harbour in such weather. By the time-table it should have arrived at ten o'clock in the morning, but Von Koren, who had gone on to the sea-front at midday and again after dinner, could see nothing through the field-glass but grey waves and rain covering the horizon.

Towards the end of the day the rain ceased and the wind began to drop perceptibly. Von Koren had already made up his mind that he would not be able to get off that day, and had settled down to play chess with Samoylenko; but after dark the orderly announced that there were lights on the sea and that a rocket had been seen.

Von Koren made haste. He put his satchel over his shoulder, and kissed Samoylenko and the deacon. Though there was not the slightest necessity, he went through the rooms again, said good-bye to the orderly and the cook, and went out into the street, feeling that he had left something behind, either at the doctor's or his lodging. In the street he walked beside Samoylenko, behind them came the deacon with a box, and last of all the orderly with two portmanteaus. Only Samoylenko and the orderly could distinguish the dim lights on the sea. The others gazed into the darkness and saw nothing. The steamer had stopped a long way from the coast.

"Make haste, make haste," Von Koren hurried them. "I am afraid it will set off."

As they passed the little house with three windows, into which Laevsky had moved soon after the duel, Von Koren could not resist peeping in at the window. Laevsky was sitting, writing, bent over the table, with his back to the window.

"I wonder at him!" said the zoologist softly, "What a screw he has put on himself!"

"Yes, one may well wonder," said Samoylenko. "He sits from morning till night, he's always at work. He works to pay off his debts. And he lives, brother, worse than a beggar!"

Half a minute of silence followed. The zoologist, the doctor, and the deacon stood at the window and went on looking at Laevsky.

"So he didn't get away from here, poor fellow," said Samoylenko. "Do you remember how hard he tried?"

"Yes, he has put a screw on himself," Von Koren repeated. "His marriage, the way he works all day long for his daily bread, a new expression in his face, and even in his walk—it's all so extraordinary that I don't know what to call it."

The zoologist took Samoylenko's sleeve and went on with emotion in his voice:

"You tell him and his wife that when I went away I was full of admiration for them and wished them all happiness . . . and I beg him, if he can, not to remember evil against me. He knows me. He knows that if I could have foreseen this change, then I might have become his best friend."

"Go in and say good-bye to him."

"No, that wouldn't do."

"Why? God knows, perhaps you'll never see him again."

The zoologist reflected, and said:

"That's true."

Samoylenko tapped softly at the window. Laevsky started and looked round.

"Vanya, Nikolay Vassilitch wants to say good-bye to you," said Samoylenko. "He is just going away."

Laevsky got up from the table, and went into the passage to open the door. Samoylenko, the zoologist, and the deacon went into the house.

"I can only come for one minute," began the zoologist, taking off his goloshes in the passage, and already wishing he had not given way to his feelings and come in, uninvited. "It is as though I were forcing myself on him," he thought, "and that's stupid."

"Forgive me for disturbing you," he said as he went into the room with Laevsky, "but I'm just going away, and I had an impulse to see you. God knows whether we shall ever meet again."

"I am very glad to see you. . . . Please come in," said Laevsky, and he awkwardly set chairs for his visitors as though he wanted to bar their way, and stood in the middle of the room, rubbing his hands.

"I should have done better to have left my audience in the street," thought

Von Koren, and he said firmly: "Don't remember evil against me, Ivan Andreitch. To forget the past is, of course, impossible—it is too painful, and I've not come here to apologize or to declare that I was not to blame. I acted sincerely, and I have not changed my conviction since then. . . . It is true that I see, to my great delight, that I was mistaken in regard to you, but it's easy to make a false step even on a smooth road, and, in fact, it's the natural human lot: if one is not mistaken in the main, one is mistaken in the details. Nobody knows the real truth."

"No, no one knows the truth," said Laevsky.

"Well, good-bye. . . . God give you all happiness."

Von Koren gave Laevsky his hand; the latter took it and bowed.

"Don't remember evil against me," said Von Koren. "Give my greetings to your wife, and say I am very sorry not to say good-bye to her."

"She is at home."

Laevsky went to the door of the next room, and said:

"Nadya, Nikolay Vassilitch wants to say good-bye to you."

Nadyezhda Fyodorovna came in; she stopped near the doorway and looked shyly at the visitors. There was a look of guilt and dismay on her face, and she held her hands like a schoolgirl receiving a scolding.

"I'm just going away, Nadyezhda Fyodorovna," said Von Koren, "and have come to say good-bye."

She held out her hand uncertainly while Laevsky bowed.

"What pitiful figures they are, though!" thought Von Koren. "The life they are living does not come easy to them. I shall be in Moscow and Petersburg; can I send you anything?" he asked.

"Oh!" said Nadyezhda Fyodorovna, and she looked anxiously at her husband. "I don't think there's anything. . . ."

"No, nothing . . ." said Laevsky, rubbing his hands. "Our greetings."

Von Koren did not know what he could or ought to say, though as he went in he thought he would say a very great deal that would be warm and good and important. He shook hands with Laevsky and his wife in silence, and left them with a depressed feeling.

"What people!" said the deacon in a low voice, as he walked behind them. "My God, what people! Of a truth, the right hand of God has planted this vine! Lord! Lord! One man vanquishes thousands and another tens of thousands. Nikolay Vassilitch," he said ecstatically, "let me tell you that to-day you have conquered the greatest of man's enemies—pride."

"Hush, deacon! Fine conquerors we are! Conquerors ought to look like eagles, while he's a pitiful figure, timid, crushed; he bows like a Chinese idol, and I, I am sad. . . ."

They heard steps behind them. It was Laevsky, hurrying after them to see him off. The orderly was standing on the quay with the two portmanteaus, and at a little distance stood four boatmen.

"There is a wind, though. . . . Brrr!" said Samoylenko. "There must be a pretty stiff storm on the sea now! You are not going off at a nice time, Kolya."

"I'm not afraid of sea-sickness."

"That's not the point. . . . I only hope these rascals won't upset you. You ought to have crossed in the agent's sloop. Where's the agent's sloop?" he shouted to the boatmen.

"It has gone, Your Excellency."

"And the Customs-house boat?"

"That's gone, too."

"Why didn't you let us know?" said Samoylenko angrily. "You dolts!"

"It's all the same, don't worry yourself . . ." said Von Koren. "Well, good-bye. God keep you."

Samoylenko embraced Van Koren and made the sign of the cross over him three times.

"Don't forget us, Kolya. . . . Write. . . . We shall look out for you next spring."

"Good-bye, deacon," said Von Koren, shaking hands with the deacon. "Thank you for your company and for your pleasant conversation. Think about the expedition."

"Oh Lord, yes! to the ends of the earth," laughed the deacon. "I've nothing against it."

Von Koren recognized Laevsky in the darkness, and held out his hand without speaking. The boatmen were by now below, holding the boat, which was beating against the piles, though the breakwater screened it from the breakers. Von Koren went down the ladder, jumped into the boat, and sat at the helm.

"Write!" Samoylenko shouted to him. "Take care of yourself!"

"No one knows the real truth," thought Laevsky, turning up the collar of his coat and thrusting his hands into his sleeves.

The boat turned briskly out of the harbour into the open sea. It vanished in the waves, but at once from a deep hollow glided up on to a high breaker, so that they could distinguish the men and even the oars. The boat moved three yards forward and was sucked two yards back.

"Write!" shouted Samoylenko; "it's devilish weather for you to go in."

"Yes, no one knows the real truth . . ." thought Laevsky, looking wearily at the dark, restless sea.

"It flings the boat back," he thought; "she makes two steps forward and one step back; but the boatmen are stubborn, they work the oars unceasingly, and are not afraid of the high waves. The boat goes on and on. Now she is out of sight, but in half an hour the boatmen will see the steamer lights distinctly, and within an hour they will be by the steamer ladder. So it is in life. . . . In the search for truth man makes two steps forward and one step back. Suffering, mistakes, and weariness of life thrust them back, but the thirst for truth and stubborn will drive them on and on. And who knows? Perhaps they will reach the real truth at last."

"Go—o—od-by—e," shouted Samoylenko.

"There's no sight or sound of them," said the deacon. "Good luck on the journey!"

It began to spot with rain.

The Virgin and the Gipsy

_B Y_

D. H. Lawrence

Editor's Note

D. H. Lawrence was born in 1885 in the town of Eastwood, near Nottingham, England, the son of an uncouth coal miner and his better-educated wife. Lawrence's childhood was oppressed by the family's poverty, his father's drinking, his mother's ambitions, and his parents' unhappy marriage. After completing his primary education, he taught school for three years; then a scholarship gave him two years at Nottingham University. He had begun to write. He taught school again near London for a time. In December 1910 his mother died; in January 1911 his first novel, *The White Peacock*, was published. Within a year he had left teaching to devote himself entirely to writing.

In early April 1912, he called on his former French professor in Nottingham, Ernest Weekley, and was smitten by his wife, Frieda. She was descended from a German aristocratic family, the von Richtofens. On May 3 she abandoned her husband and three children for Lawrence; they were later married. (After Lawrence's death, Weekley offered to remarry her; she declined.) For the rest of Lawrence's life, they wandered: Italy, Switzerland, Germany, France, Australia, England, Mexico, New Mexico.

Lawrence wrote a great many novels, stories, poems, travel sketches, letters, literary essays, and diatribes. His prophetic teachings on sex and society, on how to live, on the hidden nature of human beings, together with his extraordinary force of person, made him the center of a cult which still flourishes. Several of his stories, perhaps some of his essays, a few of his novels because of the strength of parts of them (especially the first part of the early autobiographical novel, *Sons and Lovers*) show every sign of enduring. But ranking Lawrence and his works is even harder than ranking most writers, because of the partisan zeal of his admirers and detractors both.

The Virgin and the Gipsy was written in 1926 in Spotorno, Italy, and is sometimes seen as an earlier and more successful handling of one of the themes of Lawrence's last novel, *Lady Chatterley's Lover*. The story, dedicated to Frieda, was published in 1930, shortly after Lawrence's death by tuberculosis in Vence, on the French Riviera.

The Virgin and the Gipsy

ONE

WHEN THE VICAR'S WIFE WENT OFF WITH A YOUNG AND PENNILESS MAN
the scandal knew no bounds. Her two little girls were only seven
and nine years old respectively. And the vicar was such a good
husband. True, his hair was grey. But his moustache was dark, he was handsome, and still full of furtive passion for his unrestrained and beautiful wife.

Why did she go? Why did she burst away with such an *éclat* of revulsion,
like a touch of madness?

Nobody gave any answer. Only the pious said she was a bad woman.
While some of the good women kept silent. They knew.

The two little girls never knew. Wounded, they decided that it was because their mother found them negligible.

The ill wind that blows nobody any good swept away the vicarage family
on its blast. Then lo and behold! the vicar, who was somewhat distinguished
as an essayist and a controversialist, and whose case had aroused sympathy
among the bookish men, received the living of Papplewick. The Lord had
tempered the wind of misfortune with a rectorate in the north country.

The rectory was a rather ugly stone house down by the river Papple, before you come into the village. Further on, beyond where the road crosses
the stream, were the big old stone cottonmills, once driven by water. The
road curved uphill, into the bleak stone streets of the village.

The vicarage family received decided modification, upon its transference
into the rectory. The vicar, now the rector, fetched up his old mother
and his sister, and a brother from the city. The two little girls had a very
different milieu from the old home.

The rector was now forty-seven years old; he had displayed an intense
and not very dignified grief after the flight of his wife. Sympathetic ladies
had stayed him from suicide. His hair was almost white, and he had a wild-
eyed, tragic look. You had only to look at him, to know how dreadful it all
was, and how he had been wronged.

Yet somewhere there was a false note. And some of the ladies, who had sympathised most profoundly with the vicar, secretly rather disliked the rector. There was a certain furtive self-righteousness about him, when all was said and done.

The little girls, of course, in the vague way of children, accepted the family verdict. Granny, who was over seventy and whose sight was failing, became the central figure in the house. Aunt Cissie, who was over forty, pale, pious, and gnawed by an inward worm, kept house. Uncle Fred, a stingy and grey-faced man of forty, who just lived dingily for himself, went into town every day. And the rector, of course, was the most important person, after Granny.

They called her The Mater. She was one of those physically vulgar, clever old bodies who had got her own way all her life by buttering the weaknesses of her men-folk. Very quickly she took her cue. The rector still "loved" his delinquent wife, and would "love her" till he died. Therefore hush! The rector's feeling was sacred. In his heart was enshrined the pure girl he had wedded and worshipped.

Out in the evil world, at the same time, there wandered a disreputable woman who had betrayed the rector and abandoned his little children. She was now yoked to a young and despicable man, who no doubt would bring her the degradation she deserved. Let this be clearly understood, and then hush! For in the pure loftiness of the rector's heart still bloomed the pure white snowflower of his young bride. This white snowflower did not wither. That other creature, who had gone off with that despicable young man, was none of his affair.

The Mater, who had been somewhat diminished and insignificant as a widow in a small house, now climbed into the chief arm-chair in the rectory, and planted her old bulk firmly again. She was not going to be dethroned. Astutely she gave a sigh of homage to the rector's fidelity to the pure white snowflower, while she pretended to disapprove. In sly reverence for her son's great love, she spoke no word against that nettle which flourished in the evil world, and which had once been called Mrs. Arthur Saywell. Now, thank heaven, having married again, she was no more Mrs. Arthur Saywell. No woman bore the rector's name. The pure white snowflower bloomed *in perpetuum*, without nomenclature. The family even thought of her as She-who-was-Cynthia.

All this was water on the Mater's mill. It secured her against Arthur's ever marrying again. She had him by his feeblest weakness, his skulking self-love. He had married an imperishable white snowflower. Lucky man! He had been injured! Unhappy man! He had suffered. Ah, what a heart of love! And he had—forgiven! Yes, the white snowflower was forgiven. He even had made provision in his will for her, when that other scoundrel—But hush! Don't even *think* too near to that horrid nettle in the rank outer world! She-who-was-Cynthia. Let the white snowflower bloom inaccessible on the heights of the past. The present is another story.

The children were brought up in this atmosphere of cunning self-sanctification and of unmentionability. They too, saw the snowflower on inaccessible heights. They too knew that it was throned in lone splendour aloft their lives, never to be touched.

At the same time, out of the squalid world sometimes would come a rank, evil smell of selfishness and degraded lust, the smell of that awful nettle, She-who-was-Cynthia. This nettle actually contrived, at intervals, to get a little note through to her girls, her children. And at this the silver-haired Mater shook inwardly with hate. For if She-who-was-Cynthia ever came back, there wouldn't be much left of the Mater. A secret gust of hate went from the old granny to the girls, children of that foul nettle of lust, that Cynthia who had had such an affectionate contempt for the Mater.

Mingled with all this, was the children's perfectly distinct recollection of their real home, the Vicarage in the south, and their glamorous but not very dependable mother, Cynthia. She had made a great glow, a flow of life, like a swift and dangerous sun in the home, forever coming and going. They always associated her presence with brightness, but also with danger; with glamour, but with fearful selfishness.

Now the glamour was gone, and the white snowflower, like a porcelain wreath, froze on its grave. The danger of instability, the peculiarly *danger-ous* sort of selfishness, like lions and tigers, was also gone. There was now a complete stability, in which one could perish safely.

But they were growing up. And as they grew, they became more definitely confused, more actively puzzled. The Mater, as she grew older, grew blinder. Somebody had to lead her about. She did not get up till towards midday. Yet blind or bed-ridden, she held the house.

Besides, she wasn't bed-ridden. Whenever the *men* were present, the Mater was in her throne. She was too cunning to court neglect. Especially as she had rivals.

Her great rival was the younger girl, Yvette. Yvette had some of the vague, careless blitheness of She-who-was-Cynthia. But this one was more docile. Granny perhaps had caught her in time. Perhaps!

The rector adored Yvette, and spoiled her with a doting fondness; as much as to say: am I not a soft-hearted, indulgent old boy! He liked to have weaknesses to a hair's-breadth. She knew them, this opinion of himself, and the Mater knew his and she traded on them by turning them into decorations for him, for his character. He wanted, in his own eyes, to have a fascinating character, as women want to have fascinating dresses. And the Mater cunningly put beauty-spots over his defects and deficiencies. Her mother-love gave her the clue to his weaknesses, and she hid them for him with decorations. Whereas She-who-was-Cynthia—! But don't mention *her*, in this connection. In her eyes, the rector was almost humpbacked and an idiot.

The funny thing was, Granny secretly hated Lucille, the elder girl, more than the pampered Yvette. Lucille, the uneasy and irritable, was more conscious of being under Granny's power, than was the spoilt and vague Yvette.

On the other hand, Aunt Cissie hated Yvette. She hated her very name. Aunt Cissie's life had been sacrificed to the Mater, and Aunt Cissie knew it, and the Mater knew she knew it. Yet as the years went on, it became a convention. The convention of Aunt Cissie's sacrifice was accepted by everybody, including the self-same Cissie. She prayed a good deal about it. Which also showed that she had her own private feelings somewhere, poor thing. She had ceased to be Cissie, she had lost her life and her sex. And now, she was creeping towards fifty, strange green flares of rage would come up in her, and at such times, she was insane.

But Granny held her in her power. And Aunt Cissie's one object in life was to look after The Mater.

Aunt Cissie's green flares of hellish hate would go up against all young things, sometimes. Poor thing, she prayed and tried to obtain forgiveness from heaven. But what had been done to her, *she* could not forgive, and the vitriol would spurt in her veins sometimes.

It was not as if the Mater were a warm, kindly soul. She wasn't. She only seemed it, cunningly. And the fact dawned gradually on the girls. Under her old-fashioned lace cap, under her silver hair, under the black silk of her stout, forward-bulging body, this old woman had a cunning heart, seeking forever her own female power. And through the weakness of the unfresh, stagnant men she had bred, she kept her power, as her years rolled on, from seventy to eighty, and from eighty on the new lap, towards ninety.

For in the family there was a whole tradition of "loyalty"; loyalty to one another, and especially to the Mater. The Mater, of course, was the pivot of the family. The family was her own extended ego. Naturally she covered it with her power. And her sons and daughters, being weak and disintegrated, naturally were loyal. Outside the family, what was there for them but danger and insult and ignominy? Had not the rector experienced it, in his marriage. So now, caution! Caution and loyalty, fronting the world! Let there be as much hate and friction *inside* the family, as you like. To the outer world, a stubborn fence of unison.

TWO

But it was not until the girls finally came home from school, that they felt the full weight of Granny's dear old hand on their lives. Lucille was now nearly twenty-one, and Yvette nineteen. They had been to a good girls' school, and had had a finishing year in Lausanne, and were quite the usual thing, tall young creatures with fresh, sensitive faces and bobbed hair and young-manly, deuce-take-it manners.

"What's so awfully *boring* about Papplewick," said Yvette, as they stood on the Channel boat watching the grey, grey cliffs of Dover draw near, "is that there are no *men* about. Why doesn't Daddy have some good old sports for friends? As for Uncle Fred, he's the limit!"

"Oh, you never know what will turn up," said Lucille, more philosophic.

"You jolly well know what to expect," said Yvette. "Choir on Sundays, and I hate mixed choirs. Boys' voices are *lovely*, when there are no women. And Sunday School and Girls' Friendly, and socials, all the dear old souls that enquire after Granny! Not a decent young fellow for miles."

"Oh I don't know!" said Lucille. "There's always the Framleys. And you know Gerry Somercotes *adores* you."

"Oh but I *hate* fellows who adore me!" cried Yvette, turning up her sensitive nose. "They *bore* me. They hang on like lead."

"Well what *do* you want, if you can't stand being adored? *I* think it's perfectly all right to be adored. You know you'll never marry them, so why not let them go on adoring, if it amuses them."

"Oh but I *want* to get married," cried Yvette.

"Well in that case, let them go on adoring you till you find one that you can *possibly* marry."

"I never should, that way. Nothing puts me off like an adoring fellow. They *bore* me so! They make me feel beastly."

"Oh, so they do me, if they get pressing. But at a distance, I think they're rather nice."

"I should like to fall *violently* in love."

"Oh, very likely! I shouldn't! I should hate it. Probably so would you, if it actually happened. After all, we've got to settle down a bit, before we know what we want."

"But don't you *hate* going back to Papplewick?" cried Yvette, turning up her young sensitive nose.

"No, not particularly. I suppose we shall be rather bored. I wish Daddy would get a car. I suppose we shall have to drag the old bikes out. Wouldn't you like to get up to Tansy Moor?"

"Oh, *love* it! Though it's an awful *strain*, shoving an old push-bike up those hills."

The ship was nearing the grey cliffs. It was summer, but a grey day. The two girls wore their coats with fur collars turned up, and little *chic* hats pulled down over their ears. Tall, slender, fresh-faced, naive, yet confident, too confident, in their school-girlish arrogance, they were so terribly English. They seemed so free, and were as a matter of fact so tangled and tied up, inside themselves. They seemed so dashing and unconventional, and were really so conventional, so, as it were, shut up indoors inside themselves. They looked like bold, tall young sloops, just slipping from the harbour, into the wide seas of life. And they were, as a matter of fact, two poor young rudderless lives, moving from one chain anchorage to another.

The rectory struck a chill into their hearts as they entered. It seemed ugly, and almost sordid, with the dank air of that middle-class, degenerated comfort which has ceased to be comfortable and has turned stuffy, unclean. The hard, stone house struck the girls as being unclean, they could not have said why. The shabby furniture seemed somehow sordid, nothing was fresh. Even the food at meals had that awful dreary sordidness which is so repulsive to a young thing coming from abroad. Roast beef and wet cabbage, cold mutton and mashed potatoes, sour pickles, inexcusable puddings.

Granny, who "loved a bit of pork," also had special dishes, beef-tea and rusks, or a small savoury custard. The grey-faced Aunt Cissie ate nothing at all. She would sit at table, and take a single lonely and naked boiled potato on to her plate. She never ate meat. So she sat in sordid durance, while the meal went on, and Granny quickly slobbered her portion—lucky if she spilled nothing on her protuberant stomach. The food was not appetising in itself: how could it be, when Aunt Cissie hated food herself, hated the fact of eating, and never could keep a maid-servant for three months. The girls ate with repulsion, Lucille bravely bearing up, Yvette's tender nose showing her disgust. Only the rector, white-haired, wiped his long grey moustache with his serviette, and cracked jokes. He too was getting heavy and inert, sitting in his study all day, never taking exercise. But he cracked sarcastic little jokes all the time, sitting there under the shelter of the Mater.

The country, with its steep hills and its deep, narrow valleys, was dark and gloomy, yet had a certain powerful strength of its own. Twenty miles away was the black industrialism of the north. Yet the village of Papplewick was comparatively lonely, almost lost, the life in it stony and dour. Everything was stone, with a hardness that was almost poetic, it was so unrelenting.

It was as the girls had known: they went back into the choir, they helped in the parish. But Yvette struck absolutely against Sunday School, the Band of Hope, the Girls Friendlies—indeed against all those functions that were conducted by determined old maids and obstinate, stupid elderly men. She avoided church duties as much as possible, and got away from the rectory whenever she could. The Framleys, a big, untidy, jolly family up at the Grange, were an enormous standby. And if anybody asked her out to a meal, even if a woman in one of the workmen's houses asked her to stay to tea, she accepted at once. In fact, she was rather thrilled. She liked talking to the working men, they had often such fine, hard heads. But of course they were in another world.

So the months went by. Gerry Somercotes was still an adorer. There were others, too, sons of farmers or mill-owners. Yvette really ought to have had a good time. She was always out to parties and dances, friends came for her in their motor-cars, and off she went to the city, to the afternoon dance in the chief hotel, or in the gorgeous new Palais de Danse, called the Pally.

Yet she always seemed like a creature mesmerised. She was never free to be quite jolly. Deep inside her worked an intolerable irritation, which she thought she *ought* not to feel, and which she hated feeling, thereby making it worse. She never understood at all whence it arose.

At home, she truly was irritable, and outrageously rude to Aunt Cissie. In fact Yvette's awful temper became one of the family by-words.

Lucille, always more practical, got a job in the city as private secretary to a man who needed somebody with fluent French and shorthand. She went back and forth every day, by the same train as Uncle Fred. But she never travelled with him, and wet or fine, bicycled to the station, while he went on foot.

The two girls were both determined that what they wanted was a really jolly social life. And they resented with fury that the rectory was, for their friends, impossible. There were only four rooms downstairs: the kitchen, where lived the two discontented maid-servants: the dark dining-room: the rector's study: and the big, "homely," dreary living-room or drawing-room. In the dining-room there was a gas fire. Only in the living-room was a good hot fire kept going. Because of course, here Granny reigned.

In this room the family was assembled. At evening, after dinner, Uncle Fred and the rector invariably played cross-word puzzles with Granny.

"Now, Mater, are you ready? N blank blank blank blank W: a Siamese functionary."

"Eh? Eh? M blank blank blank blank W?"

Granny was hard of hearing.

"No, Mater. Not M! N blank blank blank blank W: a Siamese functionary."

"N blank blank blank blank W: a Chinese functionary."

"SIAMESE."

"Eh?"

"SIAMESE! SIAM!"

"A Siamese functionary! Now what can that be?" said the old lady profoundly, folding her hands on her round stomach. Her two sons proceeded to make suggestions, at which she said Ah! Ah! The rector was amazingly clever at cross-word puzzles. But Fred had a certain technical vocabulary.

"This certainly is a hard nut to crack," said the old lady, when they were all stuck.

Meanwhile Lucille sat in a corner with her hands over her ears, pretending to read, and Yvette irritably made drawings, or hummed loud and exasperating tunes, to add to the family concert. Aunt Cissie continually reached for a chocolate, and her jaws worked ceaselessly. She literally lived on chocolates. Sitting in the distance, she put another into her mouth, then looked again at the parish magazine. Then she lifted her head, and saw it was time to fetch Granny's cup of Horlicks.

While she was gone, in nervous exasperation Yvette would open the window. The room was never fresh, she imagined it smelt: smelt of Granny. And Granny, who was hard of hearing, heard like a weasel when she wasn't wanted to.

"Did you open the window, Yvette? I think you might remember there are older people than yourself in the room," she said.

"It's stifling! It's unbearable! No wonder we've all of us always got colds."

"I'm sure the room is large enough, and a good fire burning." The old lady gave a little shudder. "A draught to give us all our death."

"Not a draught at all," roared Yvette. "A breath of fresh air."

The old lady shuddered again, and said:

"Indeed!"

The rector, in silence, marched to the window and firmly closed it. He did not look at his daughter meanwhile. He hated thwarting her. But she must know what's what!

The cross-word puzzles, invented by Satan himself, continued till Granny had had her Horlicks, and was to go to bed. Then came the ceremony of Goodnight! Everybody stood up. The girls went to be kissed by the blind old woman. The rector gave his arm, and Aunt Cissie followed with a candle.

But this was already nine o'clock, although Granny was really getting old, and should have been in bed sooner. But when she was in bed, she could not sleep, till Aunt Cissie came.

"You see," said Granny, "I have *never* slept alone. For fifty-four years I never slept a night without the Pater's arm round me. And when he was gone, I tried to sleep alone. But as sure as my eyes closed to sleep, my heart nearly jumped out of my body, and I lay in a palpitation. Oh, you may think what you will, but it was a fearful experience, after fifty-four years of perfect married life! I would have prayed to be taken first, but the Pater, well, no I don't think he would have been able to bear up."

So Aunt Cissie slept with Granny. And she hated it. She said *she* could never sleep. And she grew greyer and greyer, and the food in the house got worse, and Aunt Cissie had to have an operation.

But The Mater rose as ever, towards noon, and at the mid-day meal, she presided from her arm-chair, with her stomach protruding, her reddish, pendulous face, that had a sort of horrible majesty, dropping soft under the wall of her high brow, and her blue eyes peering unseeing. Her white hair was getting scanty, it was altogether a little indecent. But the rector jovially cracked his jokes to her, and she pretended to disapprove. But she was perfectly complacent, sitting in her ancient obesity, and after meals, getting the wind from her stomach, pressing her bosom with her hand as she "rifted" in gross physical complacency.

What the girls minded most was that, when they brought their young friends to the house, Granny always was there, like some awful idol of old flesh, consuming all the attention. There was only the one room for everybody. And there sat the old lady, with Aunt Cissie keeping an acrid guard over her. Everybody must be presented first to Granny: she was ready to be genial, she liked company. She had to know who everybody was, where they came from, every circumstance of their lives. And then, when she was *au fait*, she could get hold of the conversation.

Nothing could be more exasperating to the girls. "Isn't old Mrs. Saywell wonderful! She takes *such* an interest in life, at nearly ninety!"

"She does take an interest in people's affairs, if that's life," said Yvette.

Then she would immediately feel guilty. After all, it *was* wonderful to be nearly ninety, and have such a clear mind! And Granny never *actually* did anybody any harm. It was more that she was in the way. And perhaps it was rather awful to hate somebody because they were old and in the way.

Yvette immediately repented, and was nice. Granny blossomed forth into reminiscences of when she was a girl, in the little town in Buckinghamshire. She talked and talked away, and was *so* entertaining. She really *was* rather wonderful.

Then in the afternoon Lottie and Ella and Bob Framley came, with Leo Wetherell.

"Oh, come in!"—and in they all trooped to the sitting-room, where Granny, in her white cap, sat by the fire.

"Granny, this is Mr. Wetherell."

"Mr. What-did-you-say? You must excuse me, I'm a little deaf!"

Granny gave her hand to the uncomfortable young man, and gazed silently at him, sightlessly.

"You are not from our parish?" she asked him.

"Dinnington!" he shouted.

"We want to go to a picnic tomorrow, to Bonsall Head, in Leo's car. We can all squeeze in," said Ella, in a low voice.

"Did you say Bonsall Head?" asked Granny.

"Yes!"

There was a blank silence.

"Did you say you were going in a car?"

"Yes! In Mr. Wetherell's."

"I hope he's a good driver. It's a very dangerous road."

"He's a *very* good driver."

"Not a very good driver?"

"Yes! He *is* a very good driver."

"If you go to Bonsall Head, I think I must send a message to Lady Louth."

Granny always dragged in this miserable Lady Louth, when there was company.

"Oh, we shan't go that way," cried Yvette.

"Which way?" said Granny. "You must go by Heanor."

The whole party sat, as Bob expressed it, like stuffed ducks, fidgeting on their chairs.

Aunt Cissie came in—and then the maid with the tea. There was the eternal and everlasting piece of bought cake. Then appeared a plate of little fresh cakes. Aunt Cissie had actually sent to the baker's.

"Tea, Mater!"

The old lady gripped the arms of her chair. Everybody rose and stood, while she waded slowly across, on Aunt Cissie's arm, to her place at table.

During tea Lucille came in from town, from her job. She was simply worn out, with black marks under her eyes. She gave a cry, seeing all the company.

As soon as the noise had subsided, and the awkwardness was resumed, Granny said:

"You have never mentioned Mr. Wetherell to me, have you, Lucille?"

"I don't remember," said Lucille.

"You can't have done. The name is strange to me."

Yvette absently grabbed another cake, from the now almost empty plate. Aunt Cissie, who was driven almost crazy by Yvette's vague and inconsiderate ways, felt the green rage fuse in her heart. She picked up her own plate, on which was the one cake she allowed herself, and said with vitriolic politeness, offering it to Yvette:

"Won't you have mine?"

"Oh thanks!" said Yvette, starting in her angry vagueness. And with an appearance of the same insouciance, she helped herself to Aunt Cissie's cake also, adding as an afterthought: "If you're sure you don't want it."

She now had two cakes on her plate. Lucille had gone white as a ghost, bending to her tea. Aunt Cissie sat with a green look of poisonous resignation. The awkwardness was an agony.

But Granny, bulkily enthroned and unaware, only said, in the centre of the cyclone:

"If you are motoring to Bonsall Head tomorrow, Lucille, I wish you would take a message from me to Lady Louth."

"Oh!" said Lucille, giving a queer look across the table at the sightless old woman. Lady Louth was the King Charles' Head of the family, invariably produced by Granny for the benefit of visitors. "Very well!"

"She was so very kind last week. She sent her chauffeur over with a Cross-word Puzzle book for me."

"But you thanked her then," cried Yvette.

"I should like to send her a note."

"We can post it," cried Lucille.

"Oh, no! I should like you to take it. When Lady Louth called last time. . . ."

The young ones sat like a shoal of young fishes dumbly mouthing at the surface of the water, while Granny went on about Lady Louth. Aunt Cissie, the two girls knew, was still helpless, almost unconscious in a paroxysm of rage about the cake. Perhaps, poor thing, she was praying.

It was a mercy when the friends departed. But by that time the two girls were both haggard-eyed. And it was then that Yvette, looking round, suddenly saw the stony, implacable will-to-power in the old and motherly-seeming Granny. She sat there bulging backwards in her chair, impassive, her reddish, pendulous old face rather mottled, almost unconscious, but implacable, her face like a mask that hid something stony, relentless. It was the static inertia of her unsavoury power. Yet in a minute she would open her ancient mouth to find out every detail about Leo Wetherell. For the moment she was hibernating in her oldness, her agedness. But in a minute her mouth would open, her mind would flicker awake, and with her insatiable greed for life, other people's life, she would start on her quest for every detail. She was like the old toad which Yvette had watched, fascinated, as it sat on the ledge of the beehive, immediately in front of the little entrance by which the bees emerged, and which, with a demonish lightning-like snap of its pursed jaws, caught every bee as it came out to launch into the air, swallowed them one after the other, as if it could consume the whole hive-full, into its aged, bulging, purse-like wrinkledness. It had been swallowing bees as they launched into the air of spring, year after year, year after year, for generations:

But the gardener, called by Yvette, was in a rage, and killed the creature with a stone.

"'Appen tha *art* good for th' snails," he said, as he came down with the stone. "But tha 'rt none goin' ter emp'y th' bee-'ive into thy guts."

THREE

The next day was dull and low, and the roads were awful, for it had been raining for weeks, yet the young ones set off on their trip, without taking Granny's message either. They just slipped out while she was making her slow trip upstairs after lunch. Not for anything would they have called at Lady Louth's house. That widow of a knighted doctor, a harmless person indeed, had become an obnoxity in their lives.

Six young rebels, they sat very perkily in the car as they swished through the mud. Yet they had a peaked look too. After all, they had nothing really to rebel against, any of them. They were left so very free in their movements. Their parents let them do almost entirely as they liked. There wasn't really a fetter to break, nor a prison-bar to file through, nor a bolt to shatter. The keys of their lives were in their own hands. And there they dangled inert.

It is very much easier to shatter prison bars than to open undiscovered doors to life. As the younger generation finds out, somewhat to its chagrin. True, there was Granny. But poor old Granny, you couldn't actually say to her: "Lie down and die, you old woman!" She might be an old nuisance, but she never really *did* anything. It wasn't fair to hate her.

So the young people set off on their jaunt, trying to be very full of beans. They could really do as they liked. And so, of course, there was nothing to do but sit in the car and talk a lot of criticism of other people, and silly flirty gallantry that was really rather a bore. If there had only been a few "strict orders" to be disobeyed! But nothing: beyond the refusal to carry the message to Lady Louth, of which the rector would approve, because he didn't encourage King Charles' Head either.

They sang, rather scrappily, the latest would-be comic songs, as they went through the grim villages. In the great park the deer were in groups near the road, roe deer and fallow, nestling in the gloom of the afternoon under the oaks by the road, as if for the stimulus of human company.

Yvette insisted on stopping and getting out to talk to them. The girls, in their Russian boots, tramped through the damp grass, while the deer watched them with big, unfrightened eyes. The hart trotted away mildly, holding back his head, because of the weight of the horns. But the doe, balancing her big ears, did not rise from under the tree, with her half-grown young ones, till the girls were almost in touch. Then she walked lightfoot away, lifting her tail from her spotted flanks, while the young ones nimbly trotted.

"Aren't they awfully dainty and nice!" cried Yvette. "You'd wonder they could lie so cosily in this horrid wet grass."

"Well I suppose they've got to lie down *sometime*," said Lucille. "And it's *fairly* dry under the tree." She looked at the crushed grass, where the deer had lain.

Yvette went and put her hand down, to feel how it felt.

"Yes!" she said, doubtfully, "I believe it's a bit warm."

The deer had bunched again a few yards away, and were standing motionless in the gloom of the afternoon. Away below the slopes of grass and trees, beyond the swift river with its balustraded bridge, sat the huge ducal house, one or two chimneys smoking bluely. Behind it rose purplish woods.

The girls, pushing their fur collars up to their ears, dangling one long arm, stood watching in silence, their wide Russian boots protecting them from the wet grass. The great house squatted square and creamy-grey below. The deer, in little groups, were scattered under the old trees close by. It all seemed so still, so unpretentious, and so sad.

"I wonder where the Duke is now," said Ella.

"Not here, wherever he is," said Lucille. "I expect he's abroad where the sun shines."

The motor horn called from the road, and they heard Leo's voice:

"Come on boys! If we're going to get to the Head and down to Amber-dale for tea, we'd better move."

They crowded into the car again, with chilled feet, and set off through the park, past the silent spire of the church, out through the great gates and over the bridge, on into the wide, damp, stony village of Woodlinkin, where the river ran. And thence, for a long time, they stayed in the mud and dark and dampness of the valley, often with sheer rock above them; the water brawl-ing on one hand, the steep rock or dark trees on the other.

Till, through the darkness of overhanging trees, they began to climb, and Leo changed the gear. Slowly the car toiled up through the whitey-grey mud, into the stony village of Bolehill, that hung on the slope, round the old cross, with its steps, that stood where the road branched, on past the cottages whence came a wonderful smell of hot tea-cakes, and beyond, still upwards, under dripping trees and past broken slopes of bracken, always climbing. Until the cleft became shallower, and the trees finished, and the slopes on either side were bare, gloomy grass, with low dry-stone walls. They were emerging on to the Head.

The party had been silent for some time. On either side the road was grass, then a low stone fence, and the swelling curve of the hill-summit, traced with the low, dry-stone walls. Above this, the low sky.

The car ran out, under the low, grey sky, on the naked tops.

"Shall we stay a moment?" called Leo.

"Oh yes!" cried the girls.

And they scrambled out once more, to look around. They knew the place quite well. But still, if one came to the Head, one got out to look.

The hills were like the knuckles of a hand, the dales were below, between the fingers, narrow, steep, and dark. In the deeps a train was steaming, slowly pulling north: a small thing of the underworld. The noise of the engine re-echoed curiously upwards. Then came the dull, familiar sound of blasting in a quarry.

Leo, always on the go, moved quickly.

"Shall we be going?" he said. "Do we *want* to get down to Amberdale for tea? Or shall we try somewhere nearer?"

They all voted for Amberdale, for the Marquis of Grantham.

"Well, which way shall we go back? Shall we go by Codnor and over Crosshill, or shall we go by Ashborne?"

There was the usual dilemma. Then they finally decided on the Codnor top road. Off went the car, gallantly.

They were on the top of the world, now, on the back of the fist. It was naked, too, as the back of your fist, high under heaven, and dull, heavy green. Only it was veined with a network of old stone walls, dividing the fields, and broken here and there with ruins of old lead-mines and works. A sparse stone farm bristled with six naked sharp trees. In the distance was a patch of smokey grey stone, a hamlet. In some fields grey, dark sheep fed silently, somberly. But there was not a sound nor a movement. It was the roof of England, stony and arid as any roof. Beyond, below, were the shires.

" 'And see the coloured counties,' " said Yvette to herself. Here anyhow they were not coloured. A stream of rooks trailed out from nowhere. They had been walking, pecking, on a naked field that had been manured. The car ran on between the grass and the stone walls of the upland lane, and the young people were silent, looking out over the far network of stone fences, under the sky, looking for the curves downward that indicated a drop to one of the underneath, hidden dales.

Ahead was a light cart, driven by a man, and trudging along at the side was a woman, sturdy and elderly, with a pack on her back. The man in the cart had caught her up, and now was keeping pace.

The road was narrow. Leo sounded the horn sharply. The man on the cart looked round, but the woman on foot only trudged steadily, rapidly forward, without turning her head.

Yvette's heart gave a jump. The man on the cart was a gipsy, one of the black, loose-bodied, handsome sort. He remained seated on his cart, turning round and gazing at the occupants of the motor-car, from under the brim of his cap. And his pose was loose, his gaze insolent in its indifference. He had a thin black moustache under his thin, straight nose, and a big silk handkerchief of red and yellow tied round his neck. He spoke a word to the woman. She stood a second, solid, to turn round and look at the occupants of the car, which had now drawn quite close. Leo honked the horn again, imperiously. The woman, who had a grey-and-white kerchief tied round her head, turned sharply, to keep pace with the cart, whose driver also had settled back, and was lifting the reins, moving his loose, light shoulders. But still he did not pull aside.

Leo made the horn scream, as he put the brakes on and the car slowed up near the back of the cart. The gipsy turned round at the din, laughing in his dark face under his dark-green cap, and said something which they did not hear, showing white teeth under the line of black moustache, and making a gesture with his dark, loose hand.

"Get out o' the way then!" yelled Leo.

For answer, the man delicately pulled the horse to a standstill, as it curved to the side of the road. It was a good roan horse, and a good, natty, dark-green cart.

Leo, in a rage, had to jam on the brake and pull up too.

"Don't the pretty young ladies want to hear their fortunes?" said the gipsy on the cart, laughing except for his dark, watchful eyes, which went from face to face, and lingered on Yvette's young, tender face.

She met his dark eyes for a second, their level search, their insolence, their complete indifference to people like Bob and Leo, and something took fire in her breast. She thought: "He is stronger than I am! He doesn't care!"

"Oh yes! let's!" cried Lucille at once.

"Oh yes!" chorused the girls.

"I say! What about the time?" cried Leo.

"Oh bother the old time! Somebody's always dragging in time by the forelock," cried Lucille.

"Well, if you don't mind *when* we get back, *I* don't!" said Leo heroically.

The gipsy man had been sitting loosely on the side of his cart, watching the faces. He now jumped softly down from the shaft, his knees a bit stiff. He was apparently a man something over thirty, and a beau in his way. He wore a sort of shooting-jacket, double-breasted, coming only to the hips, of dark green-and-black frieze; rather tight black trousers, black boots, and a dark-green cap; with the big yellow-and-red bandanna handkerchief round his neck. His appearance was curiously elegant, and quite expensive in its gipsy style. He was handsome, too, pressing in his chin with the old, gipsy conceit, and now apparently not heeding the strangers any more, as he led his good roan horse off the road, preparing to back his cart.

The girls saw for the first time a deep recess in the side of the road, and two caravans smoking. Yvette got quickly down. They had suddenly come upon a disused quarry, cut into the slope of the road-side, and in this sudden lair, almost like a cave, were three caravans, dismantled for the winter. There was also deep at the back, a shelter built of boughs, as a stable for the horse. The grey, crude rock rose high above the caravans, and curved round towards the road. The floor was heaped chips of stone, with grasses growing among. It was a hidden, snug winter camp.

The elderly woman with the pack had gone in to one of the caravans, leaving the door open. Two children were peeping out, shewing black heads. The gipsy man gave a little call, as he backed his cart into the quarry, and an elderly man came out to help him untackle.

The gipsy himself went up the steps into the newest caravan, that had its door closed. Underneath, a tied-up dog ranged forth. It was a white hound spotted liver-coloured. It gave a low growl as Leo and Bob approached.

At the same moment, a dark-faced gipsy-woman with a pink shawl or kerchief round her head and big gold ear-rings in her ears, came down the steps of the newest caravan, swinging her flounced, voluminous green skirt. She was handsome in a bold, dark, long-faced way, just a bit wolfish. She looked like one of the bold, loping Spanish gipsies.

"Good-morning, my ladies and gentlemen," she said, eyeing the girls from her bold, predative eyes. She spoke with a certain foreign stiffness.

"Good afternoon!" said the girls.

"Which beautiful little lady like to hear her fortune? Give me her little hand?"

She was a tall woman, with a frightening way of reaching forward her neck like a menace. Her eyes went from face to face, very active, heartlessly searching out what she wanted. Meanwhile the man, apparently her husband, appeared at the top of the caravan steps smoking a pipe, and with a small, black-haired child in his arms. He stood on his limber legs, casually looking down on the group, as if from a distance, his long black lashes lifted from his full, conceited, impudent black eyes. There was something peculiarly transfusing in his stare. Yvette felt it, felt it in her knees. She pretended to be interested in the white-and-liver-coloured hound.

"How much do you want, if we all have our fortunes told?" asked Lottie Framley, as the six fresh-faced young Christians hung back rather reluctantly from this pagan pariah woman.

"All of you? ladies and gentlemen, all?" said the woman shrewdly.

"I don't want mine told! You go ahead!" cried Leo.

"Neither do I," said Bob. "You four girls."

"The four ladies?" said the gipsy woman, eyeing them shrewdly, after having looked at the boys. And she fixed her price. "Each one give me a sheeling, and a little bit more for luck? a little bit!" She smiled in a way that was more wolfish than cajoling, and the force of her will was felt, heavy as iron beneath the velvet of her words.

"All right," said Leo. "Make it a shilling a head. Don't spin it out too long."

"Oh, *you!*" cried Lucille at him. "We want to hear it *all.*"

The woman took two wooden stools, from under a caravan, and placed them near the wheel. Then she took the tall, dark Lottie Framley by the hand, and bade her sit down.

"You don't care if everybody hear?" she said, looking up curiously into Lottie's face.

Lottie blushed dark with nervousness, as the gipsy woman held her hand, and stroked her palm with hard, cruel-seeming fingers.

"Oh, I don't mind," she said.

The gipsy woman peered into the palm, tracing the lines of the hand with a hard, dark forefinger. But she seemed clean.

And slowly she told the fortune, while the others, standing listening, kept on crying out: "Oh, that's Jim Baggaley! Oh, I don't believe it! Oh, that's not true! A fair woman who lives beneath a tree! why whoever's that?" until Leo stopped them with manly warning:

"Oh, hold on, girls! You give everything away."

Lottie retired blushing and confused, and it was Ella's turn. She was much more calm and shrewd, trying to read the oracular words. Lucille kept breaking out with: Oh, I say! the gipsy man at the top of the steps stood imperturbable, without any expression at all. But his bold eyes kept staring at Yvette, she could feel them on her cheek, on her neck, and she dared not look up. But Framley would sometimes look up at him, and got a level stare back, from the handsome face of the male gipsy, from the dark conceited proud eyes. It was a peculiar look, in the eyes that belonged to the tribe of the humble: the pride of the pariah, the half-sneering challenge of the outcast, who sneered at law-abiding men, and went his own way. All the time, the gipsy man stood there, holding his child in his arms, looking on without being concerned.

Lucille was having her hand read,—"You have been across the sea, and there you met a man—a brown-haired man—but he was too old—."

"Oh, I *say!*" cried Lucille, looking round at Yvette.

But Yvette was abstracted, agitated, hardly heeding: in one of her mesmerised states.

"You will marry in a few years—not now, but a few years—perhaps four—and you will not be rich, but you will have plenty—enough—and you will go away, a long journey."

"With my husband, or without?" cried Lucille.

"With him—."

When it came to Yvette's turn, and the woman looked up boldly, cruelly, searching for a long time in her face, Yvette said nervously:

"I don't think I want mine told. No, I won't have mine told! No I won't, really!"

"You are afraid of some thing?" said the gipsy woman cruelly.

"No, it's not that—" Yvette fidgetted.

"You have some secret? You are afraid I shall say it. Come, would you like to go in the caravan, where nobody hears?"

The woman was curiously insinuating; while Yvette was always wayward, perverse. The look of perversity was on her soft, frail young face now, giving her a queer hardness.

"Yes!" she said suddenly. "Yes! I might do that!"

"Oh, I say!" cried the others. "Be a sport!"

"I don't think you'd *better!*" cried Lucille.

"Yes!" said Yvette, with that hard little way of hers. "I'll do that. I'll go in the caravan."

The gipsy woman called something to the man on the steps. He went into the caravan for a moment or two, then re-appeared, and came down the steps, setting the small child on its uncertain feet, and holding it by the hand. A dandy, in his polished black boots, tight black trousers and tight dark-green jersey, he walked slowly across, with the toddling child, to where the elderly gipsy was giving the roan horse a feed of oats, in the bough shelter between pits of grey rock, with dry bracken upon the stone-chip floor. He looked at Yvette as he passed, staring her full in the eyes, with his pariah's bold yet dishonest stare. Something hard inside her met his stare. But the surface of her body seemed to turn to water. Nevertheless, something hard in her registered the peculiar pure lines of his face, of his straight, pure nose, of his cheeks and temples. The curious dark, suave purity of all his body, outlined in the green jersey: a purity like a living sneer.

And as he loped slowly past her, on his flexible hips, it seemed to her still that he was stronger than she was. Of all the men she had ever seen, this one was the only one who was stronger than she was, in her own kind of strength, her own kind of understanding.

So, with curiosity, she followed the woman up the steps of the caravan, the skirts of her well-cut tan coat swinging and almost showing her knees, under the pale-green cloth dress. She had long, long-striding, fine legs, too slim rather than too thick, and she wore curiously-patterned pale-and-fawn stockings of fine wool, suggesting the legs of some delicate animal.

At the top of the steps she paused and turned, debonair, to the others, saying in her naïve, lordly way, so off-hand:

"I won't let her be long."

Her grey fur collar was open, showing her soft throat and pale green dress, her little, plaited tan-coloured hat came down to her ears, round her soft, fresh face. There was something soft and yet overbearing, unscrupulous, about her. She knew the gipsy man had turned to look at her. She was aware of the pure dark nape of his neck, the black hair groomed away. He watched as she entered his house.

What the gipsy told her, no one ever knew. It was a long time to wait, the others felt. Twilight was deepening on the gloom, and it was turning raw and cold. From the chimney of the second caravan came smoke and a smell of rich food. The horse was fed, a yellow blanket strapped round him, the two gipsy men talked together in the distance, in low tones. There was a peculiar feeling of silence and secrecy in that lonely, hidden quarry.

At last the caravan door opened, and Yvette emerged, bending forward and stepping with long, witch-like slim legs down the steps. There was a stooping, witch-like silence about her as she emerged on the twilight.

"Did it seem long?" she said vaguely, not looking at anybody and keeping her own counsel hard within her soft, vague waywardness. "I hope you weren't bored! Wouldn't tea be nice! Shall we go?"

"You get in!" said Bob. "I'll pay."

The gipsy-woman's full, metallic skirts of jade-green alpaca came swinging down the steps. She rose to her height, a big, triumphant-looking woman with a dark-wolf face. The pink cashmere kerchief, stamped with red roses, was slipping to one side over her black and crimped hair. She gazed at the young people in the twilight with bold arrogance.

Bob put two half-crowns in her hand.

"A little bit more, for luck, for your young lady's luck," she wheedled, like a wheedling wolf. "Another bit of silver, to bring you luck."

"You've got a shilling for luck, that's enough," said Bob calmly and quietly, as they moved away to the car.

"A little bit of silver! Just a little bit, for your luck in love!"

Yvette, with the sudden long, startling gestures of her long limbs, swung round as she was entering the car, and with long arm outstretched, strode and put something into the gipsy's hand, then stepped, bending her height, into the car.

"Prosperity to the beautiful young lady, and the gipsy's blessing on her," came the suggestive, half-sneering voice of the woman.

The engine *birred!* then *birred!* again more fiercely, and started. Leo switched on the lights, and immediately the quarry with the gipsies fell back into the blackness of night.

"Goodnight!" called Yvette's voice, as the car started. But hers was the only voice that piped up, chirpy and impudent in its nonchalance. The headlights glared down the stone lane.

"Yvette, you've got to tell us what she said to you," cried Lucille, in the teeth of Yvette's silent will *not* to be asked.

"Oh, nothing at *all* thrilling," said Yvette, with false warmth. "Just the usual old thing: a dark man who means good luck, and a fair one who means bad: and a death in the family, which if it means Granny, won't be so *very* awful: and I shall marry when I'm twenty-three, and have heaps of money and heaps of love, and two children. All sounds very nice, but it's a bit too much of a good thing, you know."

"Oh, but why did you give her more money?"

"Oh well, I wanted to! You *have* to be a bit lordly with people like that—."

FOUR

There was a terrific rumpus down at the rectory, on account of Yvette and the Window Fund. After the war, Aunt Cissie had set her heart on a stained glass window in the church, as a memorial for the men of the parish who had fallen. But the bulk of the fallen had been non-conformists, so the memorial took the form of an ugly little monument in front of the Wesleyan chapel.

This did not vanquish Aunt Cissie. She canvassed, she had bazaars, she made the girls get up amateur theatrical shows, for her precious window. Yvette, who quite liked the acting and showing-off part of it, took charge of the farce called *Mary in the Mirror,* and gathered in the proceeds, which were to be paid to the Window Fund when accounts were settled. Each of the girls was supposed to have a money-box for the Fund.

Aunt Cissie, feeling that the united sums must now almost suffice, suddenly called in Yvette's box. It contained fifteen shillings. There was a moment of green horror.

"Where is all the rest?"

"Oh!" said Yvette, casually. "I just borrowed it. It wasn't so awfully much."

"What about the three pounds thirteen for *Mary in the Mirror?*" asked Aunt Cissie, as if the jaws of Hell were yawning.

"Oh quite! I just borrowed it. I can pay it back."

Poor Aunt Cissie! The green tumour of hate burst inside her, and there was a ghastly, abnormal scene, which left Yvette shivering with fear and nervous loathing.

Even the rector was rather severe.

"If you needed money, why didn't you tell me?" he said coldly. "Have you ever been refused anything in reason?"

"I—I thought it didn't matter," stammered Yvette.

"And what have you done with the money?"

"I suppose I've spent it," said Yvette, with wide, distraught eyes and a peaked face.

"Spent it, on what?"

"I can't remember everything: stockings and things, and I gave some of it away."

Poor Yvette! Her lordly airs and ways were already hitting back at her, on the reflex. The rector was angry: his face had a snarling, doggish look, a sort of sneer. He was afraid his daughter was developing some of the rank, tainted qualities of She-who-was-Cynthia.

"You *would* do the large with somebody else's money, wouldn't you?" he said, with a cold, mongrel sort of sneer, which showed what an utter unbeliever he was, at the heart. The inferiority of a heart which has no core of warm belief in it, no pride in life. He had utterly no belief in her.

Yvette went pale, and very distant. Her pride, that frail, precious flame which everybody tried to quench, recoiled like a flame blown far away, on a cold wind, as if blown out, and her face, white now and still like a snow-drop, the white snowflower of his conceit, seemed to have no life in it, only this pure, strange abstraction.

"He has no belief in me!" she thought in her soul. "I am really nothing to him. I am nothing, only a shameful thing. Everything is shameful, everything is shameful!"

A flame of passion or rage, while it might have overwhelmed or infuriated her, would not have degraded her as did her father's unbelief, his final atti-tude of a sneer against her.

He became a little afraid, in the silence of sterile thought. After all, he needed the *appearance* of love and belief and bright life, he would never dare to face the fat worm of his own unbelief, that stirred in his heart.

"What have you to say for yourself?" he asked.

She only looked at him from that senseless snowdrop face which haunted him with fear, and gave him a helpless sense of guilt. That other one, She-who-was-Cynthia, she had looked back at him with the same numb, white fear, the fear of his degrading unbelief, the worm which was his heart's core. He *knew* his heart's core was a fat, awful worm. His dread was lest anyone else should know. His anguish of hate was against anyone who knew, and recoiled.

He saw Yvette recoiling, and immediately his manner changed to the worldly old good-humoured cynic which he affected.

"Ah well!" he said. "You have to pay it back, my girl, that's all. I will ad-vance you the money out of your allowance. But I shall charge you four per-cent a month interest. Even the devil himself must pay a percentage on his debts. Another time, if you can't trust yourself, don't handle money which isn't your own. Dishonesty isn't pretty."

Yvette remained crushed, and deflowered and humiliated. She crept about, trailing the rays of her pride. She had a revulsion even from herself. Oh, why had she ever touched the leprous money! Her whole flesh shrank as if it were defiled. Why was that? Why, why was that?

She admitted herself wrong in having spent the money. "Of course I shouldn't have done it. They are quite right to be angry," she said to herself.

But where did the horrible wincing of her flesh come from? Why did she feel she had caught some physical contagion?

"Where you're so *silly*, Yvette," Lucille lectured her: poor Lucille was in great distress—"is that you give yourself away to them all. You might *know* they'd find out. I could have raised the money for you, and saved all this bother. It's perfectly awful! But you never will think beforehand where your actions are going to land you! Fancy Aunt Cissie saying all those things to you! How *awful!* Whatever would Mamma have said, if she'd heard it?"

When things went very wrong, they thought of their mother, and despised their father and all the low brood of the Saywells. Their mother, of course, had belonged to a higher, if more dangerous and "immoral" world. More selfish, decidedly. But with a showier gesture. More unscrupulous and more easily moved to contempt: but not so humiliating.

Yvette always considered that she got her fine, delicate flesh from her mother. The Saywells were all a bit leathery, and grubby somewhere inside. But then the Saywells never let you down. Whereas the fine She-who-was-Cynthia had let the rector down with a bang, and his little children along with him. Her little children! They could not quite forgive her.

Only dimly, after the row, Yvette began to realize the other sanctity of herself, the sanctity of her sensitive, clean flesh and blood, which the Saywells with their so-called morality, succeeded in defiling. They always wanted to defile it. They were the life unbelievers. Whereas, perhaps She-who-was-Cynthia had only been a moral unbeliever.

Yvette went about dazed and peaked and confused. The rector paid in the money to Aunt Cissie, much to that lady's rage. The helpless tumour of her rage was still running. She would have liked to announce her niece's delinquency in the parish magazine. It was anguish to the destroyed woman that she could not publish the news to all the world. The selfishness! The selfishness! The selfishness!

Then the rector handed his daughter a little account with himself: her debt to him, interest thereon, the amount deducted from her small allowance. But to her credit he had placed a guinea, which was the fee he had to pay for complicity.

"As father of the culprit," he said humorously, "I am fined one guinea. And with that I wash the ashes out of my hair."

He was always generous about money. But somehow, he seemed to think that by being free about money he could absolutely call himself a generous man. Whereas he used money, even generosity, as a hold over her.

But he let the affair drop entirely. He was by this time more amused than anything, to judge from appearances. He thought still he was safe.

Aunt Cissie, however, could not get over her convulsion. One night when Yvette had gone rather early, miserably, to bed, when Lucille was away at a party, and she was lying with soft, peaked limbs aching with a sort of numbness and defilement, the door softly opened, and there stood Aunt Cissie, pushing her grey-green face through the opening of the door. Yvette started up in terror.

"Liar! Thief! Selfish little beast!" hissed the maniacal face of Aunt Cissie. "You little hypocrite! You liar! You selfish beast! You greedy little beast!"

There was such extraordinary impersonal hatred in that grey-green mask, and those frantic words, that Yvette opened her mouth to scream with hysterics. But Aunt Cissie shut the door as suddenly as she had opened it, and disappeared. Yvette leaped from her bed and turned the key. Then she crept back, half demented with fear of the squalid abnormal, half numbed with paralysis of damaged pride. And amid it all, up came a bubble of distracted laughter. It *was* so filthily ridiculous!

Aunt Cissie's behaviour did not hurt the girl so very much. It was after all somewhat fantastic. Yet hurt she was: in her limbs, in her body, in her sex, hurt. Hurt, numbed, and half destroyed, with only her nerves vibrating and jangled. And still so young, she could not conceive what was happening.

Only she lay and wished she were a gipsy. To live in a camp, in a caravan, and never set foot in a house, not know the existence of a parish, never look at a church. Her heart was hard with repugnance, against the rectory. She loathed these houses with their indoor sanitation and their bathrooms, and their extraordinary repulsiveness. She hated the rectory, and everything it implied. The whole stagnant, sewerage sort of life, where sewerage is never mentioned, but where it seems to smell from the centre of every two-legged inmate, from Granny to the servants, was foul. If gipsies had no bathrooms, at least they had no sewerage. There was fresh air. In the rectory there was *never* fresh air. And in the souls of the people, the air was stale till it stank.

Hate kindled her heart, as she lay with numbed limbs. And she thought of the words of the gipsy woman: "There is a dark man who never lived in a house. He loves you. The other people are treading on your heart. They will tread on your heart till you think it is dead. But the dark man will blow the one spark up into fire again, good fire. You will see what good fire."

Even as the woman was saying it, Yvette felt there was some duplicity somewhere. But she didn't mind. She hated with the cold, acrid hatred of a child the rectory interior, the sort of putridity in the life. She liked that big, swarthy, wolf-like gipsy-woman, with the big gold rings in her ears, the pink scarf over her wavy black hair, the tight bodice of brown velvet, the green, fan-like shirt. She liked her dusky, strong, relentless hands, that had pressed so firm, like wolf's paws, in Yvette's own soft palm. She liked her. She liked the danger and the covert fearlessness of her. She liked her covert, unyielding sex, that was immoral, but with a hard, defiant pride of its own. Nothing would ever get that woman under. She would despise the rectory and the rectory morality, utterly! She would strangle Granny with one hand. And she would have the same contempt for Daddy and for Uncle

Fred, as men, as she would have for fat old slobbery Rover, the Newfound-land dog. A great, sardonic female contempt, for such domesticated dogs, calling themselves men.

And the gipsy man himself! Yvette quivered suddenly, as if she had seen his big, bold eyes upon her, with the naked insinuation of desire in them. The absolutely naked insinuation of desire made her lie prone and powerless in the bed, as if a drug had cast her in a new, molten mould.

She never confessed to anybody that two of the ill-starred Window Fund pounds had gone to the gipsy woman. What if Daddy and Aunt Cissie knew *that!* Yvette stirred luxuriously in the bed. The thought of the gipsy had released the life of her limbs, and crystallised in her heart the hate of the rectory: so that now she felt potent, instead of impotent.

When, later, Yvette told Lucille about Aunt Cissie's dramatic interlude in the bedroom doorway, Lucille was indignant.

"Oh, hang it all!" cried she. "She might let it drop now. I should think we've heard enough about it by now! Good heavens, you'd think Aunt Cissie was a perfect bird of paradise! Daddy's dropped it, and after all, it's his business if it's anybody's. Let Aunt Cissie shut up!"

It was the very fact that the rector had dropped it, and that he again treated the vague and inconsiderate Yvette as if she were some specially-licensed being, that kept Aunt Cissie's bile flowing. The fact that Yvette really was most of the time unaware of other people's feelings, and being unaware, couldn't care about them, nearly sent Aunt Cissie mad. Why should that young creature, with a delinquent mother, go through life as a privileged being, even unaware of other people's existence, though they were under her nose.

Lucille at this time was very irritable. She seemed as if she simply went a little unbalanced, when she entered the rectory. Poor Lucille, she was so thoughtful and responsible. She did all the extra troubling, thought about doctors, medicines, servants, and all that sort of thing. She slaved con-scientiously at her job all day in town, working in a room with artificial light from ten till five. And she came home to have her nerves rubbed almost to frenzy by Granny's horrible and persistent inquisitiveness and parasitic agedness.

The affair of the Window Fund had apparently blown over, but there remained a stuffy tension in the atmosphere. The weather continued bad. Lucille stayed at home on the afternoon of her half holiday, and did herself no good by it. The rector was in his study, she and Yvette were making a dress for the latter young woman. Granny was resting on the couch.

The dress was of blue silk velours, French material, and was going to be very becoming. Lucille made Yvette try it on again: she was nervously uneasy about the hang, under the arms.

"Oh bother!" cried Yvette, stretching her long, tender, childish arms, that tended to go bluish with the cold. "Don't be so frightfully *fussy*, Lucille! It's quite all right."

"If that's all the thanks I get, slaving my half day away making dresses for you, I might as well do something for myself!"

"Well, Lucille! You know I never *asked* you! You know you can't bear it unless you *do* supervise," said Yvette, with that irritating blandness of hers, as she raised her naked elbows and peered over her shoulder into the long mirror.

"Oh yes! you never *asked* me!" cried Lucille. "As if I didn't know what you meant, when you started sighing and flouncing about."

"I!" said Yvette, with vague surprise. "Why, when did I start sighing and flouncing about?"

"Of course you know you did."

"Did I? No, I didn't know! When was it?" Yvette could put a peculiar annoyance into her mild, straying questions.

"I shan't do another thing to this frock, if you don't stand still and *stop* it," said Lucille, in her rather sonorous, burning voice.

"You know you are most awfully nagging and irritable, Lucille," said Yvette, standing as if on hot bricks.

"Now Yvette!" cried Lucille, her eyes suddenly flashing in her sister's face, with wild flashes. "Stop it at once! Why should everybody put up with your abominable and overbearing temper!"

"Well, I don't know about *my* temper," said Yvette, writhing slowly out of the half-made frock, and slipping into her dress again.

Then, with an obstinate little look on her face, she sat down again at the table, in the gloomy afternoon, and began to sew at the blue stuff. The room was littered with blue clippings, the scissors were lying on the floor, the work-basket was spilled in chaos all over the table, and a second mirror was perched perilously on the piano.

Granny, who had been in a semi-coma, called a doze, roused herself on the big, soft couch and put her cap straight.

"I don't get much peace for my nap," she said, slowly feeling her thin white hair, to see that it was in order. She had heard vague noises.

Aunt Cissie came in, fumbling in a bag for a chocolate.

"I never saw such a mess!" she said. "You'd better clear some of that litter away, Yvette."

"All right," said Yvette. "I will in a minute."

"Which means never!" sneered Aunt Cissie, suddenly darting and picking up the scissors.

There was silence for a few moments, and Lucille slowly pushed her hands in her hair, as she read a book.

"You'd better clear away, Yvette," persisted Aunt Cissie.

"I will, before tea," replied Yvette, rising once more and pulling the blue dress over her head, flourishing her long, naked arms through the sleeveless armholes. Then she went between the mirrors, to look at herself once more.

As she did so, she sent the second mirror, that she had perched carelessly on the piano, sliding with a rattle to the floor. Luckily it did not break. But everybody started badly.

"She's smashed the mirror!" cried Aunt Cissie.

"Smashed a mirror! Which mirror! Who's smashed it?" came Granny's sharp voice.

"I haven't smashed anything," came the calm voice of Yvette. "It's quite all right."

"You'd better not perch it up there again," said Lucille.

Yvette, with a little impatient shrug at all the fuss, tried making the mirror stand in another place. She was not successful.

"If one had a fire in one's own room," she said crossly, "one needn't have a lot of people fussing when one wants to sew."

"Which mirror are you moving about?" asked Granny.

"One of our own, that came from the Vicarage," said Yvette rudely.

"Don't break it in *this* house, wherever it came from," said Granny.

There was a sort of family dislike for the furniture that had belonged to She-who-was-Cynthia. It was most of it shoved into the kitchen, and the servants' bedrooms.

"Oh, *I'm* not superstitious," said Yvette, "about mirrors or any of that sort of thing."

"Perhaps you're not," said Granny. "People who never take the responsibility for their own actions usually don't care what happens."

"After all," said Yvette, "I may say it's my own looking-glass, even if I did break it."

"And I say," said Granny, "that there shall be no mirrors broken in *this* house, if we can help it; no matter who they belong to, or did belong to. Cissie, have I got my cap straight?"

Aunt Cissie went over and straightened the old lady. Yvette loudly and irritatingly trilled a tuneless tune.

"And now, Yvette, will you please clear away," said Aunt Cissie.

"Oh bother!" cried Yvette angrily. "It's simply *awful* to live with a lot of people who are always nagging and fussing over trifles."

"What people, may I ask?" said Aunt Cissie ominously.

Another row was imminent. Lucille looked up with a queer cast in her eyes. In the two girls, the blood of She-who-was-Cynthia was roused.

"Of course you may ask! You know quite well I mean the people in this beastly house," said the outrageous Yvette.

"At least," said Granny, "we don't come of half-depraved stock."

There was a second's electric pause. Then Lucille sprang from her low seat, with sparks flying from her.

"You shut up!" she shouted, in a blast full upon the mottled majesty of the old lady.

The old woman's breast began to heave with heaven knows what emotions. The pause this time, as after the thunderbolt, was icy.

Then Aunt Cissie, livid, sprang upon Lucille, pushing her like a fury.

"Go to your room!" she cried hoarsely. "Go to your room!"

And she proceeded to push the white but fiery-eyed Lucille from the room. Lucille let herself be pushed, while Aunt Cissie vociferated:

"Stay in your room till you've apologised for this!—till you've apologised to the Mater for this!"

"I shan't apologise!" came the clear voice of Lucille, from the passage, while Aunt Cissie shoved her.

Aunt Cissie drove her more wildly upstairs.

Yvette stood tall and bemused in the sitting-room, with the air of offended dignity, at the same time bemused, which was so odd on her. She still was bare-armed, in the half-made blue dress. And even *she* was half-aghast at Lucille's attack on the majesty of age. But also, she was coldly indignant against Granny's aspersion of the maternal blood in their veins.

"Of course I meant no offence," said Granny.

"Didn't you!" said Yvette coolly.

"Of course not. I only said we're not depraved, just because we happen to be superstitious about breaking mirrors."

Yvette could hardly believe her ears. Had she heard right? Was it possible! Or was Granny, at her age, just telling a barefaced lie?

Yvette knew that the old woman was telling a cool, barefaced lie. But already, so quickly, Granny believed her own statement.

The rector appeared, having left time for a lull.

"What's wrong?" he asked cautiously, genially.

"Oh, nothing!" drawled Yvette. "Lucille told Granny to shut up, when she was saying something. And Aunt Cissie drove her to her room. *Tant de bruit pour une omelette!* Though Lucille *was* a bit over the mark, that time."

The old lady couldn't quite catch what Yvette said.

"Lucille really will have to learn to control her nerves," said the old woman. "The mirror fell down, and it worried me. I said so to Yvette, and she said something about superstitions and the people in the beastly house. I told her the people in the house were not depraved, if they happened to mind when a mirror was broken. And at that Lucille flew at me and told me to shut up. It really is disgraceful how these children give way to their nerves. I know it's nothing but nerves."

Aunt Cissie had come in during this speech. At first even she was dumb. Then it seemed to her, it was as Granny had said.

"I have forbidden her to come down until she comes to apologise to the Mater," she said.

"I doubt if she'll apologise," said the calm, queenly Yvette, holding her bare arms.

"And I don't want any apology," said the old lady. "It is merely nerves. I don't know what they'll come to, if they have nerves like that, at their age! She must take Vibrofat.—I am sure Arthur would like his tea, Cissie!"

Yvette swept her sewing together, to go upstairs. And again she trilled her tune, rather shrill and tuneless. She was trembling inwardly.

"More glad rags!" said her father to her, genially.

"More glad rags!" she re-iterated sagely, as she sauntered upstairs, with her day dress over one arm. She wanted to console Lucille, and ask her how the blue stuff hung now.

At the first landing, she stood as she nearly always did, to gaze through the window that looked to the road and the bridge. Like the Lady of Shalott, she seemed always to imagine that someone would come along singing *Tirra-lirra!* or something equally intelligent, by the river.

FIVE

It was nearly tea-time. The snow-drops were out by the short drive going to the gate from the side of the house, and the gardener was pottering at the round, damp flower-beds, on the wet grass that sloped to the stream. Past the gate went the whitish muddy road, crossing the stone bridge almost immediately, and winding in a curve up to the steep, clustering, stony, smoking northern village, that perched over the grim stone mills which Yvette could see ahead down the narrow valley, their tall chimneys long and erect.

The rectory was on one side the Papple, in the rather steep valley, the village was beyond and above, further down, on the other side the swift stream. At the back of the rectory the hill went up steep, with a grove of dark, bare larches, through which the road disappeared. And immediately across from the rectory, facing the house, the river-bank rose steep and bushy, up to the sloping, dreary meadows, that sloped up again to dark hillsides of trees, with grey rock cropping out.

But from the end of the house, Yvette could only see the road curving round past the wall with its laurel hedge, down to the bridge, then up again round the shoulder to that first hard cluster of houses in Papplewick village, beyond the drystone walls of the steep fields.

She always expected *something* to come down the slant of the road from Papplewick, and she always lingered at the landing window. Often a cart came, or a motor-car, or a lorry with stone, or a laborer, or one of the servants. But never anybody who sang *Tirra-lirra!* by the river. The tirra-lirraing days seemed to have gone by.

This day, however, round the corner on the white-grey road, between the grass and the low stone walls, a roan horse came stepping bravely and briskly down-hill, driven by a man in a cap, perched on the front of his light cart. The man swayed loosely to the swing of the cart, as the horse stepped down-hill, in the silent sombreness of the afternoon. At the back of the cart, long duster-brooms of reed and feather stuck out, nodding on their stalks of cane.

Yvette stood close to the window, and put the casement-cloth curtains behind her, clutching her bare upper arms with the hands.

At the foot of the slope the horse started into a brisk trot to the bridge. The cart rattled on the stone bridge, the brooms bobbed and flustered, the driver sat as if in a kind of dream, swinging along. It was like something seen in a sleep.

But as he crossed the end of the bridge, and was passing along the rectory wall, he looked up at the grim stone house that seemed to have backed away from the gate, under the hill. Yvette moved her hands quickly on her arms.

And as quickly, from under the peak of his cap, he had seen her, his swarthy predative face was alert.

He pulled up suddenly at the white gate, still gazing upwards at the landing window; while Yvette, always clasping her cold and mottled arms, still gazed abstractedly down at him, from the window.

His head gave a little, quick jerk of signal, and he led his horse well aside, on to the grass. Then, limber and alert, he turned back the tarpaulin of the cart, fetched out various articles, pulled forth two or three of the long brooms of reed or turkey-feathers, covered the cart, and turned towards the house, looking up at Yvette as he opened the white gate.

She nodded to him, and flew to the bathroom to put on her dress, hoping she had disguised her nod so that he wouldn't be sure she had nodded. Meanwhile she heard the hoarse deep roaring of that old fool, Rover, punctuated by the yapping of that young idiot, Trixie.

She and the housemaid arrived at the same moment at the sitting-room door.

"Was it the man selling brooms?" said Yvette to the maid. "All right!" and she opened the door. "Aunt Cissie, there's a man selling brooms. Shall I go?"

"What sort of a man?" said Aunt Cissie, who was sitting at tea with the rector and the Mater: the girls having been excluded for once from the meal.

"A man with a cart," said Yvette.

"A gipsy," said the maid.

Of course Aunt Cissie rose at once. She had to look at him.

The gipsy stood at the back door, under the steep dark bank where the larches grew. The long brooms flourished from one hand, and from the other hung various objects of shining copper and brass: a saucepan, a candlestick, plates of beaten copper. The man himself was neat and dapper, almost rakish, in his dark green cap and double-breasted green check coat. But his manner was subdued, very quiet: and at the same time proud, with a touch of condescension and aloofness.

"Anything today, lady?" he said, looking at Aunt Cissie with dark, shrewd, searching eyes, but putting a very quiet tenderness into his voice.

Aunt Cissie saw how handsome he was, saw the flexible curve of his lips under the line of black moustache, and she was fluttered. The merest hint of roughness or aggression on the man's part would have made her shut the door contemptuously in his face. But he managed to insinuate such a subtle suggestion of submission into his male bearing, that she began to hesitate.

"The candlestick is lovely!" said Yvette. "Did you make it?"

And she looked up at the man with her naïve, childlike eyes, that were as capable of double meanings as his own.

"Yes lady!" He looked back into her eyes for a second, with that naked suggestion of desire which acted on her like a spell, and robbed her of her will. Her tender face seemed to go into a sleep.

"It's awfully nice!" she murmured vaguely.

Aunt Cissie began to bargain for the candlestick: which was a low, thick stem of copper, rising from a double bowl. With patient aloofness the man attended to her, without ever looking at Yvette, who leaned against the doorway and watched in a muse.

"How is your wife?" she asked him suddenly, when Aunt Cissie had gone indoors to show the candlestick to the rector, and ask him if he thought it was worth it.

The man looked fully at Yvette, and a scarcely discernible smile curled his lips. His eyes did not smile: the insinuation in them only hardened to a glare.

"She's all right. When are you coming that way again?" he murmured, in a low, caressive, intimate voice.

"Oh, I don't know," said Yvette vaguely.

"You come Fridays, when I'm there," he said. Yvette gazed over his shoulder as if she had not heard him. Aunt Cissie returned, with the candlestick and the money to pay for it. Yvette turned nonchalant away, trilling one of her broken tunes, abandoning the whole affair with a certain rudeness.

Nevertheless, hiding this time at the landing window, she stood to watch the man go. What she wanted to know, was whether he really had any power over her. She did not intend him to see her this time.

She saw him go down to the gate, with his brooms and pans, and out to the cart. He carefully stowed away his pans and his brooms, and fixed down the tarpaulin over the cart. Then with a slow, effortless spring of his flexible loins, he was on the cart again, and touching the horse with the reins. The roan horse was away at once, the cart-wheels grinding uphill, and soon the man was gone, without looking round. Gone like a dream which was only a dream, yet which she could not shake off.

"No, he hasn't any power over me!" she said to herself: rather disappointed really, because she wanted somebody, or something to have power over her.

She went up to reason with the pale and over-wrought Lucille, scolding her for getting into a state over nothing.

"What does it *matter*," she expostulated, "if you told Granny to shut up! Why, everybody ought to be told to shut up, when they're being beastly. But she didn't mean it, you know. No, she didn't mean it. And she's quite sorry she said it. There's absolutely no reason to make a fuss. Come on, let's dress ourselves up and sail down to dinner like duchesses. Let's have our own back that way. Come on, Lucille!"

There was something strange and mazy, like having cobwebs over one's face, about Yvette's vague blitheness; her queer misty side-stepping from an unpleasantness. It was cheering too. But it was like walking in one of those autumn mists, when gossamer strands blow over your face. You don't quite know where you are.

She succeeded, however, in persuading Lucille, and the girls got out their best party frocks: Lucille in green and silver, Yvette in a pale lilac colour with turquoise chenille threading. A little rouge and powder, and their best slippers, and the gardens of paradise began to blossom. Yvette hummed and looked at herself, and put on her most *dégagé* airs of one of the young marchionesses. She had an odd way of slanting her eyebrows and pursing her

lips, and to all appearances detaching herself from every earthly consideration, and floating through the cloud of her own pearl-coloured reserves. It
was amusing, and not quite convincing.

"Of course I am beautiful, Lucille," she said blandly. "And you're
perfectly lovely, now you look a bit reproachful. Of course you're the
most aristocratic of the two of us, with your nose! And now your eyes
look reproachful, that adds an appealing look, and you're perfect, perfectly
lovely. But I'm more *winning*, in a way.—Don't you agree?" She turned
with arch, complicated simplicity to Lucille.

She was truly simple in what she said. It was just what she thought. But
it gave no hint of the very different *feeling* that also preoccupied her: the
feeling that she had been looked upon, not from the outside, but from the
inside, from her secret female self. She was dressing herself up and looking
her most dazzling, just to counteract the effect that the gipsy had had on
her, when he had looked at her, and seen none of her pretty face and her
pretty ways, but just the dark, tremulous, potent secret of her virginity.

The two girls started downstairs in state when the dinner-gong rang: but
they waited till they heard the voice of the men. Then they sailed down and
into the sitting-room, Yvette preening herself in her vague, debonair way,
always a little bit absent; and Lucille shy, ready to burst into tears.

"My goodness gracious!" exclaimed Aunt Cissie, who was still wearing
her dark-brown knitted sports coat. "What an apparition! Wherever do you
think you're going?"

"We're dining with the family," said Yvette naïvely, "and we've put
on our best gewgaws in honour of the occasion."

The rector laughed aloud, and Uncle Fred said:

"The family feels itself highly honoured."

Both the elderly men were quite gallant, which was what Yvette wanted.

"Come and let me feel your dresses, do!" said Granny. "Are they your
best? It *is* a shame I can't see them."

"Tonight, Mater," said Uncle Fred, "we shall have to take the young
ladies in to dinner, and live up to the honour. Will you go with Cissie?"

"I certainly will," said Granny. "Youth and beauty must come first."

"Well, tonight Mater!" said the rector, pleased.

And he offered his arm to Lucille, while Uncle Fred escorted Yvette.

But it was a draggled, dull meal, all the same. Lucille tried to be bright
and sociable, and Yvette really was most amiable, in her vague, cobwebby
way. Dimly, at the back of her mind, she was thinking: Why are we all only
like mortal pieces of furniture? Why is nothing *important*?

That was her constant refrain, to herself: Why is nothing important?
Whether she was in church, or at a party of young people, or dancing in the
hotel in the city, the same little bubble of a question rose repeatedly on her
consciousness: Why is nothing important?

There were plenty of young men to make love to her: even devotedly.
But with impatience she had to shake them off. Why were they so unimportant?—so irritating!

She never even thought of the gipsy. He was a perfectly negligible incident. Yet the approach of Friday loomed strangely significant. "What are we doing on Friday?" she said to Lucille. To which Lucille replied that they were doing nothing. And Yvette was vexed.

Friday came, and in spite of herself she thought all day of the quarry off the road up high Bonsall Head. She wanted to be there. That was all she was conscious of. She wanted to be there. She had not even a dawning idea of going there. Besides, it was raining again. But as she sewed the blue dress, finishing it for the party up at Lambley Close, tomorrow, she just felt that her soul was up there, at the quarry, among the caravans, with the gipsies. Like one lost, or whose soul was stolen, she was not present in her body, the shell of her body. Her intrinsic body was away, at the quarry, among the caravans.

The next day, at the party, she had no idea that she was being sweet to Leo. She had no idea that she was snatching him away from the tortured Ella Framley. Not until, when she was eating her pistachio ice, he said to her:

"Why don't you and me get engaged, Yvette? I'm absolutely sure it's the right thing for us both."

Leo was a bit common, but good-natured, and well-off. Yvette quite liked him. But engaged! How perfectly silly! She felt like offering him a set of her silk underwear, to get engaged to.

"But I thought it was Ella!" she said, in wonder.

"Well! It might ha' been, but for you. It's your doings, you know! Ever since those gipsies told your fortune, I felt it was me or nobody, for you, and you or nobody, for me."

"Really!" said Yvette, simply lost in amazement. "Really!"

"Didn't you feel a bit the same?" he asked.

"Really!" Yvette kept on gasping softly, like a fish.

"You felt a bit the same, didn't you?" he said.

"What? About what?" she asked, coming to.

"About me, as I feel about you."

"Why? What? Getting engaged, you mean? I? no! Why how *could* I? I could never have dreamed of such an impossible thing."

She spoke with her usual heedless candour, utterly unoccupied with his feelings.

"What was to prevent you?" he said, a bit nettled. "I thought you did."

"Did you *really now?*" she breathed in amazement, with that soft, virgin, heedless candour which made her her admirers and her enemies.

She was so completely amazed, there was nothing for him to do but twiddle his thumbs in annoyance.

The music began, and he looked at her.

"No! I won't dance any more," she said, drawing herself up and gazing away rather loftily over the assembly, as if he did not exist. There was a touch of puzzled wonder on her brow, and her soft, dim virgin face did indeed suggest the snowdrop of her father's pathetic imagery.

"But of course *you* will dance," she said, turning to him with young condescension. "Do ask somebody to have this with you."

He rose, angry, and went down the room.

She remained soft and remote in her amazement. Expect Leo to propose to her! She might as well have expected old Rover the Newfoundland dog to propose to her. Get engaged, to any man on earth? No, good heavens, nothing more ridiculous could be imagined!

It was then, in a fleeting side-thought, that she realised that the gipsy existed. Instantly, she was indignant. Him, of all things! Him! Never!

"Now why?" she asked herself, again in hushed amazement. "Why? It's *absolutely* impossible: absolutely! So why is it?"

This was a nut to crack. She looked at the young men dancing, elbows out, hips prominent, waists elegantly in. They gave her no clue to her problem. Yet she did particularly dislike the forced elegance of the waists and the prominent hips, over which the well-tailored coats hung with such effeminate discretion.

"There is something about me which they don't see and never would see," she said angrily to herself. And at the same time, she was relieved that they didn't and couldn't. It made life so very much simpler.

And again, since she was one of the people who are conscious in visual images, she saw the dark-green jersey rolled on the black trousers of the gipsy, his fine, quick hips, alert as eyes. They were elegant. The elegance of these dancers seemed so stuffed, hips merely wadded with flesh. Leo the same, thinking himself such a fine dancer! and a fine figure of a fellow!

Then she saw the gipsy's face; the straight nose, the slender mobile lips, and the level, significant stare of the black eyes, which seemed to shoot her in some vital, undiscovered place, unerring.

She drew herself up angrily. How dare he look at her like that! So she gazed glaringly at the insipid beaux on the dancing floor. And she despised them. Just as the raggle-taggle gipsy women despise men who are not gipsies, despise their dog-like walk down the streets, she found herself despising this crowd. Where among them was the subtle, lonely, insinuating challenge that could reach her?

She did not want to mate with a house-dog.

Her sensitive nose turned up, her soft brown hair fell like a soft sheath round her tender, flower-like face, as she sat musing. She seemed so virginal. At the same time, there was a touch of the tall young virgin *witch* about her, that made the house-dog men shy off. She might metamorphose into something uncanny before you knew where you were.

This made her lonely, in spite of all the courting. Perhaps the courting only made her lonelier.

Leo, who was a sort of mastiff among the house-dogs, returned after his dance, with fresh cheery-O! courage.

"You've had a little think about it, haven't you?" he said, sitting down beside her: a comfortable, well-nourished, determined sort of fellow. She did not know why it irritated her so unreasonably, when he hitched up his trousers at the knee, over his good-sized but not very distinguished legs, and lowered himself assuredly on to a chair.

"Have I?" she said vaguely. "About what?"

"You know what about," he said. "Did you make up your mind?"

"Make up my mind about what?" she asked, innocently.

In her upper consciousness, she truly had forgotten.

"Oh!" said Leo, settling his trousers again. "About me and you getting engaged, you know." He was almost as off-hand as she.

"Oh that's *absolutely* impossible," she said, with mild amiability, as if it were some stray question among the rest. "Why, I never even thought of it again. Oh, don't talk about that sort of nonsense! That sort of thing is *absolutely* impossible," she re-iterated like a child.

"That sort of thing is, is it?" he said, with an odd smile at her calm, distant assertion. "Well what sort of thing *is* possible, then? You don't want to die an old maid, do you?"

"Oh I don't mind," she said absently.

"I do," he said.

She turned round and looked at him in wonder.

"Why?" she said. "Why should you mind if I was an old maid?"

"Every reason in the world," he said, looking up at her with a bold, meaningful smile, that wanted to make its meaning blatant, if not patent.

But instead of penetrating into some deep, secret place, and shooting her there, Leo's bold and patent smile only hit her on the outside of the body, like a tennis ball, and caused the same kind of sudden irritated reaction.

"I think this sort of thing is awfully silly," she said, with minx-like spite. "Why, you're practically engaged to—to—" she pulled herself up in time —"probably half a dozen other girls. I'm not flattered by what you've said. I should hate it if anybody knew!—Hate it!—I shan't breathe a word of it, and I hope you'll have the sense not to.—There's Ella!"

And keeping her face averted from him, she sailed away like a tall, soft flower, to join poor Ella Framley.

Leo flapped his white gloves.

"Catty little bitch!" he said to himself. But he was of the mastiff type, he rather liked the kitten to fly in his face. He began definitely to single her out.

SIX

The next week it poured again with rain. And this irritated Yvette with strange anger. She had intended it should be fine. Especially she insisted it should be fine towards the week-end. Why, she did not ask herself.

Thursday, the half-holiday, came with a hard frost, and sun. Leo arrived with his car, the usual bunch. Yvette disagreeably and unaccountably refused to go.

"No thanks, I don't feel like it," she said.

She rather enjoyed being Mary-Mary-quite-contrary.

Then she went for a walk by herself, up the frozen hills, to the Black Rocks.

The next day also came sunny and frosty. It was February, but in the north country the ground did not thaw in the sun. Yvette announced that she was going for a ride on her bicycle, and taking her lunch, as she might not be back till afternoon.

She set off, not hurrying. In spite of the frost, the sun had a touch of spring. In the park, the deer were standing in the distance, in the sunlight, to be warm. One doe, white spotted, walked slowly across the motion-less landscape.

Cycling, Yvette found it difficult to keep her hands warm, even when bodily she was quite hot. Only when she had to walk up the long hill, to the top, and there was no wind.

The upland was very bare and clear, like another world. She had climbed on to another level. She cycled slowly, a little afraid of taking the wrong lane, in the vast maze of stone fences. As she passed along the lane she thought was the right one, she heard a faint tapping noise, with a slight metallic resonance.

The gipsy man was seated on the ground with his back to the cart-shaft, hammering a copper bowl. He was in the sun, bare-headed, but wearing his green jersey. Three small children were moving quietly round, playing in the horse's shelter: the horse and cart were gone. An old woman, bent, with a kerchief round her head, was cooking over a fire of sticks. The only sound was the rapid, ringing tap-tap-tap; of the small hammer on the dull copper.

The man looked up at once, as Yvette stepped from her bicycle, but he did not move, though he ceased hammering. A delicate, barely discernible smile of triumph was on his face. The old woman looked round, keenly, from under her dirty grey hair. The man spoke a half-audible word to her, and she turned again to her fire. He looked up at Yvette.

"How are you all getting on?" she asked politely.

"All right, eh! You sit down a minute?" He turned as he sat, and pulled a stool from under the caravan for Yvette. Then, as she wheeled her bicycle to the side of the quarry, he started hammering again, with that bird-like, rapid light stroke.

Yvette went to the fire to warm her hands.

"Is this the dinner cooking?" she asked childishly, of the old gipsy, as she spread her long, tender hands, mottled red with the cold, to the embers.

"Dinner, yes!" said the old woman. "For him! And for the children."

She pointed with the long fork at the three black-eyed, staring children, who were staring at her from under their black fringes. But they were clean. Only the old woman was not clean. The quarry itself they had kept per-fectly clean.

Yvette crouched in silence, warming her hands. The man rapidly ham-mered away with intervals of silence. The old hag slowly climbed the steps to the third, oldest caravan. The children began to play again, like little wild animals, quiet and busy.

"Are they your children?" asked Yvette, rising from the fire and turning to the man.

He looked her in the eyes, and nodded.

"But where's your wife?"

"She's gone out with the basket. They're all gone out, cart and all, selling things. I don't go selling things. I make them, but I don't go selling them. Not often. I don't often."

"You make all the copper and brass things?" she said.

He nodded, and again offered her the stool. She sat down.

"You said you'd be here on Fridays," she said. "So I came this way, as it was so fine."

"Very fine day!" said the gipsy, looking at her cheek, that was still a bit blanched by the cold, and the soft hair over her reddened ear, and the long, still mottled bands on her knee.

"You get cold, riding a bicycle?" he asked.

"My hands!" she said, clasping them nervously.

"You didn't wear gloves?"

"I did, but they weren't much good."

"Cold comes through," he said.

"Yes!" she replied.

The old woman came slowly, grotesquely down the steps of the caravan, with some enamel plates.

"The dinner cooked, eh?" he called softly.

The old woman muttered something, as she spread the plates near the fire. Two pots hung from a long iron horizontal-bar, over the embers of the fire. A little pan seethed on a small iron tripod. In the sunshine, heat and vapour wavered together.

He put down his tools and the pot, and rose from the ground.

"You eat something along of us?" he asked Yette, not looking at her.

"Oh, I brought my lunch," said Yvette.

"You eat some stew?" he said. And again he called quietly, secretly to the old woman, who muttered in answer, as she slid the iron pot towards the end of the bar.

"Some beans, and some mutton in it," he said.

"Oh thanks awfully!" said Yvette. Then suddenly taking courage, added: "Well yes, just a very little, if I may."

She went across to untie her lunch from her bicycle, and he went up the steps to his own caravan. After a minute, he emerged, wiping his hands on a towel.

"You want to come up and wash your hands?" he said.

"No, I think not," she said. "They are clean."

He threw away his wash-water, and set off down the road with a high brass jug, to fetch clean water from the spring that trickled into a small pool, taking a cup to dip it with.

When he returned, he set the jug and the cup by the fire, and fetched himself a short log, to sit on. The children sat on the floor, by the fire, in a cluster, eating beans and bits of meat with spoon or fingers. The man on the log ate in silence, absorbedly. The woman made coffee in the black pot on the tripod, hobbling upstairs for the cups. There was silence in the camp.

Yvette sat on her stool, having taken off her hat and shaken her hair in the sun.

"How many children have you?" Yvette asked suddenly.

"Say five," he replied slowly, as he looked up into her eyes.

And again the bird of her heart sank down and seemed to die. Vaguely, as in a dream, she received from him the cup of coffee. She was aware only of his silent figure, sitting like a shadow there on the log, with an enamel cup in his hand, drinking his coffee in silence. Her will had departed from her limbs, he had power over her: his shadow was on her.

And he, as he blew his hot coffee, was aware of one thing only, the mysterious fruit of her virginity, her perfect tenderness in the body.

At length he put down his coffee-cup by the fire, then looked round at her. Her hair fell across her face, as she tried to sip from the hot cup. On her face was that tender look of sleep, which a nodding flower has when it is full out, like a mysterious early flower, she was full out, like a snowdrop which spreads its three white wings in a flight into the waking sleep of its brief blossoming. The waking sleep of her full-opened virginity, entranced like a snowdrop in the sunshine, was upon her.

The gipsy, supremely aware of her, waited for her like the substance of shadow, as shadow waits and is there.

At length his voice said, without breaking the spell:

"You want to go in my caravan, now, and wash your hands?"

The childlike, sleep-waking eyes of her moment of perfect virginity looked into his, unseeing. She was only aware of the dark, strange effluence of him bathing her limbs, washing her at last purely will-less. She was aware of *him*, as a dark, complete power.

"I think I might," she said.

He rose silently, then turned to speak, in a low command, to the old woman. And then again he looked at Yvette, and putting his power over her, so that she had no burden of herself, or of action.

"Come!" he said.

She followed simply, followed the silent, secret, overpowering motion of his body in front of her. It cost her nothing. She was gone in his will.

He was at the top of the steps, and she at the foot, when she became aware of an intruding sound. She stood still, at the foot of the steps. A motor-car was coming. He stood at the top of the steps, looking round strangely. The old woman harshly called something, as with rapidly increasing sound, a car rushed near. It was passing.

Then they heard the cry of a woman's voice, and the brakes on the car. It had pulled up, just beyond the quarry.

The gipsy came down the steps, having closed the door of the caravan.

"You want to put your hat on," he said to her.

Obediently she went to the stool by the fire, and took up her hat. He sat down by the cart-wheel, darkly, and took up his tools. The rapid tap-tap-tap of his hammer, rapid and angry now like the sound of a tiny machine-gun, broke out just as the voice of the woman was heard crying:

"May we warm our hands at the camp fire?"

She advanced, dressed in a sleek but bulky coat of sable fur. A man followed, in a blue great-coat; pulling off his fur gloves and pulling out a pipe.

"It looked so tempting," said the woman in the coat of many dead little animals, smiling a broad, half-condescending, half-hesitant simper, around the company.

No one said a word.

She advanced to the fire, shuddering a little inside her coat, with the cold. They had been driving in an open car.

She was a very small woman, with a rather large nose: probably a Jewess. Tiny almost as a child, in that sable coat she looked much more bulky than she should, and her wide, rather resentful brown eyes of a spoilt Jewess gazed oddly out of her expensive get-up.

She crouched over the low fire, spreading her little hands, on which diamonds and emeralds glittered.

"Ugh!" she shuddered. "Of course we ought not to have come in an open car! But my husband won't even let me say I'm cold!" She looked round at him with her large, childish, reproachful eyes, that had still the canny shrewdness of a bourgeois Jewess: a rich one, probably.

Apparently she was in love, in a Jewess's curious way, with the big, blond man. He looked back at her with his abstracted blue eyes, that seemed to have no lashes, and a small smile creased his smooth, curiously naked cheeks. The smile didn't mean anything at all.

He was a man one connects instantly with winter sports, ski-ing and skating. Athletic, unconnected with life, he slowly filled his pipe, pressing in the tobacco with long, powerful reddened finger.

The Jewess looked at him to see if she got any response from him. Nothing at all, but that odd, blank smile. She turned again to the fire, tilting her eyebrows and looking at her small, white, spread hands.

He slipped off his heavily lined coat, and appeared in one of the handsome, sharp-patterned knitted jerseys, in yellow and grey and black, over well-cut trousers, rather wide. Yes, they were both expensive! And he had a magnificent figure, an athletic, prominent chest. Like an experienced camper, he began building the fire together, quietly: like a soldier on campaign.

"D'you think they'd mind if we put some fir-cones on, to make a blaze?" he asked of Yvette, with a silent glance at the hammering gipsy.

"Love it, I should think," said Yvette, in a daze, as the spell of the gipsy slowly left her, feeling stranded and blank.

The man went to the car, and returned with a little sack of cones, from which he drew a handful.

"Mind if we make a blaze?" he called to the gipsy.

"Eh?"

"Mind if we make a blaze with a few cones?"

"You go ahead!" said the gipsy.

The man began placing the cones lightly, carefully on the red embers. And soon, one by one, they caught fire, and burned like roses of flame, with a sweet scent.

"Ah lovely! lovely!" cried the little Jewess, looking up at her man again. He looked down at her quite kindly, like the sun on ice. "Don't you love fire! Oh, I love it!" the little Jewess cried to Yvette, across the hammering.

The hammering annoyed her. She looked round with a slight frown on her fine little brows, as if she would bid the man stop. Yvette looked round too. The gipsy was bent over his copper bowl, legs apart, head down, lithe arm lifted. Already he seemed so far from her.

The man who accompanied the little Jewess strolled over to the gipsy, and stood in silence looking down on him, holding his pipe to his mouth. Now they were two men, like two strange male dogs, having to sniff one another.

"We're on our honeymoon," said the little Jewess, with an arch, resentful look at Yvette. She spoke in a rather high, defiant voice, like some bird, a jay, or a crook, calling.

"Are you really?" said Yvette.

"Yes! Before we're married! Have you heard of Simon Fawcett?"—she named a wealthy and well-known engineer of the north country. "Well, I'm Mrs. Fawcett, and he's just divorcing me!" She looked at Yvette with curious defiance and wistfulness.

"Are you really!" said Yvette.

She understood now the look of resentment and defiance in the little Jewess' big, childlike brown eyes. She was an honest little thing, but perhaps her honesty was *too* rational. Perhaps it partly explained the notorious unscrupulousness of the well-known Simon Fawcett.

"Yes! As soon as we get the divorce, I'm going to marry Major Eastwood."

Her cards were now all on the table. She was not going to deceive anybody.

Behind her, the two men were talking briefly. She glanced round, and fixed the gipsy with her big brown eyes.

He was looking up, as if shyly, at the big fellow in the sparkling jersey, who was standing pipe in mouth, man to man, looking down.

"With the horses back of Arras," said the gipsy, in a low voice.

They were talking war. The gipsy had served with the artillery teams, in the Major's own regiment.

"Ein schöner Mensch!" said the Jewess. "A handsome man, eh?"

For her, too, the gipsy was one of the common men, the Tommies.

"Quite handsome!" said Yvette.

"You are cycling?" asked the Jewess in a tone of surprise.

"Yes! Down to Papplewick. My father is rector of Papplewick: Mr. Saywell!"

"Oh!" said the Jewess. "I know! A clever writer! Very clever! I have read him."

The fir-cones were all consumed already, the fire was a tall pile now of crumbling, shattering fire-roses. The sky was clouding over for afternoon. Perhaps towards evening it would snow.

The Major came back, and slung himself into his coat.

"I thought I remembered his face" he said. "One of our grooms, A. 1. man with horses."

"Look!" cried the Jewess to Yvette. "Why don't you let us motor you down to Normanton. We live in Scoresby. We can tie the bicycle on behind."

"I think I will," said Yvette.

"Come!" called the Jewess to the peeping children, as the blond man wheeled away the bicycle. "Come! Come here!" and taking out her little purse, she held out a shilling.

"Come!" she cried. "Come and take it!"

The gipsy had laid down his work, and gone into his caravan. The old woman called hoarsely to the children, from the enclosure. The two elder children came stealing forward. The Jewess gave them the two bits of silver, a shilling and a florin, which she had in her purse, and again the hoarse voice of the unseen old woman was heard.

The gipsy descended from his caravan and strolled to the fire. The Jewess searched his face with the peculiar bourgeois boldness of her race.

"You were in the war, in Major Eastwood's regiment!" she said.

"Yes, lady!"

"Imagine you both being here now!—It's going to snow—" she looked up at the sky.

"Later on," said the man, looking at the sky.

He too had gone inaccessible. His race was very old, in its peculiar battle with established society, and had no conception of winning. Only now and then it could score.

But since the war, even the old sporting chance of scoring now and then, was pretty well quenched. There was no question of yielding. The gipsy's eyes still had their bold look: but it was hardened and directed far away, the touch of insolent intimacy was gone. He had been through the war.

He looked at Yvette.

"You're going back in the motor-car?" he said.

"Yes!" she replied, with a rather mincing mannerism. "The weather is so treacherous!"

"Treacherous weather!" he repeated, looking at the sky.

She could not tell in the least what his feelings were. In truth, she wasn't very much interested. She was rather fascinated, now, by the little Jewess, mother of two children, who was taking her wealth away from the well-known engineer and transferring it to the penniless, sporting young Major Eastwood, who must be five or six years younger than she. Rather intriguing!

The blond man returned.

"A cigarette, Charles!" cried the little Jewess, plaintively.

He took out his case, slowly, with his slow, athletic movement. Something sensitive in him made him slow, cautious, as if he had hurt himself against people. He gave a cigarette to his wife, then one to Yvette, then offered the case, quite simply, to the gipsy. The gipsy took one.

"Thank you sir!"

And he went quietly to the fire, and stooping, lit it at the red embers. Both women watched him.

"Well goodbye!" said the Jewess, with her odd bourgeois free-masonry. "Thank you for the warm fire."

"Fire is everybody's," said the gipsy.

The young child came toddling to him.

"Goodbye!" said Yvette. "I hope it won't snow for you."

"We don't mind a bit of snow," said the gipsy.

"Don't you?" said Yvette. "I should have thought you would!"

"No!" said the gipsy.

She flung her scarf royally over her shoulder, and followed the fur coat of the Jewess, which seemed to walk on little legs of its own.

SEVEN

Yvette was rather thrilled by the Eastwoods, as she called them. The little Jewess had only to wait three months now, for the final decree. She had boldly rented a small summer cottage, by the moors up at Scoresby, not far from the hills. Now it was dead winter, and she and the Major lived in comparative isolation, without any maid-servant. He had already resigned his commission in the regular army, and called himself Mr. Eastwood. In fact, they were already Mr. and Mrs. Eastwood, to the common world.

The little Jewess was thirty-six, and her two children were both over twelve years of age. The husband had agreed that she should have the custody, as soon as she was married to Eastwood.

So there they were, this queer couple, the tiny, finely-formed little Jewess with her big, resentful reproachful eyes, and her mop of carefully-barbered black, curly hair, an elegant little thing in her way; and the big, pale-eyed young man, powerful and wintry, the remnant surely of some old uncanny Danish stock: living together in a small modern house near the moors and the hills, and doing their own housework.

It was a funny household. The cottage was hired furnished, but the little Jewess had brought along her dearest pieces of furniture. She had an odd little taste for the rococo, strange curving cupboards inlaid with mother of pearl, tortoiseshell, ebony, heaven knows what; strange tall flamboyant chairs, from Italy, with sea-green brocade: astonishing saints with wind-blown, richly-coloured carven garments and pink faces: shelves of weird old Saxe and Capo di Monte figurines: and finally, a strange assortment of astonishing pictures painted on the back of glass, done, probably in the early years of the nineteenth century, or in the late eighteenth.

In this crowded and extraordinary interior she received Yvette, when the latter made a stolen visit. A whole system of stoves had been installed into the cottage, every corner was warm, almost hot. And there was the tiny rococo figurine of the Jewess herself, in a perfect little frock, and an apron, putting slices of ham on the dish, while the great snow-bird of a major, in a white sweater and grey trousers, cut bread, mixed mustard, prepared coffee, and did all the rest. He had even made the dish of jugged hare which followed the cold meat and caviare.

The silver and the china were really valuable, part of the bride's trousseau. The Major drank beer from a silver mug, the little Jewess and Yvette had champagne in lovely glasses, the Major brought in coffee. They talked away. The little Jewess had a burning indignation against her first husband. She was intensely moral, so moral, that she was a divorcée. The Major too, strange wintry bird, so powerful, handsome, too, in his way, but pale round the eyes as if he had no eyelashes, like a bird, he too had a curious indignation against life, because of the false morality. That powerful, athletic chest hid a strange, snowy sort of anger. And his tenderness for the little Jewess was based on his sense of outraged justice, the abstract morality of the north blowing him, like a strange wind, into isolation.

As the afternoon drew on, they went to the kitchen, the Major pushed back his sleeves, showing his powerful athletic white arms, and carefully, deftly washed the dishes, while the women wiped. It was not for nothing his muscles were trained. Then he went round attending to the stoves of the small house, which only needed a moment or two of care each day. And after this, he brought out the small, closed car and drove Yvette home, in the rain, depositing her at the back gate, a little wicket among the larches, through which the earthen steps sloped downwards to the house.

She was really amazed by this couple.

"Really, Lucille!" she said. "I do meet the most extraordinary people!" And she gave a detailed description.

"I think they sound rather nice!" said Lucille. "I like the Major doing the housework, and looking so frightfully Bond-streety with it all. I should think, *when they're married*, it would be rather fun knowing them."

"Yes!" said Yvette vaguely. "Yes! Yes, it would!"

The very strangeness of the connection between the tiny Jewess and that pale-eyed, athletic young officer made her think again of her gipsy, who had been utterly absent from her consciousness, but who now returned with sudden painful force.

"What is it, Lucille," she asked, "that brings people together? People like the Eastwoods, for instance? and Daddy and Mamma, so frightfully unsuitable?—and that gipsy woman who told my fortune, like a great horse, and the gipsy man, so fine and delicately cut? What is it?"

"I suppose it's sex, whatever that is," said Lucille.

"Yes, what is it? It's not really anything *common*, like common sensuality, you know, Lucille. It really isn't!"

"No, I suppose not," said Lucille. "Anyhow I suppose it needn't be."

"Because you see, the *common* fellows, you know, who make a girl feel *low*: nobody cares much about them. Nobody feels any connection with them. Yet they're supposed to be the sexual sort."

"I suppose," said Lucille, "there's the low sort of sex, and there's the other sort, that isn't low. It's frightfully complicated, really! I *loathe* common fellows. And I never feel anything *sexual*—" she laid a rather disgusted stress on the word—"for fellows who aren't common. Perhaps I haven't got any sex."

"That's just it!" said Yvette. "Perhaps neither of us has. Perhaps we haven't really *got* any sex, to connect us with men."

"How horrible it sounds: *connect us with men!*" cried Lucille, with revulsion. "Wouldn't you hate to be connected with men that way? Oh I think it's an awful pity there has to *be* sex! It would be so much better if we could still be men and women, without that sort of thing."

Yvette pondered. Far in the background was the image of the gipsy as he had looked round at her, when she had said: The weather is so treacherous. She felt rather like Peter when the cock crew, as she denied him. Or rather, she did not deny the gipsy; she didn't care about his part in the show, anyhow. It was some hidden part of herself which she denied: that part which mysteriously and unconfessedly responded to him. And it was a strange, lustrous black cock which crew in mockery of her.

"Yes!" she said vaguely. "Yes! Sex is an awful bore, you know Lucille. When you haven't got it, you feel you *ought* to have it, somehow. And when you've got it—or *if* you have it—" she lifted her head and wrinkled her nose distainfully—"you hate it."

"Oh I don't know!" cried Lucille. "I think I should *like* to be awfully in love with a man."

"You think so!" said Yvette, again wrinkling her nose. "But if you were you wouldn't."

"How do you know?" asked Lucille.

"Well, I don't really," said Yvette. "But I think so! Yes, I think so!"

"Oh, it's very likely!" said Lucille disgustedly. "And anyhow one would be sure to get out of love again, and it would be merely disgusting."

"Yes," said Yvette. "It's a problem." She hummed a little tune.

"Oh hang it all, it's not a problem for us two, yet. We're neither of us really in love, and we probably never shall be, so the problem is settled that way."

"I'm not so sure!" said Yvette sagely. "I'm not so sure. I believe, one day, I shall fall *awfully* in love."

"Probably you never will," said Lucille brutally. "That's what most old maids are thinking all the time."

Yvette looked at her sister from pensive but apparently insouciant eyes.

"Is it?" she said. "Do you really think so, Lucille? How perfectly awful for them, poor things! Why ever do they *care?*"

"Why do they?" said Lucille. "Perhaps they don't, really.—Probably it's all because people say: *Poor old girl, she couldn't catch a man.*"

"I suppose it is!" said Yvette. "They get to mind the beastly things people always do say about old maids. What a shame!"

"Anyhow we have a good time, and we do have lots of boys who make a fuss of us," said Lucille.

"Yes!" said Yvette. "Yes! But I couldn't possibly marry any of them."

"Neither could I," said Lucille. "But why shouldn't we! Why should we bother about marrying, when we have a perfectly good time with the boys who are awfully good sorts, and you must say, Yvette, awfully sporting and *decent* to us."

"Oh, they are!" said Yvette absently.

"I think it's time to think of marrying somebody," said Lucille, "when, you feel you're *not* having a good time any more. Then marry, and just settle down."

"Quite!" said Yvette.

But now, under all her bland, soft amiability, she was annoyed with Lucille. Suddenly she wanted to turn her back on Lucille.

Besides, look at the shadows under poor Lucille's eyes, and the wistfulness in the beautiful eyes themselves. Oh, if some awfully nice, kind, protective sort of man would but marry her! And if the sporting Lucille would let him!

Yvette did not tell the rector, nor Granny, about the Eastwoods. It would only have started a lot of talk which she detested. The rector wouldn't have minded, for himself, privately. But he too knew the necessity of keeping as clear as possible from that poisonous, many-headed serpent, the tongue of the people.

"But I don't *want* you to come if your father doesn't know," cried the little Jewess.

"I suppose I'll have to tell him," said Yvette. "I'm sure he doesn't mind, really. But if he knew, he'd have to, I suppose."

The young officer looked at her with an old amusement, bird-like and un-emotional, in his keen eyes. He too was by way of falling in love with Yvette. It was her peculiar virgin tenderness, and her straying, absent-minded detachment from things, which attracted him.

She was aware of what was happening, and she rather preened herself. Eastwood piqued her fancy. Such a smart young officer, awfully good class, so calm and amazing with a motor-car, and quite a champion swimmer, it was intriguing to see him quietly, calmly washing dishes, smoking his pipe, doing his job so alert and skilful. Or, with the same interested care with which he made his investigation into the mysterious inside of an automobile, concocting jugged hare in the cottage kitchen. Then going out in the icy weather and cleaning his car till it looked like a live thing, like a cat when she has licked herself. Then coming in to talk so unassumingly and respon-sively, if briefly, with the little Jewess. And apparently, never bored. Sitting at the window with his pipe, in bad weather, silent for hours, abstracted, musing, yet with his athletic body alert in its stillness.

Yvette did not flirt with him. But she *did* like him.

"But what about your future?" she asked him.

"What about it?" he said, taking his pipe from his mouth, the unemotional point of a smile in his bird's eyes.

"A career! Doesn't every man have to carve out a career?—like some huge goose with gravy?" She gazed with odd naïveté into his eyes.

"I'm perfectly all right today, and I shall be all right tomorrow," he said, with a cold, decided look. "Why shouldn't my future be continuous todays and tomorrows?"

He looked at her with unmoved searching.

"Quite!" she said. "I hate jobs, and all that side of life." But she was thinking of the Jewess's money.

To which he did not answer. His anger was of the soft, snowy sort, which comfortably muffles the soul.

They had come to the point of talking philosophically together. The little Jewess looked a bit wan. She was curiously naïve and not possessive, in her attitude to the man. Nor was she at all catty with Yvette. Only rather wan, and dumb.

Yvette, on a sudden impulse, thought she had better clear herself.

"I think life's *awfully* difficult," she said.

"Life is!" cried the Jewess.

"What's so beastly, is that one is supposed to *fall in love*, and get married!" said Yvette, curling up her nose.

"Don't you *want* to fall in love and get married?" cried the Jewess, with great glaring eyes of astounded reproach.

"No, not particularly!" said Yvette. "Especially as one feels there's nothing else to do. It's an awful chickencoop one has to run into."

"But you don't know what love is?" cried the Jewess.

"No!" said Yvette. "Do you?"

"I!" bawled the tiny Jewess. "I! My goodness, don't I!" She looked with reflective gloom at Eastwood, who was smoking his pipe, the dimples of his disconnected amusement showing on his smooth, scrupulous face. He had a very fine, smooth skin, which yet did not suffer from the weather, so that his face looked naked as a baby's. But it was not a round face: it was characteristic enough, and took queer ironical dimples, like a mask which is comic but frozen.

"Do you mean to say you don't know what love is?" insisted the Jewess.

"No!" said Yvette, with insouciant candour. "I don't believe I do! Is it awful of me, at my age?"

"Is there never any man that makes you feel quite, quite different?" said the Jewess, with another big-eyed look at Eastwood. He smoked, utterly unimplicated.

"I don't think there is," said Yvette. "Unless—yes!—unless it is that gipsy" —she had put her head pensively sideways.

"Which gipsy?" bawled the little Jewess.

"The one who was a Tommy and looked after horses in Major Eastwood's regiment in the war," said Yvette coolly.

The little Jewess gazed at Yvette with great eyes of stupor.

"You're not in love with that *gipsy!*" she said.

"Well!" said Yvette. "I don't know. He's the only one that makes me feel—different! He really is!"

"But how? How? Has he ever *said* anything to you?"

"No! No!"

"Then how? What has he done?"

"Oh, just looked at me!"

"How?"

"Well you see, I don't know. But different! Yes, different! Different, quite different from the way any man ever looked at me."

"But *how* did he look at you?" insisted the Jewess.

"Why—as if he really, but *really, desired* me," said Yvette, her meditative face looking like the bud of a flower.

"What a vile fellow! What *right* had he to look at you like that?" cried the indignant Jewess.

"A cat may look at a king," calmly interposed the Major, and now his face had the smiles of a cat's face.

"You think he oughtn't to?" asked Yvette, turning to him.

"Certainly not! A gipsy fellow, with half a dozen dirty women trailing after him! Certainly not!" cried the tiny Jewess.

"I wondered!" said Yvette. "Because it *was* rather wonderful, really! And it *was* something quite different in my life."

"I think," said the Major, taking his pipe from his mouth, "that desire is the most wonderful thing in life. Anybody who can really feel it, is a king, and I envy nobody else!" He put back his pipe.

The Jewess looked at him stupefied.

"But Charles!" she cried. "Every common low man in Halifax feels nothing else!"

He again took his pipe from his mouth.

"That's merely appetite," he said.

And he put back his pipe.

"You think the gipsy is a real thing?" Yvette asked him. He lifted his shoulders.

"It's not for me to say," he replied. "If I were you, I should know, I shouldn't be asking other people."

"Yes—but—" Yvette trailed out.

"Charles! You're wrong! How *could* it be a real thing! As if she could possibly marry him and go round in a caravan!"

"I didn't say marry him," said Charles.

"Or a love affair! Why it's monstrous! What would she think of herself! —That's not love! That's—that's prostitution!"

Charles smoked for some moments.

"That gipsy was the best man we had, with horses. Nearly died of pneumonia. I thought he *was* dead. He's a resurrected man to me. I'm a resurrected man myself, as far as that goes." He looked at Yvette. "I was buried for twenty hours under snow," he said. "And not much the worse for it, when they dug me out."

There was a frozen pause in the conversation.

"Life's awful!" said Yvette.

"They dug me out by accident," he said.

"Oh!—" Yvette trailed slowly. "It might be destiny, you know."

To which he did not answer.

EIGHT

The rector heard about Yvette's intimacy with the Eastwoods, and she was somewhat startled by the result. She had thought he wouldn't care. Verbally, in his would-be humorous fashion, he was so entirely unconventional, such a frightfully good sport. As he said himself, he was a conservative anarchist; which meant, he was like a great many more people, a mere unbeliever. The anarchy extended to his humorous talk, and his secret thinking. The conservatism based on a mongrel fear of the anarchy, controlled every action. His thoughts, secretly, were something to be scared of. Therefore, in his life, he was fanatically afraid of the unconventional.

When his conservatism and his abject sort of fear were uppermost, he always lifted his lip and bared his teeth a little, in a dog-like sneer.

"I hear your latest friends are the half-divorced Mrs. Fawcett and the *maquereau* Eastwood," he said to Yvette.

She didn't know what a *maquereau* was, but she felt the poison in the rector's fangs.

"I just know them," she said. "They're awfully nice, really. And they'll be married in about a month's time."

The rector looked at her insouciant face with hatred. Somewhere inside him, he was cowed, he had been born cowed. And those who are born cowed are natural slaves, and deep instinct makes them fear with prisonous fear those who might suddenly snap the slave's collar around their necks.

It was for this reason the rector had so abjectly curled up, who still so abject curled up before She-who-was-Cynthia: because of his slave's fear of her contempt, the contempt of a born-free nature for a base-born nature.

Yvette too had a free-born quality. She too, one day, would know him, and clap the slave's collar of her contempt round his neck.

But should she? He would fight to the death, this time, first. The slave in him was cornered this time, like a cornered rat, and with the courage of a cornered rat.

"I suppose they're your sort!" he sneered.

"Well they are, really," she said, with that blithe vagueness. "I do like them awfully. They seem so solid, you know, so honest."

"You've got a peculiar notion of honesty!" he sneered. "A young sponge going off with a woman older than himself, so that he can live on her money! The woman leaving her home and her children! I don't know where you get your idea of honesty. Not from me, I hope.—And you seem to be very well acquainted with them, considering you say you just know them. Where did you meet them?"

"When I was out bicycling. They came along in their car, and we happened to talk. She told me at once who she was, so that I shouldn't make a mistake. She *is* honest."

Poor Yvette was struggling to bear up.

"And how often have you seen them since?"

"Oh, I've just been over twice."

"Over where?"

"To their cottage in Scoresby."

He looked at her in hate, as if he could kill her. And he backed away from her, against the window-curtains of his study, like a rat at bay. Somewhere in his mind he was thinking unspeakable depravities about his daughter, as he had thought them of She-who-was-Cynthia. He was powerless against the lowest insinuations of his own mind. And these depravities which he attributed to the still-uncowed, but frightened girl in front of him, made him recoil, showing all his fangs in his handsome face.

"So you just know them, do you?" he said. "Lying is in your blood, I see. I don't believe you get it from me."

Yvette half averted her mute face, and thought of Granny's bare-faced prevarication. She did not answer.

"What takes you creeping round such couples?" he sneered. "Aren't there enough decent people in the world, for you to know? Anyone would think you were a stray dog, having to run round indecent couples, because the decent ones wouldn't have you. Have you got something worse than lying in your blood?"

"What have I got, worse than lying in my blood?" she asked. A cold deadness was coming over her. Was she abnormal, one of the semi-criminal abnormals? It made her feel cold and dead.

In his eyes, she was just brazening out the depravity that underlay her virgin, tender, birdlike face. She-who-was-Cynthia had been like this: a snow flower. And he had convulsions of sadistic horror, thinking what might be the *actual* depravity of She-who-was-Cynthia. Even his *own* love for her, which had been the lust love of the born cowed, had been a depravity, in secret, to him. So what must an illegal love be?

"You know best yourself, what you have got," he sneered. "But it is something you had best curb, and quickly, if you don't intend to finish in a criminal-lunacy asylum."

"Why?" she said, pale and muted, numbed with frozen fear. "Why criminal lunacy? What have I done?"

"That is between you and your Maker," he jeered. "I shall never ask. But certain tendencies end in criminal lunacy, unless they are curbed in time."

"Do you mean like knowing the Eastwoods?" asked Yvette, after a pause of numb fear.

"Do I mean like nosing round such people as Mrs. Fawcett, a Jewess, and ex-Major Eastwood, a man who goes off with an older woman for the sake of her money? Why yes, I do!"

"But you *can't* say that," cried Yvette. "He's an awfully simple, straightforward man."

"He is apparently one of your sort."

"Well.—In a way, I thought he was. I thought you'd like him too," she said, simply, hardly knowing what she said.

The rector backed into the curtains, as if the girl menaced him with something fearful.

"Don't say any more," he snarled, abject. "Don't say any more. You've said too much, to implicate you. I don't want to learn any more horrors."

"But what horrors?" she persisted.

The very naïveté of her unscrupulous innocence repelled him, cowed him still more.

"Say no more!" he said, in a low, hissing voice. "But I will kill you before you shall go the way of your mother."

She looked at him, as he stood there backed against the velvet curtains of his study, his face yellow, his eyes distraught like a rat's with fear and rage and hate, and a numb, frozen loneliness came over her. For her too, the meaning had gone out of everything.

It was hard to break the frozen, sterile silence that ensued. At last, however, she looked at him. And in spite of herself, beyond her own knowledge, the contempt for him was in her young, clear, baffled eyes. It fell like the slave's collar over his neck, finally.

"Do you mean I mustn't know the Eastwoods?" she said.

"You can know them if you wish," he sneered. "But you must not expect to associate with your Granny, and your Aunt Cissie, and Lucille, if you do. I cannot have *them* contaminated. Your Granny was a faithful wife and a faithful mother, if ever one existed. She has already had one shock of shame and abomination to endure. She shall never be exposed to another."

Yvette heard it all dimly, half hearing.

"I can send a note and say you disapprove," she said dimly.

"You follow your own course of action. But remember, you have to choose between clean people, and reverence for your Granny's blameless old age, and people who are unclean in their minds and their bodies."

Again there was a silence. Then she looked at him, and her face was more puzzled than anything. But somewhere at the back of her perplexity was that peculiar calm, virgin contempt of the free-born for the base-born. He, and all the Saywells, were base-born.

"All right," she said. "I'll write and say you disapprove."

He did not answer. He was partly flattered, secretly triumphant, but abjectedly.

"I have tried to keep this from your Granny and Aunt Cissie," he said. "It need not be public property, since you choose to make your friendship clandestine."

There was a dreary silence.

"All right," she said. "I'll go and write."

And she crept out of the room.

She addressed her little note to Mrs. Eastwood. "Dear Mrs. Eastwood, Daddy doesn't approve of my coming to see you. So you will understand if we have to break it off. I'm awfully sorry—." That was all.

Yet she felt a dreary blank when she had posted her letter. She was now even afraid of her own thoughts. She wanted, now, to be held against the slender, fine-shaped breast of the gipsy. She wanted him to hold her in his arms, if only for once, for once, and comfort and confirm her. She wanted to be confirmed by him, against her father, who had only a repulsive fear of her.

And at the same time she cringed and winced, so that she could hardly walk, for fear the thought was obscene, a criminal lunacy. It seemed to wound her heels as she walked, the fear. The fear, the great cold fear of the base-born, her father, everything human and swarming. Like a great bog humanity swamped her, and she sank in, weak at the knees, filled with repulsion and fear of every person she met.

She adjusted herself, however, quite rapidly to her new conception of people. She had to live. It is useless to quarrel with one's bread and butter. And to expect a great deal out of life is puerile. So, with the rapid adaptability of the post-war generation, she adjusted herself to the new facts. Her father was what he was. He would always play up to appearances. She would do the same. She too would play up to appearances.

So, underneath the blithe, gossamer-straying insouciance, a certain hardness formed, like rock crystallising in her heart. She lost her illusions in the collapse of her sympathies. Outwardly, she seemed the same. Inwardly she was hard and detached, and, unknown to herself, revengeful.

Outwardly she remained the same. It was part of her game. While circumstances remained as they were, she must remain, at least in appearance, true to what was expected of her.

But the revengefulness came out in her new vision of people. Under the rector's apparently gallant handsomeness, she saw the weak, feeble nullity. And she despised him. Yet still, in a way, she liked him too. Feelings are so complicated.

It was Granny whom she came to detest with all her soul. That obese old woman, sitting there in her blindness like some great red-blotched fungus, her neck swallowed between her heaped-up shoulders and her rolling, ancient chins, so that she was neckless as a double potato, her Yvette really hated, with that pure, sheer hatred which is almost a joy. Her hate was so clear, that while she was feeling strong, she enjoyed it.

The old woman sat with her big, reddened face pressed a little back, her lace cap perched on her thin white hair, her stub nose still assertive, and her old mouth shut like a trap. This motherly old soul, her mouth gave her away. It always had been one of the compressed sort. But in her great age, it had gone like a toad's lipless, the jaw pressing up like the lower jaw of a trap. The look Yvette most hated, was the look of that lower jaw pressing relentlessly up, with an ancient prognathous thrust, so that the snub nose in turn was forced to press upwards, and the whole face was pressed a little back, beneath the big, wall like forehead. The will, the ancient, toad-like obscene *will* in the old woman, was fearful, once you saw it: a toad-like self-will that was godless, and less than human! It belonged to the old, enduring race of toads, or tortoises. And it made one feel that Granny would never die. She would live on like these higher reptiles, in a state of semi-coma, forever.

Yvette dared not even suggest to her father that Granny was not perfect.

He would have threatened his daughter with the lunatic asylum. That was the threat he always seemed to have up his sleeve: the lunatic asylum. Exactly as if a distaste for Granny and for that horrible house of relatives was in itself a proof of lunacy, dangerous lunacy.

Yet in one of her moods of irritable depression, she once did fling out:

"How perfectly beastly, this house is! Aunt Lucy comes, and Aunt Nell, and Aunt Alice, and they make a ring like a ring of crows, with Granny and Aunt Cissie, all lifting their skirts up and warming their legs at the fire, and shutting Lucille and me out. We're nothing but outsiders in this beastly house!"

Her father glanced at her curiously. But she managed to put a petulance into her speech, and a mere cross rudeness into her look, so that he could laugh, as at a childish tantrum. Somewhere, though, he knew that she coldly, venomously meant what she said, and he was wary of her.

Her life seemed now nothing but an irritable friction against the unsavoury household of the Saywells, in which she was immersed. She loathed the rectory with a loathing that consumed her life, a loathing so strong, that she could not really go away from the place. While it endured, she was spell-bound to it, in revulsion.

She forgot the Eastwoods again. After all! what was the revolt of the little Jewess, compared to Granny and the Saywell bunch! A husband was never more than a semicasual thing! But a family!—an awful, smelly family that would never disperse, stuck half dead round the base of a fungoid old woman! How was one to cope with that?"

She did not forget the gipsy entirely. But she had no time for him. She, who was bored almost to agony, and who had nothing at all to do, she had not time to think even, seriously, of anything. Time being, after all, only the current of the soul in its flow.

She saw the gipsy twice. Once he came to the house, with things to sell. And she, watching him from the landing window, refused to go down. He saw her too, as he was putting his things back into his cart. But he too gave no sign. Being of a race that exists only to be harrying the outskirts of our society, forever hostile and living only by spoil, he was too much master to himself, and too wary, to expose himself openly to the vast and gruesome clutch of our law. He had been through the war. He had been enslaved against his will, that time.

So now, he showed himself at the rectory, and slowly, quietly busied himself at his cart outside the white gate, with that air of silent and forever-unyielding outsideness which gave him his lonely, predative grace. He knew she saw him. And she should see him unyielding, quietly hawking his copper vessels, on an old, old war-path against such as herself.

Such as herself? Perhaps he was mistaken. Her heart, in its stroke, now rang hard as his hammer upon his copper, beating against circumstances. But he struck stealthily on the outside, and she still more secretly on the inside of the establishment. She liked him. She liked the quiet, noiseless, clean-cut presence of him. She liked that mysterious endurance in him, which endures in opposition, without any idea of victory. And she liked that peculiar added relentlessness, the disillusion in hostility, which belongs to after the war. Yes, if she belonged to any side, and to any clan, it was to his. Almost she could have found in her heart to go with him, and be a pariah gipsy-woman.

But she was born inside the pale. And she liked comfort, and a certain prestige. Even as a mere rector's daughter, one did have a certain prestige. And she liked that. Also she liked to chip against the pillars of the temple, from the inside. She wanted to be safe under the temple roof. Yet she enjoyed chipping fragments off the supporting pillars. Doubtless many fragments had been whittled away from the pillars of the Philistine, before Samson pulled the temple down.

"I'm not sure one shouldn't have one's fling till one is twenty-six, and then give in, and marry!"

This was Lucille's philosophy, learned from older women. Yvette was twenty-one. It meant she had five more years in which to have this precious fling. And the fling meant, at the moment, the gipsy. The marriage, at the age of twenty-six, meant Leo or Gerry.

So, a woman could eat her cake and have her bread and butter.

Yvette, pitched in gruesome, deadlocked hostility to the Saywell household, was very old and very wise: with the agedness and the wisdom of the young, which always overleaps the agedness and the wisdom of the old, or the elderly.

The second time, she met the gipsy by accident. It was March, and sunny weather, after unheard-of rains. Celandines were yellow in the hedges, and primroses among the rocks. But still there came a smell of sulphur from faraway steel-works, out of the steel-blue sky.

And yet it was spring.

Yvette was cycling slowly along by Codnor Gate, past the lime quarries, when she saw the gipsy coming away from the door of a stone cottage. His cart stood there in the road. He was returning with his brooms and copper things, to the cart.

She got down from her bicycle. As she saw him, she loved with curious tenderness, the slim lines of his body in the green jersey, the turn of his silent face. She felt she knew him better than she knew anybody on earth, even Lucille, and belonged to him, in some way, for ever.

"Have you made anything new and nice?" she asked innocently, looking at his copper things.

"I don't think," he said, glancing back at her.

The desire was still there, still curious and naked, in his eyes. But it was more remote, the boldness was diminished. There was a tiny glint, as if he might dislike her. But this dissolved again, as he saw her looking among his bits of copper and brasswork. She searched them diligently.

There was a little oval brass plate, with a queer figure like a palm-tree beaten upon it.

"I like that," she said. "How much is it?"

"What you like," he said.

This made her nervous: he seemed off-hand, almost mocking.

"I'd rather you said," she told him, looking up at him.

"You give me what you like," he said.

"No!" she said, suddenly. "If you won't tell me I won't have it."

"All right," he said. "Two shilling."

She found half-a-crown, and he drew from his pocket a handful of silver, from which he gave her her sixpence.

"The old gipsy dreamed something about you," he said, looking at her with curious, searching eyes.

"Did she!" cried Yvette, at once interested. "What was it?"

"She said: 'Be braver in your heart, or you lose your game.' She said it this way: 'Be braver in your body, or your luck will leave you.' And she said as well: 'Listen for the voice of water.'"

Yvette was very much impressed.

"And what does it mean?" she asked.

"I asked her," he said. "She says she don't know."

"Tell me again what it was," said Yvette.

"'Be braver in your body, or your luck will go.' And: 'Listen for the voice of water.'"

He looked in silence at her soft, pondering face. Something almost like a perfume seemed to flow from her young bosom direct to him, in a grateful connection.

"I'm to be braver in my body, and I'm to listen for the voice of water! All right!" she said. "I don't understand, but perhaps I shall."

She looked at him with clear eyes. Man or woman is made up of many selves. With one self, she loved this gipsy man. With many selves, she ig-nored him or had a distaste for him.

"You're not coming up to the Head no more?" he asked.

Again she looked at him absently.

"Perhaps I will," she said, "some time. Some time!"

"Spring weather!" he said, smiling faintly and glancing round at the sun. "We're going to break camp soon, and go away."

"When?" she said.

"Perhaps next week."

"Where to?"

Again he made a move with his head.

"Perhaps up north," he said.

She looked at him.

"All right!" she said. "Perhaps I *will* come up before you go, and say goodbye! to your wife and to the old woman who sent me the message."

NINE

Yvette did not keep her promise. The few March days were lovely, and she let them slip. She had a curious reluctance always, towards taking action, or making any real move of her own. She always wanted someone else to make a move for her, as if she did not want to play her own game of life.

She lived as usual, went out to her friends, to parties, and danced with the undiminished Leo. She wanted to go up and say goodbye to the gipsies. She wanted to. And nothing prevented her.

On the Friday afternoon especially she wanted to go. It was sunny, and the last yellow crocuses down the drive were in full blaze, wide open, the first bees rolling in them. The Papple rushed under the stone bridge, uncannily full, nearly filling the arches. There was the scent of a mezereon tree.

And she felt too lazy, too lazy, too lazy. She strayed in the garden by the river, half dreamy, expecting something. While the gleam of spring sun lasted, she would be out of doors. Indoors Granny, sitting back like some awful old prelate, in her bulk of black silk and her white lace cap, was warming her feet by the fire, and hearing everything that Aunt Nell had to say. Friday was Aunt Nell's day. She usually came for lunch, and left after an early tea. So the mother and the large, rather common daughter, who was a widow at the age of forty, sat gossiping by the fire, while Aunt Cissie prowled in and out. Friday was the rector's day for going to town: it was also the housemaid's half day.

Yvette sat on a wooden seat in the garden, only a few feet above the bank of the swollen river, which rolled a strange, uncanny mass of water. The crocuses were passing in the ornamental beds, the grass was dark green where it was mown, the laurels looked a little brighter. Aunt Cissie appeared at the top of the porch steps, and called to ask if Yvette wanted that early cup of tea. Because of the river just below, Yvette could not hear what Aunt Cissie said, but she guessed, and shook her head. An early cup of tea, indoors, when the sun actually shone? No thanks!

She was conscious of her gipsy, as she sat there musing in the sun. Her soul had the half painful, half easing knack of leaving her, and straying away to some place, to somebody that had caught her imagination. Some days she would be all the Framleys, even though she did not go near them. Some days, she was all the time in spirit with the Eastwoods. And today it was the gipsies. She was up at their encampment in the quarry. She saw the man hammering his copper, lifting his head to look at the road; and the children playing in the horse-shelter: and the women, the gipsy's wife and the strong, elderly woman, coming home with their packs, along with the elderly man. For this afternoon, she felt intensely that *that* was home for her: the gipsy camp, the fire, the stool, the man with the hammer, the old crone.

It was part of her nature, to get these fits of yearning for some place she knew; to be in a certain place; with somebody who meant home to her. This afternoon it was the gipsy camp. And the man in the green jersey made it home to her. Just to be where he was, that was to be at home. The caravans, the brats, the other women: everything was natural to her, her home, as if she had been born there. She wondered if the gipsy was aware of her: if he could see her sitting on the stool by the fire; if he would lift his head and see her as she rose, looking at him slowly and significantly, turning towards the steps of his caravan. Did he know? Did he know?

Vaguely she looked up the steep of dark larch trees north of the house, where unseen the road climbed, going towards the Head. There was nothing, and her glance strayed down again. At the foot of the slope the river turned, thrown back harshly, ominously, against the low rocks across stream, then pouring past the garden to the bridge. It was unnaturally full, and whitey-muddy, and ponderous, "Listen for the voice of water," she said to herself. "No need to listen for it, if the voice means the noise!"

And again she looked at the swollen river breaking angrily as it came round the bend. Above it the black-looking kitchen garden hung and the hard-natured fruit trees. Everything was on the tilt, facing south and south-west, for the sun. Behind, above the house and the kitchen garden hung the steep little wood of withered-seeming larches. The gardener was working in the kitchen garden, high up there, by the edge of the larch-wood.

She heard a call. It was Aunt Cissie and Aunt Nell. They were on the drive, waving Goodbye! Yvette waved back. Then Aunt Cissie, pitching her voice against the waters, called:

"I shan't be long. Don't forget Granny is alone!"

"All right!" screamed Yvette rather ineffectually.

And she sat on her bench and watched the two undignified, long-coated women walk slowly over the bridge and begin the curving climb on the opposite slope, Aunt Nell carrying a sort of suit-case in which she brought a few goods for Granny and took back vegetables or whatever the rectory garden or cupboard was yielding. Slowly the two figures diminished, on the whitish, up-curving road, laboring slowly up towards Papplewick village. Aunt Cissie was going as far as the village for something.

The sun was yellowing to decline. What a pity! Oh what a pity the sunny day was going, and she would have to turn indoors, to those hateful rooms, and Granny! Aunt Cissie would be back directly: it was past five. And all the others would be arriving from town, rather irritable and tired, soon after six.

As she looked uneasily round, she heard, across the running of water, the sharp noise of a horse and cart rattling on the road hidden in the larch trees. The gardener was looking up too. Yvette turned away again, lingering, strolling by the full river a few paces, unwilling to go in; glancing up the road to see if Aunt Cissie were coming. If she saw her, she would go indoors.

She heard somebody shouting, and looked round. Down the path through the larch-trees the gipsy was bounding. The gardener, away beyond, was also running. Simultaneously she became aware of a great roar, which, before she could move, accumulated to a vast deafening snarl. The gipsy was gesticulating. She looked round, behind her.

And to her horror and amazement, round the bend of the river she saw a shaggy, tawny wave-front of water advancing like a wall of lions. The roaring sound wiped out everything. She was powerless, too amazed and wonder-struck, she wanted to see it.

Before she could think twice, it was near, a roaring cliff of water. She almost fainted with horror. She heard the scream of the gipsy, and looked up to see him bounding upon her, his black eyes starting out of his head.

"Run!" he screamed, seizing her arm.

And in the instant the first wave was washing her feet from under her, swirling, in the insane noise, which suddenly for some reason seemed like stillness, with a devouring flood over the garden. The horrible mowing of water!

The gipsy dragged her heavily, lurching, plunging, but still keeping foot-hold both of them, towards the house. She was barely conscious: as if the flood was in her soul.

There was one grass-banked terrace of the garden, near the path round the house. The gipsy clawed his way up this terrace to the dry level of the path, dragging her after him, and sprang with her past the windows to the porch steps. Before they got there, a new great surge of water came mowing, mowing trees down even, and mowed them down too.

Yvette felt herself gone in an agonising millrace of icy water, whirled, with only the fearful grip of the gipsy's hand on her wrist. They were both down and gone. She felt a dull but stunning bruise somewhere.

Then he pulled her up. He was up, streaming forth water, clinging to the stem of the great wisteria that grew against the wall, crushed against the wall by the water. Her head was above water, he held her arm till it seemed dislocated: but she could not get her footing. With a ghastly sickness like a dream, she struggled and struggled, and could not get her feet. Only his hand was locked on her wrist.

He dragged her nearer till her one hand caught his leg. He nearly went down again. But the wisteria held him, and he pulled her up to him. She clawed at him, horribly, and got to her feet, he hanging on like a man torn in two, to the wisteria trunk.

The water was above her knees. The man and she looked into each other's ghastly streaming faces.

"Get to the steps!" he screamed.

It was only just round the corner: four strides! She looked at him: she could not go. His eyes glared on her like a tiger's, and he pushed her from him. She clung to the wall, and the water seemed to abate a little. Round the corner she staggered, but staggering, reeled and was pitched up against the cornice of the balustrade of the porch steps, the man after her.

They got on to the steps, when another roar was heard amid the roar, and the wall of the house shook. Up heaved the water round their legs again, but the gipsy had opened the hall door. In they poured with the water, reeling to the stairs. And as they did so, they saw the short but strange bulk of Granny emerge in the hall, away down from the dining-room door. She had her hands lifted and clawing, as the first water swirled round her legs, and her coffin-like mouth was opened in a hoarse scream.

Yvette was blind to everything but the stairs. Blind, unconscious of everything save the steps rising beyond the water, she clambered up like a wet, shuddering cat, in a state of unconsciousness. It was not till she was on the landing, dripping and shuddering till she could not stand erect, clinging to the banisters, while the house shook and the water raved below, that she was aware of the sodden gipsy, in paroxysms of coughing at the head of the stairs, his cap gone, his black hair over his eyes, peering between his washed-down hair at the sickening heave of water below, in the hall. Yvette, fainting, looked too, and saw Granny bob up, like a strange float, her face purple, her blind blue eyes bolting, spume hissing from her mouth. One old purple hand clawed at a banister rail, and held for a moment, showing the glint of a wedding ring.

The gipsy, who had coughed himself free and pushed back his hair, said to that awful float-like face below:

"Not good enough! Not good enough!"

With a low thud like thunder, the house was struck again, and shuddered, and a strange cracking, rattling, spitting noise began. Up heaved the water like a sea. The hand was gone, all sign of anything was gone, but upheaving water.

Yvette turned in blind unconscious frenzy, staggering like a wet cat to the upper stair-case, and climbing swiftly. It was not till she was at the door of her room that she stopped, paralysed by the sound of a sickening, tearing crash while the house swayed.

"The house is coming down!" yelled the green-white face of the gipsy, in her face.

He glared into her crazed face.

"Where is the chimney? the back chimney?—which room? The chimney will stand—."

He glared with strange ferocity into her face, forcing her to understand. And she nodded with a strange, crazed poise, nodded quite serenely, saying:

"In here! In here! It's all right."

They entered her room, which had a narrow fire-place. It was a back room with two windows, one on each side the great chimney-flue. The gipsy, coughing bitterly and trembling in every limb, went to the window to look out.

Below, between the house and the steep rise of the hill, was a wild mill-race, of water rushing with refuse, including Rover's green dog-kennel. The gipsy coughed and coughed, and gazed down blankly. Tree after tree went down, mown by the water, which must have been ten feet deep.

Shuddering and pressing his sodden arms on his sodden breast, a look of resignation on his livid face, he turned to Yvette. A fearful tearing noise tore the house, then there was a deep, watery explosion. Something had gone down, some part of the house, the floor heaved and wavered beneath them. For some moments both were suspended, stupefied. Then he roused.

"Not good enough! Not good enough! This will stand. This here will stand. See that chimney! like a tower. Yes! All right! All right. You take your clothes off and go to bed. You'll die of the cold."

"It's all right! It's quite all right!" she said to him, sitting on a chair and looking up into his face with her white, insane little face, round which the hair was plastered.

"No!" he cried. "No! Take your things off and I rub you with this towel. I rub myself. If the house falls then die warm. If it don't fall, then live, not die of pneumonia."

Coughing, shuddering violently, he pulled up his jersey hem and wrestled with all his shuddering, cold-cracked might, to get off his wet, tight jersey.

"Help me!" he cried, his face muffled.

She seized the edge of the jersey, obediently, and pulled with all her might. The garment came over his head, and he stood in his braces.

"Take your things off! Rub with this towel!" he commanded ferociously, the savageness of the war on him. And like a thing obsessed, he pushed himself out of his trousers, and got out of his wet, clinging shirt, emerging slim and livid, shuddering in every fibre with cold and shock.

He seized a towel, and began quickly to rub his body, his teeth chattering like plates rattling together. Yvette dimly saw it was wise. She tried to get out of her dress. He pulled the horrible wet death-gripping thing off her, then, resuming his rubbing, went to the door, tip-toeing on the wet floor.

There he stood, naked, towel in hand, petrified. He looked west, towards where the upper landing window had been, and was looking into the sunset, over an insane sea of waters, bristling with uptorn trees and refuse. The end corner of the house, where porch had been, and the stairs, had gone. The wall had fallen, leaving the floors sticking out. The stairs had gone.

Motionless, he watched the water. A cold wind blew in upon him. He clenched his rattling teeth with a great effort of will, and turned into the room again, closing the door.

Yvette, naked, shuddering so much that she was sick, was trying to wipe herself dry.

"All right!" he cried. "All right! The water don't rise no more! All right!"

With his towel he began to rub her, himself shaking all over, but holding her gripped by the shoulder, and slowly, numbedly rubbing her tender body, even trying to rub up into some dryness the pitiful hair of her small head.

Suddenly he left off.

"Better lie in the bed," he commanded, "I want to rub myself."

His teeth went snap-snap-snap-snap, in great snaps, cutting off his words. Yvette crept shaking and semi-conscious into her bed. He, making strained efforts to hold himself still and rub himself warm, went again to the north window, to look out.

The water had risen a little. The sun had gone down, and there was a reddish glow. He rubbed his hair into a black, wet tangle, then paused for breath, in a sudden access of shuddering, then looked out again, then rubbed again on his breast, and began to cough afresh, because of the water he had swallowed. His towel was red: he had hurt himself somewhere: but he felt nothing.

There was still the strange huge noise of water, and the horrible bump of things bumping against the walls. The wind was rising with sundown, cold and hard. The house shook with explosive thuds, and weird, weird frightening noises came up.

A terror creeping over his soul, he went again to the door. The wind, roaring with the waters, blew in as he opened it. Through the awesome gap in the house he saw the world, the waters, the chaos of horrible waters, the twilight, the perfect new moon high above the sunset, a faint thing, and clouds pushing dark into the sky, on the cold, blustery wind.

Clenching his teeth again, fear mingling with resignation, or fatalism, in his soul, he went into the room and closed the door, picking up her towel to see if it were drier than his own, and less bloodstained, again rubbing his head, and going to the window.

He turned away, unable to control his spasms of shivering. Yvette had disappeared right under the bedclothes, and nothing of her was visible but a shivering mound under the white quilt. He laid his hand on this shivering mound, as if for company. It did not stop shivering.

"All right!" he said. "All right! Water's going down."

She suddenly uncovered her head and peered out at him from a white face. She peered into his greenish, curiously calm face, semi-conscious. His teeth were chattering unheeded, as he gazed down at her, his black eyes still full of the fire of life and a certain vagabond calm of fatalistic resignation.

"Warm me!" she moaned, with chattering teeth. "Warm me! I shall die of shivering."

A terrible convulsion went through her curled-up white body, enough indeed to rupture her and cause her to die.

The gipsy nodded, and took her in his arms, and held her in a clasp like a vice, to still his own shuddering. He himself was shuddering fearfully, and only semi-conscious. It was the shock.

The vice-like grip of his arms round her seemed to her the only stable point in her consciousness. It was a fearful relief to her heart, which was strained to bursting. And though his body, wrapped round her strange and lithe and powerful, like tentacles, rippled with shuddering as an electric current, still the rigid tension of the muscles that held her clenched steadied them both, and gradually the sickening violence of the shuddering, caused by shock, abated, in his body first, then in hers, and the warmth revived between them. And as it roused, their tortured, semiconscious minds became unconscious, they passed away into sleep.

TEN

The sun was shining in heaven before men were able to get across the Papple with ladders. The bridge was gone. But the flood had abated, and the house, that leaned forwards as if it were making a stiff bow to the stream, stood now in mud and wreckage, with a great heap of fallen masonry and debris at the south-west corner. Awful were the gaping mouths of rooms!

Inside, there was no sign of life. But across-stream the gardener had come to reconnoitre, and the cook appeared, thrilled with curiosity. She had escaped from the back door and up through the larches to the high-road, when she saw the gipsy bound past the house: thinking he was coming to murder somebody. At the little top gate she had found his cart standing. The gardener had led the horse away to the Red Lion up at Darley, when night had fallen.

This the men from Papplewick learned when at last they got across the stream with ladders, and to the back of the house. They were nervous, fearing a collapse of the building, whose front was all undermined and whose back was choked up. They gazed with horror at the silent shelves of the rector's rows of books, in his torn-open study; at the big brass bed-stead of Granny's room, the bed so deep and comfortably made, but one brass leg of the bed-stead perched tentatively over the torn void; at the wreckage of the maid's room upstairs. The housemaid and the cook wept. Then a man climbed in cautiously through a smashed kitchen window, into the jungle and morass of the ground floor. He found the body of the old woman: or at least he saw her foot, in its flat black slipper, muddily protruding from a mud-heap of debris. And he fled.

The gardener said he was sure that Miss Yvette was not in the house. He had seen her and the gipsy swept away. But the policeman insisted on a search, and the Framley boys rushing up at last, the ladders were roped together. Then the whole party set up a loud yell. But without result. No answer from within.

A ladder was up, Bob Framley climbed, smashed a window, and clambered into Aunt Cissie's room. The perfect homely familiarity of everything terrified him like ghosts. The house might go down any minute.

They had just got the ladder up to the top floor, when men came running from Darley, saying the old gipsy had been to the Red Lion for the horse and cart, leaving word that his son had seen Yvette at the top of the house. But by that time the policeman was smashing the window of Yvette's room.

Yvette, fast asleep, started from under the bed-clothes with a scream, as the glass flew. She clutched the sheets round her nakedness. The policeman uttered a startled yell, which he converted into a cry of: Miss Yvette! Miss Yvette! He turned round on the ladder, and shouted to the faces below.

"Miss Yvette's in bed!—in bed!"

And he perched there on the ladder, an unmarried man, clutching the window in peril, not knowing what to do.

Yvette sat up in bed, her hair in a matted tangle, and stared with wild eyes, clutching up the sheets at her naked breast. She had been so very fast asleep, that she was still not there.

The policeman, terrified at the flabby ladder, climbed into the room, saying:

"Don't be frightened, Miss! Don't you worry any more about it. You're safe now."

And Yvette, so dazed, thought he meant the gipsy. Where was the gipsy? This was the first thing in her mind. Where was her gipsy of this world's-end night?

He was gone! He was gone! And a policeman was in the room! A policeman!

She rubbed her hand over her dazed brow.

"If you'll get dressed, Miss, we can get you down to safe ground. The house is likely to fall. I suppose there's nobody in the other rooms?"

He stepped gingerly into the passage, and gazed in terror through the torn-out end of the house, and far-off saw the rector coming down in a motor-car, on the sunlit hill.

Yvette, her face gone numb and disappointed, got up quickly, closing the bed-clothes, and looked at herself a moment, then opened her drawers for clothing. She dressed herself, then looked in a mirror, and saw her matted hair with horror. Yet she did not care. The gipsy was gone, anyhow.

Her own clothes lay in a sodden heap. There was a great sodden place on the carpet where his had been, and two blood-stained filthy towels. Otherwise there was no sign of him.

She was tugging at her hair when the policeman tapped at her door. She called him to come in. He saw with relief that she was dressed and in her right senses.

"We'd better get out of the house as soon as possible, Miss," he reiterated. "It might fall any minute."

"Really!" said Yvette calmly. "Is it as bad as that?"

There were great shouts. She had to go to the window. There, below, was the rector, his arms wide open, tears streaming down his face.

"I'm perfectly all right, Daddy!" she said, with the calmness of her contradictory feelings. She would keep the gipsy a secret from him. At the same time, tears ran down her face.

"Don't you cry, Miss, don't you cry! The rector's lost his mother, but he's thanking his stars to have his daughter. We all thought you were gone as well, we did that!"

"Is Granny drowned?" said Yvette.

"I'm afraid she is, poor lady!" said the policeman, with a grave face.

Yvette wept away into her hanky, which she had had to fetch from a drawer.

"Dare you go down that ladder, Miss?" said the policeman.

Yvette looked at the sagging depth of it, and said promptly to herself: No! Not for anything!—But then she remembered the gipsy's saying: "Be braver in the body."

"Have you been in all the other rooms?" she said, in her weeping, turning to the policeman.

"Yes, Miss! But you was the only person in the house, you know, save the old lady. Cook got away in time, and Lizzie was up at her mother's. It was only you and the poor old lady we was fretting about. Do you think you dare go down that ladder?"

"Oh, yes!" said Yvette with indifference. The gipsy was gone anyway.

And now the rector in torment watched his tall, slender daughter slowly stepping backwards down the sagging ladder, the policeman, peering hero-ically from the smashed window, holding the ladder's top ends.

At the foot of the ladder Yvette appropriately fainted in her father's arms, and was borne away with him, in the car, by Bob, to the Framley home. There the poor Lucille, a ghost of ghosts, wept with relief till she had hysterics, and even Aunt Cissie cried out among her tears: "Let the old be taken and the young spared! Oh I *can't* cry for the Mater, now Yvette is spared!"

And she wept gallons.

The flood was caused by the sudden bursting of the great reservoir, up in Papple Highdale, five miles from the rectory. It was found out later that an ancient, perhaps even a Roman mine tunnel, unsuspected, undreamed of, beneath the reservoir dam, had collapsed undermining the whole dam. That was why the Papple had been, for the last day, so uncannily full. And then the dam had burst.

The rector and the two girls stayed on at the Framley's, till a new home could be found. Yvette did not attend Granny's funeral. She stayed in bed.

Telling her tale, she only told how the gipsy had got her inside the porch, and she had crawled to the stairs out of the water. It was known that he had escaped: the old gipsy had said so, when he fetched the horse and cart from the Red Lion. Yvette could tell little. She was vague, confused, she seemed hardly to remember anything. But that was just like her.

It was Bob Framley who said:

"You know, I think that gipsy deserves a medal."

The whole family was suddenly struck.

"Oh, we *ought* to thank him!" cried Lucille.

The rector himself went with Bob in the car. But the quarry was deserted. The gipsies had lifted camp and gone, no one knew whither.

And Yvette, lying in bed, moaned in her heart: Oh, I love him! I love him! I love him!—The grief over him kept her prostrate. Yet practically, she too was acquiescent in the fact of his disappearance. Her young soul knew the wisdom of it.

But after Granny's funeral, she received a little letter, dated from some unknown place.

"Dear Miss, I see in the paper you are all right after your ducking, as is the same with me. I hope I see you again one day, maybe at Tideswell cattle fair, or maybe we come that way again. I come that day to say goodbye! and I never said it, well, the water give no time, but I live in hopes. Your obdt. servant Joe Boswell."

And only then she realised that he had a name.

Red Leaves

B Y

William Faulkner

Editor's Note

William Faulkner was born in 1897 in New Albany, Mississippi. (To the family name, Falkner, the *u* was added in 1924 by the printer who set up his first book, *The Marble Faun*, a book of imitative verses.) His great-grandfather had been a legendary figure in northern Mississippi: he was twice acquitted of murder charges; in the Civil War he was the colonel of a group of raiders; he owned a railroad, and was killed by his former railroad partner after defeating him for a seat in the state legislature. His grandfather was a banker and an Assistant United States Attorney. When William was five, his family moved to Oxford, where his father ran a livery stable and a hardware store. William left high school, a poor student, after the tenth grade. During World War I, he was rejected by the U.S. Army for being underweight and only five feet five, but he joined the Royal Flying Corps in Canada and was demobilized a second lieutenant. As a veteran he was allowed to enroll at the University of Mississippi in Oxford, but stayed for only a year. During the twenties he wandered a good deal and wrote a lot. In 1929 he published his first good book, *The Sound and the Fury*, married, and settled down in Oxford to write.

During the next thirteen years he published his chief books: *These Thirteen* (1931, a collection of stories including "Red Leaves"), *Light in August* (1932), *Absalom, Absalom!* (1936), *The Hamlet* (1940), and *Go Down, Moses* (1942). Recognition of his merit came sooner in Europe than in America; in 1946 not one of his books was in print in the United States; in 1950 he was awarded the Nobel Prize. In 1957 he was writer in residence at the University of Virginia, in Charlottesville. In 1962 he died of a heart attack in Oxford.

Red Leaves

I

THE TWO INDIANS CROSSED THE PLANTATION TOWARD THE SLAVE QUARTERS. Neat with whitewash, of baked soft brick, the two rows of houses in which lived the slaves belonging to the clan, faced one another across the mild shade of the lane marked and scored with naked feet and with a few homemade toys mute in the dust. There was no sign of life.

"I know what we will find," the first Indian said.

"What we will not find," the second said. Although it was noon, the lane was vacant, the doors of the cabins empty and quiet; no cooking smoke rose from any of the chinked and plastered chimneys.

"Yes. It happened like this when the father of him who is now the Man died."

"You mean, of him who was the Man."

"Yao."

The first Indian's name was Three Basket. He was perhaps sixty. They were both squat men, a little solid, burgherlike; paunchy, with big heads, big, broad, dust-colored faces of a certain blurred serenity like carved heads on a ruined wall in Siam or Sumatra, looming out of a mist. The sun had done it, the violent sun, the violent shade. Their hair looked like sedge grass on burnt-over land. Clamped through one ear Three Basket wore an enameled snuffbox.

"I have said all the time that this is not the good way. In the old days there were no quarters, no Negroes. A man's time was his own then. He had time. Now he must spend most of it finding work for them who prefer sweating to do."

"They are like horses and dogs."

"They are like nothing in this sensible world. Nothing contents them save sweat. They are worse than the white people."

"It is not as though the Man himself had to find work for them to do."

"You said it. I do not like slavery. It is not the good way. In the old days, there was the good way. But not now."

"You do not remember the old way either."

"I have listened to them who do. And I have tried this way. Man was not made to sweat."

"That's so. See what it has done to their flesh."

"Yes. Black. It has a bitter taste, too."

"You have eaten of it?"

"Once. I was young then, and more hardy in the appetite than now. Now it is different with me."

"Yes. They are too valuable to eat now."

"There is a bitter taste to the flesh which I do not like."

"They are too valuable to eat, anyway, when the white men will give horses for them."

They entered the lane. The mute, meager toys—the fetish-shaped objects made of wood and rags and feathers—lay in the dust about the patinaed doorsteps, among bones and broken gourd dishes. But there was no sound from any cabin, no face in any door; had not been since yesterday, when Issetibbeha died. But they already knew what they would find.

It was in the central cabin, a house a little larger than the others, where at certain phases of the moon the Negroes would gather to begin their ceremonies before removing after nightfall to the creek bottom, where they kept the drums. In this room they kept the minor accessories, the cryptic ornaments, the ceremonial records which consisted of sticks daubed with red clay in symbols. It had a hearth in the center of the floor, beneath a hole in the roof, with a few cold wood ashes and a suspended iron pot. The window shutters were closed; when the two Indians entered, after the abashless sunlight they could distinguish nothing with the eyes save a movement, shadow, out of which eyeballs rolled, so that the place appeared to be full of Negroes. The two Indians stood in the door.

"Yao," Basket said. "I said this is not the good way."

"I don't think I want to be here," the second said.

"That is black man's fear which you smell. It does not smell as ours does."

"I don't think I want to be here."

"Your fear has an odor too."

"Maybe it is Issetibbeha which we smell."

"Yao. He knows. He knows what we will find here. He knew when he died what we should find here today." Out of the rank twilight of the room the eyes, the smell, of Negroes rolled about them. "I am Three Basket, whom you know," Basket said into the room. "We are come from the Man. He whom we seek is gone?" The Negroes said nothing. The smell of them, of their bodies, seemed to ebb and flux in the still hot air. They seemed to be musing as one upon something remote, inscrutable. They were like a single octopus. They were like the roots of a huge tree uncovered, the earth broken momentarily upon the writhen, thick, fetid tangle of its lightless and outraged life. "Come," Basket said. "You know our errand. Is he whom we seek gone?"

"They are thinking something," the second said. "I do not want to be here."

"They are knowing something," Basket said.

"They are hiding him, you think?"

"No. He is gone. He has been gone since last night. It happened like this before, when the grandfather of him who is now the Man died. It took us three days to catch him. For three days Doom lay above the ground, saying, 'I see my horse and my dog. But I do not see my slave. What have you done with him that you will not permit me to lie quiet?'"

"They do not like to die."

"Yao. They cling. It makes trouble for us, always. A people without honor and without decorum. Always a trouble."

"I do not like it here."

"Nor do I. But then, they are savages; they cannot be expected to regard usage. That is why I say that this way is a bad way."

"Yao. They cling. They would even rather work in the sun than to enter the earth with a chief. But he is gone."

The Negroes had said nothing, made no sound. The white eyeballs rolled, wild, subdued; the smell was rank, violent. "Yes, they fear," the second said. "What shall we do now?"

"Let us go and talk with the Man."

"Will Moketubbe listen?"

"What can he do? He will not like to. But he is the Man now."

"Yao. He is the Man. He can wear the shoes with the red heels all the time now." They turned and went out. There was no door in the door frame. There were no doors in any of the cabins.

"He did that anyway," Basket said.

"Behind Issetibbeha's back. But now they are his shoes, since he is the Man."

"Yao. Issetibbeha did not like it. I have heard. I know that he said to Moketubbe: 'When you are the Man, the shoes will be yours. But until then, they are my shoes.' But now Moketubbe is the Man; he can wear them."

"Yao," the second said. "He is the Man now. He used to wear the shoes behind Issetibbeha's back, and it was not known if Issetibbeha knew this or not. And then Issetibbeha became dead, who was not old, and the shoes are Moketubbe's, since he is the Man now. What do you think of that?"

"I don't think about it," Basket said. "Do you?"

"No," the second said.

"Good," Basket said. "You are wise."

II

The house sat on a knoll, surrounded by oak trees. The front of it was one story in height, composed of the deck house of a steamboat which had gone ashore and which Doom, Issetibbeha's father, had dismantled with his slaves and hauled on cypress rollers twelve miles home overland. It took them five months. His house consisted at the time of one brick wall. He set the steamboat broadside on to the wall, where now the chipped and flaked gilding of the rococo cornices arched in faint splendor above the gilt lettering of the stateroom names above the jalousied doors.

Doom had been born merely a subchief, a Mingo, one of three children on the mother's side of the family. He made a journey—he was a young man then and New Orleans was a European city—from north Mississippi to New Orleans by keel boat, where he met the Chevalier Sœur Blonde de Vitry, a man whose social position, on its face, was as equivocal as Doom's own. In New Orleans, among the gamblers and cutthroats of the river front, Doom, under the tutelage of his patron, passed as the chief, the Man, the hereditary owner of that land which belonged to the male side of the family; it was the Chevalier de Vitry who spoke of him as *l'Homme* or *de l'Homme*, and hence Doom.

They were seen everywhere together—the Indian, the squat man with a bold, inscrutable, underbred face, and the Parisian, the expatriate, the friend, it was said, of Carondelet and the intimate of General Wilkinson. Then they disappeared, the two of them, vanishing from their old equivocal haunts and leaving behind them the legend of the sums which Doom was believed to have won, and some tale about a young woman, daughter of a fairly well-to-do West Indian family, the son and brother of whom sought Doom with a pistol about his old haunts for some time after his disappearance.

Six months later the young woman herself disappeared, boarding the Saint Louis packet, which put in one night at a wood landing on the north Mississippi side, where the woman, accompanied by a Negro maid, got off. Four Indians met her with a horse and wagon, and they traveled for three days, slowly, since she was already big with child, to the plantation, where she found that Doom was now chief. He never told her how he accomplished it, save that his uncle and his cousin had died suddenly. Before that time the house had consisted of a brick wall built by shiftless slaves, against which was propped a thatched lean-to divided into rooms and littered with bones and refuse, set in the center of ten thousand acres of matchless parklike forest where deer grazed like domestic cattle. Doom and the woman were married there a short time before Issetibbeha was born, by a combination itinerant minister and slave trader who arrived on a mule, to the saddle of which was lashed a cotton umbrella and a three-gallon demijohn of whiskey. After that, Doom began to acquire more slaves and to cultivate some of his land, as the white people did. But he never had enough for them to do. In utter idleness the majority of them led lives transplanted whole out of African jungles, save on the occasions when, entertaining guests, Doom coursed them with dogs.

When Doom died, Issetibbeha, his son, was nineteen. He became proprietor of the land and of the quintupled herd of blacks for which he had no use at all. Though the title of Man rested with him, there was a hierarchy of cousins and uncles who ruled the clan and who finally gathered in squatting conclave over the Negro question, squatting profoundly beneath the golden names above the doors of the steamboat.

"We cannot eat them," one said.

"Why not?"

"There are too many of them."

"That's true," a third said. "Once we started, we should have to eat them all. And that much flesh diet is not good for man."

"Perhaps they will be like deer flesh. That cannot hurt you."

"We might kill a few of them and not eat them," Issetibbeha said.

They looked at him for a while. "What for?" one said.

"That is true," a second said. "We cannot do that. They are too valuable; remember all the bother they have caused us, finding things for them to do. We must do as the white men do."

"How is that?" Issetibbeha said.

"Raise more Negroes by clearing more land to make corn to feed them, then sell them. We will clear the land and plant it with food and raise Negroes and sell them to the white men for money."

"But what will we do with this money?" a third said.

They thought for a while.

"We will see," the first said. They squatted, profound, grave.

"It means work," the third said.

"Let the Negroes do it," the first said.

"Yao. Let them. To sweat is bad. It is damp. It opens the pores."

"And then the night air enters."

"Yao. Let the Negroes do it. They appear to like sweating."

So they cleared the land with the Negroes and planted it in grain. Up to that time the slaves had lived in a huge pen with a lean-to roof over one corner, like a pen for pigs. But now they began to build quarters, cabins, putting the young Negroes in the cabins in pairs to mate; five years later Issetibbeha sold forty head to a Memphis trader, and he took the money and went abroad upon it, his maternal uncle from New Orleans conducting the trip. At that time the Chevalier Sœur Blonde de Vitry was an old man in Paris, in a toupee and a corset and a careful, toothless old face fixed in a grimace quizzical and profoundly tragic. He borrowed three hundred dollars from Issetibbeha and in return he introduced him into certain circles; a year later Issetibbeha returned home with a gilt bed, a pair of girandoles by whose light it was said that Pompadour arranged her hair while Louis smirked at his mirrored face across her powdered shoulder, and a pair of slippers with red heels. They were too small for him, since he had not worn shoes at all until he reached New Orleans on his way abroad.

He brought the slippers home in tissue paper and kept them in the remaining pocket of a pair of saddlebags filled with cedar shavings, save when he took them out on occasion for his son, Moketubbe, to play with. At three years of age Moketubbe had a broad, flat, Mongolian face that appeared to exist in a complete and unfathomable lethargy, until confronted by the slippers.

Moketubbe's mother was a comely girl whom Issetibbeha had seen one day working in her shift in a melon patch. He stopped and watched her for a while—the broad, solid thighs, the sound back, the serene face. He was on his way to the creek to fish that day, but he didn't go any farther; perhaps while he stood there watching the unaware girl he may have remembered his own mother, the city woman, the fugitive with her fans and laces and her Negro blood, and all the tawdry shabbiness of that sorry affair. Within the year Moketubbe was born; even at three he could not get his feet into the slippers. Watching him in the still, hot afternoons as he struggled with the slippers with a certain monstrous repudiation of fact, Issetibbeha laughed quietly to himself. He laughed at Moketubbe's antics with the shoes for several years, because Moketubbe did not give up trying to put them on until he was sixteen. Then he quit. Or Issetibbeha thought he had. But he had merely quit trying in Issetibbeha's presence. Issetibbeha's newest wife told him that Moketubbe had stolen and hidden the shoes. Issetibbeha quit laughing then, and he sent the woman away, so that he was alone. "Yao," he said. "I too like being alive, it seems." He sent for Moketubbe. "I give them to you," he said.

Moketubbe was twenty-five then, unmarried. Issetibbeha was not tall, but he was taller by six inches than his son and almost a hundred pounds lighter. Moketubbe was already diseased with flesh, with a pale, broad, inert face and dropsical hands and feet. "They are yours now," Issetibbeha said, watching him. Moketubbe had looked at him once when he entered, a glance brief, discreet, veiled.

"Thanks," he said.

Issetibbeha looked at him. He could never tell if Moketubbe saw anything, looked at anything. "Why will it not be the same if I give the slippers to you?"

"Thanks," Moketubbe said. Issetibbeha was using snuff at the time; a white man had shown him how to put the powder into his lip and scour it against his teeth with a twig of gum or of alphea.

"Well," he said, " a man cannot live forever." He looked at his son, then his gaze went blank in turn, unseeing, and he mused for an instant. You could not tell what he was thinking, save that he said half aloud: "Yao. But Doom's uncle had no shoes with red heels." He looked at his son again, fat, inert. "Beneath all that, a man might think of doing anything and it not be known until too late." He sat in a splint chair hammocked with deer thongs. "He cannot even get them on; he and I are both frustrated by the same gross meat which he wears. He cannot even get them on. But is that my fault?"

He lived for five years longer, then he died. He was sick one night, and though the doctor came in a skunk-skin vest and burned sticks, Issetibbeha died before noon.

That was yesterday; the grave was dug, and for twelve hours now the People had been coming in wagons and carriages and on horseback and afoot, to eat the baked dog and the succotash and the yams cooked in ashes and to attend the funeral.

III

"It will be three days," Basket said, as he and the other Indian returned to the house. "It will be three days and the food will not be enough; I have seen it before."

The second Indian's name was Louis Berry. "He will smell too, in this weather."

"Yao. They are nothing but a trouble and a care."

"Maybe it will not take three days."

"They run far. Yao. We will smell this Man before he enters the earth. You watch and see if I am not right."

They approached the house.

"He can wear the shoes now," Berry said. "He can wear them now in man's sight."

"He cannot wear them for a while yet," Basket said. Berry looked at him. "He will lead the hunt."

"Moketubbe?" Berry said. "Do you think he will? A man to whom even talking is travail?"

"What else can he do? It is his own father who will soon begin to smell."

"That is true," Berry said. "There is even yet a price he must pay for the shoes. Yao. He has truly bought them. What do you think?"

"What do you think?"

"What do you think?"

"I think nothing."

"Nor do I. Issetibbeha will not need the shoes now. Let Moketubbe have them; Issetibbeha will not care."

"Yao. Man must die."

"Yao. Let him; there is still the Man."

The bark roof of the porch was supported by peeled cypress poles, high above the texas of the steamboat, shading an unfloored banquette where on the trodden earth mules and horses were tethered in bad weather. On the forward end of the steamboat's deck sat an old man and two women. One of the women was dressing a fowl, the other was shelling corn. The old man was talking. He was barefoot, in a long linen frock coat and a beaver hat.

"This world is going to the dogs," he said. "It is being ruined by white men. We got along fine for years and years, before the white men foisted their Negroes upon us. In the old days the old men sat in the shade and ate stewed deer's flesh and corn and smoked tobacco and talked of honor and grave affairs; now what do we do? Even the old wear themselves into the grave taking care of them that like sweating." When Basket and Berry crossed the deck he ceased and looked up at them. His eyes were querulous, bleared; his face was myriad with tiny wrinkles. "He is fled also," he said.

"Yes," Berry said, "he is gone."

"I knew it. I told them so. It will take three weeks, like when Doom died. You watch and see."

"It was three days, not three weeks," Berry said.

"Were you there?"

"No," Berry said. "But I have heard."

"Well, I was there," the old man said. "For three whole weeks, through the swamps and the briers—" They went on and left him talking.

What had been the saloon of the steamboat was now a shell, rotting slowly; the polished mahogany, the carving glinting momentarily and fading through the mold in figures cabalistic and profound; the gutted windows were like cataracted eyes. It contained a few sacks of seed or grain, and the fore part of the running gear of a barouche, to the axle of which two C-springs rusted in graceful curves, supporting nothing. In one corner a fox cub ran steadily and soundlessly up and down a willow cage; three scrawny gamecocks moved in the dust, and the place was pocked and marked with their dried droppings.

They passed through the brick wall and entered a big room of chinked logs. It contained the hinder part of the barouche, and the dismantled body lying on its side, the window slatted over with willow withes, through which protruded the heads, the still, beady, outraged eyes and frayed combs of still more game chickens. It was floored with packed clay; in one corner leaned a crude plow and two hand-hewn boat paddles. From the ceiling, suspended by four deer thongs, hung the gilt bed which Issetibbeha had fetched from Paris. It had neither mattress nor springs, the frame criss-crossed now by a neat hammocking of thongs.

Issetibbeha had tried to have his newest wife, the young one, sleep in the bed. He was congenitally short of breath himself, and he passed the nights half reclining in his splint chair. He would see her to bed and, later, wakeful, sleeping as he did but three or four hours a night, he would sit in the darkness and simulate slumber and listen to her sneak infinitesimally from the gilt and ribboned bed, to lie on a quilt pallet on the floor until just before daylight. Then she would enter the bed quietly again and in turn simulate slumber, while in the darkness beside her Issetibbeha quietly laughed and laughed.

The girandoles were lashed by thongs to two sticks propped in a corner where a ten-gallon whiskey keg lay also. There was a clay hearth; facing it, in the splint chair, Moketubbe sat. He was maybe an inch better than five feet tall, and he weighed two hundred and fifty pounds. He wore a broad-cloth coat and no shirt, his round, smooth copper balloon of belly swelling above the bottom piece of a suit of linen underwear. On his feet were the slippers with the red heels. Behind his chair stood a stripling with a punkah-like fan made of fringed paper. Moketubbe sat motionless, with his broad, yellow face with its closed eyes and flat nostrils, his flipperlike arms extended. On his face was an expression profound, tragic, and inert. He did not open his eyes when Basket and Berry came in.

"He has worn them since daylight?" Basket said.

"Since daylight," the stripling said. The fan did not cease. "You can see."

"Yao," Basket said. "We can see." Moketubbe did not move. He looked like an effigy, like a Malay god in frock coat, drawers, naked chest, the trivial scarlet-heeled shoes.

"I wouldn't disturb him, if I were you," the stripling said.

"Not if I were you," Basket said. He and Berry squatted. The stripling moved the fan steadily. "O Man," Basket said, "listen." Moketubbe did not move. "He is gone," Basket said.

"I told you so," the stripling said. "I knew he would flee. I told you."

"Yao," Basket said. "You are not the first to tell us afterward what we should have known before. Why is it that some of you wise men took no steps yesterday to prevent this?"

"He does not wish to die," Berry said.

"Why should he not wish it?" Basket said.

"Because he must die some day is no reason," the stripling said. "That would not convince me either, old man."

"Hold your tongue," Berry said.

"For twenty years," Basket said, "while others of his race sweat in the fields, he served the Man in the shade. Why should he not wish to die, since he did not wish to sweat?"

"And it will be quick," Berry said. "It will not take long."

"Catch him and tell him that," the stripling said.

"Hush," Berry said. They squatted, watching Moketubbe's face. He might have been dead himself. It was as though he were cased so in flesh that even breathing took place too deep within him to show.

"Listen, O Man," Basket said. "Issetibbeha is dead. He waits. His dog and his horse we have. But his slave has fled. The one who held the pot for him, who ate of his food, from his dish, is fled. Issetibbeha waits."

"Yao," Berry said.

"This is not the first time," Basket said. "This happened when Doom, thy grandfather, lay waiting at the door of the earth. He lay waiting three days, saying, 'Where is my Negro?' And Issetibbeha, thy father, answered, 'I will find him. Rest; I will bring him to you so that you may begin the journey.' "

"Yao," Berry said.

Moketubbe had not moved, had not opened his eyes.

"For three days Issetibbeha hunted in the bottom," Basket said. "He did not even return home for food, until the Negro was with him; then he said to Doom, his father, 'Here is thy dog, thy horse, thy Negro; rest.' Issetibbeha, who is dead since yesterday, said it. And now Issetibbeha's Negro is fled. His horse and his dog wait with him, but his Negro is fled."

"Yao," Berry said.

Moketubbe had not moved. His eyes were closed; upon his supine monstrous shape there was a colossal inertia, something profoundly immobile, beyond and impervious to flesh. They watched his face, squatting.

"When thy father was newly the Man, this happened," Basket said. "And it was Issetibbeha who brought back the slave to where his father waited to enter the earth." Moketubbe's face had not moved, his eyes had not moved. After a while Basket said, "Remove the shoes."

The stripling removed the shoes. Moketubbe began to pant, his bare chest moving deep, as though he were rising from beyond his unfathomed flesh back into life, like up from the water, the sea. But his eyes had not opened yet.

Berry said, "He will lead the hunt."

"Yao," Basket said. "He is the Man. He will lead the hunt."

IV

All that day the Negro, Issetibbeha's body servant, hidden in the barn, watched Issetibbeha's dying. He was forty, a Guinea man. He had a flat nose, a close, small head; the inside corners of his eyes showed red a little, and his prominent gums were a pale bluish red above his square, broad teeth. He had been taken at fourteen by a trader off Kamerun, before his teeth had been filed. He had been Issetibbeha's body servant for twenty-three years.

On the day before, the day on which Issetibbeha lay sick, he returned to the quarters at dusk. In that unhurried hour the smoke of the cooking fires blew slowly across the street from door to door, carrying into the opposite one the smell of the identical meat and bread. The women tended them; the men were gathered at the head of the lane, watching him as he came down the slope from the house, putting his naked feet down carefully in a strange dust. To the waiting men his eyeballs were a little luminous.

"Issetibbeha is not dead yet," the headman said.

"Not dead," the body servant said. "Who not dead?"

In the dusk they had faces like his, the different ages, the thoughts sealed inscrutable behind faces like the death masks of apes. The smell of the fires, the cooking, blew sharp and slow across the strange dusk, as from another world, above the lane and the pickaninnies naked in the dust.

"If he lives past sundown, he will live until day break," one said.

"Who says?"

"Talk says."

"Yao. Talk says. We know but one thing." They looked at the body servant as he stood among them, his eyeballs a little luminous. He was breathing slow and deep. His chest was bare; he was sweating a little. "He knows. He knows it."

"Let us let the drums talk."

"Yao. Let the drums tell it."

The drums began after dark. They kept them hidden in the creek bottom. They were made of hollowed cypress knees, and the Negroes kept them hidden; why, none knew. They were buried in the mud on the bank of a slough; a lad of fourteen guarded them. He was undersized, and a mute; he squatted in the mud there all day, clouded over with mosquitoes, naked save for the mud with which he coated himself against the mosquitoes, and about his neck a fiber bag containing a pig's rib to which black shreds of flesh still adhered, and two scaly barks on a wire. He slobbered onto his clutched knees, drooling; now and then Indians came noiselessly out of the bushes behind him and stood there and contemplated him for a while and went away, and he never knew it.

From the loft of the stable where he lay hidden until dark and after, the Negro could hear the drums. They were three miles away, but he could hear them as though they were in the barn itself below him, thudding and thudding. It was as though he could see the fire too, and the black limbs turning into and out of the flames in copper gleams. Only there would be no fire. There would be no more light there than where he lay in the dusty loft, with the whispering arpeggios of rat feet along the warm and immemorial axsquared rafters. The only fire there would be the smudge against mosquitoes where the women with nursing children crouched, their heavy, sluggish breasts nippled full and smooth into the mouths of men children; contemplative, oblivious of the drumming, since a fire would signify life.

There was a fire in the steamboat, where Issetibbeha lay dying among his wives, beneath the lashed girandoles and the suspended bed. He could see the smoke, and just before sunset he saw the doctor come out, in a waistcoat made of skunk skins, and set fire to two clay-daubed sticks at the bows of the boat deck. "So he is not dead yet," the Negro said into the whispering gloom of the loft, answering himself; he could hear the two voices, himself and himself:

"Who not dead?"

"You are dead."

"Yao, I am dead," he said quietly. He wished to be where the drums were. He imagined himself springing out of the bushes, leaping among the drums on his bare, lean, greasy, invisible limbs. But he could not do that, because man leaped past life, into where death was; he dashed into death and did not die because when death took a man, it took him just this side of the end of living. It was when death overran him from behind, still in life. The thin whisper of rat feet died in fainting gusts along the rafters. Once he had eaten rat. He was a boy then, but just come to America. They had lived ninety days in a three-foot-high 'tween deck in tropic latitudes, hearing from topside the drunken New England captain intoning aloud from a book which he did not recognize for ten years afterward to be the Bible. Squatting in the stable so, he had watched the rat, civilized, by association with man reft of its inherent cunning of limb and eye; he had caught it without difficulty, with scarce a movement of his hand, and he ate it slowly, wondering how any of the rats had escaped so long. At that time he was still wearing the single white garment which the trader, a deacon in the Unitarian church, had given him, and he spoke then only his native tongue.

He was naked now, save for a pair of dungaree pants brought by Indians from white men, and an amulet slung on a thong about his hips. The amulet consisted of one half of a mother-of-pearl lorgnon which Issetibbeha had brought back from Paris, and the skull of a cottonmouth moccasin. He had killed the snake himself and eaten it, save the poison head. He lay in the loft, watching the house, the steamboat, listening to the drums, thinking of himself among the drums.

He lay there all night. The next morning he saw the doctor come out, in his skunk vest, and get on his mule and ride away, and he became quite still and watched the final dust from beneath the mule's delicate feet die away, and then he found that he was still breathing and it seemed strange to him that he still breathed air, still needed air. Then he lay and watched quietly, waiting to move, his eyeballs a little luminous, but with a quiet light, and his breathing light and regular, and saw Louis Berry come out and look at the sky. It was good light then, and already five Indians squatted in their Sunday clothes along the steamboat deck; by noon there were twenty-five there. That afternoon they dug the trench in which the meat would be baked, and the yams; by that time there were almost a hundred guests—decorous, quiet, patient in their stiff European finery—and he watched Berry lead Issetibbeha's mare from the stable and tie her to a tree, and then he watched Berry emerge from the house with the old hound which lay beside Issetibbeha's chair. He tied the hound to the tree too, and it sat there, looking gravely about at the faces. Then it began to howl. It was still howling at sundown, when the Negro climbed down the back wall of the barn and entered the spring branch, where it was already dusk. He began to run then. He could hear the hound howling behind him, and near the spring, already running, he passed another Negro. The two men, the one motionless and the other running, looked for an instant at each other as though across an actual boundary between two different worlds. He ran on into full darkness, mouth closed, fists doubled, his broad nostrils bellowing steadily.

He ran on in the darkness. He knew the country well, because he had hunted it often with Issetibbeha, following on his mule the course of the fox or the cat beside Issetibbeha's mare; he knew it as well as did the men who would pursue him. He saw them for the first time shortly before sunset of the second day. He had run thirty miles then, up the creek bottom, before doubling back; lying in a pawpaw thicket he saw the pursuit for the first time. There were two of them, in shirts and straw hats, carrying their neatly rolled trousers under their arms, and they had no weapons. They were middle-aged, paunchy, and they could not have moved very fast anyway; it would be twelve hours before they could return to where he lay watching them. "So I will have until midnight to rest," he said. He was near enough to the plantation to smell the cooking fires, and he thought how he ought to be hungry, since he had not eaten in thirty hours. "But it is more important to rest," he told himself. He continued to tell himself that, lying in the pawpaw thicket, because the effort of resting, the need and the haste to rest, made his heart thud the same as the running had done. It was as though he had forgot how to rest, as though the six hours were not long enough to do it in, to remember again how to do it.

As soon as dark came he moved again. He had thought to keep going steadily and quietly through the night, since there was nowhere for him to go, but as soon as he moved he began to run at top speed, breasting his panting chest, his broad-flaring nostrils through the choked and whipping darkness. He ran for an hour, lost by then, without direction, when suddenly he stopped, and after a time his thudding heart unraveled from the sound of the drums. By the sound they were not two miles away; he followed the sound until he could smell the smudge fire and taste the acrid smoke. When he stood among them the drums did not cease; only the headman came to him where he stood in the drifting smudge, panting, his nostrils flaring and pulsing, the hushed glare of his ceaseless eyeballs in his mud-daubed face as though they were worked from lungs.

"We have expected thee," the headman said. "Go, now."

"Go?"

"Eat, and go. The dead may not consort with the living; thou knowest that."

"Yao. I know that." They did not look at one another. The drums had not ceased.

"Wilt thou eat?" the headman said.

"I am not hungry. I caught a rabbit this afternoon, and ate while I lay hidden."

"Take some cooked meat with thee, then."

He accepted the cooked meat, wrapped in leaves, and entered the creek bottom again; after a while the sound of the drums ceased. He walked steadily until daybreak. "I have twelve hours," he said. "Maybe more, since the trail was followed by night." He squatted and ate the meat and wiped his hands on his thighs. Then he rose and removed the dungaree pants and squatted again beside a slough and coated himself with mud—face, arms, body and legs—and squatted again, clasping his knees, his head bowed. When it was light enough to see, he moved back into the swamp and squatted again and went to sleep so. He did not dream at all. It was well that he moved, for, waking suddenly in broad daylight and the high sun, he saw the two Indians. They still carried their neatly rolled trousers; they stood opposite the place where he lay hidden, paunchy, thick, soft-looking, a little ludicrous in their straw hats and shirt tails.

"This is wearying work," one said.

"I'd rather be at home in the shade myself," the other said. "But there is the Man waiting at the door to the earth."

"Yao." They looked quietly about; stooping, one of them removed from his shirt tail a clot of cockleburs. "Damn that Negro," he said.

"Yao. When have they ever been anything but a trial and a care to us?"

In the early afternoon, from the top of a tree, the Negro looked down into the plantation. He could see Issetibbeha's body in a hammock between the two trees where the horse and the dog were tethered, and the concourse about the steamboat was filled with wagons and horses and mules, with carts and saddle-horses, while in bright clumps the women and the smaller children and the old men squatted about the long trench where the smoke from the barbecuing meat blew slow and thick. The men and the big boys would all be down there in the creek bottom behind him, on the trail, their Sunday clothes rolled carefully up and wedged into tree crotches. There was a clump of men near the door to the house, to the saloon of the steamboat, though, and he watched them, and after a while he saw them bring Moketubbe out in a litter made of buckskin and persimmon poles; high hidden in his leafed nook the Negro, the quarry, looked quietly down upon his irrevocable doom with an expression as profound as Moketubbe's own. "Yao," he said quietly. "He will go then. That man whose body has been dead for fifteen years, he will go also."

In the middle of the afternoon he came face to face with an Indian. They were both on a footlog across a slough—the Negro gaunt, lean, hard, tireless and desperate; the Indian thick, soft-looking, the apparent embodiment of the ultimate and the supreme reluctance and inertia. The Indian made no move, no sound; he stood on the log and watched the Negro plunge into the slough and swim ashore and crash away into the undergrowth.

Just before sunset he lay behind a down log. Up the log in slow procession moved a line of ants. He caught them and ate them slowly, with a kind of detachment, like that of a dinner guest eating salted nuts from a dish. They too had a salt taste, engendering a salivary reaction out of all proportion. He ate them slowly, watching the unbroken line move up the log and into oblivious doom with a steady and terrific undeviation. He had eaten nothing else all day; in his caked mud mask his eyes rolled in reddened rims. At sunset, creeping along the creek bank toward where he had spotted a frog, a cottonmouth moccasin slashed him suddenly across the forearm with a thick, sluggish blow. It struck clumsily, leaving two long slashes across his arm like two razor slashes, and half sprawled with its own momentum and rage, it appeared for the moment utterly helpless with its own awkwardness and choleric anger. "Olé, Grandfather," the Negro said. He touched its head and watched it slash him again across his arm, and again, with thick, raking, awkward blows. "It's that I do not wish to die," he said. Then he said it again—"It's that I do not wish to die"—in a quiet tone, of slow and low amaze, as though it were something that, until the words had said themselves, he found that he had not known, or had not known the depth and extent of his desire.

V

Moketubbe took the slippers with him. He could not wear them very long while in motion, not even in the litter where he was slung reclining, so they rested upon a square of fawnskin upon his lap—the cracked, frail slippers a little shapeless now, with their scaled patent-leather surface and buckleless tongues and scarlet heels, lying upon the supine, obese shape just barely alive, carried through swamp and brier by swinging relays of men who bore steadily all day long the crime and its object, on the business of the slain. To Moketubbe it must have been as though, himself immortal, he were being carried rapidly through hell by doomed spirits which, alive, had contemplated his disaster, and, dead, were oblivious partners to his damnation.

After resting for a while, the litter propped in the center of the squatting circle and Moketubbe motionless in it, with closed eyes and his face at once peaceful for the instant and filled with inescapable foreknowledge, he could wear the slippers for a while. The stripling put them on him, forcing his big, tender, dropsical feet into them; whereupon into his face came again that expression, tragic, passive, and profoundly attentive, which dyspeptics wear. Then they went on. He made no move, no sound, inert in the rhythmic litter out of some reserve of inertia, or maybe of some kingly virtue such as courage or fortitude. After a time they set the litter down and looked at him, at the yellow face like that of an idol, beaded over with sweat. Then Three Basket or Louis Berry would say: "Take them off. Honor has been served." They would remove the shoes. Moketubbe's face would not alter, but only then would his breathing become perceptible, going in and out of his pale lips with a faint ah-ah-ah sound, and they would squat again while the couriers and the runners came up.

"Not yet?"

"Not yet. He is going east. By sunset he will reach Mouth of Tippah. Then he will turn back. We may take him tomorrow."

"Let us hope so. It will not be too soon."

"Yao. It has been three days now."

"When Doom died, it took only three days."

"But that was an old man. This one is young."

"Yao. A good race. If he is taken tomorrow, I will win a horse."

"May you win it."

"Yao. This work is not pleasant."

That was the day on which the food gave out at the plantation. The guests returned home and came back the next day with more food, enough for a week longer. On that day Issetibbeha began to smell; they could smell him for a long way up and down the bottom when it got hot toward noon and the wind blew. But they didn't capture the Negro on that day, nor on the next. It was about dusk on the sixth day when the couriers came up to the litter; they had found blood. "He has injured himself."

"Not bad, I hope," Basket said. "We cannot send with Issetibbeha one who will be of no service to him."

"Nor whom Issetibbeha himself will have to nurse and care for," Berry said.

"We do not know," the courier said. "He has hidden himself. He has crept back into the swamp. We have left pickets."

They trotted with the litter now. The place where the Negro had crept into the swamp was an hour away. In the hurry and excitement they had forgotten that Moketubbe still wore the slippers; when they reached the place Moketubbe had fainted. They removed the slippers and brought him to.

With dark, they formed a circle about the swamp. They squatted, clouded over with gnats and mosquitoes; the evening star burned low and close down the west, and the constellations began to wheel overhead. "We will give him time," they said. "Tomorrow is just another name for today."

"Yao. Let him have time." Then they ceased, and gazed as one into the darkness where the swamp lay. After a while the noise ceased, and soon the courier came out of the darkness.

"He tried to break out."

"But you turned him back?"

"He turned back. We feared for a moment, the three of us. We could smell him creeping in the darkness, and we could smell something else, which we did not know. That was why we feared, until he told us. He said to slay him there, since it would be dark and he would not have to see the face when it came. But it was not that which we smelled; he told us what it was. A snake had struck him. That was two days ago. The arm swelled, and it smelled bad. But it was not that which we smelled then, because the swelling had gone down and his arm was no longer than that of a child. He showed us. We felt the arm, all of us did; it was no larger than that of a child. He said to give him a hatchet so he could chop the arm off. But tomorrow is today also."

"Yao. Tomorrow is today."

"We feared for a while. Then he went back into the swamp."

"That is good."

"Yao. We feared. Shall I tell the Man?"

"I will see," Basket said. He went away. The courier squatted, telling again about the Negro. Basket returned. "The Man says that it is good. Return to your post."

The courier crept away. They squatted about the litter; now and then they slept. Sometime after midnight the Negro waked them. He began to shout and talk to himself, his voice coming sharp and sudden out of the darkness, then he fell silent. Dawn came; a white crane flapped slowly across the jonquil sky. Basket was awake. "Let us go now," he said. "It is today."

Two Indians entered the swamp, their movements noisy. Before they reached the Negro they stopped, because he began to sing. They could see him, naked and mud-caked, sitting on a log, singing. They squatted silently a short distance away, until he finished. He was chanting something in his own language, his face lifted to the rising sun. His voice was clear, full, with a quality wild and sad. "Let him have time," the Indians said, squatting, patient, waiting. He ceased and they approached. He looked back and up at them through the cracked mud mask. His eyes were bloodshot, his lips cracked upon his square short teeth. The mask of mud appeared to be loose on his face, as if he might have lost flesh since he put it there; he held his left arm close to his breast. From the elbow down it was caked and shapeless with black mud. They could smell him, a rank smell. He watched them quietly until one touched him on the arm. "Come," the Indian said. "You ran well. Do not be ashamed."

VI

As they neared the plantation in the tainted bright morning, the Negro's eyes began to roll a little, like those of a horse. The smoke from the cooking pit blew low along the earth and upon the squatting and waiting guests about the yard and upon the steamboat deck, in their bright, stiff, harsh finery; the women, the children, the old men. They had sent couriers along the bottom, and another on ahead, and Issetibbeha's body had already been removed to where the grave waited, along with the horse and the dog, though they could still smell him in death about the house where he had lived in life. The guests were beginning to move toward the grave when the bearers of Moketubbe's litter mounted the slope.

The Negro was the tallest there, his high, close, mudcaked head looming above them all. He was breathing hard, as though the desperate effort of the six suspended and desperate days had capitulated upon him at once; although they walked slowly, his naked scarred chest rose and fell above the close-clutched left arm. He looked this way and that continuously, as if he were not seeing, as though sight never quite caught up with the looking. His mouth was open a little upon his big white teeth; he began to pant. The already moving guests halted, pausing, looking back, some with pieces of meat in their hands, as the Negro looked about at their faces with his wild, restrained, unceasing eyes.

"Will you eat first?" Basket said. He had to say it twice.

"Yes," the Negro said. "That's it. I want to eat."

The throng had begun to press back toward the center; the word passed to the outermost: "He will eat first."

They reached the steamboat. "Sit down," Basket said. The Negro sat on the edge of the deck. He was still panting, his chest rising and falling, his head ceaseless with its white eyeballs, turning from side to side. It was as if the inability to see came from within, from hopelessness, not from absence of vision. They brought food and watched quietly as he tried to eat it. He put the food into his mouth and chewed it, but chewing, the half-masticated matter began to emerge from the corners of his mouth and to drool down his chin, onto his chest, and after a while he stopped chewing and sat there, naked, covered with dried mud, the plate on his knees, and his mouth filled with a mass of chewed food, open, his eyes wide and unceasing, panting and panting. They watched him, patient, implacable, waiting.

"Come," Basket said at last.

"It's water I want," the Negro said. "I want water."

The well was a little way down the slope toward the quarters. The slope lay dappled with the shadows of noon, of that peaceful hour when, Issetibbeha napping in his chair and waiting for the noon meal and the long afternoon to sleep in, the Negro, the body servant, would be free. He would sit in the kitchen door then, talking with the women that prepared the food. Beyond the kitchen the lane between the quarters would be quiet, peaceful, with the women talking to one another across the lane and the smoke of the dinner fires blowing upon the pickaninnies like ebony toys in the dust.

"Come," Basket said.

The Negro walked among them, taller than any. The guests were moving on toward where Issetibbeha and the horse and the dog waited. The Negro walked with his high ceaseless head, his panting chest. "Come," Basket said. "You wanted water."

"Yes," the Negro said. "Yes," He looked back at the house, then down to the quarters, where today no fire burned, no face showed in any door, no pickaninny in the dust, panting. "It struck me here, raking me across this arm; once, twice, three times. I said, 'Olé, Grandfather.'"

"Come now," Basket said. The Negro was still going through the motion of walking, his knee action high, his head high, as though he were on a treadmill. His eyeballs had a wild, restrained glare, like those of a horse. "You wanted water," Basket said. "Here it is."

There was a gourd in the well. They dipped it full and gave it to the Negro, and they watched him try to drink. His eyes had not ceased rolling as he tilted the gourd slowly against his caked face. They could watch his throat working and the bright water cascading from either side of the gourd, down his chin and breast. Then the water stopped. "Come," Basket said.

"Wait," the Negro said. He dipped the gourd again and tilted it against his face, beneath his ceaseless eyes. Again they watched his throat working and the unswallowed water sheathing broken and myriad down his chin, channeling his caked chest. They waited, patient, grave, decorous, implacable; clansman and guest and kin. Then the water ceased, though still the empty gourd tilted higher and higher, and still his black throat aped the vain motion of his frustrated swallowing. A piece of water-loosened mud carried away from his chest and broke at his muddy feet, and in the empty gourd they could hear his breath: ah-ah-ah.

"Come," Basket said, taking the gourd from the Negro and hanging it back in the well.

Seize the Day

B Y

Saul Bellow

Editor's Note

Saul Bellow was born in 1915 in Lachine, Quebec, and moved to Chicago at the age of nine. He attended the Universities of Chicago, Wisconsin, and Northwestern. He worked at a variety of jobs and on the WPA Writers' Project. Most of his life he has received his livelihood from his writing, from teaching literature (Princeton, Bard, New York University, Minnesota, New School, and Chicago), and from fellowships and awards (Guggenheim, Academy of Arts and Letters, Ford). He is on the Committee on Social Thought. He has published four novels: *Dangling Man* (1944), *The Victim* (1947), *The Adventures of Augie March* (1953), and *Henderson the Rain King* (1959). He has published many essays and stories in magazines and for three years was chief editor of a magazine, *The Noble Savage*. In 1956, "Seize the Day" was published in *The Partisan Review*, and also in a volume entitled *Seize the Day*, along with three short stories and a one-act play. His fiction has received higher critical praise than that of any other American writer of his generation.

Seize the Day

I

WHEN IT CAME TO CONCEALING HIS TROUBLES, TOMMY WILHELM WAS not less capable than the next fellow. So at least he thought, and there was a certain amount of evidence to back him up. He had once been an actor—no, not quite, an extra—and he knew what acting should be. Also, he was smoking a cigar, and when a man is smoking a cigar, wearing a hat, he has an advantage; it is harder to find out how he feels. He came from the twenty-third floor down to the lobby on the mezzanine to collect his mail before breakfast, and he believed—he hoped—that he looked passably well: doing all right. It was a matter of sheer hope, because there was not much that he could add to his present effort. On the fourteenth floor he looked for his father to enter the elevator; they often met at this hour, on the way to breakfast. If he worried about his appearance it was mainly for his old father's sake. But there was no stop on the fourteenth, and the elevator sank and sank. Then the smooth door opened and the great dark red uneven carpet that covered the lobby billowed toward Wilhelm's feet. In the foreground the lobby was dark, sleepy. French drapes like sails kept out the sun, but three high, narrow windows were open, and in the blue air Wilhelm saw a pigeon about to light on the great chain that supported the marquee of the movie house directly underneath the lobby. For one moment he heard the wings beating strongly.

Most of the guests at the Hotel Gloriana were past the age of retirement. Along Broadway in the Seventies, Eighties, and Nineties, a great part of New York's vast population of old men and women lives. Unless the weather is too cold or wet they fill the benches about the tiny railed parks and along the subway gratings from Verdi Square to Columbia University, they crowd the shops and cafeterias, the dime stores, the tea-rooms, the bakeries, the beauty parlors, the reading rooms and club rooms. Among these old people at the Gloriana, Wilhelm felt out of place. He was comparatively young, in his middle forties, large and blond, with big shoulders; his back was heavy and strong, if already a little stooped or thickened. After breakfast the old guests sat down on the green leather armchairs and sofas in the lobby and began to gossip and look into the papers; they had nothing to do but wait out the day. But Wilhelm was used to an active life and liked to go out energetically in the morning. And for several months, because he had no position, he had kept up his morale by rising early; he was shaved and in the lobby by eight o'clock. He bought the paper and some cigars and drank a Coca-Cola or two before he went in to breakfast with his father. After breakfast—out, out, out to attend to business. The getting out had in itself become the chief business. But he had realized that he could not keep this up much longer, and today he was afraid. He was aware that his routine was about to break up and he sensed that a huge trouble long presaged but till now formless was due. Before evening, he'd know.

Nevertheless he followed his daily course and crossed the lobby.

Rubin, the man at the newsstand, had poor eyes. They may not have been actually weak but they were poor in expression, with lacy lids that furled down at the corners. He dressed well. It didn't seem necessary—he was behind the counter most of the time—but he dressed very well. He had on a rich brown suit; the cuffs embarrassed the hairs on his small hands. He wore a Countess Mara painted necktie. As Wilhelm approached, Rubin did not see him; he was looking out dreamily at the Hotel Ansonia, which was visible from his corner, several blocks away. The Ansonia, the neighborhood's great landmark, was built by Stanford White. It looks like a baroque palace from Prague or Munich enlarged a hundred times, with towers, domes, huge swells and bubbles of metal gone green from exposure, iron fretwork and festoons. Black television antennae are densely planted on its round summits. Under the changes of weather it may look like marble or like sea water, black as slate in the fog, white as tufa in sunlight. This morning it looked like the image of itself reflected in deep water, white and cumulous above, with cavernous distortions underneath. Together, the two men gazed at it.

Then Rubin said, "Your dad is in to breakfast already, the old gentleman."

"Oh, yes? Ahead of me today?"

"That's a real knocked-out shirt you got on," said Rubin. "Where's it from, Saks?"

"No, it's a Jack Fagman—Chicago."

Even when his spirits were low, Wilhelm could still wrinkle his forehead in a pleasing way. Some of the slow, silent movements of his face were very attractive. He went back a step, as if to stand away from himself and get a better look at his shirt. His glance was comic, a comment upon his untidiness. He liked to wear good clothes, but once he had put it on each article appeared to go its own way. Wilhelm, laughing, panted a little; his teeth were small; his cheeks when he laughed and puffed grew round, and he looked much younger than his years. In the old days when he was a college freshman and wore a raccoon coat and a beanie on his large blond head his father used to say that, big as he was, he could charm a bird out of a tree. Wilhelm had great charm still.

"I like this dove-gray color," he said in his sociable, good-natured way. "It isn't washable. You have to send it to the cleaner. It never smells as good as washed. But it's a nice shirt. It cost sixteen, eighteen bucks."

This shirt had not been bought by Wilhelm; it was a present from his boss—his former boss, with whom he had had a falling out. But there was no reason why he should tell Rubin the history of it. Although perhaps Rubin knew—Rubin was the kind of man who knew, and knew and knew. Wilhelm also knew many things about Rubin, for that matter, about Rubin's wife and Rubin's business, Rubin's health. None of these could be mentioned, and the great weight of the unspoken left them little to talk about.

"Well, y'lookin' pretty sharp today," Rubin said.

And Wilhelm said gladly, "Am I? Do you really think so?" He could not believe it. He saw his reflection in the glass cupboard full of cigar boxes, among the grand seals and paper damask and the gold-embossed portraits of famous men, García, Edward the Seventh, Cyrus the Great. You had to allow for the darkness and deformations of the glass, but he thought he didn't look too good. A wide wrinkle like a comprehensive bracket sign was written upon his forehead, the point between his brows, and there were patches of brown on his dark blond skin. He began to be half amused at the shadow of his own marveling, troubled, desirous eyes, and his nostrils and his lips. Fair-haired hippopotamus!—that was how he looked to himself. He saw a big round face, a wide, flourishing red mouth, stump teeth. And the hat, too; and the cigar, too. I should have done hard labor all my life, he reflected. Hard honest labor that tires you out and makes you sleep. I'd have worked off my energy and felt better. Instead, I had to distinguish myself—yet.

He had put forth plenty of effort, but that was not the same as working hard, was it? And if as a young man he had got off to a bad start it was due to this very same face. Early in the nineteen-thirties, because of his striking looks, he had been very briefly considered star material, and he had gone to Hollywood. There for seven years, stubbornly, he had tried to become a screen artist. Long before that time his ambition or delusion had ended, but through pride and perhaps also through laziness he had remained in California. At last he turned to other things, but those seven years of persistence and defeat had unfitted him somehow for trades and businesses, and then it was too late to go into one of the professions. He had been slow to mature, and he had lost ground, and so he hadn't been able to get rid of his energy and he was convinced that this energy itself had done him the greatest harm.

"I didn't see you at the gin game last night," said Rubin.

"I had to miss it. How did it go?"

For the last few weeks Wilhelm had played gin almost nightly, but yesterday he had felt that he couldn't afford to lose any more. He had never won. Not once. And while the losses were small they weren't gains, were they? They were losses. He was tired of losing, and tired also of the company, and so he had gone by himself to the movies.

"Oh," said Rubin, "it went okay. Carl made a chump of himself yelling at the guys. This time Doctor Tamkin didn't let him get away with it. He told him the psychological reason why."

"What was the reason?"

Rubin said, "I can't quote him. Who could? You know the way Tamkin talks. Don't ask me. Do you want the *Trib?* Aren't you going to look at the closing quotations?"

"It won't help much to look. I know what they were yesterday at three," said Wilhelm. "But I suppose I better had get the paper." It seemed necessary for him to lift one shoulder in order to put his hand into his jacket pocket. There, among little packets of pills and crushed cigarette butts and strings of cellophane, the red tapes of packages which he sometimes used as dental floss, he recalled that he had dropped some pennies.

"That doesn't sound so good," said Rubin. He meant to be conversationally playful, but his voice had no tone and his eyes, slack and lid-blinded, turned elsewhere. He didn't want to hear. It was all the same to him. Maybe he already knew, being the sort of man who knew and knew.

No, it wasn't good. Wilhelm held three orders of lard in the commodities market. He and Dr. Tamkin had bought this lard together four days ago at 12.96, and the price at once began to fall and was still falling. In the mail this morning there was sure to be a call for additional margin payment. One came every day.

The psychologist, Dr. Tamkin, had got him into this. Tamkin lived at the Gloriana and attended the card game. He had explained to Wilhelm that you could speculate in commodities at one of the uptown branches of a good Wall Street house without making the full deposit of margin legally required. It was up to the branch manager. If he knew you—and all the branch managers knew Tamkin—he would allow you to make short-term purchases. You needed only to open a small account.

"The whole secret of this type of speculation," Tamkin had told him, "is in the alertness. You have to act fast—buy it and sell it; sell it and buy in again. But quick! Get to the window and have them wire Chicago at just the right second. Strike and strike again! Then get out the same day. In no time at all you turn over fifteen, twenty thousand dollars' worth of soy beans, coffee, corn, hides, wheat, cotton." Obviously the doctor understood the market well. Otherwise he could not make it sound so simple. "People lose because they are greedy and can't get out when it starts to go up. They gamble, but I do it scientifically. This is not guesswork. You must take a few points and get out. Why, ye gods!" said Dr. Tamkin with his bulging eyes, his bald head, and his drooping lip. "Have you stopped to think how much dough people are making in the market?"

Wilhelm with a quick shift from gloomy attention to the panting laugh which entirely changed his face had said, "Ho, have I ever! What do you think? Who doesn't know it's way beyond nineteen-twenty-eight—twenty-nine and still on the rise? Who hasn't read the Fulbright investigation? There's money everywhere. Everyone is shoveling it in. Money is—is—"

"And can you rest—can you sit still while this is going on?" said Dr. Tamkin. "I confess to you I can't. I think about people, just because they have a few bucks to invest, making fortunes. They have no sense, they have no talent, they just have the extra dough and it makes them more dough. I get so worked up and tormented and restless, so restless! I haven't even been able to practice my profession. With all this money around you don't want to be a fool while everyone else is making. I know guys who make five, ten thousand a week just by fooling around. I know a guy at the Hotel Pierre. There's nothing to him, but he has a whole case of Mumm's champagne at lunch. I know another guy on Central Park South— But what's the use of talking. They make millions. They have smart lawyers who get them out of taxes by a thousand schemes."

"Whereas I got taken," said Wilhelm. "My wife refused to sign a joint return. One fairly good year and I got into the thirty-two-per-cent bracket and was stripped bare. What of all my bad years?"

"It's a businessmen's government," said Dr. Tamkin. "You can be sure that these men making five thousand a week—"

"I don't need that sort of money," Wilhelm had said. "But oh! if I could only work out a little steady income from this. Not much. I don't ask much. But how badly I need—! I'd be so grateful if you'd show me how to work it."

"Sure I will. *I* do it regularly. I'll bring you my receipts if you like. And do you want to know something? I approve of your attitude very much. You want to avoid catching the money fever. This type of activity is filled with hostile feeling and lust. You should see what it does to some of these fellows. They go on the market with murder in their hearts."

"What's that I once heard a guy say?" Wilhelm remarked. "A man is only as good as what he loves."

"That's it—just it," Tamkin said. "You don't have to go about it their way. There's also a calm and rational, a psychological approach."

Wilhelm's father, old Dr. Adler, lived in an entirely different world from his son, but he had warned him once against Dr. Tamkin. Rather casually—he was a very bland old man—he said, "Wilky, perhaps you listen too much to this Tamkin. He's interesting to talk to. I don't doubt it. I think he's pretty common but he's a persuasive man. However, I don't know how reliable he may be."

It made Wilhelm profoundly bitter that his father should speak to him with such detachment about his welfare. Dr. Adler liked to appear affable. Affable! His own son, his one and only son, could not speak his mind or ease his heart to him. I wouldn't turn to Tamkin, he thought, if I could turn to him. At least Tamkin sympathizes with me and tries to give me a hand, whereas Dad doesn't want to be disturbed.

Old Dr. Adler had retired from practice; he had a considerable fortune and could easily have helped his son. Recently Wilhelm had told him, "Father—it so happens that I'm in a bad way now. I hate to have to say it. You realize that I'd rather have good news to bring you. But it's true. And since it's true, Dad— What else am I supposed to say? It's true."

Another father might have appreciated how difficult this confession was— so much bad luck, weariness, weakness, and failure. Wilhelm had tried to copy the old man's tone and made himself sound gentlemanly, low-voiced, tasteful. He didn't allow his voice to tremble; he made no stupid gesture. But the doctor had no answer. He only nodded. You might have told him that Seattle was near Puget Sound, or that the Giants and Dodgers were playing a night game, so little was he moved from his expression of healthy, handsome, good-humored old age. He behaved toward his son as he had formerly done toward his patients, and it was a great grief to Wilhelm; it was almost too much to bear. Couldn't he see—couldn't he feel? Had he lost his family sense?

Greatly hurt, Wilhelm struggled however to be fair. Old people are bound to change, he said. They have hard things to think about. They must prepare for where they are going. They can't live by the old schedule any longer and all their perspectives change, and other people become alike, kin and acquaintances. Dad is no longer the same person, Wilhelm reflected. He was thirty-two when I was born, and now he's going on eighty. Further-more, it's time I stopped feeling like a kid toward him, a small son.

The handsome old doctor stood well above the other old people in the hotel. He was idolized by everyone. This was what people said: "That's old Professor Adler, who used to teach internal medicine. He was a diagnos-tician, one of the best in New York, and had a tremendous practice. Isn't he a wonderful-looking old guy? It's a pleasure to see such a fine old sci-entist, clean and immaculate. He stands straight and understands every single thing you say. He still has all his buttons. You can discuss any subject with him." The clerks, the elevator operators, the telephone girls and waitresses and chambermaids, the management flattered and pampered him. That was what he wanted. He had always been a vain man. To see how his father loved himself sometimes made Wilhelm madly indignant.

He folded over the *Tribune* with its heavy, black, crashing sensational print and read without recognizing any of the words, for his mind was still on his father's vanity. The doctor had created his own praise. People were primed and did not know it. And what did he need praise for? In a hotel where everyone was busy and contacts were so brief and had such small weight, how could it satisfy him? He could be in people's thoughts here and there for a moment; in and then out. He could never matter much to them. Wilhelm let out a long, hard breath and raised the brows of his round and somewhat circular eyes. He stared beyond the thick borders of the paper.

. . . love that well which thou must leave ere long.

Involuntary memory brought him this line. At first he thought it referred to his father, but then he understood that it was for himself, rather. *He* should love that well. "This thou perceivest, which makes *thy* love more strong." Under Dr. Tamkin's influence Wilhelm had recently begun to remember the poems he used to read. Dr. Tamkin knew, or said he knew, the great English poets and once in a while he mentioned a poem of his own. It was a long time since anyone had spoken to Wilhelm about this sort of thing. He didn't like to think about his college days, but if there was one course that now made sense it was Literature I. The textbook was Lieder and Lovett's *British Poetry and Prose,* a black heavy book with thin pages. Did I read that? he asked himself. Yes, he had read it and there was one accomplishment at least he could recall with pleasure. He had read "Yet once more, O ye laurels." How pure this was to say! It was beautiful.

> Sunk though he be beneath the wat'ry floor . . .

Such things had always swayed him, and now the power of such words was far, far greater.

Wilhelm respected the truth, but he could lie and one of the things he lied often about was his education. He said he was an alumnus of Penn State; in fact he had left school before his sophomore year was finished. His sister Catherine had a B.S. degree. Wilhelm's late mother was a graduate of Bryn Mawr. He was the only member of the family who had no education. This was another sore point. His father was ashamed of him.

But he had heard the old man bragging to another old man, saying, "My son is a sales executive. He didn't have the patience to finish school. But he does all right for himself. His income is up in the five figures somewhere."

"What—thirty, forty thousand?" said his stooped old friend.

"Well, he needs at least that much for his style of life. Yes, he needs that."

Despite his troubles, Wilhelm almost laughed. Why, that boasting old hypocrite. He knew the sales executive was no more. For many weeks there had been no executive, no sales, no income. But how we love looking fine in the eyes of the world—how beautiful are the old when they are doing a snow job! It's Dad, thought Wilhelm, who is the salesman. He's selling me. *He* should have gone on the road.

But what of the truth? Ah, the truth was that there were problems, and of these problems his father wanted no part. His father was ashamed of him. The truth, Wilhelm thought, was very awkward. He pressed his lips together, and his tongue went soft; it pained him far at the back, in the cords and throat, and a knot of ill formed in his chest. Dad never was a pal to me when I was young, he reflected. He was at the office or the hospital, or lecturing. He expected me to look out for myself and never gave me much thought. Now he looks down on me. And maybe in some respects he's right.

No wonder Wilhelm delayed the moment when he would have to go into the dining room. He had moved to the end of Rubin's counter. He had opened the *Tribune;* the fresh pages drooped from his hands; the cigar was smoked out and the hat did not defend him. He was wrong to suppose that he was more capable than the next fellow when it came to concealing his troubles. They were clearly written out upon his face. He wasn't even aware of it.

There was the matter of the different names, which, in the hotel, came up frequently. "Are you Doctor Adler's son?" "Yes, but my name is Tommy Wilhelm." And the doctor would say, "My son and I use different monikers. I uphold tradition. He's for the new." The Tommy was Wilhelm's own invention. He adopted it when he went to Hollywood, and dropped the Adler. Hollywood was his own idea, too. He used to pretend that it had all been the doing of a certain talent scout named Maurice Venice. But the scout had never made him a definite offer of a studio connection. He had approached him, but the results of the screen tests had not been good. After the test Wilhelm took the initiative and pressed Maurice Venice until he got him to say, "Well, I suppose you might make it out there." On the strength of this Wilhelm had left college and had gone to California.

Someone had said, and Wilhelm agreed with the saying, that in Los Angeles all the loose objects in the country were collected, as if America had been tilted and everything that wasn't tightly screwed down had slid into Southern California. He himself had been one of these loose objects. Sometimes he told people, "I was too mature for college. I was a big boy, you see. Well, I thought, when do you start to become a man?" After he had driven a painted flivver and had worn a yellow slicker with slogans on it, and played illegal poker, and gone out on Coke dates, he had *had* college. He wanted to try something new and quarreled with his parents about his career. And then a letter came from Maurice Venice.

The story of the scout was long and intricate and there were several versions of it. The truth about it was never told. Wilhelm had lied first boastfully and then out of charity to himself. But his memory was good, he could still separate what he had invented from the actual happenings, and this morning he found it necessary as he stood by Rubin's showcase with his *Tribune* to recall the crazy course of the true events.

I didn't seem even to realize that there was a depression. How could I have been such a jerk as not to prepare for anything and just go on luck and inspiration? With round gray eyes expanded and his large shapely lips closed in severity toward himself he forced open all that had been hidden. Dad I couldn't affect one way or another. Mama was the one who tried to stop me, and we carried on and yelled and pleaded. The more I lied the louder I raised my voice, and charged—like a hippopotamus. Poor Mother! How I disappointed her. Rubin heard Wilhelm give a broken sigh as he stood with the forgotten *Tribune* crushed under his arm.

When Wilhelm was aware that Rubin watched him, loitering and idle, apparently not knowing what to do with himself this morning, he turned to the Coca-Cola machine. He swallowed hard at the Coke bottle and coughed over it, but he ignored his coughing, for he was still thinking, his eyes upcast and his lips closed behind his hand. By a peculiar twist of habit he wore his coat collar turned up always, as though there were a wind. It never lay flat. But on his broad back, stooped with its own weight, its strength warped almost into deformity, the collar of his sports coat appeared anyway to be no wider than a ribbon.

He was listening to the sound of his own voice as he explained, twenty-five years ago in the living room on West End Avenue, "But Mother, if I don't pan out as an actor I can still go back to school."

But she was afraid he was going to destroy himself. She said, "Wilky, Dad could make it easy for you if you wanted to go into medicine." To remember this stifled him.

"I can't bear hospitals. Besides, I might make a mistake and hurt someone or even kill a patient. I couldn't stand that. Besides, I haven't got that sort of brains."

Then his mother had made the mistake of mentioning her nephew Artie, Wilhelm's cousin, who was an honor student at Columbia in math and languages. That dark little gloomy Artie with his disgusting narrow face, and his moles and self-sniffing ways and his unclean table manners, the boring habit he had of conjugating verbs when you went for a walk with him. "Roumanian is an easy language. You just add a *tl* to everything." He was now a professor, this same Artie with whom Wilhelm had played near the soldiers' and sailors' monument on Riverside Drive. Not that to be a professor was in itself so great. How could anyone bear to know so many languages? And Artie also had to remain Artie, which was a bad deal. But perhaps success had changed him. Now that he had a place in the world perhaps he was better. Did Artie love his languages, and live for them, or was he also, in his heart, cynical? So many people nowadays were. No one seemed satisfied, and Wilhelm was especially horrified by the cynicism of successful people. Cynicism was bread and meat to everyone. And irony, too. Maybe it couldn't be helped. It was probably even necessary. Wilhelm, however, feared it intensely. Whenever at the end of the day he was unusually fatigued he attributed it to cynicism. Too much of the world's business done. Too much falsity. He had various words to express the effect this had on him. Chicken! Unclean! Congestion! he exclaimed in his heart. Rat race! Phony! Murder! Play the Game! Buggers!

At first the letter from the talent scout was nothing but a flattering sort of joke. Wilhelm's picture in the college paper when he was running for class treasurer was seen by Maurice Venice, who wrote to him about a screen test. Wilhelm at once took the train to New York. He found the scout to be huge and oxlike, so stout that his arms seemed caught from beneath in a grip of flesh and fat; it looked as though it must be positively painful. He had little hair. Yet he enjoyed a healthy complexion. His breath was noisy and his voice rather difficult and husky because of the fat in his throat. He had on a double-breasted suit of the type then known as the pillbox; it was chalk-striped, pink on blue; the trousers hugged his ankles.

They met and shook hands and sat down. Together these two big men dwarfed the tiny Broadway office and made the furnishings look like toys. Wilhelm had the color of a Golden Grimes apple when he was well, and then his thick blond hair had been vigorous and his wide shoulders unwarped; he was leaner in the jaws, his eyes fresher and wider; his legs were then still awkward but he was impressively handsome. And he was about to make his first great mistake. Like, he sometimes thought, I was going to pick up a weapon and strike myself a blow with it.

Looming over the desk in the small office darkened by overbuilt midtown —sheer walls, gray spaces, dry lagoons of tar and pebbles—Maurice Venice proceeded to establish his credentials. He said, "My letter was on the regular stationery, but maybe you want to check on me?"

"Who, *me?*" said Wilhelm. "Why?"

"There's guys who think I'm in a racket and make a charge for the test. I don't ask a cent. I'm no agent. There ain't no commission."

"I never even thought of it," said Wilhelm. Was there perhaps something fishy about this Maurice Venice? He protested too much.

In his husky, fat-weakened voice he finally challenged Wilhelm, "If you're not sure, you can call the the distributor and find out who I am, Maurice Venice."

Wilhelm wondered at him. "Why shouldn't I be sure? Of course I am."

"Because I can see the way you size me up, and because this is a dinky office. Like you don't believe me. Go ahead. Call. I won't care if you're cautious. I mean it. There's quite a few people who doubt me at first. They can't really believe that fame and fortune are going to hit 'em."

"But I tell you I do believe you," Wilhelm had said, and bent inward to accommodate the pressure of his warm, panting laugh. It was purely nervous. His neck was ruddy and neatly shaved about the ears—he was fresh from the barbershop; his face anxiously glowed with his desire to make a pleasing impression. It was all wasted on Venice, who was just as concerned about the impression *he* was making.

"If you're surprised, I'll just show you what I mean," Venice had said. "It was about fifteen months ago right in this identical same office when I saw a beautiful thing in the paper. It wasn't even a photo but a drawing, a brassière ad, but I knew right away that this was star material. I called up the paper to ask who the girl was, they gave me the name of the advertising agency; I phoned the agency and they gave me the name of the artist; I got hold of the artist and he gave me the number of the model agency. Finally, finally I got her number and phoned her and said, 'This is Maurice Venice, scout for Kaskaskia Films.' So right away she says, 'Yah, so's your old lady.' Well, when I saw I wasn't getting nowhere with her I said to her, 'Well, miss. I don't blame you. You're a very beautiful thing and must have a dozen admirers after you all the time, boy friends who like to call and pull your leg and give a tease. But as I happen to be a very busy fellow and don't have the time to horse around or argue, I tell you what to do. Here's my number, and here's the number of the Kaskaskia Distributors, Inc. Ask them who am I, Maurice Venice. The scout.' She did it. A little while later she phoned me back, all apologies and excuses, but I didn't want to embarrass her and get off on the wrong foot with an artist. I know better than to do that. So I told her it was a natural precaution, never mind. I wanted to run a screen test right away. Because I seldom am wrong about talent. If I see it, it's there. Get that, please. And do you know who that little girl is today?"

"No," Wilhelm said eagerly. "Who is she?"

Venice said impressively, " 'Nita Christenberry."

Wilhelm sat utterly blank. This was failure. He didn't know the name, and Venice was waiting for his response and would be angry.

And in fact Venice had been offended. He said, "What's the matter with you! Don't you read a magazine? She's a starlet."

"I'm sorry," Wilhelm answered. "I'm at school and don't have time to keep up. If I don't know her, it doesn't mean a thing. She made a big hit, I'll bet."

"You can say that again. Here's a photo of her." He handed Wilhelm some pictures. She was a bathing beauty—short, the usual breasts, hips, and smooth thighs. Yes, quite good, as Wilhelm recalled. She stood on high heels and wore a Spanish comb and mantilla. In her hand was a fan.

He had said, "She looks awfully peppy."

"Isn't she a divine girl? And what personality! Not just another broad in the show business, believe me." He had a surprise for Wilhelm. "I have found happiness with her," he said.

"You have?" said Wilhelm, slow to understand.

"Yes, boy, we're engaged."

Wilhelm saw another photograph, taken on the beach. Venice was dressed in a terry-cloth beach outfit, and he and the girl, cheek to cheek, were looking into the camera. Below, in white ink, was written "Love at Malibu Colony."

"I'm sure you'll be very happy. I wish you—"

"I *know*," said Venice firmly, "I'm going to be happy. When I saw that drawing, the breath of fate breathed on me. I felt it over my entire body."

"Say, it strikes a bell suddenly," Wilhelm had said. "Aren't you related to Martial Venice the producer?"

Venice was either a nephew of the producer or the son of a first cousin. Decidedly he had not made good. It was easy enough for Wilhelm to see this now. The office was so poor, and Venice bragged so nervously and identified himself so scrupulously—the poor guy. He was the obscure failure of an aggressive and powerful clan. As such he had the greatest sympathy from Wilhelm.

Venice had said, "Now I suppose you want to know where you come in. I seen your school paper, by accident. You take quite a remarkable picture."

"It can't be so much," said Wilhelm, more panting than laughing.

"You don't want to tell me my business," Venice said. "Leave it to me. I studied up on this."

"I never imagined—Well, what kind of roles do you think I'd fit?"

"All this time that we've been talking, I've been watching. Don't think I haven't. You remind me of someone. Let's see who it can be—one of the great old-timers. Is it Milton Sills? No, that's not the one. Conway Tearle, Jack Mulhall? George Bancroft? No, his face was ruggeder. One thing I can tell you, though, a George Raft type you're not—those tough, smooth, black little characters."

"No, I wouldn't seem to be."

"No, you're not that flyweight type, with the fists, from a nightclub, and the glamorous sideburns, doing the tango or the bolero. Not Edward G. Robinson, either—I'm thinking aloud. Or the Cagney fly-in-your-face role, a cabbie, with that mouth and those punches."

"I realize that."

"Not suave like William Powell, or a lyric juvenile like Buddy Rogers. I suppose you don't play the sax? No. But—"

"But what?"

"I have you placed as the type that loses the girl to the George Raft type or the William Powell type. You are steady, faithful, you get stood up. The older women would know better. The mothers are on your side. With what they been through, if it was up to them, they'd take you in a minute. You're very sympathetic, even the young girls feel that. You'd make a good provider. But they go more for the other types. It's as clear as anything."

This was not how Wilhelm saw himself. And as he surveyed the old ground he recognized now that he had been not only confused but hurt. Why, he thought, he cast me even then for a loser.

Wilhelm had said, with half a mind to be defiant, "Is that your opinion?"

It never occurred to Venice that a man might object to stardom in such a role. "Here is your chance," he said. "Now you're just in college. What are you studying?" He snapped his fingers. "Stuff." Wilhelm himself felt this way about it. "You may plug along fifty years before you get anywheres. This way, in one jump, the world knows who you are. You become a name like Roosevelt, Swanson. From east to west, out to China, into South America. This is no bunk. You become a lover to the whole world. The world wants it, needs it. One fellow smiles, a billion people also smile. One fellow cries, the other billion sob with him. Listen, bud—" Venice had pulled himself together to make an effort. On his imagination there was some great weight which he could not discharge. He wanted Wilhelm, too, to feel it. He twisted his large, clean, well-meaning, rather foolish features as though he were their unwilling captive, and said in his choked, fate-obstructed voice, "Listen, everywhere there are people trying hard, miserable, in trouble, downcast, tired, trying and trying. They need a break, right? A break through, a help, luck or sympathy."

"That certainly is the truth," said Wilhelm. He had seized the feeling and he waited for Venice to go on. But Venice had no more to say; he had concluded. He gave Wilhelm several pages of blue hectographed script, stapled together, and told him to prepare for the screen test. "Study your lines in front of a mirror," he said. "Let yourself go. The part should take ahold of you. Don't be afraid to make faces and be emotional. Shoot the works. Because when you start to act you're no more an ordinary person, and those things don't apply to you. You don't behave the same way as the average."

And so Wilhelm had never returned to Penn State. His roommate sent his things to New York for him, and the school authorities had to write to Dr. Adler to find out what had happened.

Still, for three months Wilhelm delayed his trip to California. He wanted to start out with the blessings of his family, but they were never given. He quarreled with his parents and his sister. And then, when he was best aware of the risks and knew a hundred reasons against going and had made himself sick with fear, he left home. This was typical of Wilhelm. After much thought and hesitation and debate he invariably took the course he had rejected innumerable times. Ten such decisions made up the history of his life. He had decided that it would be a bad mistake to go to Hollywood, and then he went. He had made up his mind not to marry his wife, but ran off and got married. He had resolved not to invest money with Tamkin, and then had given him a check.

But Wilhelm had been eager for life to start. College was merely another delay. Venice had approached him and said that the world had named Wilhelm to shine before it. He was to be freed from the anxious and narrow life of the average. Moreover, Venice had claimed that he never made a mistake. His instinct for talent was infallible, he said.

But when Venice saw the results of the screen test he did a quick about-face. In those days Wilhelm had had a speech difficulty. It was not a true stammer, it was a thickness of speech which the sound track exaggerated. The film showed that he had many peculiarities, otherwise unnoticeable. When he shrugged, his hands drew up within his sleeves. The vault of his chest was huge, but he really didn't look strong under the lights. Though he called himself a hippopotamus, he more nearly resembled a bear. His walk was bearlike, quick and rather soft, toes turned inward, as though his shoes were an impediment. About one thing Venice had been right. Wilhelm was photogenic, and his wavy blond hair (now graying) came out well, but after the test Venice refused to encourage him. He tried to get rid of him. He couldn't afford to take a chance on him, he had made too many mistakes already and lived in fear of his powerful relatives.

Wilhelm had told his parents, "Venice says I owe it to myself to go." How ashamed he was now of this lie! He had begged Venice not to give him up. He had said, "Can't you help me out? It would kill me to go back to school now."

Then when he reached the Coast he learned that a recommendation from Maurice Venice was the kiss of death. Venice needed help and charity more than he, Wilhelm, ever had. A few years later when Wilhelm was down on his luck and working as an orderly in a Los Angeles hospital, he saw Venice's picture in the papers. He was under indictment for pandering. Closely following the trial, Wilhelm found out that Venice had indeed been employed by Kaskaskia Films but that he had evidently made use of the connection to organize a ring of call girls. Then what did he want with me? Wilhelm had cried to himself. He was unwilling to believe anything very bad about Venice. Perhaps he was foolish and unlucky, a fall guy, a dupe, a sucker. You didn't give a man fifteen years in prison for that. Wilhelm often thought that he might write him a letter to say how sorry he was. He remembered the breath of fate and Venice's certainty that he would be happy. 'Nita Christenberry was sentenced to three years. Wilhelm recognized her although she had changed her name.

By that time Wihelm too had taken his new name. In California he became Tommy Wilhelm. Dr. Adler would not accept the change. Today he still called his son Wilky, as he had done for more than forty years. Well, now, Wilhelm was thinking, the paper crowded in disarray under his arm, there's really very little that a man can change at will. He can't change his lungs, or nerves, or constitution or temperament. They're not under his control. When he's young and strong and impulsive and dissatisfied with the way things are he wants to rearrange them to assert his freedom. He can't overthrow the government or be differently born; he only has a little scope and maybe a foreboding, too, that essentially you can't change. Nevertheless, he makes a gesture and becomes Tommy Wilhelm. Wilhelm had always had a great longing to be Tommy. He had never, however, succeeded in feeling like Tommy, and in his soul had always remained Wilky. When he was drunk he reproached himself horribly as Wilky. "You fool, you clunk, you Wilky!" he called himself. He thought that it was a good thing perhaps that he had not become a success as Tommy since that would not have been a genuine success. Wilhelm would have feared that not he but Tommy had brought it off, cheating Wilky of his birthright. Yes, it had been a stupid thing to do, but it was his imperfect judgment at the age of twenty which should be blamed. He had cast off his father's name, and with it his father's opinion of him. It was, he knew it was, his bid for liberty. Adler being in his mind the title of the species, Tommy the freedom of the person. But Wilky was his inescapable self.

In middle age you no longer thought such thoughts about free choice. Then it came over you that from one grandfather you had inherited such and such a head of hair which looked like honey when it whitens or sugars in the jar; from another, broad thick shoulders; an oddity of speech from one uncle, and small teeth from another, and the gray eyes with darkness diffused even into the whites, and a wide-lipped mouth like a statue from Peru. Wandering races have such looks, the bones of one tribe, the skin of another. From his mother he had gotten sensitive feelings, a soft heart, a brooding nature, a tendency to be confused under pressure.

The changed name was a mistake, and he would admit it as freely as you liked. But this mistake couldn't be undone now, so why must his father continually remind him how he had sinned? It was too late. He would have to go back to the pathetic day when the sin was committed. And where was that day? Past and dead. Whose humiliating memories were these? His and not his father's. What had he to think back on that he could call good? Very, very little. You had to forgive. First, to forgive yourself, and then general forgiveness. Didn't he suffer from his mistakes far more than his father could?

"Oh, God," Wilhelm prayed. "Let me out of my trouble. Let me out of my thoughts, and let me do something better with myself. For all the time I have wasted I am very sorry. Let me out of this clutch and into a different life. For I am all balled up. Have mercy."

II

The mail.

The clerk who gave it to him did not care what sort of appearance he made this morning. He only glanced at him from under his brows, upward, as the letters changed hands. Why should the hotel people waste courtesies on him? They had his number. The clerk knew that he was handing him, along with the letters, a bill for his rent. Wihelm assumed a look that removed him from all such things. But it was bad. To pay the bill he would have to withdraw money from his brokerage account, and the account was being watched because of the drop in lard. According to the *Tribune's* figures lard was still twenty points below last year's level. There were government price supports. Wilhelm didn't know how these worked but he understood that the farmer was protected and that the SEC kept an eye on the market and therefore he believed that lard would rise again and he wasn't greatly worried as yet. But in the meantime his father might have offered to pick up his hotel tab. Why didn't he? What a selfish old man he was! He saw his son's hardships; he could so easily help him. How little it would mean to him, and how much to Wilhelm! Where was the old man's heart? Maybe, thought Wilhelm, I was sentimental in the past and exaggerated his kindliness—warm family life. It may never have been there.

Not long ago his father had said to him in his usual affable, pleasant way, "Well, Wilky, here we are under the same roof again, after all these years."

Wilhelm was glad for an instant. At last they would talk over old times. But he was also on guard against insinuations. Wasn't his father saying, "Why are you here in a hotel with me and not at home in Brooklyn with your wife and two boys? You're neither a widower nor a bachelor. You have brought me all your confusions. What do you expect me to do with them?"

So Wilhelm studied the remark for a bit, then said, "The roof is twenty-six stories up. But how many years has it been?"

"That's what I was asking you."

"Gosh, Dad, I'm not sure. Wasn't it the year Mother died? What year was that?"

He asked this question with an innocent frown on his Golden Grimes, dark blond face. *What year was it!* As though he didn't know the year, the month, the day, the very hour of his mother's death.

"Wasn't it nineteen-thirty-one?" said Dr. Adler.

"Oh, was it?" said Wilhelm. And in hiding the sadness and the overwhelming irony of the question he gave a nervous shiver and wagged his head and felt the ends of his collar rapidly.

"Do you know?" his father said. "You must realize, an old fellow's memory becomes unreliable. It was in winter, that I'm sure of. Nineteen-thirty-two?"

Yes, it was age. Don't make an issue of it, Wilhelm advised himself. If you were to ask the old doctor in what year he had interned, he'd tell you correctly. All the same, don't make an issue. Don't quarrel with your own father. Have pity on an old man's failings.

"I believe the year was closer to nineteen-thirty-four, Dad," he said.

But Dr. Adler was thinking. Why the devil can't he stand still when we're talking? He's either hoisting his pants up and down by the pockets or jittering with his feet. A regular mountain of tics, he's getting to be. Wilhelm had a habit of moving his feet back and forth as though, hurrying into a house, he had to clean his shoes first on the doormat.

Then Wilhelm had said, "Yes, that was the beginning of the end, wasn't it, Father?"

Wilhelm often astonished Dr. Adler. Beginning of the end? What could he mean—what was he fishing for? Whose end? The end of family life? The old man was puzzled but he would not give Wilhelm an opening to introduce his complaints. He had learned that it was better not to take up Wilhelm's strange challenges. So he merely agreed pleasantly, for he was a master of social behavior, and said, "It was an awful misfortune for us all."

He thought, What business has he to complain to *me* of his mother's death?

Face to face they had stood, each declaring himself silently after his own way. It was: it was not, the beginning of the end—*some* end.

Unaware of anything odd in his doing it, for he did it all the time, Wilhelm had pinched out the coal of his cigarette and dropped the butt in his pocket, where there were many more. And as he gazed at his father the little finger of his right hand began to twitch and tremble; of that he was unconscious, too.

And yet Wilhelm believed that when he put his mind to it he could have perfect and even distinguished manners, outdoing his father. Despite the slight thickness in his speech—it amounted almost to a stammer when he started the same phrase over several times in his effort to eliminate the thick sound—he could be fluent. Otherwise he would never have made a good salesman. He claimed also that he was a good listener. When he listened he made a tight mouth and rolled his eyes thoughtfully. He would soon tire and begin to utter short, loud, impatient breaths, and he would say, "Oh yes . . . yes . . . yes. I couldn't agree more." When he was forced to differ he would declare, "Well, I'm not sure. I don't really see it that way. I'm of two minds about it." He would never willingly hurt any man's feelings.

But in conversation with his father he was apt to lose control of himself. After any talk with Dr. Adler, Wilhelm generally felt dissatisfied, and his dissatisfaction reached its greatest intensity when they discussed family matters. Ostensibly he had been trying to help the old man to remember a date, but in reality he meant to tell him, "You were set free when Ma died. You wanted to forget her. You'd like to get rid of Catherine, too. Me, too. You're not kidding anyone"—Wilhelm striving to put this across, and the old man not having it. In the end he was left struggling, while his father seemed unmoved.

And then once more Wilhelm had said to himself, "But man! you're not a kid. Even then you weren't a kid!" He looked down over the front of his big, indecently big, spoiled body. He was beginning to lose his shape, his gut was fat, and he looked like a hippopotamus. His younger son called him "a hummuspotamus"; that was little Paul. And here he was still struggling with his old dad, filled with ancient grievances. Instead of saying, "Good-by, youth! Oh, good-by those marvelous, foolish wasted days. What a big clunk I was—I *am*."

Wilhelm was still paying heavily for his mistakes. His wife Margaret would not give him a divorce, and he had to support her and the two children. She would regularly agree to divorce him, and then think things over again and set new and more difficult conditions. No court would have awarded her the amounts he paid. One of today's letters, as he had expected, was from her. For the first time he had sent her a postdated check, and she protested. She also enclosed bills for the boys' educational insurance policies, due next week. Wilhelm's mother-in-law had taken out these policies in Beverly Hills, and since her death two years ago he had to pay the premiums. Why couldn't she have minded her own business! They were his kids, and he took care of them and always would. He had planned to set up a trust fund. But that was on his former expectations. Now he had to rethink the future, because of the money problem. Meanwhile, here were the bills to be paid. When he saw the two sums punched out so neatly on the cards he cursed the company and its IBM equipment. His heart and his head were congested with anger. Everyone was supposed to have money. It was nothing to the company. It published pictures of funerals in the magazines and frightened the suckers, and then punched out little holes, and the customers would lie awake to think out ways to raise the dough. They'd be ashamed not to have it. They couldn't let a great company down, either, and they got the scratch. In the old days a man was put in prison for debt, but there were subtler things now. They made it a shame not to have money and set everybody to work.

Well, and what else had Margaret sent him? He tore the envelope open with his thumb, swearing that he would send any other bills back to her. There was, luckily, nothing more. He put the hole-punched cards in his pocket. Didn't Margaret know that he was nearly at the end of his rope? Of course. Her instinct told her that this was her opportunity, and she was giving him the works.

He went into the dining room, which was under Austro-Hungarian management at the Hotel Gloriana. It was run like a European establishment. The pastries were excellent, especially the strudel. He often had apple strudel and coffee in the afternoon.

As soon as he entered he saw his father's small head in the sunny bay at the farther end, and heard his precise voice. It was with an odd sort of perilous expression that Wilhelm crossed the dining room.

Dr. Adler liked to sit in a corner that looked across Broadway down to the Hudson and New Jersey. On the other side of the street was a super-modern cafeteria with gold and purple mosaic columns. On the second floor a private-eye school, a dental laboratory, a reducing parlor, a veteran's club, and a Hebrew school shared the space. The old man was sprinkling sugar on his strawberries. Small hoops of brilliance were cast by the water glasses on the white tablecloth, despite a faint murkiness in the sunshine. It was early summer, and the long window was turned inward; a moth was on the pane; the putty was broken and the white enamel on the frames was streaming with wrinkles.

"Ha, Wilky," said the old man to his tardy son. "You haven't met our neighbor Mr. Perls, have you? From the fifteenth floor."

"How d'do," Wilhelm said. He did not welcome this stranger; he began at once to find fault with him. Mr. Perls carried a heavy cane with a crutch tip. Dyed hair, a skinny forehead—these were not reasons for bias. Nor was it Mr. Perls's fault that Dr. Adler was using him, not wishing to have breakfast with his son alone. But a gruffer voice within Wilhelm spoke, asking, "Who is this damn frazzle-faced herring with his dyed hair and his fish teeth and this drippy mustache? Another one of Dad's German friends. Where does he collect all these guys? What is the stuff on his teeth? I never saw such pointed crowns. Are they stainless steel, or a kind of silver? How can a human face get into this condition. Uch!" Staring with his widely spaced gray eyes, Wilhelm sat, his broad back stooped under the sports jacket. He clasped his hands on the table with an implication of suppliance. Then he began to relent a little toward Mr. Perls, beginning at the teeth. Each of those crowns represented a tooth ground to the quick, and estimating a man's grief with his teeth as two per cent of the total, and adding to that his flight from Germany and the probable origin of his wincing wrinkles, not to be confused with the wrinkles of his smile, it came to a sizable load.

"Mr. Perls was a hosiery wholesaler," said Dr. Adler.

"Is this the son you told me was in the selling line?" said Mr. Perls.

Dr. Adler replied, "I have only this one son. One daughter. She was a medical technician before she got married—anesthetist. At one time she had an important position in Mount Sinai."

He couldn't mention his children without boasting. In Wilhelm's opinion, there was little to boast of. Catherine, like Wilhelm, was big and fair-haired. She had married a court reporter who had a pretty hard time of it. She had taken a professional name, too—Philippa. At forty she was still ambitious to become a painter. Wilhelm didn't venture to criticize her work. It didn't do much to him, he said, but then he was no critic. Anyway, he and his sister were generally on the outs and he didn't often see her paintings. She worked very hard, but there were fifty thousand people in New York with paints and brushes, each practically a law unto himself. It was the Tower of Babel in paint. *He* didn't want to go far into this. Things were chaotic all over.

Dr. Adler thought that Wilhelm looked particularly untidy this morning —unrested, too, his eyes red-rimmed from excessive smoking. He was breathing through his mouth and he was evidently much distracted and rolled his red-shot eyes barbarously. As usual, his coat collar was turned up as though he had had to go out in the rain. When he went to business he pulled himself together a little; otherwise he let himself go and looked like hell.

"What's the matter, Wilky, didn't you sleep last night?"

"Not very much."

"You take too many pills of every kind—first stimulants and then depressants, anodynes followed by analeptics, until the poor organism doesn't know what's happened. Then the luminal won't put people to sleep, and the Pervitin or Benzedrine won't wake them. God knows! These things get to be as serious as poisons, and yet everyone puts all their faith in them."

"No, Dad, it's not the pills. It's that I'm not used to New York any more. For a native, that's very peculiar, isn't it? It was never so noisy at night as now, and every little thing is a strain. Like the alternate parking. You have to run out at eight to move your car. And where can you put it? If you forget for a minute they tow you away. Then some fool puts advertising leaflets under your windshield wiper and you have heart failure a block away because you think you've got a ticket. When you do get stung with a ticket, you can't argue. You haven't got a chance in court and the city wants the revenue."

"But in your line you have to have a car, eh?" said Mr. Perls.

"Lord knows why any lunatic would want one in the city who didn't need it for his livelihood."

Wilhelm's old Pontiac was parked in the street. Formerly, when on an expense account, he had always put it up in a garage. Now he was afraid to move the car from Riverside Drive lest he lose his space, and he used it only on Saturdays when the Dodgers were playing in Ebbets Field and he took his boys to the game. Last Saturday, when the Dodgers were out of town, he had gone out to visit his mother's grave.

Dr. Adler had refused to go along. He couldn't bear his son's driving. Forgetfully, Wilhelm traveled for miles in second gear; he was seldom in the right lane and he neither gave signals nor watched for lights. The upholstery of his Pontiac was filthy with grease and ashes. One cigarette burned in the ashtray, another in his hand, a third on the floor with maps and other waste paper and Coca-Cola bottles. He dreamed at the wheel or argued and gestured, and therefore the old doctor would not ride with him.

Then Wilhelm had come back from the cemetery angry because the stone bench between his mother's and his grandmother's graves had been over-turned and broken by vandals. "Those damn teen-age hoodlums get worse and worse," he said. "Why, they must have used a sledge-hammer to break the seat smack in half like that. If I could catch one of them!" He wanted the doctor to pay for a new seat, but his father was cool to the idea. He said he was going to have himself cremated.

Mr. Perls said, "I don't blame you if you get no sleep up where you are." His voice was tuned somewhat sharp, as though he were slightly deaf. "Don't you have Parigi the singing teacher there? God, they have some queer elements in this hotel. On which floor is that Estonian woman with all her cats and dogs? They should have made her leave long ago."

"They've moved her down to twelve," said Dr. Adler.

Wilhelm ordered a large Coca-Cola with his breakfast. Working in secret at the small envelopes in his pocket, he found two pills by touch. Much fingering had worn and weakened the paper. Under cover of a napkin he swallowed a Phenaphen sedative and a Unicap, but the doctor was sharp-eyed and said, "Wilky, what are you taking now?"

"Just my vitamin pills." He put his cigar butt in an ashtray on the table behind him, for his father did not like the odor. Then he drank his Coca-Cola.

"That's what you drink for breakfast, and not orange juice?" said Mr. Perls. He seemed to sense that he would not lose Dr. Adler's favor by taking an ironic tone with his son.

"The caffeine stimulates brain activity," said the old doctor. "It does all kinds of things to the respiratory center."

"It's just a habit of the road, that's all," Wilhelm said. "If you drive around long enough it turns your brains, your stomach, and everything else."

His father explained, "Wilky used to be with the Rojax Corporation. He was their northeastern sales representative for a good many years but recently ended the connection."

"Yes," said Wilhelm, "I was with them from the end of the war." He sipped the Coca-Cola and chewed the ice, glancing at one and the other with his attitude of large, shaky, patient dignity. The waitress set two boiled eggs before him.

"What kind of line does this Rojax company manufacture?" said Mr. Perls.

"Kiddies' furniture. Little chairs, rockers, tables, Jungle-Gyms, slides, swings, seesaws."

Wilhelm let his father do the explaining. Large and stiffbacked, he tried to sit patiently, but his feet were abnormally restless. All right! His father had to impress Mr. Perls? He would go along once more, and play his part. Fine! He would play along and help his father maintain his style. Style was the main consideration. That was just fine!

"I was with the Rojax Corporation for almost ten years," he said. "We parted ways because they wanted me to share my territory. They took a son-in-law into the business—a new fellow. It was his idea."

To himself, Wilhelm said, Now God alone can tell why I have to lay my whole life bare to this blasted herring here. I'm sure nobody else does it. Other people keep their business to themselves. Not me.

He continued, "But the rationalization was that it was too big a territory for one man. I had a monopoly. That wasn't so. The real reason was that they had gotten to the place where they would have to make me an officer of the corporation. Vice presidency. I was in line for it, but instead this son-in-low got in, and—"

Dr. Adler thought Wilhelm was discussing his grievances much too openly and said, "My son's income was up in the five figures."

As soon as money was mentioned, Mr. Perls's voice grew eagerly sharper. "Yes? What, the thirty-two-per-cent bracket? Higher even, I guess?" He asked for a hint, and he named the figures not idly but with a sort of hugging relish. Uch! How they love money, thought Wilhelm. They adore money! Holy money! Beautiful money! It was getting so that people were feeble-minded about everything except money. While if you didn't have it you were a dummy, a dummy! You had to excuse yourself from the face of the earth. Chicken! that's what it was. The world's business. If only he could find a way out of it.

Such thinking brought on the usual congestion. It would grow into a fit of passion if he allowed it to continue. Therefore he stopped talking and began to eat.

Before he struck the egg with his spoon he dried the moisture with his napkin. Then he battered it (in his father's opinion) more than was necessary. A faint grime was left by his fingers on the white of the egg after he had picked away the shell. Dr. Adler saw it with silent repugnance. What a Wilky he had given to the world! Why, he didn't even wash his hands in the morning. He used an electric razor so that he didn't have to touch water. The doctor couldn't bear Wilky's dirty habits. Only once—and never again, he swore—had he visited his room. Wilhelm, in pajamas and stockings had sat on his bed, drinking gin from a coffee mug and rooting for the Dodgers on television. "That's two and two on you, Duke. Come on—hit it, now." He came down on the mattress—bam! The bed looked kicked to pieces. Then he drank the gin as though it were tea, and urged his team on with his fist. The smell of dirty clothes was outrageous. By the bedside lay a quart bottle and foolish magazines and mystery stories for the hours of insomnia. Wilhelm lived in worse filth than a savage. When the Doctor spoke to him about this he answered, "Well, I have no wife to look after my things." And who—*who!*—had done the leaving? Not Margaret. The Doctor was certain that she wanted him back.

Wilhelm drank his coffee with a trembling hand. In his full face his abused bloodshot gray eyes, moved back and forth. Jerkily he set his cup back and put half the length of a cigarette into his mouth; he seemed to hold it with his teeth, as though it were a cigar.

"I can't let them get away with it," he said. "It's also a question of morale."

His father corrected him. "Don't you mean a moral question, Wilky?"

"I mean that, too. I have to do something to protect myself. I was promised executive standing." Correction before a stranger mortified him, and his dark blond face changed color, more pale, and then more dark. He went on talking to Perls but his eyes spied on his father. "I was the one who opened the territory for them. I could go back for one of their competitors and take away their customers. *My* customers. Morale enters into it because they've tried to take away my confidence."

"Would you offer a different line to the same people?" Mr. Perls wondered.

"Why not? I know what's wrong with the Rojax product."

"Nonsense," said his father. "Just nonsense and kid's talk, Wilky. You're only looking for trouble and embarrassment that way. What would you gain by such a silly feud? You have to think about making a living and meeting your obligations."

Hot and bitter, Wilhelm said with pride, while his feet moved angrily under the table, "I don't have to be told about my obligations. I've been meeting them for years. In more than twenty years I've never had a penny of help from anybody. I preferred to dig a ditch on the WPA but never asked anyone to meet my obligations for me."

"Wilky has had all kinds of experiences," said Dr. Adler.

The old doctor's face had a wholesome reddish and almost translucent color, like a ripe apricot. The wrinkles beside his ears were deep because the skin conformed so tightly to his bones. With all his might, he was a healthy and fine small old man. He wore a white vest of a light check pattern. His hearing-aid doodad was in the pocket. An unusual shirt of red and black stripes covered his chest. He bought his clothes in a college shop farther uptown. Wilhelm thought he had no business to get himself up like a jockey, out of respect for his profession.

"Well," said Mr. Perls. "I can understand how you feel. You want to fight it out. By a certain time of life, to have to start all over again can't be a pleasure, though a good man can always do it. But anyway you want to keep on with a business you know already, and not have to meet a whole lot of new contacts."

Wilhelm again thought, Why does it have to be me and my life that's discussed, and not him and his life? He would never allow it. But I am an idiot. I have no reserve. To me it can be done. I talk. I must ask for it. Everybody wants to have intimate conversations, but the smart fellows don't give out, only the fools. The smart fellows talk intimately about the fools, and examine them all over and give them advice. Why do I allow it? The hint about his age had hurt him. No, you can't admit it's as good as ever, he conceded. Things do give out.

"In the meanwhile," Dr. Adler said, "Wilky is taking it easy and considering various propositions. Isn't that so?"

"More or less," said Wilhelm. He suffered his father to increase Mr. Perls's respect for him. The WPA ditch had brought the family into contempt. He was a little tired. The spirit, the peculiar burden of his existence lay upon him like an accretion, a load, a hump. In any moment of quiet, when sheer fatigue prevented him from struggling, he was apt to feel this mysterious weight, this growth or collection of nameless things which it was the business of his life to carry about. That must be what a man was for. This large, odd, excited, fleshy, blond, abrupt personality named Wilhelm, or Tommy, was here, present, in the present—Dr. Tamkin had been putting into his mind many suggestions about the present moment, the here and now—this Wilky, or Tommy Wilhelm, forty-four years old, father of two sons, at present living in the Hotel Gloriana, was assigned to be the carrier of a load which was his own self, his characteristic self. There was no figure or estimate for the value of this load. But it is probably exaggerated by the subject, T. W. Who is a visionary sort of animal. Who has to believe that he can know why he exists. Though he has never seriously tried to find out why.

Mr. Perls said, "If he wants time to think things over and have a rest, why doesn't he run down to Florida for a while? Off season it's cheap and quiet. Fairyland. The mangoes are just coming in. I got two acres down there. You'd think you were in India."

Mr. Perls utterly astonished Wilhelm when he spoke of fairyland with a foreign accent. Mangoes—India? What did he mean, India?

"Once upon a time," said Wilhelm, "I did some public-relations work for a big hotel down in Cuba. If I could get them a notice in Leonard Lyons or one of the other columns it might be good for another holiday there, gratis. I haven't had a vacation for a long time, and I could stand a rest after going so hard. You know that's true, Father." He meant that his father knew how deep the crisis was becoming; how badly he was strapped for money; and that he could not rest but would be crushed if he stumbled; and that his obligations would destroy him. He couldn't falter. He thought, The money! When I had it, I flowed money. They bled it away from me. I hemorrhaged money. But now it's almost all gone, and where am I supposed to turn for more?

He said, "As a matter of fact, Father, I am tired as hell."

But Mr. Perls began to smile and said, "I understand from Doctor Tamkin that you're going into some kind of investment with him, partners."

"You know, he's a very ingenious fellow," said Dr. Adler. "I really enjoy hearing him go on. I wonder if he really is a medical doctor."

"Isn't he?" said Perls. "Everybody thinks he is. He talks about his patients. Doesn't he write prescriptions?"

"I don't really know what he does," said Dr. Adler. "He's a cunning man."

"He's a psychologist, I understand," said Wilhelm.

"I don't know what sort of psychologist or psychiatrist he may be," said his father. "He's a little vague. It's growing into a major industry, and a very expensive one. Fellows have to hold down very big jobs in order to pay those fees. Anyway, this Tamkin is clever. He never said he practiced here, but I believe he was a doctor in California. They don't seem to have much legislation out there to cover these things, and I hear a thousand dollars will get you a degree from a Los Angeles correspondence school. He gives the impression of knowing something about chemistry, and things like hypnotism. I wouldn't trust him, though."

"And why wouldn't you?" Wilhelm demanded.

"Because he's probably a liar. Do you believe he invented all the things he claims?"

Mr. Perls was grinning.

"He was written up in *Fortune*," said Wilhelm. "Yes, in *Fortune* magazine. He showed me the article. I've seen his clippings."

"That doesn't make him legitimate," said Dr. Adler. "It might have been another Tamkin. Make no mistake, he's an operator. Perhaps even crazy."

"Crazy, you say?"

Mr. Perls put in, "He could be both sane and crazy. In these days nobody can tell for sure which is which."

"An electrical device for truck drivers to wear in their caps," said Dr. Adler, describing one of Tamkin's proposed inventions. "To wake them with a shock when they begin to be drowsy at the wheel. It's triggered by the change in blood-pressure when they start to doze."

"It doesn't sound like such an impossible thing to me," said Wilhelm.

Mr. Perls said, "To me he described an underwater suit so a man could walk on the bed of the Hudson in case of an atomic attack. He said he could walk to Albany in it."

"Ha, ha, ha, ha, ha!" cried Dr. Adler in his old man's voice. "Tamkin's Folly. You could go on a camping trip under Niagara Falls."

"This is just his kind of fantasy," said Wilhelm. "It doesn't mean a thing. Inventors are supposed to be like that. I get funny ideas myself. Everybody wants to make something. Any American does."

But his father ignored this and said to Perls, "What other inventions did he describe?"

While the frazzle-faced Mr. Perls and his father in the unseemly, monkey-striped shirt were laughing, Wilhelm could not restrain himself and joined in with his own panting laugh. But he was in despair. They were laughing at the man to whom he had given a power of attorney over his last seven hundred dollars to speculate for him in the commodities market. They had bought all that lard. It had to rise today. By ten o'clock, or half-past ten, trading would be active, and he would see.

III

Between white tablecloths and glassware and glancing silver ware, through overfull light, the long figure of Mr. Perls went away into the darkness of the lobby. He thrust with his cane, and dragged a large built-up shoe which Wilhelm had not included in his estimate of troubles. Dr. Adler wanted to talk about him. "There's a poor man," he said, "with a bone condition which is gradually breaking him up."

"One of those progressive diseases?" said Wilhelm.

"Very bad. I've learned," the doctor told him, "to keep my sympathy for the real ailments. This Perls is more to be pitied than any man I know."

Wilhelm understood he was being put on notice and did not express his opinion. He ate and ate. He did not hurry but kept putting food on his plate until he had gone through the muffins and his father's strawberries, and then some pieces of bacon that were left; he had several cups of coffee, and when he was finished he sat gigantically in a state of arrest and didn't seem to know what he should do next.

For a while father and son were uncommonly still. Wilhelm's preparations to please Dr. Adler had failed completely, for the old man kept thinking, You'd never guess he had a clean upbringing, and, What a dirty devil this son of mine is. Why can't he try to sweeten his appearance a little? Why does he want to drag himself like this? And he makes himself look so idealistic.

Wilhelm sat, mountainous. He was not really so slovenly as his father found him to be. In some aspects he even had a certain delicacy. His mouth, though broad, had a fine outline, and his brow and his gradually incurved nose, dignity, and in his blond hair there was white but there were also shades of gold and chestnut. When he was with the Rojax Corporation Wilhelm had kept a small apartment in Roxbury, two rooms in a large house with a small porch and garden, and on mornings of leisure, in late spring weather like this, he used to sit expanded in a wicker chair with the sunlight pouring through the weave, and sunlight through the slug-eaten holes of the young hollyhocks and as deeply as the grass allowed into small flowers. This peace (he forgot that that time had had its troubles, too), this peace was gone. It must not have belonged to him, really, for to be here in New York with his old father was more genuinely like his life. He was well aware that he didn't stand a chance of getting sympathy from his father, who said he kept his for real ailments. Moreover, he advised himself repeatedly not to discuss his vexatious problems with him, for his father, with some justice, wanted to be left in peace. Wilhelm also knew that when he began to talk about these things he made himself feel worse, he became congested with them and worked himself into a clutch. Therefore he warned himself, Lay off, pal. It'll only be an aggravation. From a deeper source, however, came other promptings. If he didn't keep his troubles before him he risked losing them altogether, and he knew by experience that this was worse. And furthermore, he could not succeed in excusing his father on the ground of old age. No. No, he could not. I am his son, he thought. He is my father. He is as much father as I am son—old or not. Affirming this, though in complete silence, he sat, and, sitting, he kept his father at the table with him.

"Wilky," said the old man, "have you gone down to the baths here yet?"

"No, Dad, not yet."

"Well, you know the Gloriana has one of the finest pools in New York. Eighty feet, blue tile. It's a beauty."

Wilhelm had seen it. On the way to the gin game you passed the stairway to the pool. He did not care for the odor of the wall-locked and chlorinated water.

"You ought to investigate the Russian and Turkish baths, and the sunlamps and massage. I don't hold with sunlamps. But the massage does a world of good, and there's nothing better than hydrotherapy when you come right down to it. Simple water has a calming effect and would do you more good than all the barbiturates and alcohol in the world."

Wilhelm reflected that this advice was as far as his father's help and sympathy would extend.

"I thought," he said, "that the water cure was for lunatics."

The doctor received this as one of his son's jokes and said with a smile,

"Well, it won't turn a sane man into a lunatic. It does a great deal for me. I couldn't live without my massages and steam."

"You're probably right. I ought to try it one of these days. Yesterday, late in the afternoon, my head was about to bust and I just had to have a little air, so I walked around the reservoir, and I sat down for a while in a playground. It rests me to watch the kids play potsy and skiprope."

The doctor said with approval, "Well, now, that's more like the idea."

"It's the end of the lilacs," said Wilhelm. "When they burn it's the beginning of summer. At least, in the city. Around the time of year when the candy stores take down the windows and start to sell sodas on the sidewalk. But even though I was raised here, Dad, I can't take city life any more, and I miss the country. There's too much push here for me. It works me up too much. I take things too hard. I wonder why you never retired to a quieter place."

The doctor opened his small hand on the table in a gesture so old and so typical that Wilhelm felt it like an actual touch upon the foundations of his life. "I am a city boy myself, you must remember," Dr. Adler explained. "But if you find the city so hard on you, you ought to get out."

"I'll do that," said Wilhelm, "as soon as I can make the right connection. Meanwhile—"

His father interrupted, "Meanwhile I suggest you cut down on drugs."

"You exaggerate that, Dad. I don't really— I give myself a little boost against—" He almost pronounced the word "misery" but he kept his resolution not to complain.

The doctor, however, fell into the error of pushing his advice too hard. It was all he had to give his son and he gave it once more. "Water and exercise," he said.

He wants a young, smart, successful son, thought Wilhelm, and he said, "Oh, Father, it's nice of you to give me this medical advice, but steam isn't going to cure what ails me."

The doctor measurably drew back, warned by the sudden weak strain of Wilhelm's voice and all that the droop of his face, the swell of his belly against the restraint of his belt intimated.

"Some new business?" he asked unwillingly.

Wilhelm made a great preliminary summary which involved the whole of his body. He drew and held a long breath, and his color changed and his eyes swam. "New?" he said.

"You make too much of your problems," said the doctor. "They ought not to be turned into a career. Concentrate on real troubles—fatal sickness, accidents." The old man's whole manner said, Wilky, don't start this on me. I have a right to be spared.

Wilhelm himself prayed for restraint; he knew this weakness of his and fought it. He knew, also, his father's character. And he began mildly, "As far as the fatal part of it goes, everyone on this side of the grave is the same distance from death. No, I guess my trouble is not exactly new. I've got to pay premiums on two policies for the boys. Margaret sent them to me. She unloads everything on me. Her mother left her an income. She won't even file a joint tax return. I get stuck. Etcetera. But you've heard the whole story before."

"I certainly have," said the old man. "And I've told you to stop giving her so much money."

Wilhelm worked his lips in silence before he could speak. The congestion was growing. "Oh, but my kids, Father. My kids. I love them. I don't want them to lack anything."

The doctor said with a half-deaf benevolence, "Well, naturally. And she, I'll bet, is the beneficiary of that policy."

"Let her be. I'd sooner die myself before I collected a cent of such money."

"Ah yes." The old man sighed. He did not like the mention of death. "Did I tell you that your sister Catherine—Philippa—is after me again."

"What for?"

"She wants to rent a gallery for an exhibition."

Stiffly fair-minded, Wilhelm said, "Well, of course that's up to you, Father."

The round-headed old man with his fine, feather-white, ferny hair said, "No, Wilky. There's not a thing on those canvases. I don't believe it; it's a case of the emperor's clothes. I may be old enough for my second childhood, but at least the first is well behind me. I was glad enough to buy crayons for her when she was four. But now she's a woman of forty and too old to be encouraged in her delusions. She's no painter."

"I wouldn't go so far as to call her a born artist," said Wilhelm, "but you can't blame her for trying something worth while."

"Let her husband pamper her."

Wilhelm had done his best to be just to his sister, and he had sincerely meant to spare his father, but the old man's tight, benevolent deafness had it's usual effect on him. He said, "When it comes to women and money, I'm completely in the dark. What makes Margaret act like this?"

"She's showing you that you can't make it without her," said the doctor. "She aims to bring you back by financial force."

"But if she ruins me, Dad, how can she expect me to come back? No, I have a sense of honor. What you don't see is that she's trying to put an end to me."

His father stared. To him this was absurd. And Wilhelm thought, Once a guy starts to slip, he figures he might as well be a clunk. A real big clunk. He even takes pride in it. But there's nothing to be proud of—hey, boy? Nothing. I don't blame Dad for his attitude. And it's no cause for pride.

"I don't understand that. But if you feel like this why don't you settle with her once and for all?"

"What do you mean, Dad?" said Wilhelm, surprised. "I thought I told you. Do you think I'm not willing to settle? Four years ago when we broke up I gave her everything—goods, furniture, savings. I tried to show good will, but I didn't get anywhere. Why when I wanted Scissors, the dog, because the animal and I were so attached to each other—it was bad enough to leave the kids—she absolutely refused me. Not that she cared a damn about the animal. I don't think you've seen him. He's an Australian sheep dog. They usually have one blank or whitish eye which gives a misleading look, but they're the gentlest dogs and have unusual delicacy about eating or talking. Let me at least have the companionship of this animal. Never." Wilhelm was greatly moved. He wiped his face at all corners with his napkin. Dr. Adler felt that his son was indulging himself too much in his emotions.

"Whenever she can hit me, she hits, and she seems to live for that alone. And she demands more and more, and still more. Two years ago she wanted to go back to college and get another degree. It increased my burden but I thought it would be wiser in the end if she got a better job through it. But still she takes as much from me as before. Next thing she'll want to be a Doctor of Philosophy. She says the women in her family live long, and I'll have to pay and pay for the rest of my life."

The doctor said impatiently, "Well, these are details, not principles. Just details which you can leave out. The dog! You're mixing up all kinds of irrelevant things. Go to a good lawyer."

"But I've already told you, Dad. I got a lawyer, and she got one, too, and both of them talk and send me bills, and I eat my heart out. Oh, Dad, Dad, what a hole I'm in!" said Wilhelm in utter misery. "The lawyers—see?— draw up an agreement, and she says okay on Monday and wants more money on Tuesday. And it begins again."

"I always thought she was a strange kind of woman," said Dr. Adler. He felt that by disliking Margaret from the first and disapproving of the marriage he had done all that he could be expected to do.

"Strange, Father? I'll show you what she's like." Wilhelm took hold of his broad throat with brown-stained fingers and bitten nails and began to choke himself.

"What are you doing?" cried the old man.

"I'm showing you what she does to me."

"Stop that—stop it!" the old man said and tapped the table commandingly.

"Well, Dad, she hates me. I feel that she's strangling me. I can't catch my breath. She just has fixed herself on me to kill me. She can do it at long distance. One of these days I'll be struck down by suffocation or apoplexy because of her. I just can't catch my breath."

"Take your hands off your throat, you foolish man," said his father. "Stop this bunk. Don't expect me to believe in all kinds of voodoo."

"If that's what you want to call it, all right." His face flamed and paled and swelled and his breath was laborious.

"But I'm telling you that from the time I met her I've been a slave. The Emancipation Proclamation was only for colored people. A husband like me is a slave, with an iron collar. The churches go up to Albany and supervise the law. They won't have divorces. The court says, 'You want to be free.

Then you have to work twice as hard—twice, at least! Work! you bum.' So then guys kill each other for the buck, and they may be free of a wife who hates them but they are sold to the company. The company knows a guy has got to have his salary, and takes full advantage of him. Don't talk to me about being free. A rich man may be free on an income of a million net. A poor man may be free because nobody cares what he does. But a fellow in my position has to sweat it out until he drops dead."

His father replied to this, "Wilky, it's entirely your own fault. You don't have to allow it."

Stopped in his eloquence, Wilhelm could not speak for a while. Dumb and incompetent, he struggled for breath and frowned with effort into his father's face.

"I don't understand your problems," said the old man. "I never had any like them."

By now Wilhelm had lost his head and he waved his hands and said over and over, "Oh, Dad, don't give me that stuff, don't give me that. Please don't give me that sort of thing."

"It's true," said his father. "I come from a different world. Your mother and I led an entirely different life."

"Oh, how can you compare Mother," Wilhelm said. "Mother was a help to you. Did she harm you ever?"

"There's no need to carry on like an opera, Wilky," said the doctor. "This is only your side of things."

"What? It's the truth," said Wilhelm.

The old man could not be persuaded and shook his round head and drew his vest down over the gilded shirt, and leaned back with a completeness of style that made this look, to anyone out of hearing, like an ordinary conversation between a middle-aged man and his respected father. Wilhelm towered and swayed, big and sloven, with his gray eyes red-shot and his honey-colored hair twisted in flaming shapes upward. Injustice made him angry, made him beg. But he wanted an understanding with his father, and he tried to capitulate to him. He said, "You can't compare Mother and Margaret, and neither can you and I be compared, because you, Dad, were a success. And a success—is a success. I never made a success."

The doctor's old face lost all of its composure and became hard and angry. His small breast rose sharply under the red and black shirt and he said, "Yes. Because of hard work. I was not self-indulgent, not lazy. My old man sold dry goods in Williamsburg. We were nothing, do you understand? I knew I couldn't afford to waste my chances."

"I wouldn't admit for one minute that I was lazy," said Wilhelm. "If anything, I tried too hard. I admit I made many mistakes. Like I thought I shouldn't do things you had done already. Study chemistry. You had done it already. It was in the family."

His father continued, "I didn't run around with fifty women, either. I was not a Hollywood star. I didn't have time to go to Cuba for a vacation. I stayed at home and took care of my children."

Oh, thought Wilhelm, eyes turning upward. Why did I come here in the first place, to live near him? New York is like a gas. The colors are running. My head feels so tight, I don't know what I'm doing. He thinks I want to take away his money or that I envy him. He doesn't see what I want.

"Dad," Wilhelm said aloud, "you're being very unfair. It's true the movies was a false step. But I love my boys. I didn't abandon them. I left Margaret because I had to."

"Why did you have to?"

"Well—" said Wilhelm, struggling to condense his many reasons into a few plain words. "I had to—I had to."

With sudden and surprising bluntness his father said, "Did you have bed-trouble with her? Then you should have stuck it out. Sooner or later everyone has it. Normal people stay with it. It passes. But you wouldn't, so now you pay for your stupid romantic notions. Have I made my view clear?"

It was very clear. Wilhelm seemed to hear it repeated from various sides and inclined his head different ways, and listened and thought. Finally he said, "I guess that's the medical standpoint. You may be right. I just couldn't live with Margaret. I wanted to stick it out, but I was getting very sick. She was one way and I was another. She wouldn't be like me, so I tried to be like her, and I couldn't do it."

"Are you sure she didn't tell *you* to go?" the doctor said.

"I wish she had. I'd be in a better position now. No, it was me. I didn't want to leave, but I couldn't stay. Somebody had to take the initiative. I did. Now I'm the fall guy too."

Pushing aside in advance all the objections that his son would make, the doctor said, "Why did you lose your job with Rojax?"

"I didn't, I've told you."

"You're lying. You wouldn't have ended the connection. You need the money too badly. But you must have got into trouble." The small old man spoke concisely and with great strength. "Since you have to talk and can't let it alone, tell the truth. Was there a scandal—a woman?"

Wilhelm fiercely defended himself. "No, Dad, there wasn't any woman. I told you how it was."

"Maybe it was a man, then," the old man said wickedly.

Shocked, Wilhelm stared at him with burning pallor and dry lips. His skin looked a little yellow. "I don't think you know what you're talking about," he answered after a moment. "You shouldn't let your imagination run so free. Since you've been living here on Broadway you must think you understand life, up to date. You ought to know your own son a little better. Let's drop that, now."

"All right, Wilky, I'll withdraw it. But something must have happened in Roxbury nevertheless. You'll never go back. You're just talking wildly about representing a rival company. You won't. You've done something to spoil your reputation, I think. But you've got girl friends who are expecting you back, isn't that so?"

"I take a lady out now and then while on the road," said Wilhelm. "I'm not a monk."

"No one special? Are you sure you haven't gotten into complications?"

He had tried to unburden himself and instead, Wilhelm thought, he had to undergo an inquisition to prove himself worthy of a sympathetic word. Because his father believed that he did all kinds of gross things.

"There is a woman in Roxbury that I went with. We fell in love and wanted to marry, but she got tired of waiting for my divorce. Margaret figured that. On top of which the girl was a Catholic and I had to go with her to the priest and make an explanation."

Neither did this last confession touch Dr. Adler's sympathies or sway his calm old head or affect the color of his complexion.

"No, no, no, no; all wrong," he said.

Again Wilhelm cautioned himself. Remember his age. He is no longer the same person. He can't bear trouble. I'm so choked up and congested anyway I can't see straight. Will I ever get out of the woods, and recover my balance? You're never the same afterward. Trouble rusts out the system.

"You really *want* a divorce?" said the old man.

"For the price I pay I should be getting something."

"In that case," Dr. Adler said, "it seems to me no normal person would stand for such treatment from a woman."

"Ah, Father, Father!" said Wilhelm. "It's always the same thing with you. Look how you lead me on. You always start out to help me with my problems, and be sympathetic and so forth. It gets my hopes up and I begin to be grateful. But before we're through I'm a hundred times more depressed than before. Why is that? You have no sympathy. You want to shift all the blame on to me. Maybe you're wise to do it." Wilhelm was beginning to lose himself. "All you seem to think about is your death. Well, I'm sorry. But I'm going to die too. And I'm your son. It isn't my fault in the first place. There ought to be a right way to do this, and be fair to each other. But what I want to know is, why do you start up with me if you're not going to help me? What do you want to know about my problems for, Father? So you can lay the whole responsibility on me—so that you won't have to help me? D'you want me to comfort you for having such a son?" Wilhelm had a great knot of wrong tied tight within his chest, and tears approached his eyes but he didn't let them out. He looked shabby enough as it was. His voice was thick and hazy, and he was stammering and could not bring his awful feelings forth.

"You have some purpose of your own," said the doctor, "in acting so unreasonable. What do you want from me? What do you expect?"

"What do I expect?" said Wilhelm. He felt as though he were unable to recover something. Like a ball in the surf, washed beyond reach, his self-control was going out. "I expect *help!*" The words escaped him in a loud, wild, frantic cry and startled the old man, and two or three breakfasters within hearing glanced their way. Wilhelm's hair, the color of whitened honey, rose dense and tall with the expansion of his face, and he said, "When

I suffer—you aren't even sorry. That's because you have no affection for me, and you don't want any part of me."

"Why must I like the way you behave? No, I don't like it," said Dr. Adler.

"All right. You want me to change myself. But suppose I could do it—what would I become? What could I? Let's suppose that all my life I have had the wrong ideas about myself and wasn't what I thought I was. And wasn't even careful to take a few precautions, as most people do—like a woodchuck has a few exits to his tunnel. But what shall I do now? More than half my life is over. More than half. And now you tell me I'm not even normal."

The old man too had lost his calm. "You cry about being helped," he said. "When you thought you had to go into the service I sent a check to Margaret every month. As a family man you could have had an exemption. But no! The war couldn't be fought without you and you had to get yourself drafted and be an office-boy in the Pacific theater. Any clerk could have done what you did. You could find nothing better to become than a GI."

Wilhelm was going to reply, and half raised his bearish figure from the chair, his fingers spread and whitened by their grip on the table, but the old man would not let him begin. He said, "I see other elderly people here with children who aren't much good, and they keep backing them and holding them up at a great sacrifice. But I'm not going to make that mistake. It doesn't enter your mind that when I die—a year, two years from now—you'll still be here. I do think of it."

He had intended to say that he had a right to be left in peace. Instead he gave Wilhelm the impression that he meant it was not fair for the better man of the two, and the more useful, the more admired, to leave the world first. Perhaps he meant that, too—a little; but he would not under other circumstances have come out with it so flatly.

"Father," said Wilhelm with an unusual openness of appeal. "Don't you think I know how you feel? I have pity. I want you to live on and on. If you outlive me, that's perfectly okay by me." As his father did not answer this avowal and turned away his glance, Wilhelm suddenly burst out, "No, but you hate me. And if I had money you wouldn't. By God, you have to admit it. The money makes the difference. Then we would be a fine father and son, if I was a credit to you—so you could boast and brag about me all over the hotel. But I'm not the right type of son. I'm too old, I'm too old and too unlucky."

His father said, "I can't give you any money. There would be no end to it if I started. You and your sister would take every last buck from me. I'm still alive, not dead. I am still here. Life isn't over yet. I am as much alive as you or anyone. And I want nobody on my back. Get off! And I give you the same advice, Wilky. Carry nobody on your back."

"Just keep your money," said Wilhelm miserably. "Keep it and enjoy it yourself. That's the ticket!"

IV

Ass! Idiot! Wild boar! Dumb mule! Slave! Lousy, wallowing hippopotamus! Wilhelm called himself as his bending legs carried him from the dining
room. His pride! His inflamed feelings! His begging and feebleness! And
trading insults with his old father—and spreading confusion over everything.
Oh, how poor, contemptible, and ridiculous he was! When he remembered
how he had said, with great reproof, "You ought to know your own son"—
why, how corny and abominable it was.

He could not get out of the sharply brilliant dining room fast enough. He
was horribly worked up; his neck and shoulders, his entire chest ached as
though they had been tightly tied with ropes. He smelled the salt odor of
tears in his nose.

But at the same time, since there were depths in Wilhelm not unsuspected
by himself, he received a suggestion from some remote element in his
thoughts that the business of life, the real business—to carry his peculiar
burden, to feel shame and impotence, to taste these quelled tears—the only
important business, the highest business was being done. Maybe the making
of mistakes expressed the very purpose of his life and the essence of his being
here. Maybe he was supposed to make them and suffer from them on this
earth. And though he had raised himself above Mr. Perls and his father because they adored money, still they were called to act energetically and this
was better than to yell and cry, pray and beg, poke and blunder and go by
fits and starts and fall upon the thorns of life. And finally sink beneath that
watery floor—would that be tough luck, or would it be good riddance?

But he raged once more against his father. Other people with money,
while they're still alive, want to see it do some good. Granted, he shouldn't
support me. But have I ever asked him to do that? Have I ever asked for
dough at all, either for Margaret or for the kids or for myself? It isn't the
money, but only the assistance; not even assistance, but just the feeling.
But he may be trying to teach me that a grown man should be cured of such
feeling. Feeling got me in dutch at Rojax. I had the *feeling* that I belonged
to the firm, and my *feelings* were hurt when they put Gerber in over me.
Dad thinks I'm too simple. But I'm not so simple as he thinks. What about
his feelings? He doesn't forget death for one single second, and that's what
makes him like this. And not only is death on his mind but through money
he forces me to think about it, too. It gives him power over me. He forces
me that way, he himself, and then he's sore. If he was poor, I could care for
him and show it. The way I *could* care, too, if I only had a chance. He'd see
how much love and respect I had in me. It would make him a different man,
too. He'd put his hands on me and give me his blessing.

Someone in a gray straw hat with a wide cocoa-colored band spoke to
Wilhelm in the lobby. The light was dusky, splotched with red underfoot;
green, the leather furniture; yellow, the indirect lighting.

"Hey, Tommy. Say, there."

"Excuse me," said Wilhelm, trying to reach a house phone. But this was
Dr. Tamkin, whom he was just about to call.

"You have a very obsessional look on your face," said Dr. Tamkin.

Wilhelm thought, Here he is, Here he is. If I could only figure this guy out.

"Oh," he said to Tamkin. "Have I got such a look? Well, whatever it is, you name it and I'm sure to have it."

The sight of Dr. Tamkin brought his quarrel with his father to a close. He found himself flowing into another channel.

"What are we doing?" he said. "What's going to happen to lard today?"

"Don't worry yourself about that. All we have to do is hold on to it and it's sure to go up. But what's made you so hot under the collar, Wilhelm?"

"Oh, one of those family situations." This was the moment to take a new look at Tamkin, and he viewed him closely but gained nothing by the new effort. It was conceivable that Tamkin was everything that he claimed to be, and all the gossip false. But was he a scientific man, or not? If he was not, this might be a case for the district attorney's office to investigate. Was he a liar? That was a delicate question. Even a liar might be trustworthy in some ways. Could he trust Tamkin—could he? He feverishly, fruitlessly sought an answer.

But the time for this question was past, and he had to trust him now. After a long struggle to come to a decision, he had given him the money. Practical judgment was in abeyance. He had worn himself out, and the decision was no decision. How had this happened? But how had his Hollywood career begun? It was not because of Maurice Venice, who turned out to be a pimp. It was because Wilhelm himself was ripe for the mistake. His marriage, too, had been like that. Through such decisions somehow his life had taken form. And so, from the moment when he tasted the peculiar flavor of fatality in Dr. Tamkin, he could no longer keep back the money.

Five days ago Tamkin had said, "Meet me tomorrow, and we'll go to the market." Wilhelm, therefore, had had to go. At eleven o'clock they had walked to the brokerage office. On the way, Tamkin broke the news to Wilhelm that though this was an equal partnership he couldn't put up his half of the money just yet; it was tied up for a week or so in one of his patents. Today he would be two hundred dollars short; next week, he'd make it up. But neither of them needed an income from the market, of course. This was only a sporting proposition anyhow, Tamkin said. Wilhelm had to answer, "Of course." It was too late to withdraw. What else could he do? Then came the formal part of the transaction, and it was frightening. The very shade of green of Tamkin's check looked wrong; it was a false, disheartening color. His handwriting was peculiar, even monstrous; the e's were like i's, the t's and l's the same, and the h's like wasps' bellies. He wrote like a fourth-grader. Scientists, however, dealt mostly in symbols; they printed. This was Wilhelm's explanation.

Dr. Tamkin had given him his check for three hundred dollars. Wilhelm, in a blinded and convulsed aberration, pressed and pressed to try to kill the trembling of his hand as he wrote out his check for a thousand. He set his lips tight, crouched with his huge back over the table, and wrote with crumbling, terrified fingers, knowing that if Tamkin's check bounced his own would not be honored either. His sole cleverness was to set the date ahead by one day to give the green check time to clear.

Next he had signed a power of attorney, allowing Tamkin to speculate with his money, and this was an even more frightening document. Tamkin had never said a word about it, but here they were and it had to be done.

After delivering his signatures, the only precaution Wilhelm took was to come back to the manager of the brokerage office and ask him privately, "Uh, about Doctor Tamkin. We were in here a few minutes ago, remember?"

That day had been a weeping, smoky one and Wilhelm had gotten away from Tamkin on the pretext of having to run to the post office. Tamkin had gone to lunch alone, and here was Wilhelm, back again, breathless, his hat dripping, needlessly asking the manager if he remembered.

"Yes, sir, I know," the manager had said. He was a cold, mild, lean German who dressed correctly and around his neck wore a pair of opera glasses with which he read the board. He was an extremely correct person except that he never shaved in the morning, not caring, probably, how he looked to the fumblers and the old people and the operators and the gamblers and the idlers of Broadway uptown. The market closed at three. Maybe, Wilhelm guessed, he had a thick beard and took a lady out to dinner later and wanted to look fresh-shaven.

"Just a question," said Wilhelm. "A few minutes ago I signed a power of attorney so Doctor Tamkin could invest for me. You gave me the blanks."

"Yes, sir, I remember."

"Now this is what I want to know," Wilhelm had said. "I'm no lawyer and I only gave the paper a glance. Does this give Doctor Tamkin power of attorney over any other assets of mine—money, or property?"

The rain had dribbled from Wilhelm's deformed, transparent raincoat; the buttons of his shirt, which always seemed tiny, were partly broken, in pearly quarters of the moon, and some of the dark, thick golden hairs that grew on his belly stood out. It was the manager's business to conceal his opinion of him; he was shrewd, gray, correct (although unshaven) and had little to say except on matters that came to his desk. He must have recognized in Wilhelm a man who reflected long and then made the decision he had rejected twenty separate times. Silvery, cool, level, long-profiled, experienced, indifferent, observant, with unshaven refinement, he scarcely looked at Wilhelm, who trembled with fearful awkwardness. The manager's face, low-colored, long-nostriled, acted as a unit of perception; his eyes merely did their reduced share. Here was a man, like Rubin, who knew and knew and knew. He, a foreigner, knew; Wilhelm, in the city of his birth, was ignorant.

The manager had said, "No, sir, it does not give him."

"Only over the funds I deposited with you?"

"Yes, that is right, sir."

"Thank you, that's what I wanted to find out," Wilhelm had said, grateful.

The answer comforted him. However, the question had no value. None at all. For Wilhelm had no other assets. He had given Tamkin his last money. There wasn't enough of it to cover his obligations anyway, and Wilhelm had reckoned that he might as well go bankrupt now as next month. "Either broke or rich," was how he had figured, and that formula had encouraged him to make the gamble. Well, not rich; he did not expect that, but perhaps Tamkin might really show him how to earn what he needed in the market. By now, however, he had forgotten his own reckoning and was aware only that he stood to lose his seven hundred dollars to the last cent.

Dr. Tamkin took the attitude that they were a pair of gentlemen experimenting with lard and grain futures. The money, a few hundred dollars, meant nothing much to either of them. He said to Wilhelm, "Watch. You'll get a big kick out of this and wonder why more people don't go into it. You think the Wall Street guys are so smart—geniuses? That's because most of us are psychologically afraid to think about the details. Tell me this. When you're on the road, and you don't understand what goes on under the hood of your car, you'll worry what'll happen if something goes wrong with the engine. Am I wrong?" No, he was right. "Well," said Dr. Tamkin with an expression of quiet triumph about his mouth, almost the suggestion of a jeer. "It's the same psychological principle, Wilhelm. They are rich because you don't understand what goes on. But it's no mystery, and by putting in a little money and applying certain principles of observation, you begin to grasp it. It can't be studied in the abstract. You have to take a specimen risk so that you feel the process, the money-flow, the whole complex. To know how it feels to be a seaweed you have to get in the water. In a very short time we'll take out a hundred-per-cent profit." Thus Wilhelm had had to pretend at the outset that his interest in the market was theoretical.

"Well," said Tamkin when he met him now in the lobby, "what's the problem, what is this family situation? Tell me." He put himself forward as the keen mental scientist. Whenever this happened Wilhelm didn't know what to reply. No matter what he said or did it seemed that Dr. Tamkin saw through him.

"I had some words with my dad."

Dr. Tamkin found nothing extraordinary in this. "It's the eternal same story," he said. "The elemental conflict of parent and child. It won't end, ever. Even with a fine old gentleman like your dad."

"I don't suppose it will. I've never been able to get anywhere with him. He objects to my feelings. He thinks they're sordid. I upset him and he gets mad at me. But maybe all old men are alike."

"Sons, too. Take it from one of them," said Dr. Tamkin. "All the same, you should be proud of such a fine old patriarch of a father. It should give you hope. The longer he lives, the longer your life-expectancy becomes."

Wilhelm answered, brooding, "I guess so. But I think I inherit more from my mother's side, and she died in her fifties."

"A problem arose between a young fellow I'm treating and his dad—I just had a consultation," said Dr. Tamkin as he removed his dark gray hat.

"So early in the morning?" said Wilhelm with suspicion.

"Over the telephone, of course."

What a creature Tamkin was when he took off his hat! The indirect light showed the many complexities of his bald skull, his gull's nose, his rather handsome eyebrows, his vain mustache, his deceiver's brown eyes. His figure was stocky, rigid, short in the neck, so that the large ball of the occiput touched his collar. His bones were peculiarly formed, as though twisted twice where the ordinary human bone was turned only once, and his shoulders rose in two pagoda-like points. At midbody he was thick. He stood pigeon-toed, a sign perhaps that he was devious or had much to hide. The skin of his hands was aging, and his nails were moonless, concave, clawlike, and they appeared loose. His eyes were as brown as beaver fur and full of strange lines. The two large brown naked balls looked thoughtful—but were they? And honest—but was Dr. Tamkin honest? There was a hypnotic power in his eyes, but this was not always of the same strength, nor was Wilhelm convinced that it was completely natural. He felt that Tamkin tried to make his eyes deliberately conspicuous, with studied art, and that he brought forth his hypnotic effect by an exertion. Occasionally it failed or drooped, and when this happened the sense of his face passed downward to his heavy (possibly foolish?) red underlip.

Wilhelm wanted to talk about the lard holdings, but Dr. Tamkin said, "This father-and-son case of mine would be instructive to you. It's a different psychological type completely than your dad. This man's father thinks that he isn't his son."

"Why not?"

"Because he has found out something about the mother carrying on with a friend of the family for twenty-five years."

"Well, what do you know!" said Wilhelm. His silent thought was, Pure bull. Nothing but bull!

"You must note how interesting the woman is, too. She has two husbands. Whose are the kids? The fellow detected her and she gave a signed confession that two of the four children were not the father's."

"It's amazing," said Wilhelm, but he said it in a rather distant way. He was always hearing such stories from Dr. Tamkin. If you were to believe Tamkin, most of the world was like this. Everybody in the hotel had a mental disorder, a secret history, a concealed disease. The wife of Rubin at the newsstand was supposed to be kept by Carl, the yelling, loud-mouthed gin-rummy player. The wife of Frank in the barbershop had disappeared with a GI while he was waiting for her to disembark at the French Lines pier. Everyone was like the faces on a playing card, upside down either way. Every public figure had a character-neurosis. Maddest of all were the businessmen, the heartless, flaunting, boisterous business class who ruled this country with their hard manners and their bold lies and their absurd words that nobody could believe. They were crazier than anyone. They spread the plague. Wilhelm, thinking of the Rojax Corporation, was inclined to agree that many businessmen were insane. And he supposed that Tamkin, for all his peculiarities, spoke a kind of truth and did some people a sort of good. It confirmed Wilhelm's suspicions to hear that there was a plague, and he said, "I couldn't agree with you more. They trade on anything, they steal everything, they're cynical right to the bones."

"You have to realize," said Tamkin, speaking of his patient, or his client, "that the mother's confession isn't good. It's a confession of duress. I try to tell the young fellow he shouldn't worry about a phony confession. But what does it help him if I am rational with him?"

"No?" said Wilhelm, intensely nervous. "I think we ought to go over to the market. It'll be opening pretty soon."

"Oh, come on," said Tamkin. "It isn't even nine o'clock, and there isn't much trading the first hour anyway. Things don't get hot in Chicago until half-past ten, and they're an hour behind us, don't forget. Anyway, I say lard will go up, and it will. Take my word. I've made a study of the guilt-aggression cycle which is behind it. I ought to know *something* about that. Straighten your collar."

"But meantime," said Wilhelm, "we have taken a licking this week. Are you sure your insight is at its best? Maybe when it isn't we should lay off and wait."

"Don't you realize," Dr. Tamkin told him, "you can't march in a straight line to the victory? You fluctuate toward it. From Euclid to Newton there was straight lines. The modern age analyzes the wavers. On my own accounts, I took a licking in hides and coffee. But I have confidence. I'm sure I'll outguess them." He gave Wilhelm a narrow smile, friendly, calming, shrewd, and wizard-like, patronizing, secret, potent. He saw his fears and smiled at them. "It's something," he remarked, "to see how the competition-factor will manifest itself in different individuals."

"So? Let's go over."

"But I haven't had my breakfast yet."

"I've had mine."

"Come, have a cup of coffee."

"I wouldn't want to meet my dad." Looking through the glass doors, Wilhelm saw that his father had left by the other exit. Wilhelm thought, He didn't want to run into me, either. He said to Dr. Tamkin, "Okay, I'll sit with you, but let's hurry it up because I'd like to get to the market while there's still a place to sit. Everybody and his uncle gets in ahead of you."

"I want to tell you about this boy and his dad. It's highly absorbing. The father was a nudist. Everybody went naked in the house. Maybe the woman found men *with* clothes attractive. Her husband didn't believe in cutting his hair, either. He practiced dentistry. In his office he wore riding pants and a pair of boots, and he wore a green eyeshade."

"Oh, come off it," said Wilhelm.

"This is a true case history."

Without warning, Wilhelm began to laugh. He himself had had no premonition of his change of humor. His face became warm and pleasant, and he forgot his father, his anxieties; he panted bearlike, happily, through his teeth. "This sounds like a horse-dentist. He wouldn't have to put on pants to treat a horse. Now what else are you going to tell me? Did the wife play the mandolin? Does the boy join the cavalry? Oh, Tamkin, you really are a killer-diller."

"Oh, you think I'm trying to amuse you," said Tamkin. "That's because you aren't familiar with my outlook. I deal in facts. Facts always are sensational. I'll say that a second time. Facts *always!* are sensational."

Wilhelm was reluctant to part with his good mood. The doctor had little sense of humor. He was looking at him earnestly.

"I'd bet you any amount of money," said Tamkin, "that the facts about you are sensational."

"Oh—ha, ha! You want them? You can sell them to a true confession magazine."

"People forget how sensational the things are that they do. They don't see it on themselves. It blends into the background of their daily life."

Wilhelm smiled. "Are you sure this boy tells you the truth?"

"Yes, because I've known the whole family for years."

"And you do psychological work with your own friends? I didn't know that was allowed."

"Well, I'm a radical in the profession. I have to do good wherever I can."

Wilhelm's face became ponderous again and pale. His whitened gold hair lay heavy on his head, and he clasped uneasy fingers on the table. Sensational, but oddly enough, dull, too. Now how do you figure that out? It blends with the background. Funny but unfunny. True but false. Casual but laborious, Tamkin was. Wilhelm was most suspicious of him when he took his driest tone.

"With me," said Dr. Tamkin, "I am at my most efficient when I don't need the fee. When I only love. Without a financial reward. I remove myself from the social influence. Especially money. The spiritual compensation is what I look for. Bringing people into the here-and-now. The real universe. That's the present moment. The past is no good to us. The future is full of anxiety. Only the present is real—the here-and-now. Seize the day."

"Well," said Wilhelm, his earnestness returning. "I know you are a very unusual man. I like what you say about here-and-now. Are all the people who come to see you personal friends and patients too? Like that tall handsome girl, the one who always wears those beautiful broomstick skirts and belts?"

"She was an epileptic, and a most bad and serious pathology, too. I'm curing her successfully. She hasn't had a seizure in six months, and she used to have one every week."

"And that young cameraman, the one who showed us those movies from the jungles of Brazil, isn't he related to her?"

"Her brother. He's under my care, too. He has some terrible tendencies, which are to be expected when you have an epileptic sibling. I came into their lives when they needed help desperately, and took hold of them. A certain man forty years older than she had her in his control and used to give her fits by suggestion whenever she tried to leave him. If you only knew one per cent of what goes on in the city of New York! You see, I understand what it is when the lonely person begins to feel like an animal. When the night comes and he feels like howling from his window like a wolf. I'm taking complete care of that young fellow and his sister. I have to steady him down or he'll go from Brazil to Australia the next day. The way I keep him in the here-and-now is by teaching him Greek."

This was a complete surprise! "What, do you know Greek?"

"A friend of mine taught me when I was in Cairo. I studied Aristotle with him to keep from being idle."

Wilhelm tried to take in these new claims and examine them. Howling from the window like a wolf when night comes sounded genuine to him. That was something really to think about. But the Greek! He realized that Tamkin was watching to see how he took it. More elements were continually being added. A few days ago Tamkin had hinted that he had once been in the underworld, one of the Detroit Purple Gang. He was once head of a mental clinic in Toledo. He had worked with a Polish inventor on an unsinkable ship. He was a technical consultant in the field of television. In the life of a man of genius, all of these things might happen. But had they happened to Tamkin? Was he a genius? He often said that he had attended some of the Egyptian royal family as a psychiatrist. "But everybody is alike, common or aristocrat," he told Wilhelm. "The aristocrat knows less about life."

An Egyptian princess whom he had treated in California, for horrible disorders he had described to Wilhelm, retained him to come back to the old country with her, and there he had had many of her friends and relatives under his care. They turned over a villa on the Nile to him. "For ethical reasons, I can't tell you many of the details about them," he said—but Wilhelm had already heard all these details, and strange and shocking they were, if true. *If* true—he could not be free from doubt. For instance, the general who had to wear ladies' silk stockings and stand otherwise naked before the mirror—and all the rest. Listening to the doctor when he was so strangely factual, Wilhelm had to translate his words into his own language, and he could not translate fast enough or find terms to fit what he heard.

"Those Egyptian big shots invested in the market, too, for the heck of it. What did they need extra money for? By association, I almost became a millionaire myself, and if I had played it smart there's no telling what might have happened. I could have been the ambassador." The American? The Egyptian ambassador? "A friend of mine tipped me off on the cotton. I made a heavy purchase of it. I didn't have that kind of money, but everybody there knew me. It never entered their minds that a person of their social circle didn't have dough. The sale was made on the phone. Then, while the cotton shipment was at sea, the price tripled. When the stuff suddenly became so valuable all hell broke loose on the world cotton market, they looked to see who was the owner of this big shipment. Me! They investigated my credit and found out I was a mere doctor, and they canceled. This was illegal. I sued them. But as I didn't have the money to fight them I sold the suit to a Wall Street lawyer for twenty thousand dollars. He fought it and was winning. They settled with him out of court for more than a million. But on the way back from Cairo, flying, there was a crash. All on board died. I have this guilt on my conscience, of being the murderer of that lawyer. Although he was a crook."

Wilhelm thought, I must be a real jerk to sit and listen to such impossible stories. I guess I am a sucker for people who talk about the deeper things of life, even the way he does.

"We scientific men speak of irrational guilt, Wilhelm," said Dr. Tamkin, as if Wilhelm were a pupil in his class. "But in such a situation, because of the money, I wished him harm. I realize it. This isn't the time to describe all the details, but the money made me guilty. *M*oney and *M*urder both begin with *M*. *M*achinery. *M*ischief."

Wilhelm, his mind thinking for him at random, said, "What about *M*ercy? *M*ilk-of-human-kindness?"

"One fact should be clear to you by now. Money-making is aggression. That's the whole thing. The functionalistic explanation is the only one. People come to the market to kill. They say, 'I'm going to make a killing.' It's not accidental. Only they haven't got the genuine courage to kill, and they erect a symbol of it. The money. They make a killing by a fantasy. Now, counting and number is always a sadistic activity. Like hitting. In the Bible, the Jews wouldn't allow you to count them. They knew it was sadistic."

"I don't understand what you mean," said Wilhelm. A strange uneasiness tore at him. The day was growing too warm and his head felt dim. "What makes them want to kill?"

"By and by, you'll get the drift," Dr. Tamkin assured him. His amazing eyes had some of the rich dryness of a brown fur. Innumerable crystalline hairs of spicules of light glittered in their bold surfaces. "You can't understand without first spending years on the study of the ultimates of human and animal behavior, the deep chemical, organismic, and spiritual secrets of life. I am a psychological poet."

"If you're this kind of poet," said Wilhelm, whose fingers in his pocket were feeling in the little envelopes for the Phenaphen capsules, "what are you doing on the market?"

"That's a good question. Maybe I am better at speculation because I don't care. Basically, I don't wish hard enough for money, and therefore I come with a cool head to it."

Wilhelm thought, Oh, sure! That's an answer, is it? I bet that if I took a strong attitude he'd back down on everything. He'd grovel in front of me. The way he looks at me on the sly, to see if I'm being taken in! He swallowed his Phenaphen pill with a long gulp of water. The rims of his eyes grew red as it went down. And then he felt calmer.

"Let me see if I can give you an answer that will satisfy you," said Dr. Tamkin. His flapjacks were set before him. He spread the butter on them, poured on brown maple syrup, quartered them, and began to eat with hard, active, muscular jaws which sometimes gave a creak at the hinges. He pressed the handle of his knife against his chest and said, "In here, the human bosom —mine, yours, everybody's—there isn't just one soul. There's a lot of souls. But there are two main ones, the real soul and a pretender soul. Now! Every man realizes that he has to love something or somebody. He feels that he must go outward. 'If thou canst not love, what art thou?' Are you with me?"

"Yes, Doc, I think so," said Wilhelm listening—a little skeptically but nonetheless hard.

" 'What are thou?' Nothing. That's the answer. Nothing. In the heart of hearts—Nothing! So of course you can't stand that and want to be Something, and you try. But instead of being this Something, the man puts it over on everybody instead. You can't be that strict to yourself. You love a *little*. Like you have a dog" (*Scissors!*) "or give some money to a charity drive. Now that isn't love, is it? What is it? Egotism, pure and simple. It's a way to love the pretender soul. Vanity. Only vanity, is what it is. And social control. The interest of the pretender soul is the same as the interest of the social life, the society mechanism. This is the main tragedy of human life. Oh, it is terrible! Terrible! You are not free. Your own betrayer is inside of you and sells you out. You have to obey him like a slave. He makes you work like a horse. And for what? For who?"

"Yes, for what?" The doctor's words caught Wilhelm's heart. "I couldn't agree more," he said. "When do we get free?"

"The purpose is to keep the whole thing going. The true soul is the one that pays the price. It suffers and gets sick, and it realizes that the pretender can't be loved. Because the pretender is a lie. The true soul loves the truth. And when the true soul feels like this, it wants to kill the pretender. The love has turned into hate. Then you become dangerous. A killer. You have to kill the deceiver."

"Does this happen to everybody?"

The doctor answered simply, "Yes, to everybody. Of course, for simplification purposes, I have spoken of the soul; it isn't a scientific term, but it helps you to understand it. Whenever the slayer slays, he wants to slay the soul in him which has gypped and deceived him. Who is his enemy? Him. And his lover? Also. Therefore, all suicide is murder, and all murder is suicide. It's the one and identical phenomenon. Biologically, the pretender soul takes away the energy of the true soul and makes it feeble, like a parasite. It happens unconsciously, unawaringly, in the depths of the organism. Ever take up parasitology?"

"No, it's my dad who's the doctor."

"You should read a book about it."

Wilhelm said, "But this means that the world is full of murderers. So it's not the world. It's a kind of hell."

"Sure," the doctor said. "At least a kind of purgatory. You walk on the bodies. They are all around. I can hear them cry *de profundis* and wring their hands. I hear them, poor human beasts. I can't help hearing. And my eyes are open to it. I have to cry, too. This is the human tragedy-comedy."

Wilhelm tried to capture his vision. And again the doctor looked untrust-worthy to him, and he doubted him. "Well," he said, "there are also kind, ordinary, helpful people. They're—out in the country. All over. What kind of morbid stuff do you read, anyway?" The doctor's room was full of books.

"I read the best of literature, science and philosophy," Dr. Tamkin said. Wilhelm had observed that in his room even the TV aerial was set upon a pile of volumes. "Korzybski, Aristotle, Freud, W. H. Sheldon, and all the great poets. You answer me like a layman. You haven't applied your mind strictly to this."

"Very interesting," said Wilhelm. He was aware that he hadn't applied his mind strictly to anything. "You don't have to think I'm a dummy, though. I have ideas, too." A glance at the clock told him that the market would soon open. They could spare a few minutes yet. There were still more things he wanted to hear from Tamkin. He realized that Tamkin spoke faultily, but then scientific men were not always strictly literate. It was the description of the two souls that had awed him. In Tommy he saw the pre-tender. And even Wilky might not be himself. Might the name of his true soul be the one by which his old grandfather had called him—Velvel? The name of a soul, however, must be only that—soul. What did it look like? Does my soul look like me? Is there a soul that looks like Dad? Like Tamkin? Where does the true soul get its strength? Why does it have to love truth? Wilhelm was tormented, but tried to be oblivious to his torment. Secretly, he prayed the doctor would give him some useful advice and transform his life. "Yes, I understand you," he said. "It isn't lost on me."

"I never said you weren't intelligent, but only you just haven't made a study of it all. As a matter of fact you're a profound personality with very profound creative capacities but also disturbances. I've been concerned with you, and for some time I've been treating you."

"Without my knowing it? I haven't felt you doing anything. What do you mean? I don't think I like being treated without my knowledge. I'm of two minds. What's the matter, don't you think I'm normal?" And he really was divided in mind. That the doctor cared about him pleased him. This was what he craved, that someone should care about him, wish him well. Kind-ness, mercy, he wanted. But—and here he retracted his heavy shoulders in his peculiar way, drawing his hands up into his sleeves; his feet moved un-easily under the table—but he was worried, too, and even somewhat in-dignant. For what right had Tamkin to meddle without being asked? What kind of privileged life did this man lead? He took other people's money and speculated with it. Everybody came under his care. No one could have secrets from him.

The doctor looked at him with his deadly brown, heavy, impenetrable eyes, his naked shining head, his red hanging underlip, and said, "You have lots of guilt in you."

Wilhelm helplessly admitted, as he felt the heat rise to his wide face, "Yes, I think so too. But personally," he added, "I don't feel like a murderer. I always try to lay off. It's the others who get me. You know—make me feel oppressed. And if you don't mind, and it's all the same to you, I would rather know it when you start to treat me. And now, Tamkin, for Christ's sake, they're putting out the lunch menus already. Will you sign the check, and let's go!"

Tamkin did as he asked, and they rose. They were passing the book-keeper's desk when he took out a substantial bundle of onionskin papers and said, "These are receipts of the transactions. Duplicates. You'd better keep them as the account is in your name and you'll need them for income taxes. And here is a copy of a poem I wrote yesterday."

"I have to leave something at the desk for my father," Wilhelm said, and he put his hotel bill in an envelope with a note. *Dear Dad, Please carry me this month, Yours, W.* He watched the clerk with his sullen pug's profile and his stiff-necked look push the envelope into his father's box.

"May I ask you really why you and your dad had words?" said Dr. Tamkin, who had hung back, waiting.

"It was about my future," said Wilhelm. He hurried down the stairs with swift steps, like a tower in motion, his hands in his trousers pockets. He was ashamed to discuss the matter. "He says there's a reason why I can't go back to my old territory, and there is. I told everybody I was going to be an officer of the corporation. And I was supposed to. It was promised. But then they welshed because of the son-in-law. I bragged and made myself look big."

"If you was humble enough, you could go back. But it doesn't make much difference. We'll make you a good living on the market."

They came into the sunshine of upper Broadway, not clear but throbbing through the dust and fumes, a false air of gas visible at eye-level as it spurted from the bursting buses. From old habit, Wilhelm turned up the collar of his jacket.

"Just a technical question," Wilhelm said. "What happens if your losses are bigger than your deposit?"

"Don't worry. They have ultra-modern electronic bookkeeping machinery, and it won't let you get in debt. It puts you out automatically. But I want you to read this poem. You haven't read it yet."

Light as a locust, a helicopter bringing mail from Newark Airport to La Guardia sprang over the city in a long leap.

The paper Wilhelm unfolded had ruled borders in red ink. He read:

MECHANISM VS FUNCTIONALISM
ISM VS HISM

If thee thyself couldst only see
Thy greatness that is and yet to be,
Thou would feel joy-beauty-what ecstasy.
They are at thy feet, earth-moon-sea, the trinity.

Why-forth then dost thou tarry
And partake thee only of the crust
And skim the earth's surface narry
When all creations art thy just?

Seek ye then that which art not there
In thine own glory let thyself rest.
Witness. Thy power is not bare.
Thou art King. Thou art at thy best.

Look then right before thee.
Open thine eyes and see.
At the foot of Mt. Serenity
Is thy cradle to eternity.

Utterly confused, Wilhelm said to himself explosively, What kind of mishmash, claptrap is this! What does he want from me? Damn him to hell, he might as well hit me on the head, and lay me out, kill me. What does he give me this for? What's the purpose? Is it a deliberate test? Does he want to mix me up? He's already got me mixed up completely. I was never good at riddles. Kiss those seven hundred bucks good-by, and call it one more mistake in a long line of mistakes—Oh, Mama, what a line! He stood near the shining window of a fancy fruit store, holding Tamkin's paper, rather dazed, as though a charge of photographer's flash powder had gone up in his eyes.

But he's waiting for my reaction. I have to say something to him about his poem. It really is no joke. What will I tell him? Who is this King? The poem is written *to* someone. But who? I can't even bring myself to talk. I feel too choked and strangled. With all the books he reads, how come the guy is so illiterate? And why do people just naturally assume that you'll know what they're talking about? No. I don't know, and nobody knows. The planets don't, the stars don't, infinite space doesn't. It doesn't square with Planck's Constant or anything else. So what's the good of it? Where's the need of it? What does he mean here by Mount Serenity? Could it be a figure of speech for Mount Everest? As he says people are all committing suicide, maybe those guys who climbed Everest were only trying to kill themselves, and if we want peace we should stay at the foot of the mountain. In the here-and-now. But it's also here-and-now on the slope, and on the top, where they climbed to seize the day. Surface narry is something he can't mean, I don't believe. I'm about to start foaming at the mouth. "Thy cradle . . ." *Who* is resting in his cradle—in his glory? My thoughts are at an end. I feel the wall. No more. So ——k it all! The money and everything. Take it away! When I have the money they eat me alive, like those piranha fish in the movie about the Brazilian jungle. It was hideous when they ate up that Brahma bull in the river. He turned pale, just like clay, and in five minutes nothing was left except the skeleton still in one piece, floating away. When I haven't got it any more, at least they'll let me alone.

"Well, what do you think of this?" said Dr. Tamkin. He gave a special sort of wise smile, as though Wilhelm must now see what kind of man he was dealing with.

"Nice. Very nice. Have you been writing long?"

"I've been developing this line of thought for years and years. You follow it all the way?"

"I'm trying to figure out who this Thou is."

"Thou? Thou is you."

"Me! Why? This applies to *me?*"

"Why shouldn't it apply to you. You were in my mind when I composed it. Of course, the hero of the poem is sick humanity. If it would open its eyes it would be great."

"Yes, but how do I get into this?"

"The main idea of the poem is *con*struct or *de*struct. There is no ground in between. Mechanism is *de*struct. Money of course is *de*struct. When the last grave is dug, the gravedigger will have to be paid. If you could have confidence in nature you would not have to fear. It would keep you up. Creative is nature. Rapid. Lavish. Inspirational. It shapes leaves. It rolls the waters of the earth. Man is the chief of this. All creations are his just inheritance. You don't know what you've got within you. A person either creates or he destroys. There is no neutrality . . ."

"I realized you were no beginner," said Wilhelm with propriety. "I have only one criticism to make. I think 'whyforth' is wrong. You should write 'Wherefore then dost thou . . .' " And he reflected, So? I took a gamble. It'll have to be a miracle, though, to save me. My money will be gone, then it won't be able to destruct me. He can't just take and lose it, though. He's in it, too. I think he's in a bad way himself. He must be. I'm sure because, come to think of it, he sweated blood when he signed that check. But what have I let myself in for? The waters of the earth are going to roll over me.

V

Patiently, in the window of the fruit store, a man with a scoop spread crushed ice between his rows of vegetables. There were also Persian melons, lilacs, tulips with radiant black at the middle. The many street noises came back after a little while from the caves of the sky. Crossing the tide of Broadway traffic, Wilhelm was saying to himself, The reason Tamkin lectures me is that somebody has lectured him, and the reason for the poem is that he wants to give me good advice. Everybody seems to know something. Even fellows like Tamkin. Many people know what to do, but how many can do it?

He believed that he must, that he could and would recover the good things, the happy things, the easy tranquil things of life. He had made mistakes, but he could overlook these. He had been a fool, but that could be forgiven. The time wasted—must be relinquished. What else could one do about it? Things were too complex, but they might be reduced to simplicity again. Recovery was possible. First he had to get out of the city. No, first he had to pull out his money. . . .

From the carnival of the street—pushcarts, accordion and fiddle, shoeshine, begging, the dust going round like a woman on stilts—they entered the narrow crowded theater of the brokerage office. From front to back it was filled with the Broadway crowd. But how was lard doing this morning? From the rear of the hall Wilhelm tried to read the tiny figures. The German manager was looking through his binoculars. Tamkin placed himself on Wilhelm's left and covered his conspicuous bald head. "The guy'll ask me about the margin," he muttered. They passed, however, unobserved. "Look, the lard has held its place," he said.

Tamkin's eyes must be very sharp to read the figures over so many heads and at this distance—another respect in which he was unusual.

The room was always crowded. Everyone talked. Only at the front could you hear the flutter of the wheels within the board. Teletyped news items crossed the illuminated screen above.

"Lard. Now what about rye?" said Tamkin, rising on his toes. Here he was a different man, active and impatient. He parted people who stood in his way. His face turned resolute, and on either side of his mouth odd bulges formed under his mustache. Already he was pointing out to Wilhelm the appearance of a new pattern on the board. "There's something up today," he said.

"Then why'd you take so long with breakfast?" said Wilhelm.

There were no reserved seats in the room, only customary ones. Tamkin always sat in the second row, on the commodities side of the aisle. Some of his acquaintances kept their hats on the chairs for him.

"Thanks. Thanks," said Tamkin, and he told Wilhelm, "I fixed it up yesterday."

"That was a smart thought," said Wilhelm. They sat down.

With folded hands, by the wall, sat an old Chinese businessman in a seersucker coat. Smooth and fat, he wore a white Vandyke. One day Wilhelm had seen him on Riverside Drive pushing two little girls along in a baby carriage—his grandchildren. Then there were two women in their fifties, supposed to be sisters, shrewd and able money-makers, according to Tamkin. They had never a word to say to Wilhelm. But they would chat with Tamkin. Tamkin talked to everyone.

Wilhelm sat between Mr. Rowland, who was elderly, and Mr. Rappaport, who was very old. Yesterday Rowland had told him that in the year 1908, when he was a junior at Harvard, his mother had given him twenty shares of steel for his birthday, and then he had started to read the financial news and had never practiced law but instead followed the market for the rest of his life. Now he speculated only in soy beans, of which he had made a specialty. By his conservative method, said Tamkin, he cleared two hundred a week. Small potatoes, but then he was a bachelor, retired, and didn't need money.

"Without dependents," said Tamkin. "He doesn't have the problems that you and I do."

Did Tamkin have dependents? He had everything that it was possible for a man to have—science, Greek, chemistry, poetry, and now dependents too. That beautiful girl with epilepsy, perhaps. He often said that she was a pure, marvelous, spiritual child who had no knowledge of the world. He protected her, and, if he was not lying, adored her. And if you encouraged Tamkin by believing him, or even if you refrained from questioning him, his hints became more daring. Sometimes he said that he paid for her music lessons. Sometimes he seemed to have footed the bill for the brother's camera expedition to Brazil. And he spoke of paying for the support of the orphaned child of a dead sweetheart. These hints, made dully as asides, grew by repetition into sensational claims.

"For myself, I don't need much," said Tamkin. "But a man can't live for himself and I need the money for certain important things. What do you figure you have to have, to get by?"

"Not less than fifteen grand, after taxes. That's for my wife and the two boys."

"Isn't there anybody else?" said Tamkin with a shrewdness almost cruel. But his look grew more sympathetic as Wilhelm stumbled, not willing to recall another grief.

"Well—there was. But it wasn't a money matter."

"I should hope!" said Tamkin. "If love is love, it's free. Fifteen grand, though, isn't too much for a man of your intelligence to ask out of life. Fools, hard-hearted criminals, and murderers have millions to squander. They burn up the world—oil, coal, wood, metal, and soil, and suck even the air and the sky. They consume, and they give back no benefit. A man like you, humble for life, who wants to feel and live, has trouble—not wanting," said Tamkin in his parenthetical fashion, "to exchange an ounce of soul for a pound of social power—he'll never make it without help in a world like this. But don't you worry." Wilhelm grasped at this assurance. "Just you never mind. We'll go easily beyond your figure."

Dr. Tamkin gave Wilhelm comfort. He often said that he had made as much as a thousand a week in commodities. Wilhelm had examined the receipts, but until this moment it had never occurred to him that there must be debit slips too; he had been shown only the credits.

"But fifteen grand is not an ambitious figure," Tamkin was telling him. "For that you don't have to wear yourself out on the road, dealing with narrow-minded people. A lot of them don't like Jews, either, I suppose?"

"I can't afford to notice. I'm lucky when I have my occupation. Tamkin, do you mean you can save our money?"

"Oh, did I forget to mention what I did before closing yesterday? You see, I closed out one of the lard contracts and bought a hedge of December rye. The rye is up three points already and takes some of the sting out. But lard will go up, too."

"Where? God, yes, you're right," said Wilhelm, eager, and got to his feet to look. New hope freshened his heart. "Why didn't you tell me before?"

And Tamkin, smiling like a benevolent magician, said, "You must learn to have trust. The slump in lard can't last. And just take a look at eggs. Didn't I predict they couldn't go any lower? They're rising and rising. If we had taken eggs we'd be far ahead."

"Then why didn't we take them?"

"We were just about to. I had a buying order in at .24, but the tide turned at .26¼ and we barely missed. Never mind. Lard will go back to last year's levels."

Maybe. But when? Wilhelm could not allow his hopes to grow too strong. However, for a little while he could breathe more easily. Late-morning trading was getting active. The shining numbers whirred on the board, which sounded like a huge cage of artificial birds. Lard fluctuated between two points, but rye slowly climbed.

He closed his strained, greatly earnest eyes briefly and nodded his Buddha's head, too large to suffer such uncertainties. For several moments of peace he was removed to his small yard in Roxbury.

He breathed in the sugar of the pure morning.

He heard the long phrases of the birds.

No enemy wanted his life.

Wilhelm thought, I will get out of here. I don't belong in New York any more. And he sighed like a sleeper.

Tamkin said, "Excuse me," and left his seat. He could not sit still in the room but passed back and forth between the stocks and commodities sections. He knew dozens of people and was continually engaging in discussions. Was he giving advice, gathering information, or giving it, or practicing— whatever mysterious profession he practiced? Hypnotism? Perhaps he could put people in a trance while he talked to them. What a rare, peculiar bird he was, with those pointed shoulders, that bare head, his loose nails, almost claws, and those brown, soft, deadly, heavy eyes.

He spoke of things that mattered, and as very few people did this he could take you by surprise, excite you, move you. Maybe he wished to do good, maybe give himself a lift to a higher level, maybe believe his own prophecies, maybe touch his own heart. Who could tell? He had picked up a lot of strange ideas; Wilhelm could only suspect, he could not say with certainty, that Tamkin hadn't made them his own.

Now Tamkin and he were equal partners, but Tamkin had put up only three hundred dollars. Suppose he did this not only once but five times; then an investment of fifteen hundred dollars gave him five thousand to speculate with. If he had power of attorney in every case, he could shift the money from one account to another. No, the German probably kept an eye on him. Nevertheless it was possible. Calculations like this made Wilhelm feel ill. Obviously Tamkin was a plunger. But how did he get by? He must be in his fifties. How did he support himself? Five years in Egypt; Hollywood before that; Michigan; Ohio; Chicago. A man of fifty has supported himself for at least thirty years. You could be sure that Tamkin had never worked in a factory or in an office. How did he make it? His taste in clothes was horrible, but he didn't buy cheap things. He wore corduroy or velvet shirts from Clyde's, painted neckties, striped socks. There was a slightly acid or pasty smell about his person; for a doctor, he didn't bathe much. Also, Dr. Tamkin had a good room at the Gloriana and had had it for about a year. But so was Wilhelm himself a guest, with an unpaid bill at present in his father's box. Did the beautiful girl with the skirts and belts pay him? Was he defrauding his so-called patients? So many questions impossible to answer could not be asked about an honest man. Nor perhaps about a sane man. Was

Tamkin a lunatic, then? That sick Mr. Perls at breakfast had said that there was no easy way to tell the sane from the mad, and he was right about that in any big city and especially in New York—the end of the world, with its complexity and machinery, bricks and tubes, wires and stones, holes and heights. And was everybody crazy here? What sort of people did you see? Every other man spoke a language entirely his own, which he had figured out by private thinking; he had his own ideas and peculiar ways. If you wanted to talk about a glass of water, you had to start back with God creating the heavens and earth; the apple; Abraham; Moses and Jesus; Rome; the Middle Ages; gunpowder; the Revolution; back to Newton; up to Einstein; then war and Lenin and Hitler. After reviewing this and getting it all straight again you could proceed to talk about a glass of water. "I'm fainting, please get me a little water." You were lucky even then to make yourself understood. And this happened over and over and over with everyone you met. You had to translate and translate, explain and explain, back and forth, and it was the punishment of hell itself not to understand or be understood, not to know the crazy from the sane, the wise from the fools, the young from the old or the sick from the well. The fathers were no fathers and the sons no sons. You had to talk with yourself in the daytime and reason with yourself at night. Who else was there to talk to in a city like New York?

A queer look came over Wilhelm's face with its eyes turned up and his silent mouth with its high upper lip. He went several degrees further—when you are like this, dreaming that everybody is outcast, you realize that this must be one of the small matters. There is a larger body, and from this you cannot be separated. The glass of water fades out. You do not go from simple *a* and simple *b* to the great *x* and *y*, nor does it matter whether you agree about the glass but, far beneath such details, what Tamkin would call the real soul says plain and understandable things to everyone. There sons and fathers are themselves, and a glass of water is only an ornament; it makes a hoop of brightness on the cloth; it is an angel's mouth. There truth for everybody may be found, and confusion is only—only temporary, thought Wilhelm.

The idea of this larger body had been planted in him a few days ago beneath Times Square, when he had gone downtown to pick up tickets for the baseball game on Saturday (a doubleheader at the Polo Grounds). He was going through an underground corridor, a place he had always hated and hated more than ever now. On the walls between the advertisements were words in chalk: "Sin No More," and "Do Not Eat the Pig," he had particularly noticed. And in the dark tunnel, in the haste, heat, and darkness which disfigure and make freaks and fragments of nose and eyes and teeth, all of a sudden, unsought, a general love for all these imperfect and lurid-looking people burst out in Wilhelm's breast. He loved them. One and all, he passionately loved them. They were his brothers and his sisters. He was imperfect and disfigured himself, but what difference did that make if he was united with them by this blaze of love? And as he walked he began to say, "Oh my brothers—my brothers and my sisters," blessing them all as well as himself.

So what did it matter how many languages there were, or how hard it was to describe a glass of water? Or matter that a few minutes later he didn't feel anything like a brother toward the man who sold him the tickets?

On that very same afternoon he didn't hold so high an opinion of this same onrush of loving kindness. What did it come to? As they had the capacity and must use it once in a while, people were bound to have such involuntary feelings. It was only another one of those subway things. Like having a hard-on at random. But today, his day of reckoning, he consulted his memory again and thought, I must go back to that. That's the right clue and may do me the most good. Something very big. Truth, like.

The old fellow on the right, Mr. Rappaport, was nearly blind and kept asking Wilhelm, "What's the new figure on November wheat? Give me July soy beans too." When you told him he didn't say thank you. He said, "Okay," instead, or, "Check," and turned away until he needed you again. He was very old, older even than Dr. Adler, and if you believed Tamkin he had once been the Rockefeller of the chicken business and had retired with a large fortune.

Wilhelm had a queer feeling about the chicken industry, that it was sinister. On the road, he frequently passed chicken farms. Those big, rambling, wooden buildings out in the neglected fields; they were like prisons. The lights burned all night in them to cheat the poor hens into laying. Then the slaughter. Pile all the coops of the slaughtered on end, and in one week they'd go higher than Mount Everest or Mount Serenity. The blood filling the Gulf of Mexico. The chicken shit, acid, burning the earth.

How old—old this Mr. Rappaport was! Purple stains were buried in the flesh of his nose, and the cartilage of his ear was twisted like a cabbage heart. Beyond remedy by glasses, his eyes were smoky and faded.

"Read me that soy-bean figure now, boy," he said, and Wilhelm did. He thought perhaps the old man might give him a tip, or some useful advice or information about Tamkin. But no. He only wrote memoranda on a pad, and put the pad in his pocket. He let no one see what he had written. And Wilhelm thought this was the way a man who had grown rich by the murder of millions of animals, little chickens, would act. If there was a life to come he might have to answer for the killing of all those chickens. What if they all were waiting? But if there was a life to come, everybody would have to answer. But if there was a life to come, the chickens themselves would be all right.

Well! What stupid ideas he was having this morning. Phooey!

Finally old Rappaport did address a few remarks to Wilhelm. He asked him whether he had reserved his seat in the synagogue for Yom Kippur.

"No," said Wilhelm.

"Well, you better hurry up if you expect to say *Yiskor* for your parents. I never miss."

And Wilhelm thought, Yes, I suppose I should say a prayer for Mother once in a while. His mother had belonged to the Reform congregation. His father had no religion. At the cemetery Wilhelm had paid a man to say a prayer for her. He was among the tombs and he wanted to be tipped for the *El molai rachamin*. "Thou God of Mercy," Wilhelm thought that meant. *B'gan Aden*—"in Paradise." Singing, they drew it out. *B'gan Ay–den*. The broken bench beside the grave made him wish to do something. Wilhelm often prayed in his own manner. He did not go to the synagogue but he would occasionally perform certain devotions, according to his feelings. Now he reflected, In Dad's eyes I am the wrong kind of Jew. He doesn't like the way I act. Only he is the right kind of Jew. Whatever you are, it always turns out to be the wrong kind.

Mr. Rappaport grumbled and whiffed at his long cigar, and the board, like a swarm of electrical bees, whirred.

"Since you were in the chicken business, I thought you'd speculate in eggs, Mr. Rappaport." Wilhelm, with his warm, panting laugh, sought to charm the old man.

"Oh. Yeah. Loyalty, hey?" said old Rappaport. "I should stick to them. I spent a lot of time amongst chickens. I got to be an expert chicken-sexer. When the chick hatches you have to tell the boys from the girls. It's not easy. You need long, long experience. What do you think, it's a joke? A whole industry depends on it. Yes, now and then I buy a contract eggs. What have you got today?"

Wilhelm said anxiously, "Lard. Rye."

"Buy? Sell?"

"Bought."

"Uh," said the old man. Wilhelm could not determine what he meant by this. But of course you couldn't expect him to make himself any clearer. It was not in the code to give information to anyone. Sick with desire, Wilhelm waited for Mr. Rappaport to make an exception in his case. Just this once! Because it was critical. Silently, by a sort of telepathic concentration, he begged the old man to speak the single word that would save him, give him the merest sign. "Oh, please—please help," he nearly said. If Rappaport would close one eye, or lay his head to one side, or raise his finger and point to a column in the paper or to a figure on his pad. A hint! A hint!

A long perfect ash formed on the end of the cigar, the white ghost of the leaf with all its veins and its fainter pungency. It was ignored, in its beauty, by the old man. For it was beautiful. Wilhelm he ignored as well.

Then Tamkin said to him, "Wilhelm, look at the jump our rye just took."

December rye climbed three points as they tensely watched; the tumblers raced and the machine's lights buzzed.

"A point and a half more, and we can cover the lard losses," said Tamkin. He showed him his calculations on the margin of the *Times*.

"I think you should put in the selling order now. Let's get out with a small loss."

"Get out now? Nothing doing."

"Why not? Why should we wait?"

"Because," said Tamkin with a smiling, almost openly scoffing look, "you've got to keep your nerve when the market starts to go places. Now's when you can make something."

"I'd get out while the getting's good."

"No, you shouldn't lose your head like this. It's obvious to me what the mechanism is, back in the Chicago market. There's a short supply of December rye. Look, it's just gone up another quarter. We should ride it."

"I'm losing my taste for the gamble," said Wilhelm. "You can't feel safe when it goes up so fast. It's liable to come down just as quick."

Dryly, as though he were dealing with a child, Tamkin told him in a tone of tiring patience, "Now listen, Tommy. I have it diagnosed right. If you wish I should sell I can give the sell order. But this is the difference between healthiness and pathology. One is objective, doesn't change his mind every minute, enjoys the risk element. But that's not the neurotic character. The neurotic character—"

"Damn it, Tamkin!" said Wilhelm roughly. "Cut that out. I don't like it. Leave my character out of consideration. Don't pull any more of that stuff on me. I tell you I don't like it."

Tamkin therefore went no further; he backed down. "I meant," he said, softer, "that as a salesman you are basically an artist type. The seller is in the visionary sphere of the business function. And then you're an actor, too."

"No matter what type I am—" An angry and yet weak sweetness rose into Wilhelm's throat. He coughed as though he had the flu. It was twenty years since he had appeared on the screen as an extra. He blew the bagpipes in a film called *Annie Laurie*. Annie had come to warn the young Laird; he would not believe her and called the bagpipers to drown her out. He made fun of her while she wrung her hands. Wilhelm, in a kilt, barelegged, blew and blew and blew and not a sound came out. Of course all the music was recorded. He fell sick with the flu after that and still suffered sometimes from chest weakness.

"Something stuck in your throat?" said Tamkin. "I think maybe you are too disturbed to think clearly. You should try some of my 'here-and-now' mental exercises. It stops you from thinking so much about the future and the past and cuts down confusion."

"Yes, yes, yes, yes," said Wilhelm, his eyes fixed on December rye.

"Nature only knows one thing, and that's the present. Present, present, eternal present, like a big, huge, giant wave—colossal, bright and beautiful, full of life and death, climbing into the sky, standing in the seas. You must go along with the actual, the Here-and-Now, the glory—"

. . . chest weakness, Wilhelm's recollection went on. Margaret nursed him. They had had two rooms of furniture, which was later seized. She sat on the bed and read to him. He made her read for days, and she read stories, poetry, everything in the house. He felt dizzy, stifled when he tried to smoke. They had him wear a flannel vest.

> Come then, Sorrow!
> Sweetest Sorrow!
> Like an own babe I nurse thee on my breast!

Why did he remember that? Why?

"You have to pick out something that's in the actual, immediate present moment," said Tamkin. "And say to yourself here-and-now, here-and-now, here-and-now. 'Where am I?' 'Here.' 'When is it?' 'Now.' Take an object or a person. Anybody. 'Here and now I see a person.' 'Here and now I see a man.' 'Here and now I see a man sitting on a chair.' Take me, for instance. Don't let your mind wander. 'Here and now I see a man in a brown suit. Here and now I see a corduroy shirt.' You have to narrow it down, one item at a time, and not let your imagination shoot ahead. Be in the present. Grasp the hour, the moment, the instant."

Is he trying to hypnotize or con me? Wilhelm wondered. To take my mind off selling? But even if I'm back at seven hundred bucks, then where am I?

As if in prayer, his lids coming down with raised veins, frayed out, on his significant eyes, Tamkin said, " 'Here and now I see a button. Here and now I see the thread that sews the button. Here and now I see the green thread.' " Inch by inch he contemplated himself in order to show Wilhelm how calm it would make him. But Wilhelm was hearing Margaret's voice as she read, somewhat unwillingly,

> Come then, Sorrow!
>   .   .   .   .
> I thought to leave thee,
> And deceive thee,
> But now of all the world I love thee best.

Then Mr. Rappaport's old hand pressed his thigh, and he said, "What's my wheat? Those damn guys are blocking the way. I can't see."

VI

Rye was still ahead when they went out to lunch, and lard was holding its own.

They ate in the cafeteria with the gilded front. There was the same art inside as outside. The food looked sumptuous. Whole fishes were framed like pictures with carrots, and the salads were like terraced landscapes or like Mexican pyramids; slices of lemon and onion and radishes were like sun and moon and stars; the cream pies were about a foot thick and the cakes swollen as if sleepers had baked them in their dreams.

"What'll you have?" said Tamkin.

"Not much. I ate a big breakfast. I'll find a table. Bring me some yogurt and crackers and a cup of tea. I don't want to spend much time over lunch."

Tamkin said, "You've got to eat."

Finding an empty place at this hour was not easy. The old people idled and gossiped over their coffee. The elderly ladies were rouged and mascaraed and hennaed and used blue hair rinse and eye shadow and wore costume jewelry, and many of them were proud and stared at you with expressions that did not belong to their age. Were there no longer any respectable old ladies who knitted and cooked and looked after their grandchildren? Wilhelm's grandmother had dressed him in a sailor suit and danced him on her knee, blew on the porridge for him and said, "Admiral, you must eat." But what was the use of remembering this so late in the day?

He managed to find a table, and Dr. Tamkin came along with a tray piled with plates and cups. He had Yankee pot roast, purple cabbage, potatoes, a big slice of watermelon, and two cups of coffee. Wilhelm could not even swallow his yogurt. His chest pained him still.

At once Tamkin involved him in a lengthy discussion. Did he do it to stall Wilhelm and prevent him from selling out the rye—or to recover the ground lost when he had made Wilhelm angry by hints about the neurotic character? Or did he have no purpose except to talk?

"I think you worry a lot too much about what your wife and your father will say. Do they matter so much?"

Wilhelm replied, "A person can become tired of looking himself over and trying to fix himself up. You can spend the entire second half of your life recovering from the mistakes of the first half."

"I believe your dad told me he had some money to leave you."

"He probably does have something."

"A lot?"

"Who can tell," said Wilhelm guardedly.

"You ought to think over what you'll do with it."

"I may be too feeble to do anything by the time I get it. If I get anything."

"A thing like this you ought to plan out carefully. Invest it properly." He began to unfold schemes whereby you bought bonds, and used the bonds as security to buy something else and thereby earned twelve per cent safely on your money. Wilhelm failed to follow the details. Tamkin said, "if he made you a gift now, you wouldn't have to pay the inheritance taxes."

Bitterly, Wilhelm told him, "My father's death blots out all other considerations from his mind. He forces me to think about it, too. Then he hates me because he succeeds. When I get desperate—of course I think about money. But I don't want anything to happen to him. I certainly don't want him to die." Tamkin's brown eyes glittered shrewdly at him. "You don't believe it. Maybe it's not psychological. But on my word of honor. A joke is a joke, but I don't want to joke about stuff like this. When he dies, I'll be robbed, like. I'll have no more father."

"You love your old man?"

Wilhelm grasped at this. "Of course, of course I love him. My father. My mother—" As he said this there was a great pull at the very center of his soul. When a fish strikes the line you feel the live force in your hand. A mysterious being beneath the water, driven by hunger, has taken the hook and rushes away and fights, writhing. Wilhelm never identified what struck within him. It did not reveal itself. It got away.

And Tamkin, the confuser of the imagination, began to tell, or to fabricate, the strange history of *his* father. "He was a great singer," he said. "He left us five kids because he fell in love with an opera soprano. I never held it

against him, but admired the way he followed the life-principle. I wanted to
do the same. Because of unhappiness, at a certain age, the brain starts to die
back." (True, true! thought Wilhelm) "Twenty years later I was doing ex-
periments in Eastman Kodak, Rochester, and I found the old fellow. He had
five more children." (False, false!) "He wept; he was ashamed. I had nothing
against him. I naturally felt strange."

"My dad is something of a stranger to me, too," said Wilhelm, and he
began to muse. Where is the familiar person he used to be? Or I used to be?
Catherine—she won't even talk to me any more, my own sister. It may not
be so much my trouble that Papa turns his back on as my confusion. It's too
much. The ruins of life, and on top of that confusion—chaos and old night.
Is it an easier farewell for Dad if we don't part friends? He should maybe
do it angrily—"Blast you with my curse!" And why, Wilhelm further asked,
should he or anybody else pity me; or why should I be pitied sooner than
another fellow? It is my childish mind that thinks people are ready to give it
just because you need it.

Then Wilhelm began to think about his own two sons and to wonder how
he appeared to them, and what they would think of him. Right now he had
an advantage through baseball. When he went to fetch them, to go to Ebbets
Field, though, he was not himself. He put on a front but he felt as if he had
swallowed a fistful of sand. The strange, familiar house, horribly awkward;
the dog, Scissors, rolled over on his back and barked and whined. Wilhelm
acted as if there were nothing irregular, but a weary heaviness came over
him. On the way to Flatbush he would think up anecdotes about old Pig-
town and Charlie Ebbets for the boys and reminiscences of the old stars, but
it was very heavy going. They did not know how much he cared for them.
No. It hurt him greatly and he blamed Margaret for turning them against
him. She wanted to ruin him, while she wore the mask of kindness. Up in
Roxbury he had to go and explain to the priest, who was not sympathetic.
They don't care about individuals, their rules come first. Olive said she
would marry him outside the Church when he was divorced. But Margaret
would not let go. Olive's father was a pretty decent old guy, an osteopath,
and he understood what it was all about. Finally he said, "See here, I have to
advise Olive. She is asking me. I am mostly a freethinker myself, but the girl
has to live in this town." And by now Wilhelm and Olive had had a great
many troubles and she was beginning to dread his days in Roxbury, she said.
He trembled at offending this small, pretty, dark girl whom he adored.
When she would get up late on Sunday morning she would wake him almost
in tears at being late for Mass. He would try to help her hitch her garters
and smooth out her slip and dress and even put on her hat with shaky hands;
then he would rush her to church and drive in second gear in his forgetful
way, trying to apologize and to calm her. She got out a block from church
to avoid gossip. Even so she loved him, and she would have married him if
he had obtained the divorce. But Margaret must have sensed this. Margaret
would tell him he did not really want a divorce; he was afraid of it. He
cried, "Take everything I've got, Margaret. Let me go to Reno. Don't you

want to marry again?" No. She went out with other men, but took his money. She lived in order to punish him.

Dr. Tamkin told Wilhelm, "Your dad is jealous of you."

Wilhelm smiled. "Of *me?* That's rich."

"Sure. People are always jealous of a man who leaves his wife."

"Oh," said Wilhelm scornfully. "When it comes to wives he wouldn't have to envy me."

"Yes, and your wife envies you, too. She thinks, He's free and goes with young women. Is she getting old?"

"Not exactly old," said Wilhelm, whom the mention of his wife made sad. Twenty years ago, in a neat blue wool suit, in a soft hat made of the same cloth—he could plainly see her. He stooped his yellow head and looked under the hat at her clear, simple face, her living eyes moving, her straight small nose, her jaw beautifully, painfully clear in its form. It was a cool day, but he smelled the odor of pines in the sun, in the granite canyon. Just south of Santa Barbara, this was.

"She's forty-some years old," he said.

"I was married to a lush," said Tamkin. "A painful alcoholic. I couldn't take her out to dinner because she'd say she was going to the ladies' toilet and disappear into the bar. I'd ask the bartenders they shouldn't serve her. But I loved her deeply. She was the most spiritual woman of my entire experience."

"Where is she now?"

"Drowned," said Tamkin. "At Provincetown, Cape Cod. It must have been a suicide. She was that way—suicidal. I tried everything in my power to cure her. Because," said Tamkin, "my real calling is to be a healer. I get wounded. I suffer from it. I would like to escape from the sicknesses of others, but I can't. I am only on loan to myself, so to speak. I belong to humanity."

Liar! Wilhelm inwardly called him. Nasty lies. He invented a woman and killed her off and then called himself a healer, and made himself so earnest he looked like a bad-natured sheep. He's a puffed-up little bogus and humbug with smelly feet. A doctor! A doctor would wash himself. He believes he's making a terrific impression, and he practically invites you to take off your hat when he talks about himself; and he thinks he has an imagination, but he hasn't, neither is he smart.

Then what am I doing with him here, and why did I give him the seven hundred dollars? thought Wilhelm.

Oh, this was a day of reckoning. It was a day, he thought, on which, willing or not, he would take a good close look at the truth. He breathed hard and his misshapen hat came low upon his congested dark blond face. A rude look. Tamkin was a charlatan, and furthermore he was desperate. And furthermore, Wilhelm had always known this about him. But he appeared to have worked it out at the back of his mind that Tamkin for thirty or forty years had gotten through many a tight place, that he would get through this crisis too and bring him, Wilhelm, to safety also. And Wilhelm realized that he was on Tamkin's back. It made him feel that he had virtually left the ground and was riding upon the other man. He was in the air. It was for Tamkin to take the steps.

The doctor, if he was a doctor, did not look anxious. But then his face did not have much variety. Talking always about spontaneous emotion and open receptors and free impulses, he was about as expressive as a pincushion. When his hypnotic spell failed, his big underlip made him look weak-minded. Fear stared from his eyes, sometimes, so humble as to make you sorry for him. Once or twice Wilhelm had seen that look. Like a dog, he thought. Perhaps he didn't look it now, but he was very nervous. Wilhelm knew, but he could not afford to recognize this too openly. The doctor needed a little room, a little time. He should not be pressed now. So Tamkin went on, telling his tales.

Wilhelm said to himself, I am on his back—his back. I gambled seven hundred bucks, so I must take this ride. I have to go along with him. It's too late. I can't get off.

"You know," Tamkin said, "that blind old man Rappaport—he's pretty close to totally blind—is one of the most interesting personalities around here. If you could only get him to tell his true story. It's fascinating. This is what he told me. You often hear about bigamists with a secret life. But this old man never hid anything from anybody. He's a regular patriarch. Now, I'll tell you what he did. He had two whole families, separate and apart, one in Williamsburg and the other in the Bronx. The two wives knew about each other. The wife in the Bronx was younger; she's close to seventy now. When he got sore at one wife he went to live with the other one. Meanwhile he ran his chicken business in New Jersey. By one wife he had four kids, and by the other six. They're all grown, but they never have met their half-brothers and sisters and don't want to. The whole bunch of them are listed in the telephone book."

"I can't believe it," said Wilhelm.

"He told me this himself. And do you know what else? While he had his eyesight he used to read a lot, but the only books he would read were by Theodore Roosevelt. He had a set in each of the places where he lived, and he brought his kids up on those books."

"Please," said Wilhelm, "don't feed me any more of this stuff, will you? Kindly do not—"

"In telling you this," said Tamkin with one of his hypnotic subtleties, "I do have a motive. I want you to see how some people free themselves from morbid guilt feelings and follow their instincts. Innately, the female knows how to cripple by sickening a man with guilt. It is a very special *destruct*, and she sends her curse to make a fellow impotent. As if she says, 'Unless I allow it, you will never more be a man.' But men like my old dad or Mr. Rappaport answer, 'Woman, what art thou to me?' You can't do that yet. You're a halfway case. You want to follow your instinct, but you're too worried still. For instance, about your kids—"

"Now look here," said Wilhelm, stamping his feet. "One thing! Don't bring up my boys. Just lay off."

"I was only going to say that they are better off than with conflicts in the home."

"I'm deprived of my children." Wilhelm bit his lip. It was too late to turn away. The anguish struck him. "I pay and pay. I never see them. They grow up without me. She makes them like herself. She'll bring them up to be my enemies. Please let's not talk about this."

But Tamkin said, "Why do you let her make you suffer so? It defeats the original object in leaving her. Don't play her game. Now, Wilhelm, I'm trying to do you some good. I want to tell you, don't marry suffering. Some people do. They get married to it, and sleep and eat together, just as husband and wife. If they go with joy they think it's adultery."

When Wilhelm heard this he had, in spite of himself, to admit that there was a great deal in Tamkin's words. Yes, thought Wilhelm, suffering is the only kind of life they are sure they can have, and if they quit suffering they're afraid they'll have nothing. He knows it. This time the faker knows what he's talking about.

Looking at Tamkin he believed he saw all this confessed from his usually barren face. Yes, yes, he too. One hundred falsehoods, but at last one truth. Howling like a wolf from the city window. No one can bear it any more. Everyone is so full of it that at last everybody must proclaim it. It! It!

Then suddenly Wilhelm rose and said, "That's enough of this. Tamkin, let's go back to the market."

"I haven't finished my melon."

"Never mind that. You've had enough to eat. I want to go back."

Dr. Tamkin slid the two checks across the table. "Who paid yesterday? It's your turn, I think."

It was not until they were leaving the cafeteria that Wilhelm remembered definitely that he had paid yesterday too. But it wasn't worth arguing about.

Tamkin kept repeating as they walked down the street that there were many who were dedicated to suffering. But he told Wilhelm, "I'm optimistic in your case, and I have seen a world of maladjustment. There's hope for you. You don't really want to destroy yourself. You're trying hard to keep your feelings open, Wilhelm. I can see it. Seven per cent of this country is committing suicide by alcohol. Another three, maybe, narcotics. Another sixty just fading away into dust by boredom. Twenty more who have sold their souls to the Devil. Then there's a small percentage of those who want to live. That's the only significant thing in the whole world of today. Those are the only two classes of people there are. Some want to live, but the great majority don't." This fantastic Tamkin began to surpass himself. "They don't. Or else, why these wars? I'll tell you more," he said. "The love of the dying amounts to one thing; they want you to die with them. It's because they love you. Make no mistake."

True, true! thought Wilhelm, profoundly moved by these revelations. How does he know these things? How can he be such a jerk, and even perhaps an operator, a swindler, and understand so well what gives? I believe what he says. It simplifies much—everything. People are dropping like flies. I am trying to stay alive and work too hard at it. That's what's turning my brains. This working hard defeats its own end. At what point should I start over? Let me go back a ways and try once more.

Only a few hundred yards separated the cafeteria from the broker's, and within that short space Wilhelm turned again, in measurable degrees, from these wide considerations to the problems of the moment. The closer he approached to the market, the more Wilhelm had to think about money.

They passed the newsreel theater where the ragged shoeshine kids called after them. The same old bearded man with his bandaged beggar face and his tiny ragged feet and the old press clipping on his fiddle case to prove he had once been a concert violinist, pointed his bow at Wilhelm, saying, "You!" Wilhelm went by with worried eyes, bent on crossing Seventy-second Street. In full tumult the great afternoon current raced for Columbus Circle, where the mouth of midtown stood open and the skyscrapers gave back the yellow fire of the sun.

As they approached the polished stone front of the new office building, Dr. Tamkin said, "Well, isn't that old Rappaport by the door? I think he should carry a white cane, but he will never admit there's a single thing the matter with his eyes."

Mr. Rappaport did not stand well; his knees were sunk, while his pelvis only half filled his trousers. His suspenders held them, gaping.

He stopped Wilhelm with an extended hand, having somehow recognized him. In his deep voice he commanded him, "Take me to the cigar store."

"You want me—? Tamkin!" Wilhelm whispered, "You take him."

Tamkin shook his head. "He wants you. Don't refuse the old gentleman." Significantly he said in a lower voice. "This minute is another instance of the 'here-and-now.' You have to live in this very minute, and you don't want to. A man asks you for help. Don't think of the market. It won't run away. Show your respect to the old boy. Go ahead. That may be more valuable."

"Take me," said the old chicken merchant again.

Greatly annoyed, Wilhelm wrinkled his face at Tamkin. He took the old man's big but light elbow at the bone. "Well, let's step on it," he said. "Or wait—I want to have a look at the board first to see how we're doing."

But Tamkin had already started Mr. Rappaport forward. He was walking, and he scolded Wilhelm, saying, "Don't leave me standing in the middle of the sidewalk. I'm afraid to get knocked over."

"Let's get a move on. Come." Wilhelm urged him as Tamkin went into the broker's.

The traffic seemed to come down Broadway out of the sky, where the hot spokes of the sun rolled from the south. Hot, stony odors rose from the subway grating in the street.

"These teen-age hoodlums worry me. I'm ascared of these Puerto Rican kids, and these young characters who take dope," said Mr. Rappaport. "They go around all hopped up."

"Hoodlums?" said Wilhelm. "I went to the cemetery and my mother's stone bench was split. I could have broken somebody's neck for that. Which store do you go to?"

"Across Broadway. That La Magnita sign next door to the Automat."

"What's the matter with this store here on this side?"

"They don't carry my brand, that's what's the matter."

Wilhelm cursed, but checked the words.

"What are you talking?"

"Those damn taxis," said Wilhelm. "They want to run everybody down."

They entered the cool, odorous shop. Mr. Rappaport put away his large cigars with great care in various pockets while Wilhelm muttered, "Come on, you old creeper. What a poky old character! The whole world waits on him." Rappaport did not offer Wilhelm a cigar, but, holding one up, he asked, "What do you say at the size of these, huh? They're Churchill-type cigars."

He barely crawls along, thought Wilhelm. His pants are dropping off because he hasn't got enough flesh for them to stick to. He's almost blind, and covered with spots, but this old man still makes money in the market. Is loaded with dough, probably. And I bet he doesn't give his children any. Some of them must be in their fifties. This is what keeps middle-aged men as children. He's master over the dough. Think—just think! Who controls everything? Old men of this type. Without needs. They don't need therefore they have. I need, therefore I don't have. That would be too easy.

"I'm older even than Churchill," said Rapapport.

Now he wanted to talk! But if you asked him a question in the market, he couldn't be bothered to answer.

"I bet you are," said Wilhelm. "Come, let's get going."

"I was a fighter, too, like Churchill," said the old man. "When we licked Spain I went into the Navy. Yes, I was a gob that time. What did I have to lose? Nothing. After the battle of San Juan Hill, Teddy Roosevelt kicked me off the beach."

"Come, watch the curb," said Wilhelm.

"I was curious and wanted to see what went on. I didn't have no business there, but I took a boat and rowed myself to the beach. Two of our guys was dead, layin' under the American flag to keep the flies off. So I says to the guy on duty, there, who was the sentry, 'Let's have a look at these guys. I want to see what went on here,' and he says, 'Naw,' but I talked him into it. So he took off the flag and there were these two tall guys, both gentlemen, lying in their boots. They was very tall. The two of them had long mustaches. They were high-society boys. I think one of them was called Fish, from up the Hudson, a big-shot family. When I looked up, there was Teddy Roosevelt, with his hat off, and he was looking at these fellows, the only ones who got killed there. Then he says to me, 'What's the Navy want here? Have you got orders?' 'No, sir,' I says to him. 'Well, get the hell off the beach, then.'"

Old Rappaport was very proud of this memory. "Everything he said had such snap, such class. Man! I love that Teddy Roosevelt," he said, "I love him!"

Ah, what people are! He is almost not with us, and his life is nearly gone, but T. R. once yelled at him, so he loves him. I guess it is love, too. Wilhelm smiled. So maybe the rest of Tamkin's story was true, about the ten children and the wives and the telephone directory.

He said, "Come on, come on, Mr. Rappaport," and hurried the old man back by the large hollow elbow; he gripped it through the thin cotton cloth. Re-entering the brokerage office where under the lights the tumblers were speeding with the clack of drumsticks upon wooden blocks, more than ever resembling a Chinese theater, Wilhelm strained his eyes to see the board.

The lard figures were unfamiliar. That amount couldn't be lard! They must have put the figures in the wrong slot. He traced the line back to the margin. It was down to .19, and had dropped twenty points since noon. And what about the contract of rye? It had sunk back to its earlier position, and they had lost their chance to sell.

Old Mr. Rappaport said to Wilhelm, "Read me my wheat figure."

"Oh, leave me alone for a minute," he said, and positively hid his face from the old man behind one hand. He looked for Tamkin, Tamkin's bald head, or Tamkin with his gray straw and the cocoa-colored band. He couldn't see him. Where was he? The seats next to Rowland were taken by strangers. He thrust himself over the one on the aisle, Mr. Rappaport's former place, and pushed at the back of the chair until the new occupant, a red-headed man with a thin, determined face, leaned forward to get out of his way but would not surrender the seat. "Where's Tamkin?" Wilhelm asked Rowland.

"Gee, I don't know. Is anything wrong?"

"You must have seen him. He came in a while back."

"No, but I didn't."

Wilhelm fumbled out a pencil from the top pocket of his coat and began to make calculations. His very fingers were numb, and in his agitation he was afraid he made mistakes with the decimal points and went over the subtraction and multiplication like a schoolboy at an exam. His heart, accustomed to many sorts of crisis, was now in a new panic. And, as he had dreaded, he was wiped out. It was unnecessary to ask the German manager. He could see for himself that the electronic bookkeeping device must have closed him out. The manager probably had known that Tamkin wasn't to be trusted, and on that first day he might have warned him. But you couldn't expect him to interfere.

"You get hit?" said Mr. Rowland.

And Wilhelm, quite coolly, said, "Oh, it could have been worse, I guess." He put the piece of paper into his pocket with its cigarette butts and packets of pills. The lie helped him out—although, for a moment, he was afraid he would cry. But he hardened himself. The hardening effort made a violent, vertical pain go through his chest, like that caused by a pocket of air under the collar bones. To the old chicken millionaire, who by this time had become acquainted with the drop in rye and lard, he also denied that anything serious had happened. "It's just one of those temporary slumps. Nothing to be scared about," he said, and remained in possession of himself. His need to

cry, like someone in a crowd, pushed and jostled and abused him from behind, and Wilhelm did not dare turn. He said to himself, I will not cry in
front of these people. I'll be damned if I'll break down in front of them like
a kid, even though I never expect to see them again. No! No! And yet his
unshed tears rose and rose and he looked like a man about to drown. But
when they talked to him, he answered very distinctly. He tried to speak
proudly.

". . . going away?" he heard Rowland ask.

"What?"

"I thought you might be going away too. Tamkin said he was going to
Maine this summer for his vacation."

"Oh, going away?"

Wilhelm broke off and went to look for Tamkin in the men's toilet.
Across the corridor was the room where the machinery of the board was
housed. It hummed and whirred like mechanical birds, and the tubes glittered
in the dark. A couple of businessmen with cigarettes in their fingers were
having a conversation in the lavatory. At the top of the closet door sat a
gray straw hat with a cocoa-colored band. "Tamkin," said Wilhelm. He tried
to identify the feet below the door. "Are you in there, Doctor Tamkin?"
he said with stifled anger. "Answer me. It's Wilhelm."

The hat was taken down, the latch lifted, and a stranger came out who
looked at him with annoyance.

"You waiting?" said one of the businessmen. He was warning Wilhelm
that he was out of turn.

"Me? Not me," said Wilhelm. "I'm looking for a fellow."

Bitterly angry, he said to himself that Tamkin would pay him the two
hundred dollars at least, his share of the original deposit. "And before he
takes the train to Maine, too. Before he spends a penny on vacation—that
liar! We went into this as equal partners."

VII

I was the man beneath; Tamkin was on my back, and I thought I was on
his. He made me carry him, too, besides Margaret. Like this they ride on me
with hoofs and claws. Tear me to pieces, stamp on me and break my bones.

Once more the hoary old fiddler pointed his bow at Wilhelm as he hurried
by. Wilhelm rejected his begging and denied the omen. He dodged heavily
through traffic and with his quick, small steps ran up the lower stairway of
the Gloriana Hotel with its dark-tinted mirrors, kind to people's defects.
From the lobby he phoned Tamkin's room, and when no one answered he
took the elevator up. A rouged woman in her fifties with a mink stole led
three tiny dogs on a leash, high-strung creatures with prominent black eyes,
like dwarf deer, and legs like twigs. This was the eccentric Estonian lady
who had been moved with her pets to the twelfth floor.

She identified Wilhelm. "You are Doctor Adler's son," she said.

Formally, he nodded.

"I am a dear friend of your father."

He stood in the corner and would not meet her glance, and she thought he was snubbing her and made a mental note to speak of it to the doctor.

The linen-wagon stood at Tamkin's door, and the chambermaid's key with its big brass tongue was in the lock.

"Has Doctor Tamkin been here?" he asked her.

"No, I haven't seen him."

Wilhelm came in, however, to look around. He examined the photos on the desk, trying to connect the faces with the strange people in Tamkin's stories. Big, heavy volumes were stacked under the double-pronged TV aerial. *Science and Sanity*, he read, and there were several books of poetry. The *Wall Street Journal* hung in separate sheets from the bed-table under the weight of the silver water jug. A bathrobe with lightning streaks of red and white was laid across the foot of the bed with a pair of expensive batik pajamas. It was a box of a room, but from the windows you saw the river as far uptown as the bridge, as far downtown as Hoboken. What lay between was deep, azure, dirty, complex, crystal, rusty, with the red bones of new apartments rising on the bluffs of New Jersey, and huge liners in their berths, the tugs with matted beards of cordage. Even the brackish tidal river smell rose this high, like the smell of mop water. From every side he heard pianos, and the voices of men and women singing scales and opera, all mixed, and the sounds of pigeons on the ledges.

Again Wilhelm took the phone. "Can you locate Doctor Tamkin in the lobby for me?" he asked. And when the operator reported that she could not, Wilhelm gave the number of his father's room, but Dr. Adler was not in either. "Well, please give me the masseur. I say the massage room. Don't you understand me? The men's health club. Yes, Max Schilper's—how am I supposed to know the name of it?"

There a strange voice said, "Toktor Adler?" It was the old Czech prize-fighter with the deformed nose and ears who was attendant down there and gave out soap, sheets, and sandals. He went away. A hollow endless silence followed. Wilhelm flickered the receiver with his nails, whistled into it, but could not summon either the attendant or the operator.

The maid saw him examining the bottles of pills on Tamkin's table and seemed suspicious of him. He was running low on Phenaphen pills and was looking for something else. But he swallowed one of his own tablets and went out and rang again for the elevator. He went down to the health club. Through the steamy windows, when he emerged, he saw the reflection of the swimming pool swirling green at the bottom of the lowest stairway. He went through the locker-room curtains. Two men wrapped in towels were playing Ping-pong. They were awkward and the ball bounded high. The Negro in the toilet was shining shoes. He did not know Dr. Adler by name, and Wilhelm descended to the massage room. On the tables naked men were lying. It was not a brightly lighted place, and it was very hot, and under the white faint moons of the ceiling shone pale skins. Calendar pictures of pretty girls dressed in tiny fringes were pinned on the wall. On the first table, eyes deeply shut in heavy silent luxury lay a man with a full square beard and short legs, stocky and black-haired. He might have been an orthodox Russian. Wrapped in a sheet, waiting, the man beside him was newly shaved and red from the steambath. He had a big happy face and was dreaming. And after him was an athlete, strikingly muscled, powerful and young, with a strong white curve to his genital and a half-angry smile on his mouth. Dr. Adler was on the fourth table, and Wilhelm stood over his father's pale, slight body. His ribs were narrow and small, his belly round, white, and high. It had its own being, like something separate. His thighs were weak, the muscles of his arms had fallen, his throat was creased.

The masseur in his undershirt bent and whispered in his ear, "It's your son," and Dr. Adler opened his eyes into Wilhelm's face. At once he saw the trouble in it, and by an instantaneous reflex he removed himself from the danger of contagion, and he said serenely, "Well, have you taken my advice, Wilky?"

"Oh, Dad," said Wilhelm.

"To take a swim and get a massage?"

"Did you get my note?" said Wilhelm.

"Yes, but I'm afraid you'll have to ask somebody else, because I can't. I had no idea you were so low on funds. How did you let it happen? Didn't you lay anything aside?"

"Oh, please, Dad," said Wilhelm, almost bringing his hands together in a clasp.

"I'm sorry," said the doctor. "I really am. But I have set up a rule. I've thought about it, I believe it is a good rule, and I don't want to change it. You haven't acted wisely. What's the matter?"

"Everything. Just everything. What isn't? I did have a little, but I haven't been very smart."

"You took some gamble? You lost it? Was it Tamkin? I told you, Wilky, not to build on that Tamkin. Did you? I suspect—"

"Yes, Dad, I'm afraid I trusted him."

Dr. Adler surrendered his arm to the masseur, who was using wintergreen oil.

"Trusted! And got taken?"

"I'm afraid I kind of—" Wilhelm glanced at the masseur but he was absorbed in his work. He probably did not listen to conversations. "I did. I might as well say it. I should have listened to you."

"Well, I won't remind you how often I warned you. It must be very painful."

"Yes, Father, it is."

"I don't know how many times you have to be burned in order to learn something. The same mistakes, over and over."

"I couldn't agree with you more," said Wilhelm with a face of despair. "You're so right, Father. It's the same mistakes, and I get burned again and again. I can't seem to—I'm stupid, Dad, I just can't breathe. My chest is all up—I feel choked. I just simply can't catch my breath."

He stared at his father's nakedness. Presently he became aware that Dr. Adler was making an effort to keep his temper. He was on the verge of an explosion. Wilhelm hung his face and said, "Nobody likes bad luck, eh Dad?"

"So! It's bad luck, now. A minute ago it was stupidity."

"It is stupidity—it's some of both. It's true that I can't learn. But I—"

"I don't want to listen to the details," said his father. "And I want you to understand that I'm too old to take on new burdens. I'm just too old to do it. And people who will just wait for help—must *wait* for help. They have got to stop waiting."

"It isn't all a question of money—there are other things a father can give to a son." He lifted up his gray eyes and his nostrils grew wide with a look of suffering appeal that stirred his father even more deeply against him.

He warningly said to him, "Look out, Wilky, you're tiring my patience very much."

"I try not to. But one word from you, just a word, would go a long way. I've never asked you for very much. But you are not a kind man, Father. You don't give the little bit I beg you for."

He recognized that his father was now furiously angry. Dr. Adler started to say something, and then raised himself and gathered the sheet over him as he did so. His mouth opened, wide, dark, twisted, and he said to Wilhelm, "You want to make yourself into my cross. But I am not going to pick up a cross. I'll see you dead, Wilky, by Christ, before I let you do that to me."

"Father, listen! Listen!"

"Go away from me now. It's torture for me to look at you, you slob!" cried Dr. Adler.

Wilhelm's blood rose up madly, in anger equal to his father's, but then it sank down and left him helplessly captive to misery. He said stiffly, and with a strange sort of formality, "Okay, Dad. That'll be enough. That's about all we should say." And he stalked out heavily by the door adjacent to the swimming pool and the steam room, and labored up two long flights from the basement. Once more he took the elevator to the lobby on the mezzanine.

He inquired at the desk for Dr. Tamkin.

The clerk said, "No, I haven't seen him. But I think there's something in the box for you."

"Me? Give it here," said Wilhelm and opened a telephone message from his wife. It read, "Please phone Mrs. Wilhelm on return. Urgent."

Whenever he received an urgent message from his wife he was always thrown into a great fear for the children. He ran to the phone booth, spilled out the change from his pockets onto the little curved steel shelf under the telephone, and dialed the Digby number.

"Yes?" said his wife. Scissors barked in the parlor.

"Margaret?"

"Yes, hello." They never exchanged any other greeting. She instantly knew his voice.

"The boys all right?"

"They're out on their bicycles. Why shouldn't they be all right? Scissors, quiet!"

"Your message scared me," he said. "I wish you wouldn't make 'urgent' so common."

"I had something to tell you."

Her familiar unbending voice awakened in him a kind of hungry longing, not for Margaret but for the peace he had once known.

"You sent me a postdated check," she said. "I can't allow that. It's already five days past the first. You dated your check for the twelfth."

"Well, I have no money. I haven't got it. You can't send me to prison for that. I'll be lucky if I can raise it by the twelfth."

She answered, "You better get it, Tommy."

"Yes? What for?" he said. "Tell me. For the sake of what? To tell lies about me to everyone? You—"

She cut him off. "You know what for. I've got the boys to bring up."

Wilhelm in the narrow booth broke into a heavy sweat. He dropped his head and shrugged while with his fingers he arranged nickels, dimes, and quarters in rows. "I'm doing my best," he said. "I've had some bad luck. As a matter of fact, it's been so bad that I don't know where I am. I couldn't tell you what day of the week this is. I can't think straight. I'd better not even try. This has been one of those days, Margaret. May I never live to go through another like it. I mean that with all my heart. So I'm not going to try to do any thinking today. Tomorrow I'm going to see some guys. One is a sales manager. The other is in television. But not to act," he hastily added. "On the business end."

"That's just some more of your talk, Tommy," she said. "You ought to patch things up with Rojax Corporation. They'd take you back. You've got to stop thinking like a youngster."

"What do you mean?"

"Well," she said, measured and unbending, remorselessly unbending, "you still think like a youngster. But you can't do that any more. Every other day you want to make a new start. But in eighteen years you'll be eligible for retirement. Nobody wants to hire a new man of your age."

"I know. But listen, you don't have to sound so hard. I can't get on my knees to them. And really you don't have to sound so hard. I haven't done you so much harm."

"Tommy, I have to chase you and ask you for money that you owe us, and I hate it."

She hated also to be told that her voice was hard.

"I'm making an effort to control myself," she told him.

He could picture her, her graying bangs cut with strict fixity above her pretty, decisive face. She prided herself on being fair-minded. We could not bear, he thought, to know what we do. Even though blood is spilled. Even though the breath of life is taken from someone's nostrils. This is the way of the weak; quiet and fair. And then smash! They smash!

"Rojax take me back? I'd have to crawl back. They don't need me. After so many years I should have got stock in the firm. How can I support the three of you, and live myself, on half the territory? And why should I even try when you won't lift a finger to help? I sent you back to school, didn't I? At that time you said—"

His voice was rising. She did not like that and intercepted him. "You misunderstood me," she said.

"You must realize you're killing me. You can't be as blind as all that. Thou shalt not kill! Don't you remember that?"

She said, "You're just raving now. When you calm down it'll be different. I have great confidence in your earning ability."

"Margaret, you don't grasp the situation. You'll have to get a job."

"Absolutely not. I'm not going to have two young children running loose."

"They're not babies," Wilhelm said. "Tommy is fourteen. Paulie is going to be ten."

"Look," Margaret said in her deliberate manner. "We can't continue this conversation if you're going to yell so, Tommy. They're at a dangerous age. There are teen-aged gangs—the parents working, or the families broken up."

Once again she was reminding him that it was he who had left her. She had the bringing up of the children as her burden, while he must expect to pay the price of his freedom.

Freedom! he thought with consuming bitterness. Ashes in his mouth, not freedom. Give me my children. For they are mine too.

Can you be the woman I lived with? he started to say. Have you forgotten that we slept so long together? Must you now deal with me like this, and have no mercy?

He would be better off with Margaret again than he was today. This was what she wanted to make him feel, and she drove it home. "Are you in misery?" she was saying. "But you have deserved it." And he could not return to her any more than he could beg Rojax to take him back. If it cost him his life, he could not. Margaret had ruined him with Olive. She hit him and hit him, beat him, battered him, wanted to beat the very life out of him.

"Margaret, I want you please to reconsider about work. You have that degree now. Why did I pay your tuition?"

"Because it seemed practical. But it isn't. Growing boys need parental authority and a home."

He begged her, "Margaret, go easy on me. You ought to. I'm at the end of my rope and feel that I'm suffocating. You don't want to be responsible for a person's destruction. You've got to let up. I feel I'm about to burst." His face had expanded. He struck a blow upon the tin and wood and nails of the wall of the booth. "You've got to let me breathe. If I should keel over, what then? And it's something I can never understand about you. How you can treat someone like this whom you lived with so long. Who gave you the best of himself. Who tried. Who loved you." Merely to pronounce the word "love" made him tremble.

"Ah," she said with a sharp breath. "Now we're coming to it. How did you imagine it was going to be—big shot? Everything made smooth for you? I thought you were leading up to this."

She had not, perhaps, intended to reply as harshly as she did, but she brooded a great deal and now she could not forbear to punish him and make him feel pains like those she had to undergo.

He struck the wall again, this time with his knuckles, and he had scarcely enough air in his lungs to speak in a whisper, because his heart pushed upward with a frightful pressure. He got up and stamped his feet in the narrow enclosure.

"Haven't I always done my best?" he yelled, though his voice sounded weak and thin to his own ears. "Everything comes from me and nothing back again to me. There's no law that'll punish this, but you are committing a crime against me. Before God—and that's no joke. I mean that. Before God! Sooner or later the boys will know it."

In a firm tone, levelly, Margaret said to him, "I won't stand to be howled at. When you can speak normally and have something sensible to say I'll listen. But not to this." She hung up.

Wilhelm tried to tear the apparatus from the wall. He ground his teeth and seized the black box with insane digging fingers and made a stifled cry and pulled. Then he saw an elderly lady staring through the glass door, utterly appalled by him, and he ran from the booth, leaving a large amount of change on the shelf. He hurried down the stairs and into the street.

On Broadway it was still bright afternoon and the gassy air was almost motionless under the leaden spokes of sunlight, and sawdust footprints lay about the doorways of butcher shops and fruit stores. And the great, great crowd, the inexhaustible current of millions of every race and kind pouring out, pressing round, of every age, of every genius, possessors of every human secret, antique and future, in every face the refinement of one particular motive or essence—*I labor, I spend, I strive, I design, I love, I cling, I uphold, I give way, I envy, I long, I scorn, I die, I hide, I want.* Faster, much faster than any man could make the tally. The sidewalks were wider than any causeway; the street itself was immense, and it quaked and gleamed and it seemed to Wilhelm to throb at the last limit of endurance. And although the sunlight appeared like a broad tissue, its actual weight made him feel like a drunkard.

"I'll get a divorce if it's the last thing I do," he swore. "As for Dad— As for Dad— I'll have to sell the car for junk and pay the hotel. I'll have to go on my knees to Olive and say, 'Stand by me a while. Don't let her win. Olive!'" And he thought, I'll try to start again with Olive. In fact, I must. Olive loves me. Olive—

Beside a row of limousines near the curb he thought he saw Dr. Tamkin. Of course he had been mistaken before about the hat with the cocoa-colored band and didn't want to make the same mistake twice. But wasn't that Tamkin who was speaking so earnestly, with pointed shoulders, to someone under the canopy of the funeral parlor? For this was a huge funeral. He looked for the singular face under the dark gray, fashionable hatbrim. There were two open cars filled with flowers, and a policeman tried to keep a path open to pedestrians. Right at the canopy-pole, now wasn't that that damned Tamkin talking away with a solemn face, gesticulating with an open hand?

"Tamkin!" shouted Wilhelm, going forward. But he was pushed to the side by a policeman clutching his nightstick at both ends, like a rolling pin. Wilhelm was even farther from Tamkin now, and swore under his breath at the cop who continued to press him back, back, belly and ribs, saying, "Keep it moving there, please," his face red with impatient sweat, his brows like red fur. Wilhelm said to him haughtily. "You shouldn't push people like this."

The policeman, however, was not really to blame. He had been ordered to keep a way clear. Wilhelm was moved forward by the pressure of the crowd.

He cried, "Tamkin!"

But Tamkin was gone. Or rather, it was he himself who was carried from the street into the chapel. The pressure ended inside, where it was dark and cool. The flow of fan-driven air dried his face, which he wiped hard with his handkerchief to stop the slight salt itch. He gave a sigh when he heard the organ notes that stirred and breathed from the pipes and he saw people in the pews. Men in formal clothes and black homburgs strode softly back and forth on the cork floor, up and down the center aisle. The white of the stained glass was like mother-of-pearl, the blue of the Star of David like velvet ribbon.

Well, thought Wilhelm, if that was Tamkin outside I might as well wait for him here where it's cool. Funny, he never mentioned he had a funeral to go to today. But that's just like the guy.

But within a few minutes he had forgotten Tamkin. He stood along the wall with others and looked toward the coffin and the slow line that was moving past it, gazing at the face of the dead. Presently he too was in this line, and slowly, slowly, foot by foot, the beating of his heart anxious, thick, frightening, but somehow also rich, he neared the coffin and paused for his turn, and gazed down. He caught his breath when he looked at the corpse, and his face swelled, his eyes shone hugely with instant tears.

The dead man was gray-haired. He had two large waves of gray hair at the front. But he was not old. His face was long, and he had a bony nose, slightly, delicately twisted. His brows were raised as though he had sunk into the final thought. Now at last he was with it, after the end of all distractions, and when his flesh was no longer flesh. And by this meditative look Wilhelm was so struck that he could not go away. In spite of the tinge of horror, and then the splash of heartsickness that he felt, he could not go. He stepped out of line and remained beside the coffin; his eyes filled silently and through his still tears he studied the man as the line of visitors moved with veiled looks past the satin coffin toward the standing bank of lilies, lilacs, roses. With great stifling sorrow, almost admiration, Wilhelm nodded and nodded. On the surface, the dead man with his formal shirt and his tie and silk lapels and his powdered skin looked so proper; only a little beneath so—black, Wilhelm thought, so fallen in the eyes.

Standing a little apart, Wilhelm began to cry. He cried at first softly and from sentiment, but soon from deeper feeling. He sobbed loudly and his face grew distorted and hot, and the tears stung his skin. A man—another human creature, was what first went through his thoughts, but other and different things were torn from him. What'll I do? I'm stripped and kicked out. . . . Oh, Father, what do I ask of you? What'll I do about the kids—Tommy, Paul? My children. And Olive? My dear! Why, why, why—you must protect me against that devil who wants my life. If you want it, then kill me. Take, take it, take it from me."

Soon he was past words, past reason, coherence. He could not stop. The source of all tears had suddenly sprung open within him, black, deep, and hot, and they were pouring out and convulsed his body, bending his stubborn head, bowing his shoulders, twisting his face, crippling the very hands with which he held the handkerchief. His efforts to collect himself were useless. The great knot of ill and grief in his throat swelled upward and he gave in utterly and held his face and wept. He cried with all his heart.

He, alone of all the people in the chapel, was sobbing. No one knew who he was.

One woman said, "Is that perhaps the cousin from New Orleans they were expecting?"

"It must be somebody real close to carry on so."

"Oh my, oh my! To be mourned like that," said one man and looked at Wilhelm's heavy shaken shoulders, his clutched face and whitened fair hair, with wide, glinting, jealous eyes.

"The man's brother, maybe?"

"Oh, I doubt that very much," said another bystander. "They're not alike at all. Night and day."

The flowers and lights fused ecstatically in Wilhelm's blind, wet eyes; the heavy sea-like music came up to his ears. It poured into him where he had hidden himself in the center of a crowd by the great and happy oblivion of tears. He heard it and sank deeper than sorrow, through torn sobs and cries toward the consummation of his heart's ultimate need.

About the Editor

GEORGE P. ELLIOTT is Professor of English at Syracuse University. He went to college at the University of California and received his M.A. from there in 1941. From 1947 to 1955 he taught at Saint Mary's College, California. He has also taught at the University of California, Cornell University, Barnard College, and the Writers' Workshop of the State University of Iowa.

Mr. Elliott is the editor of the anthology, *Fifteen Modern American Poets* (1956), and the author of several score poems, stories, and essays which have appeared in magazines. Ten of his stories were collected in *Among the Dangs* (1961). His published books include two novels, *Parktilden Village* (1958) and *David Knudsen* (1962), a narrative poem, *Fever and Chills* (1961), and a book of essays, *A Piece of Lettuce* (1964).

A Note on the Type

The text of this book was set on the Linotype in Janson, a recutting made direct from type cast from matrices long thought to have been made by the Dutchman Anton Janson, who was a practicing type founder in Leipzig during the years 1668–87. However, it has been conclusively demonstrated that these types are actually the work of Nicholas Kis (1650–1702), a Hungarian, who most probably learned his trade from the master Dutch type founder Dirk Voskens. The type is an excellent example of the influential and sturdy Dutch types that prevailed in England up to the time William Caslon developed his own incomparable designs from these Dutch faces.